GREYSHIRT: INDIGO SUNSET

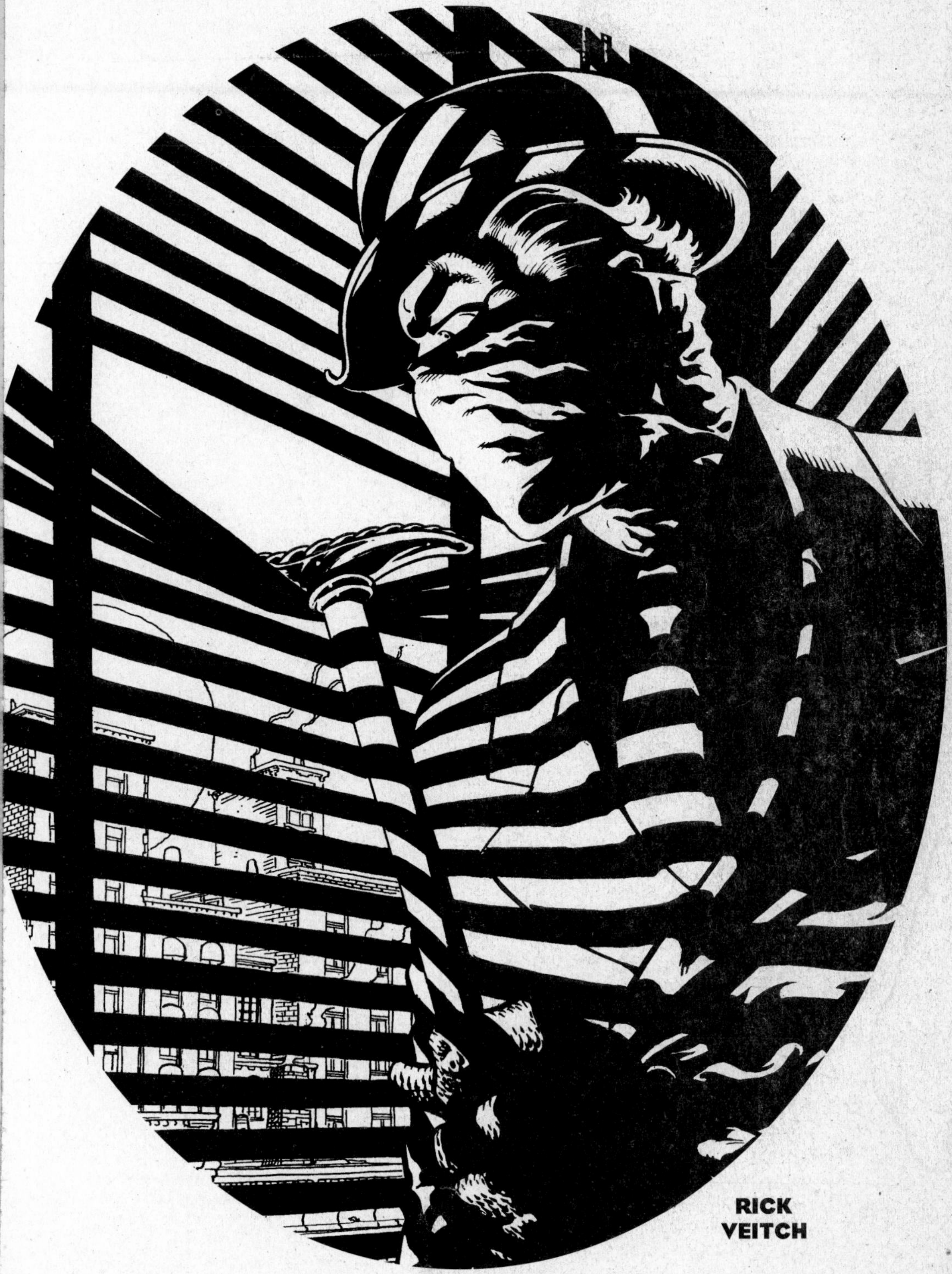

RICK
VEITCH

JIM LEE
EDITORIAL DIRECTOR

JOHN NEE
VP AND GENERAL MANAGER

SCOTT DUNBIER
GROUP EDITOR

KRISTY QUINN
NEAL POZNER
ASSISTANT EDITORS

GREYSHIRT: INDIGO SUNSET PUBLISHED BY AMERICA'S BEST COMICS, LLC. ISBN 1-56389-909-4.

GREYSHIRT
INDIGO SUNSET

RICK VEITCH
WRITER / ARTIST

ADDITIONAL MATERIAL BY

HILARY BARTA
INKER

FRANK CHO
ARTIST

DAVE GIBBONS
WRITER

RUSS HEATH
ARTIST

DAVID LLOYD
ARTIST

JOHN SEVERIN
ARTIST

AL WILLIAMSON
INKER

WILDSTORM FX
COLORS

TODD KLEIN
LETTERING, LOGOS & DESIGN

ALAN MOORE
CONSULTANT / PREFACE

GREYSHIRT CREATED BY ALAN MOORE & RICK VEITCH

AMERICA'S BEST COMICS

PREFACE

If the comic industry is ever on fire, someone please make sure to save Rick Veitch. Firstly because he's almost certain to be asleep and will never make it out on his own, and secondly because in some eerie and unfathomable way, every comic book panel ever committed to pulp has imprinted itself upon this man's more-than-usually-twisted DNA. Save Rick Veitch from the flames, even rescue some organic scrap of him, and we can probably regenerate the entire history of the medium from, say, a toenail or something. If you should get a choice of body parts to carry out of this hypothetical medium-wide inferno, then take my advice and go for the brain. That way we'll have a chance of finding out how it worked so well while being made only from some form of super-absorptive cotton wool capable of soaking up every splash of imagery, dribble of atmosphere or word-spill that Veitch has ever waded through.

Curt Swan silverings or Kirby kracklefests, gunslingers or G.I.s, furry funsters or fashion floozies, there remains no obscure corner or cobwebbed and discarded genre of comic book history that this creator has not poked, prodded or pitched his tent in for a while. Nuances of ambience and flavor, as delicate as the paper-fungus bouquet lifting from a back-issue box, are hardwired into the Veitch cortex and can be resurrected intact at the flick of a neuron, the twitch of a Rapidograph. The tone of a specific long-misplaced anthology story or mood from a half-remembered run of now-tattered covers may be summoned through the artist's Ouija board, made to parade before the slack-jawed séance audience, all at the drop of a waterlogged Bob Powell hat. Not until the advent of grim, gallant *Greyshirt* in *TOMORROW STORIES*, however, had the once-mighty but lately derelict crime comic genre played host to the artist's wandering eye and eclectic enthusiasms.

Against the largely Veitch-invented gas-lit backdrop of Indigo City, our *Greyshirt* presented the opportunity for spontaneous and often improvised fantasy-dramas or comedies, for self-contained set-pieces often revolving around some experimental storytelling notion in the hope of at least *trying* to be as inventive in terms of the medium as Will Eisner's *Spirit* had been forty or fifty years before. Nostalgic touches and furnishings were wedded to an unmistakably progressive sensibility, in the hope of something genuinely new emerging as a result, and over the thus-far dozen issues of *TOMORROW STORIES* Veitch has treated us to a masterly array of breathtaking new riffs upon what is undeniably a timeworn instrument.

It's only in the wholly self-started *GREYSHIRT: INDIGO SUNSET* series, however, that we see the mad intricacy of undiluted Veitch at full throttle. While the star-studded pageant of guest talent parading through the short, independent stories featured here is a treat for the connoisseur, it is in the main "Young Greyshirt" narrative that the comic medium's best-kept secret shows off his most ingenious moves and structures. Characters or ideas hurled into the original *TOMORROW STORIES* episodes without a moment's thought and in unconnected disarray are here enlarged upon and given histories, woven carefully together in a storyline which seems so natural you'd almost swear that those earlier short features had been written with this grand end-tying climax in mind. Persons previously given a minor role during one specific page of a *Greyshirt* tale in *TOMORROW STORIES* are herein realized as vital players in a larger narrative, their personalities expanded, provided with more dimensions and complexities than their original walk-on part had allowed or demanded.

This being a Rick Veitch joint, though, there's clearly a lot more going on than can be seen from the not-so-simple mechanics of the plot. In the subtle stream of inspiration and allusion running through *INDIGO SUNSET* we find touches of John Stanley or Dan DeCarlo next to fond riffing on Charles Biro's crime comics or Jack Kirby's mobster and romance masterpieces. The stories here are a high-octane history of American pulp crime, of Dr. Frederick Wertham's worst nightmares: bloody rubouts and preening psychopaths. Dames with hearts of gold and dazzling headlights. Delinquent love and carmine-lipped betrayal. Rick Veitch is one of the most genuinely innovative talents ever to grace mainstream comics, and in *GREYSHIRT: INDIGO SUNSET* he treats his fans to a two-fisted burning-rubber trawl through the banned, beloved and just plain bad neighborhoods of funny-book felony. Now get in the back seat and keep that smart mouth buttoned, pal. You too, sister.

You're going for a ride.

Alan Moore,
Northampton,
October 2002

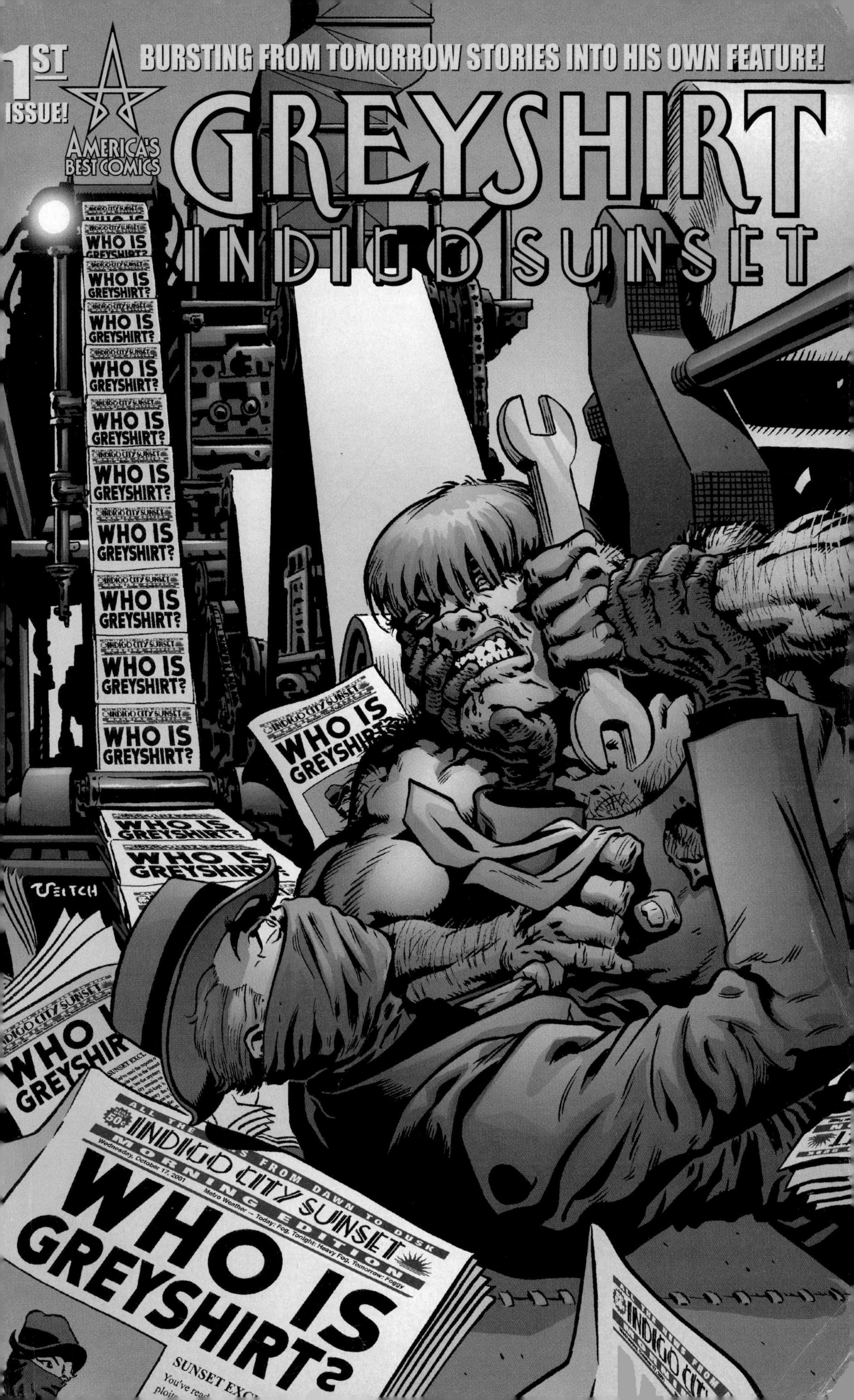
1ST ISSUE!
AMERICA'S BEST COMICS
BURSTING FROM TOMORROW STORIES INTO HIS OWN FEATURE!
GREYSHIRT
INDIGO SUNSET
INDIGO CITY SUNSET
WHO IS GREYSHIRT?
VEITCH
ALL THE NEWS FROM DAWN TO DUSK
50¢
INDIGO CITY SUNSET
MORNING EDITION
Wednesday, October 17, 2001
Metro Weather – Today: Fog. Tonight: Heavy Fog. Tomorrow: Foggy
WHO IS GREYSHIRT?

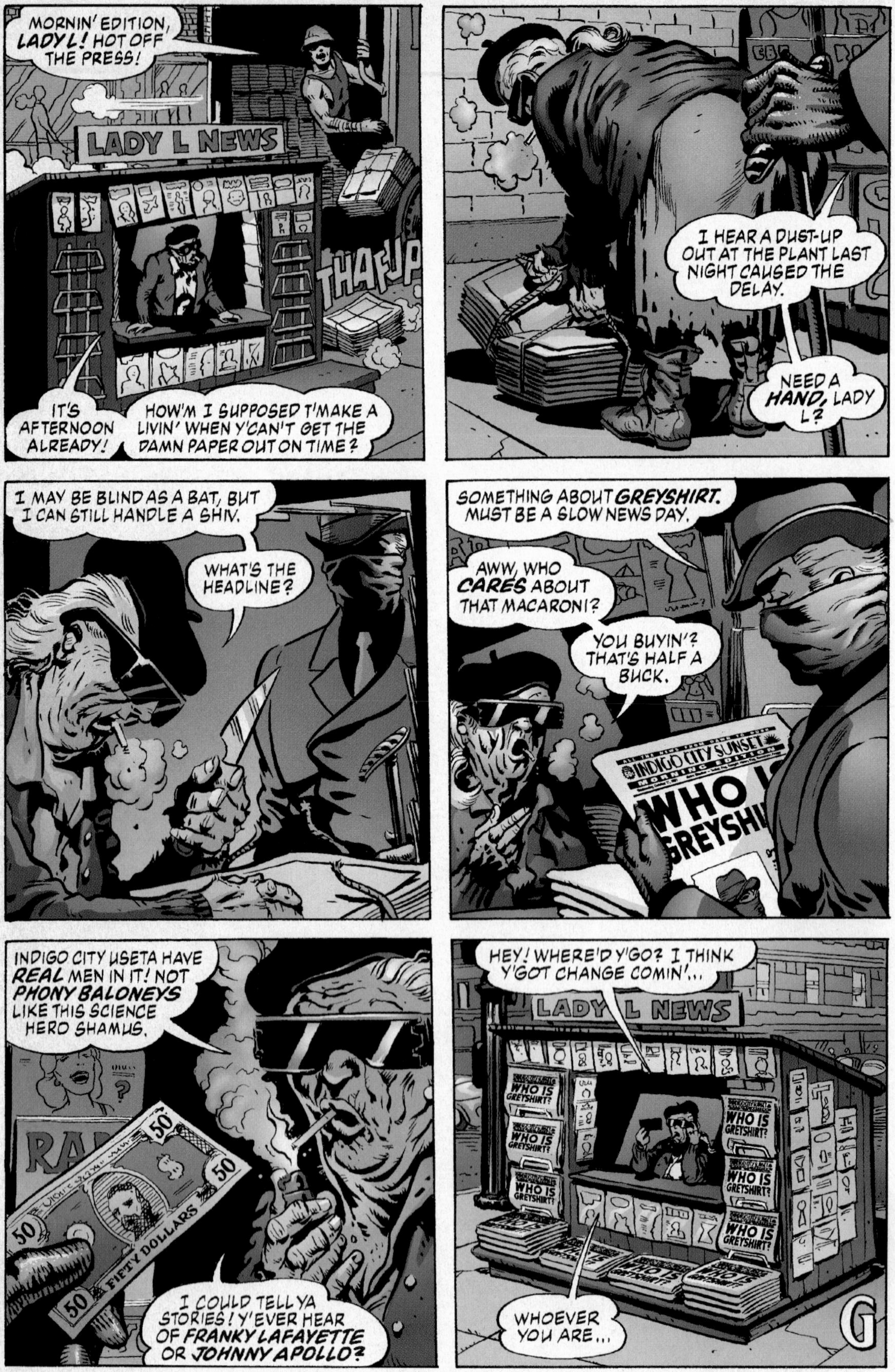
MORNIN' EDITION, LADY L! HOT OFF THE PRESS!
LADY L NEWS
THAFUP
IT'S AFTERNOON ALREADY!
HOW'M I SUPPOSED T'MAKE A LIVIN' WHEN Y'CAN'T GET THE DAMN PAPER OUT ON TIME?
I HEAR A DUST-UP OUT AT THE PLANT LAST NIGHT CAUSED THE DELAY.
NEED A HAND, LADY L?
I MAY BE BLIND AS A BAT, BUT I CAN STILL HANDLE A SHIV.
WHAT'S THE HEADLINE?
SOMETHING ABOUT GREYSHIRT. MUST BE A SLOW NEWS DAY.
AWW, WHO CARES ABOUT THAT MACARONI?
YOU BUYIN'? THAT'S HALF A BUCK.
INDIGO CITY SUNSET
MORNING EDITION
WHO IS GREYSHI
INDIGO CITY USETA HAVE REAL MEN IN IT! NOT PHONY BALONEYS LIKE THIS SCIENCE HERO SHAMUS.
50
FIFTY DOLLARS
I COULD TELL YA STORIES! Y'EVER HEAR OF FRANKY LAFAYETTE OR JOHNNY APOLLO?
HEY! WHERE'D Y'GO? I THINK Y'GOT CHANGE COMIN'...
LADY L NEWS
WHO IS GREYSHIRT?
WHOEVER YOU ARE...

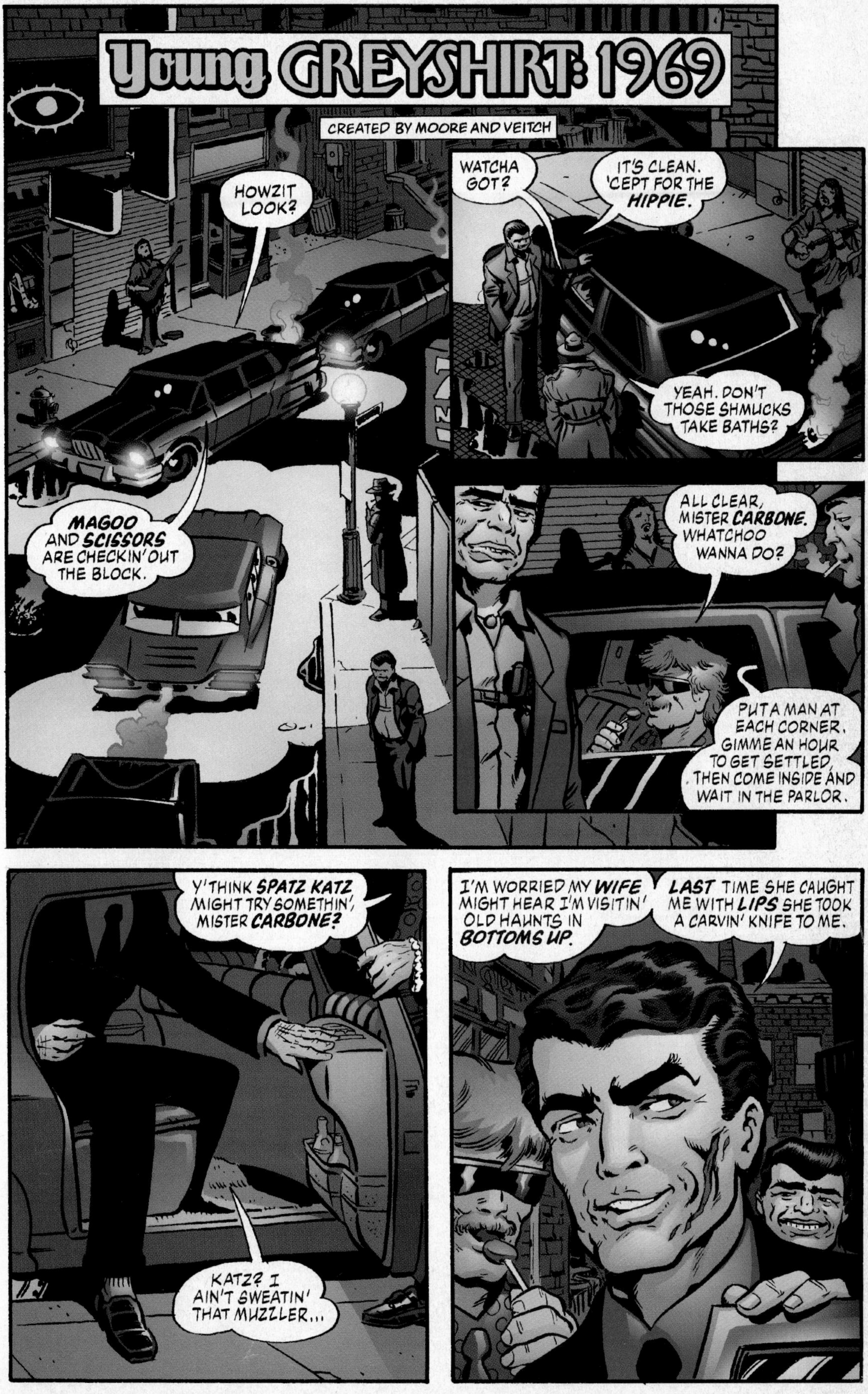
Young GREYSHIRT: 1969
CREATED BY MOORE AND VEITCH
HOWZIT LOOK?
MAGOO AND SCISSORS ARE CHECKIN' OUT THE BLOCK.
WATCHA GOT?
IT'S CLEAN. 'CEPT FOR THE HIPPIE.
YEAH. DON'T THOSE SHMUCKS TAKE BATHS?
ALL CLEAR, MISTER CARBONE. WHATCHOO WANNA DO?
PUT A MAN AT EACH CORNER. GIMME AN HOUR TO GET SETTLED, THEN COME INSIDE AND WAIT IN THE PARLOR.
Y'THINK SPATZ KATZ MIGHT TRY SOMETHIN', MISTER CARBONE?
KATZ? I AIN'T SWEATIN' THAT MUZZLER...
I'M WORRIED MY WIFE MIGHT HEAR I'M VISITIN' OLD HAUNTS IN BOTTOMS UP.
LAST TIME SHE CAUGHT ME WITH LIPS SHE TOOK A CARVIN' KNIFE TO ME.

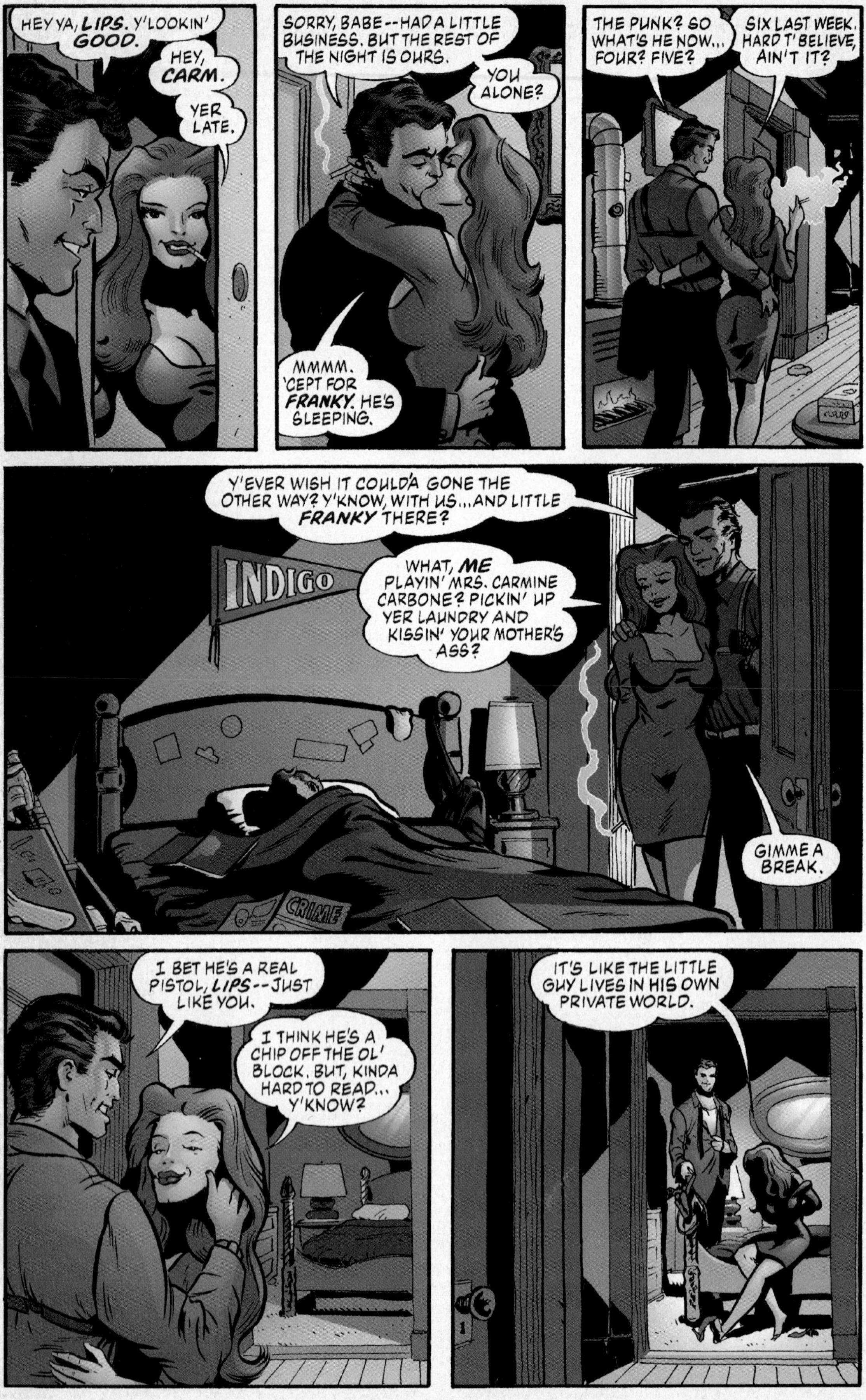
HEY YA, LIPS. Y'LOOKIN' GOOD.
HEY, CARM.
YER LATE.
SORRY, BABE--HAD A LITTLE BUSINESS. BUT THE REST OF THE NIGHT IS OURS.
YOU ALONE?
MMMM. 'CEPT FOR FRANKY. HE'S SLEEPING.
THE PUNK? SO WHAT'S HE NOW... FOUR? FIVE?
SIX LAST WEEK. HARD T' BELIEVE, AIN'T IT?
Y'EVER WISH IT COULD'A GONE THE OTHER WAY? Y'KNOW, WITH US... AND LITTLE FRANKY THERE?
INDIGO
WHAT, ME PLAYIN' MRS. CARMINE CARBONE? PICKIN' UP YER LAUNDRY AND KISSIN' YOUR MOTHER'S ASS?
GIMME A BREAK.
CRIME
I BET HE'S A REAL PISTOL, LIPS--JUST LIKE YOU.
I THINK HE'S A CHIP OFF THE OL' BLOCK. BUT, KINDA HARD TO READ... Y'KNOW?
IT'S LIKE THE LITTLE GUY LIVES IN HIS OWN PRIVATE WORLD.

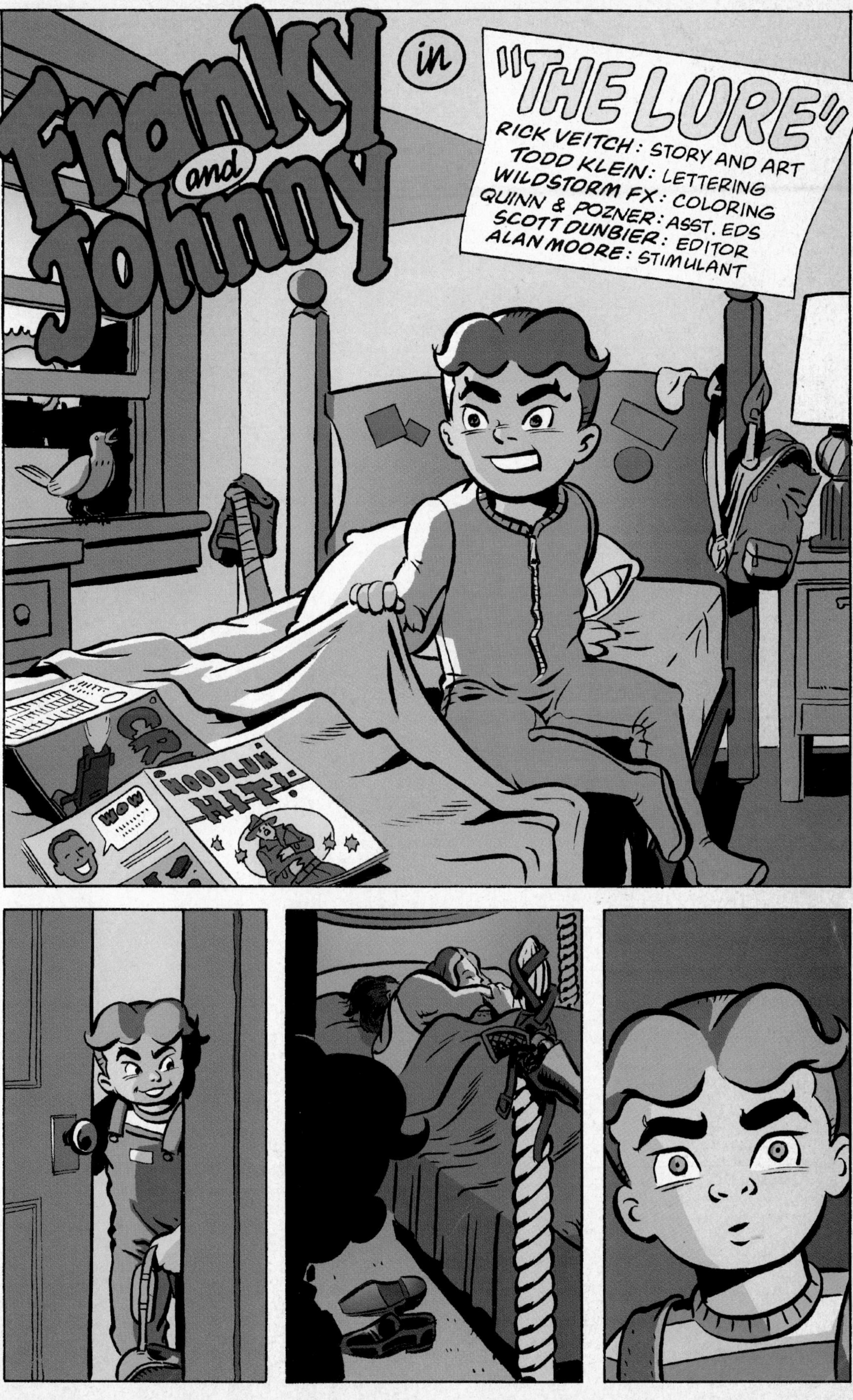
Franky and Johnny in
"THE LURE"
RICK VEITCH: STORY AND ART
TODD KLEIN: LETTERING
WILDSTORM FX: COLORING
QUINN & POZNER: ASST. EDS
SCOTT DUNBIER: EDITOR
ALAN MOORE: STIMULANT
WOW
HOODLUM HIT!

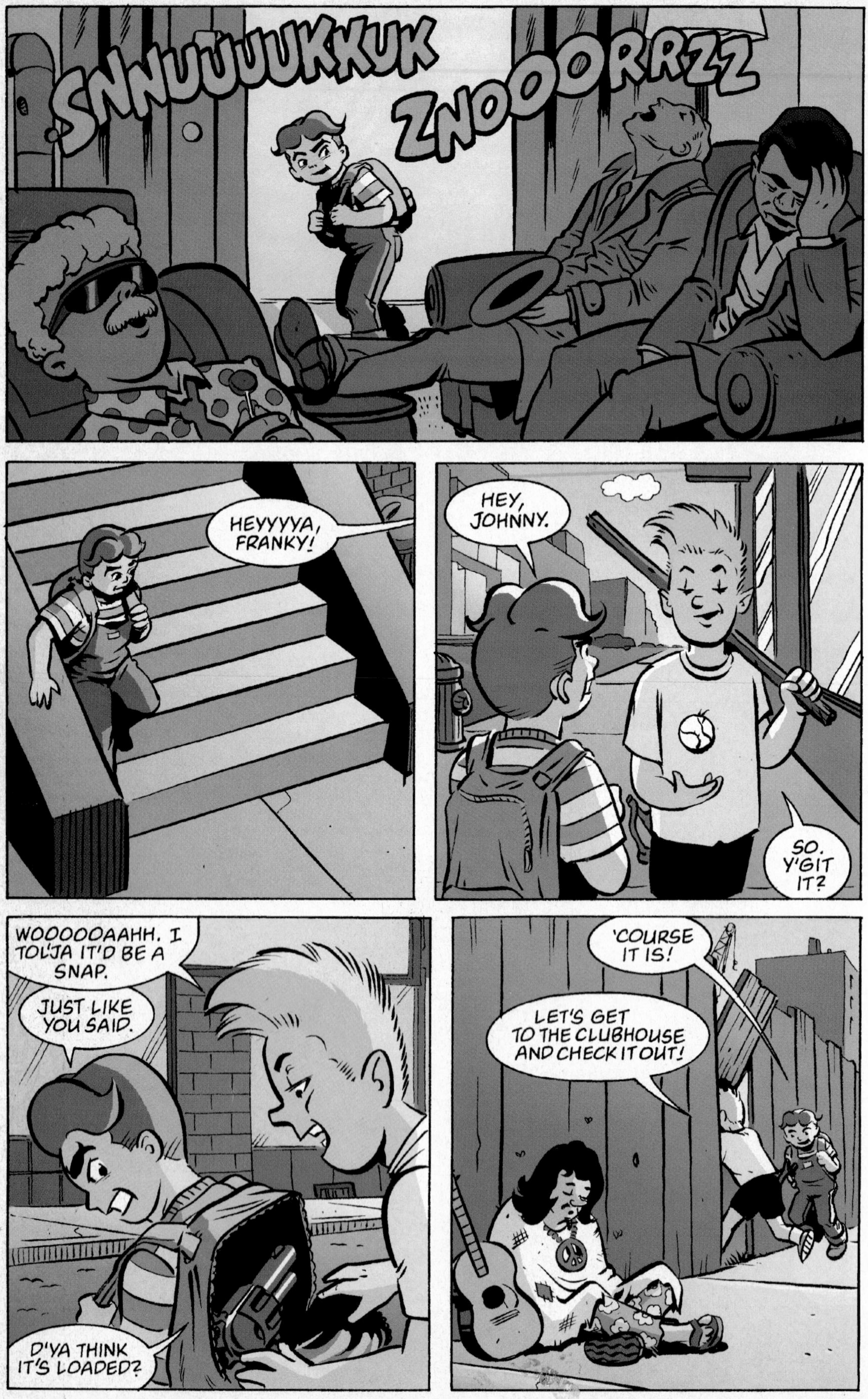
SNNUUUUKKKUK
ZNOOOORRZZ
HEYYYYA, FRANKY!
HEY, JOHNNY.
SO. Y'GIT IT?
WOOOOOAAHH. I TOL'JA IT'D BE A SNAP.
JUST LIKE YOU SAID.
D'YA THINK IT'S LOADED?
'COURSE IT IS!
LET'S GET TO THE CLUBHOUSE AND CHECK IT OUT!

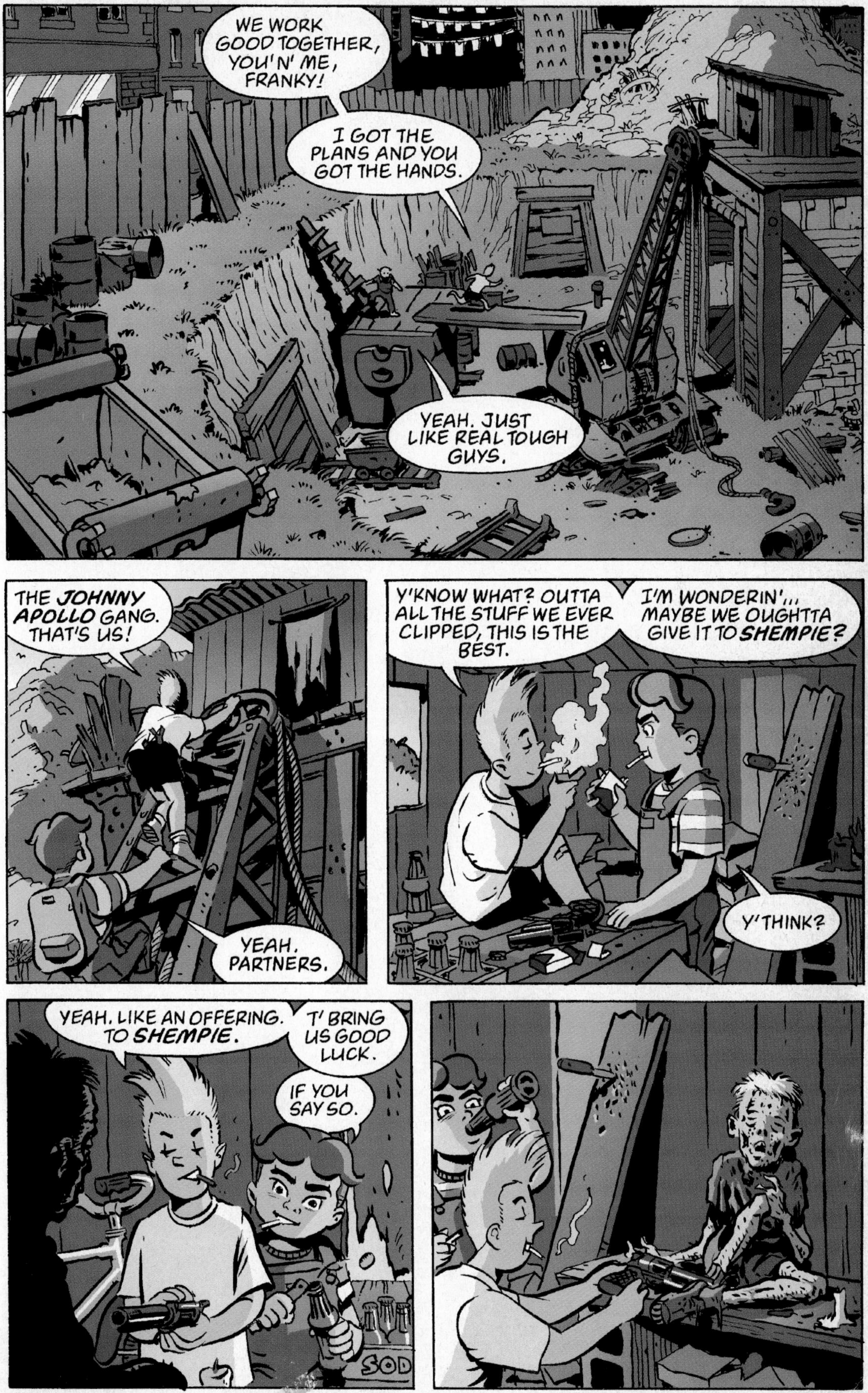
WE WORK GOOD TOGETHER, YOU'N' ME, FRANKY!
I GOT THE PLANS AND YOU GOT THE HANDS.
YEAH. JUST LIKE REAL TOUGH GUYS.
THE JOHNNY APOLLO GANG. THAT'S US!
YEAH. PARTNERS.
Y'KNOW WHAT? OUTTA ALL THE STUFF WE EVER CLIPPED, THIS IS THE BEST.
I'M WONDERIN'... MAYBE WE OUGHTTA GIVE IT TO SHEMPIE?
Y'THINK?
YEAH. LIKE AN OFFERING. TO SHEMPIE.
T' BRING US GOOD LUCK.
IF YOU SAY SO.
SOD

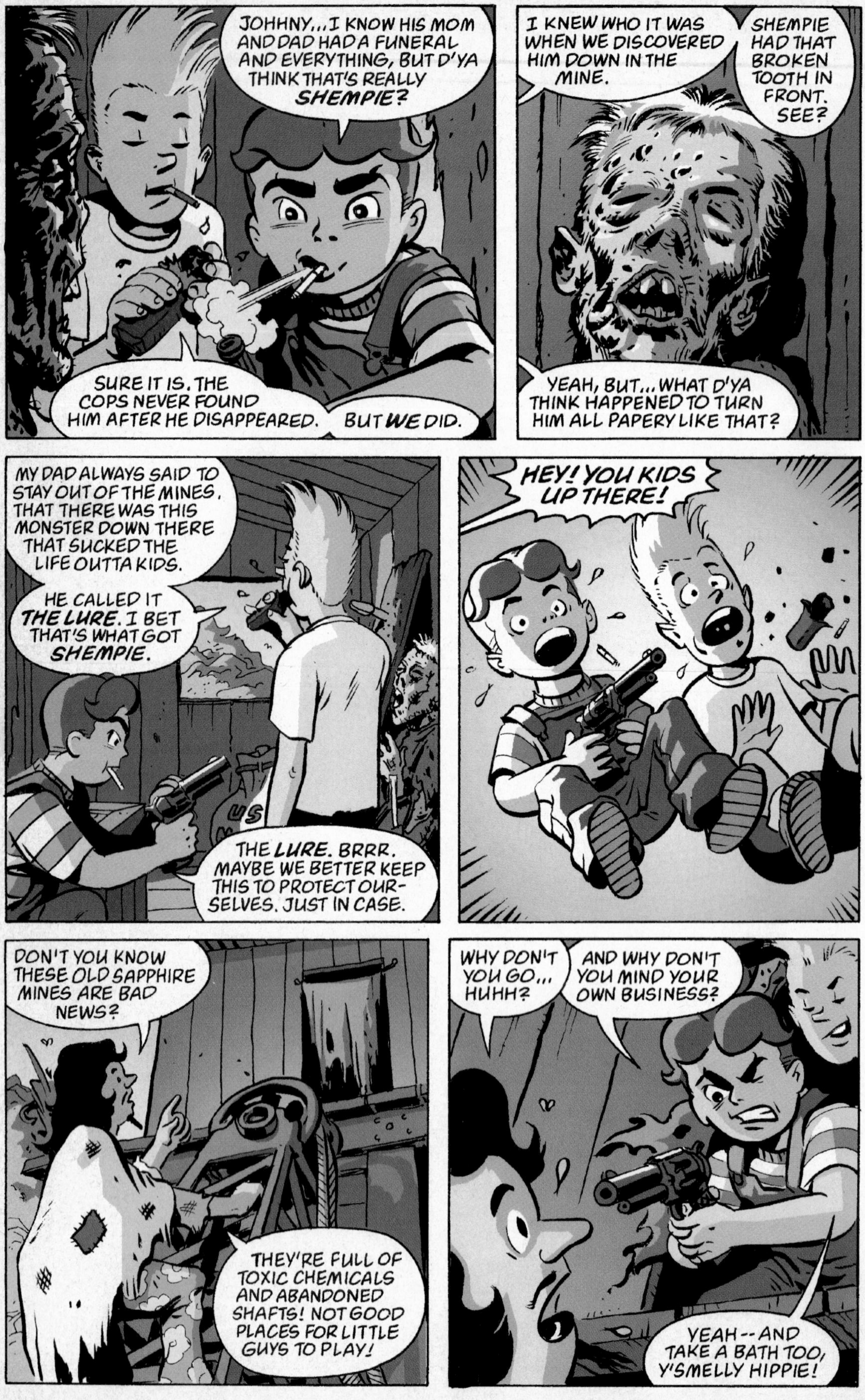
JOHNNY... I KNOW HIS MOM AND DAD HAD A FUNERAL AND EVERYTHING, BUT D'YA THINK THAT'S REALLY SHEMPIE?
SURE IT IS. THE COPS NEVER FOUND HIM AFTER HE DISAPPEARED.
BUT WE DID.
I KNEW WHO IT WAS WHEN WE DISCOVERED HIM DOWN IN THE MINE.
SHEMPIE HAD THAT BROKEN TOOTH IN FRONT. SEE?
YEAH, BUT... WHAT D'YA THINK HAPPENED TO TURN HIM ALL PAPERY LIKE THAT?
MY DAD ALWAYS SAID TO STAY OUT OF THE MINES. THAT THERE WAS THIS MONSTER DOWN THERE THAT SUCKED THE LIFE OUTTA KIDS.
HE CALLED IT THE LURE. I BET THAT'S WHAT GOT SHEMPIE.
THE LURE. BRRR. MAYBE WE BETTER KEEP THIS TO PROTECT OURSELVES. JUST IN CASE.
HEY! YOU KIDS UP THERE!
DON'T YOU KNOW THESE OLD SAPPHIRE MINES ARE BAD NEWS?
THEY'RE FULL OF TOXIC CHEMICALS AND ABANDONED SHAFTS! NOT GOOD PLACES FOR LITTLE GUYS TO PLAY!
WHY DON'T YOU GO... HUHH?
AND WHY DON'T YOU MIND YOUR OWN BUSINESS?
YEAH -- AND TAKE A BATH TOO, Y'SMELLY HIPPIE!

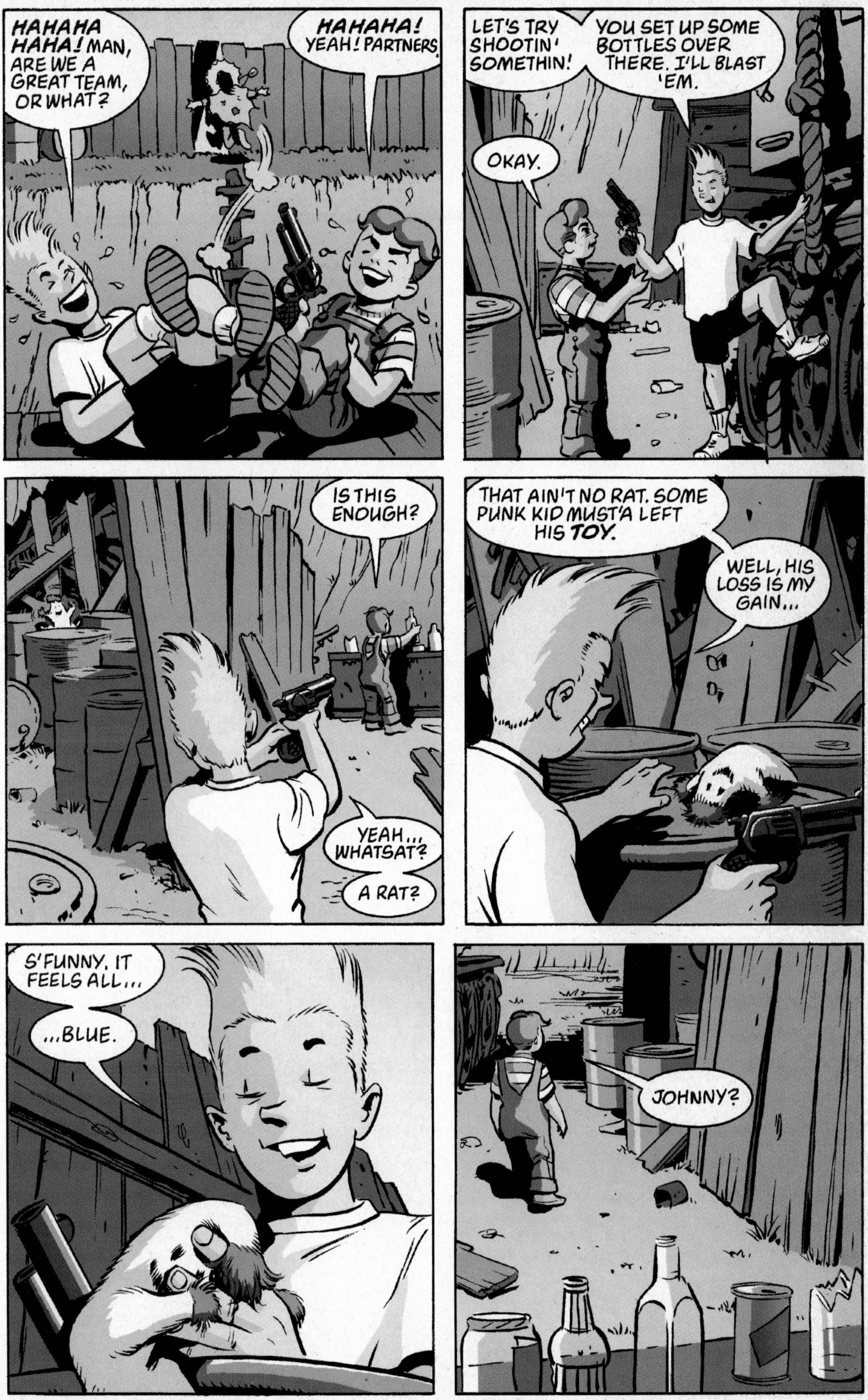
HAHAHA HAHA! MAN, ARE WE A GREAT TEAM, OR WHAT?
HAHAHA! YEAH! PARTNERS!
LET'S TRY SHOOTIN' SOMETHIN!
YOU SET UP SOME BOTTLES OVER THERE. I'LL BLAST 'EM.
OKAY.
IS THIS ENOUGH?
YEAH... WHATSAT?
A RAT?
THAT AIN'T NO RAT. SOME PUNK KID MUST'A LEFT HIS TOY.
WELL, HIS LOSS IS MY GAIN...
S'FUNNY. IT FEELS ALL...
...BLUE.
JOHNNY?

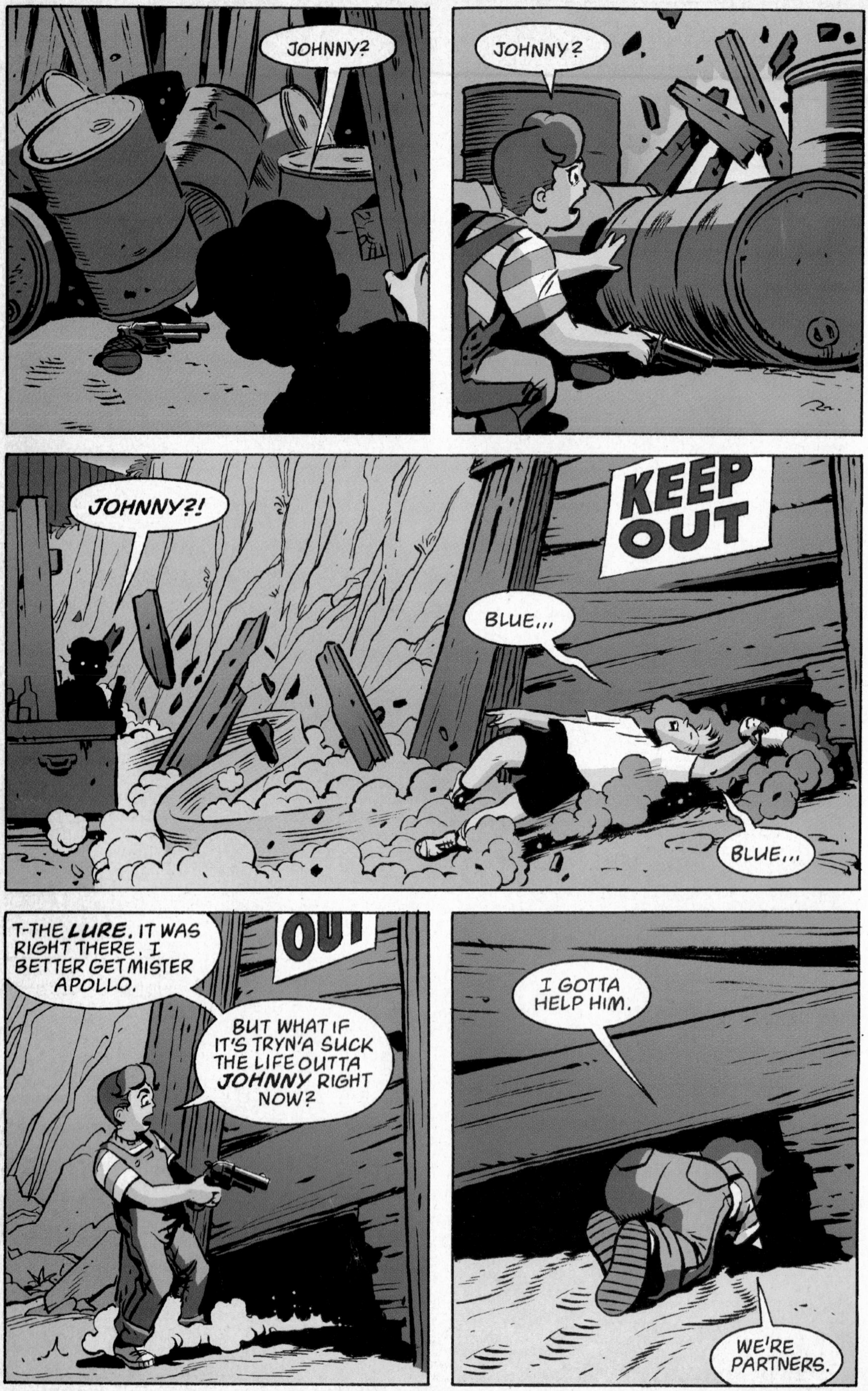
JOHNNY?
JOHNNY?
JOHNNY?!
KEEP OUT
BLUE...
BLUE...
T-THE **LURE**. IT WAS RIGHT THERE. I BETTER GET MISTER APOLLO.
BUT WHAT IF IT'S TRYN'A SUCK THE LIFE OUTTA **JOHNNY** RIGHT NOW?
OUT
I GOTTA HELP HIM.
WE'RE PARTNERS.

AWRIGHT-- WHICH ONE OF YOU DIPSTICKS TOOK MY ROSCOE?

HUNH? WHAT'CHA TALKIN' ABOUT, BOSS?

FRANKY'S GONE, TOO!

HEY, LIPS! THAT KID OF YOURS AND HIS FRIEND JUST PULLED A GUN ON ME OVER AT THE MINE.

CARM-- WE GOTTA FIND HIM!

I'M ON IT. C'MON, BOYS!

FRANKEEEE?! ARE YOU UP THERE?

HERE'S HIS TRACKS, LEADING RIGHT INTO THE MINE.

S'FUNNY. LOOKS LIKE SOME SORT OF BIG SNAKE WAS SLITHERIN' AROUND HERE TOO.

MY OLD MAN USED TO TALK ABOUT THIS SERPENT THING THAT LIVED DOWN IN THE TUNNELS. IT'D DANGLE THIS BAIT AND HYPNOTIZE THE MINERS...

AND SUCK THE LIFE OUT OF 'EM? COME ON--THE LURE'S NOTHIN' BUT AN OLD INDIAN TALE.

NO, IT AIN'T.

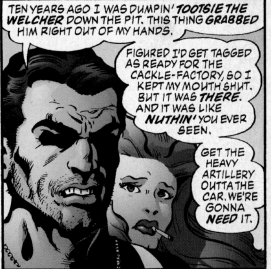

TEN YEARS AGO I WAS DUMPIN' TOOTSIE THE WELCHER DOWN THE PIT. THIS THING GRABBED HIM RIGHT OUT OF MY HANDS.

FIGURED I'D GET TAGGED AS READY FOR THE CACKLE-FACTORY, SO I KEPT MY MOUTH SHUT. BUT IT WAS THERE. AND IT WAS LIKE NUTHIN' YOU EVER SEEN.

GET THE HEAVY ARTILLERY OUTTA THE CAR. WE'RE GONNA NEED IT.

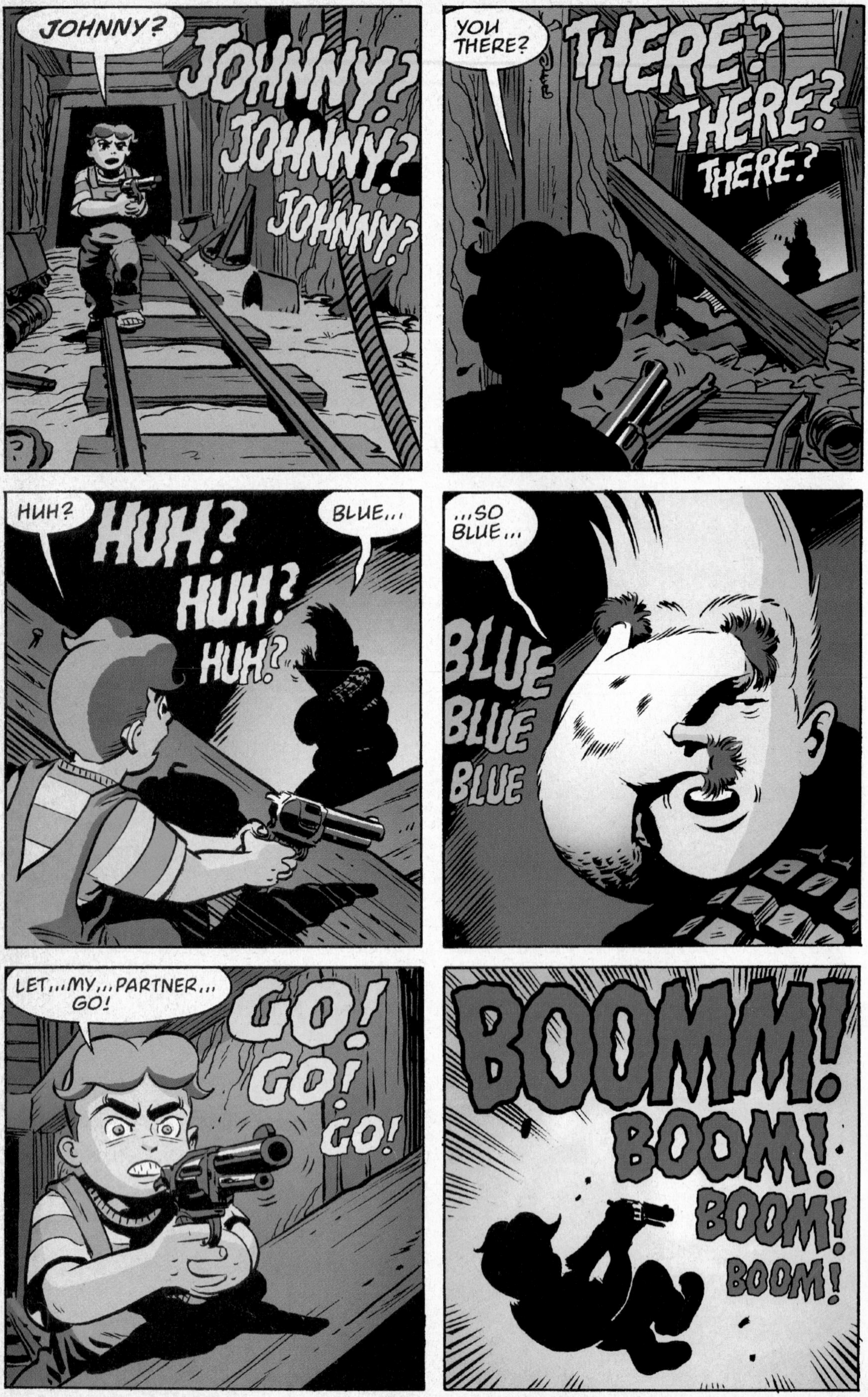
JOHNNY?
JOHNNY? JOHNNY? JOHNNY?
YOU THERE?
THERE? THERE? THERE?
HUH?
HUH? HUH? HUH?
BLUE...
...SO BLUE...
BLUE BLUE BLUE
LET...MY...PARTNER... GO!
GO! GO! GO!
BOOMM! BOOM! BOOM! BOOM!

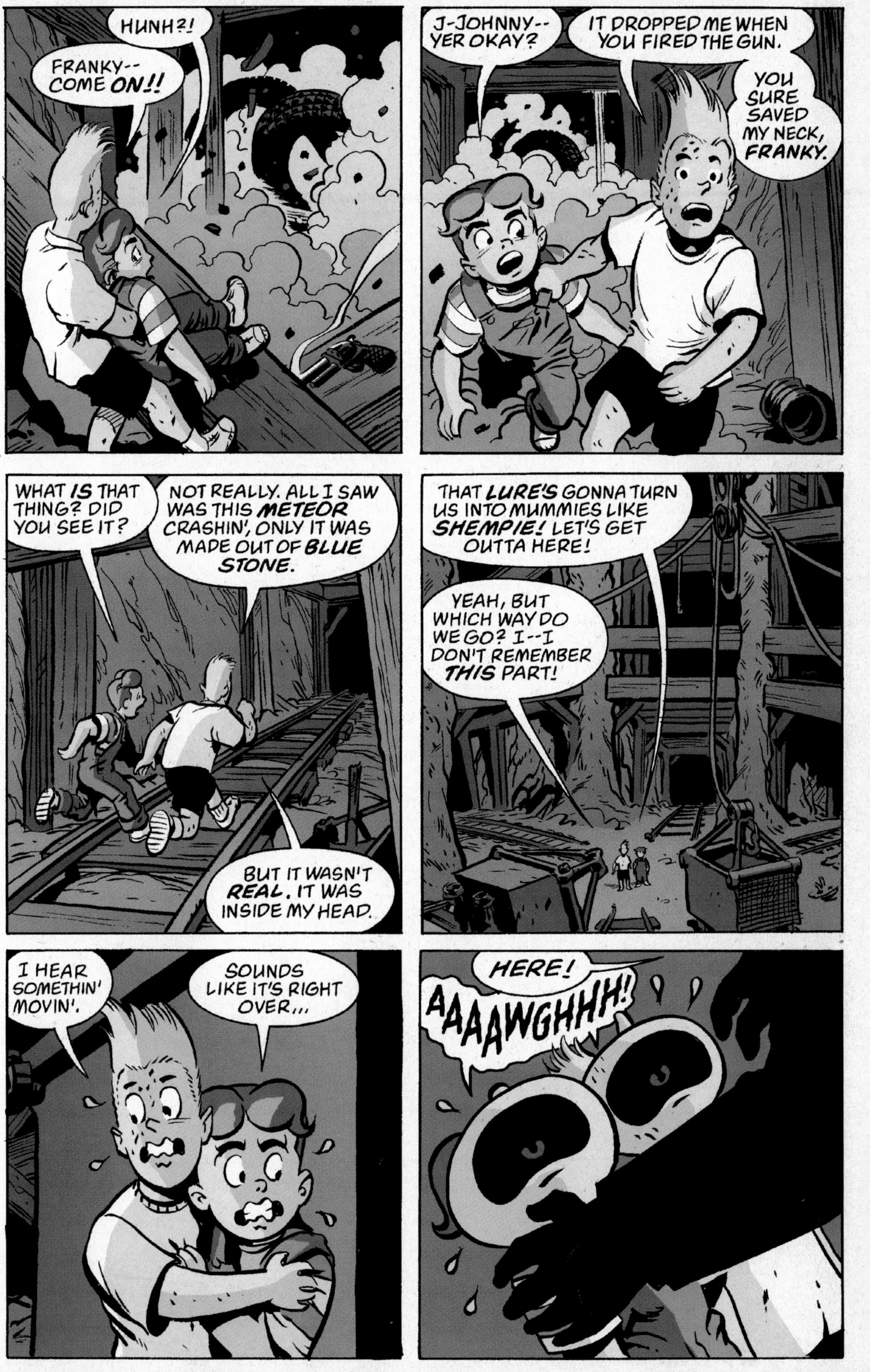

HUNH?!
FRANKY-- COME ON!!
J-JOHNNY-- YER OKAY?
IT DROPPED ME WHEN YOU FIRED THE GUN.
YOU SURE SAVED MY NECK, FRANKY.
WHAT IS THAT THING? DID YOU SEE IT?
NOT REALLY. ALL I SAW WAS THIS METEOR CRASHIN', ONLY IT WAS MADE OUT OF BLUE STONE.
BUT IT WASN'T REAL. IT WAS INSIDE MY HEAD.
THAT LURE'S GONNA TURN US INTO MUMMIES LIKE SHEMPIE! LET'S GET OUTTA HERE!
YEAH, BUT WHICH WAY DO WE GO? I--I DON'T REMEMBER THIS PART!
I HEAR SOMETHIN' MOVIN'.
SOUNDS LIKE IT'S RIGHT OVER...
HERE!
AAAAWGHHH!

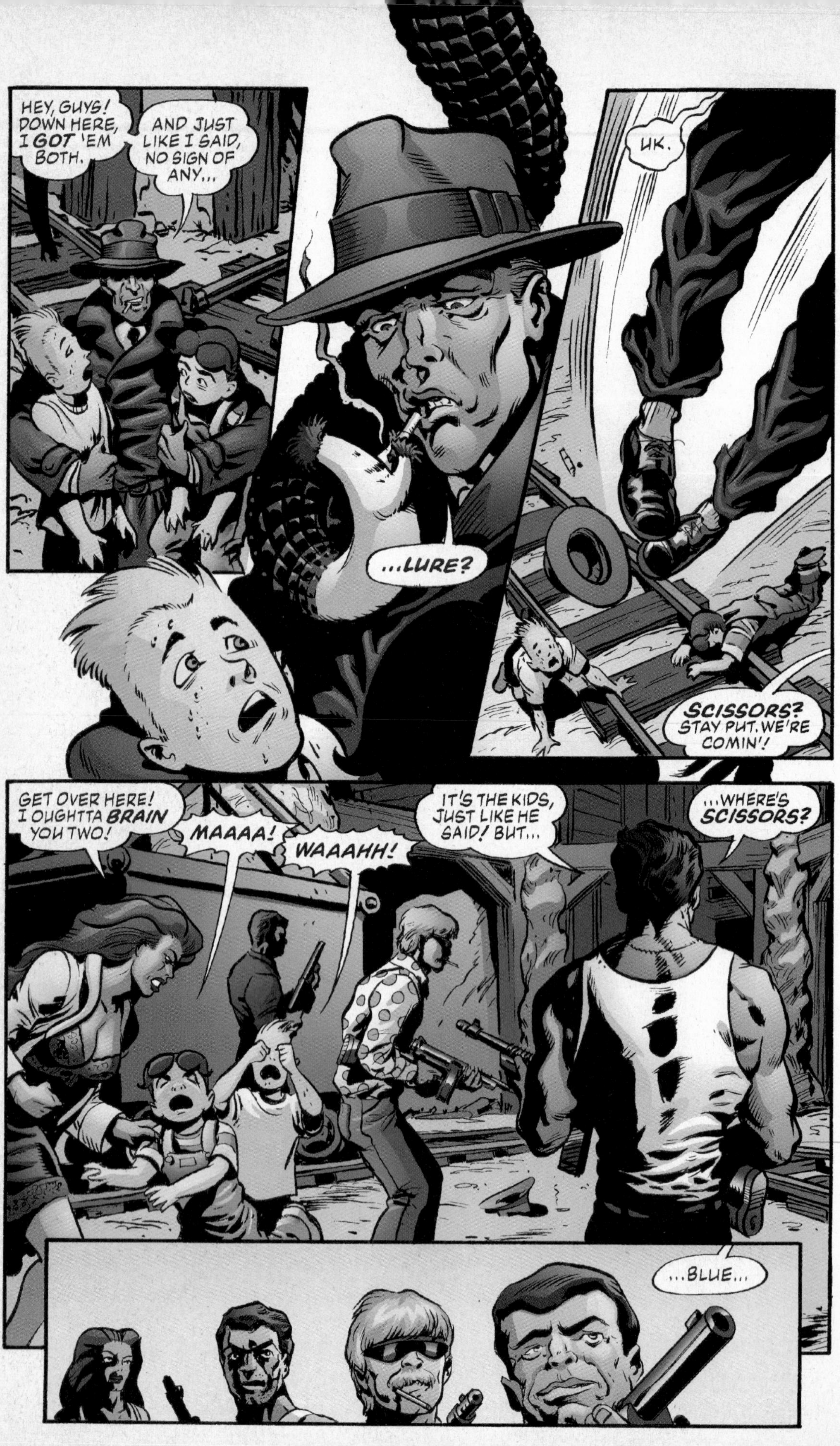
HEY, GUYS! DOWN HERE, I GOT 'EM BOTH.
AND JUST LIKE I SAID, NO SIGN OF ANY...
...LURE?
UK.
SCISSORS? STAY PUT. WE'RE COMIN'!
GET OVER HERE! I OUGHTTA BRAIN YOU TWO!
MAAAA!
WAAAHH!
IT'S THE KIDS, JUST LIKE HE SAID! BUT...
...WHERE'S SCISSORS?
...BLUE...

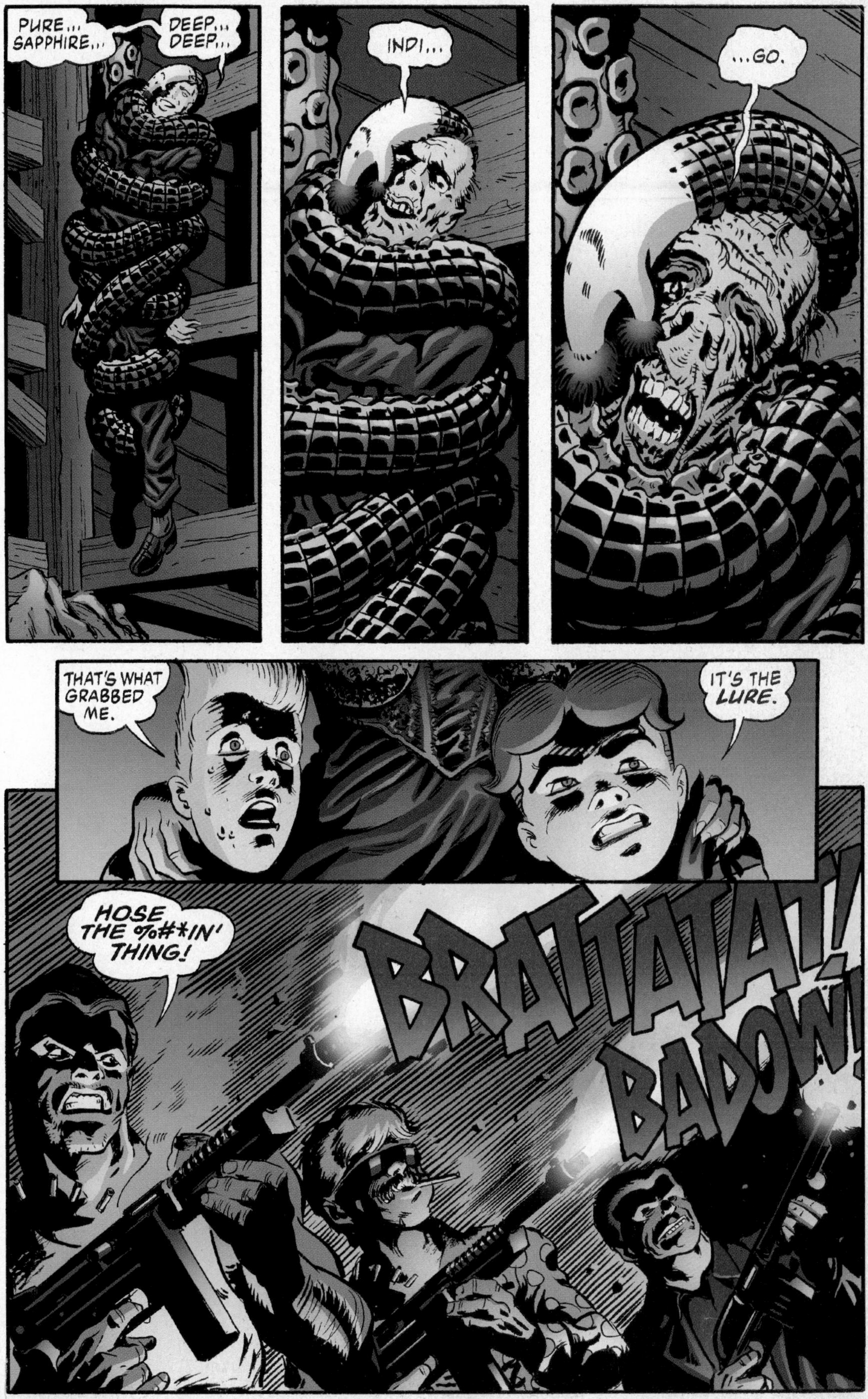
PURE... SAPPHIRE...
DEEP... DEEP...
INDI...
...GO.
THAT'S WHAT GRABBED ME.
IT'S THE LURE.
HOSE THE %#*IN' THING!
BRATTATAT!!
BADOW!!

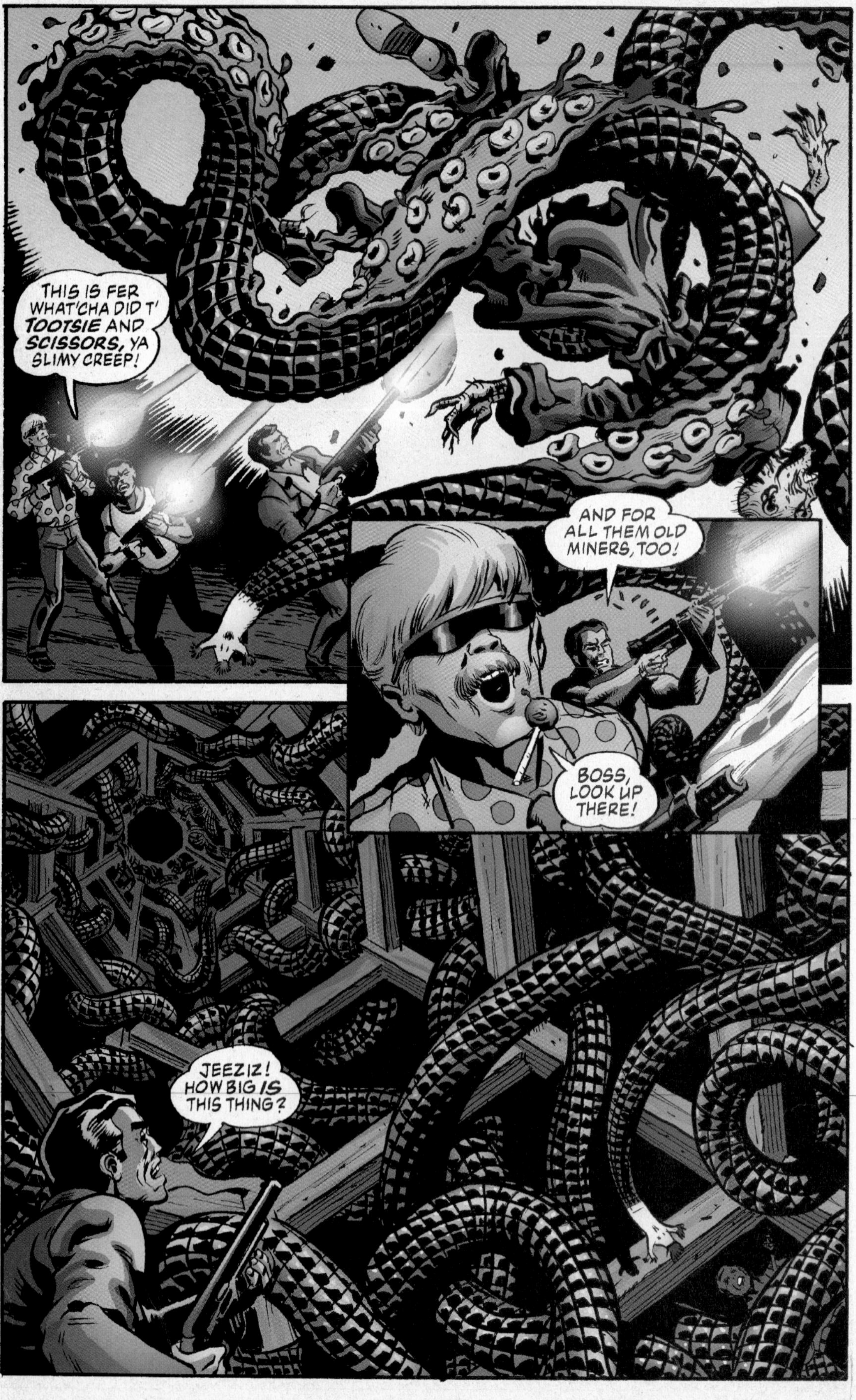
THIS IS FER WHAT'CHA DID T' *TOOTSIE* AND *SCISSORS,* YA SLIMY CREEP!
AND FOR ALL THEM OLD MINERS, TOO!
BOSS, LOOK UP THERE!
JEEZIZ! HOW BIG *IS* THIS THING?

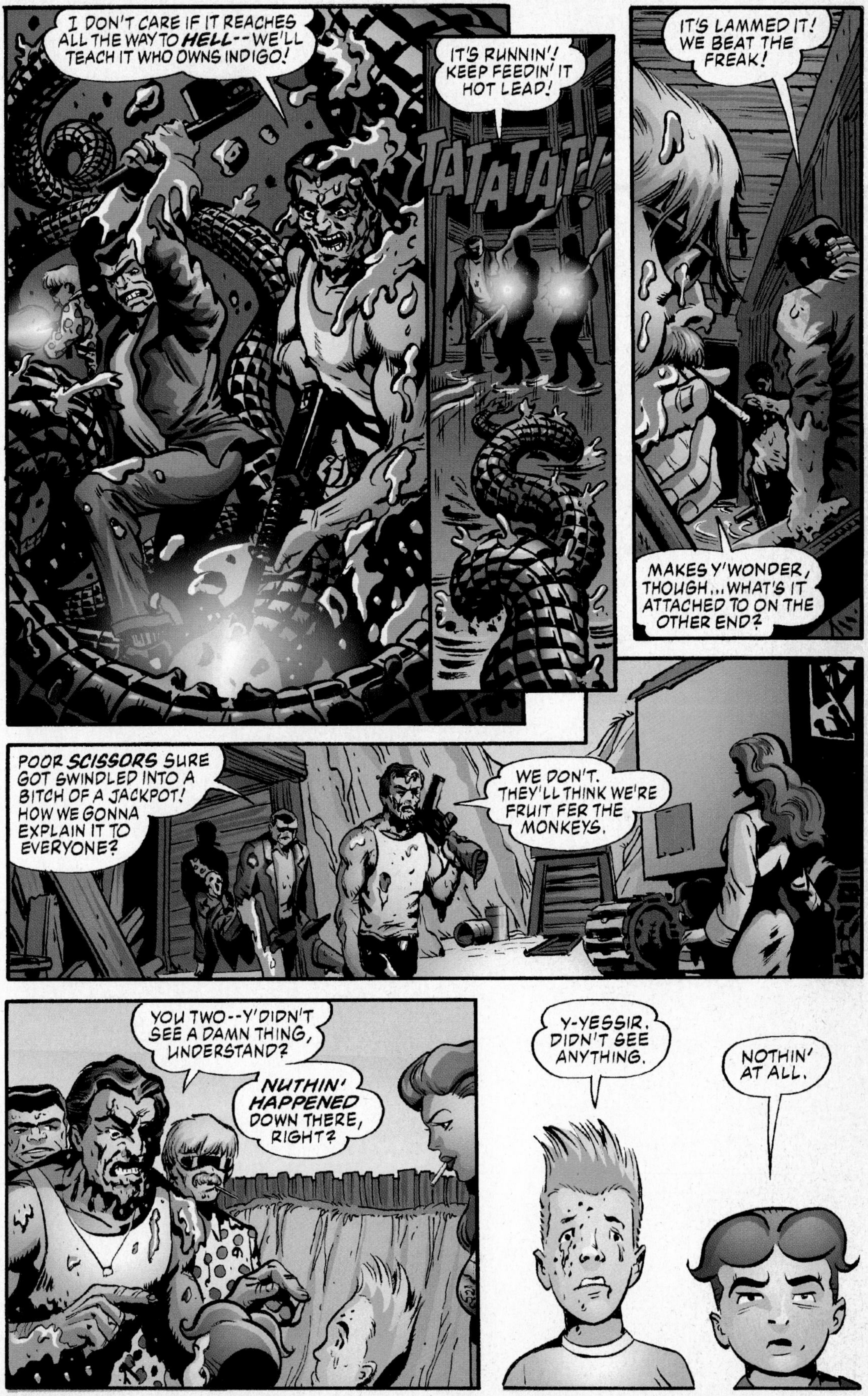
I DON'T CARE IF IT REACHES ALL THE WAY TO HELL--WE'LL TEACH IT WHO OWNS INDIGO!
IT'S RUNNIN'! KEEP FEEDIN' IT HOT LEAD!
TATATAT!
IT'S LAMMED IT! WE BEAT THE FREAK!
MAKES Y'WONDER, THOUGH... WHAT'S IT ATTACHED TO ON THE OTHER END?
POOR SCISSORS SURE GOT SWINDLED INTO A BITCH OF A JACKPOT! HOW WE GONNA EXPLAIN IT TO EVERYONE?
WE DON'T. THEY'LL THINK WE'RE FRUIT FER THE MONKEYS.
YOU TWO--Y'DIDN'T SEE A DAMN THING, UNDERSTAND?
NUTHIN' HAPPENED DOWN THERE, RIGHT?
Y-YESSIR. DIDN'T SEE ANYTHING.
NOTHIN' AT ALL.

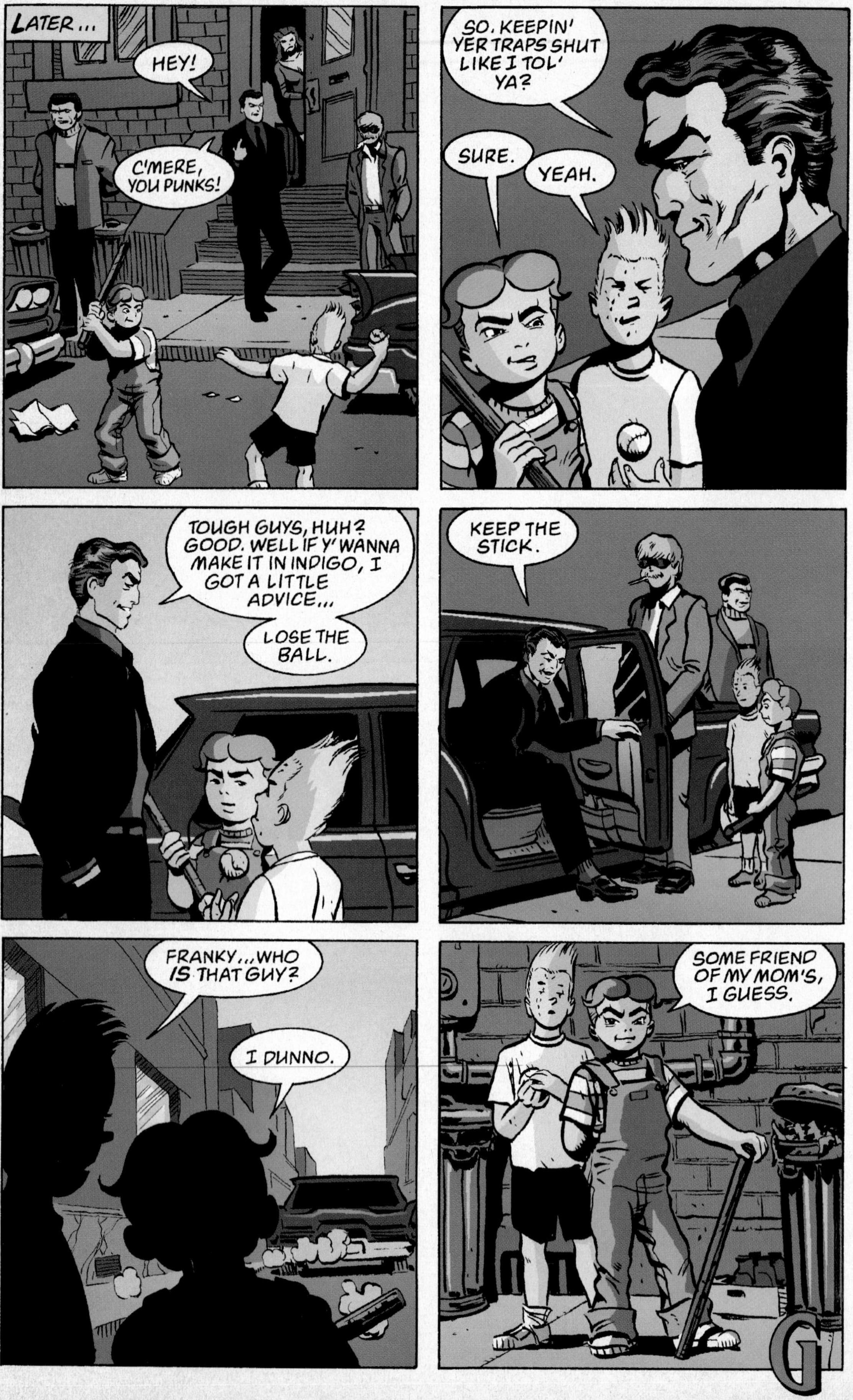
LATER...
HEY!
C'MERE, YOU PUNKS!
SO, KEEPIN' YER TRAPS SHUT LIKE I TOL' YA?
SURE.
YEAH.
TOUGH GUYS, HUH? GOOD. WELL IF Y' WANNA MAKE IT IN INDIGO, I GOT A LITTLE ADVICE...
LOSE THE BALL.
KEEP THE STICK.
FRANKY...WHO IS THAT GUY?
I DUNNO.
SOME FRIEND OF MY MOM'S, I GUESS.
G

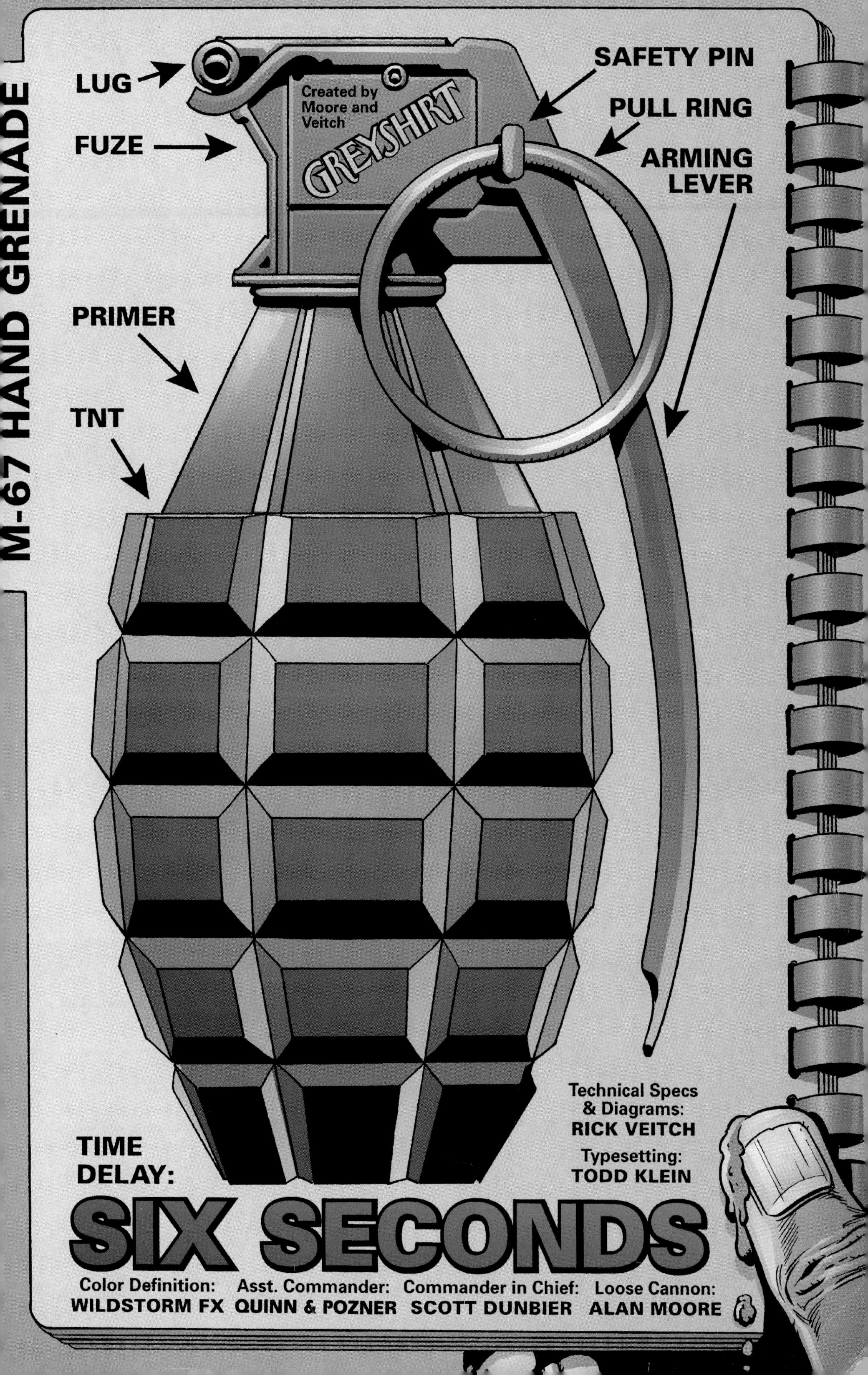

M-67 HAND GRENADE
LUG
FUZE
Created by Moore and Veitch
GREYSHIRT
SAFETY PIN
PULL RING
ARMING LEVER
PRIMER
TNT
TIME DELAY:
SIX SECONDS
Technical Specs & Diagrams: RICK VEITCH
Typesetting: TODD KLEIN
Color Definition: WILDSTORM FX
Asst. Commander: QUINN & POZNER
Commander in Chief: SCOTT DUNBIER
Loose Cannon: ALAN MOORE

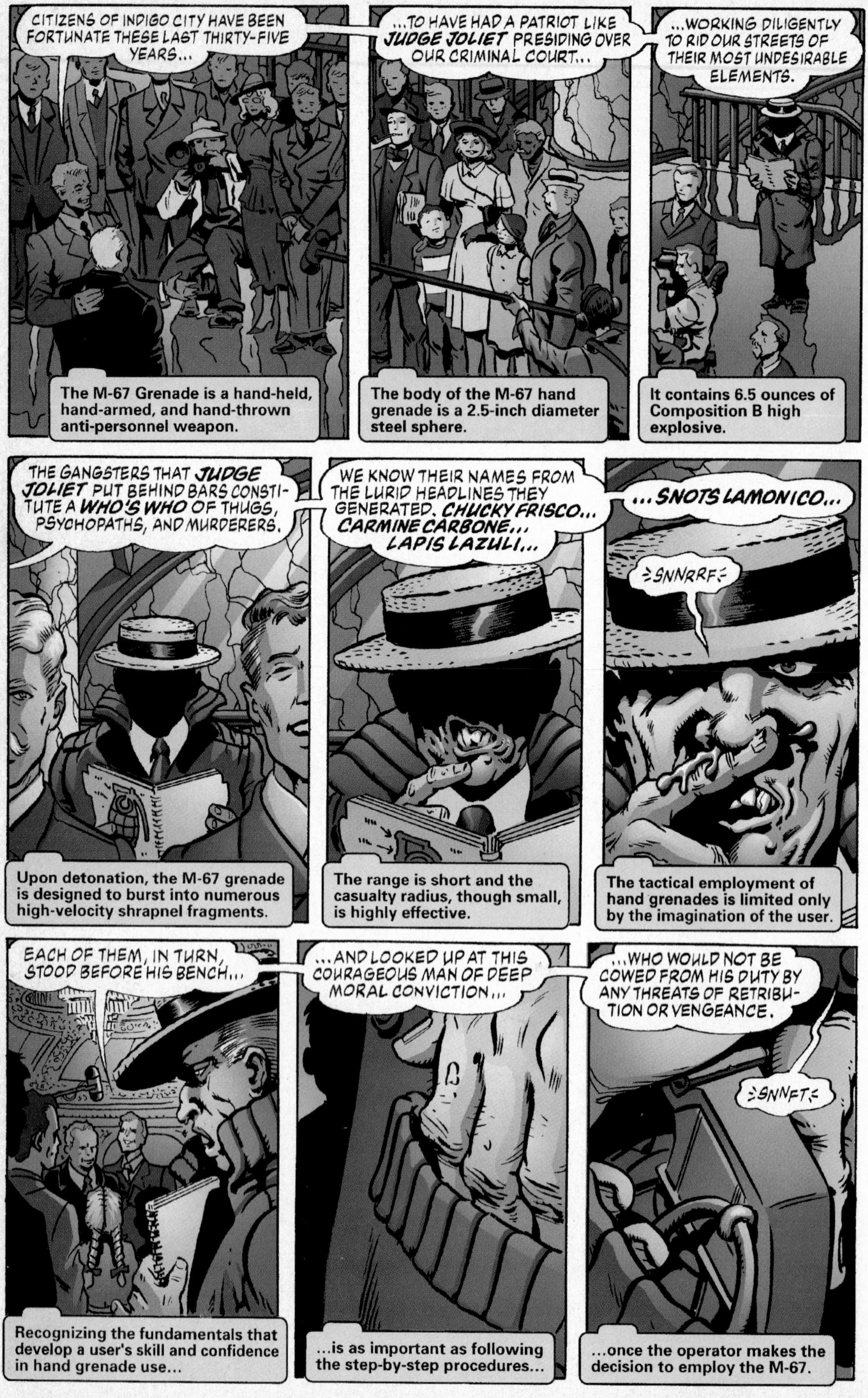
CITIZENS OF INDIGO CITY HAVE BEEN FORTUNATE THESE LAST THIRTY-FIVE YEARS...
...TO HAVE HAD A PATRIOT LIKE JUDGE JOLIET PRESIDING OVER OUR CRIMINAL COURT...
...WORKING DILIGENTLY TO RID OUR STREETS OF THEIR MOST UNDESIRABLE ELEMENTS.
The M-67 Grenade is a hand-held, hand-armed, and hand-thrown anti-personnel weapon.
The body of the M-67 hand grenade is a 2.5-inch diameter steel sphere.
It contains 6.5 ounces of Composition B high explosive.
THE GANGSTERS THAT JUDGE JOLIET PUT BEHIND BARS CONSTITUTE A WHO'S WHO OF THUGS, PSYCHOPATHS, AND MURDERERS.
WE KNOW THEIR NAMES FROM THE LURID HEADLINES THEY GENERATED. CHUCKY FRISCO... CARMINE CARBONE... LAPIS LAZULI...
...SNOTS LAMONICO...
SNNRRF
Upon detonation, the M-67 grenade is designed to burst into numerous high-velocity shrapnel fragments.
The range is short and the casualty radius, though small, is highly effective.
The tactical employment of hand grenades is limited only by the imagination of the user.
EACH OF THEM, IN TURN, STOOD BEFORE HIS BENCH...
...AND LOOKED UP AT THIS COURAGEOUS MAN OF DEEP MORAL CONVICTION...
...WHO WOULD NOT BE COWED FROM HIS DUTY BY ANY THREATS OF RETRIBUTION OR VENGEANCE.
SNNFT
Recognizing the fundamentals that develop a user's skill and confidence in hand grenade use...
...is as important as following the step-by-step procedures...
...once the operator makes the decision to employ the M-67.

JUDGE JOLIET, AS MAYOR OF INDIGO CITY, I'D LIKE TO TAKE THIS OPPORTUNITY...

Grip the M-67 grenade in your throwing hand.

...TO EXPRESS THE SINCERE GRATITUDE FELT BY ALL INDIGOIANS...

Observe the target to mentally establish the distance between your position and the target area.

...AND TO SHOW OUR DEEP APPRECIATION FOR ALL YOUR WISE AND EXTRAORDINARY EFFORTS...

≤SNNF.≥

The user should locate a protected area to minimize his own exposure to the effects of the M-67.

...AND EXEMPLARY LIFE OF CIVIC DUTY,,,

Grasp the pull ring with the index or middle finger of your non-throwing hand.

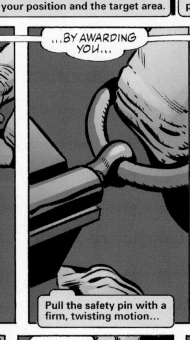

...BY AWARDING YOU...

Pull the safety pin with a firm, twisting motion...

...THE HIGHEST HONOR...

...until it separates from the fuze mechanism.

...WE CAN BESTOW.

≤SNNIFF.≥

Using the proper grip...

PLEASE ACCEPT...

...raise the fuze lever.

...THE SAPPHIRE CITIZEN AWARD.

The M-67 is now fully armed...

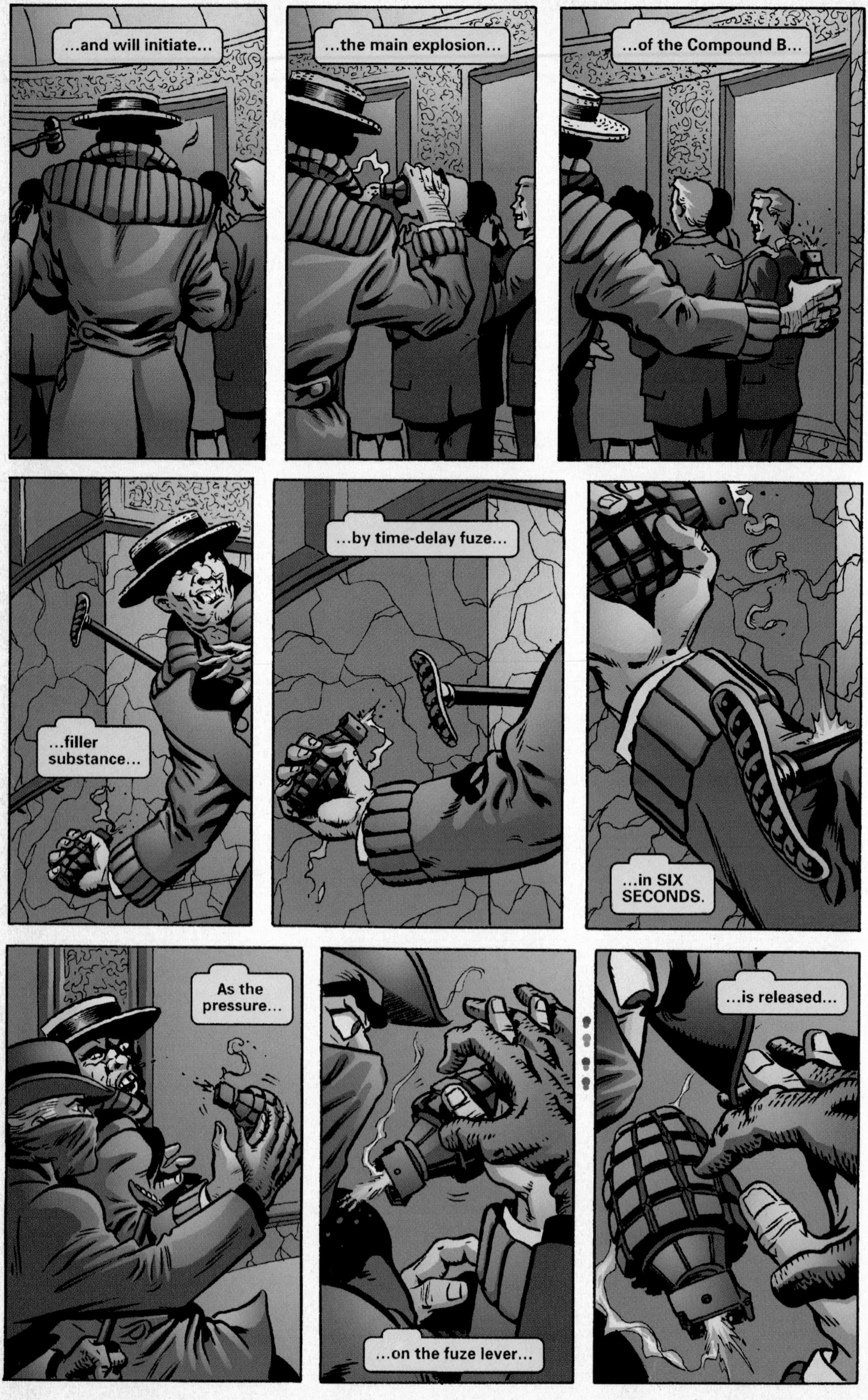
...and will initiate...
...the main explosion...
...of the Compound B...
...filler substance...
...by time-delay fuze...
...in SIX SECONDS.
As the pressure...
...on the fuze lever...
...is released...

...the striker...

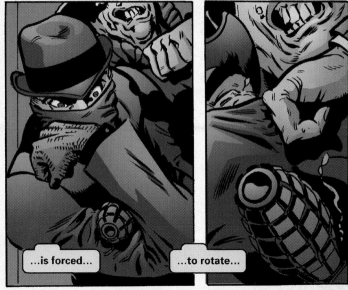

...is forced...

...to rotate...

...on its axis...

...detonating...

...the primer...

...which in turn...

...ignites...

...the time delay mechanism.

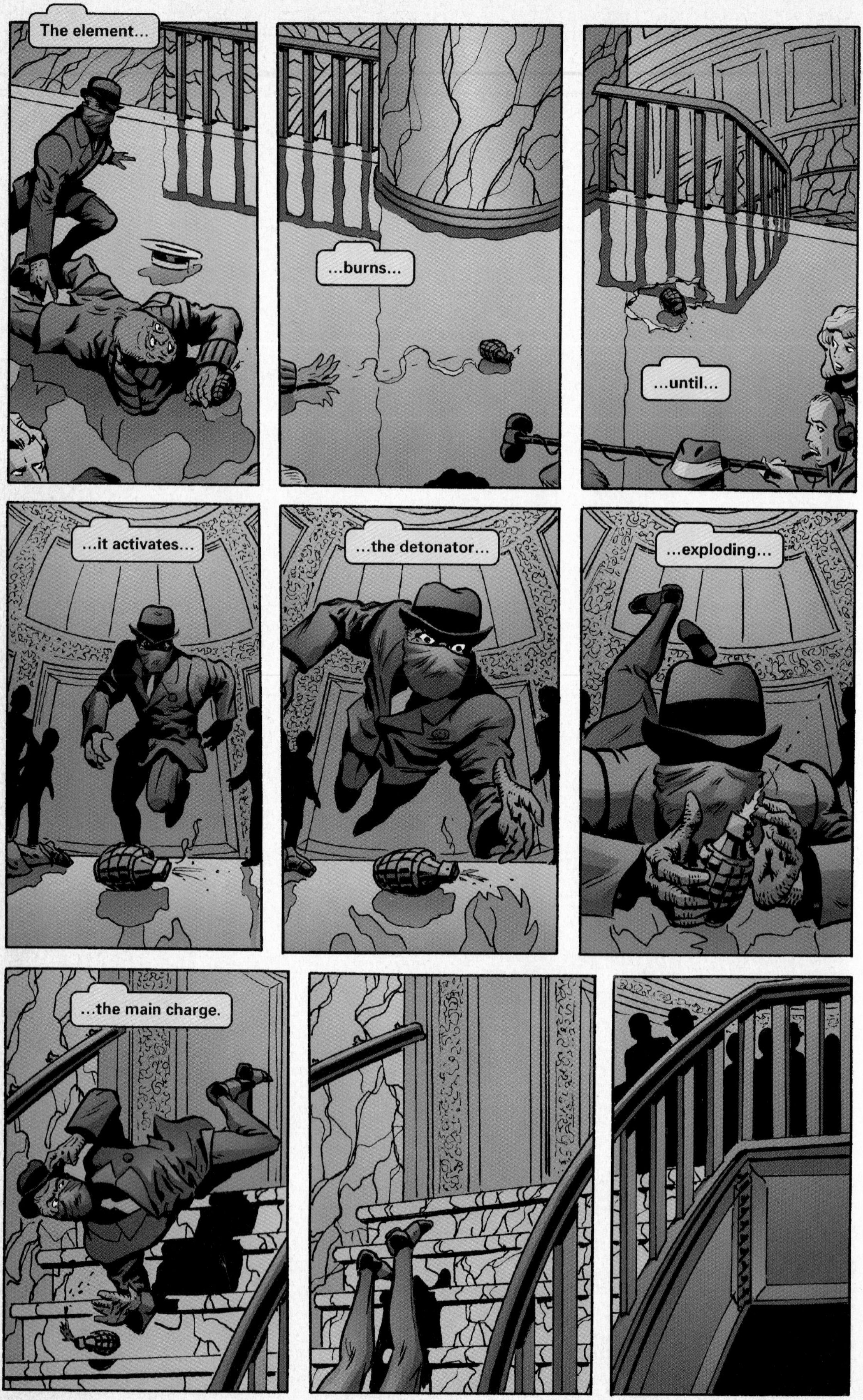

The element...
...burns...
...until...
...it activates...
...the detonator...
...exploding...
...the main charge.

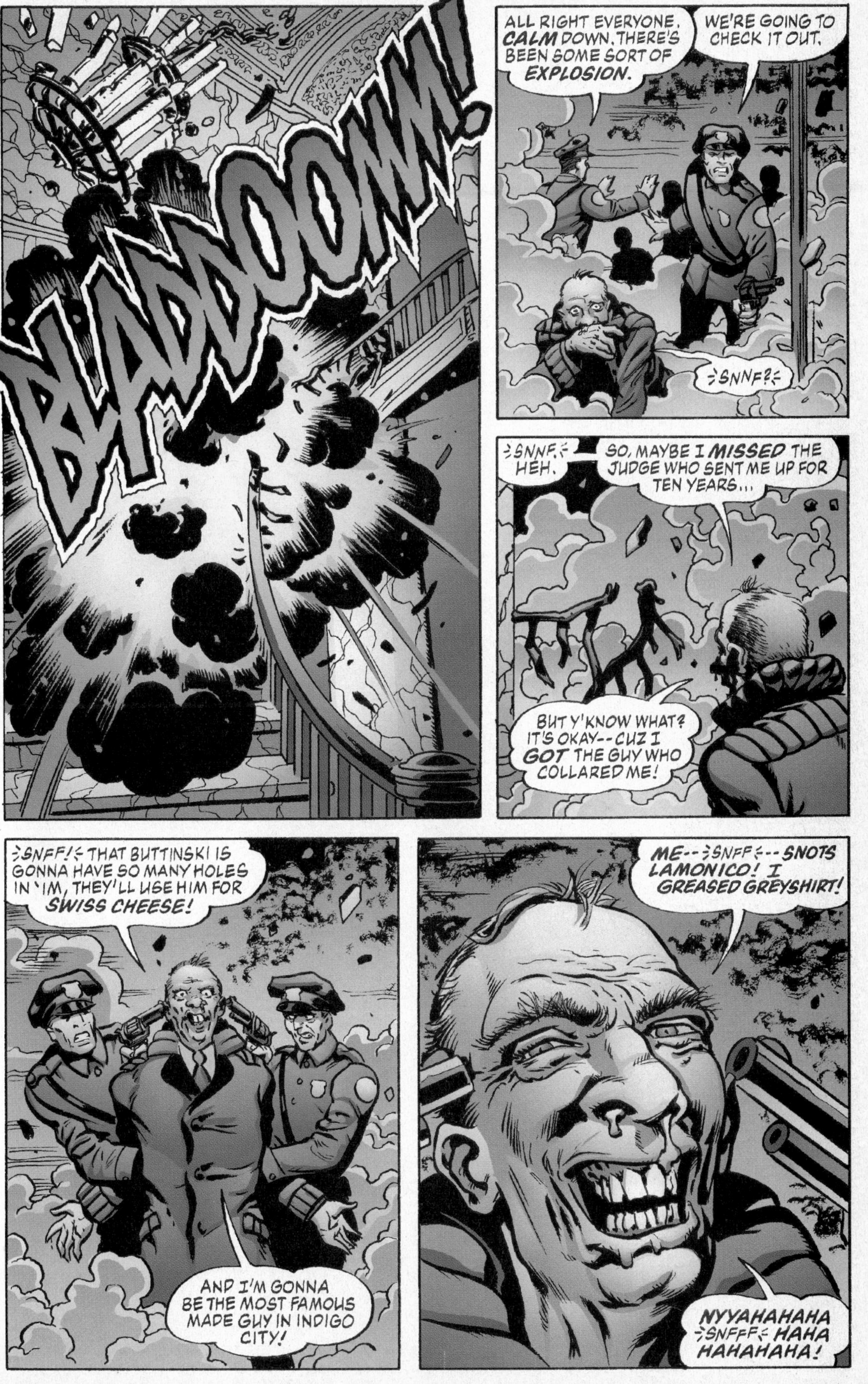
BLADDOOMM!
ALL RIGHT EVERYONE. CALM DOWN. THERE'S BEEN SOME SORT OF EXPLOSION.
WE'RE GOING TO CHECK IT OUT.
SNNF?
SNNF. HEH.
SO, MAYBE I MISSED THE JUDGE WHO SENT ME UP FOR TEN YEARS...
BUT Y'KNOW WHAT? IT'S OKAY--CUZ I GOT THE GUY WHO COLLARED ME!
SNFF! THAT BUTTINSKI IS GONNA HAVE SO MANY HOLES IN 'IM, THEY'LL USE HIM FOR SWISS CHEESE!
AND I'M GONNA BE THE MOST FAMOUS MADE GUY IN INDIGO CITY!
ME--SNFF--SNOTS LAMONICO! I GREASED GREYSHIRT!
NYYAHAHAHA SNFFF HAHA HAHAHAHA!

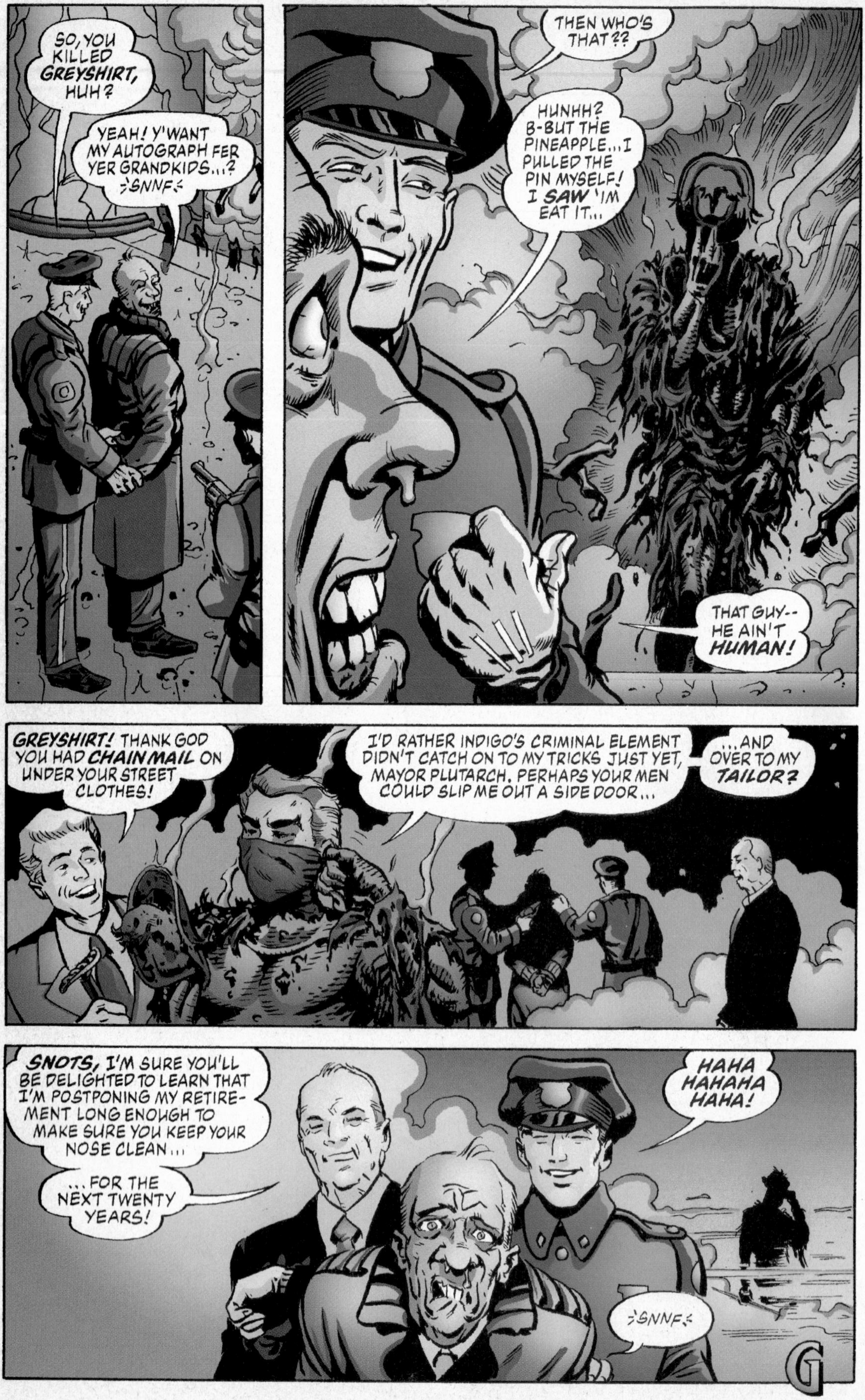
SO, YOU KILLED GREYSHIRT, HUH?
YEAH! Y'WANT MY AUTOGRAPH FER YER GRANDKIDS...? ⩥SNNF⩤
THEN WHO'S THAT??
HUNHH? B-BUT THE PINEAPPLE... I PULLED THE PIN MYSELF! I SAW 'IM EAT IT...
THAT GUY-- HE AIN'T HUMAN!
GREYSHIRT! THANK GOD YOU HAD CHAIN MAIL ON UNDER YOUR STREET CLOTHES!
I'D RATHER INDIGO'S CRIMINAL ELEMENT DIDN'T CATCH ON TO MY TRICKS JUST YET, MAYOR PLUTARCH. PERHAPS YOUR MEN COULD SLIP ME OUT A SIDE DOOR...
...AND OVER TO MY TAILOR?
SNOTS, I'M SURE YOU'LL BE DELIGHTED TO LEARN THAT I'M POSTPONING MY RETIREMENT LONG ENOUGH TO MAKE SURE YOU KEEP YOUR NOSE CLEAN...
...FOR THE NEXT TWENTY YEARS!
HAHA HAHAHA HAHA!
⩥SNNF⩤

ALL THE NEWS FROM DAWN TO DUSK

STILL ONLY 50¢

INDIGO CITY SUNSET

AFTERNOON CITY EDITION

Wednesday, October 17, 2001 — Metro Weather – Today: Fog, Tonight: Heavy Fog, Tomorrow: Foggy

MOM'S LAMENT:

THE LURE TOOK MY BABY!

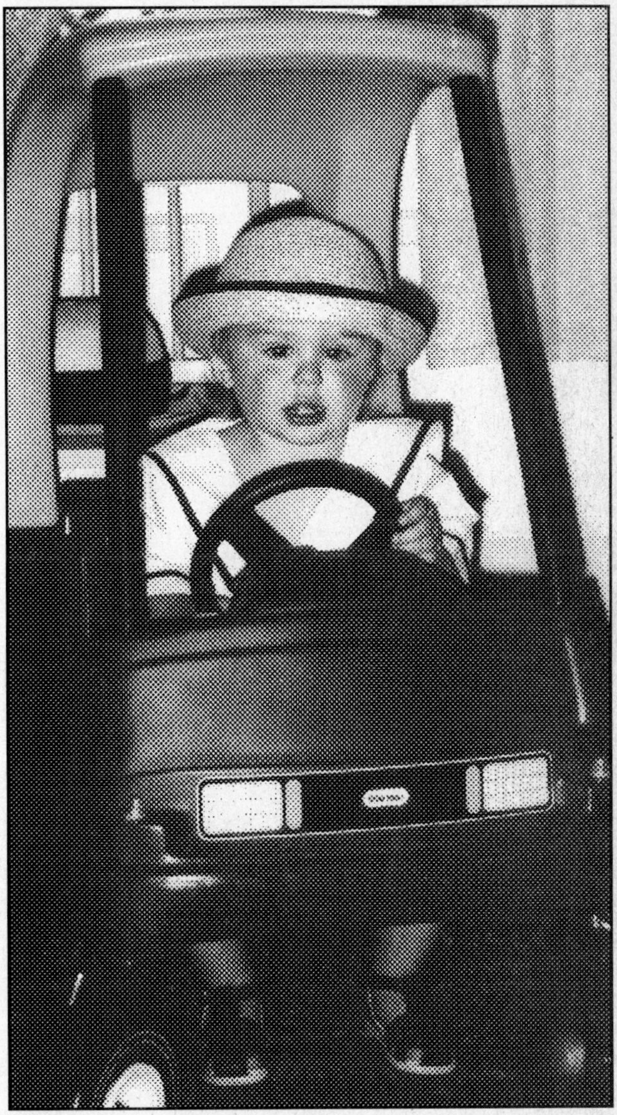

Indigo City: Rescue workers searched through the night after a distraught mother called 911 and reported her toddler missing in the vicinity of the old #11 mine in the Bottoms Up district. Like many of the abandoned mines in the city, the site's long history of tragedy has led to renewed fears that a monster inhabits the warrens of mine shafts sunk beneath Indigo.

FULL COVERAGE: Pages 2 and 3

INSIDE: Gangster Guide to Indigo City's most notorious Rogues!

BOTTOMS UP MINE TRAGEDY

"...I TURNED SHE WAS GONE!"

**EXCLUSIVE TO THE SUNSET
BY GEEKUS CROW**

Indigo City's randy old Bottoms Up district was the scene of intense activity last night as yet another child vanished near the abandoned #11 mine. Stephanie Rotunda, 3 years old, was the fourth youngster in as many months to disappear without a trace near one of the hundreds of abandoned mining sites that perforate the city.

Fire Chief Matthew L'Estrange told reporters that the search would continue through today, but held out little hope that the missing child would be found. "Those damn mines are full of drop-offs and cave-ins. And if they don't getcha', then the gas pockets will.

Some kid wanders down there and its like looking for an aphid in an anthill."

The girl's mother, an unemployed street person, Roxanne Rotunda, said she had taken the child into the fenced-off mine site in a search for empty deposit bottles. "Sometimes the older kids sneak in and drink the soda pop they've stolen from the Whiz-Chek. I turned my back for only a second and then I heard her giggle and whisper somethin' like 'blue.' When I turned around my little girl was gone!"

Mayor Plato Plutarch, responding to renewed criticism that the city hasn't moved quickly enough to safeguard the decaying mine sites, reminded reporters of the immensity of the problem. "When Indigo's economy was being built on sapphires and natural gas, the city was erected right over the mines themselves! We're talking

tens of thousands of decrepit shafts, most of them sunk before there were even historical records. The rest are tied up in claims and deeds that date back to before the Civil War."

The Mayor made it clear that the city has strict ordinances mandating that the sites be fenced off and barriers erected at the mouths of the shafts themselves, but expressed frustration with citizens who ignore the danger and penetrate the barricades. "The bottom line is any palisade can be breached by someone intent on getting through it. If a parent is crazy enough to drag their kid into a sealed-off and abandoned mining site, whose fault is that?"

The City Council will no doubt debate whether new restrictions should be in order when it meets next week. Meanwhile the search for little Stephie goes on at old mine #11.

SCIENTIST POO-POOS "THE LURE" AS

Says study of Indigo's archaeological past proves monster can't exist

Casper Chamberry, who heads up the Archaeology Department at Indigo City University, reacts to questions about The Lure with a hearty belly-laugh. Chamberry, who has been studying the underlying geological strata of the whole Crater Bay area for forty years, says The Lure is "nothing

but an old wives' tale!"

He points to the well-documented scientific evidence concerning the creation of the area's geology 20 million years ago when a rogue asteroid consisting of pure sapphire collided with the Earth, creating a huge impact crater that would ultimately fill with seawater and become Crater Bay.

"The impact of this asteroid, which was probably the size of a modern aircraft carrier, would have caused a massive explosion and filled the atmosphere with a tremendous amount of debris," says Chamberry. "Without question an impact of this magnitude

would have killed all life for thousands of miles in each direction. And the fossil record rules out any unknown species of dinosaur somehow surviving down there for 20 million years."

But what really makes it an open and shut case is what the air is like down in the deepest parts of the tunnels. "As every Indigoan knows when they turn on their lights or start their cars, our area is naturally blessed with rich methane deposits," says Chamberry. "With our drillers blasting to find new deposits and pump fresh energy to Indigo, some of that methane escapes and settles into the bottom sections of

BOTTOMS UP MINE TRAGEDY

MY BACK AND

Frantic searchers find no trace of missing child

OLD WIVES TALE

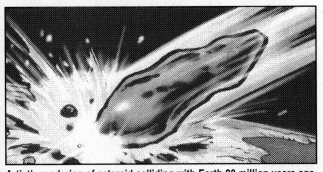

Artist's rendering of asteroid colliding with Earth 20 million years ago.

the old mines, creating an atmosphere no warm or cold blooded oxygen-breathing animal could survive. If somehow there was such a thing as The Lure, even as late as a few hundred years ago, it would have been driven out as the methane took over, just as our mining crews had to abandon their hunt for sapphire."

Fears of Monster under Indigo re-surface with latest disappearance

Neighbors in the Bottoms Up district talk of another danger associated with the mine that the city has long refused to recognize. Whenever someone goes missing, there is inevitably fearful whispering about "The Lure," a monstrous creature which many citizens of Indigo are ready to swear lives in the crumbling shafts.

Cranford Shaugnessy, at 104 the oldest resident of Bottoms Up, tells The Sunset, "Oh, they know it's down there. They just can't say so because it would cause a panic in the streets." Crawford, who is old enough to remember when many of the mines were still bustling with activity said, "The Lure has been picking off miners and kids since I was a boy, and my parents told me it had been around as long as they and their parents could remember. They say it's this big old octopus thing with a little ding-a-ling on the end. It'd catch an old-timer's attention with the tip, then hypnotize 'em and drain 'em dry!"

The myth appears to have started with Native American tribal beliefs in the Crater Bay area. Local Indians were known to leave offerings of deer and buffalo to appease a snake-god called Kwani-tuk, who they believed reached to the center of the earth. When the extensive sapphire deposits around the bay were discovered by early European settlers, full-scale mining began, and stories of a monster that sucked the life out of unwitting miners became part of the lore of the young Indigo City.

Since then, parents have frightened their children with stories about The Lure, who is said to snatch children who go near the mines. Generations of parents have used the technique to traumatize their kids into avoiding the dangerous mine shafts, and the process has led to a deeply held belief that The Lure exists and is waiting to drag victims down into the beehive of tunnels beneath the city.

While no photos or physical evidence have ever been produced, many point to serpentine tracks that can be seen leading into some of the old mine openings. The idea that these tracks have been left by a monstrous snake is "absurd," says Indigo City Historian Wesley Scott. "Hydraulics were used extensively in mining operations all through this century. The tracks were in fact dug by miners dragging their heavy hoses down into the mines."

PRESSROOM SHOWDOWN

Morning Edition delayed as Greyshirt corners wife-beater at Sunset Printing Plant

The mighty chattering presses of the INDIGO CITY SUNSET fell silent early this morning in the wake of a violent struggle between authorities and Pressman third class Clem "Coppernob" Grockle. The incident began when Greyshirt arrived at the Sunset plant with two officers of the Indigo City Police and a warrant for Grockle's arrest. Grockle's wife had charged her 6-foot 8-inch husband with assault after she was brought to the Indigo City Hospital by ambulance last night, suffering from injuries received after repeated blows to the head.

Witnesses at the plant said that when Greyshirt and the police attempted to take Grockle into custody, the Pressman flew into a rage and attacked the group with a heavy wrench, succeeding in putting both officers out of commission before they could even draw

their weapons. Greyshirt struggled with Grockle, but was no match for the Pressman's great strength, which seemed fueled by a rage that was beyond control.

The Indigo Avenger appeared to absorb a number of vicious punches before he was thrown onto the collating machine, sending freshly printed copies of the SUNSET spewing onto the pressroom floor. Ironically, the front page story on this morning's edition read, "WHO IS GREYSHIRT?", although the valiant Science Hero had his hands too full to notice the bizarre juxtaposition.

The fracas might have ended with a wrench to Greyshirt's skull if Grockle hadn't miscalculated and gotten his arm caught in the huge and swiftly moving paper rolls that feed the hungry press. In a horrifying instant, the beefy assailant was swept into the rollers

and crushed to a pulpy froth in the jaws of the high-speed machine. A few hundred copies of today's SUNSET poured off the press with bits of Grockle mashed into the newsprint before the run could be stopped.

When presented with a souvenir edition of the SUNSET, stained with the still-warm remains of Grockle, Greyshirt was heard to quip, "Now we know what's black and white and red all over."

LOOTERS ROB GRAVE OF SAPPHIRE SCIENCE VILLAIN

Weird corpse of Lapis Lazuli worth millions

The fresh grave of one of Indigo City's strangest criminals was found violated and robbed this week, according to officials at the vast Indigo City Cemetery. Maintenance crews said they discovered a hole full of rainwater and

rose petals where the remains of executed criminal Lavern Lazuli had been interred only days before. The bizarre blue Science Villain's remains were nowhere to be found.

Laverne "Lapis" Lazuli was a beautiful young Indigo City socialite, whose fixation with sapphires ended in tragedy after an experimental ray device turned her flesh into living sapphire. Scientists were never able to explain how the process worked or why she remained alive after the one-of-a-kind machine backfired on her.

What is known is that Lazuli went on a crime spree of unparalleled dimension, robbing dozens of gem shipments and killing anyone who got in her way. She is credited with the theft of the immense

"Heart of Krishna" sapphire and the kidnapping of Tucker "Baby Einstein" Pinkus. Despite intense efforts over the course of ten years, neither Indigo City's Police nor any of the city's Science Heroes were able to bring the homicidal maniac to justice.

Lazuli's luck ran out when she murdered her reputed lover, mob boss Alberto "Little Jupiter" Dominguez and was captured by Greyshirt at the scene of the crime. After being found guilty of first degree murder, Judge Joliet sentenced her to die in the gas chamber and just two weeks ago the sentence was carried out. Indigo City Police speculate that grave robbers were after Lazuli's sapphire body, which they estimate to be worth millions on the black market.

INDIGO POOP SCOOP!

BY IDLE DISH

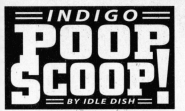

POW! ZAP! BAM!

An itty-bitty tweety bird has been singing into the POOP SCOOP'S ear about the "King of Pow! Art" Andy Savanah. Filthy rich Andy, who hit the art world jackpot with his oversized paintings of comic book panels, has been a regular on the Indigo night life circuit for years, but tongues have been wagging that Andy has been riding on his laurels too long. Insiders say he hasn't mounted a showing of new stuff in ages. Some wags even suggest the King's fortunes have dwindled to the point he's given up betting on his beloved Roller Smash.

Well, the POOP SCOOP can reveal that the great arteest is right now holed up in his million-dollar mansion, slapping paint on a brand-new series of canvasses for an unnamed patron. We hear he'll be returning to familiar territory, blowing up panels from the very same crude gangster comics that made him a household word. Wasn't it the Good Lord who said, "And someday the lowest shall be made highest?"

GANGSTERS ARE SUDDENLY "IN!"

The POOP SCOOP hears that Indigo may be in the running as the location for the filming of a monster-budget Hollywood spectacular later this year. We have it on good authority that the Mayor's office is feverishly putting together a package of tax breaks and police assistance to nail the deal. With election year coming, a little Hollywood pork will go a long way to helping fulfill some of Mayor Plutarch's campaign pledges. Whispers out of City Hall mention FANMAN Productions, which has one of the biggest hits of the current TV season with "THE CARBONES." Expect this new project to follow through with the gangster theme, which is certainly becoming tres chic again.

WHICH BARELY DRESSED Indigo City Science Heroine had customers eating out of her hand at the PURPLE PEOPLE EATER LOUNGE last night? Witnesses say one bastion of Indigo maleness went so far as to remove his clothing and howl like a dog for the mystery maiden's attention. The POOP SCOOP could have told the love-sick Romeo he was wasting his time. This particular belle only has eyes for her chauffeur!

THE SHOW MUST GO ON!

It may have garnered lukewarm reviews from critics, but GREYSHIRT: THE MUSICAL provided some new pizzazz that shocked and delighted audiences at a matinee showing last week. The lead role, usually sung and danced with uninspired aplomb by veteran hoofer ROBERT FROTH, was taken over by a surprise understudy. One playgoer, familiar with the personalities involved, said FROTH was definitely replaced by the real GREYSHIRT for one performance. The Science Hero appeared on stage unannounced, playing himself with a flair that reminded many of GENE KELLY in his prime. While no one knows exactly why Indigo's best-dressed mystery man pulled the stunt, there was an appeal to the Indigo Avenger's favorite charity at intermission.

ASK DR. SYNTAX

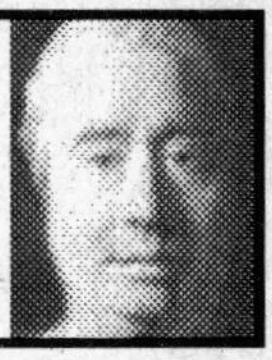

Daughter's Choice has Parents Fearful

Dear Dr. Syntax: Our daughter, Julie (not her real name) met Duke (not his real nickname) a few months ago. Duke dresses in flashy suits with extra wide shoulders and sharp lapels. He doesn't seem to have a real job but pulls a huge roll of bills out of his pocket whenever he purchases something. He drives up in a different brand-new expensive car every few weeks. He also routinely carries a large pistol on a shoulder holster and often gets up to look out the windows as if he were expecting something might happen. Ever since she got involved with Duke, Julie has been a changed person. She insists we call her by Duke's favorite nickname for her, "Tonsils," and has begun to dress in low-cut, skin-tight red or black. We tried to discuss our concerns with them, but Duke became enraged and pistol-whipped my husband. He told us we better "keep our traps shut or there wouldn't be a next time." Our daughter is a full-grown adult and we don't wish to get in the way of her choices, but we're at a loss for what to do. — Perplexed

Dear Perplexed: Young people often like to experiment with colorful nicknames. The best strategy is to go along with your daughter's wishes. Besides, "Tonsils" is cute and original.

Dear Dr. Syntax: I've always been a big fan of Indigo City's Science Heroes and follow the news reports of their exploits closely. I'm especially interested in The Cobweb, who has taken on an increasingly symbolic importance in my life. I find myself dreaming of the Belle of Indigo almost every night. I constantly follow women on the street who remind me of her. Often when I'm alone, I carry on imaginary discussions with Cobweb in which she tells me the secrets of the universe. Sometimes these talks turn into vivid fantasies of a personal nature. Last week, on an impulse, I burned all the clothes in my wife's closet and refilled it with Cobweb-licensed items from the Science Hero Style line of clothing. So far my wife has refused to wear any of them. How can I convince her how important this is to me? — Hung Up

Dear Hung Up: Imaginative people often incorporate role playing into their relationships and you appear to have joined the growing number of Indigoans who've embraced the "Science Hero Style" movement with gusto. Tell your wife that by asking her to emulate vigilante attitudes, speech patterns and dress, you are just being playful. Perhaps if you acted like a terrified and helpless victim you'd find your wife more inclined to go along with the fun.

INDIGO CITY SUNSET, WEDNESDAY, OCTOBER 17, 2001

SUNSET COMICS

MUSSEL BEACH **By Squid Pro Quo**

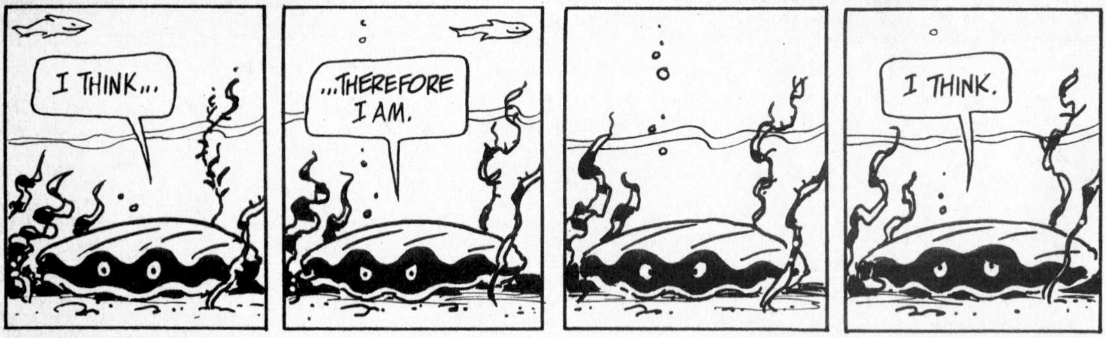

I THINK...
...THEREFORE I AM.
I THINK.

HARRY GEE **By Chet Ghoulash**

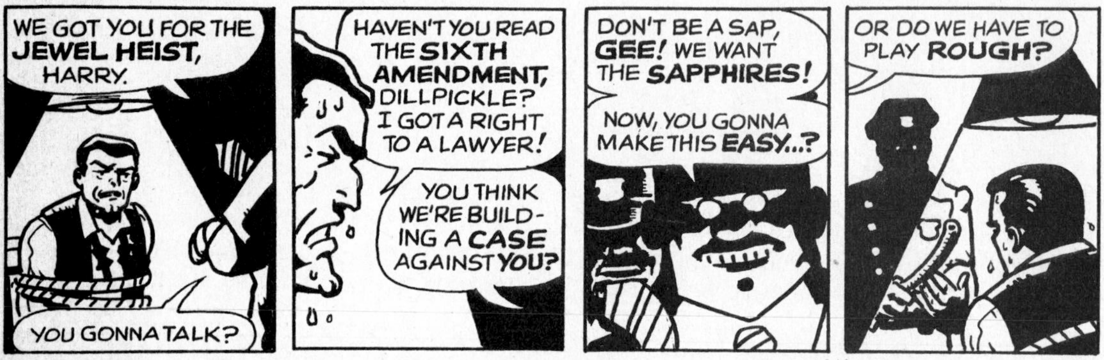

WE GOT YOU FOR THE JEWEL HEIST, HARRY.
YOU GONNA TALK?
HAVEN'T YOU READ THE SIXTH AMENDMENT, DILLPICKLE? I GOT A RIGHT TO A LAWYER!
YOU THINK WE'RE BUILDING A CASE AGAINST YOU?
DON'T BE A SAP, GEE! WE WANT THE SAPPHIRES!
NOW, YOU GONNA MAKE THIS EASY...?
OR DO WE HAVE TO PLAY ROUGH?

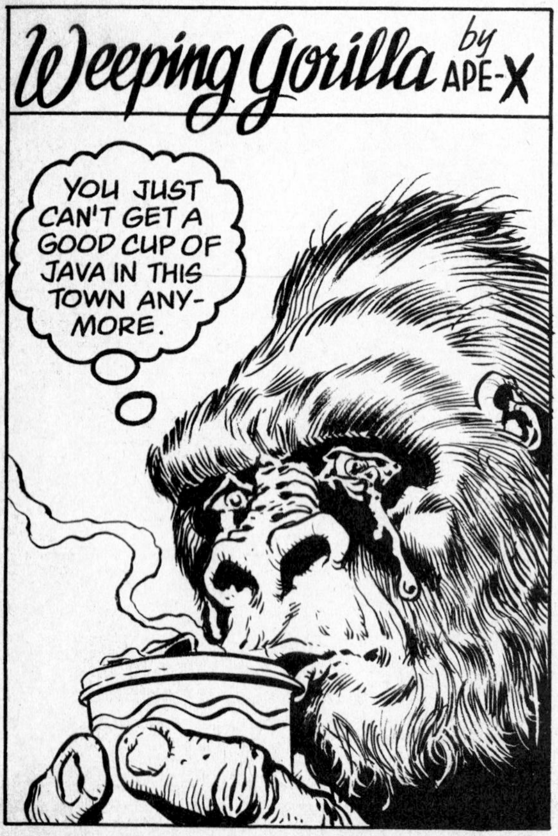

Weeping Gorilla by APE-X
YOU JUST CAN'T GET A GOOD CUP OF JAVA IN THIS TOWN ANY-MORE.

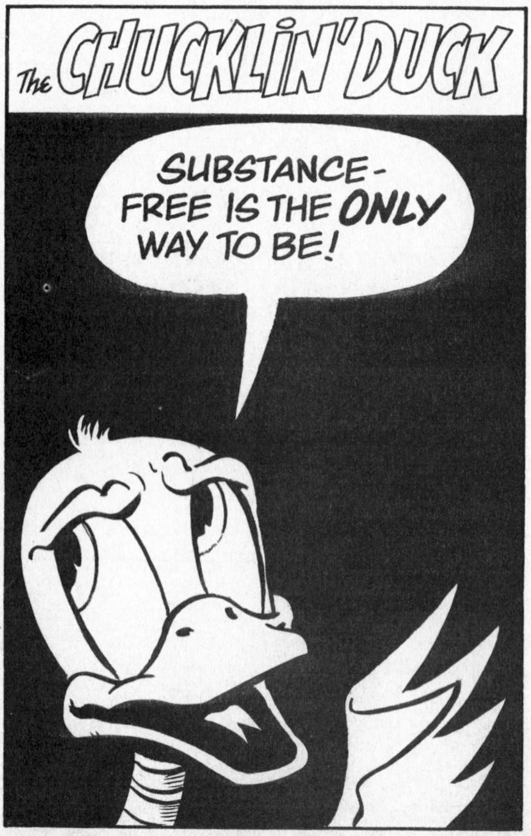

The CHUCKLIN' DUCK
SUBSTANCE-FREE IS THE ONLY WAY TO BE!

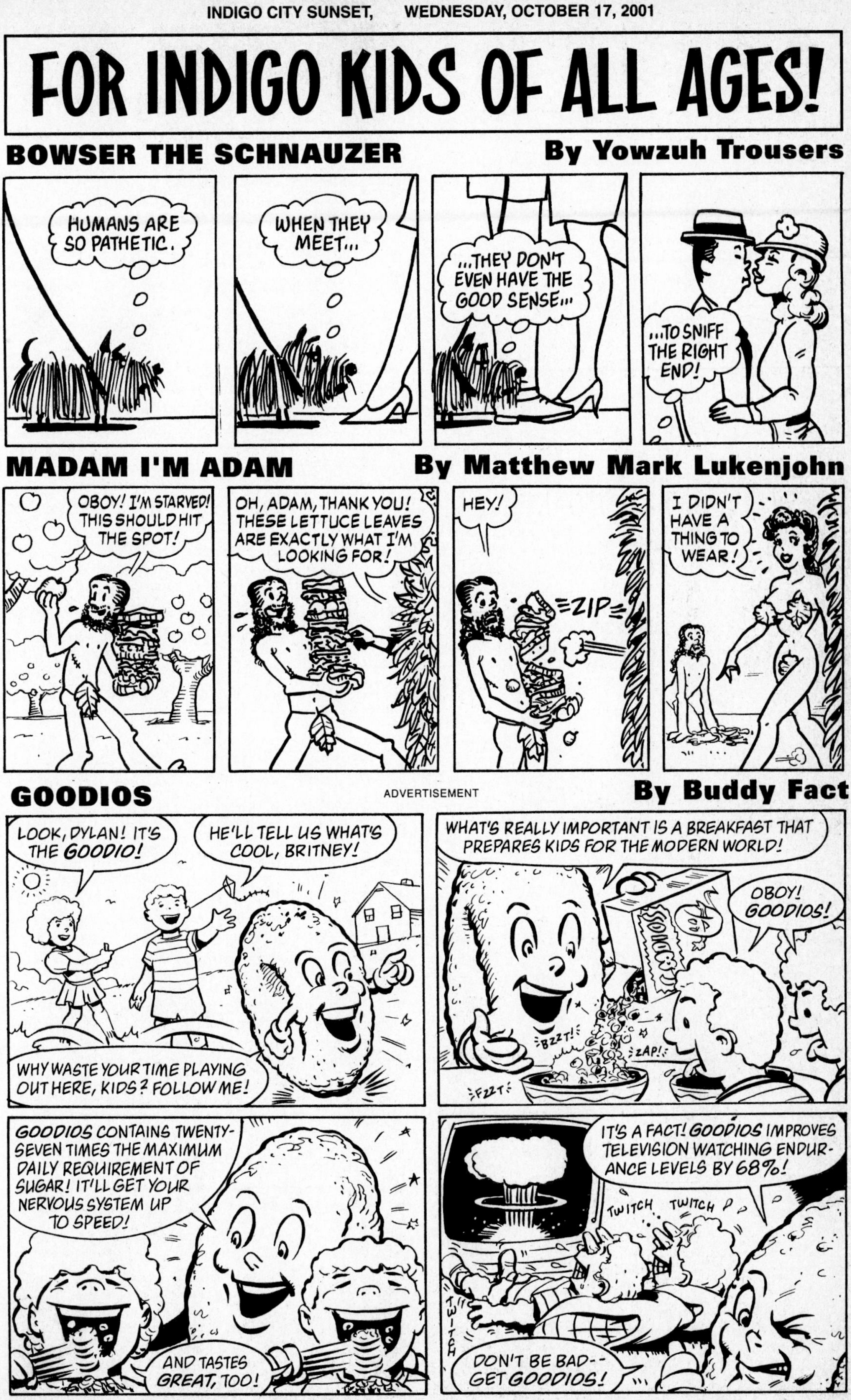
INDIGO CITY SUNSET, WEDNESDAY, OCTOBER 17, 2001
FOR INDIGO KIDS OF ALL AGES!
BOWSER THE SCHNAUZER
By Yowzuh Trousers
HUMANS ARE SO PATHETIC.
WHEN THEY MEET...
...THEY DON'T EVEN HAVE THE GOOD SENSE...
...TO SNIFF THE RIGHT END!
MADAM I'M ADAM
By Matthew Mark Lukenjohn
OBOY! I'M STARVED! THIS SHOULD HIT THE SPOT!
OH, ADAM, THANK YOU! THESE LETTUCE LEAVES ARE EXACTLY WHAT I'M LOOKING FOR!
HEY!
ZIP
I DIDN'T HAVE A THING TO WEAR!
GOODIOS
ADVERTISEMENT
By Buddy Fact
LOOK, DYLAN! IT'S THE GOODIO!
HE'LL TELL US WHAT'S COOL, BRITNEY!
WHY WASTE YOUR TIME PLAYING OUT HERE, KIDS? FOLLOW ME!
WHAT'S REALLY IMPORTANT IS A BREAKFAST THAT PREPARES KIDS FOR THE MODERN WORLD!
OBOY! GOODIOS!
BZZT!
ZAP!
FZZT
GOODIOS CONTAINS TWENTY-SEVEN TIMES THE MAXIMUM DAILY REQUIREMENT OF SUGAR! IT'LL GET YOUR NERVOUS SYSTEM UP TO SPEED!
AND TASTES GREAT, TOO!
IT'S A FACT! GOODIOS IMPROVES TELEVISION WATCHING ENDURANCE LEVELS BY 68%!
TWITCH TWITCH
TWITCH
DON'T BE BAD-- GET GOODIOS!

INDIGOPINION

The Lure is a Mom's Best Friend

Growing up in Indigo City, we will always remember THE LURE. Every chance they got, our parents chilled us with stories of the hideous monster that preyed on little children like ourselves. Gruesome descriptions of what happened to young fools who strayed near the abandoned mines were a daily ritual for us and The Lure that lived in our imaginations was far more fearsome than any poor creature that might actually make its home beneath Indigo City.

Our parents' strategy was simple: to scare the living bejeeziz out of us so we wouldn't go anywhere near the hundreds of dangerous mining sites that dot the city. At the time, we didn't quite understand the obvious relish our parents displayed while relating how they knew for a fact that some little child just our age on the other side of town was snatched by this fearsome bugaboo. But today, we are happy to report that the constant embellishment, at least in our case, worked like a charm. You couldn't have paid us all the sapphires in Indigo City to enter those abandoned shafts.

With yesterday's tragic news of another child lost in the #11 mine in the Bottoms Up district, calls have again gone up from a concerned citizenry to remove the danger of these old sites. But we think Mayor Plutarch has it exactly right when he says there is only so much the city can do if citizens insist on breaking into fenced-off areas. Mines are a fact of life in Indigo and are not going away. Everyone knows they should be avoided like the plague.

Parents, of course, might worry about the safety and sensibility of their children when they are out of sight or earshot. To them, The Lure is the perfect helper to keep little Jack and Jill from going down into the mines. If your own ghoulish tales of foolish trespassers sucked dry aren't enough to put the fear of God into your kids, back them up with the fanciful descriptions of Indigo's most famous monster that have been passed down in our history books.

In 1806, Greylock, of the Pennacook Indians, described a snake "that reached to the center of the Earth" to the first settlers. He advised it had to be fed regularly, and that humans were its food of choice. Locals soon found abundant sapphires in caves dotting the bay and figured out why Greylock, who understood things about human nature, was advising them to avoid the place.

Big John Cerulean, who founded the first professional mining operation in Indigo Junction, claimed to have seen the creature with his own eyes and even named it. Cerulean swore the thing wasn't a serpent at all, but a single tentacle, with thousands of hungry suckers on it. He said it lured miners with a little tassel on the tentacle's end, hypnotizing them with visions of sapphire fields before inhaling the juice out of them, leaving nothing but dry, papery husks. By the time his competitors realized they were having their legs pulled, Big John had laid claim to the richest strikes in Indigo and made his first fortune. And of course when he himself went missing, the local authorities blamed The Lure rather than any of Big John's host of enemies.

Since those Wild West days, every disappearance for a hundred miles has been blamed on the poor old Lure, a fact that hasn't been lost on Indigo's criminal element. More than a few gangsters' victims have been taken for a ride down those tunnels and never seen again.

We say, its time to view The Lure in a new and positive light. Indigo's scariest monster isn't something to hide in the closet or under the bed. For parents, The Lure's the best thing to happen to Indigo City since the asteroid hit!

— Victer Kich

SUNSET LETTERS

To the editor,

Citizens concerned with Indigo's disappearing architectural past should be outraged that the city has slated the Katz Building for demolition this summer. Built by fabled gangster Seymour 'Spatz' Katz during his salad days in the late 1930s, the building boasts some of the most interesting Art Deco touches seen in Indigo. Katz continued to operate his dwindling criminal empire from the building right into his eighties as the place fell into ruin around him. He died in a fall from the top floor last year. While I agree with the Police Chief that the demolition "will be a good opportunity to see where the bodies are buried," all Indigo should mourn the loss of this historical treasure.

I. M. A. Peapod
Diadem Circle

To the editor,

As the proud owner/operator of an Indigo City taxicab, I wanted to complain about the harsh realities of dealing with the police in this city. A few months ago, I was involved in a bizarre situation which ended with me helping apprehend a wanted gangster by the name of Chucky Frisco. When I delivered the criminal to the station, instead of a medal or a reward, the cops wrote me a citation because my medallion tax wasn't paid. All I can say is that the next time I see some sort of crime being perpetrated, I'm driving right on by!

Arthur Raveson
Vapor Street

To whom it may concern,

Needed: information on any musical compositions, recorded, published or unpublished, by Victor Crescendo, scientist/musician born in 1914, lived most of his life in Indigo City. Disappeared 2000. Daughter's name: Roseanne Crescendo. Reward.

Tucker Pinkus
Dept. of String Theory Studies
Livermore National Laboratory

Send letters to Sunset Letters, 888 Prospect St., Suite 240, La Jolla, CA 92037, or email sunset@wildstorm.com. We reserve the right to edit and condense all letters.

THE INDIGO CITY SUNSET
VOLUME 161, NUMBER 753

JIM LEE: Editorial Director
JOHN NEE: VP & General Manager
SCOTT DUNBIER: Group Editor

Victer Kich, City Editor
Chick Rivet, Sports Editor
Ted Lodnik, Production
Link Detoid, Designer

Main Office: 555-2800
Customer Service: 555-2820
News Tips: 555-2822
Home Delivery: 555-2828

THE BEST "GAME" IN TOWN!

SUNSET SPORTS

Wednesday, October 17, 2001 WORLD SERIES COMMENTARY PAGE 72

JO-JO RAGES AT "BLIND" REFS: "WE SHOULD'VE BUSTED THEIR BEARINGS!"

Roller Queen says Growlers still have Play-off shot after loss to Neopolis

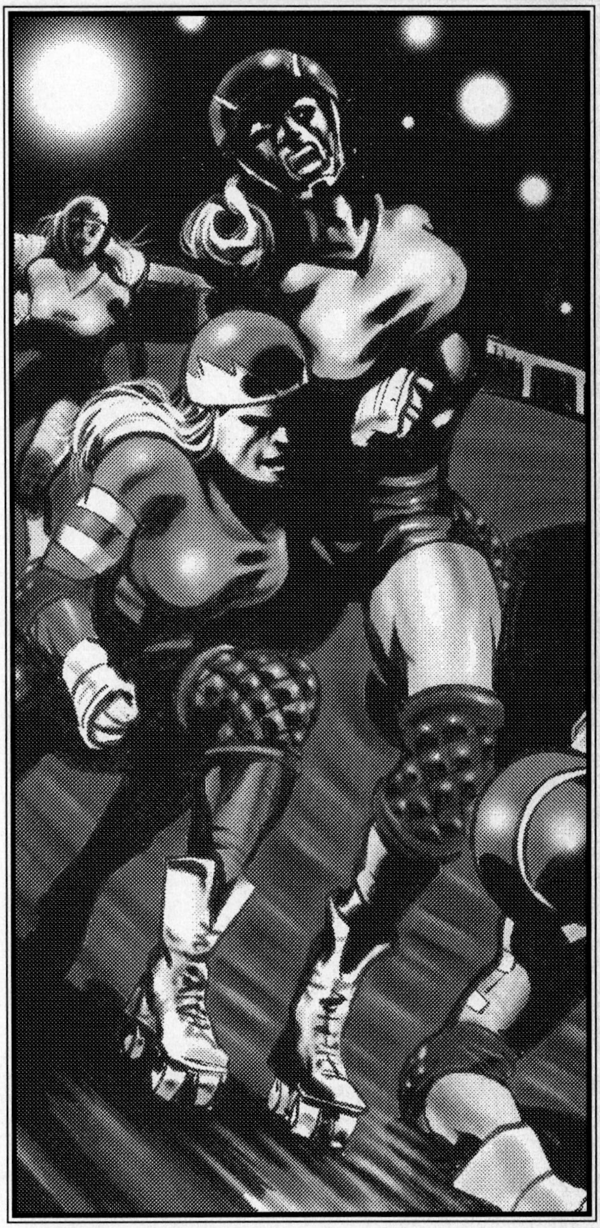

Following the Indigo City Growlers' embarrassing rout beneath the wheels of the Neopolis Nozzles last night at the Growlerdrome, Captain Jo-Jo Manchester asserted that her team was not out of the running for this year's playoffs by a long shot. Blaming the Nozzles' near mastery of the wooden oval last night on bad refereeing, the star jammer said, "How are we gonna compete against some freak that changes his molecular structure or turns into flamin' hot lava? The refs are supposed to keep an eye on those Neopolis yo-yos and penalize 'em when they see 'em use their powers. Well, last night the refs suddenly developed a mysterious case of glaucoma, you ask me!"

FULL STORY: PAGE 74, PLUS ALL THE LATEST SCORES

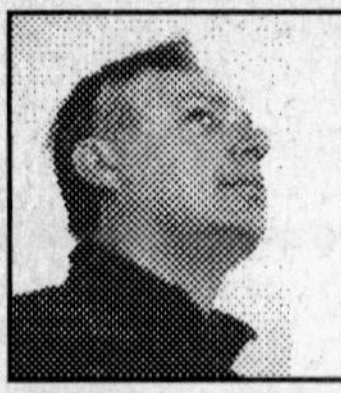

RICK VEITCH
Writer-Artist pouts: "I'm not just another pretty face!" Page 8

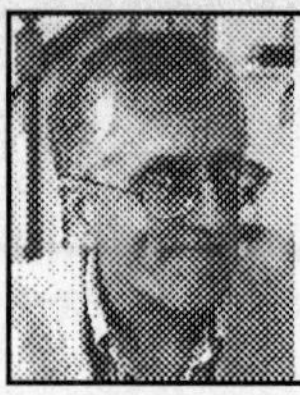

TODD KLEIN
Beloved Letterer's Corrupted Font Agony! Page 28

WILDSTORM FX COLORS: HUE AND CRY FUROR

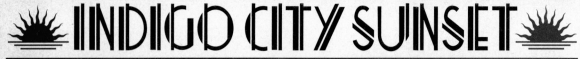

ALL THE NEWS FROM DAWN TO DUSK

INDIGO CITY SUNSET

AFTERNOON CITY EDITION

Wednesday, October 17, 2001 Metro Weather – Today: Fog, Tonight: Heavy Fog, Tomorrow: Foggy

BACK PAGE EXTRA:

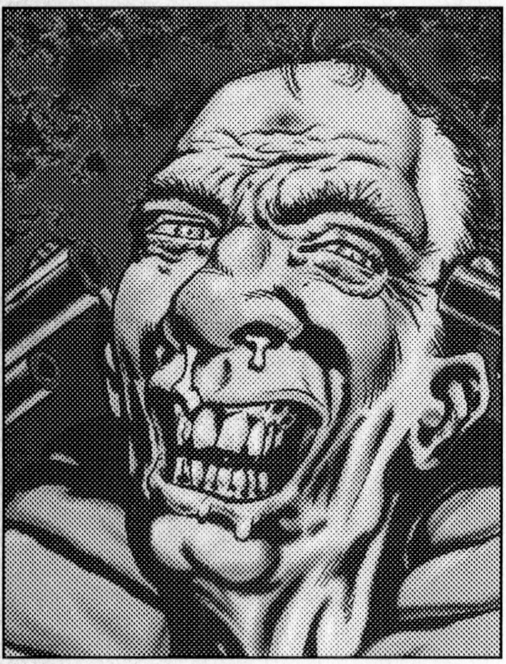

Snots Lamonico crows in triumph moments after a grenade blast apparently tore into the Indigo Avenger.

"I GREASED GREYSHIRT!"

Mystery Man Missing after Assassination Attempt on Judge Joliet!

MAYOR'S OFFICE MUM ON MID-TOWN GRENADE ATTACK

Special to The Sunset by Geekus Crow

The marbled halls of justice at the Indigo City Courthouse were rocked by exploding fury this morning, when an ex-convict attempted to strike down the crusading judge who sentenced him to prison nine years ago. Reputed gangster GARDNER LAMONICO, known in Indigo's seedier districts as "SNOTS," succeeded in penetrating tight security at the old Courthouse carrying an army surplus anti-personnel grenade. His target was Judge Joliet, who was scheduled to be presented with the prestigious Sapphire City Award in the main lobby by Mayor Plutarch.

Details are sketchy, but witnesses said GREYSHIRT was on the scene and struggled with Lamonico just before the deadly device detonated. One eye-witness said the Science Hero "was definitely caught in the blast," but the Mayor's office had not released an official statement at press time. CONTINUED INSIDE

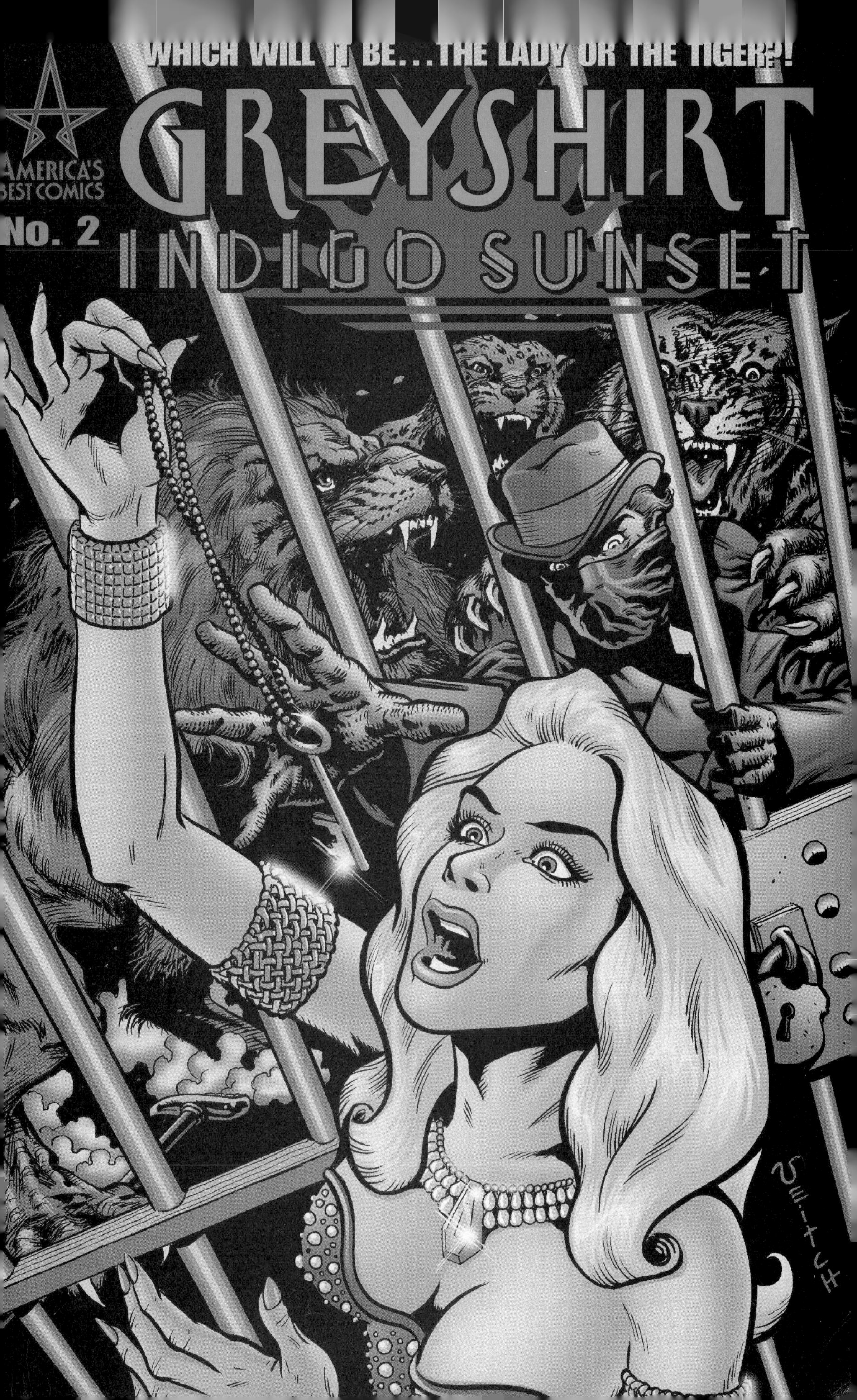

WHICH WILL IT BE...THE LADY OR THE TIGER?!
GREYSHIRT
INDIGO SUNSET
AMERICA'S BEST COMICS
No. 2
VEITCH

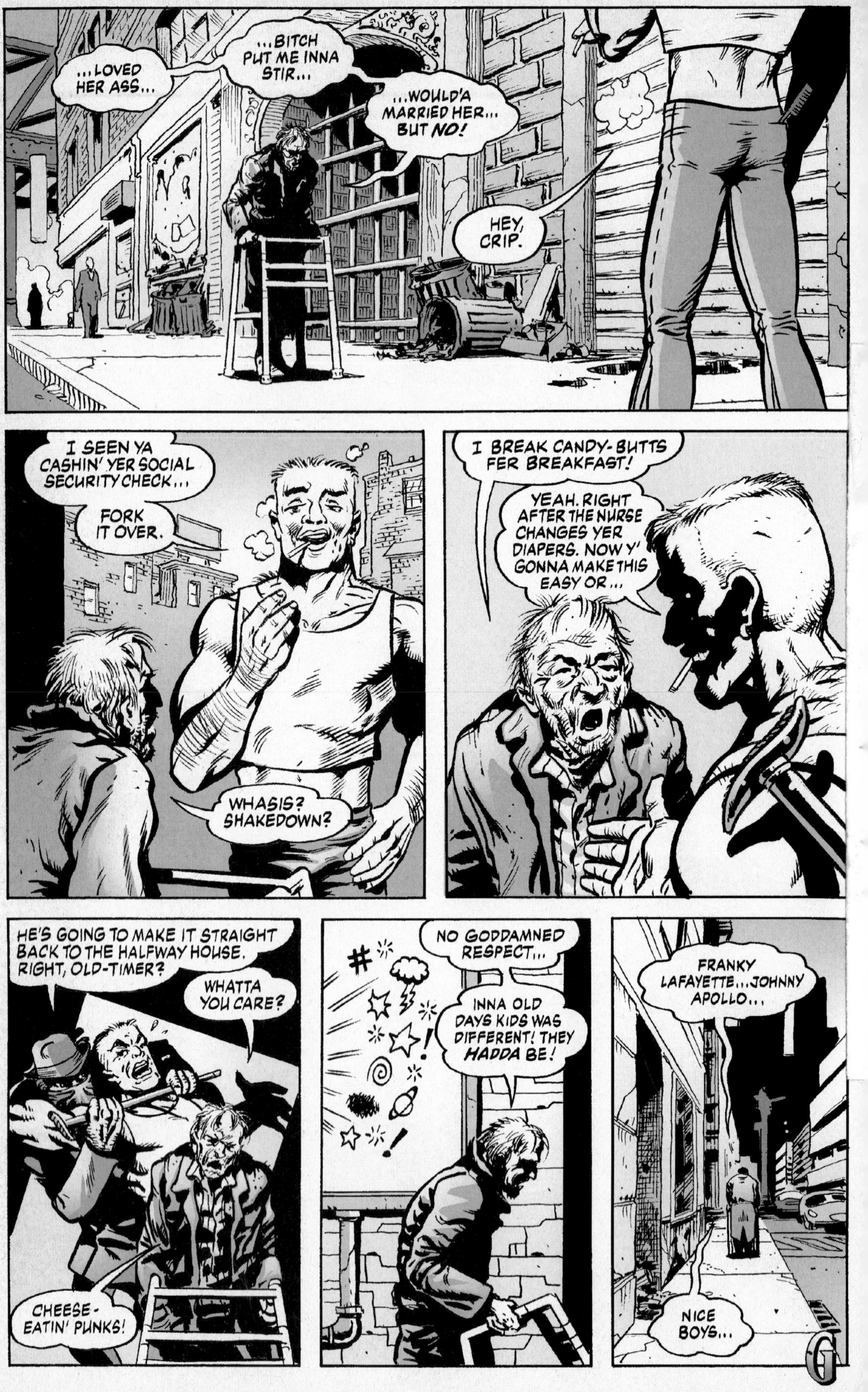
...LOVED HER ASS...
...BITCH PUT ME INNA STIR...
...WOULD'A MARRIED HER... BUT *NO!*
HEY, CRIP.
I SEEN YA CASHIN' YER SOCIAL SECURITY CHECK...
FORK IT OVER.
WHASIS? SHAKEDOWN?
I BREAK CANDY-BUTTS FER BREAKFAST!
YEAH. RIGHT AFTER THE NURSE CHANGES YER DIAPERS. NOW Y' GONNA MAKE THIS EASY OR...
HE'S GOING TO MAKE IT STRAIGHT BACK TO THE HALFWAY HOUSE. RIGHT, OLD-TIMER?
WHATTA YOU CARE?
CHEESE-EATIN' PUNKS!
NO GODDAMNED RESPECT...
INNA OLD DAYS KIDS WAS DIFFERENT! THEY *HADDA* BE!
FRANKY LAFAYETTE...JOHNNY APOLLO...
NICE BOYS...

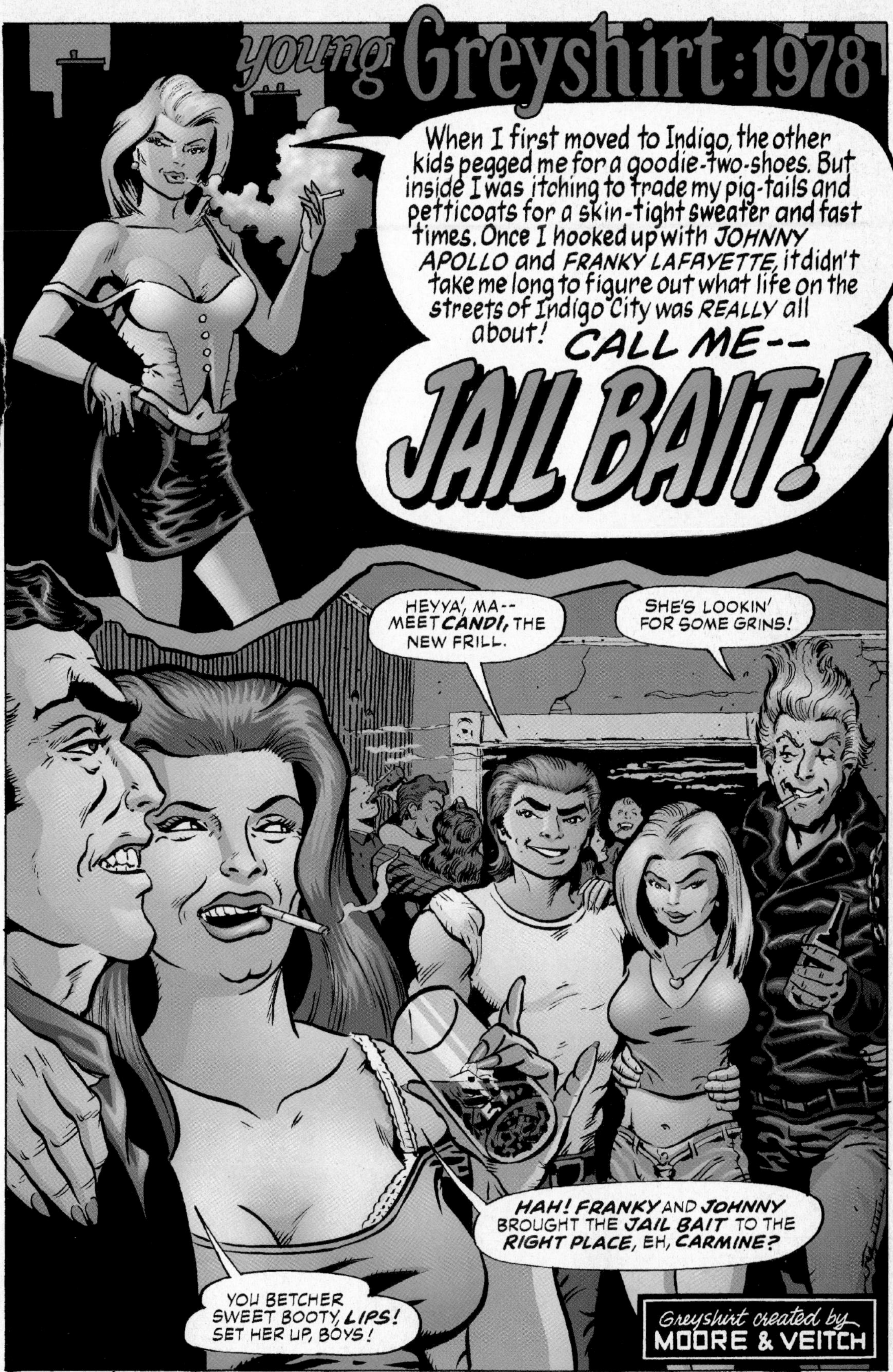
young Greyshirt: 1978
When I first moved to Indigo, the other kids pegged me for a goodie-two-shoes. But inside I was itching to trade my pig-tails and petticoats for a skin-tight sweater and fast times. Once I hooked up with JOHNNY APOLLO and FRANKY LAFAYETTE, it didn't take me long to figure out what life on the streets of Indigo City was REALLY all about! CALL ME--
JAIL BAIT!
HEYYA', MA-- MEET CANDI, THE NEW FRILL.
SHE'S LOOKIN' FOR SOME GRINS!
HAH! FRANKY AND JOHNNY BROUGHT THE JAIL BAIT TO THE RIGHT PLACE, EH, CARMINE?
YOU BETCHER SWEET BOOTY, LIPS! SET HER UP, BOYS!
Greyshirt created by MOORE & VEITCH

Hearts & Flowers: RICK VEITCH Love Letters: TODD KLEIN Red Roses: WILDSTORM FX Hugs: POZNER & QUINN Kisses: SCOTT DUNBIER Love 'em & Leave 'em: ALAN MOORE

"MY FOLKS WERE POOR AND WE MOVED AROUND A LOT; SO BY THE TIME I WAS SWEET SIXTEEN I'D KNOWN EVERY LOW RENT DISTRICT FROM MILLENNIUM CITY TO QUEERWATER, KANSAS. WHEN WE FINALLY HIT INDIGO, ALL I WANTED WAS A TICKET OUT."

PLATO? YOU HAVE YOUR REPORT ON MEDIEVAL WEAPONRY READY?

AS ALWAYS, *MR. FAFNER!*

WATCH THIS!

"MY TARGET OF OPPORTUNITY WAS THE CLASS PRESIDENT, *PLATO PLUTARCH.* SURE, HE WAS DULL AS DISH-WATER, BUT HE WAS DIFFERENT FROM THE SCRUFFS AND ROWDIES."

I'LL BE COVERING THE STRATEGIC IMPACT OF *CHAIN MAIL,* WHICH EMERGED AS THE DOMINANT FORM OF PERSONAL DEFENSE IN 8TH CENTURY BRITAIN.

GET READY!

"HE HAD A *FUTURE!*"

CHAIN MAIL WAS INTRO-DUCED BY THE *GREY-SHIRTS,* AND THE EDGE IT GAVE THE CLAN OVER THEIR ENEMIES CHANGED THE BALANCE OF POWER IN...

OOOOP! YOU LOST SOME-THING, PLATO. LET ME GET IT...

BINGO!

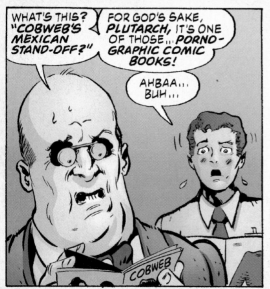

WHAT'S THIS? "*COBWEB'S MEXICAN STAND-OFF?*"

FOR GOD'S SAKE, PLUTARCH, IT'S ONE OF THOSE... *PORNO-GRAPHIC COMIC BOOKS!*

AHBAA... BUH...

COBWEB

"BUT THOSE ROWDIES *DID* SEEM TO HAVE A LOT MORE FUN...OFTEN AT *PLATO'S* EXPENSE."

NO BUTS! WE'LL SEE WHAT THE *PRINCIPAL* SAYS ABOUT OUR TOP HONOR STUDENT BRINGING A *TIJUANA BIBLE* TO SCHOOL!

≥SNICKER!≤ AM I GREAT OR AM I *GREAT?*

HAHA! YOU'RE THE *KING,* JOHNNY.

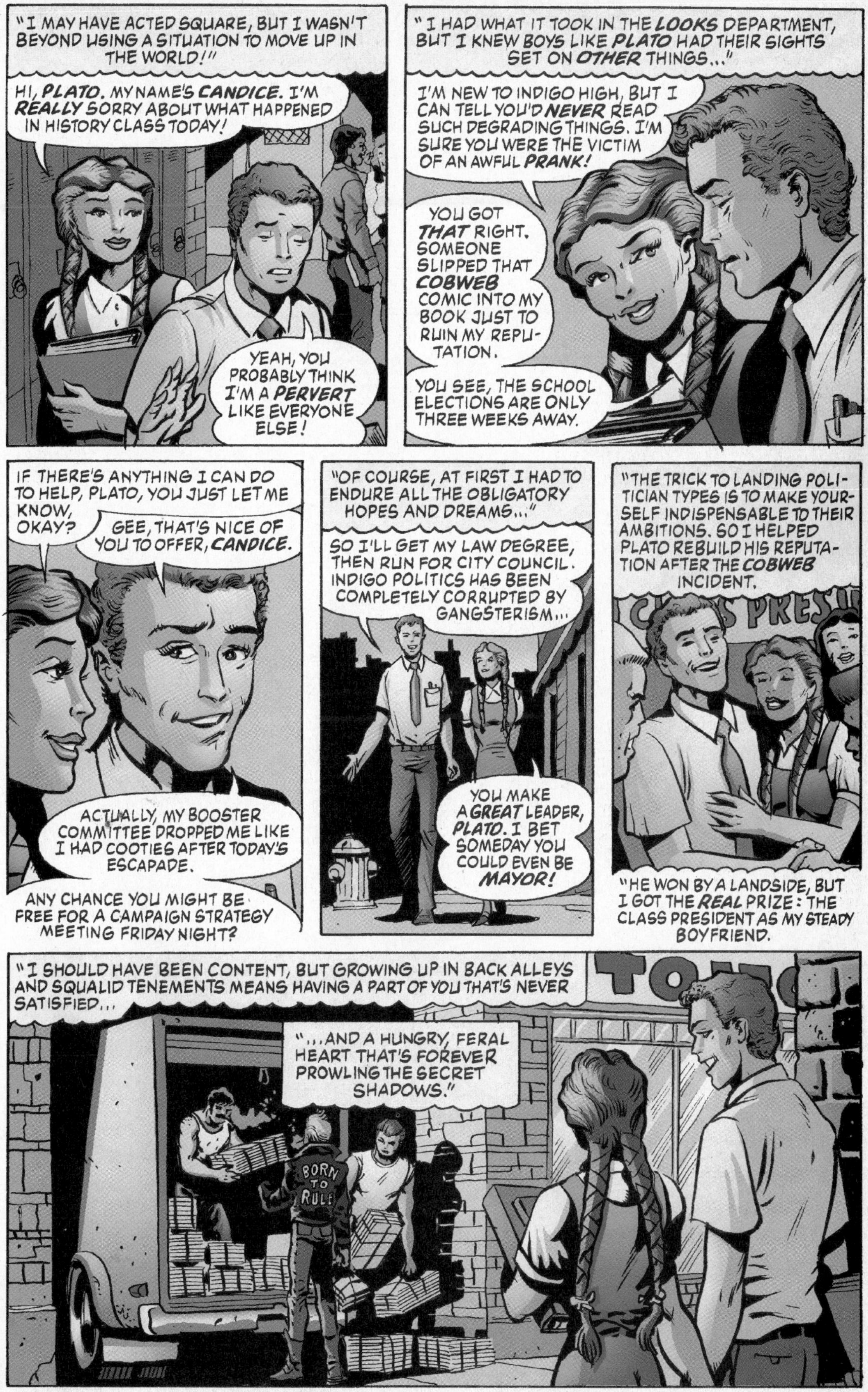
"I MAY HAVE ACTED SQUARE, BUT I WASN'T BEYOND USING A SITUATION TO MOVE UP IN THE WORLD!"
HI, PLATO. MY NAME'S CANDICE. I'M REALLY SORRY ABOUT WHAT HAPPENED IN HISTORY CLASS TODAY!
YEAH, YOU PROBABLY THINK I'M A PERVERT LIKE EVERYONE ELSE!
"I HAD WHAT IT TOOK IN THE LOOKS DEPARTMENT, BUT I KNEW BOYS LIKE PLATO HAD THEIR SIGHTS SET ON OTHER THINGS..."
I'M NEW TO INDIGO HIGH, BUT I CAN TELL YOU'D NEVER READ SUCH DEGRADING THINGS. I'M SURE YOU WERE THE VICTIM OF AN AWFUL PRANK!
YOU GOT THAT RIGHT. SOMEONE SLIPPED THAT COBWEB COMIC INTO MY BOOK JUST TO RUIN MY REPUTATION.
YOU SEE, THE SCHOOL ELECTIONS ARE ONLY THREE WEEKS AWAY.
IF THERE'S ANYTHING I CAN DO TO HELP, PLATO, YOU JUST LET ME KNOW, OKAY?
GEE, THAT'S NICE OF YOU TO OFFER, CANDICE.
ACTUALLY, MY BOOSTER COMMITTEE DROPPED ME LIKE I HAD COOTIES AFTER TODAY'S ESCAPADE.
ANY CHANCE YOU MIGHT BE FREE FOR A CAMPAIGN STRATEGY MEETING FRIDAY NIGHT?
"OF COURSE, AT FIRST I HAD TO ENDURE ALL THE OBLIGATORY HOPES AND DREAMS..."
SO I'LL GET MY LAW DEGREE, THEN RUN FOR CITY COUNCIL. INDIGO POLITICS HAS BEEN COMPLETELY CORRUPTED BY GANGSTERISM...
YOU MAKE A GREAT LEADER, PLATO. I BET SOMEDAY YOU COULD EVEN BE MAYOR!
"THE TRICK TO LANDING POLITICIAN TYPES IS TO MAKE YOURSELF INDISPENSABLE TO THEIR AMBITIONS. SO I HELPED PLATO REBUILD HIS REPUTATION AFTER THE COBWEB INCIDENT.
"HE WON BY A LANDSIDE, BUT I GOT THE REAL PRIZE: THE CLASS PRESIDENT AS MY STEADY BOYFRIEND.
"I SHOULD HAVE BEEN CONTENT, BUT GROWING UP IN BACK ALLEYS AND SQUALID TENEMENTS MEANS HAVING A PART OF YOU THAT'S NEVER SATISFIED...
"...AND A HUNGRY, FERAL HEART THAT'S FOREVER PROWLING THE SECRET SHADOWS."
BORN TO RULE

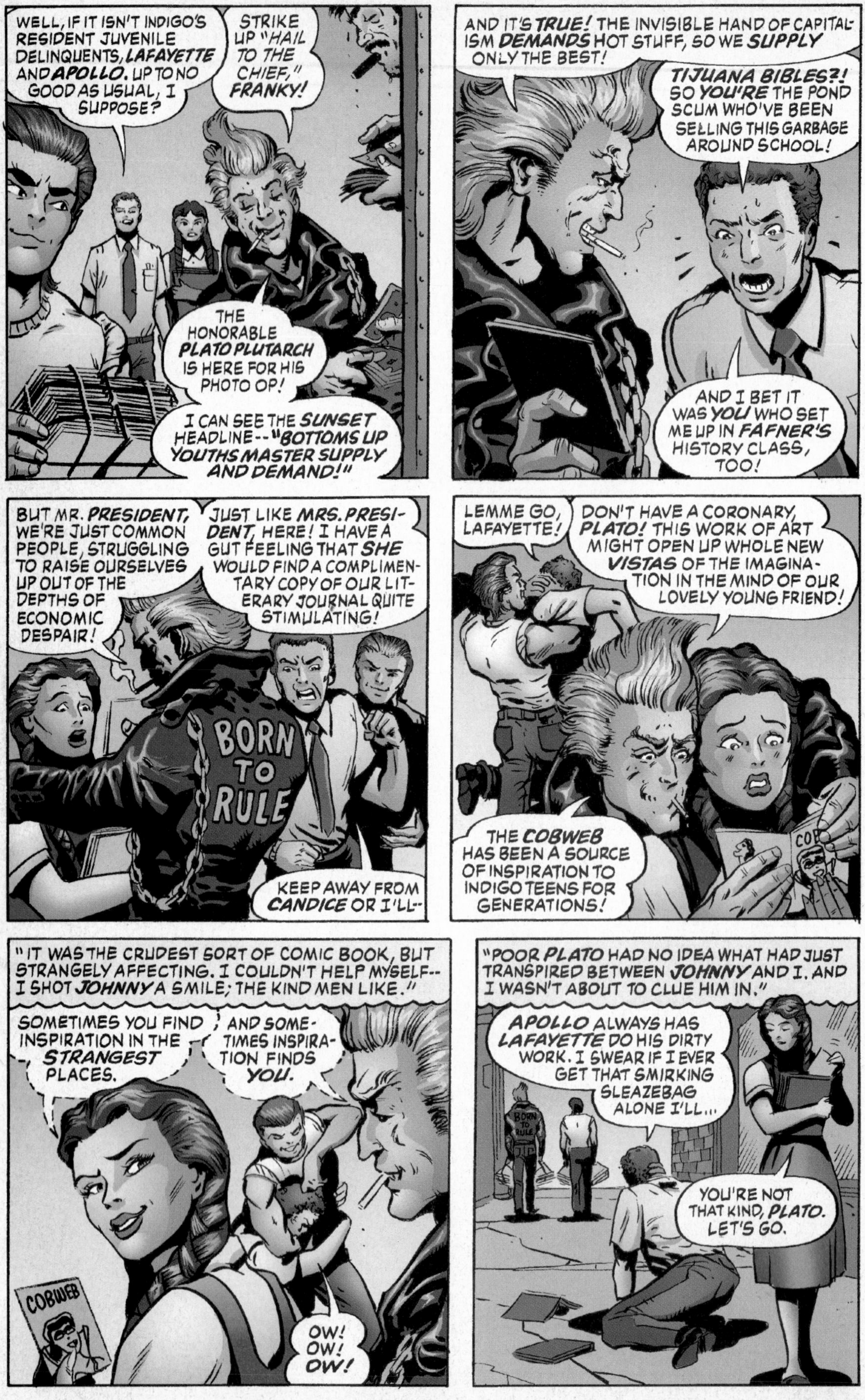
WELL, IF IT ISN'T INDIGO'S RESIDENT JUVENILE DELINQUENTS, LAFAYETTE AND APOLLO. UP TO NO GOOD AS USUAL, I SUPPOSE?
STRIKE UP "HAIL TO THE CHIEF," FRANKY!
THE HONORABLE PLATO PLUTARCH IS HERE FOR HIS PHOTO OP!
I CAN SEE THE SUNSET HEADLINE--"BOTTOMS UP YOUTHS MASTER SUPPLY AND DEMAND!"
AND IT'S TRUE! THE INVISIBLE HAND OF CAPITALISM DEMANDS HOT STUFF, SO WE SUPPLY ONLY THE BEST!
TIJUANA BIBLES?! SO YOU'RE THE POND SCUM WHO'VE BEEN SELLING THIS GARBAGE AROUND SCHOOL!
AND I BET IT WAS YOU WHO SET ME UP IN FAFNER'S HISTORY CLASS, TOO!
BUT MR. PRESIDENT, WE'RE JUST COMMON PEOPLE, STRUGGLING TO RAISE OURSELVES UP OUT OF THE DEPTHS OF ECONOMIC DESPAIR!
JUST LIKE MRS. PRESIDENT, HERE! I HAVE A GUT FEELING THAT SHE WOULD FIND A COMPLIMENTARY COPY OF OUR LITERARY JOURNAL QUITE STIMULATING!
BORN TO RULE
KEEP AWAY FROM CANDICE OR I'LL--
LEMME GO, LAFAYETTE!
DON'T HAVE A CORONARY, PLATO! THIS WORK OF ART MIGHT OPEN UP WHOLE NEW VISTAS OF THE IMAGINATION IN THE MIND OF OUR LOVELY YOUNG FRIEND!
THE COBWEB HAS BEEN A SOURCE OF INSPIRATION TO INDIGO TEENS FOR GENERATIONS!
"IT WAS THE CRUDEST SORT OF COMIC BOOK, BUT STRANGELY AFFECTING. I COULDN'T HELP MYSELF-- I SHOT JOHNNY A SMILE; THE KIND MEN LIKE."
SOMETIMES YOU FIND INSPIRATION IN THE STRANGEST PLACES.
AND SOMETIMES INSPIRATION FINDS YOU.
COBWEB
OW! OW! OW!
"POOR PLATO HAD NO IDEA WHAT HAD JUST TRANSPIRED BETWEEN JOHNNY AND I. AND I WASN'T ABOUT TO CLUE HIM IN."
APOLLO ALWAYS HAS LAFAYETTE DO HIS DIRTY WORK. I SWEAR IF I EVER GET THAT SMIRKING SLEAZEBAG ALONE I'LL...
YOU'RE NOT THAT KIND, PLATO. LET'S GO.

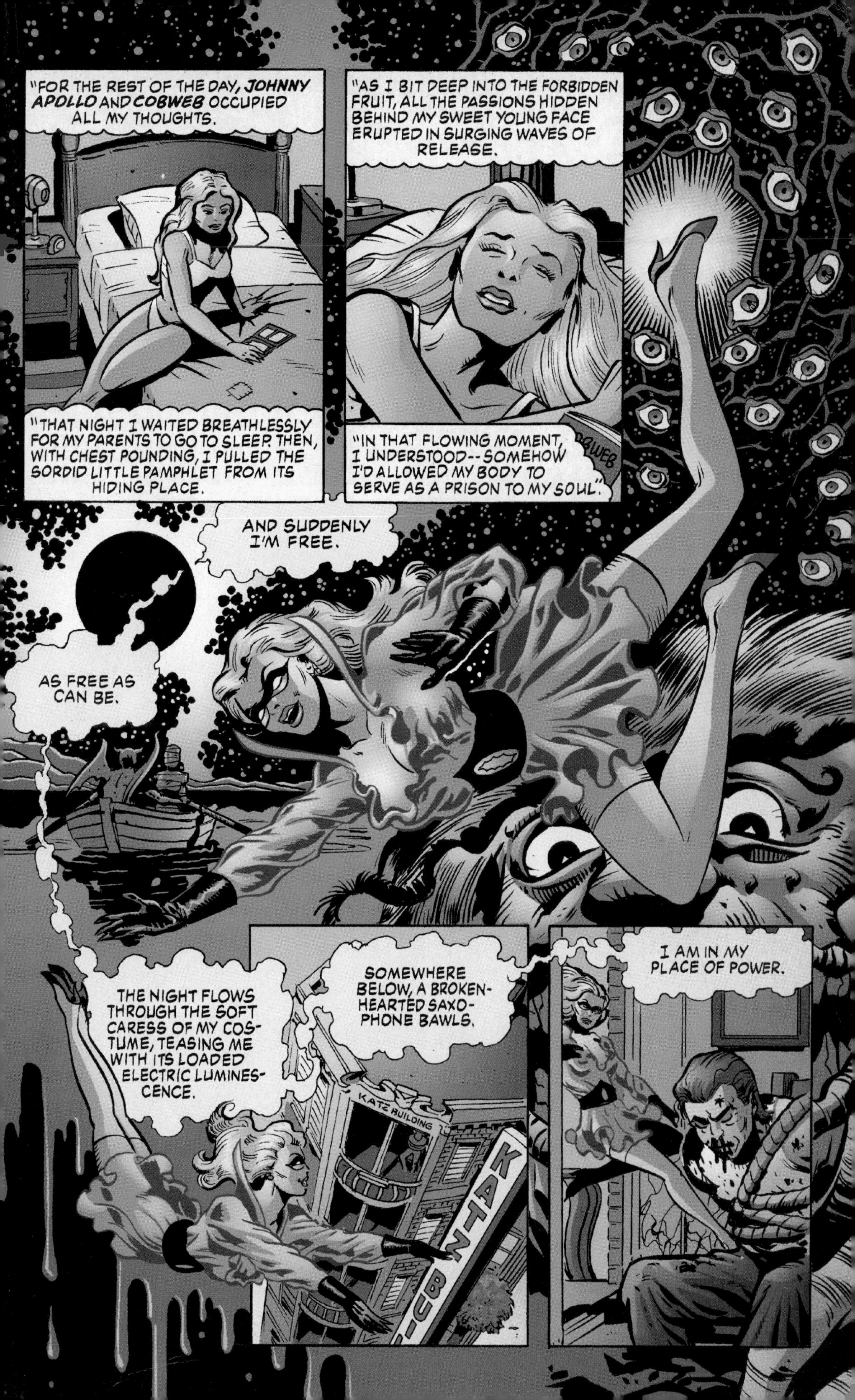
"FOR THE REST OF THE DAY, JOHNNY APOLLO AND COBWEB OCCUPIED ALL MY THOUGHTS.
"THAT NIGHT I WAITED BREATHLESSLY FOR MY PARENTS TO GO TO SLEEP. THEN, WITH CHEST POUNDING, I PULLED THE SORDID LITTLE PAMPHLET FROM ITS HIDING PLACE.
"AS I BIT DEEP INTO THE FORBIDDEN FRUIT, ALL THE PASSIONS HIDDEN BEHIND MY SWEET YOUNG FACE ERUPTED IN SURGING WAVES OF RELEASE.
"IN THAT FLOWING MOMENT, I UNDERSTOOD-- SOMEHOW I'D ALLOWED MY BODY TO SERVE AS A PRISON TO MY SOUL".
AND SUDDENLY I'M FREE.
AS FREE AS CAN BE.
THE NIGHT FLOWS THROUGH THE SOFT CARESS OF MY COSTUME, TEASING ME WITH ITS LOADED ELECTRIC LUMINESCENCE.
SOMEWHERE BELOW, A BROKEN-HEARTED SAXOPHONE BAWLS.
KATZ BUILDING
I AM IN MY PLACE OF POWER.

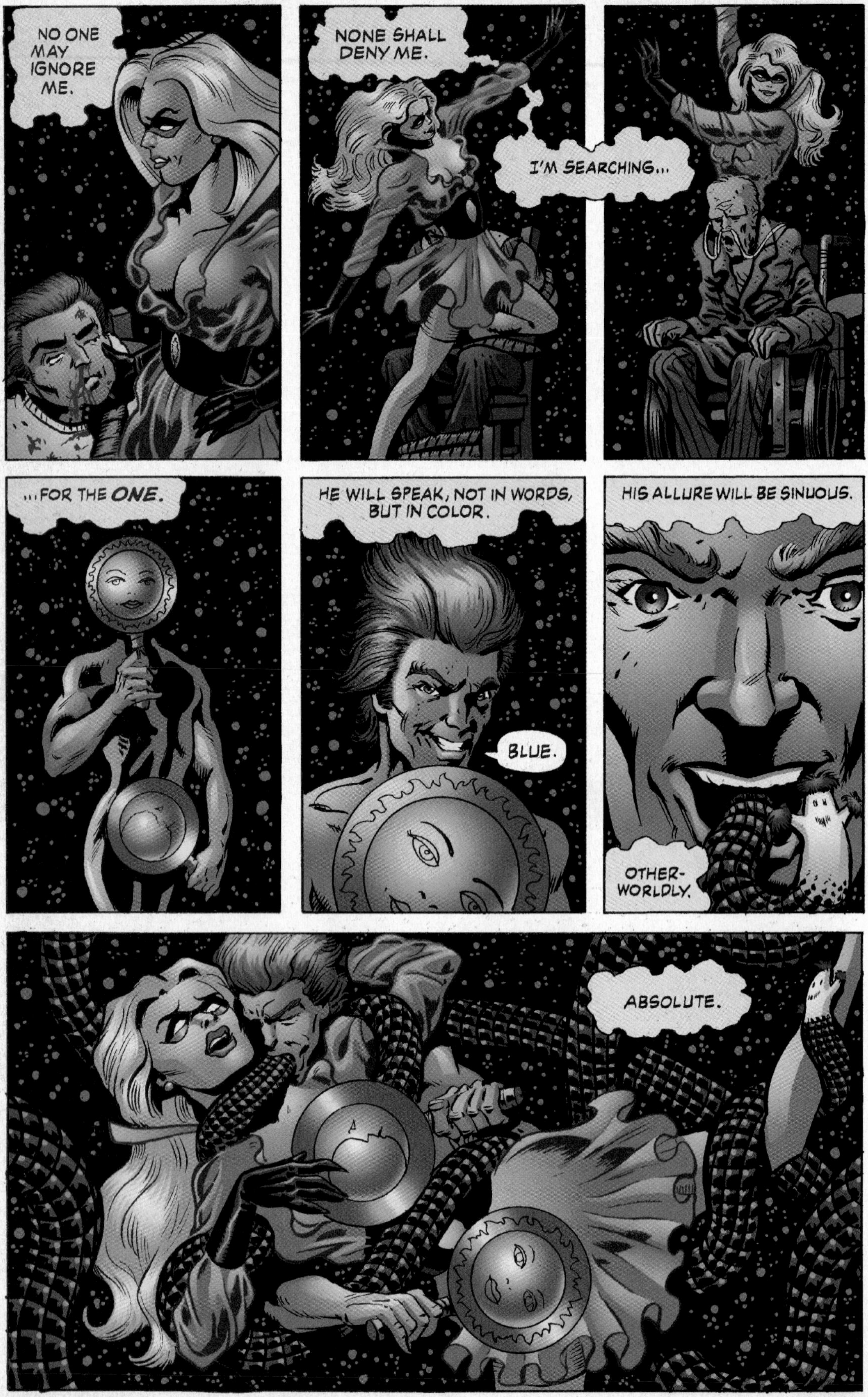
NO ONE MAY IGNORE ME.
NONE SHALL DENY ME.
I'M SEARCHING...
...FOR THE ONE.
HE WILL SPEAK, NOT IN WORDS, BUT IN COLOR.
BLUE.
HIS ALLURE WILL BE SINUOUS.
OTHER-WORLDLY.
ABSOLUTE.

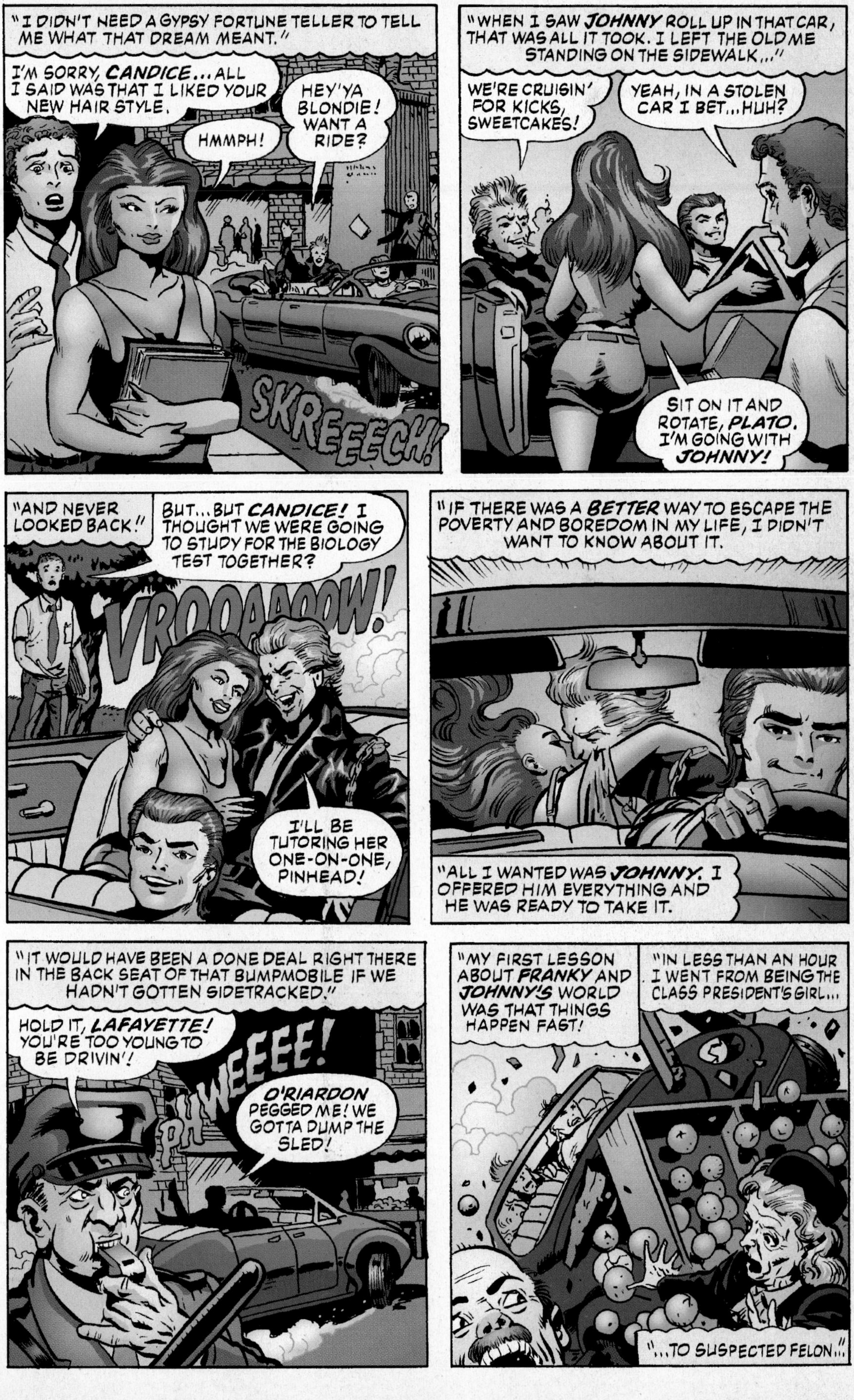
"I DIDN'T NEED A GYPSY FORTUNE TELLER TO TELL ME WHAT THAT DREAM MEANT."
I'M SORRY, CANDICE... ALL I SAID WAS THAT I LIKED YOUR NEW HAIR STYLE.
HMMPH!
HEY'YA BLONDIE! WANT A RIDE?
SKREEEECH!
"WHEN I SAW JOHNNY ROLL UP IN THAT CAR, THAT WAS ALL IT TOOK. I LEFT THE OLD ME STANDING ON THE SIDEWALK..."
WE'RE CRUISIN' FOR KICKS, SWEETCAKES!
YEAH, IN A STOLEN CAR I BET... HUH?
SIT ON IT AND ROTATE, PLATO. I'M GOING WITH JOHNNY!
"AND NEVER LOOKED BACK."
BUT... BUT CANDICE! I THOUGHT WE WERE GOING TO STUDY FOR THE BIOLOGY TEST TOGETHER?
VROOAAOOW!
I'LL BE TUTORING HER ONE-ON-ONE, PINHEAD!
"IF THERE WAS A BETTER WAY TO ESCAPE THE POVERTY AND BOREDOM IN MY LIFE, I DIDN'T WANT TO KNOW ABOUT IT.
"ALL I WANTED WAS JOHNNY. I OFFERED HIM EVERYTHING AND HE WAS READY TO TAKE IT.
"IT WOULD HAVE BEEN A DONE DEAL RIGHT THERE IN THE BACK SEAT OF THAT BUMPMOBILE IF WE HADN'T GOTTEN SIDETRACKED."
HOLD IT, LAFAYETTE! YOU'RE TOO YOUNG TO BE DRIVIN'!
PHWEEEEE!
O'RIARDON PEGGED ME! WE GOTTA DUMP THE SLED!
"MY FIRST LESSON ABOUT FRANKY AND JOHNNY'S WORLD WAS THAT THINGS HAPPEN FAST!
"IN LESS THAN AN HOUR I WENT FROM BEING THE CLASS PRESIDENT'S GIRL...
"...TO SUSPECTED FELON."

"...TO FUGITIVE FROM JUSTICE..."

WE'LL GIVE 'EM THE SLIP IN THE ALLEYS THEN HOLE UP AT MA'S PLACE!

"...TO HAVING THE TIME OF MY LIFE."

HAHAHA! DID YOU SEE THE LOOK ON O'RIARDON'S FACE?

HAHA ¿GASP¿ HAHAHA! THAT WAS FUN! LET'S DO IT AGAIN!

SOUNDS LIKE MA'S HAVIN' A PARTY. C'MON IN.

"MY SECOND LESSON TAUGHT ME HOW A REAL WOMAN GETS AHEAD IN INDIGO."

LOOK WHO JUST WALTZED IN, LIPS! IT'S THE PUNKS-- WITH FRESH JAIL BAIT TOO!

HEY, MA. HEY, CARM. MEET JOHNNY'S NEW SQUEEZE, CANDI.

HAH! Y'NEVER LET MY AGE SLOW YOU DOWN, CARMINE!

SHE'S OUR KINDA PEOPLE.

I'M THINKIN' YOU TWO ARE OLD ENOUGH TO HELP ME OUT ON SOMETHIN'. I WANNA MAKE TROUBLE FOR MY COMPETITION, Y'KNOW?

WHATTAYA DRINKIN'? BEER?

WE'RE YOUR BOYS, MR. CARBONE!

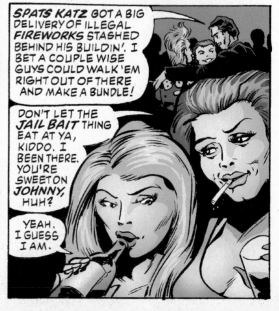

SPATS KATZ GOT A BIG DELIVERY OF ILLEGAL FIREWORKS STASHED BEHIND HIS BUILDIN'. I BET A COUPLE WISE GUYS COULD WALK 'EM RIGHT OUT OF THERE AND MAKE A BUNDLE!

DON'T LET THE JAIL BAIT THING EAT AT YA, KIDDO. I BEEN THERE. YOU'RE SWEET ON JOHNNY, HUH?

YEAH, I GUESS I AM.

HE'S A LITTLE FLAKY. NEVER WAS RIGHT AFTER *FRANKY* AND HIM GOT LOST DOWN IN THE MINE TEN YEARS AGO.

YOU FIXED? PROBABLY NOT, RIGHT? I'LL GETCHA WHAT YOU NEED.

THANKS... I JUST WANT TO HAVE SOME *FUN*, Y'KNOW.

NO ONE HAS TO EXPLAIN *FUN* TO *LIPS LAFAYETTE.* THING IS, IF YOU WANT TO KEEP THE GOOD TIMES ROLLIN', Y'NEED TO AIM A LITTLE *HIGHER.*

JOHNNY'S A GOOD KID, AND I *LOVE* MY *FRANKY* --BUT IN INDIGO, LITTLE FISH LIKE THEM EITHER GET SWALLOWED OR SENT UP THE RIVER.

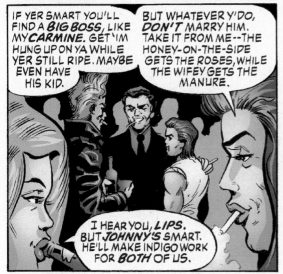

IF YER SMART YOU'LL FIND A *BIG BOSS*, LIKE MY *CARMINE.* GET 'IM HUNG UP ON YA WHILE YER STILL RIPE. MAYBE EVEN HAVE HIS KID.

BUT WHATEVER Y'DO, *DON'T* MARRY HIM. TAKE IT FROM ME--THE HONEY-ON-THE-SIDE GETS THE ROSES, WHILE THE WIFEY GETS THE MANURE.

I HEAR YOU, *LIPS.* BUT *JOHNNY'S* SMART. HE'LL MAKE INDIGO WORK FOR *BOTH* OF US.

"*JOHNNY* AND I GOT AS TIGHT AS TWO PEOPLE CAN GET, BUT I EXPECTED THE SKY TO BE THE LIMIT..."

IT FITS YOU IN *ALL* THE RIGHT PLACES, BUT IT'S KIND OF *EXPENSIVE.* I'M NOT SURE HOW MUCH DOUGH I GOT LEFT AFTER THE BEAUTY PARLOR AND SHOE STORE...

BUT *JOHNNY,* I THOUGHT *MR. CARBONE* SET YOU UP WITH THAT *FIREWORKS* HEIST?

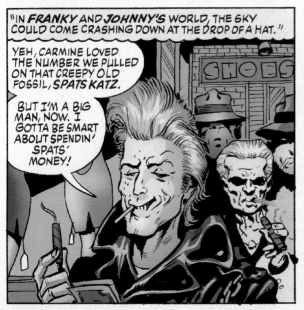

"IN *FRANKY* AND *JOHNNY'S* WORLD, THE SKY COULD COME CRASHING DOWN AT THE *DROP OF A HAT.*"

YEH, CARMINE LOVED THE NUMBER WE PULLED ON THAT CREEPY OLD FOSSIL, *SPATS KATZ.*

BUT I'M A BIG MAN, NOW. I GOTTA BE SMART ABOUT SPENDIN' *SPATS'* MONEY!

I THINK ANY THIEVING PUNK WHO'D DENY YOU THAT DRESS DESERVES TO BE BEATEN WITHIN AN INCH OF HIS LIFE.

MAY I?

SPATS! I WAS JUST KIDDIN'! OOOFT! MR. KATZ, PLEASE, I... UNNNFF!! AAAAGHH!!

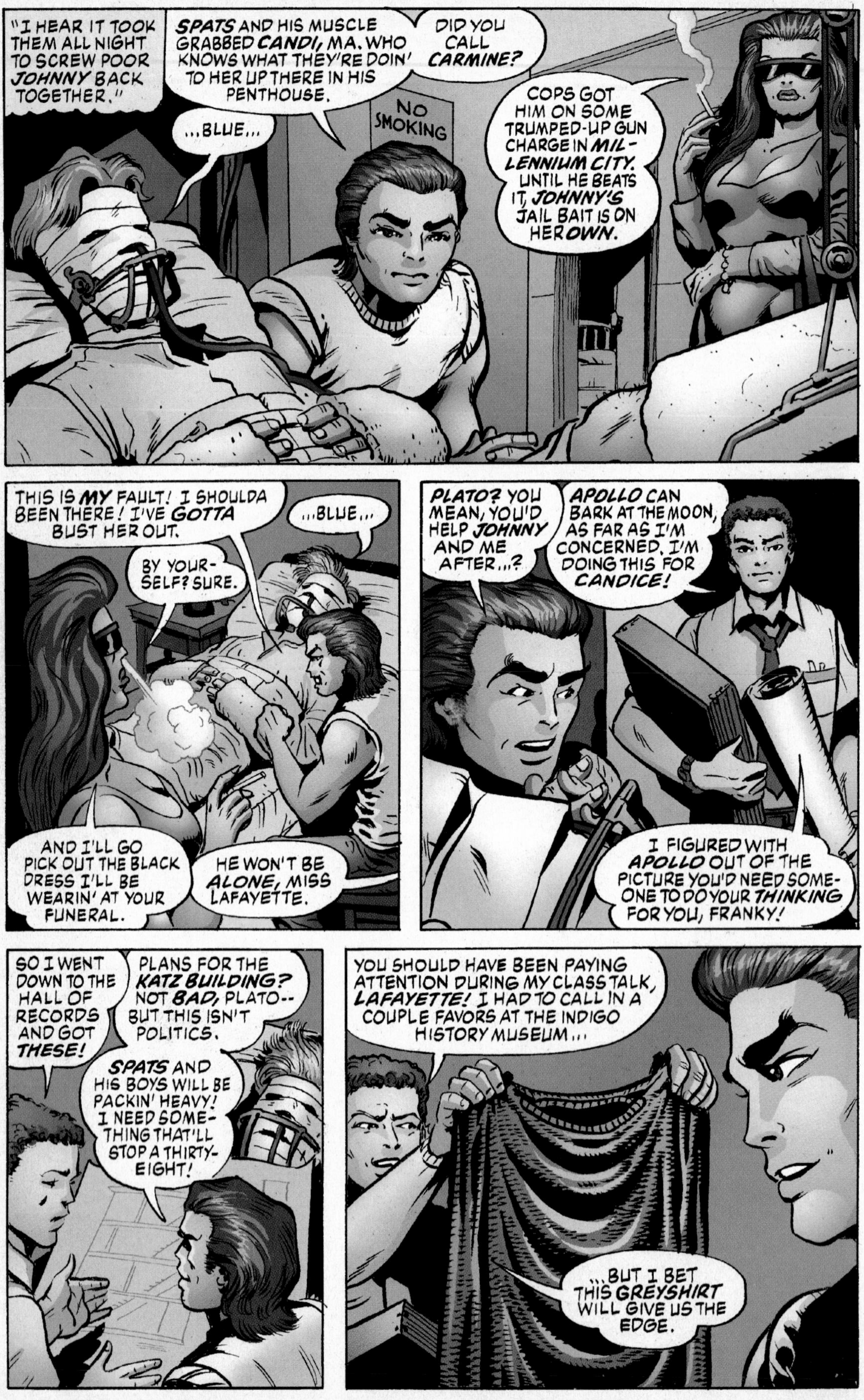
"I HEAR IT TOOK THEM ALL NIGHT TO SCREW POOR JOHNNY BACK TOGETHER."
SPATS AND HIS MUSCLE GRABBED CANDI, MA. WHO KNOWS WHAT THEY'RE DOIN' TO HER UP THERE IN HIS PENTHOUSE.
DID YOU CALL CARMINE?
...BLUE...
NO SMOKING
COPS GOT HIM ON SOME TRUMPED-UP GUN CHARGE IN MILLENNIUM CITY. UNTIL HE BEATS IT, JOHNNY'S JAIL BAIT IS ON HER OWN.
THIS IS MY FAULT! I SHOULDA BEEN THERE! I'VE GOTTA BUST HER OUT.
...BLUE...
BY YOURSELF? SURE.
AND I'LL GO PICK OUT THE BLACK DRESS I'LL BE WEARIN' AT YOUR FUNERAL.
HE WON'T BE ALONE, MISS LAFAYETTE.
PLATO? YOU MEAN, YOU'D HELP JOHNNY AND ME AFTER...?
APOLLO CAN BARK AT THE MOON, AS FAR AS I'M CONCERNED. I'M DOING THIS FOR CANDICE!
I FIGURED WITH APOLLO OUT OF THE PICTURE YOU'D NEED SOMEONE TO DO YOUR THINKING FOR YOU, FRANKY!
SO I WENT DOWN TO THE HALL OF RECORDS AND GOT THESE!
PLANS FOR THE KATZ BUILDING? NOT BAD, PLATO-- BUT THIS ISN'T POLITICS.
SPATS AND HIS BOYS WILL BE PACKIN' HEAVY! I NEED SOMETHING THAT'LL STOP A THIRTY-EIGHT!
YOU SHOULD HAVE BEEN PAYING ATTENTION DURING MY CLASS TALK, LAFAYETTE! I HAD TO CALL IN A COUPLE FAVORS AT THE INDIGO HISTORY MUSEUM...
...BUT I BET THIS GREYSHIRT WILL GIVE US THE EDGE.

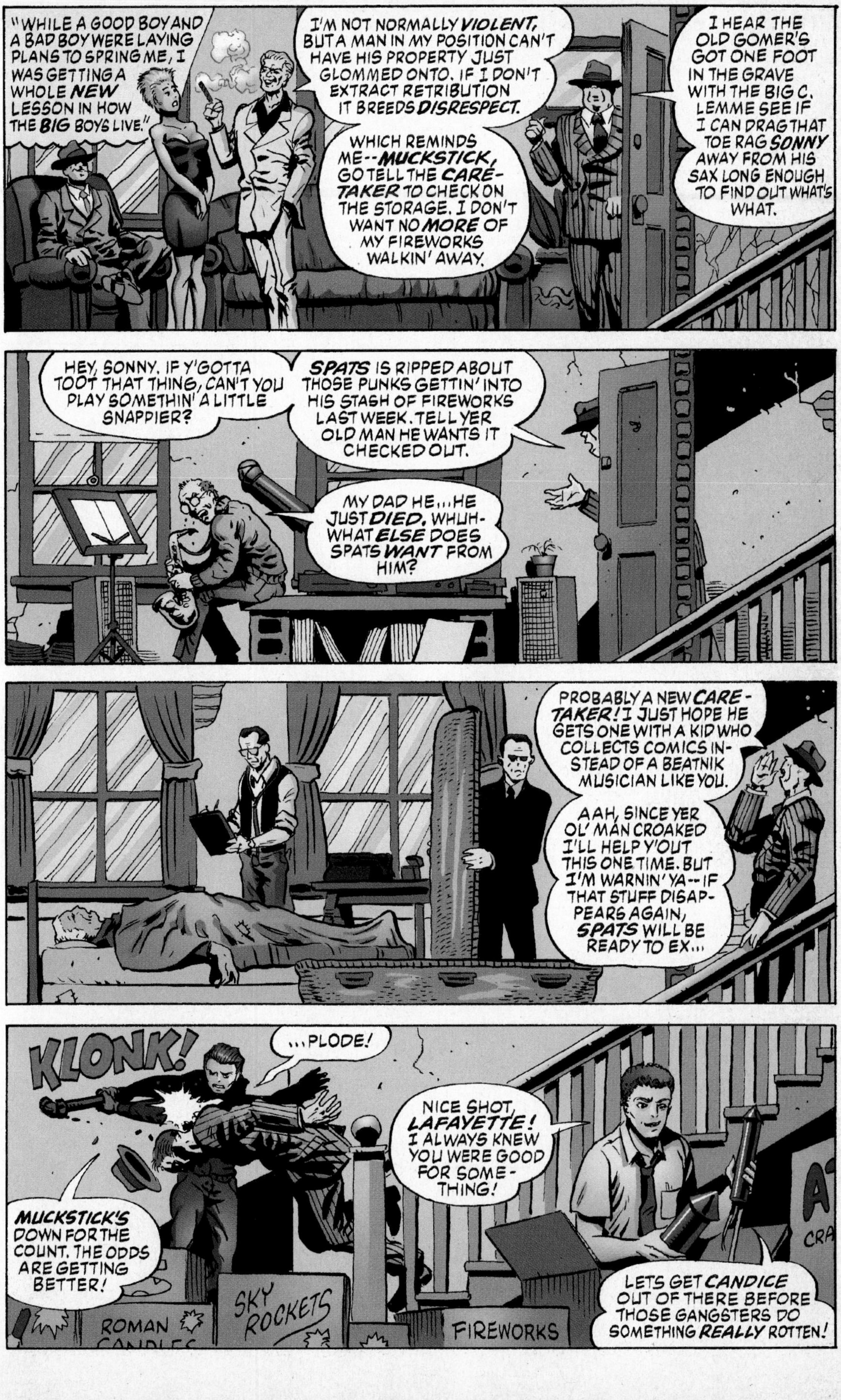
"WHILE A GOOD BOY AND A BAD BOY WERE LAYING PLANS TO SPRING ME, I WAS GETTING A WHOLE NEW LESSON IN HOW THE BIG BOYS LIVE."
I'M NOT NORMALLY VIOLENT, BUT A MAN IN MY POSITION CAN'T HAVE HIS PROPERTY JUST GLOMMED ONTO. IF I DON'T EXTRACT RETRIBUTION IT BREEDS DISRESPECT.
WHICH REMINDS ME--MUCKSTICK, GO TELL THE CARE-TAKER TO CHECK ON THE STORAGE. I DON'T WANT NO MORE OF MY FIREWORKS WALKIN' AWAY.
I HEAR THE OLD GOMER'S GOT ONE FOOT IN THE GRAVE WITH THE BIG C. LEMME SEE IF I CAN DRAG THAT TOE RAG SONNY AWAY FROM HIS SAX LONG ENOUGH TO FIND OUT WHAT'S WHAT.
HEY, SONNY. IF Y'GOTTA TOOT THAT THING, CAN'T YOU PLAY SOMETHIN' A LITTLE SNAPPIER?
SPATS IS RIPPED ABOUT THOSE PUNKS GETTIN' INTO HIS STASH OF FIREWORKS LAST WEEK. TELL YER OLD MAN HE WANTS IT CHECKED OUT.
MY DAD HE... HE JUST DIED. WHUH-WHAT ELSE DOES SPATS WANT FROM HIM?
PROBABLY A NEW CARE-TAKER! I JUST HOPE HE GETS ONE WITH A KID WHO COLLECTS COMICS IN-STEAD OF A BEATNIK MUSICIAN LIKE YOU.
AAH, SINCE YER OL' MAN CROAKED I'LL HELP Y'OUT THIS ONE TIME. BUT I'M WARNIN' YA--IF THAT STUFF DISAP-PEARS AGAIN, SPATS WILL BE READY TO EX...
KLONK!
...PLODE!
NICE SHOT, LAFAYETTE! I ALWAYS KNEW YOU WERE GOOD FOR SOME-THING!
MUCKSTICK'S DOWN FOR THE COUNT. THE ODDS ARE GETTING BETTER!
LETS GET CANDICE OUT OF THERE BEFORE THOSE GANGSTERS DO SOMETHING REALLY ROTTEN!
SKY ROCKETS
ROMAN CANDLES
FIREWORKS

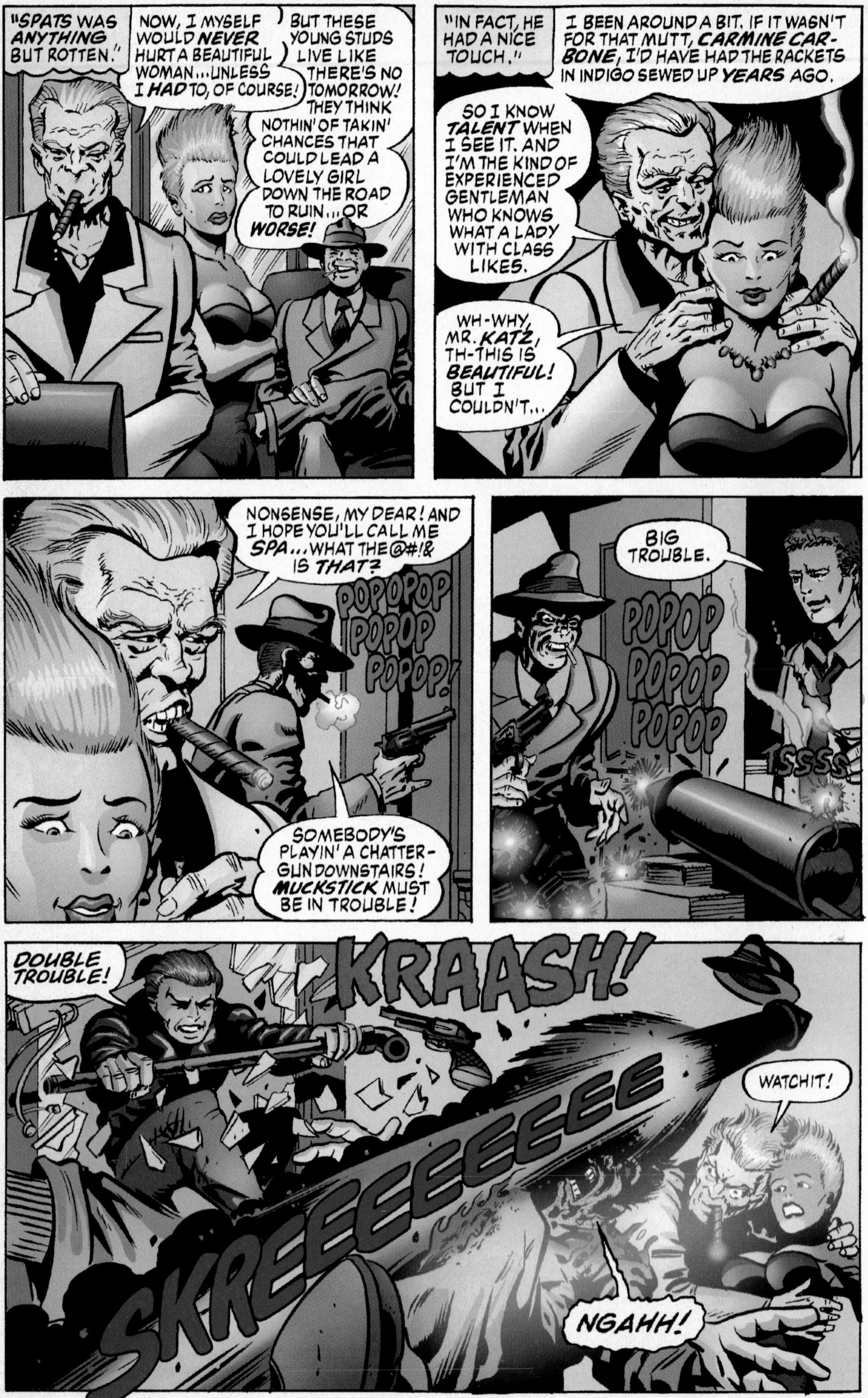
"SPATS WAS ANYTHING BUT ROTTEN."
NOW, I MYSELF WOULD NEVER HURT A BEAUTIFUL WOMAN... UNLESS I HAD TO, OF COURSE!
BUT THESE YOUNG STUDS LIVE LIKE THERE'S NO TOMORROW! THEY THINK NOTHIN' OF TAKIN' CHANCES THAT COULD LEAD A LOVELY GIRL DOWN THE ROAD TO RUIN... OR WORSE!
"IN FACT, HE HAD A NICE TOUCH."
I BEEN AROUND A BIT. IF IT WASN'T FOR THAT MUTT, CARMINE CARBONE, I'D HAVE HAD THE RACKETS IN INDIGO SEWED UP YEARS AGO.
SO I KNOW TALENT WHEN I SEE IT. AND I'M THE KIND OF EXPERIENCED GENTLEMAN WHO KNOWS WHAT A LADY WITH CLASS LIKES.
WH-WHY, MR. KATZ, TH-THIS IS BEAUTIFUL! BUT I COULDN'T...
NONSENSE, MY DEAR! AND I HOPE YOU'LL CALL ME SPA... WHAT THE @#!& IS THAT?
POPOPOP POPOP POPOP!
SOMEBODY'S PLAYIN' A CHATTER-GUN DOWNSTAIRS! MUCKSTICK MUST BE IN TROUBLE!
BIG TROUBLE.
POPOP POPOP POPOP
ISSSS
DOUBLE TROUBLE!
KRAASH!
SKREEEEEEEEEE
WATCHIT!
NGAHH!

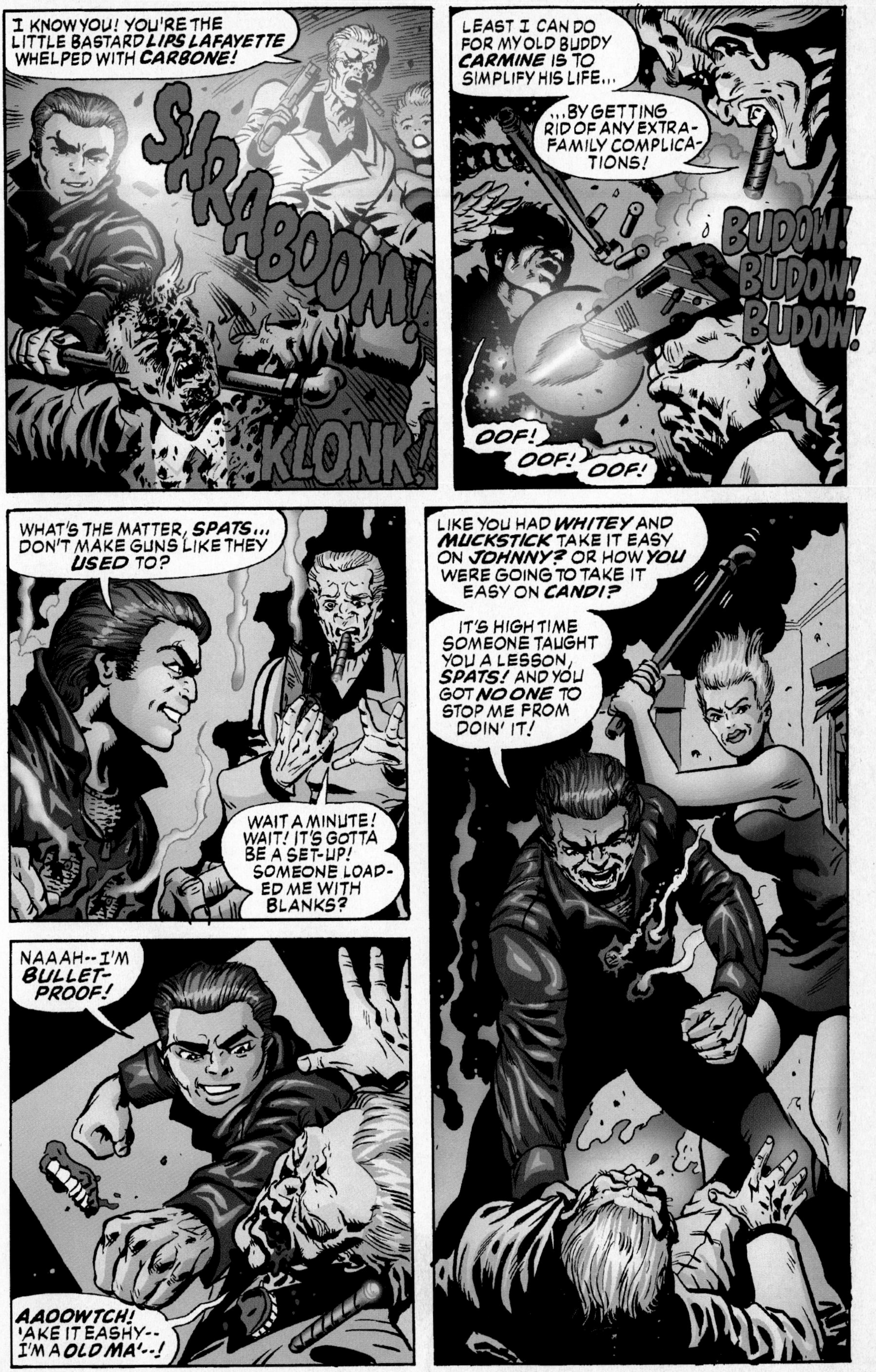
I KNOW YOU! YOU'RE THE LITTLE BASTARD LIPS LAFAYETTE WHELPED WITH CARBONE!
SHRABOOM!
KLONK!
LEAST I CAN DO FOR MY OLD BUDDY CARMINE IS TO SIMPLIFY HIS LIFE...
...BY GETTING RID OF ANY EXTRA-FAMILY COMPLICATIONS!
BUDOW! BUDOW! BUDOW!
OOF! OOF! OOF!
WHAT'S THE MATTER, SPATS... DON'T MAKE GUNS LIKE THEY USED TO?
WAIT A MINUTE! WAIT! IT'S GOTTA BE A SET-UP! SOMEONE LOADED ME WITH BLANKS?
NAAAH--I'M BULLET-PROOF!
AAOOWTCH! 'AKE IT EASHY--I'M A OLD MA'--!
LIKE YOU HAD WHITEY AND MUCKSTICK TAKE IT EASY ON JOHNNY? OR HOW YOU WERE GOING TO TAKE IT EASY ON CANDI?
IT'S HIGH TIME SOMEONE TAUGHT YOU A LESSON, SPATS! AND YOU GOT NO ONE TO STOP ME FROM DOIN' IT!

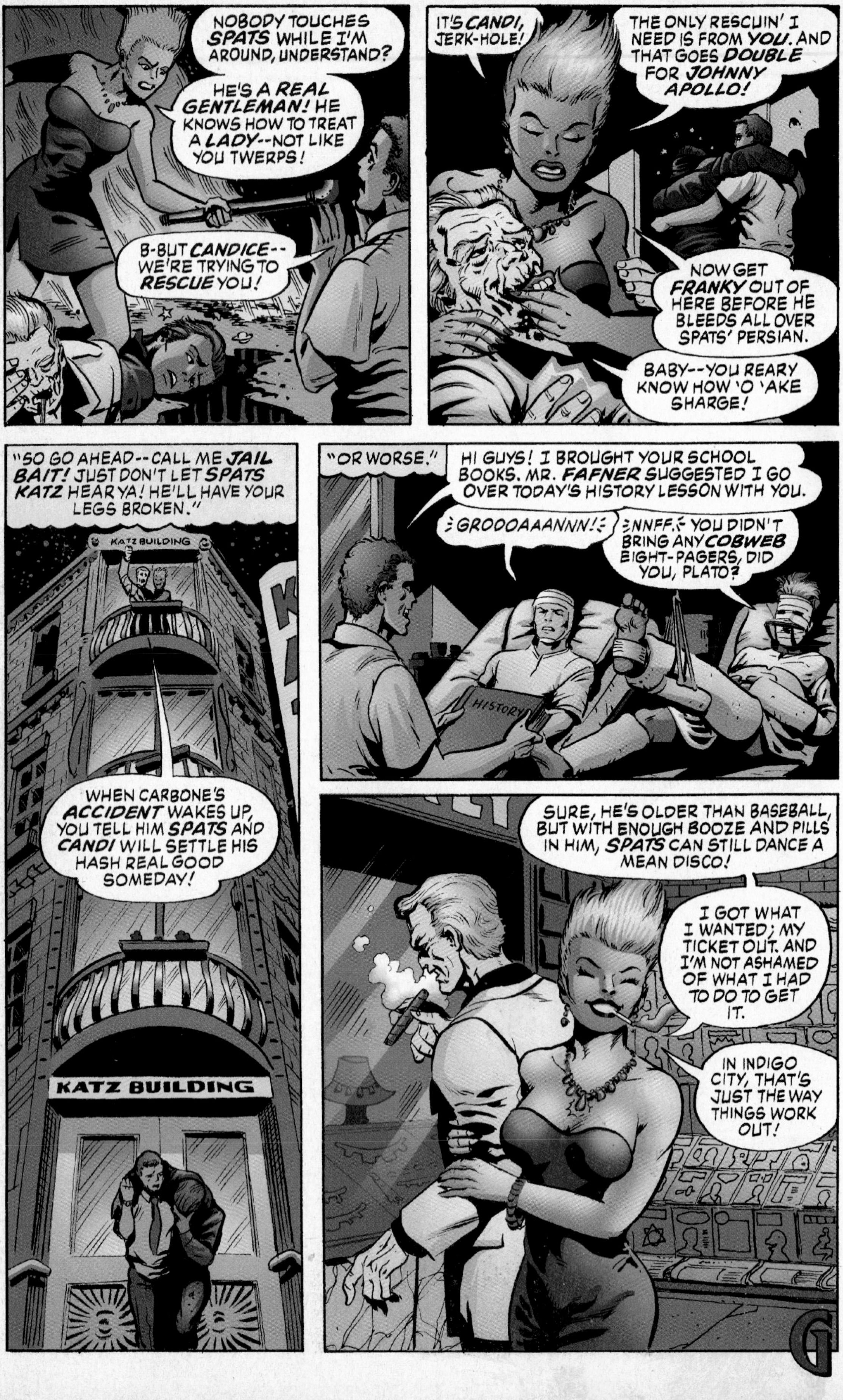
NOBODY TOUCHES SPATS WHILE I'M AROUND, UNDERSTAND?
HE'S A REAL GENTLEMAN! HE KNOWS HOW TO TREAT A LADY--NOT LIKE YOU TWERPS!
B-BUT CANDICE--WE'RE TRYING TO RESCUE YOU!
IT'S CANDI, JERK-HOLE!
THE ONLY RESCUIN' I NEED IS FROM YOU. AND THAT GOES DOUBLE FOR JOHNNY APOLLO!
NOW GET FRANKY OUT OF HERE BEFORE HE BLEEDS ALL OVER SPATS' PERSIAN.
BABY--YOU REARY KNOW HOW 'O 'AKE SHARGE!
"SO GO AHEAD--CALL ME JAIL BAIT! JUST DON'T LET SPATS KATZ HEAR YA! HE'LL HAVE YOUR LEGS BROKEN."
KATZ BUILDING
WHEN CARBONE'S ACCIDENT WAKES UP, YOU TELL HIM SPATS AND CANDI WILL SETTLE HIS HASH REAL GOOD SOMEDAY!
KATZ BUILDING
"OR WORSE."
HI GUYS! I BROUGHT YOUR SCHOOL BOOKS. MR. FAFNER SUGGESTED I GO OVER TODAY'S HISTORY LESSON WITH YOU.
GROOOAAANNN!
SNNFF. YOU DIDN'T BRING ANY COBWEB EIGHT-PAGERS, DID YOU, PLATO?
HISTORY
SURE, HE'S OLDER THAN BASEBALL, BUT WITH ENOUGH BOOZE AND PILLS IN HIM, SPATS CAN STILL DANCE A MEAN DISCO!
I GOT WHAT I WANTED; MY TICKET OUT. AND I'M NOT ASHAMED OF WHAT I HAD TO DO TO GET IT.
IN INDIGO CITY, THAT'S JUST THE WAY THINGS WORK OUT!

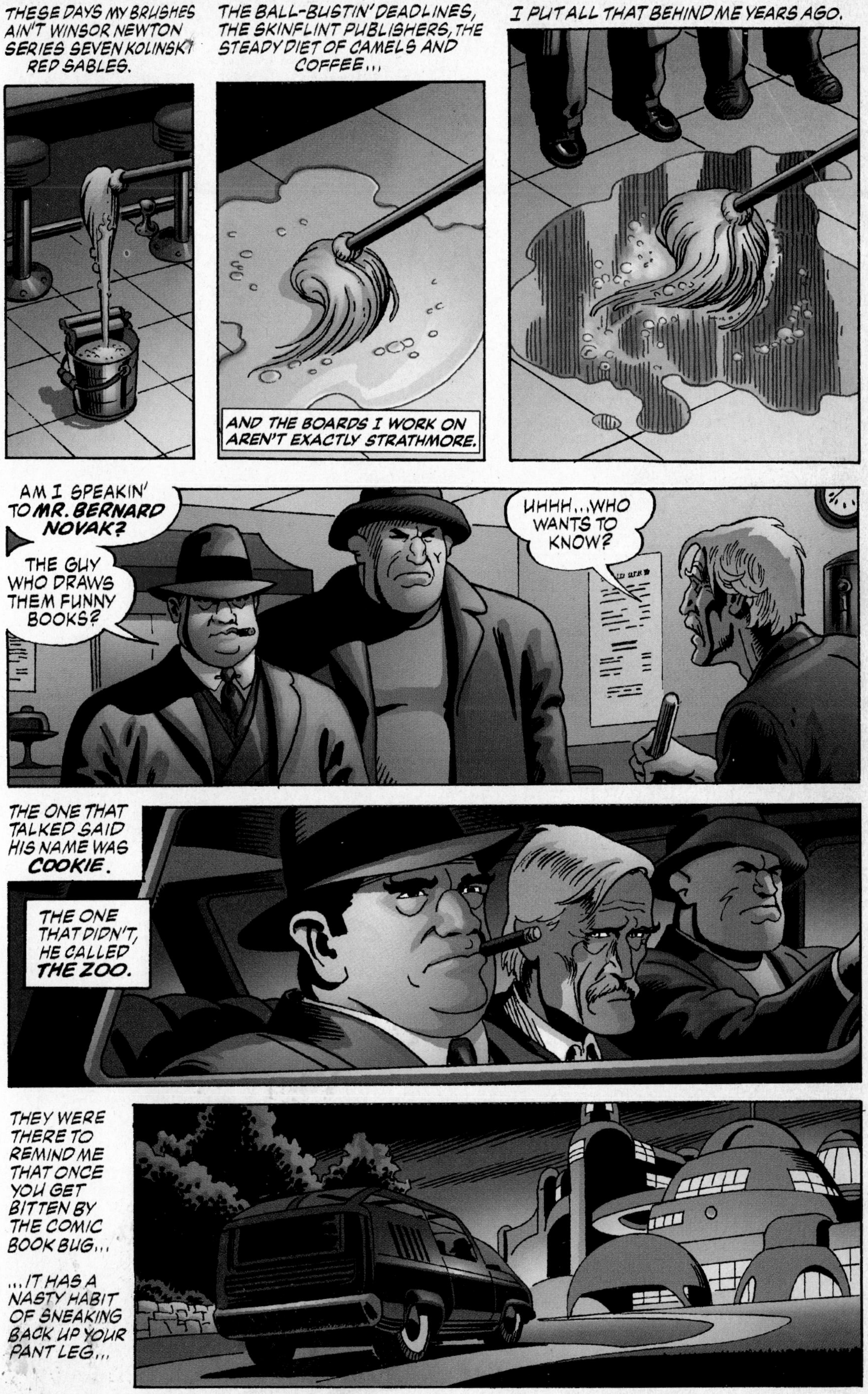
THESE DAYS MY BRUSHES AIN'T WINSOR NEWTON SERIES SEVEN KOLINSKI RED SABLES.
THE BALL-BUSTIN' DEADLINES, THE SKINFLINT PUBLISHERS, THE STEADY DIET OF CAMELS AND COFFEE...
AND THE BOARDS I WORK ON AREN'T EXACTLY STRATHMORE.
I PUT ALL THAT BEHIND ME YEARS AGO.
AM I SPEAKIN' TO MR. BERNARD NOVAK?
THE GUY WHO DRAWS THEM FUNNY BOOKS?
UHHH...WHO WANTS TO KNOW?
THE ONE THAT TALKED SAID HIS NAME WAS COOKIE.
THE ONE THAT DIDN'T, HE CALLED THE ZOO.
THEY WERE THERE TO REMIND ME THAT ONCE YOU GET BITTEN BY THE COMIC BOOK BUG...
...IT HAS A NASTY HABIT OF SNEAKING BACK UP YOUR PANT LEG...

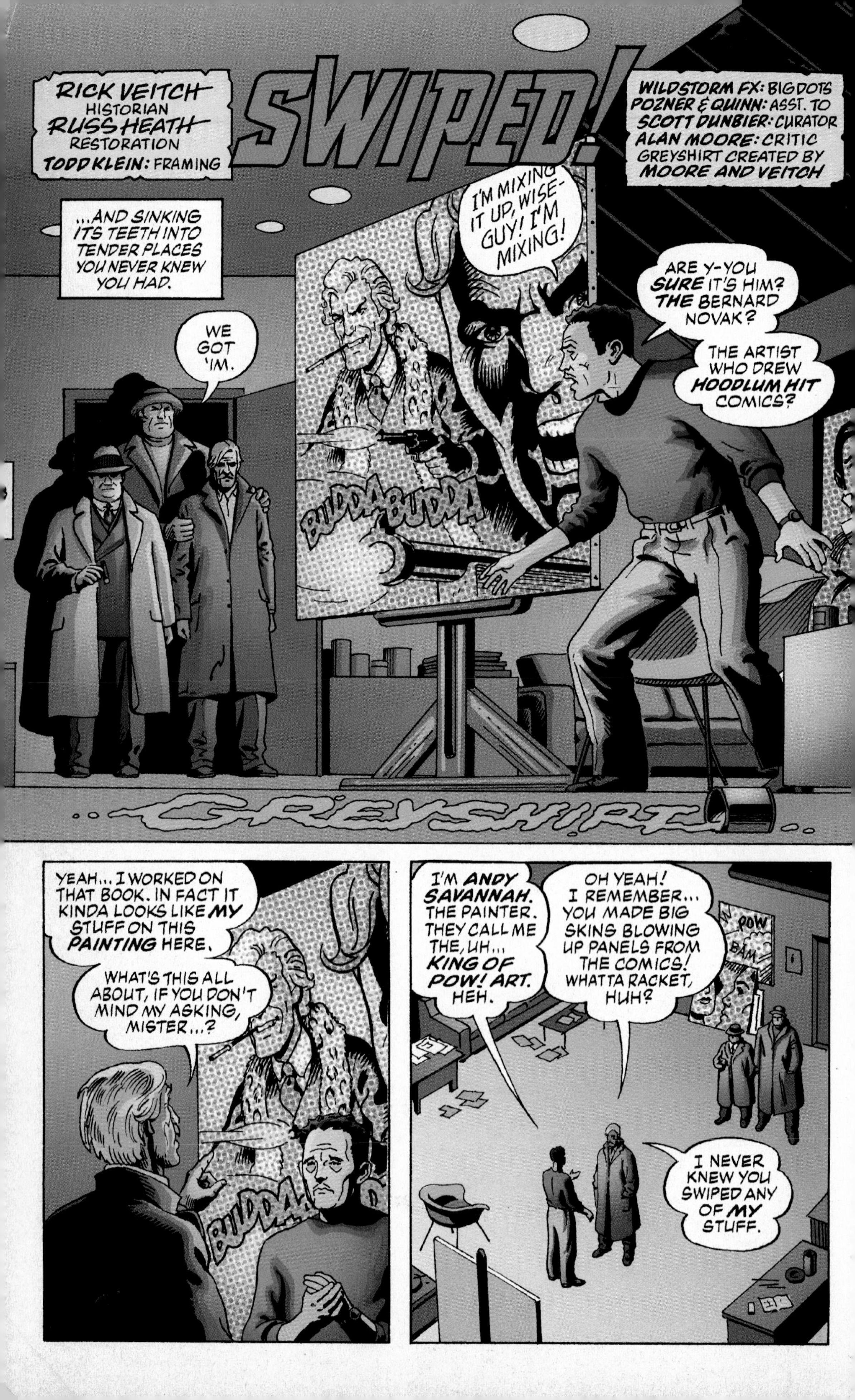
RICK VEITCH HISTORIAN
RUSS HEATH RESTORATION
TODD KLEIN: FRAMING
SWIPED!
WILDSTORM FX: BIGDOTS
POZNER & QUINN: ASST. TO
SCOTT DUNBIER: CURATOR
ALAN MOORE: CRITIC
GREYSHIRT CREATED BY MOORE AND VEITCH
...AND SINKING ITS TEETH INTO TENDER PLACES YOU NEVER KNEW YOU HAD.
I'M MIXING IT UP, WISE-GUY! I'M MIXING!
ARE Y-YOU SURE IT'S HIM? THE BERNARD NOVAK?
THE ARTIST WHO DREW HOODLUM HIT COMICS?
WE GOT 'IM.
BUDDA BUDDA
GREYSHIRT
YEAH... I WORKED ON THAT BOOK. IN FACT IT KINDA LOOKS LIKE MY STUFF ON THIS PAINTING HERE.
WHAT'S THIS ALL ABOUT, IF YOU DON'T MIND MY ASKING, MISTER...?
BUDDA
I'M ANDY SAVANNAH. THE PAINTER. THEY CALL ME THE, UH... KING OF POW! ART. HEH.
OH YEAH! I REMEMBER... YOU MADE BIG SKINS BLOWING UP PANELS FROM THE COMICS! WHATTA RACKET, HUH?
POW
BAM
I NEVER KNEW YOU SWIPED ANY OF MY STUFF.

JEEKERS, THESE *ALL* LOOK LIKE THEY'RE MINE.

I *DON'T* STEAL, MR. NOVAK. I *REINTERPRET* THE SOURCE MATERIAL IN A NEW MEDIUM. OR AT LEAST I *USED* TO...

I--I HAVEN'T MADE A NEW PAINTING IN *TEN YEARS*...

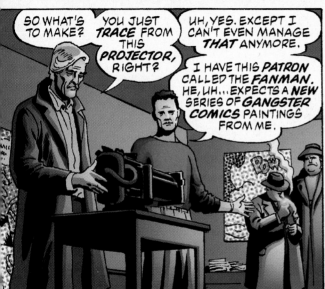

SO WHAT'S TO MAKE?

YOU JUST *TRACE* FROM THIS *PROJECTOR*, RIGHT?

UH, YES. EXCEPT I CAN'T EVEN MANAGE *THAT* ANYMORE.

I HAVE THIS *PATRON* CALLED THE *FANMAN*. HE, UH...EXPECTS A *NEW* SERIES OF *GANGSTER COMICS* PAINTINGS FROM ME.

OR HE ORDERS *COOKIE* AND *THE ZOO* TO BREAK YOUR LEGS?

OR WORSE.

LISTEN, BERNARD... I--I JUST NEED SOMEONE TO *ASSIST* ME. SOMEONE *FAMILIAR* WITH THE IDIOM...

AND IF I DON'T?

HEY! YER A *PRO*, RIGHT?

THE BOSS'LL PAY, AT *LEAST* AS MUCH AS YOUSE WUZ MAKIN' SWABBIN' THE DECK BACK AT THAT GREASY SPOON.

YOU GETCHER MONEY. THE *FANMAN* GETS HIS *ANDY SAVANNAH* PAINTINGS.

EVERYBODY'S HAPPY, RIGHT?

SO THAT'S HOW I GOT BACK INTO COMICS...

I'M AFRAID YOUR PROJECTOR'S GOT MORE PROBLEMS THAN LI'L ABNER'S GOT HILLBILLIES.

YOU SEE? IT'S *HOPELESS!* WHEN THEY COME BACK AND DON'T FIND A NEW PAINTING, I'M *MINCEMEAT!*

WELL, WE CAN ALWAYS FALL BACK ON TALENT.

YOU SAY WE *GOTTA* USE THESE GANGSTER COMICS?

YES. MY FIRST PAINTINGS WERE ALL TAKEN FROM ... ER, INSPIRED BY *HOODLUM HIT.*

THERE WAS A SERIES YOU DID CALLED *"FRANKY AND JOHNNY,"* BASED ON TWO REAL GANGSTERS HERE IN INDIGO CITY.

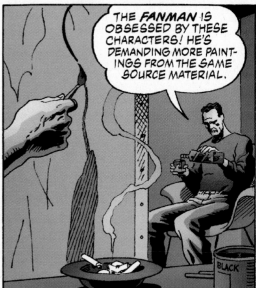

THE *FANMAN* IS OBSESSED BY THESE CHARACTERS! HE'S DEMANDING MORE PAINTINGS FROM THE SAME SOURCE MATERIAL.

BLACK

I NEVER SHOULD HAVE BET ON THE *ROLLER SMASH.* BORROWED ALL THAT MONEY FROM HIM. GOT IN SO DEEP.

FLESH

NOW HIS GOONS ARE GOING TO GIVE ME THE *JIMMY HOFFA* TREATMENT!

MAYBE NOT. CHECK THIS OUT.

WHATCHA THINK?

MY GOD... IT'S ...IT'S... BRILLIANT!

HEHHEH. IF I DO SAY SO MYSELF.

YOU'RE STILL THE KING, JOHNNY!

IT'S THE BEST THING I'VE DONE IN YEARS. EXCEPT MAYBE FOR THE COLOR ON THE FLESH DOTS.

YOU HAVEN'T MIXED THE RED AND THE WHITE CORRECTLY...

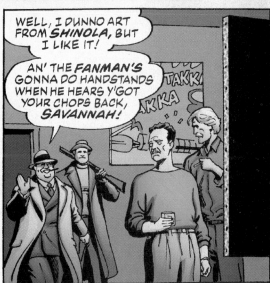

WELL, I DUNNO ART FROM SHINOLA, BUT I LIKE IT!

AN' THE FANMAN'S GONNA DO HANDSTANDS WHEN HE HEARS Y'GOT YOUR CHOPS BACK, SAVANNAH!

WELL, WHAT DID HE EXPECT FROM THE KING OF POW! ART?

NOW THAT I'M ROLLING AGAIN, YOU CAN TELL HIM HE'LL HAVE THE WHOLE SERIES IN SIX MONTHS.

UHHHM... NO.

ME AND THE ZOO GOT ANOTHER PROBLEM CLIENT TO ATTEND TO RIGHT NOW. WE'LL BE BACK TO PICK UP ALL THE PAINTINGS AT THE END OF THE WEEK.

Y'GOT A PROBLEM WIT DAT?

NOPE.

I WAS ALWAYS PRETTY GOOD WITH **DEADLINES**. ESPECIALLY THE DROP-DEAD VARIETY. SO I GRABBED A MOLDY COPY OF **HOODLUM HIT** AND GOT RIGHT TO WORK.

IT WAS WEIRD REWORKING PANELS FROM MY OLD JOBS. STILL, BLOWN UP TO THAT SIZE, THE STUFF HAD A POWERFUL PRIMAL QUALITY THAT I DUG.

I KEPT TELLIN' MYSELF I DIDN'T MIND HIM HOGGING ALL THE CREDIT. I FIGURED SOMEONE, SOMEDAY, WOULD RESEARCH HIS SOURCE MATERIAL AND MAYBE I'D MERIT A FOOTNOTE IN THE HISTORY BOOKS.

SAVANNAH COULDN'T MAKE HIMSELF SCARCE FAST ENOUGH FOR ME.

YES. **YES!** I LIKE IT EXCEPT... THE COLOR ON THE FLESH DOTS IS STILL OFF.

LOOK AT MY OLDER PAINTINGS. IT'S ALL IN THE **MIX!**

I NEVER THOUGHT FRANKY WOULD RAT ME OUT!

AT LEAST UNTIL **SAVANNAH** AND HIS ART CROWD FRIENDS WOULD SHOW UP.

ANDY, YOU STILL SERVE UP THE MOST **DELICIOUS** IRONIC INVERSION!

YOU TRANSMUTE CLICHED, STYLIZED PAP INTO A MASTERPIECE OF DISASSOCIATION!

I ONLY WISH MY **HELPER** COULD MIX THE FLESH TONES AS DIRECTED.

IN THE MEANTIME, HE SURE MADE IT HARD TO FEEL FLATTERED BY THE SWIPE.

SUCH VULGAR ELEGANCE! I'D GIVE **ANYTHING** TO ASSIST THE MAN WHO RECREATED THE LOWEST FORM OF POPULAR CULTURE IN HIS OWN IMAGE!

ACTUALLY, MY DEAR, I'M **LOOKING** FOR SOMEONE TO MIX MY FLESH TONES FOR ME.

K RAK

OKAY, LITTLE BUDDY--FOR INDIGO CITY!

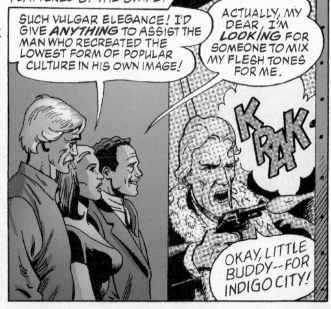

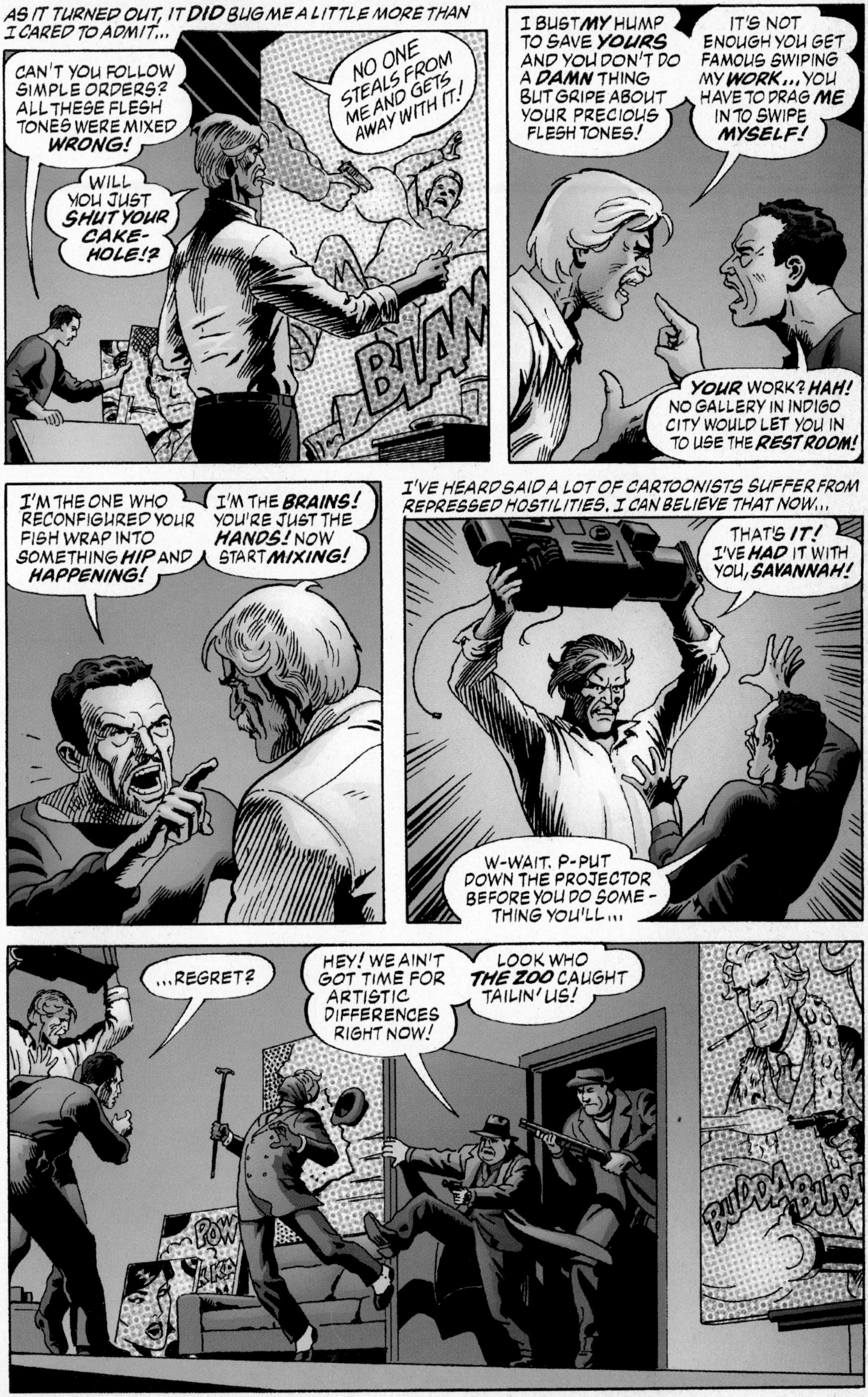
AS IT TURNED OUT, IT DID BUG ME A LITTLE MORE THAN I CARED TO ADMIT...
CAN'T YOU FOLLOW SIMPLE ORDERS? ALL THESE FLESH TONES WERE MIXED WRONG!
NO ONE STEALS FROM ME AND GETS AWAY WITH IT!
WILL YOU JUST SHUT YOUR CAKE-HOLE!?
BLAM
I BUST MY HUMP TO SAVE YOURS AND YOU DON'T DO A DAMN THING BUT GRIPE ABOUT YOUR PRECIOUS FLESH TONES!
IT'S NOT ENOUGH YOU GET FAMOUS SWIPING MY WORK... YOU HAVE TO DRAG ME IN TO SWIPE MYSELF!
YOUR WORK? HAH! NO GALLERY IN INDIGO CITY WOULD LET YOU IN TO USE THE REST ROOM!
I'M THE ONE WHO RECONFIGURED YOUR FISH WRAP INTO SOMETHING HIP AND HAPPENING!
I'M THE BRAINS! YOU'RE JUST THE HANDS! NOW START MIXING!
I'VE HEARD SAID A LOT OF CARTOONISTS SUFFER FROM REPRESSED HOSTILITIES. I CAN BELIEVE THAT NOW...
THAT'S IT! I'VE HAD IT WITH YOU, SAVANNAH!
W-WAIT. P-PUT DOWN THE PROJECTOR BEFORE YOU DO SOME-THING YOU'LL...
...REGRET?
HEY! WE AIN'T GOT TIME FOR ARTISTIC DIFFERENCES RIGHT NOW!
LOOK WHO THE ZOO CAUGHT TAILIN' US!
POW

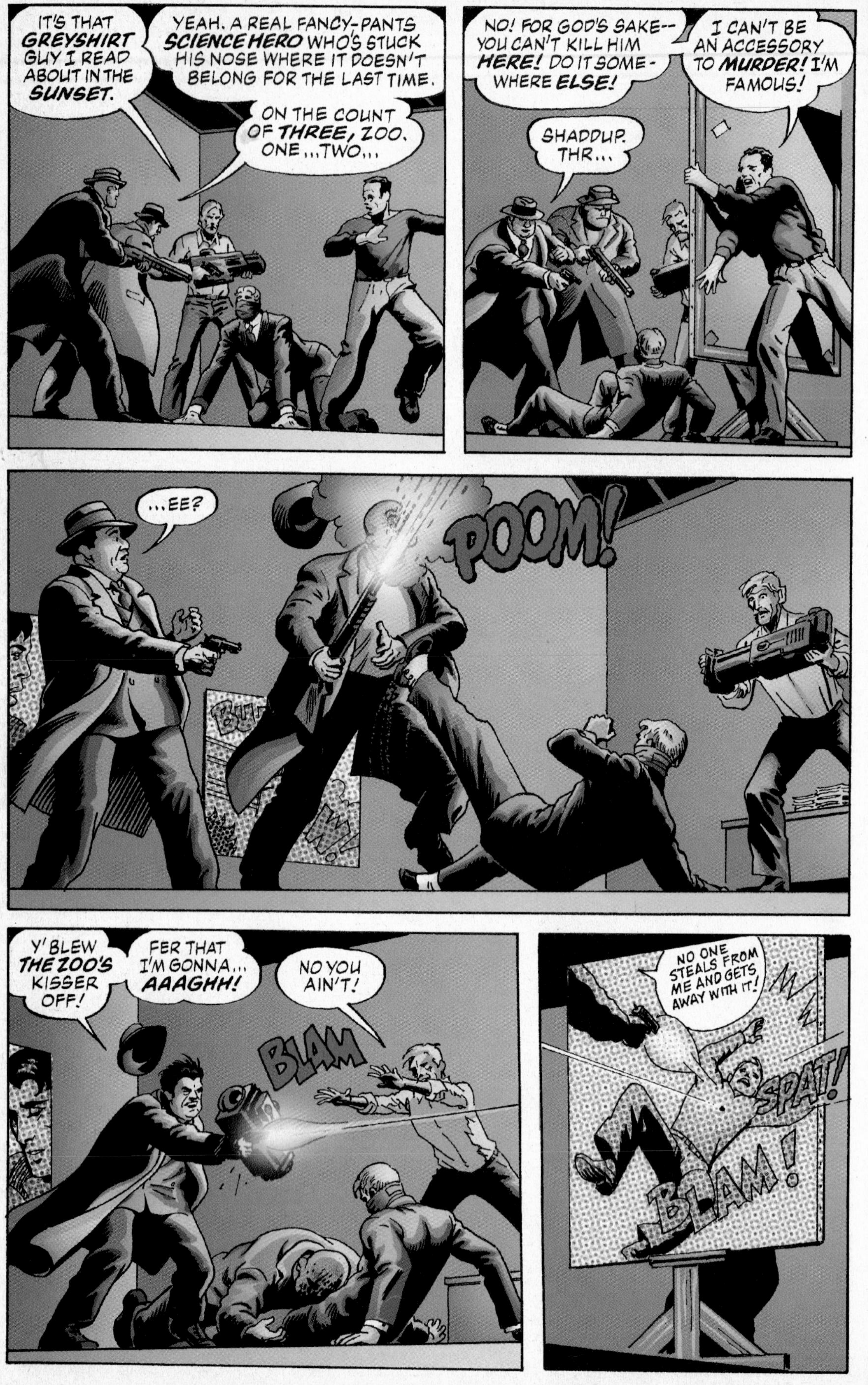
IT'S THAT GREYSHIRT GUY I READ ABOUT IN THE SUNSET.
YEAH. A REAL FANCY-PANTS SCIENCE HERO WHO'S STUCK HIS NOSE WHERE IT DOESN'T BELONG FOR THE LAST TIME.
ON THE COUNT OF THREE, ZOO. ONE... TWO...
NO! FOR GOD'S SAKE-- YOU CAN'T KILL HIM HERE! DO IT SOME-WHERE ELSE!
I CAN'T BE AN ACCESSORY TO MURDER! I'M FAMOUS!
SHADDUP. THR...
...EE?
POOM!
Y'BLEW THE ZOO'S KISSER OFF!
FER THAT I'M GONNA... AAAGHH!
NO YOU AIN'T!
BLAM
NO ONE STEALS FROM ME AND GETS AWAY WITH IT!
SPAT!
BLAM!

THE ZOO WON'T MISS THOSE BOYISH GOOD LOOKS WHERE HE'S GOING.

BUT A CUSTOM NOSE JOB WILL DO WONDERS FOR *YOUR* PRISON SOCIAL LIFE.

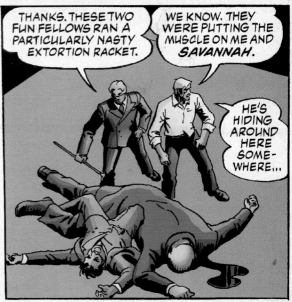

THANKS. THESE TWO FUN FELLOWS RAN A PARTICULARLY NASTY EXTORTION RACKET.

WE KNOW. THEY WERE PUTTING THE MUSCLE ON ME AND *SAVANNAH*.

HE'S HIDING AROUND HERE SOME-WHERE...

SAVANNAH?

STEALS FROM ME AND GETS AWAY WITH IT!

BLAM!

OH GOD! LOOK AT ALL THE *BLOOD*! SAVANNAH CAUGHT THE STRAY BULLET!

TOUGH BREAK. WRONG PLACE, WRONG TIME.

WHAT'S UP WITH THESE *PAINTINGS* ANYWAY?

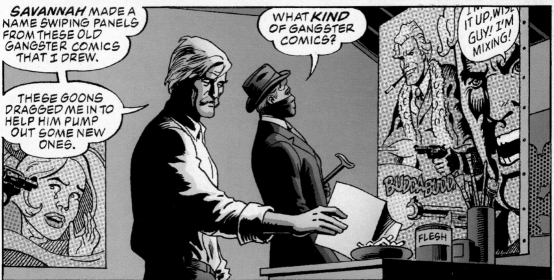

SAVANNAH MADE A NAME SWIPING PANELS FROM THESE OLD GANGSTER COMICS THAT I DREW.

THESE GOONS DRAGGED ME IN TO HELP HIM PUMP OUT SOME NEW ONES.

WHAT *KIND* OF GANGSTER COMICS?

IT UP, WISE GUY! I'M MIXING!

BUDDA-BUDDA!

FLESH

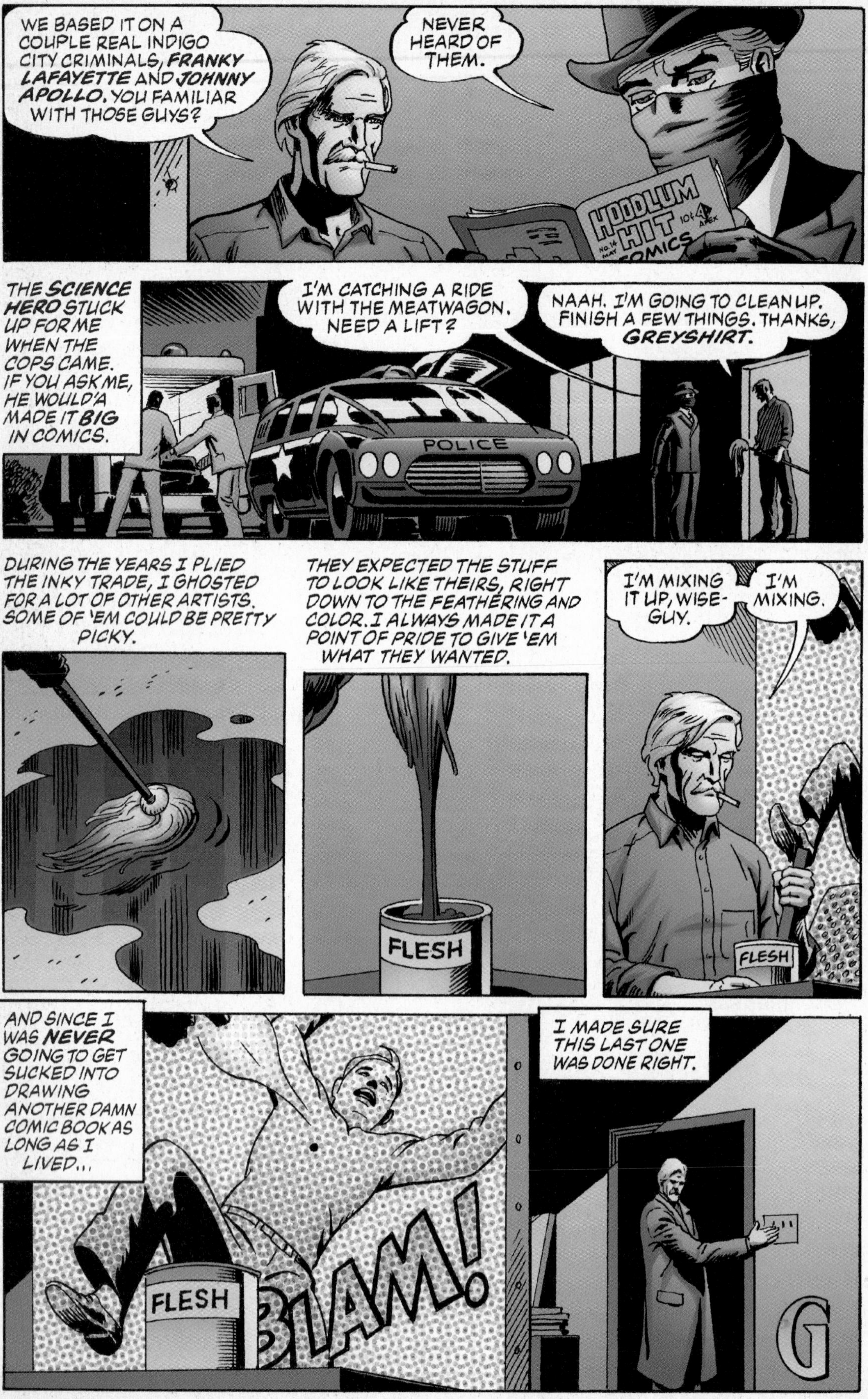
WE BASED IT ON A COUPLE REAL INDIGO CITY CRIMINALS, FRANKY LAFAYETTE AND JOHNNY APOLLO. YOU FAMILIAR WITH THOSE GUYS?
NEVER HEARD OF THEM.
HOODLUM HIT COMICS
THE SCIENCE HERO STUCK UP FOR ME WHEN THE COPS CAME. IF YOU ASK ME, HE WOULD'A MADE IT BIG IN COMICS.
I'M CATCHING A RIDE WITH THE MEATWAGON. NEED A LIFT?
NAAH. I'M GOING TO CLEAN UP. FINISH A FEW THINGS. THANKS, GREYSHIRT.
POLICE
DURING THE YEARS I PLIED THE INKY TRADE, I GHOSTED FOR A LOT OF OTHER ARTISTS. SOME OF 'EM COULD BE PRETTY PICKY.
THEY EXPECTED THE STUFF TO LOOK LIKE THEIRS, RIGHT DOWN TO THE FEATHERING AND COLOR. I ALWAYS MADE IT A POINT OF PRIDE TO GIVE 'EM WHAT THEY WANTED.
FLESH
I'M MIXING IT UP, WISE-GUY.
I'M MIXING.
FLESH
AND SINCE I WAS NEVER GOING TO GET SUCKED INTO DRAWING ANOTHER DAMN COMIC BOOK AS LONG AS I LIVED...
FLESH
BLAM!
I MADE SURE THIS LAST ONE WAS DONE RIGHT.
G

ALL THE NEWS FROM DAWN TO DUSK

NOW 60¢

INDIGO CITY SUNSET

AFTERNOON CITY EDITION

Monday, November 19, 2001 Metro Weather – Today: Misty, Tonight: Fog Creeping In, Tomorrow: Low-lying Fog

BRING IN THE CLOWNS!

GREYSHIRT COLLARS CIRCUS SLAVERS!

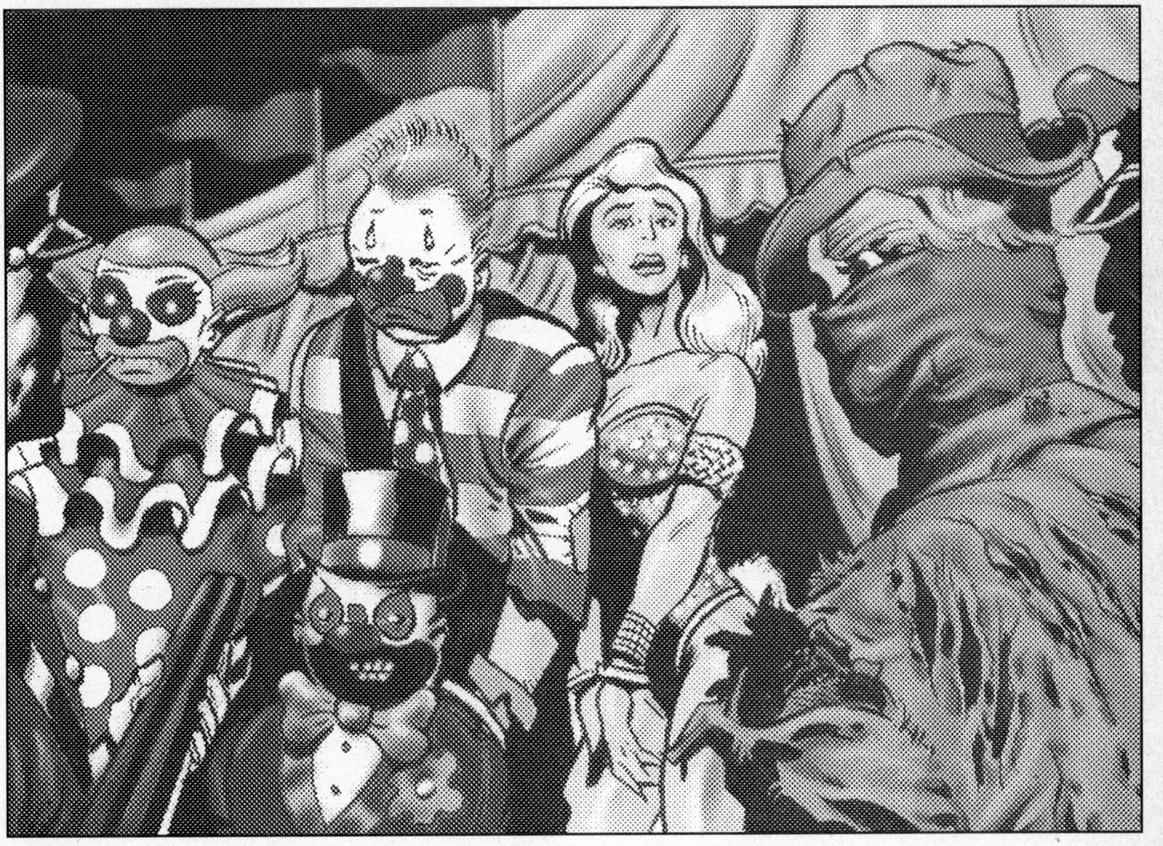

Indigo City: The big top hit rock bottom last night, after GREYSHIRT cracked a three ring circus of crime preying on innocent Indigo children. Kids hoping to escape to a life of adventure by running away with the circus, instead found themselves slapped in chains and sold as slaves in the Far East. Sources tell the SUNSET that the INDIGO AVENGER fought off man-eating tigers during the daring rescue.

FULL COVERAGE: Pages 2 and 3

EXCLUSIVE: FanMan To Film "FRANKY AND JOHNNY" in Indigo! Page 18

CIRCUS OF SLAVES

HELLO CRUEL

**EXCLUSIVE TO
THE SUNSET BY
GEEKUS CROW**

The cream pie of justice gave one of the creepiest crime rings in recent Indigo history a full facial last night, when GREYSHIRT cracked a group of international slave traders operating under the guise of a happy-go-lucky circus. The group included clowns, strong men, trapeze artists, animal trainers and even a curvaceous blonde sword swallower; all of whom had long records with Interpol for a variety of unsavory crimes.

The gang rolled into Indigo last week, billed as the 'Jingle Jangle Circus,' staging an old-fashioned parade complete with animals, firebreathers and a bevy of clowns that had every kid in the city bubbling with excitement. The group performed benefit shows for local hospitals and orphanages, earning an official 'Thank You' from the Mayor's office.

Mayor Plato Plutarch's opinion of the group had changed 360 degrees by this morning as he commended GREYSHIRT for saving a score of the city's poorer children from a terrifying fate. "GREYSHIRT has earned special status in this city for his unswerving mission of cleaning up the various criminal elements that plague us. But this time, at great personal risk, he has saved our children as well. The Indigo Avenger has proved himself, once again, to be our greatest protector. I look forward to the official dedication of the GREYSHIRT statue next month."

The slavers' plans were undone when 11-year-old Vinny Shinblind joined a group of other disadvantaged youngsters from the randy Bottoms Up district of Indigo, who had been offered jobs with the circus and planned to run away with it when it left town. Apparently the children were promised training in the circus arts as high wire aerialists, magicians and clowns.

When the kids arrived at the appointed time, they were escorted into a secret compartment underneath the tiger cages by circus stuntmen, where they were chained and gagged. But before the group was put in cuffs, the resourceful young Shinblind was able to hide in a magician's cabinet, where he heard the ringleader, a sword swallower known as Gargles Gomorrah, making plans to whisk the group to a foreign-registered freighter waiting down at the Indigo docks. Shinblind succeeded in escaping the circus grounds unnoticed and quickly notified his parents.

SCULPTOR DETAILS GREYSHIRT

Tribute to Indigo Avenger to be unveiled next month!

The city's long awaited tribute to GREYSHIRT is close to completion and on track for its official unveiling next month. The life sized granite likeness of Indigo's Silver Science Hero is undergoing its finishing touches in the studio of sculptor, Fargo Fergussen, as city crews rush to prepare the site in Propane Square.

Fergussen told the SUNSET that he was "Delighted and honored to create a fitting expression of Indigo's debt to the Dandified Detective," but was overheard by this reporter at a recent fundraiser expressing a markedly different opinion. Fergussen, who originally hails from Neopolis, remarked, "In my town, he'd be laughed off the street. I mean, the guy has no special powers and waltzes around in an Edwardian suit instead of a real costume."

The monument has been subject to a long and controversial battle between City Hall and the City Zoning Commission, which originally opposed it. A statue lionizing GREYSHIRT was seen as a tacit approval of vigilantism by some city authorities. The dispute led Mayor Plutarch to charge that the Zoning Commission was itself corrupted by the gangster element. He went on to appoint GREYSHIRT a "Special Deputy" in the Indigo City Police Department.

Eventually, what won over the City were GREYSHIRT's heroic exploits, which made headlines

CIRCUS OF SLAVES

WORLD!

Sadistic Slaverunners posed as happy circus clowns to snare unsuspecting kids!

But, even before word got out on the streets of Bottoms Up, GREYSHIRT was already on the case, tipped off to the scheme by his own confidential sources. While the frantic parents were contacting the police, the lone GREYSHIRT had already infiltrated the circus and fallen into a deadly trap the plotters had laid for anyone who caught on to them.

Wide eyed kids who witnessed the rescue told the SUNSET that when GREYSHIRT tried to release them from under the tiger cage he was locked inside by Gargles Gomorrah. Laughing wickedly, Gomorrah released two ferocious big cats, who immediately pounced on the unarmed crimefighter, dragging him down beneath their fury. The kidnap victims claimed that the Indigo Avenger, using only his bare hands against razor sharp claws and huge fangs, was somehow able to overpower the ravenous beasts. By the time the police arrived on the scene, GREYSHIRT had turned the tables on his captors, locking Gomorrah and many of her clown-faced cohorts in the monkey

house.

When questioned by reporters, GREYSHIRT said, "Those clowns may have been laughing on the outside, but they're going to be crying from the inside of a cell-block at the Federal Penitentiary!"

MONUMENT!

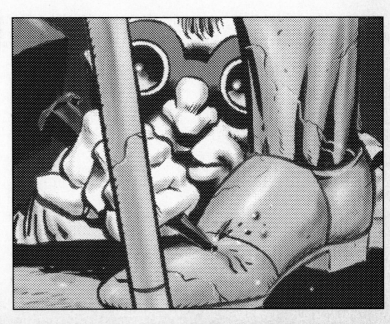

regularly in a town that thrives on them. After GREYSHIRT stopped the Robot Ape menace of Dr. Heinrich Claw and saved the kidnapped Baby Einstein, the city gratefully authorized the funds and designated the land for the project.

City crews were busy yesterday, preparing custom lighting fixtures to make the statue stand out, even at night. Parks chief Golgotha Quill told the SUNSET, "We want this monument to cast a long shadow, just like GREYSHIRT's presence in the city falls across Indigo's criminal element."

IT'S OFFICIAL! FANMAN TO FILM HERE!

"Carbones" leap to silver screen will use authentic Indigo locations!

The Mayor's office and FanMan Productions made the shotgun marriage between Indigo City and Hollywood official yesterday, jointly announcing an agreement that will bring the hit TV show "THE CARBONES" to the big screen. Principle filming of the green-lighted production will begin on location in Indigo City early in 2002, with a huge sound stage being erected in the ruins of the old Indigo Central Train Station.

"THE CARBONES: FRANKY AND JOHNNY" spins off from FanMan Productions' monster cable network hit based upon Indigo's colorful organized crime families of the past. The film is said to detail the friendship between Franky Lafayette, illegitimate son of mob boss Carmine Carbone, and his best friend Johnny Apollo. The release of the film will coincide with the end of the current second series timeline, which is set in the late 1970s and early 80s. While the TV series is focused on the two gangsters' teenage years, film viewers can expect to be brought to the edge of their seats with the falling out and final violent showdown between Lafayette and Apollo after they became the most feared criminal partnership in the city. Both mobsters were blown to atoms in a fiery explosion set off during a gunfight in the old Indigo Central Station in 1990.

Mayor Plato Plutarch, whose crusade against gangsterism in Indigo has consumed much of his incumbency, rejected a reporter's suggestion that city support of the filming constituted any sort of approval of the criminal lifestyle. "I haven't read the script, but I've been assured that it will reflect the true characters of Johnny Apollo and Franky Lafayette. Remember, I went to high school with those two low-lifes, so I know what kind of vicious punks they really were. I will resist any attempt to rehabilitate their memories or glorify their chosen vocation. The message of this film, which culminates in the immolation deaths of both Lafayette and Apollo, is 'Crime doesn't pay!'"

A spokesperson for FanMan productions described the financial benefits to the city in allowing for the filming, estimating it will add 3,000 jobs and as much as $40 million to the city's depressed economy.

FanMan Productions is a relatively new film studio, brought to prominence by its success with "THE CARBONES." A privately held company, little is known about its owners.

"Carbones" stars Kenneth Fury and Trevor Alexander will reprise their roles as Johnny Apollo and Franky Lafayette in FanMan's upcoming flick, "FRANKY AND JOHNNY."

BIZARRE RAT KINGS DISCOVERED!

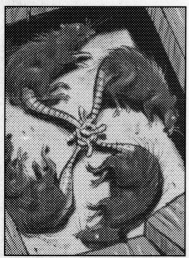

File this one under "Indigo Oddities." A Jewel Street family that heard scratching in the walls thought they had mice. They called in the local exterminator, who pulled up the floor, and discovered the problem was a bit more serious and a lot more strange. Technicians discovered over a dozen "Rat Kings," groups of rats whose tails have inexplicably become snarled together, huddled in the joists of the house.

While the "Rat King" phenomena is rare, it is not unheard of and a number of cases have been reported over the years, although scientists have no rational explanation as to why or how the rodents become entwined.

In this case, the confusion has been compounded by the number of rat kings discovered and the shapes that they took. Workers reported that the rat kings held to rigid formations that were in the shape of swastikas. Head exterminator, Rubin Holiday, told the SUNSET that "No matter how many times we moved 'em, the vicious little buggers just marched right back into swastika formations. Never seen nuthin' like it."

Specimens have been preserved at the Indigo Institute for future study.

INDIGO POOP SCOOP!

BY IDLE DISH

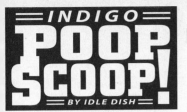

EVEN PIGEONS NEED A PLACE TO GO!

With all the various controversies swirling around the city's attempt to honor GREYSHIRT with a monument, wags are wondering why the normally cautious Mayor Plutarch has remained so solidly behind the expensive gesture. First it was finding funds in the always strapped city budget, then bullying the zoning board into agreeing to its placement, then the controversial hiring of the head of the zoning board's brother-in-law to carve the piece. Now, we hear the residents around Propane Square, where the statue is to be erected this month, are up in arms about a plan to install expensive lighting that will cast the INDIGO AVENGER's shadow as high as ten stories tall on surrounding buildings. We hear residents are complaining that the lights will shine up into their apartment windows all night long and are forming a committee to force the mayor to retool this part of the project. And what does GREYSHIRT himself think of the project? The POOP SCOOP had a chance to ask the BEAU BRUMMEL OF BLUEBURG that very question at his recent courtroom appearance at the trial of Lapis Lazuli. GREYSHIRT seemed to be in an uncharacteristically reflective mood that day and told the SCOOP, "If it somehow inspires one guilty criminal to make a single slip up, then it's all right by me."

GANGSTERS EVERYWHERE!

POOP SCOOP readers knew it a month ago, but the Mayor's announcement of a deal with FanMan Productions to film "THE CARBONES: FRANKY AND JOHNNY" here in Indigo makes everything nice and official. Things should get interesting here in the CERULEAN CITY once stars like Kenneth Fury and Trevor Alexander start showing up at local nightspots. The SCOOP is most interested in finding out the skinny on FanMan Productions, which up to now has been a mysterious and unknown presence in Indigo. Other than his involvement in the recent POW! ART show that ended in tragedy, little is known about the man pulling the levers at this year's hottest production company.

WHO is the teen-age dot-com billionaire who recently outfitted a 75-foot yacht with a posse of beautiful women and has taken to plying the waters of Crater Bay looking for people to party hearty with? We'd be remiss if we didn't warn any potential party animals that these girls have received extensive training in hand-to-hand combat as well as the geisha arts. What kind of bacchanal bashes are this boy billionaire and his bodacious babes throwing? And why hasn't the POOP SCOOP been invited?

WHICH transparently togged Indigo City Science Heroine will be donating her closet full of high heels to this year's Indigo Ball Auction? Word is that, not only does the collection makes Imelda Marcos' look beggarly, but that every pair in it is purple!

ASK DR. SYNTAX

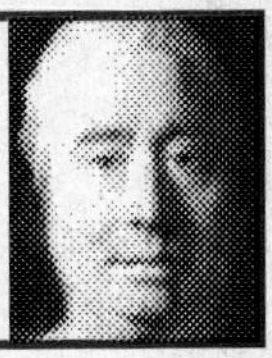

Tradition-minded Broad Won't Spare Rod

Dear Doctor Syntax: My main squeeze and I disagree about one thing. My filly firmly believes in hitting, slapping and punching as a way to get respect from a spouse. She says that when she mouths off, I should pull back and belt her a good one up side the head. And when I don't listen to her, she'll bust a lamp over my noggin without even thinking twice.

Both of us were brought up in homes where corporal punishment was expected, but I'm not sure I agree that we should continue to practice the old way of doing things. While it seems to work in the short term, in the long term the wear and tear can be expensive. Last month her dental bills alone were over a thousand bucks and my ears have been continually ringing since she caught me with that whiskey bottle.

Am I getting soft? — Knuckles

Dear Knuckles: While a good talking to is usually sufficient to put one's point across, sometimes a little love tap or two is required to get a mate's full attention. Still, marring dental work or permanently causing hearing loss is not recommended if the relationship is meant to last over a lifetime. We suggest that in the future both partners agree to avoid the head and face when the situation calls for a strong physical statement.

Dear Doctor Syntax: I've got an obsessive ex-boyfriend. We dated briefly a year ago and once I realized what a nutcase he was, I refused to go out with him or answer his endless phone calls. I've started seeing another guy and we've enjoyed an intimate physical relationship on a regular basis. But my obsessed ex has been sneaking into the back alley of my apartment building and eavesdropping on us. My new boyfriend and I hear him in the shadows of the alley right below my bedroom window almost every night. The thing is, we found we get a kick out of him being down there and have taken to keeping the lights on so he can see our silhouettes on the shade.

Are we being too cruel? — Exhibitionist

Dear Exhibitionist, Because of Indigo's colorful past it's always been a city where anything goes. If your obsessive ex doesn't like what he sees, he's free to leave his place in the shadows. As long as no one gets hurt, what's the harm?

SUNSET COMICS

MUSSEL BEACH By Squid Pro Quo

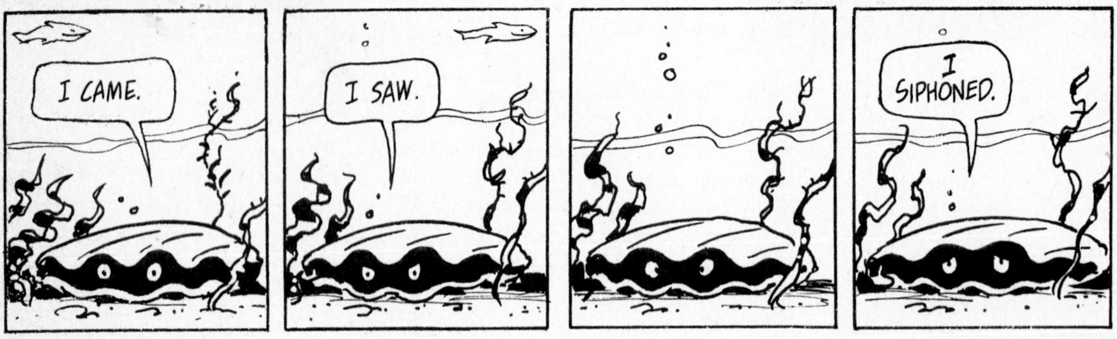
I CAME.
I SAW.
I SIPHONED.

HARRY GEE By Chet Ghoulash

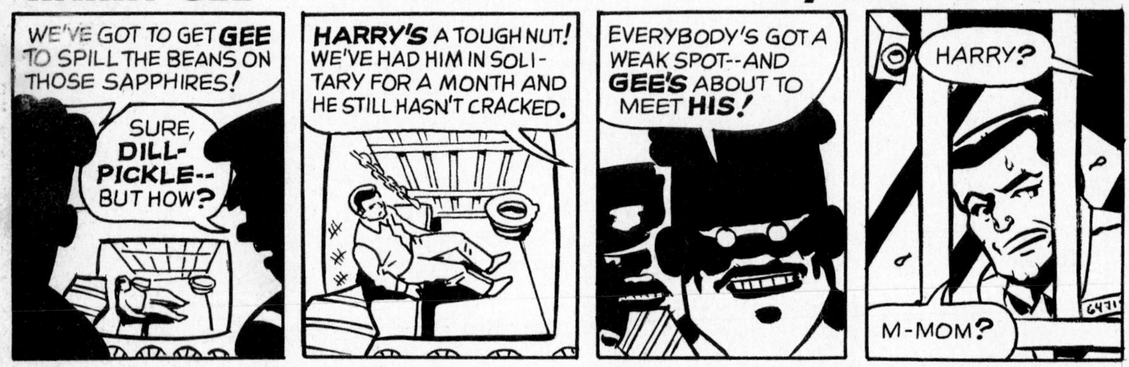
WE'VE GOT TO GET GEE TO SPILL THE BEANS ON THOSE SAPPHIRES!
SURE, DILL-PICKLE-- BUT HOW?
HARRY'S A TOUGH NUT! WE'VE HAD HIM IN SOLI-TARY FOR A MONTH AND HE STILL HASN'T CRACKED.
EVERYBODY'S GOT A WEAK SPOT--AND GEE'S ABOUT TO MEET HIS!
HARRY?
M-MOM?

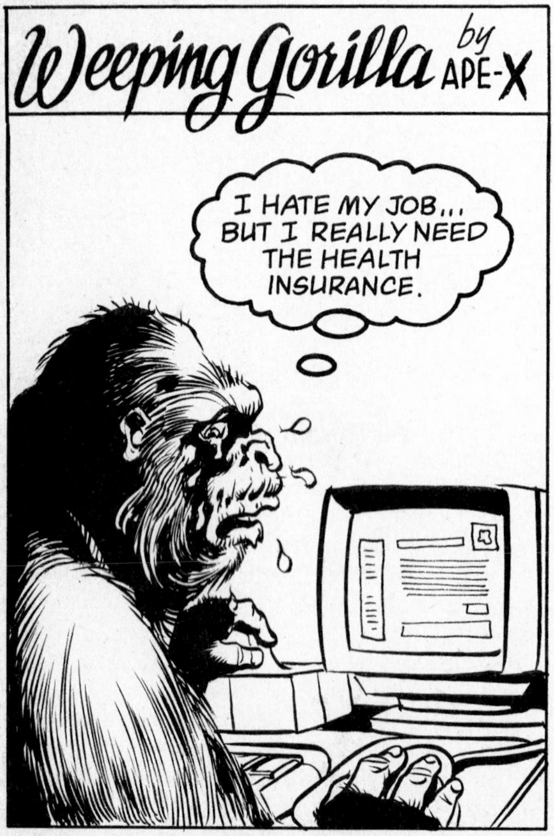
Weeping Gorilla by APE-X
I HATE MY JOB... BUT I REALLY NEED THE HEALTH INSURANCE.

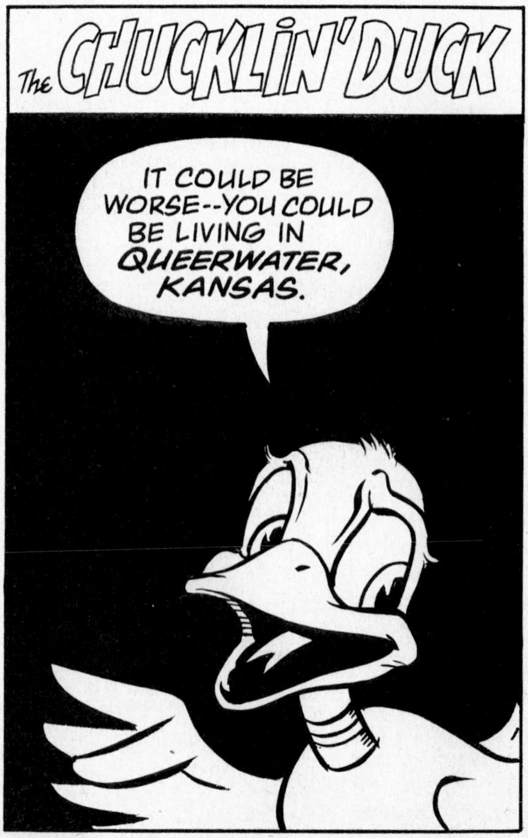
The CHUCKLIN' DUCK
IT COULD BE WORSE--YOU COULD BE LIVING IN QUEERWATER, KANSAS.

FOR INDIGO KIDS OF ALL AGES!

BOWSER THE SCHNAUZER **By Yowzuh Trousers**

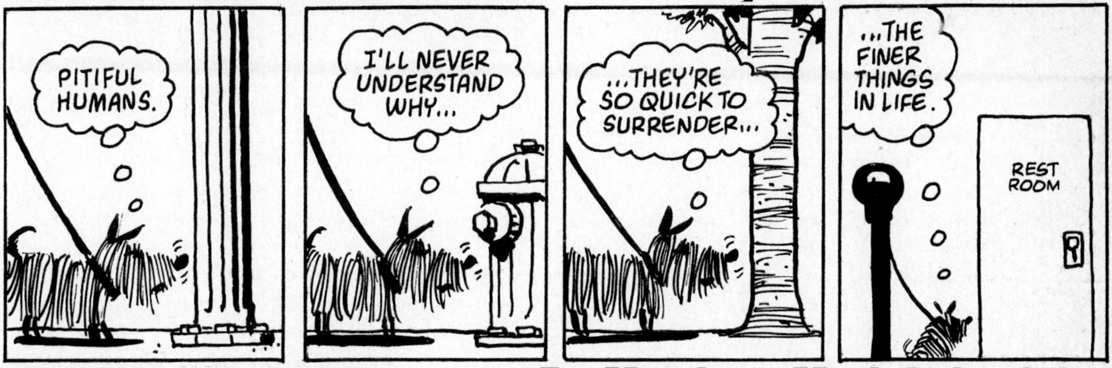
PITIFUL HUMANS.
I'LL NEVER UNDERSTAND WHY...
...THEY'RE SO QUICK TO SURRENDER...
...THE FINER THINGS IN LIFE.
REST ROOM

MADAM I'M ADAM **By Matthew Mark Lukenjohn**

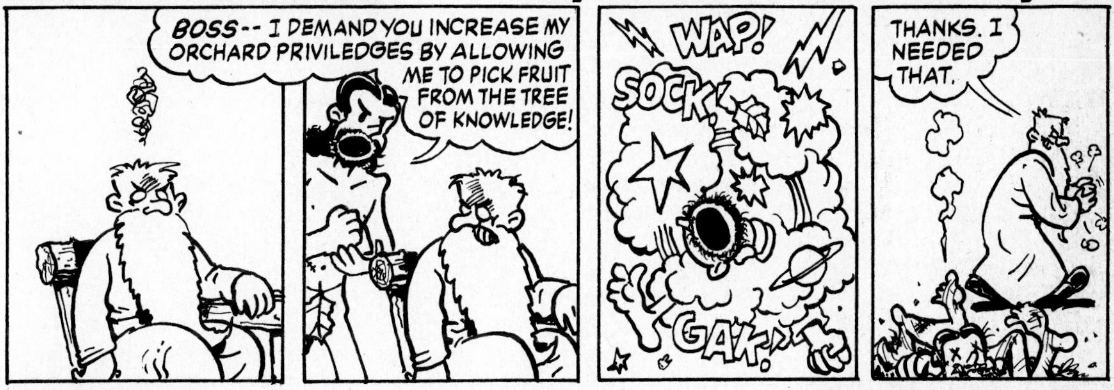
BOSS -- I DEMAND YOU INCREASE MY ORCHARD PRIVILEDGES BY ALLOWING ME TO PICK FRUIT FROM THE TREE OF KNOWLEDGE!
WAP!
SOCK!
GAK!
THANKS. I NEEDED THAT.

GOODIOS ADVERTISEMENT **By Buddy Fact**

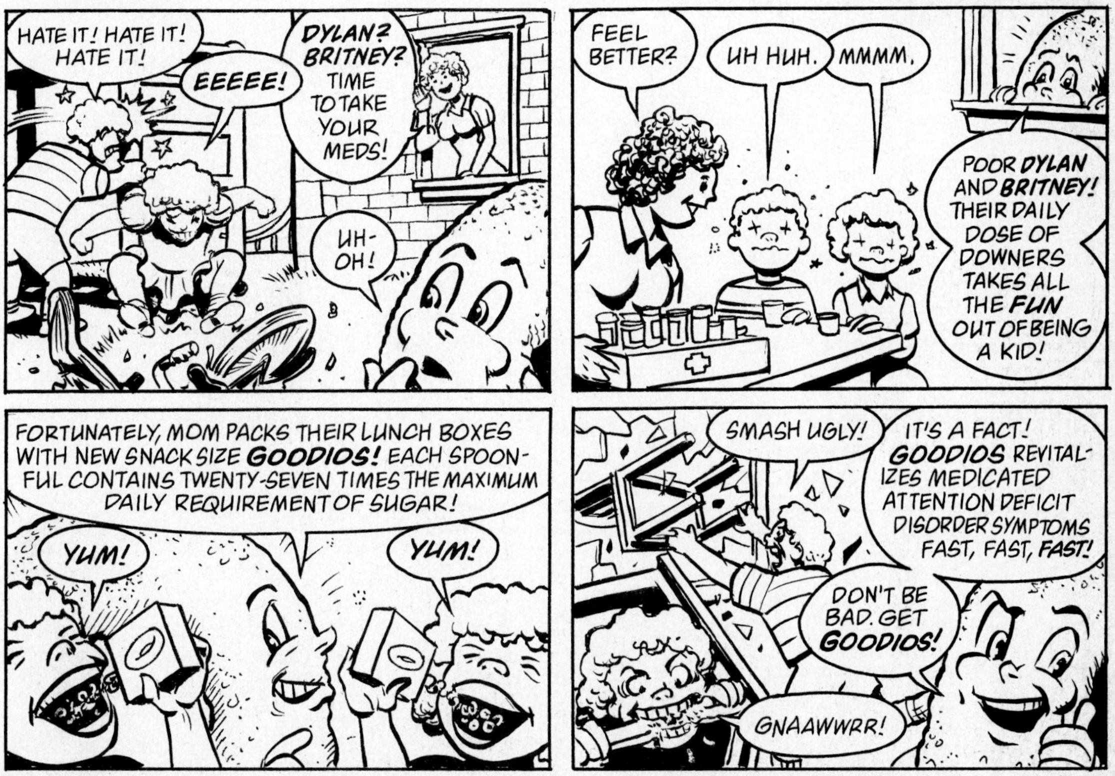
HATE IT! HATE IT! HATE IT!
EEEEE!
DYLAN? BRITNEY? TIME TO TAKE YOUR MEDS!
UH-OH!
FEEL BETTER?
UH HUH.
MMMM.
POOR DYLAN AND BRITNEY! THEIR DAILY DOSE OF DOWNERS TAKES ALL THE FUN OUT OF BEING A KID!
FORTUNATELY, MOM PACKS THEIR LUNCH BOXES WITH NEW SNACK SIZE GOODIOS! EACH SPOONFUL CONTAINS TWENTY-SEVEN TIMES THE MAXIMUM DAILY REQUIREMENT OF SUGAR!
YUM!
YUM!
SMASH UGLY!
IT'S A FACT! GOODIOS REVITALIZES MEDICATED ATTENTION DEFICIT DISORDER SYMPTOMS FAST, FAST, FAST!
DON'T BE BAD. GET GOODIOS!
GNAAWWRR!

THE PURPLE PULSE

SUNSET Arts & Leisure

"BELLE OF INDIGO" TEASES!

COBWEB Documentary asks more questions than it answers! PULSE RATE: ★★★½

A new documentary biography of ageless Science Heroine, THE COBWEB, screening tonight at the OPAL THEATER, should be an eye opener for younger fans of the Translucent Temptress. Today's fanatic GenABC'ers might be shocked to know that the object of their current fascination is at least old enough to be their grandmother. And, if what the filmmakers suggest is true, she may even be old enough to be their grandmother's grandmother!

While COBWEB's more recent exploits, such as her long-running battles with Octavia Price, a.k.a. the Money Spider, and bizarre adventures in Mondo Gowando have received extensive coverage in the SUNSET, some of the historical references unearthed by the filmmaker Ken Blaze will be new to even hard core COBWEB extremists. Beginning with Claudette Sequin's risqué 19th century pulp adventure novels of "La Toile, Mistress of Villainy," whose woodcuts were inspiration for Georges Delcourt's Surrealist masterpiece, *"La Toile dans le Chateau des Larmes,"* various COBWEB femme fatales have appeared in any number of anonymously-written pulp stories and on hundreds of calendar illustrations. Probably the best known (at least to any red blooded boy who grew up in Indigo City) are the infamous pornographic comic strips that could be found in every locker in Indigo High. The filmmakers trace the history of these so-called "Tijuana Bibles" from a few out-of-work Indigo cartoonists, to cheap printing shops just across the Mexican border, to industrious teen gangs that imported and sold the 8-pagers to legions of eager young boys (and, as it turns out, some eager young girls too). These days more than a few older aficionados are paying thousands of dollars apiece to purchase rare edition collector COBWEB items on Internet auction sites.

But "BELLE OF INDIGO" rises above simple trivia and nostalgia when it begins to ask the hard questions concerning the era of AMERICA'S BEST HEROES. The true identity of the real COBWEB who fought crime in the ABH in the 1960s, and obviously was inspired by the various pop culture COBWEBS preceding her, has never been discovered. But comparison computer analysis of photos of the 60s vintage COBWEB and the current Vermilion Vixen fail to detect any significant differences in facial structure or body type. Rumors of an anti-aging serum have circulated for years and make for sensational copy, but no one really knows the secret of COBWEB's longevity.

Blaze's patented visual technique of panning across still photographs and artwork keeps the early portions of the documentary lively, and the interview with TOM STRONG, discussing the early days of AMERICA'S BEST HEROES, is easily worth the price of admission. Also of interest, in a freakish sort of way, is the interview with heiress Laurel Lakeland, who bankrolls a COBWEB fan magazine titled *"Come Into My Parlor."* Rumor has it she has endured extensive plastic surgery in an attempt to sculpt her features to resemble those of the science heroine. But Lakeland says it best when she remarks that "Part of every girl in Indigo City wants to be COBWEB. There are scads of us trying to get the classic look down as authentically as we can. The current COBWEB is just the hostess with the mostest! I think she's divine!"

So do we and so will filmgoers who take in "BELLE OF INDIGO."

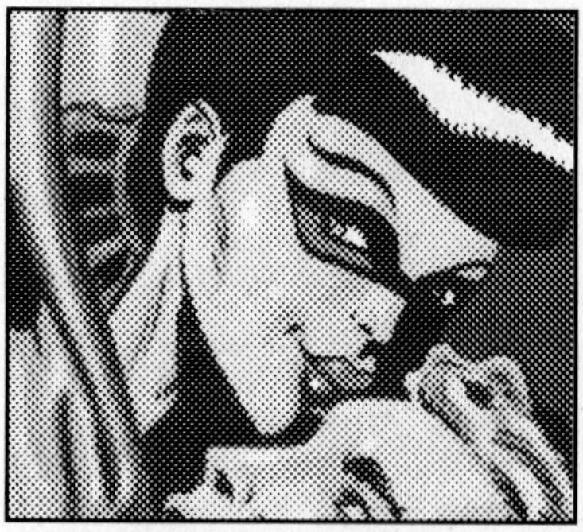

"THE CARBONES" Season Two: An offer Indigo viewers can't refuse! PULSE RATE: ★★★★★

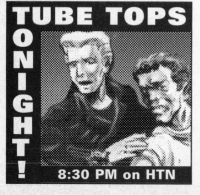

TUBE TOPS TONIGHT!

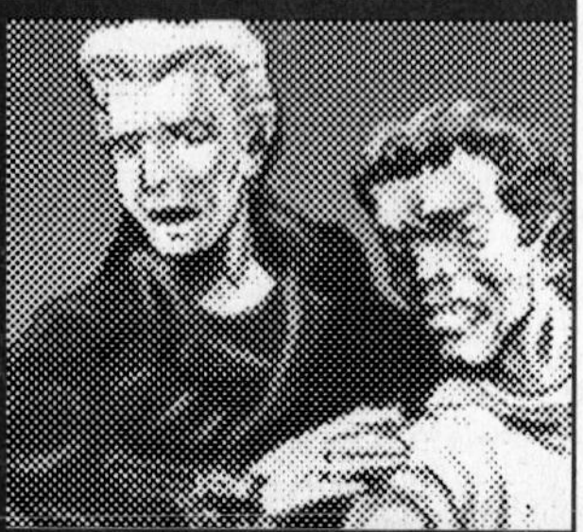

8:30 PM on HTN

The second season of FanMan Productions' hit show launches tonight with Carmine hiring his illegitimate son Franky to pull a heist on rival mob boss, Spats Katz. Johnny Apollo tries to talk sense to his hot-headed friend Franky, but gets caught by Katz and unfairly blamed for Franky's crime spree. Meanwhile, Franky's mother, Lips, succeeds in poisoning Candi's feelings for Johnny.

This Shakespearean retelling of the epic story of Indigo's most infamous organized crime families continues to define the cutting edge of cable television. Trevor Alexander's Franky is the tough-talking rat we love to despise, while Heather Ritz brings a smoldering presence rarely seen on the small screen to her Lips Lafayette. But who can resist rooting for Kenneth Fury's touching portrayal of a misunderstood gangster with a heart of gold, Johnny Apollo?

Get Away in a Bumpmobile!

Today's BUMPMOBILE builds on a heritage as wild and untamed as Indigo's own. Feel the surge as a standard 60,000 BTU natural gas powerplant leaves pursuers in the dust. Lead the pack with a wide-shouldered stance and cab forward styling that demands respect as it signals who's the boss. Optional tinted bullet-proof glass provides security and anonymity in a world of chumps and suckers. Strap on some Indigo attitude with the all-new ***BUMPMOBILE for 2002!***

Value Priced at $399/month*!

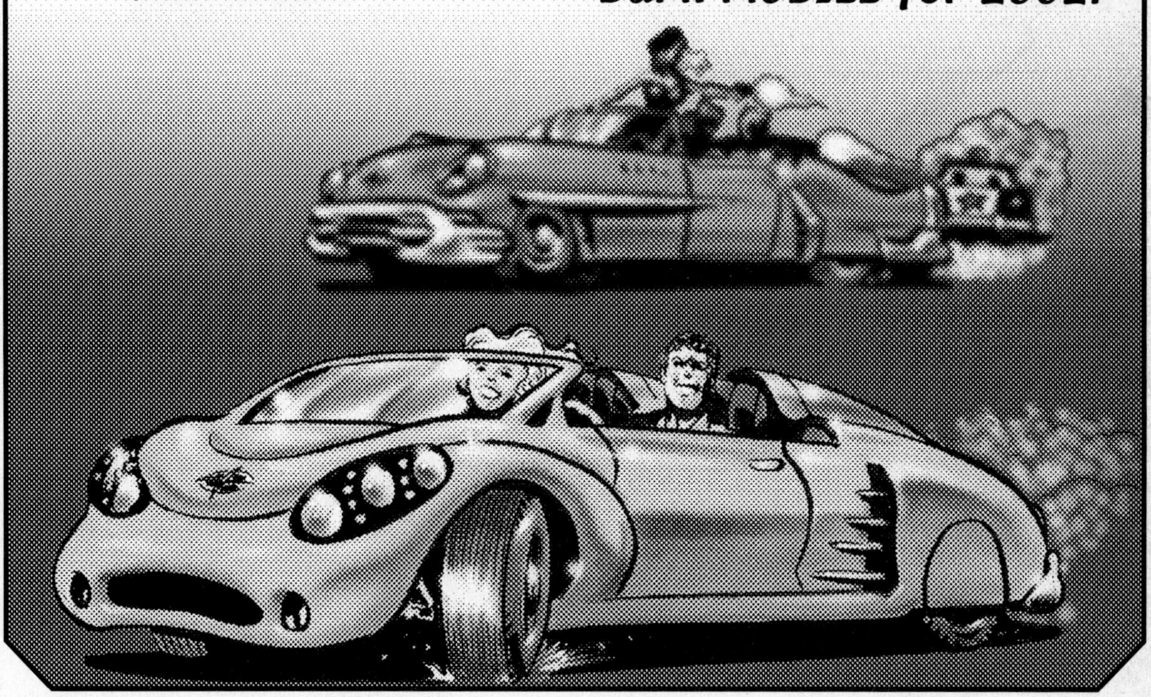

Dishonest Dan Dicer Says:

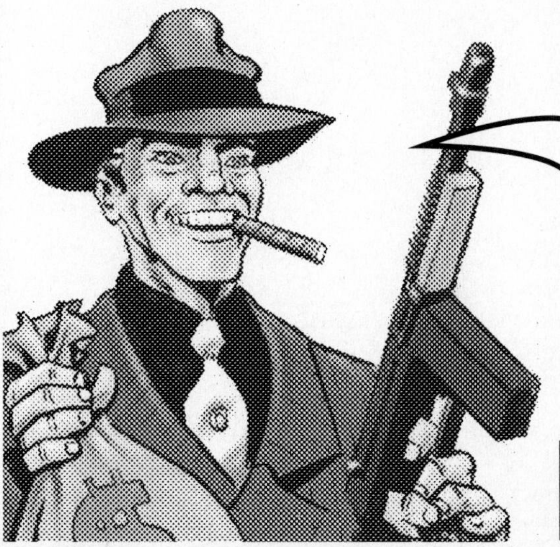

WE'RE ROBBING THE COMPETITION BLIND!

These deals oughtta be declared illegal! Come on down and break into our huge selection of new and new-to-you BUMPMOBILES. Credit problems? NO PROBLEM! Cut us in on your next heist and escape with style in a BUMPMOBILE from Dicer's Crater Bay Car Emporium!

CRATER BAY EXPRESSWAY, EXIT 46
PHONE: 1-YOU-DIRTYRAT

*Must present ad to take advantage of pricing. All vehicles sold cosmetically as is. All queries:

JIM LEE Editorial Director
JOHN NEE VP & General Manager
SCOTT DUNBIER Group Editor

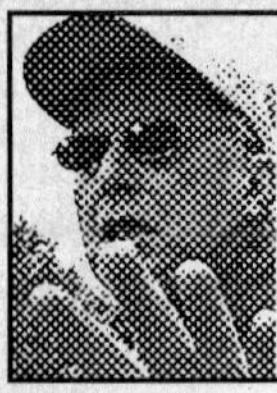

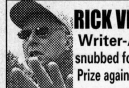

RICK VEITCH
Writer-Artist snubbed for Nobel Prize again! Page 7

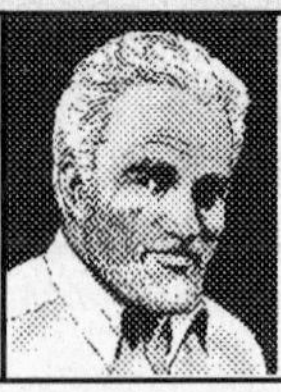

RUSS HEATH
Indigo Artist is Comeback Kid! Page 8

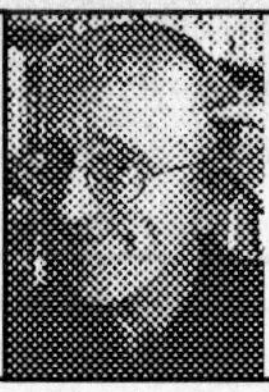

TODD KLEIN
His Inkstained Struggle for fine Lettering! Page 9

OFF-COLOR REMARKS HIT WILD-STORM FX!

ALL THE NEWS FROM DAWN TO DUSK

INDIGO CITY SUNSET

AFTERNOON CITY EDITION

Monday, November 19, 2001   Metro Weather – Today: Misty, Tonight: Fog Creeping In, Tomorrow: Low-lying Fog

BACK PAGE EXTRA:

Mayor Declares Pow! Art:

MENACE TO PUBLIC HEALTH!

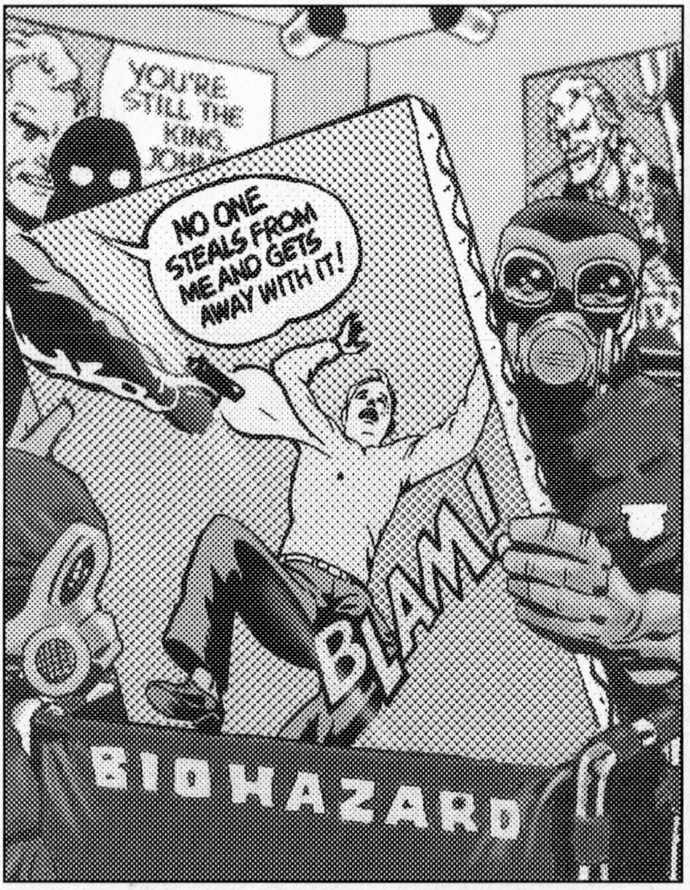
YOU'RE STILL THE KING
NO ONE STEALS FROM ME AND GETS AWAY WITH IT!
BLAM!!
BIOHAZARD

PUKE PATROL CLEANS UP AFTER ARTISTIC EXCESS

Special to The Sunset
by Geekus Crow

Indigo City Public Health officials, clad in protective gear, descended on the Lakeland Museum of Contemporary Art last night with urgent orders from Mayor Plato Plutarch to remove a recently acquired painting by Any Savannah, the once-notorious Indigo gadfly and erstwhile "King of Pow! Art."

The move followed a grisly discovery that had the highly insular Indigo City art world on edge and checking alibis.

CONTINUED INSIDE.

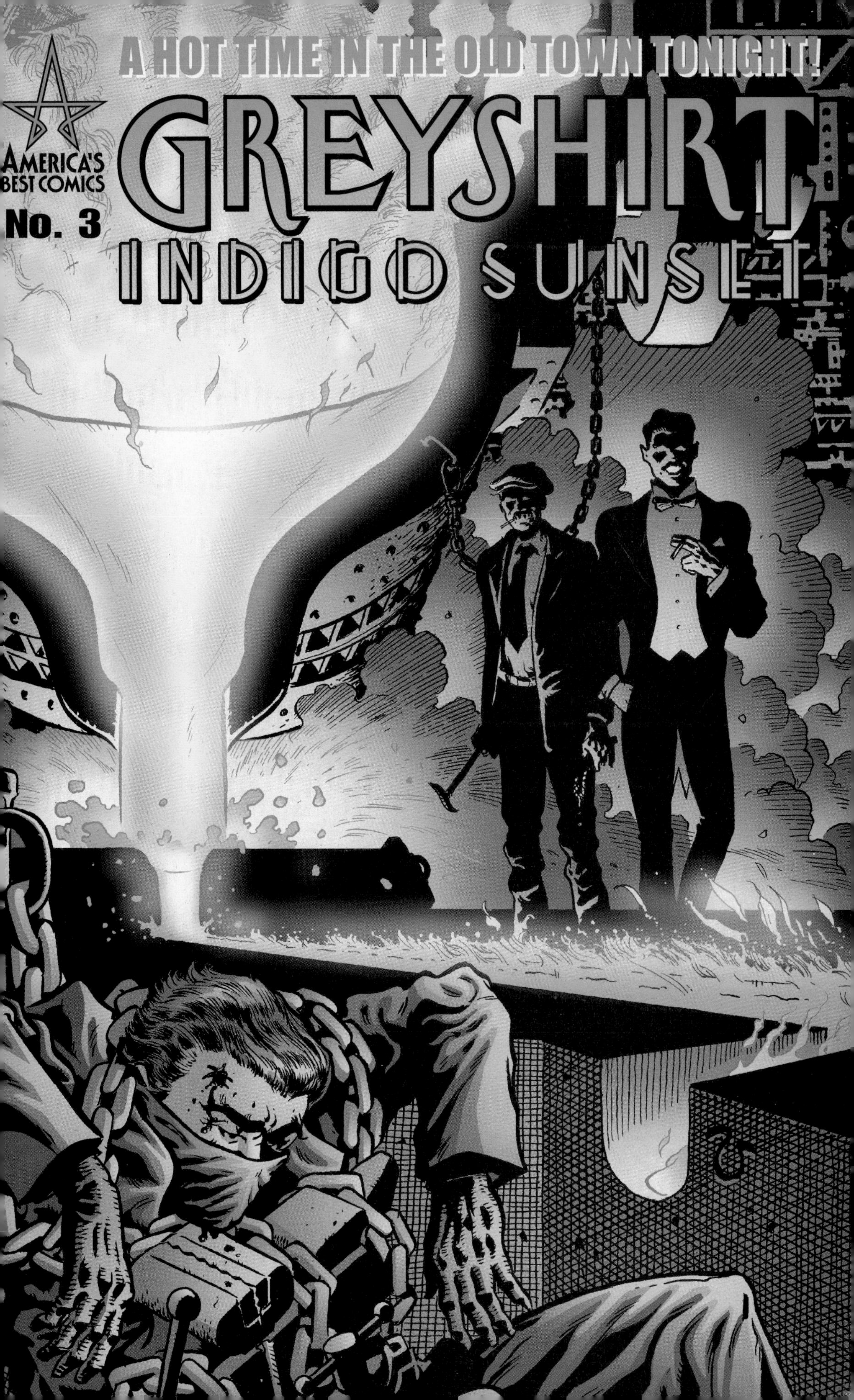
A HOT TIME IN THE OLD TOWN TONIGHT!
AMERICA'S BEST COMICS
No. 3
GREYSHIRT
INDIGO SUNSET

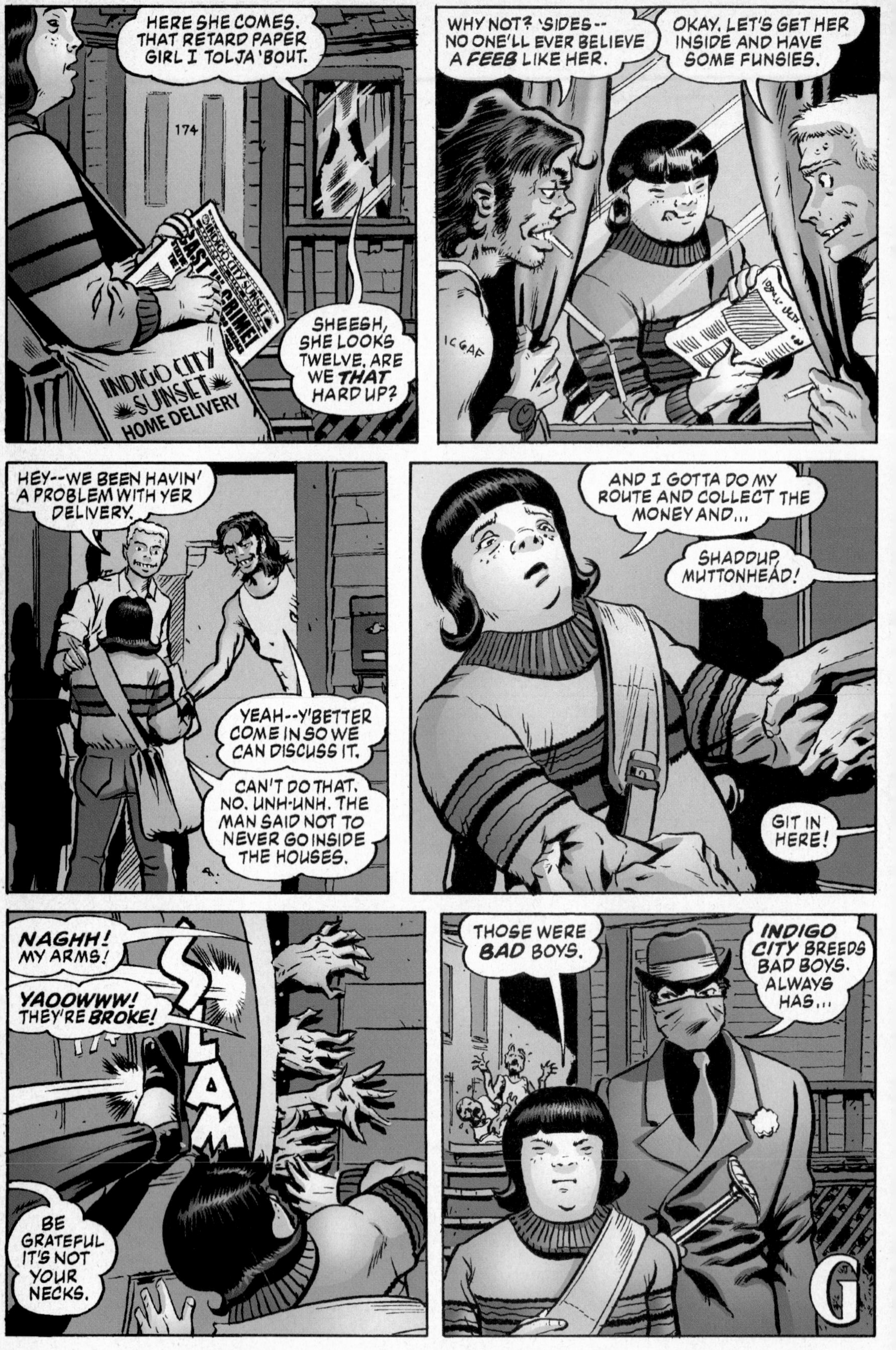
HERE SHE COMES. THAT RETARD PAPER GIRL I TOLJA 'BOUT.
174
INDIGO CITY SUNSET HOME DELIVERY
SHEESH, SHE LOOKS TWELVE. ARE WE *THAT* HARD UP?
WHY NOT? 'SIDES-- NO ONE'LL EVER BELIEVE A *FEEB* LIKE HER.
OKAY. LET'S GET HER INSIDE AND HAVE SOME FUNSIES.
HEY--WE BEEN HAVIN' A PROBLEM WITH YER DELIVERY.
YEAH--Y'BETTER COME IN SO WE CAN DISCUSS IT.
CAN'T DO THAT. NO. UNH-UNH. THE MAN SAID NOT TO NEVER GO INSIDE THE HOUSES.
AND I GOTTA DO MY ROUTE AND COLLECT THE MONEY AND...
SHADDUP, MUTTONHEAD!
GIT IN HERE!
NAGHH! MY ARMS!
YAOOWWW! THEY'RE *BROKE!*
SLAM
BE GRATEFUL IT'S NOT YOUR NECKS.
THOSE WERE *BAD* BOYS.
INDIGO CITY BREEDS BAD BOYS. ALWAYS HAS...
G

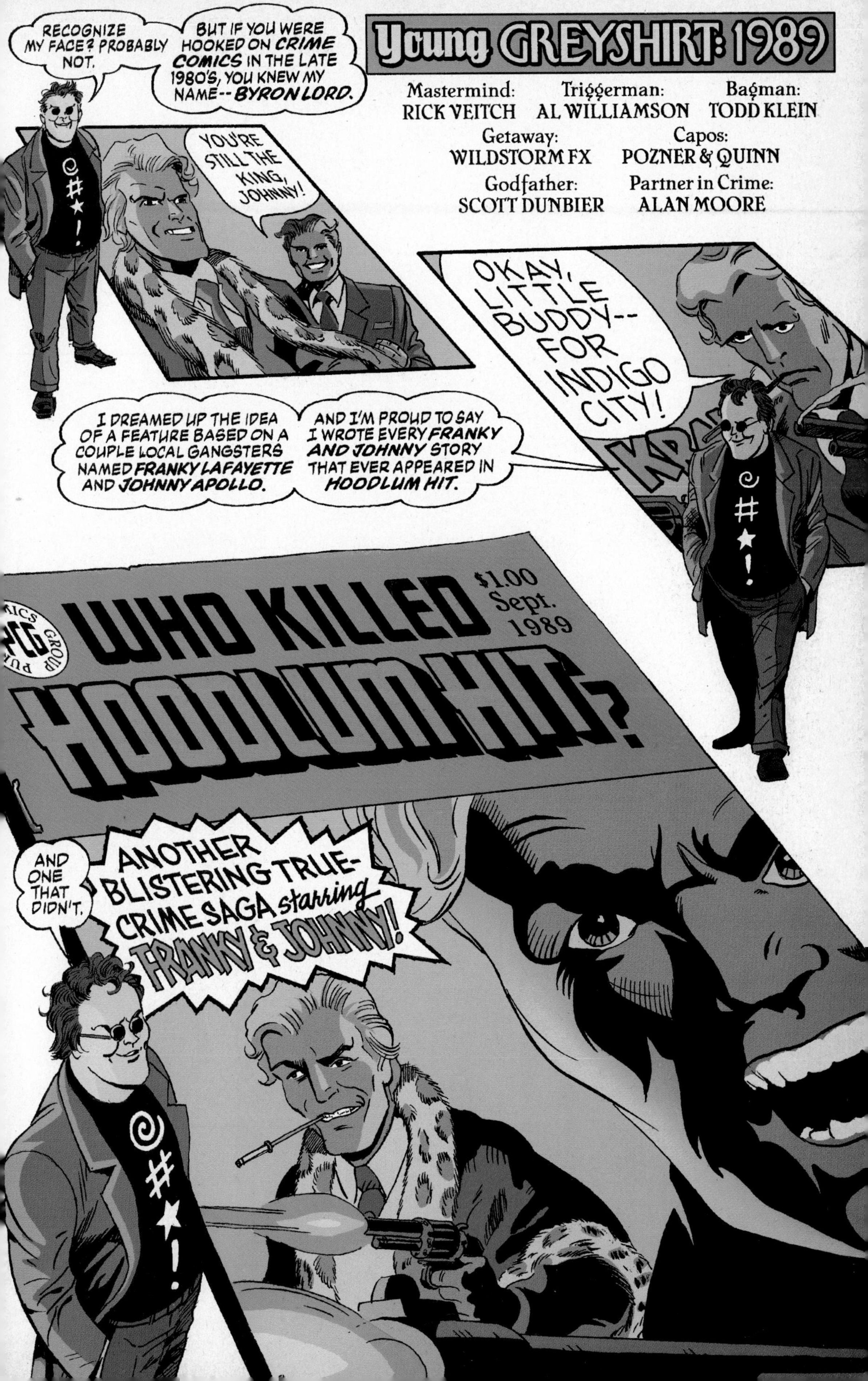

RECOGNIZE MY FACE? PROBABLY NOT.
BUT IF YOU WERE HOOKED ON CRIME COMICS IN THE LATE 1980'S, YOU KNEW MY NAME-- BYRON LORD.
Young GREYSHIRT: 1989
Mastermind: RICK VEITCH
Triggerman: AL WILLIAMSON
Bagman: TODD KLEIN
Getaway: WILDSTORM FX
Capos: POZNER & QUINN
Godfather: SCOTT DUNBIER
Partner in Crime: ALAN MOORE
YOU'RE STILL THE KING, JOHNNY!
OKAY, LITTLE BUDDY-- FOR INDIGO CITY!
I DREAMED UP THE IDEA OF A FEATURE BASED ON A COUPLE LOCAL GANGSTERS NAMED FRANKY LAFAYETTE AND JOHNNY APOLLO.
AND I'M PROUD TO SAY I WROTE EVERY FRANKY AND JOHNNY STORY THAT EVER APPEARED IN HOODLUM HIT.
$1.00 Sept. 1989
WHO KILLED HOODLUM HIT?
AND ONE THAT DIDN'T.
ANOTHER BLISTERING TRUE-CRIME SAGA starring FRANKY & JOHNNY!

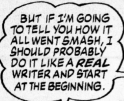

BUT IF I'M GOING TO TELL YOU HOW IT ALL WENT SMASH, I SHOULD PROBABLY DO IT LIKE A *REAL* WRITER AND START AT THE BEGINNING.

BERNIE NOVAK WAS DELIVERING HIS LATEST AND, AS IT TURNED OUT, FINAL *HOODLUM HIT* JOB TO MY OFFICE UP AT *PURPLE COMICS...*

WHATTAYA *MEAN* IT'S NOT *GORY* ENOUGH?

PURPLE COMICS HOME OF **HOODLUM HIT** Comics!

IT'S A *CRIME COMIC*, BERNIE! WE GOTTA SHOW THE BLOOD AND ENTRAILS. RUB THE READERS' NOSES RIGHT *IN* IT!

I *KNOW* HOW THIS WORKS, *BERN*. PEOPLE *LOVE* THE GRAND GUIGNOL SHTICK.

CAN'T YOU PUNCH UP THE EXIT WOUNDS A LITTLE, JUST FOR ME?

I SWEAR--THIS BIZ IS GONNA DRIVE ME *BERSERK* SOMEDAY, YOU GOT SCRIPT?

I WISH!

LAFAYETTE AND *APOLLO* HAVE BEEN LAYING LOW, LOOKS LIKE I'M GOING TO HAVE TO FALL BACK ON TALENT THIS ISSUE.

THERE'S SOMETHIN' IN TODAY'S *SUNSET* ABOUT *CARMINE CARBONE* GETTING POPPED BY THE BOYS IN BLUE...

LEMME SEE!

INDIGO CITY SUNSET ...ONE NABBED!

FRANKY AND *JOHNNY* ARE ALLIED WITH *CARBONE* AGAINST *SPATS KATZ!* BERNIE, YOU'RE A LIFE-SAVER!

DON'T FORGET THE ENTRAILS! I'LL SEND THESE CORRECTIONS OVER BY *INDIGO EXPRESS* THIS AFTERNOON.

INDIGO CITY SUNSET CARBONE NABBED!

BRIINNGG!

PURPLE COMICS. BYRON LORD SPEAKING...

SO, YOU THE GUY WHO WRITES THOSE *HOODLUM HIT* FUNNYBOOKS ABOUT *FRANKY* AND *JOHNNY?*

IT WAS A WOMAN'S VOICE.

THE KIND WRITERS LIKE ME USUALLY DESCRIBE AS A "HUSKY WHISPER!"

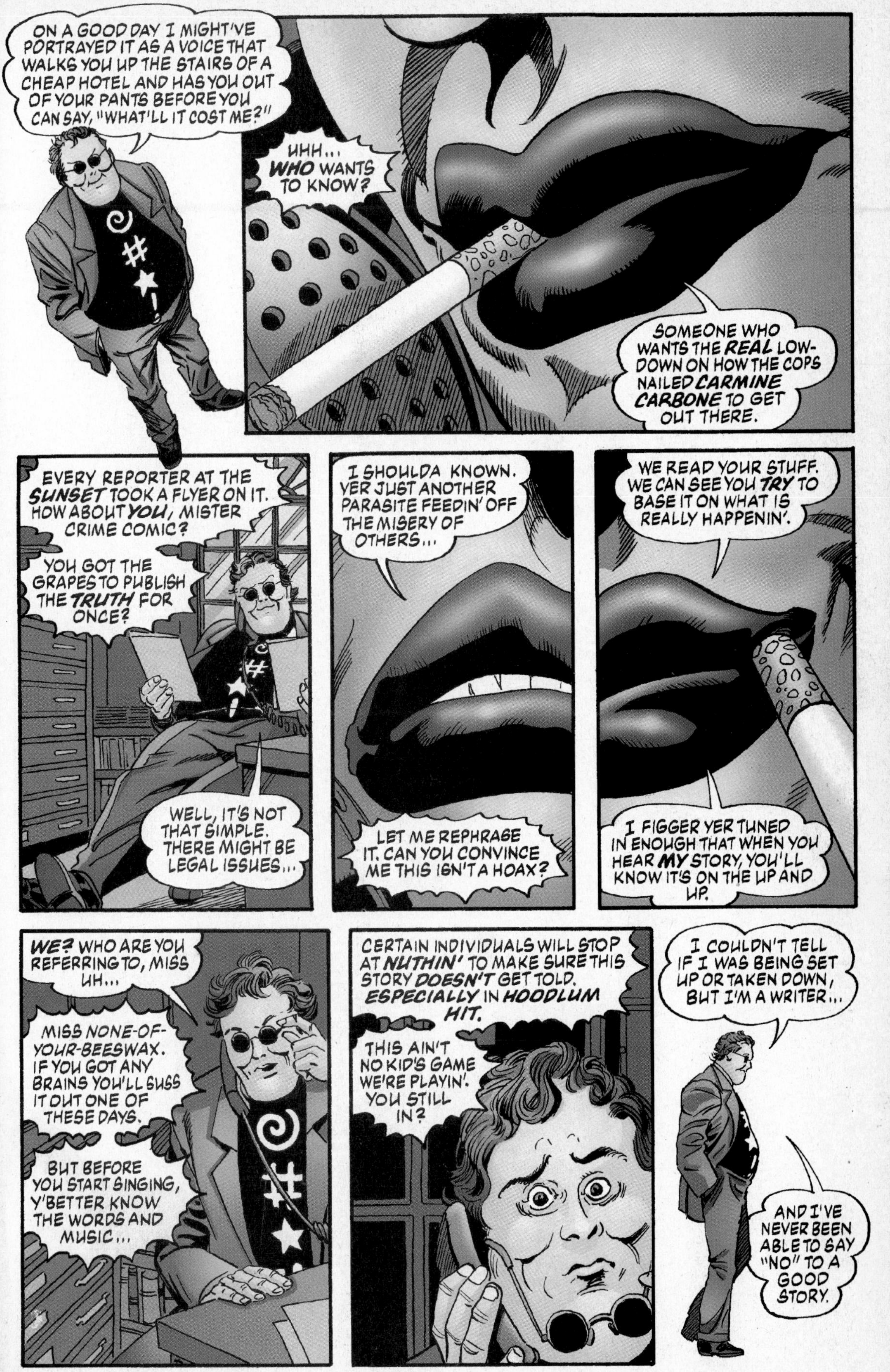

ON A GOOD DAY I MIGHT'VE PORTRAYED IT AS A VOICE THAT WALKS YOU UP THE STAIRS OF A CHEAP HOTEL AND HAS YOU OUT OF YOUR PANTS BEFORE YOU CAN SAY, "WHAT'LL IT COST ME?"
UHH... WHO WANTS TO KNOW?
SOMEONE WHO WANTS THE REAL LOW-DOWN ON HOW THE COPS NAILED CARMINE CARBONE TO GET OUT THERE.
EVERY REPORTER AT THE SUNSET TOOK A FLYER ON IT. HOW ABOUT YOU, MISTER CRIME COMIC?
YOU GOT THE GRAPES TO PUBLISH THE TRUTH FOR ONCE?
WELL, IT'S NOT THAT SIMPLE. THERE MIGHT BE LEGAL ISSUES...
I SHOULDA KNOWN. YER JUST ANOTHER PARASITE FEEDIN' OFF THE MISERY OF OTHERS...
LET ME REPHRASE IT. CAN YOU CONVINCE ME THIS ISN'T A HOAX?
WE READ YOUR STUFF. WE CAN SEE YOU TRY TO BASE IT ON WHAT IS REALLY HAPPENIN'.
I FIGGER YER TUNED IN ENOUGH THAT WHEN YOU HEAR MY STORY, YOU'LL KNOW IT'S ON THE UP AND UP.
WE? WHO ARE YOU REFERRING TO, MISS UH...
MISS NONE-OF-YOUR-BEESWAX. IF YOU GOT ANY BRAINS YOU'LL SUSS IT OUT ONE OF THESE DAYS.
BUT BEFORE YOU START SINGING, Y'BETTER KNOW THE WORDS AND MUSIC...
CERTAIN INDIVIDUALS WILL STOP AT NUTHIN' TO MAKE SURE THIS STORY DOESN'T GET TOLD. ESPECIALLY IN HOODLUM HIT.
THIS AIN'T NO KID'S GAME WE'RE PLAYIN'. YOU STILL IN?
I COULDN'T TELL IF I WAS BEING SET UP OR TAKEN DOWN, BUT I'M A WRITER...
AND I'VE NEVER BEEN ABLE TO SAY "NO" TO A GOOD STORY.

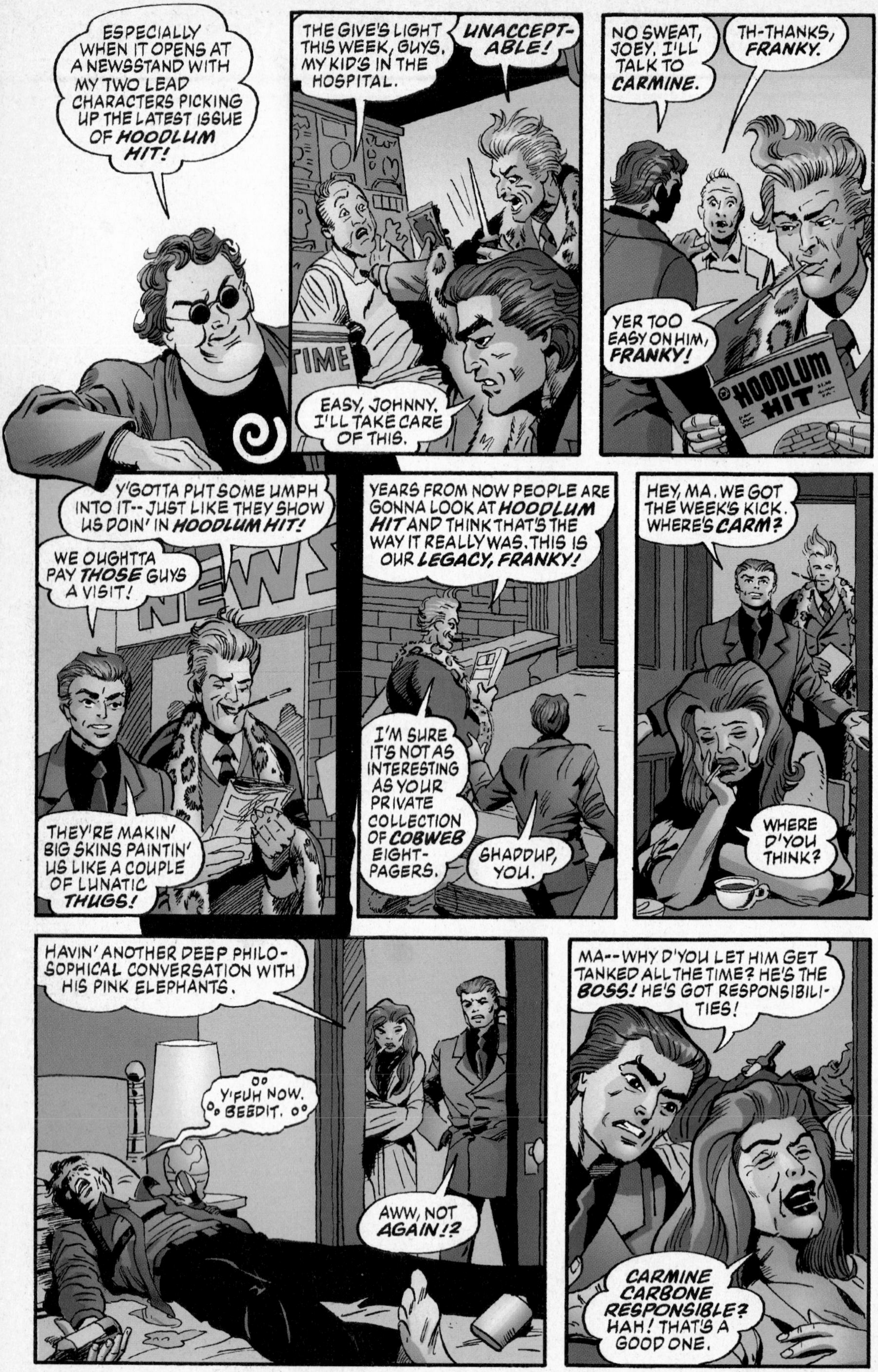

ESPECIALLY WHEN IT OPENS AT A NEWSSTAND WITH MY TWO LEAD CHARACTERS PICKING UP THE LATEST ISSUE OF HOODLUM HIT!
THE GIVE'S LIGHT THIS WEEK, GUYS. MY KID'S IN THE HOSPITAL.
UNACCEPTABLE!
TIME
EASY, JOHNNY. I'LL TAKE CARE OF THIS.
NO SWEAT, JOEY. I'LL TALK TO CARMINE.
TH-THANKS, FRANKY.
YER TOO EASY ON HIM, FRANKY!
HOODLUM HIT
Y'GOTTA PUT SOME UMPH INTO IT-- JUST LIKE THEY SHOW US DOIN' IN HOODLUM HIT!
WE OUGHTTA PAY THOSE GUYS A VISIT!
NEWS
THEY'RE MAKIN' BIG SKINS PAINTIN' US LIKE A COUPLE OF LUNATIC THUGS!
YEARS FROM NOW PEOPLE ARE GONNA LOOK AT HOODLUM HIT AND THINK THAT'S THE WAY IT REALLY WAS. THIS IS OUR LEGACY, FRANKY!
I'M SURE IT'S NOT AS INTERESTING AS YOUR PRIVATE COLLECTION OF COBWEB EIGHT-PAGERS.
SHADDUP, YOU.
HEY, MA. WE GOT THE WEEK'S KICK. WHERE'S CARM?
WHERE D'YOU THINK?
HAVIN' ANOTHER DEEP PHILOSOPHICAL CONVERSATION WITH HIS PINK ELEPHANTS.
Y'FUH NOW. BEEDIT.
AWW, NOT AGAIN!?
MA-- WHY D'YOU LET HIM GET TANKED ALL THE TIME? HE'S THE BOSS! HE'S GOT RESPONSIBILITIES!
CARMINE CARBONE RESPONSIBLE? HAH! THAT'S A GOOD ONE.

IF WORD GETS OUT ABOUT HOW LOW *CARMINE'S* SUNK, *SPATS KATZ* IS GONNA BE SMELLIN' BLOOD.

CARM'S YOUR OLD MAN, *FRANKY*. MAYBE IT'S TIME YOU STEPPED IN AND FILLED HIS SHOES.

I DON'T *WANT* IT, JOHNNY. I NEVER HAVE.

MAYBE THERE'S ANOTHER WAY.

BUT I GOTTA PROTECT HIM.

YOU GET HIM CLEANED UP. I'LL CHECK THE BUZZ ON THE STREET.

LIGHTEN UP, *LIPS.* EVERYTHING'S GONNA BE JAKE.

DON'T TAKE ME ON YER SLEIGH-RIDE, *JOHNNY.* I WASN'T BORN IN *QUEERWATER,* Y'KNOW.

CARM'S LET THE PANTHER-JUICE GET THE BEST OF HIM.

HE'S BOOZE-BLIND. AND YOU KNOW WHAT *THAT* MEANS IN *INDIGO.*

SOMEBODY'LL SEE A PROFIT IN TAKIN' HIM DOWN. MAYBE *SPATS.* MAYBE *CHUCKY FRISCO*...

HELL-- IT COULD EVEN BE *YOU.*

C'MON! DON'T TALK LIKE THAT! I'M JUST ABOUT *FAMILY!*

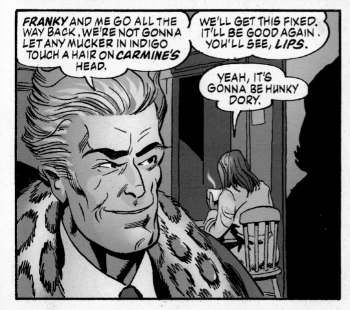

FRANKY AND ME GO ALL THE WAY BACK. WE'RE NOT GONNA LET ANY MUCKER IN INDIGO TOUCH A HAIR ON *CARMINE'S* HEAD.

WE'LL GET THIS FIXED. IT'LL BE GOOD AGAIN. YOU'LL SEE, *LIPS.*

YEAH, IT'S GONNA BE HUNKY DORY.

JUST LIKE IN THE FUNNY BOOKS.

HOODLUM HIT COMICS

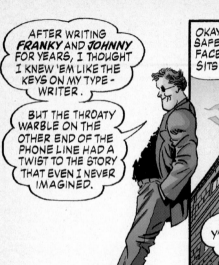

AFTER WRITING *FRANKY* AND *JOHNNY* FOR YEARS, I THOUGHT I KNEW 'EM LIKE THE KEYS ON MY TYPEWRITER.

BUT THE THROATY WARBLE ON THE OTHER END OF THE PHONE LINE HAD A TWIST TO THE STORY THAT EVEN I NEVER IMAGINED.

OKAY-- I GUARANTEED YOUR SAFETY SO WE COULD MEET FACE T' FACE, BUT *CANDI* SITS IN ON EVERYTHING.

WHATEVER Y'GOT--IT BETTER BE GOOD.

KATZ BUILDING

CARMINE CARBONE'S HEAD ON A PLATE GOOD ENOUGH?

THAT SHMUCK'S BEEN STEPPIN' ON MY WINGTIPS FOR THIRTY YEARS! WHAT MAKES Y'THINK YOU CAN PROVIDE WHAT MY BEST PEOPLE COULDN'T?

MAYBE I CAN'T. BUT IF I DELIVER, I GET HALF HIS RACKETS NOW AND THE REST WHEN YOU RETIRE.

I COULD LIVE WITH THAT. BUT, WHAT HAPPENS TO HIS BASTICH?

I THOUGHT YOU AN' *FRANKY* WERE PARTNERS.

EVERYBODY KNOWS *FRANKY'S* TOO SOFT FOR THIS BUSINESS.

I FIGURE IF HE'S DEAD WEIGHT...

...THEN WE'RE NOT PARTNERS ANY MORE, RIGHT?

I LIKE YER WAY OF THINKIN', *APOLLO*. HOW ABOUT YOU, *CANDI?*

JOHNNY'S GOT WHAT IT *TAKES*, SPATS. I SAY LET'S DO IT.

OKAY. DEAL. I'M HEADIN' DOWNTOWN TO TIP THE TROOPS ABOUT A CHANGIN' OF THE GUARD.

CANDI-- YOU MAKE OUR NEW FRIEND FEEL RIGHT AT HOME.

SURE, SPATS.

I CAN GET INTO THAT.

BIG TIME.

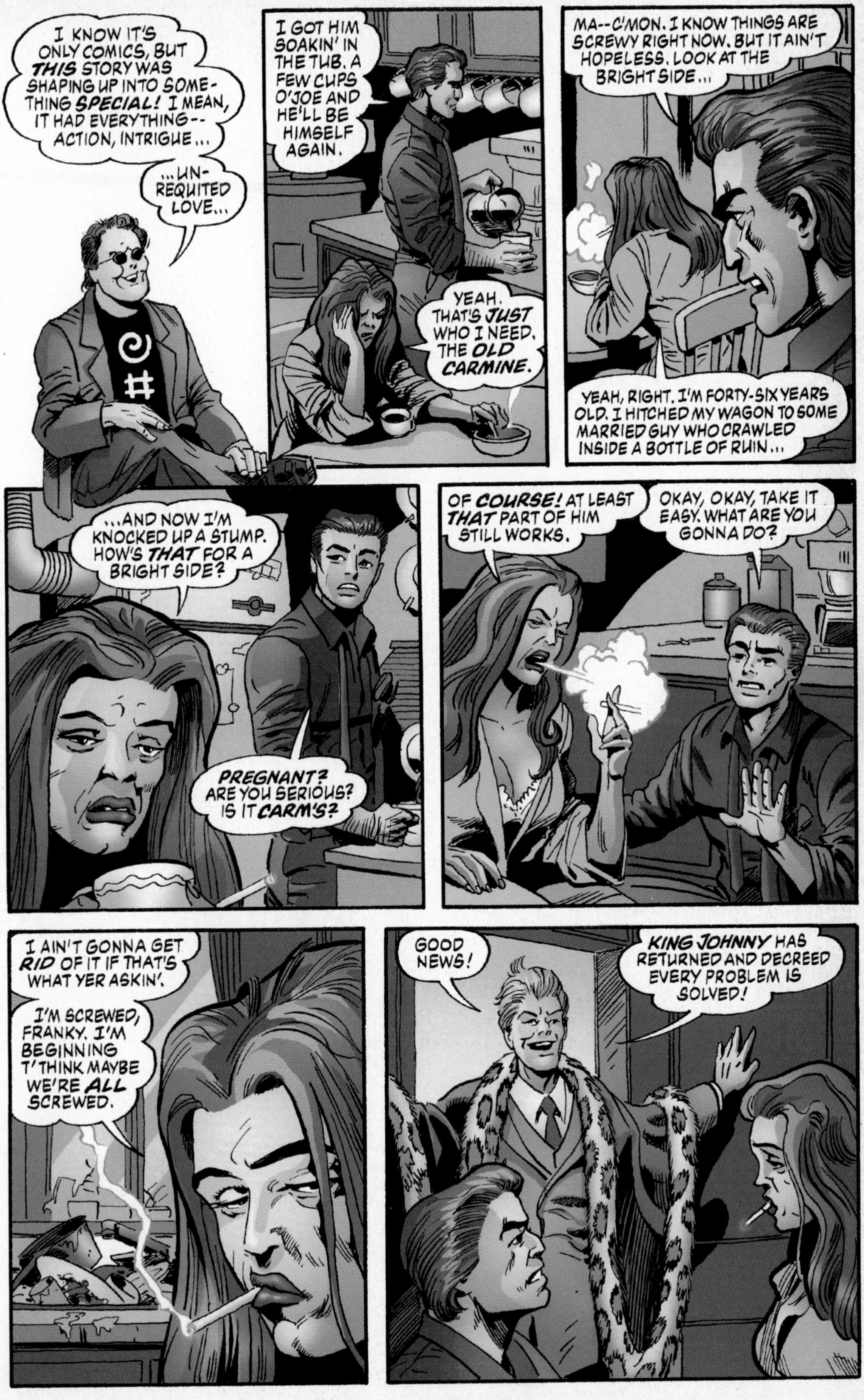

I KNOW IT'S ONLY COMICS, BUT THIS STORY WAS SHAPING UP INTO SOMETHING SPECIAL! I MEAN, IT HAD EVERYTHING-- ACTION, INTRIGUE...
...UN-REQUITED LOVE...
I GOT HIM SOAKIN' IN THE TUB. A FEW CUPS O'JOE AND HE'LL BE HIMSELF AGAIN.
YEAH. THAT'S JUST WHO I NEED. THE OLD CARMINE.
MA--C'MON. I KNOW THINGS ARE SCREWY RIGHT NOW. BUT IT AIN'T HOPELESS. LOOK AT THE BRIGHT SIDE...
YEAH, RIGHT. I'M FORTY-SIX YEARS OLD. I HITCHED MY WAGON TO SOME MARRIED GUY WHO CRAWLED INSIDE A BOTTLE OF RUIN...
...AND NOW I'M KNOCKED UP A STUMP. HOW'S THAT FOR A BRIGHT SIDE?
PREGNANT? ARE YOU SERIOUS? IS IT CARM'S?
OF COURSE! AT LEAST THAT PART OF HIM STILL WORKS.
OKAY, OKAY, TAKE IT EASY. WHAT ARE YOU GONNA DO?
I AIN'T GONNA GET RID OF IT IF THAT'S WHAT YER ASKIN'.
I'M SCREWED, FRANKY. I'M BEGINNING T'THINK MAYBE WE'RE ALL SCREWED.
GOOD NEWS!
KING JOHNNY HAS RETURNED AND DECREED EVERY PROBLEM IS SOLVED!

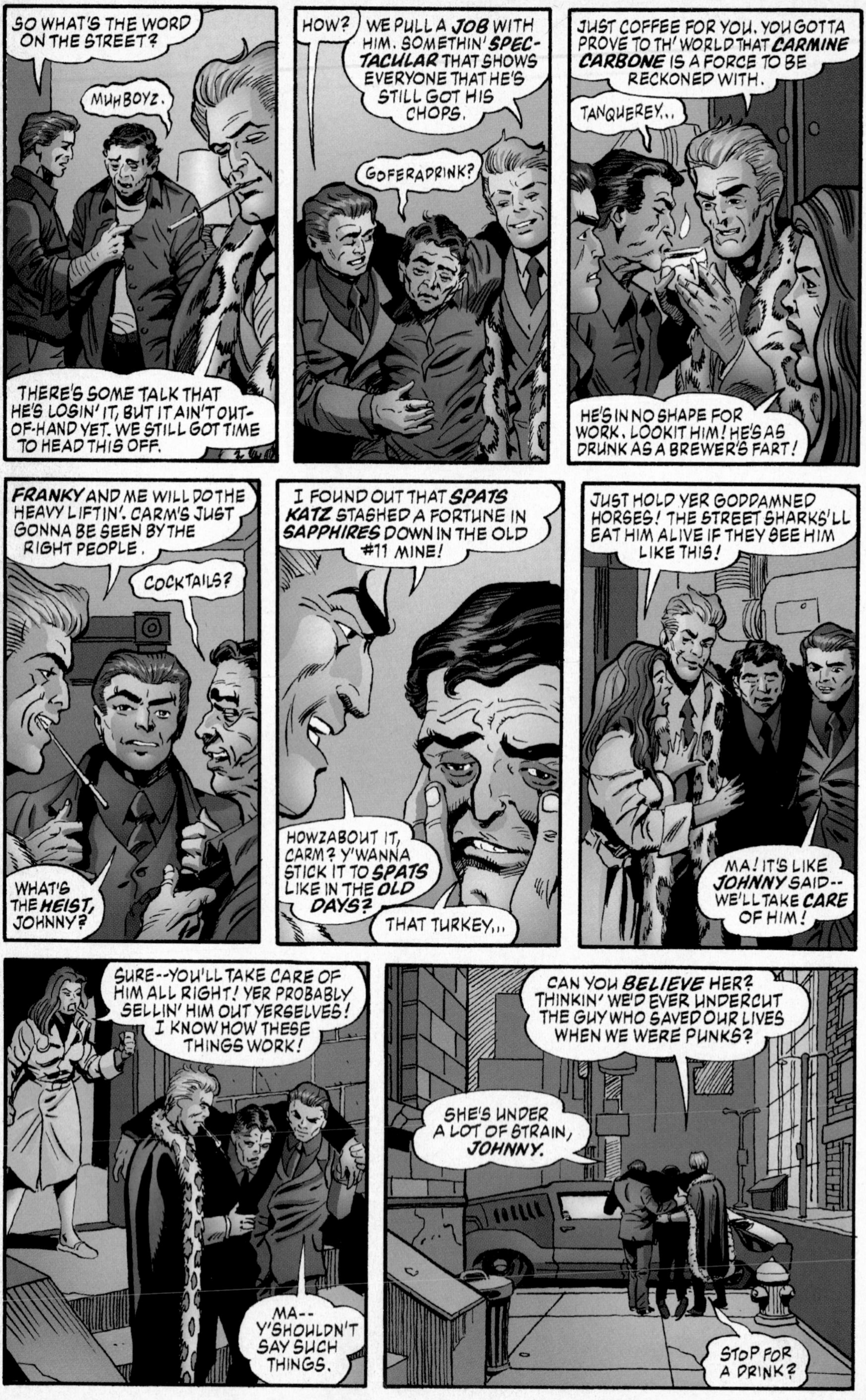

SO WHAT'S THE WORD ON THE STREET?
MUHBOYZ.
THERE'S SOME TALK THAT HE'S LOSIN' IT, BUT IT AIN'T OUT-OF-HAND YET. WE STILL GOT TIME TO HEAD THIS OFF.
HOW?
WE PULL A JOB WITH HIM. SOMETHIN' SPECTACULAR THAT SHOWS EVERYONE THAT HE'S STILL GOT HIS CHOPS.
GOFERADRINK?
JUST COFFEE FOR YOU. YOU GOTTA PROVE TO TH' WORLD THAT CARMINE CARBONE IS A FORCE TO BE RECKONED WITH.
TANQUEREY...
HE'S IN NO SHAPE FOR WORK. LOOKIT HIM! HE'S AS DRUNK AS A BREWER'S FART!
FRANKY AND ME WILL DO THE HEAVY LIFTIN'. CARM'S JUST GONNA BE SEEN BY THE RIGHT PEOPLE.
COCKTAILS?
WHAT'S THE HEIST, JOHNNY?
I FOUND OUT THAT SPATS KATZ STASHED A FORTUNE IN SAPPHIRES DOWN IN THE OLD #11 MINE!
HOWZABOUT IT, CARM? Y'WANNA STICK IT TO SPATS LIKE IN THE OLD DAYS?
THAT TURKEY...
JUST HOLD YER GODDAMNED HORSES! THE STREET SHARKS'LL EAT HIM ALIVE IF THEY SEE HIM LIKE THIS!
MA! IT'S LIKE JOHNNY SAID-- WE'LL TAKE CARE OF HIM!
SURE--YOU'LL TAKE CARE OF HIM ALL RIGHT! YER PROBABLY SELLIN' HIM OUT YERSELVES! I KNOW HOW THESE THINGS WORK!
MA-- Y'SHOULDN'T SAY SUCH THINGS.
CAN YOU BELIEVE HER? THINKIN' WE'D EVER UNDERCUT THE GUY WHO SAVED OUR LIVES WHEN WE WERE PUNKS?
SHE'S UNDER A LOT OF STRAIN, JOHNNY.
STOP FOR A DRINK?

THE BEST STORIES PICK UP ENERGY LIKE WEATHER SYSTEMS MOVING OVER LARGE BODIES OF WATER.

AND MY *WRITER'S BAROMETER* WAS DROPPING FAST ON THIS ONE.

SO THE CONNIVING OLD CREEP KEEPS HIS GOODS DOWN HERE IN THE MINES?

SPATS IS NO FOOL. HE KNOWS EVERYONE'S TERRIFIED OF THE *LURE.*

GOOD REASON FOR THAT. REMEMBER?

WHAT--THAT LITTLE RUCKUS WITH *SHEMPY* WHEN WE WAS KIDS?

CARMINE TOLD US NOTHIN' HAPPENED DOWN HERE. RIGHT, *CARM?*

FRUIT FER THE MONKEYS...

I'M NO FAN OF THE ACID WASTE PITS >KOF< DOWN HERE EITHER.

THAT'S WHERE YOU AND I DIFFER, FRANKY BOY.

I FEEL RIGHT AT HOME!

WHOK!

WATCH OUT!

RRUMMMBLE KRAASH!

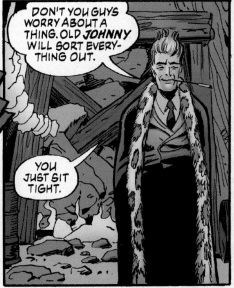

DON'T YOU GUYS WORRY ABOUT A THING. OLD *JOHNNY* WILL SORT EVERYTHING OUT.

YOU JUST SIT TIGHT.

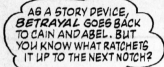

AS A STORY DEVICE, *BETRAYAL* GOES BACK TO CAIN AND ABEL. BUT YOU KNOW WHAT RATCHETS IT UP TO THE NEXT NOTCH?

THE INTENDED VICTIM SOMEHOW SURVIVING.

I'M COMIN', *CARM.* I'LL GET YOU OUT...

AAUUUNGHH. WHY BOTHER?

SOUNDS LIKE THE ADRENALINE IS BRINGING YOU OUT OF YOUR BOOZE STUPOR. THAT'S AN IMPROVEMENT.

DOESN'T MATTER. IT'S HOPELESS...

FIND *JOHNNY* IF Y'CAN. SAVE YER OWN SKIN.

GUYS LIKE ME... WE ALWAYS END UP LIKE RATS IN A TRAP. G-GOES WITH THE TERRITORY.

LEMME SEE IF I CAN ≥MMMMPH≥ CHANGE THAT.

WHAT'S *THAT?!*

OH GOD... IT'S THE #@%&IN' *LURE!*

DON'T LET IT *GET* ME, FRANKY!

I'M ON IT.

I THOUGHT...WE ALREADY TAUGHT THIS SNAKE IN THE GRASS... WHO OWNS *INDIGO!*

KA POW POW POW!

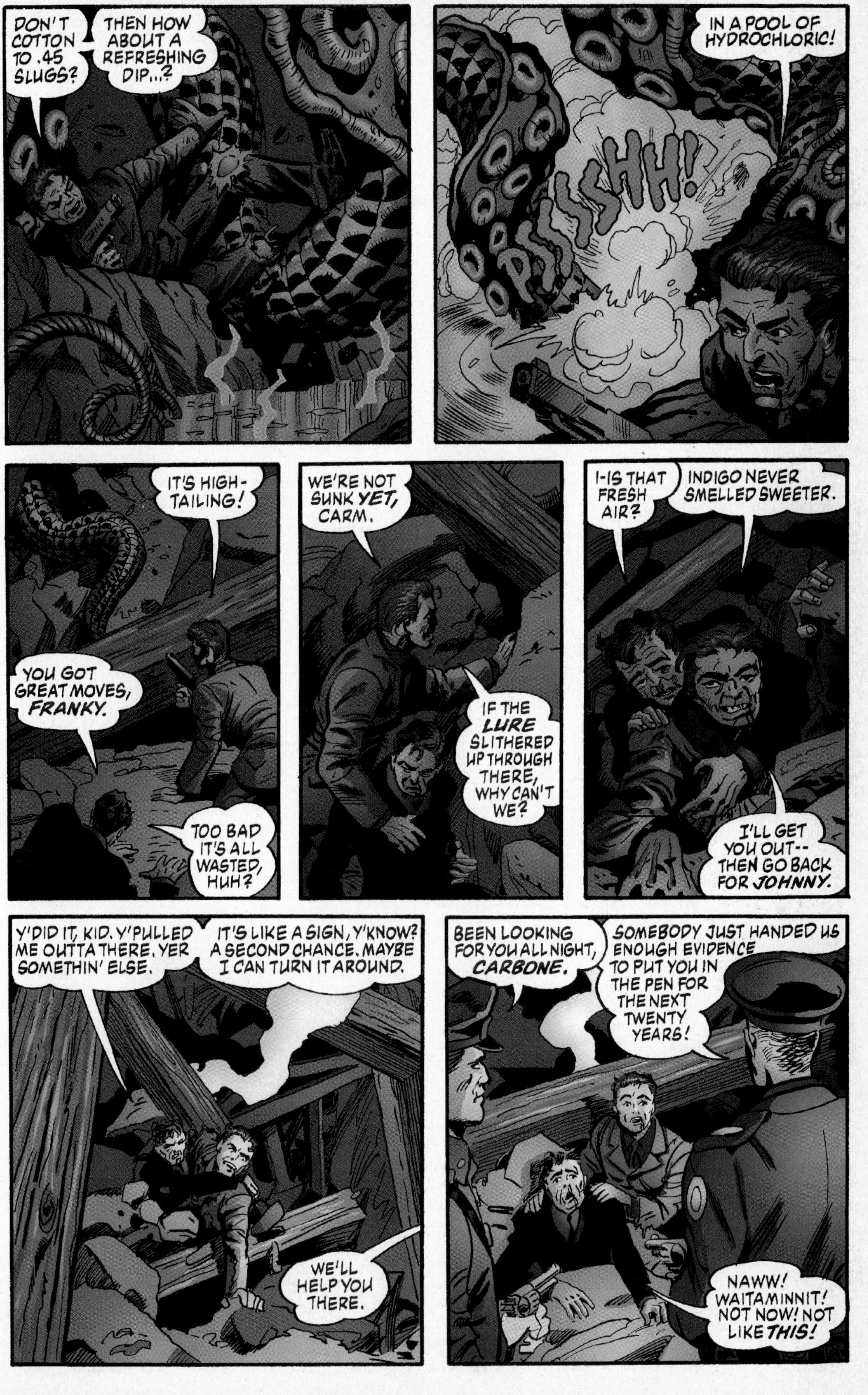
DON'T COTTON TO .45 SLUGS?
THEN HOW ABOUT A REFRESHING DIP...?
IN A POOL OF HYDROCHLORIC!
PSSSSHH!
IT'S HIGH-TAILING!
YOU GOT GREAT MOVES, FRANKY.
TOO BAD IT'S ALL WASTED, HUH?
WE'RE NOT SUNK YET, CARM.
IF THE LURE SLITHERED UP THROUGH THERE, WHY CAN'T WE?
I-IS THAT FRESH AIR?
INDIGO NEVER SMELLED SWEETER.
I'LL GET YOU OUT-- THEN GO BACK FOR JOHNNY.
Y'DID IT, KID. Y'PULLED ME OUTTA THERE. YER SOMETHIN' ELSE.
IT'S LIKE A SIGN, Y'KNOW? A SECOND CHANCE. MAYBE I CAN TURN IT AROUND.
WE'LL HELP YOU THERE.
BEEN LOOKING FOR YOU ALL NIGHT, CARBONE.
SOMEBODY JUST HANDED US ENOUGH EVIDENCE TO PUT YOU IN THE PEN FOR THE NEXT TWENTY YEARS!
NAWW! WAITAMINNIT! NOT NOW! NOT LIKE THIS!

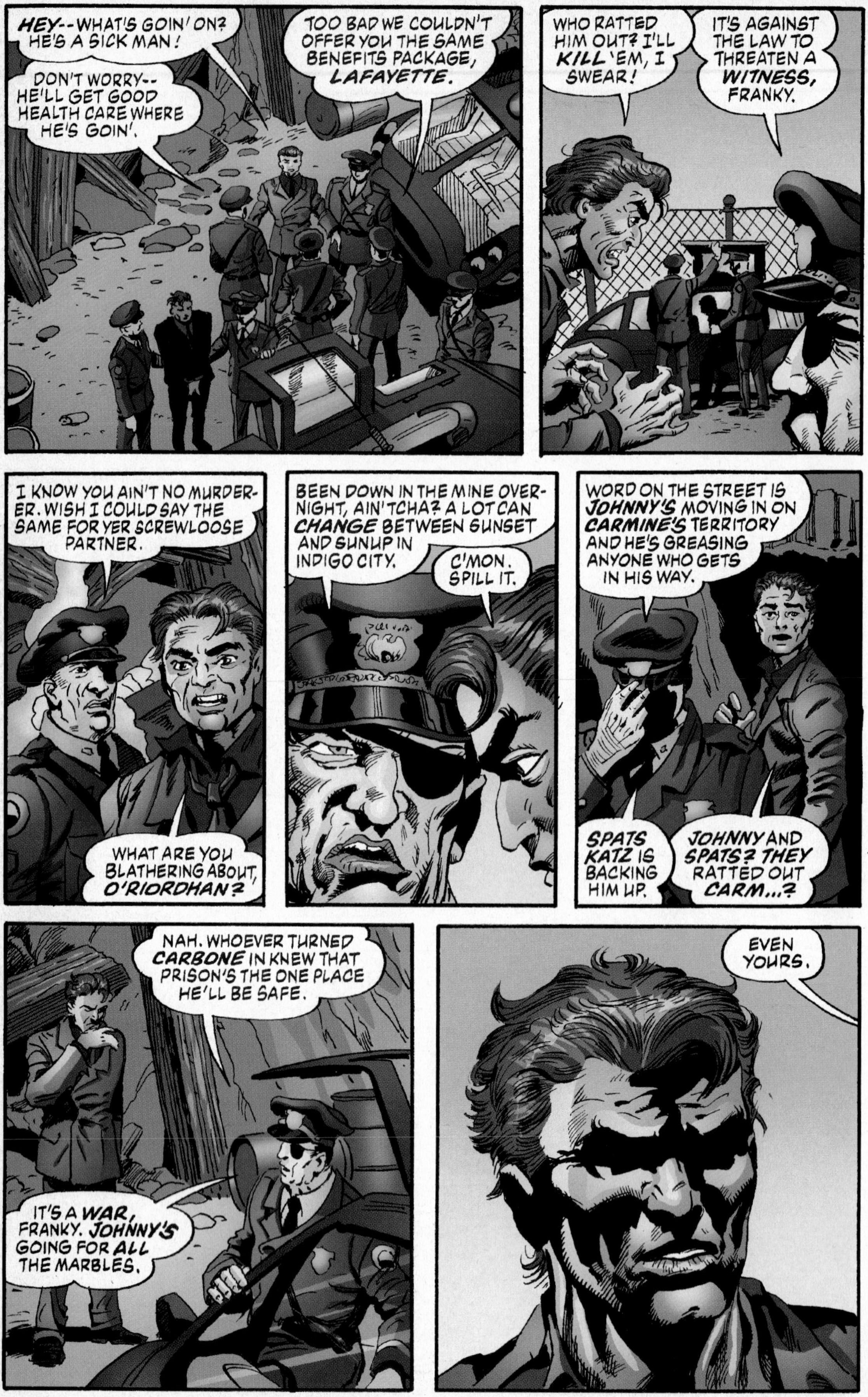
HEY--WHAT'S GOIN' ON? HE'S A SICK MAN!
DON'T WORRY-- HE'LL GET GOOD HEALTH CARE WHERE HE'S GOIN'.
TOO BAD WE COULDN'T OFFER YOU THE SAME BENEFITS PACKAGE, LAFAYETTE.
WHO RATTED HIM OUT? I'LL KILL 'EM, I SWEAR!
IT'S AGAINST THE LAW TO THREATEN A WITNESS, FRANKY.
I KNOW YOU AIN'T NO MURDERER. WISH I COULD SAY THE SAME FOR YER SCREWLOOSE PARTNER.
WHAT ARE YOU BLATHERING ABOUT, O'RIORDHAN?
BEEN DOWN IN THE MINE OVERNIGHT, AIN'TCHA? A LOT CAN CHANGE BETWEEN SUNSET AND SUNUP IN INDIGO CITY.
C'MON. SPILL IT.
WORD ON THE STREET IS JOHNNY'S MOVING IN ON CARMINE'S TERRITORY AND HE'S GREASING ANYONE WHO GETS IN HIS WAY.
SPATS KATZ IS BACKING HIM UP.
JOHNNY AND SPATS? THEY RATTED OUT CARM...?
NAH. WHOEVER TURNED CARBONE IN KNEW THAT PRISON'S THE ONE PLACE HE'LL BE SAFE.
IT'S A WAR, FRANKY. JOHNNY'S GOING FOR ALL THE MARBLES.
EVEN YOURS.

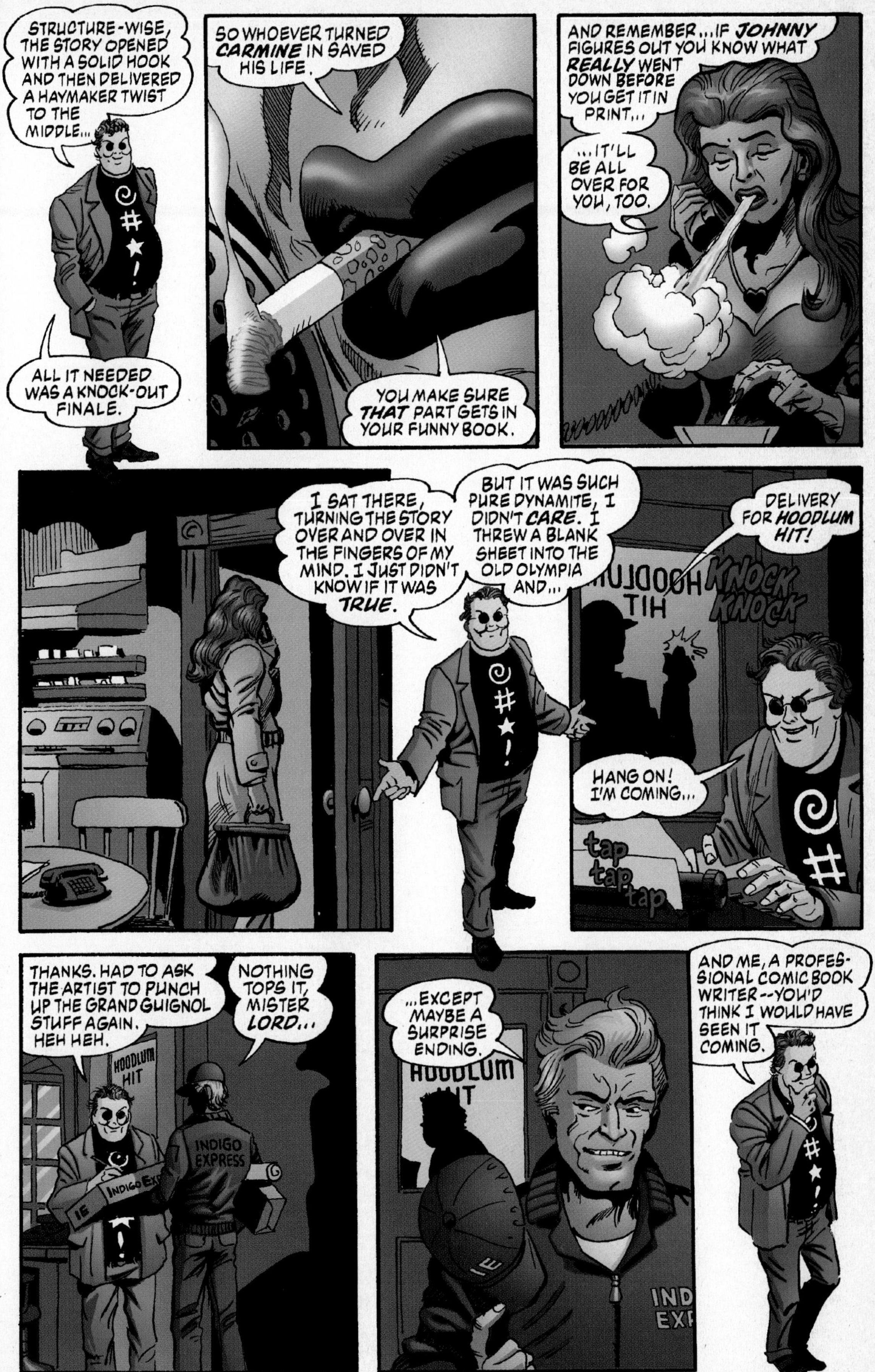
STRUCTURE-WISE, THE STORY OPENED WITH A SOLID HOOK AND THEN DELIVERED A HAYMAKER TWIST TO THE MIDDLE...
ALL IT NEEDED WAS A KNOCK-OUT FINALE.
SO WHOEVER TURNED CARMINE IN SAVED HIS LIFE.
YOU MAKE SURE THAT PART GETS IN YOUR FUNNY BOOK.
AND REMEMBER... IF JOHNNY FIGURES OUT YOU KNOW WHAT REALLY WENT DOWN BEFORE YOU GET IT IN PRINT...
...IT'LL BE ALL OVER FOR YOU, TOO.
I SAT THERE, TURNING THE STORY OVER AND OVER IN THE FINGERS OF MY MIND. I JUST DIDN'T KNOW IF IT WAS TRUE.
BUT IT WAS SUCH PURE DYNAMITE, I DIDN'T CARE. I THREW A BLANK SHEET INTO THE OLD OLYMPIA AND...
DELIVERY FOR HOODLUM HIT!
HOODLUM HIT
KNOCK KNOCK
HANG ON! I'M COMING...
tap tap tap
THANKS. HAD TO ASK THE ARTIST TO PUNCH UP THE GRAND GUIGNOL STUFF AGAIN. HEH HEH.
NOTHING TOPS IT, MISTER LORD...
HOODLUM HIT
INDIGO EXPRESS
...EXCEPT MAYBE A SURPRISE ENDING.
HOODLUM HIT
AND ME, A PROFESSIONAL COMIC BOOK WRITER--YOU'D THINK I WOULD HAVE SEEN IT COMING.

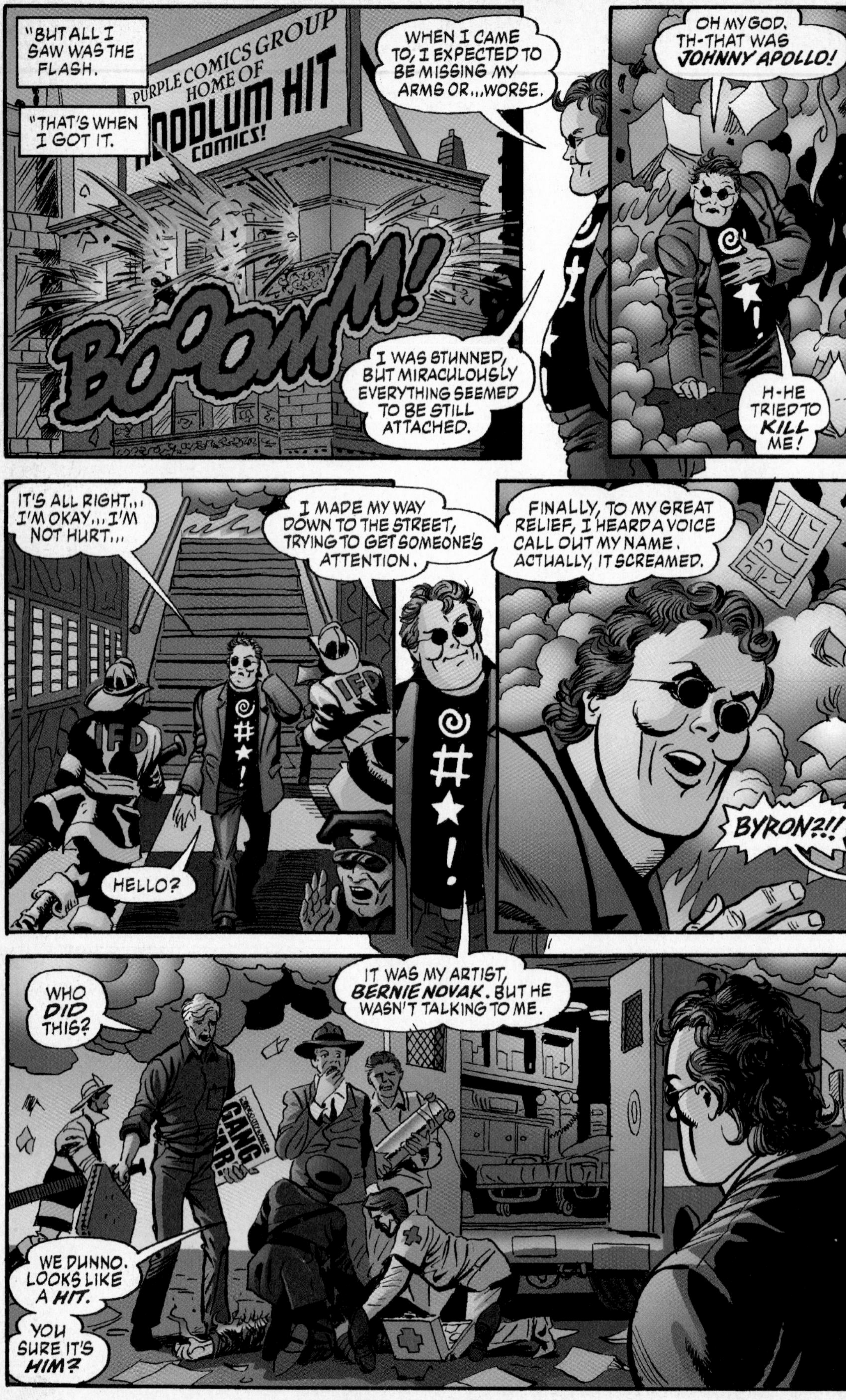
"BUT ALL I SAW WAS THE FLASH.
"THAT'S WHEN I GOT IT.
PURPLE COMICS GROUP HOME OF HOODLUM HIT COMICS!
BOOOM!
WHEN I CAME TO, I EXPECTED TO BE MISSING MY ARMS OR...WORSE.
I WAS STUNNED, BUT MIRACULOUSLY EVERYTHING SEEMED TO BE STILL ATTACHED.
OH MY GOD. TH-THAT WAS **JOHNNY APOLLO!**
H-HE TRIED TO **KILL** ME!
IT'S ALL RIGHT... I'M OKAY... I'M NOT HURT...
HELLO?
I MADE MY WAY DOWN TO THE STREET, TRYING TO GET SOMEONE'S ATTENTION.
FINALLY, TO MY GREAT RELIEF, I HEARD A VOICE CALL OUT MY NAME. ACTUALLY, IT SCREAMED.
BYRON?!!
IT WAS MY ARTIST, **BERNIE NOVAK**. BUT HE WASN'T TALKING TO ME.
WHO **DID** THIS?
WE DUNNO. LOOKS LIKE A **HIT**.
YOU SURE IT'S **HIM?**

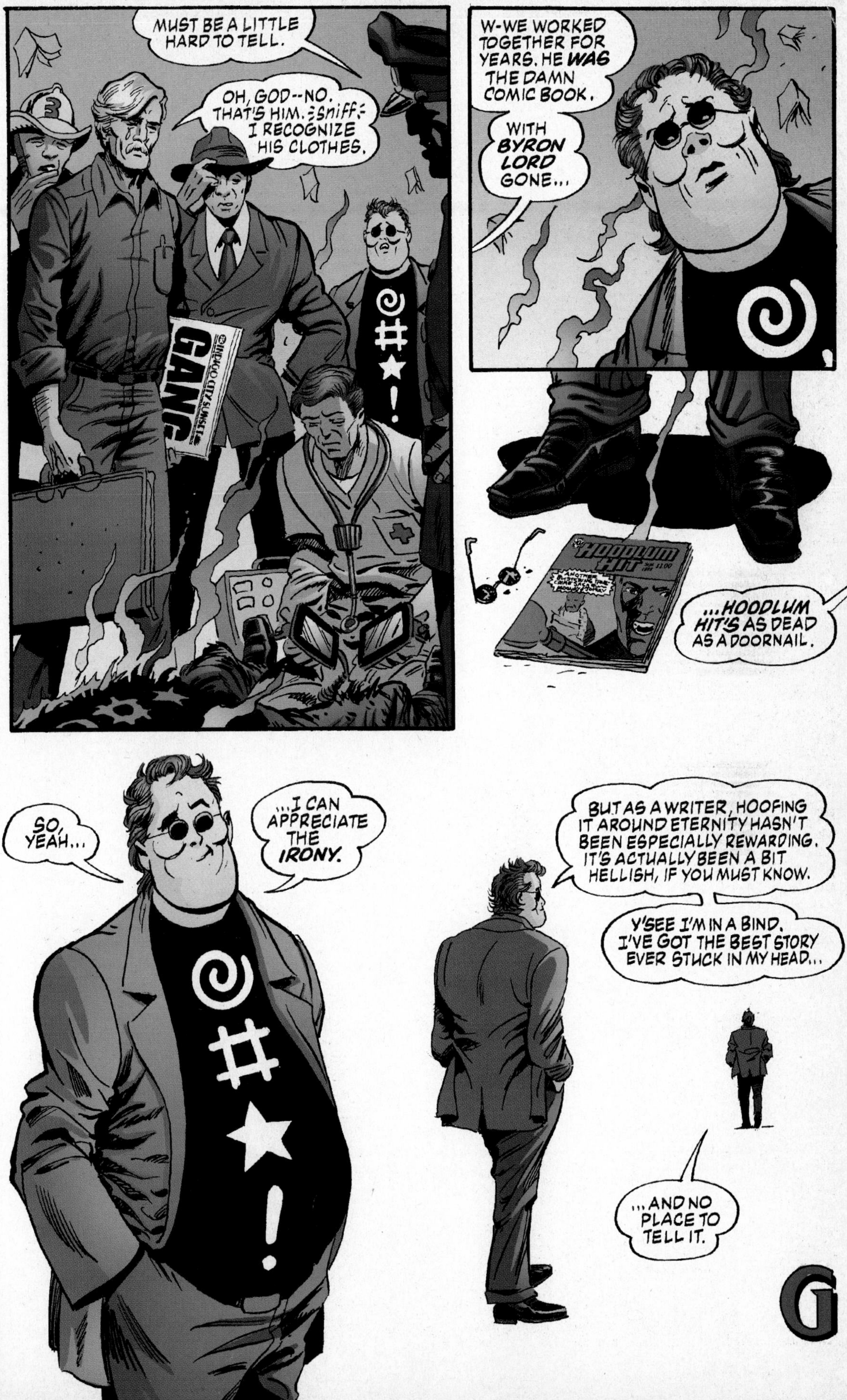
MUST BE A LITTLE HARD TO TELL.
OH, GOD--NO. THAT'S HIM. -SNIFF- I RECOGNIZE HIS CLOTHES.
W-WE WORKED TOGETHER FOR YEARS. HE WAS THE DAMN COMIC BOOK.
WITH BYRON LORD GONE...
...HOODLUM HIT'S AS DEAD AS A DOORNAIL.
SO, YEAH...
...I CAN APPRECIATE THE IRONY.
BUT AS A WRITER, HOOFING IT AROUND ETERNITY HASN'T BEEN ESPECIALLY REWARDING. IT'S ACTUALLY BEEN A BIT HELLISH, IF YOU MUST KNOW.
Y'SEE I'M IN A BIND. I'VE GOT THE BEST STORY EVER STUCK IN MY HEAD...
...AND NO PLACE TO TELL IT.

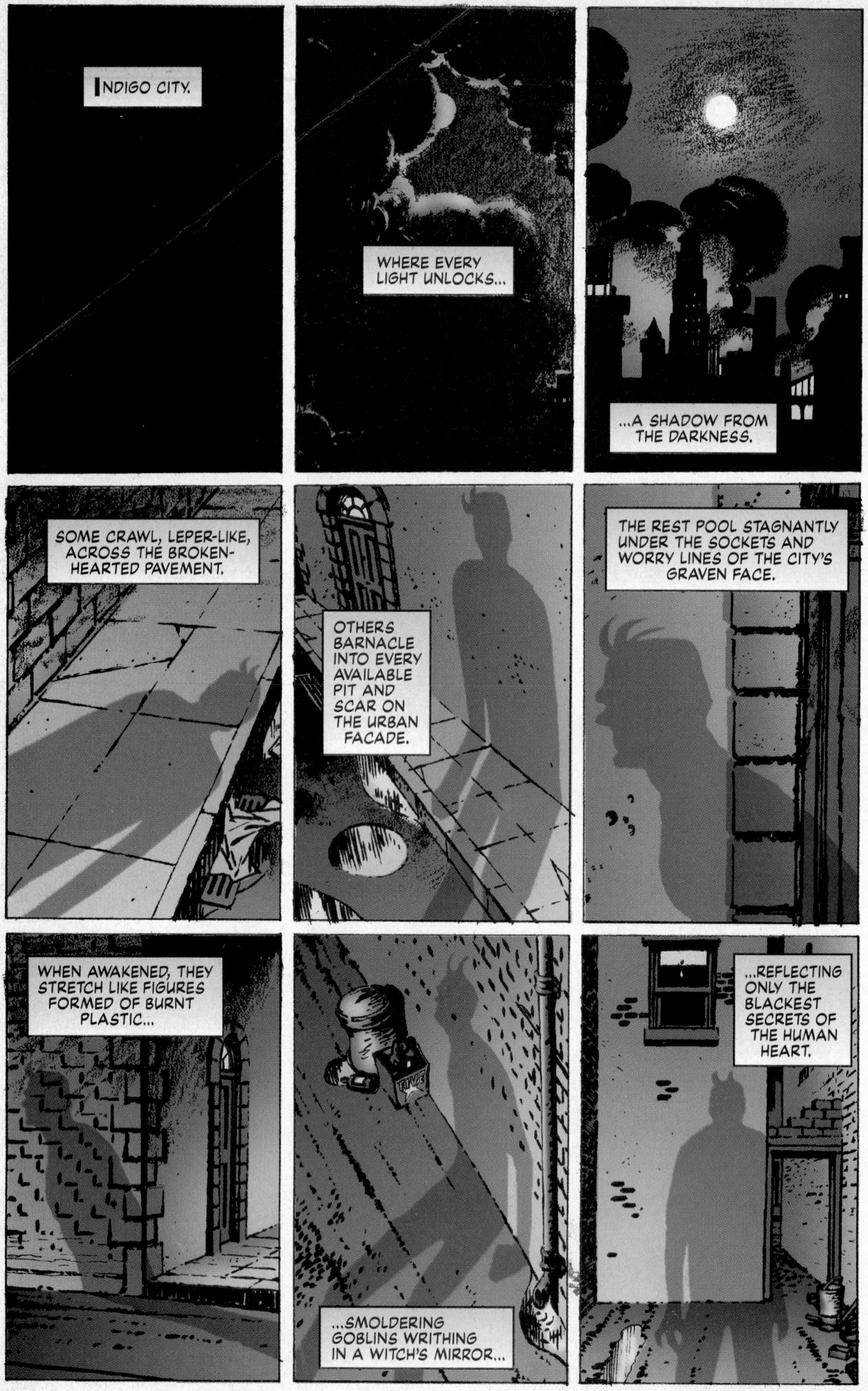
INDIGO CITY.
WHERE EVERY LIGHT UNLOCKS...
...A SHADOW FROM THE DARKNESS.
SOME CRAWL, LEPER-LIKE, ACROSS THE BROKEN-HEARTED PAVEMENT.
OTHERS BARNACLE INTO EVERY AVAILABLE PIT AND SCAR ON THE URBAN FACADE.
THE REST POOL STAGNANTLY UNDER THE SOCKETS AND WORRY LINES OF THE CITY'S GRAVEN FACE.
WHEN AWAKENED, THEY STRETCH LIKE FIGURES FORMED OF BURNT PLASTIC...
...SMOLDERING GOBLINS WRITHING IN A WITCH'S MIRROR...
...REFLECTING ONLY THE BLACKEST SECRETS OF THE HUMAN HEART.

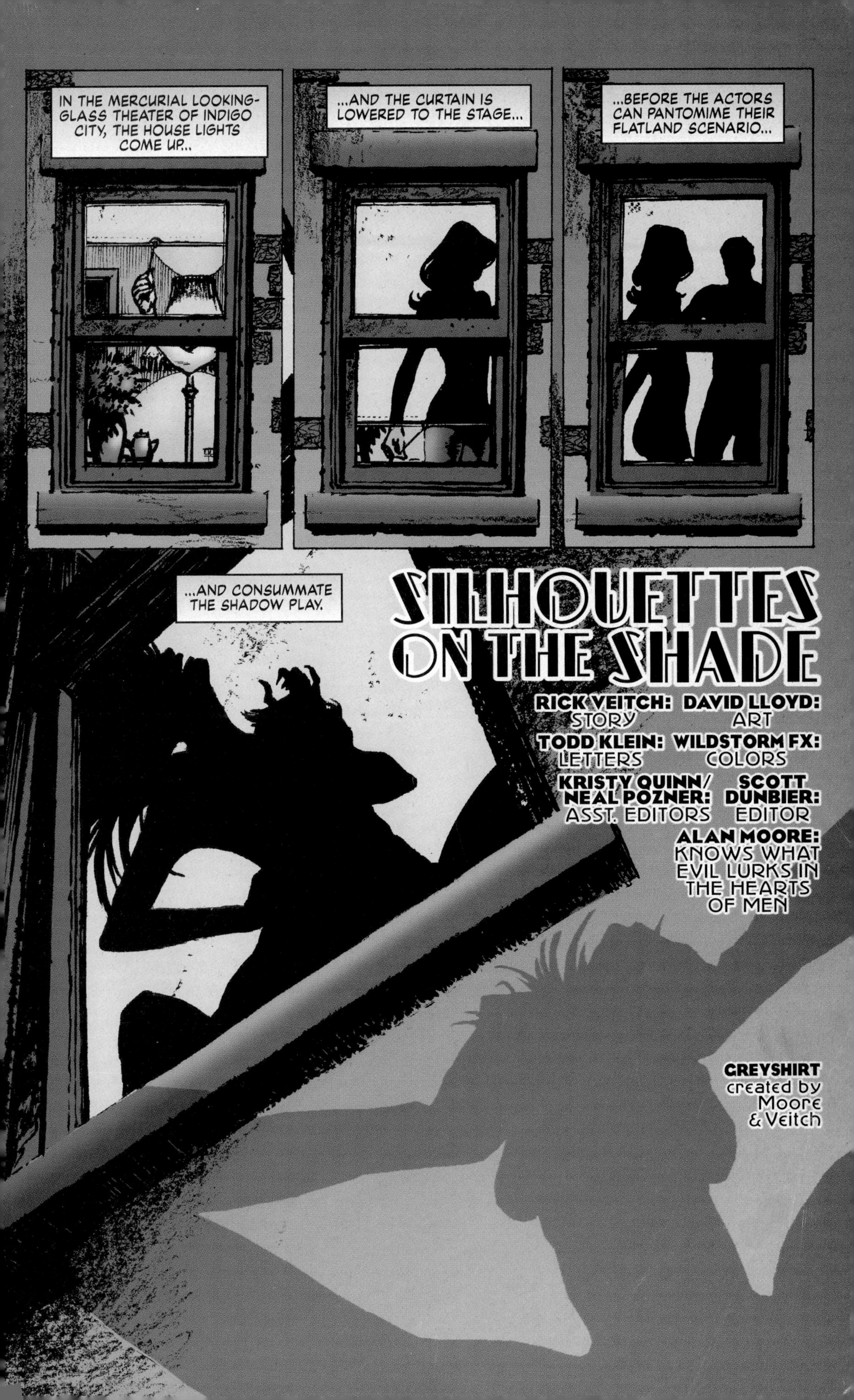
IN THE MERCURIAL LOOKING-GLASS THEATER OF INDIGO CITY, THE HOUSE LIGHTS COME UP...
...AND THE CURTAIN IS LOWERED TO THE STAGE...
...BEFORE THE ACTORS CAN PANTOMIME THEIR FLATLAND SCENARIO...
...AND CONSUMMATE THE SHADOW PLAY.
SILHOUETTES ON THE SHADE
RICK VEITCH: STORY
DAVID LLOYD: ART
TODD KLEIN: LETTERS
WILDSTORM FX: COLORS
KRISTY QUINN/ NEAL POZNER: ASST. EDITORS
SCOTT DUNBIER: EDITOR
ALAN MOORE: KNOWS WHAT EVIL LURKS IN THE HEARTS OF MEN
GREYSHIRT created by Moore & Veitch

CASTING LONG, ELECTRIC CORONA TENDRILS OF WORLDS ECLIPSED BY NEMESIS MOONS...

...THEY DETONATE LIKE ANTI-MATTER AGAINST THE IRON GRAY CHAINS OF LIGHT AND REASON...

IN INDIGO CITY, DARK IMPULSES LEAP UNBIDDEN FROM THE GHOSTLY PENUMBRA.

...REVEALING ONLY EMPTY SHADOWS.

IN INDIGO CITY, CARBONIC PATTERNS CAN EXPAND AND EXPLODE AT IMPOSSIBLE ANGLES...

...AND X-RAYS OFTEN ALCHEMIZE GEOMETRY IN A MOCKING CAULDRON OF CHAOS.

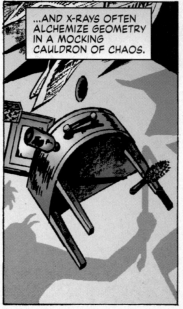

HERE, EVEN SHADOWS HAVE THEIR SHADOWS.

LIKE GREAT GALACTIC VOIDS IN-HALING LIGHT WITH THE DEATH RATTLES OF DYING STARS...

...THE INKY DEPTHS OF INDIGO QUAVER HOPELESSLY LIKE A FETID, AIRLESS CALCUTTA LOCK-UP.

HERE LOOMS THE SHADOW OF DEATH...

...WIELDED BY THE LEFT HAND OF DARKNESS.

BUT EVEN IN THIS GHASTLY GAS-LIT GOTHAM, THE DEAD OF NIGHT MUST FINALLY GIVE WAY...

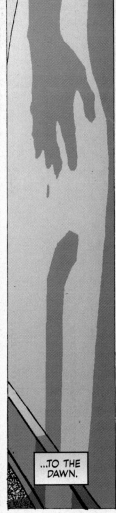

...TO THE DAWN.

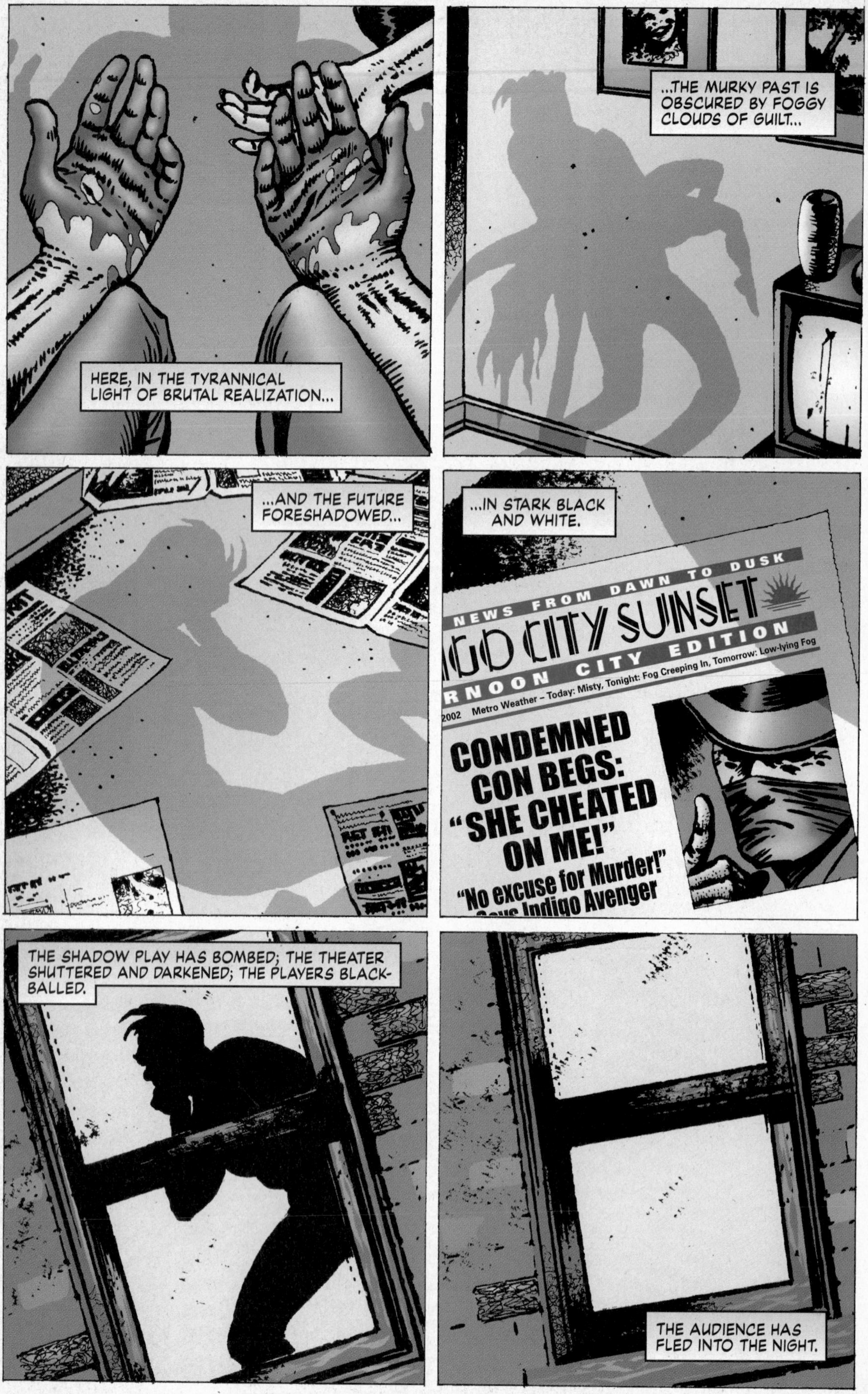

HERE, IN THE TYRANNICAL LIGHT OF BRUTAL REALIZATION...
...THE MURKY PAST IS OBSCURED BY FOGGY CLOUDS OF GUILT...
...AND THE FUTURE FORESHADOWED...
...IN STARK BLACK AND WHITE.
NEWS FROM DAWN TO DUSK
IGO CITY SUNSET
RNOON CITY EDITION
2002 Metro Weather – Today: Misty, Tonight: Fog Creeping In, Tomorrow: Low-lying Fog
CONDEMNED CON BEGS: "SHE CHEATED ON ME!"
"No excuse for Murder!"
Indigo Avenger
THE SHADOW PLAY HAS BOMBED; THE THEATER SHUTTERED AND DARKENED; THE PLAYERS BLACK-BALLED.
THE AUDIENCE HAS FLED INTO THE NIGHT.

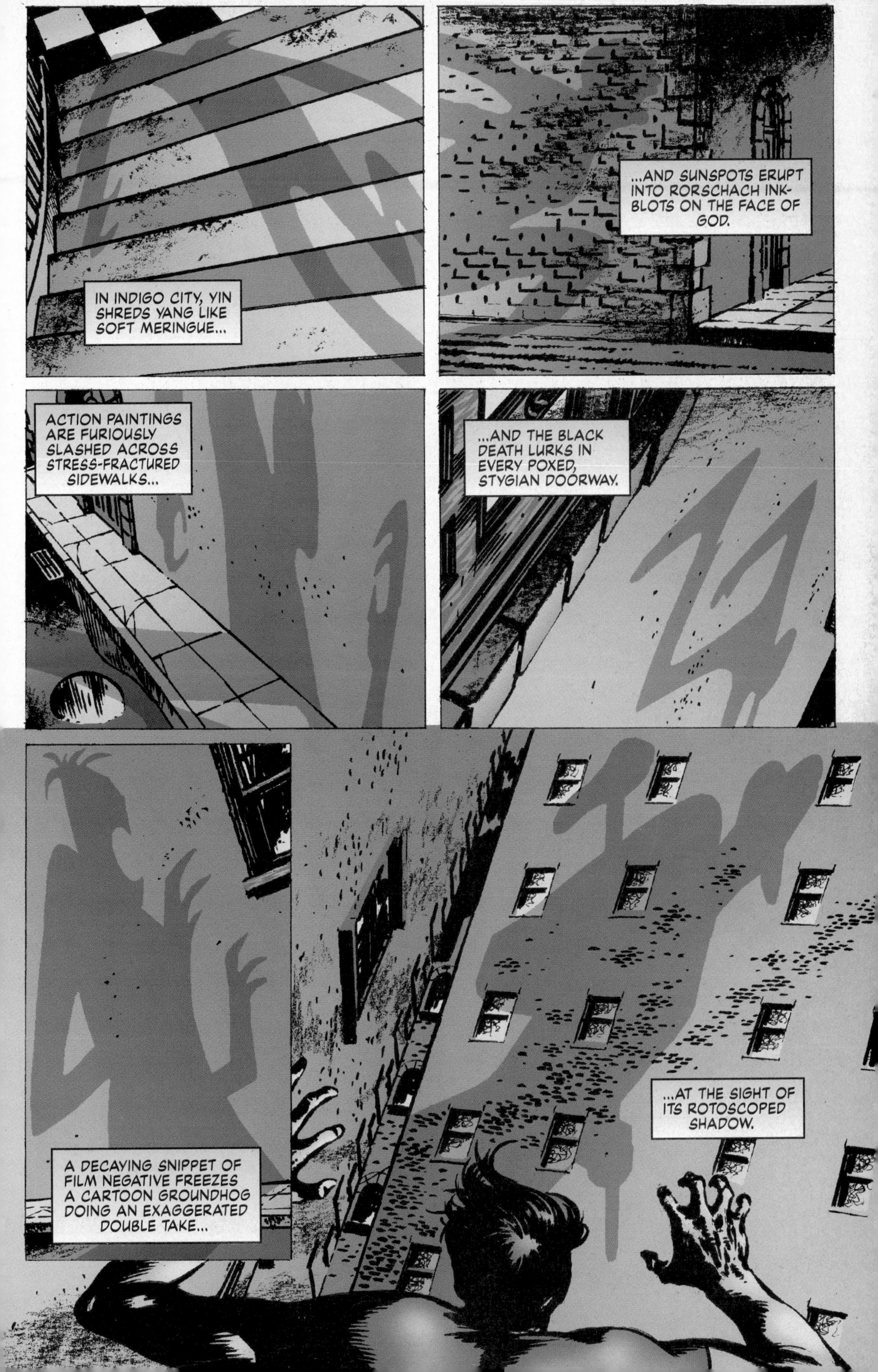
IN INDIGO CITY, YIN SHREDS YANG LIKE SOFT MERINGUE...
...AND SUNSPOTS ERUPT INTO RORSCHACH INK-BLOTS ON THE FACE OF GOD.
ACTION PAINTINGS ARE FURIOUSLY SLASHED ACROSS STRESS-FRACTURED SIDEWALKS...
...AND THE BLACK DEATH LURKS IN EVERY POXED, STYGIAN DOORWAY.
A DECAYING SNIPPET OF FILM NEGATIVE FREEZES A CARTOON GROUNDHOG DOING AN EXAGGERATED DOUBLE TAKE...
...AT THE SIGHT OF ITS ROTOSCOPED SHADOW.

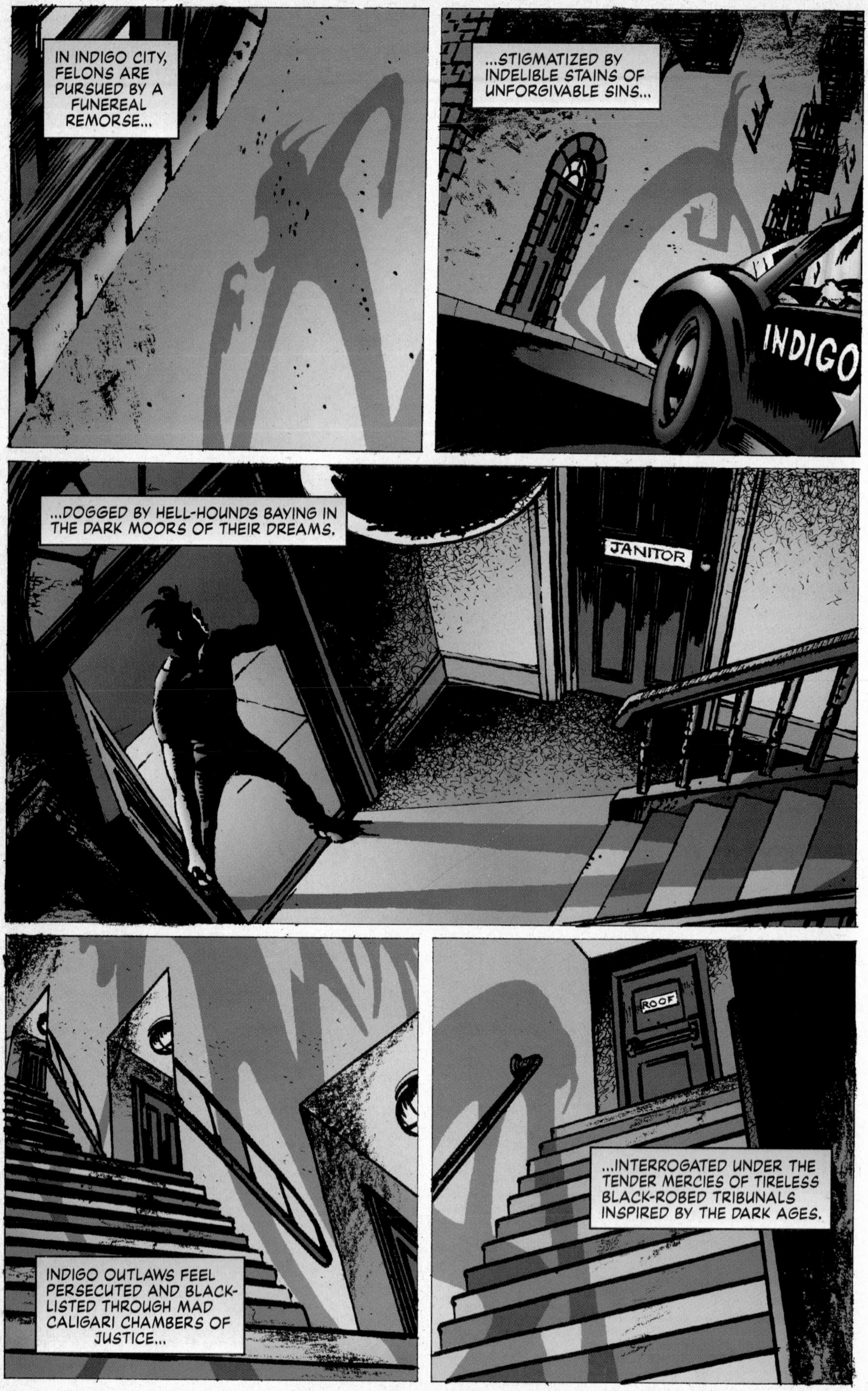
IN INDIGO CITY, FELONS ARE PURSUED BY A FUNEREAL REMORSE...
...STIGMATIZED BY INDELIBLE STAINS OF UNFORGIVABLE SINS...
INDIGO
...DOGGED BY HELL-HOUNDS BAYING IN THE DARK MOORS OF THEIR DREAMS.
JANITOR
INDIGO OUTLAWS FEEL PERSECUTED AND BLACK-LISTED THROUGH MAD CALIGARI CHAMBERS OF JUSTICE...
ROOF
...INTERROGATED UNDER THE TENDER MERCIES OF TIRELESS BLACK-ROBED TRIBUNALS INSPIRED BY THE DARK AGES.

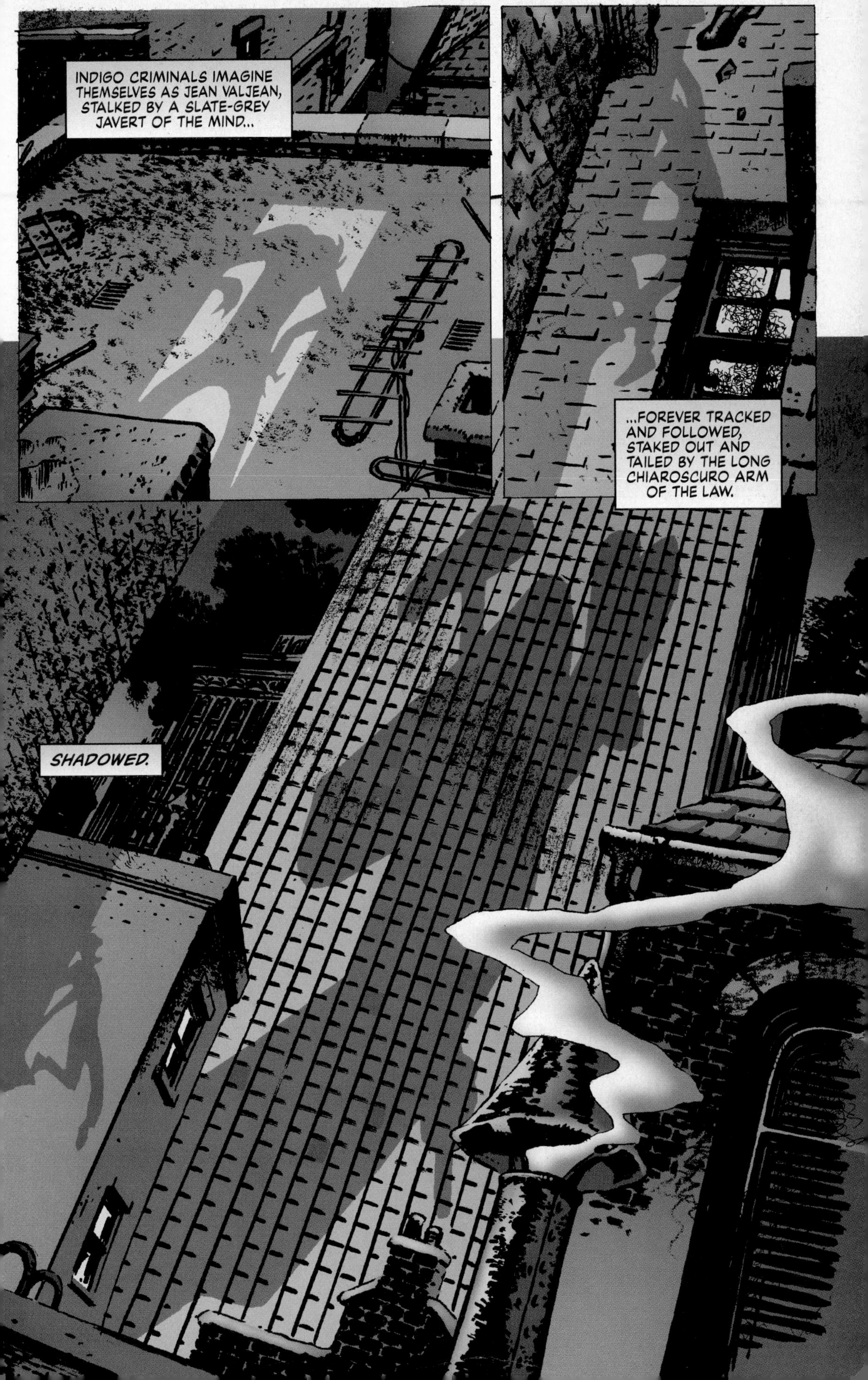

INDIGO CRIMINALS IMAGINE THEMSELVES AS JEAN VALJEAN, STALKED BY A SLATE-GREY JAVERT OF THE MIND...
...FOREVER TRACKED AND FOLLOWED, STAKED OUT AND TAILED BY THE LONG CHIAROSCURO ARM OF THE LAW.
SHADOWED.

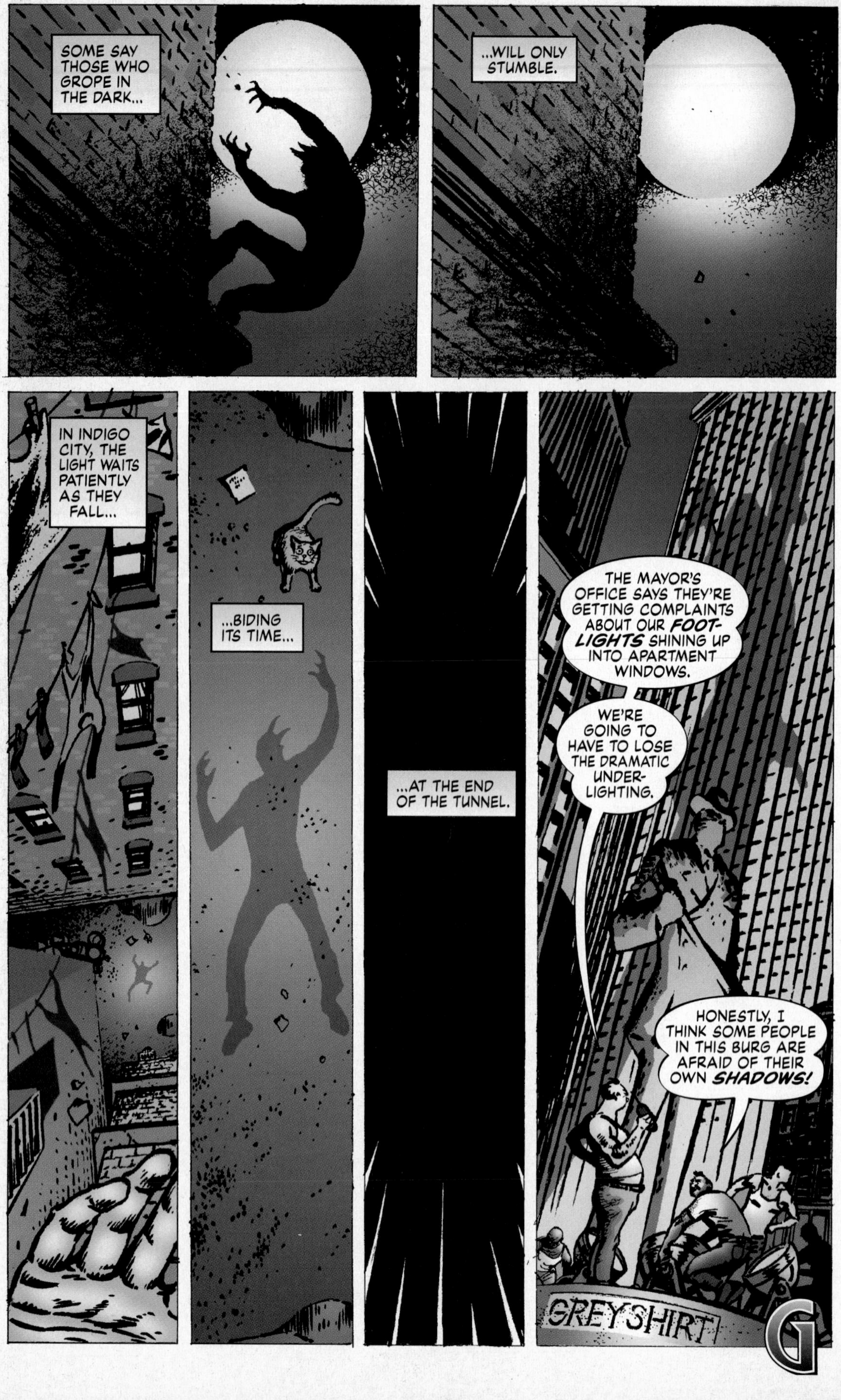
SOME SAY THOSE WHO GROPE IN THE DARK...
...WILL ONLY STUMBLE.
IN INDIGO CITY, THE LIGHT WAITS PATIENTLY AS THEY FALL...
...BIDING ITS TIME...
...AT THE END OF THE TUNNEL.
THE MAYOR'S OFFICE SAYS THEY'RE GETTING COMPLAINTS ABOUT OUR FOOT-LIGHTS SHINING UP INTO APARTMENT WINDOWS.
WE'RE GOING TO HAVE TO LOSE THE DRAMATIC UNDER-LIGHTING.
HONESTLY, I THINK SOME PEOPLE IN THIS BURG ARE AFRAID OF THEIR OWN SHADOWS!
GREYSHIRT

ALL THE NEWS FROM DAWN TO DUSK

STILL 60¢

INDIGO CITY SUNSET

AFTERNOON CITY EDITION

Wednesday, December 19, 2001 Metro Weather – Today: Hazy, Tonight: Murky, Tomorrow: Smoggy

CAST IN CRIME!

STATUESQUE SCIENCE HERO BREAKS THE MOLD OF FOUNDRY FELONS!

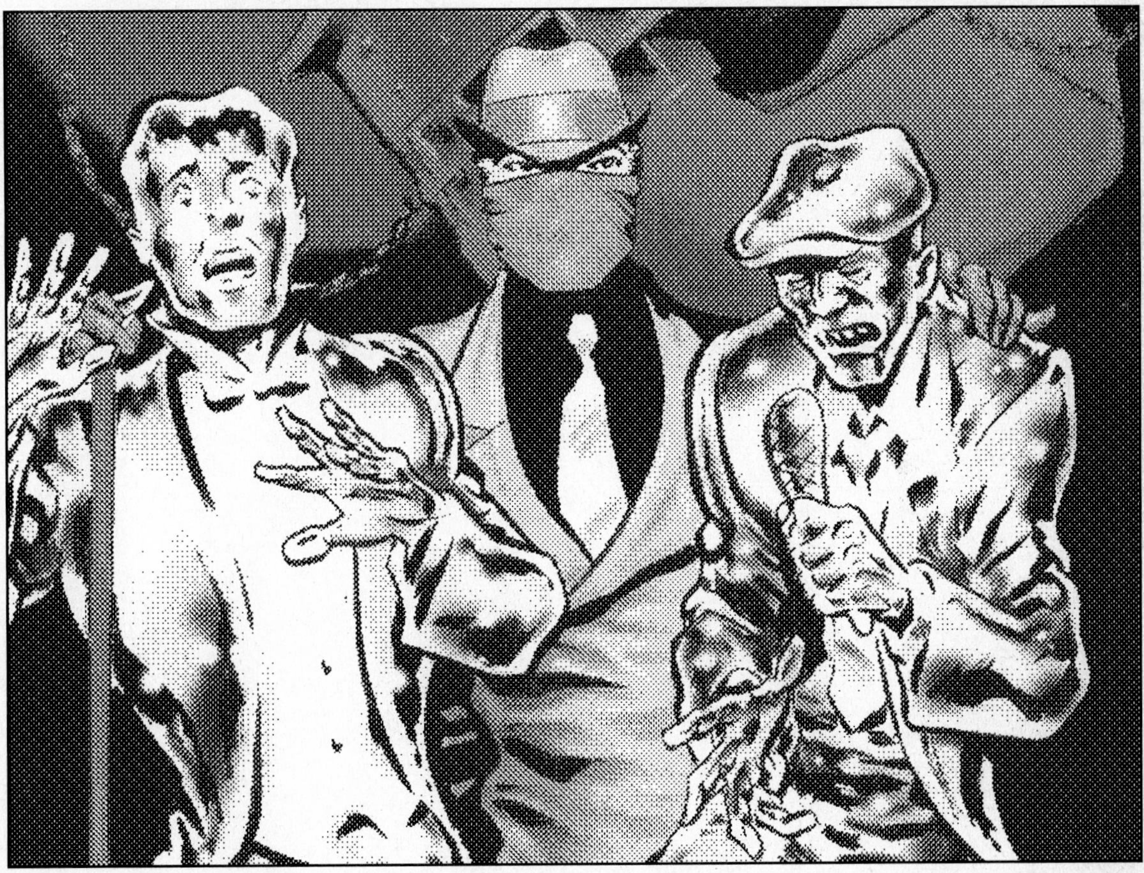

Indigo City: Cobalt Forge seemed like a model Indigo City business. It boasted ownership by a well-to-do family with long-time ties to local government and had produced some of the most famous monuments in the city. No one suspected what was concealed in the foundry's exquisite bronze statuary until GREYSHIRT unwittingly stumbled on their decades-old grisly secret.

FULL COVERAGE: Pages 2 and 3

INSIDE: Who's Haunting HOODLUM HIT Offices? Page 28

FREEZE FRAME FELONS!

BUSTED IN BRONZE!

**Coleman Kinkerdeen IV,
President of Cobalt Forge**

SPECIAL TO THE SUNSET BY SKEETER BACKENBEATER

GREYSHIRT sculpted another model case yesterday when he cracked an insidious group of paid assassins who had used one of Indigo's oldest and most highly respected businesses as a front for its murderous activities over a seventy-year period.

According to officials in the mayor's office, who briefed reporters on condition of anonymity, authorities were alerted earlier this week when a local recycling center reported a strange odor emanating from a cracked bronze statue that had been scheduled to be melted down after being donated to charity. Tests conducted by the Coroner's Office indicated that the statue, which had a date of 1956, contained human remains. Police immediately contacted the Cobalt Forge, which had originally cast the piece forty-five years ago.

When informed of the situation by police, the Cobalt Forge CEO COLEMAN KINKERDEEN IV, offered full cooperation and ordered his office to do a complete check on the history of the piece. A search of the files indicated that a worker in the foundry, one MORTIMER REPTILE, had accidentally fallen into the molten bronze vats and been incinerated the morning before the piece was cast in 1956. Authorities were thus convinced that somehow pieces of the luckless Reptile had ended up inside the bust and the investigation was closed.

Which is how things would have been left had not GREYSHIRT been following up leads on the disappearance of an Indigo City mobster's ex-girlfriend. All indications were that stripper CHINA BARTELLE had been murdered by her ex-lover CARLOS SOLARE, except that there was no trace of her body. Checking telephone logs, GREYSHIRT was able to ascertain that the crime lord had made a number of phone calls to the office of the Cobalt Forge in the days immediately before Bartelle's disappearance.

Acting on his characteristic combination of intuition and stubborn stick-to-it-ivness, GREYSHIRT slipped into the massive Cobalt Forge foundry as a black tie dinner celebrating Indigo City's blue-bloods was in full swing at the Kinkerdeen Mansion up on the hill overlooking the complex. GREYSHIRT immediately executed a surreptitious search of the Cobalt Forge offices and turned up what appeared to be a duplicate set of books containing a second history of each piece as it was cast. The Indigo Avenger was just beginning to study the documents, looking for discrepancies from those the police had been given, when he heard a noise on the foundry floor.

Slipping out of the office and concealing himself behind a bubbling vat of molten bronze, GREYSHIRT watched as a scruffy workman, later identified as ALBERT BINORAT, met a large limousine as it backed up to a darkened loading dock. GREYSHIRT observed Binorat and a gangster unloading a dead body and dropping it in one of the many molds waiting to be filled. As GREYSHIRT watched in horror, Binorat casually threw the switch of the big vat and molten bronze poured down the sluice and into the mold, entombing the corpse.

GREYSHIRT was putting two and two together when he was struck from behind by an unseen assailant. When he regained consciousness, he found himself bound with chains and dumped into one of the empty molds. Standing above him were the scruffy Binorat and Coleman Kinkerdeen IV himself, who had slipped out of his dinner party up at the mansion to assist in the casting of the corpse, and who had come upon the hiding GREYSHIRT, before cold-cocking him with a spanner.

Kinkerdeen proceeded to mock the helpless GREYSHIRT, saying he usually didn't like to get his hands dirty but was prepared to suffer the indignity if it meant disposing of the Indigo Avenger once and for all. Kinkerdeen proceeded to tell the struggling Science Hero the history of Cobalt Forge, confessing how his family had allied itself with Indigo's organized crime during the Great Depression. He bragged about how much money the family had made getting rid of gangsters' murder victims by entombing them inside the company's cast bronzes. Kinkerdeen then detailed how GREYSHIRT himself was about to become a victim of the process, chuckling that the only difference would be that the Indigo Avenger would be alive when the super-heated molten metal poured over him.

As it developed, taking the time to crow was a fatal mistake for Kinkerdeen as it gave GREYSHIRT a chance to pick the lock that bound his chains. Just as the boiling bronze began to flood the mold, the indefatigable Science Hero swung the chain and succeeded in entangling both Kinkerdeen and his henchman,

FREEZE FRAME FELONS!

Greyshirt's latest a work of art!

Binorat. A brief struggle ensued that ended with the two criminals falling into the vats full of molten metal and being entombed themselves.

When Indigo police arrived, a check of the books GREYSHIRT had found revealed a seventy year scheme, implicating three generations of Kinkerdeens as accessories to many unsolved murders in law enforcement files.

Posing with the grotesque effigies depicting the final death screams of the entombed criminals, GREYSHIRT quipped, "I may not know art, but I know what I like!"

SCANDAL SHUTTERS COMPANY THAT HELPED BUILD CITY!

Kinkerdeen family was authentic Indigo blue blood!

The Cobalt Forge, implicated in a seventy year scheme to thwart justice, is one of the city's oldest businesses, having been founded by Coleman Kinkerdeen in 1894. Coming from his native Scotland, where his family had operated a forge going back to medieval times, the elder Kinkerdeen was part of a generation of immigrants who settled in the untamed mining town of Indigo Junction, building solid businesses that helped set the foundation for the modern metropolis of Indigo City.

The Forge has been owned and operated by the Kinkerdeens, who are among Indigo's most highly respected families, since its doors opened 107 years ago. Kinkerdeens have been active in the social and political life of the city as well as the national scene. Orion Kinkerdeen served in the United States Senate and Mr. and Mrs. Metron Kinkerdeen went down on the *Titanic*.

But it was Coleman Kinkerdeen Jr. who made a pact with the devil during the Great Depression. Apparently, under threat of financial ruin, Kinkerdeen cut a deal with Indigo's gangster elite offering a fool-proof method of getting rid of murder victims. His son, Coleman Kinkerdeen III and grandson, Coleman Kinkerdeen IV all inherited the mantle and continued the grisly work right up until last night when GREYSHIRT put an end to the family's history of crime, adding the figures of Kinkerdeen and Binorat to his gallery of rogues.

WHO'S HAUNTING PURPLE COMICS?

Sunset reporter hears ghostly typing, heavy footsteps!

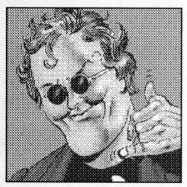

**Special to the Sunset
by Geekus Crow**

It's been seven years since Indigo City's venerable PURPLE COMICS company upgraded their offices with modern computer systems and whisper-quiet word processors. So why do writers, editors, secretaries and even night watchmen swear they hear an old-style typewriter clacking away at all hours of the day and night? Is it the fevered imaginations of comic book geeks playing tricks, or is there someone with serious unfinished business tapping out a message to comics fans everywhere?

To find out once and for all, this reporter recently spent a night in the PURPLE COMICS offices and yes, I did hear typing, coming out of nowhere. The tapping of type-writer keys was often joined by a squeaking office chair, ghostly sighs and what sounded like a person scratching their head and biting their nails. This symphony of sound effects would be regularly interrupted by heavy footsteps walking across the hall and what sounded like vending machines being operated. At least twenty-seven trips to these invisible "vending machines" were heard by this reporter in the course of one night. Workers said that section of the office had been a snack area before renovations in 1990.

PURPLE COMICS had its hey-day in the 1980s when it published HOODLUM HIT, a wildly successful comic book that chronicled fictionalized adventures of two local gangsters, FRANKY LAFAYETTE and JOHNNY APOLLO. The offices were bombed in 1989, killing the author of the series, BYRON LORD, and ending publication of the lurid crime stories. The murder of LORD, never solved, was the subject of intense speculation that it had been carried out by LAFAYETTE and APOLLO, perhaps angered by the use of their names and likenesses in HOODLUM HIT. The two gangsters were themselves blown to bits in the infamous explosion of a fuel depot under Indigo's abandoned Central Station a few days after LORD's death. The company bounced back in the early nineties and is now a successful publisher of horror comics such as VERBOTEN! and PARADE OF GORE.

Most PURPLE COMICS employees agree that the ghostly presence in their midst is that of murdered comics scribe, BYRON LORD. Long-time night watchman TREVOR PECKSNIFF told the Sunset, "BYRON used to sit up there every night, banging away on his old Olympia and sucking down soda pops and candy bars. When I hear those noises today I think to myself, that's Byron! Still strugglin' with this month's HOODLUM HIT."

The Sunset tracked down BERNARD NOVAK, the artist who illustrated LORD's scripts for the FRANKY AND JOHNNY feature. Novak, now a janitor at the MISS MAUVE DINER, refused comment other than to say, "I've had a belly-full of gangsters and comic books, thank you very much!"

PURPLE COMICS PUBLISHING LTD was recently purchased by FANMAN PRODUCTIONS, which is said to be contemplating a relaunch of HOODLUM HIT to coincide with the film release of *THE CARBONES: FRANKY AND JOHNNY*. If HOODLUM HIT comics grace the newsstands of Indigo once again, maybe BYRON LORD will finally get some much-deserved rest.

FABLED "STAR OF INDIGO" COMING HOME!

Sapphire said to inspire true love!

The mythical STAR OF INDIGO, a fabulous twenty-six pound star sapphire that rivals the "HEART OF KRISHNA" in size and purity, will be returning to Indigo City next month. The Indigo Museum of Natural History announced an arrangement with the Kremlin that will bring the much-traveled jewel back to the area for the first time since it was unearthed here by Aztecs over 800 years ago.

The STAR OF INDIGO has been proven to be part of the huge deposits of sapphire left in the Indigo City area when the Earth collided with an asteroid made of the pure gemstone twenty million years ago, creating Crater Bay.

Historians say the jewel passed through the hands of a number of colorful characters, while popular myth claims the gem possesses magical powers that lead complete strangers to fall in love in its vicinity. The first known depiction of such properties comes in the memoirs of a Spanish Conquistador; one BERNARD DIAZ DEL CASTILLO, who claimed he experienced recognition with a native woman as he attempted to plunder the stone from the palace of Montezuma in 1519.

The Museum of Natural History expects large crowds of Indigoans to visit the exhibit, with many no doubt hoping to meet their soul mates before the Star of Indigo! Chief O'Riardon of the Indigo City Police said he's putting on full time guards to protect the priceless jewel from Indigo's criminal element.

INDIGO POOP SCOOP! BY IDLE DISH

FRANKY AND JOHNNY HYSTERIA HITS INDIGO!

Filming on FANMAN PRODUCTIONS' $100 million extravaganza "THE CARBONES: FRANKY AND JOHNNY" is only half finished but it's clear the mood in Indigo Town is head over heels for her two most infamous sons, FRANKY LAFAYETTE and JOHNNY APOLLO. Gangster styles with wide lapels and shoulder pads grace the windows of downtown's finest men's clothing stores, while the Moll Look is burning up runways all across the fashion district. Sales of BUMPMOBILES have gone through the roof since their new "GETAWAY" ad campaign launched last month. And STANLEY AND THE STALEMATES' rendition of *FRANKY AND JOHNNY,* which was first released years ago, is suddenly back climbing the charts. Stanley's modernized lyrics of the old folk ballad tell the story of the Tyrant Twins' final shootout. And now comes rumors that the comic book that started it all, HOODLUM HIT, is set for relaunch in the next few months. Can life get any sweeter?

YOU CAN'T KEEP A GOOD GANGSTER DOWN!

So says kooky heiress Laurel Lakeland, whose family's billions created the Lakeland Museum of Contemporary Art. Mayor Plato Plutarch shut down the facility when it was discovered that one of Andy Savannah's POW! ART pieces had been partially painted with human blood, but we hear Lakeland, a large contributor to the Mayor's election committee, made a personal appeal to hizzonner that couldn't be refused! We're told that thanks to the Lady Of The Lakeland's creative lobbying, the museum was open the next day and has since seen attendance skyrocket!

FANNING THE FLAMES!

The POOP SCOOP has it on good authority that the mysterious FANMAN himself paid a visit to the PURPLE COMICS offices last week to seal his purchase of the venerable comic book company for his FANMAN PRODUCTIONS. We call him "mysterious" because we're told no one knows the producer's true identity. Even spookier, say those in the know, is that when he does appear at meetings, the executive holds an ornate fan in front of his face; thus the "FANMAN" monicker! The SCOOP is trying to get the POOP on whether Sunset photographer Riccardo Veitichello's recent broken nose and slipped disc had anything to do with his attempt to get a shot of the reclusive producer. We'll have all the latest on that story soon!

ASK DR. SYNTAX

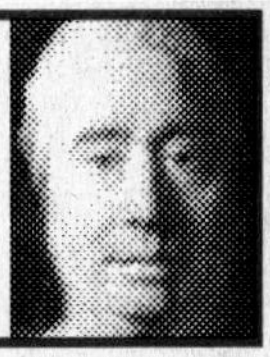

Husband's Long-time Affair Cheated Wife of Life

Dear Doctor Syntax: I've been married for thirty-five years. I am active in my church and community. Everyone thinks my marriage has been a perfect one. However, they are mistaken.

My husband, who I'll call Red, had a long-running affair with an old flame from the Bottoms Up district. When I first heard of it in the 1960s, I lost my temper and attacked Red with a kitchen knife. He was left with a large scar on his face for the rest of his life. This year, I hired an investigator who found out that Red's philandering went on for the length of our marriage. I also learned he had two children by her before they finally split up in 1989.

Red is old and feeble now, suffering from health problems. He's in a halfway house for elderly convicts. Fortunately, I was able to get control of our finances when he was incarcerated, and I want for nothing, but I'm still angry at his decades of philandering behind my back. Should I have him whacked? — Red's Wife

Dear Red's Wife: Is it really worth risking a murder rap? Why not just hire some tough in the neighborhood of his halfway house to harass him regularly? Instruct the hooligan to steal your husband's Social Security check and generally make what little he has left of life completely miserable. Remember; don't get mad--get even!

Dear Doctor Syntax: About a year ago, I was married to this guy who I was really tired of. He was a butcher whose only saving grace was the big life insurance policy he kept. I decided to get rid of him and tricked a young kid into thinking my husband wanted to chop off my hands. The kid was nice; a real thoughtful type, but wet behind the ears. Anyway, the scam went off without a hitch and the kid blew away my husband and ended up sentenced to life in the state pen. I got off scot-free, collected on the insurance and moved to the Bahamas. The thing is, every once in a while I think of the sweet kid sitting in a cell for the rest of his life trying to figure out what happened. It weighs on my thoughts some times. Should I clue him in? — Kid Gloves

Dear Kid Gloves: Scam victims who understand they've been screwed over should be considered extremely dangerous, even if doing life in prison. There is always the possibility of parole or jail break and then you could find yourself on the receiving end of pent-up anger and revenge. A thoughtful card or gift during the holidays designed to keep the rube thinking that you are innocent of any wrongdoing is the way to go.

SUNSET COMICS

MUSSEL BEACH **By Squid Pro Quo**

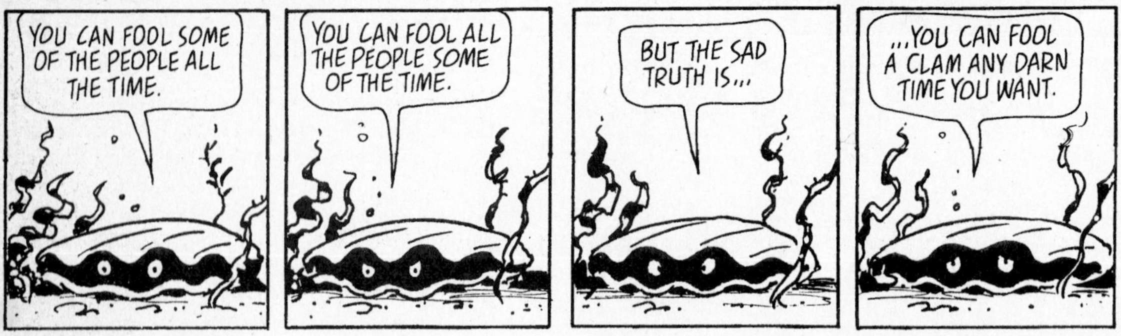
YOU CAN FOOL SOME OF THE PEOPLE ALL THE TIME.
YOU CAN FOOL ALL THE PEOPLE SOME OF THE TIME.
BUT THE SAD TRUTH IS...
...YOU CAN FOOL A CLAM ANY DARN TIME YOU WANT.

HARRY GEE **By Chet Ghoulash**

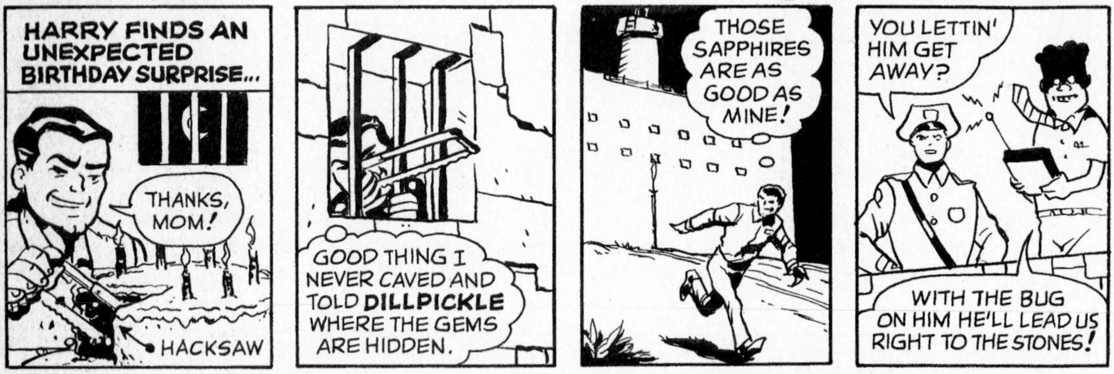
HARRY FINDS AN UNEXPECTED BIRTHDAY SURPRISE...
THANKS, MOM!
HACKSAW
GOOD THING I NEVER CAVED AND TOLD DILLPICKLE WHERE THE GEMS ARE HIDDEN.
THOSE SAPPHIRES ARE AS GOOD AS MINE!
YOU LETTIN' HIM GET AWAY?
WITH THE BUG ON HIM HE'LL LEAD US RIGHT TO THE STONES!

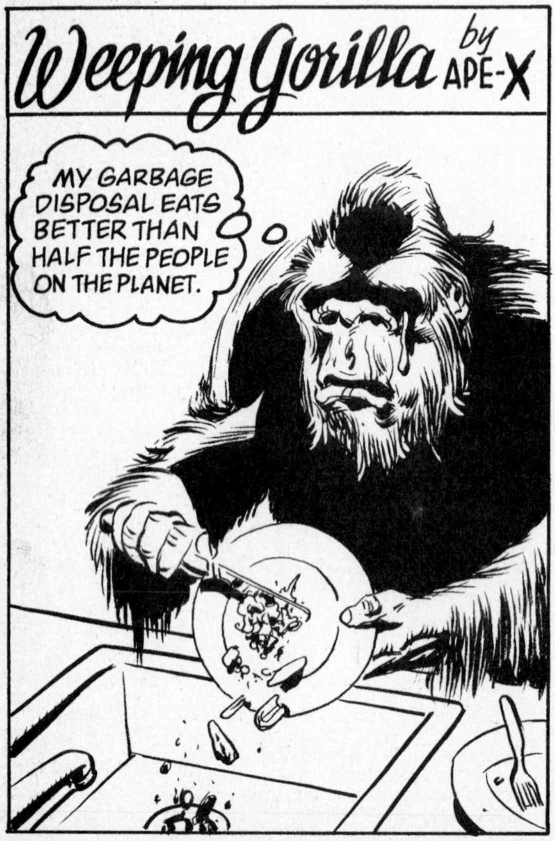
Weeping Gorilla by APE-X
MY GARBAGE DISPOSAL EATS BETTER THAN HALF THE PEOPLE ON THE PLANET.

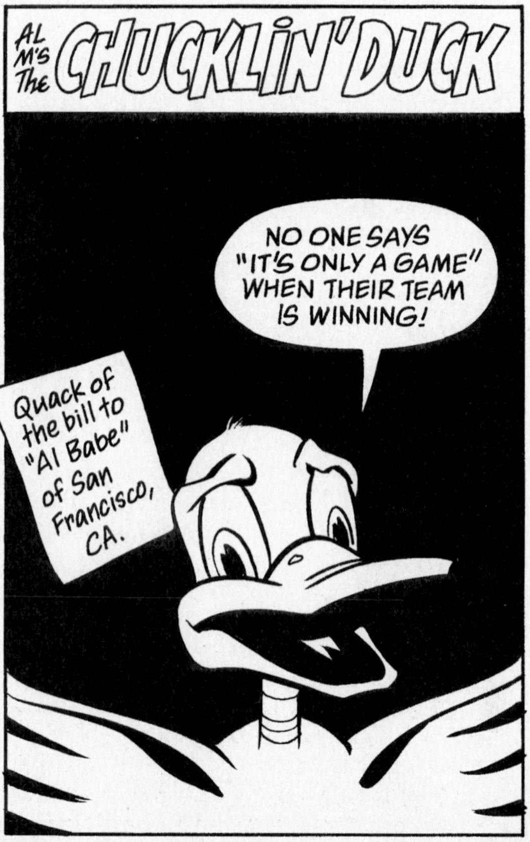
AL M's The CHUCKLIN' DUCK
NO ONE SAYS "IT'S ONLY A GAME" WHEN THEIR TEAM IS WINNING!
Quack of the bill to "Al Babe" of San Francisco, CA.

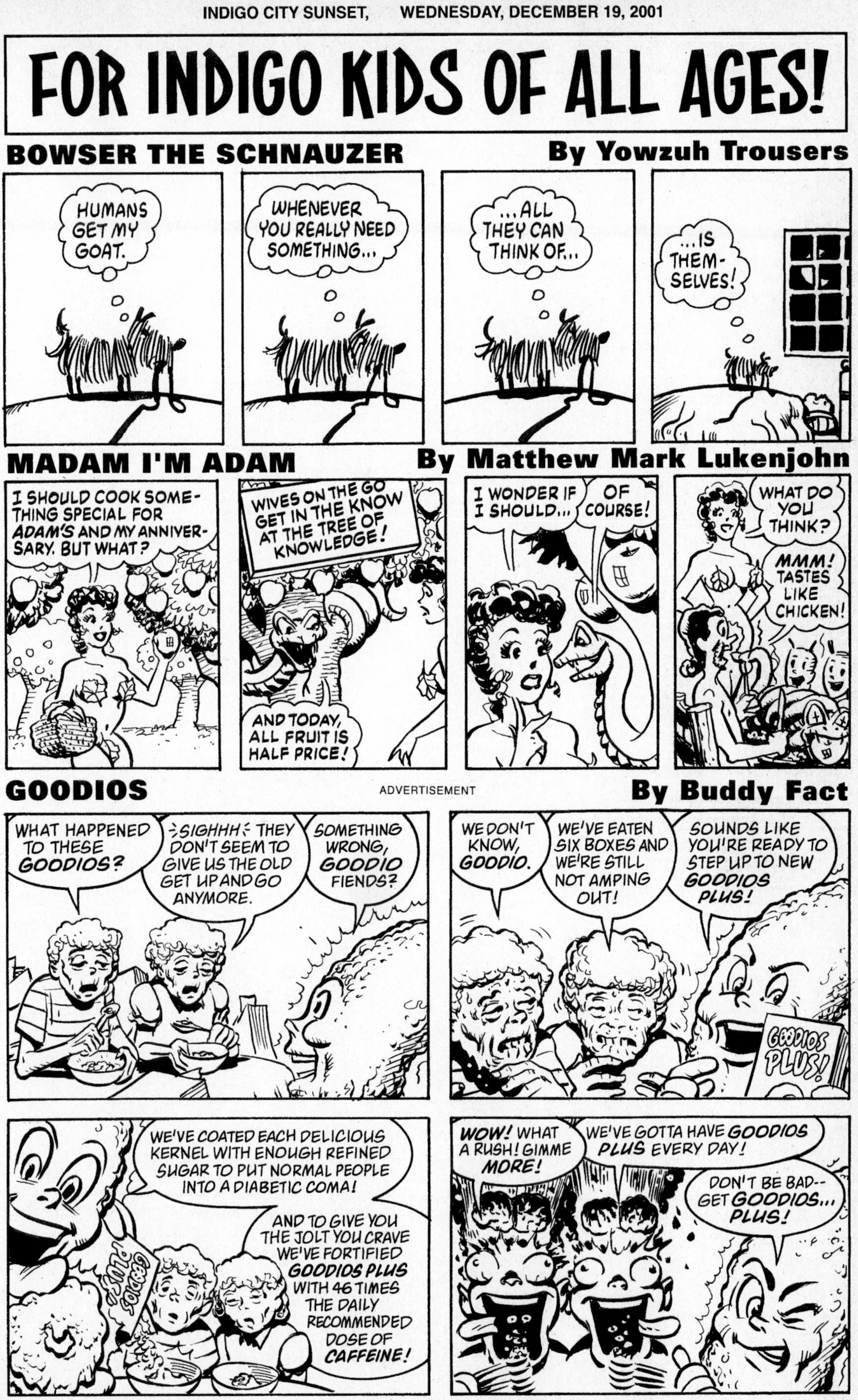

INDIGO CITY SUNSET, WEDNESDAY, DECEMBER 19, 2001
FOR INDIGO KIDS OF ALL AGES!
BOWSER THE SCHNAUZER
By Yowzuh Trousers
HUMANS GET MY GOAT.
WHENEVER YOU REALLY NEED SOMETHING...
...ALL THEY CAN THINK OF...
...IS THEM-SELVES!
MADAM I'M ADAM
By Matthew Mark Lukenjohn
I SHOULD COOK SOME-THING SPECIAL FOR ADAM'S AND MY ANNIVER-SARY. BUT WHAT?
WIVES ON THE GO GET IN THE KNOW AT THE TREE OF KNOWLEDGE!
AND TODAY, ALL FRUIT IS HALF PRICE!
I WONDER IF I SHOULD...
OF COURSE!
WHAT DO YOU THINK?
MMM! TASTES LIKE CHICKEN!
GOODIOS
ADVERTISEMENT
By Buddy Fact
WHAT HAPPENED TO THESE GOODIOS?
SIGHHH THEY DON'T SEEM TO GIVE US THE OLD GET UP AND GO ANYMORE.
SOMETHING WRONG, GOODIO FIENDS?
WE DON'T KNOW, GOODIO.
WE'VE EATEN SIX BOXES AND WE'RE STILL NOT AMPING OUT!
SOUNDS LIKE YOU'RE READY TO STEP UP TO NEW GOODIOS PLUS!
GOODIOS PLUS!
WE'VE COATED EACH DELICIOUS KERNEL WITH ENOUGH REFINED SUGAR TO PUT NORMAL PEOPLE INTO A DIABETIC COMA!
AND TO GIVE YOU THE JOLT YOU CRAVE WE'VE FORTIFIED GOODIOS PLUS WITH 46 TIMES THE DAILY RECOMMENDED DOSE OF CAFFEINE!
GOODIOS PLUS
WOW! WHAT A RUSH! GIMME MORE!
WE'VE GOTTA HAVE GOODIOS PLUS EVERY DAY!
DON'T BE BAD-- GET GOODIOS... PLUS!

INDIGO CITY SUNSET, WEDNESDAY, DECEMBER 19, 2001

SUNSET CLASSIFIEDS To place an ad call 555-5674 Visa/MC welcomed

The Indigo City Sunset takes no responsibility for the legality of any goods or services offered.

LOST AND FOUND

LOST: Kitten. Orange tabby. Last seen going into mine shaft in Bottoms Up. 555 2314

LOST: Vicinity of #11 mine in Bottoms Up district. Small poodle. Answers to 'Fifi.' 555 8873

LOST: Great Dane. Bottoms Up, last seen near abandoned mine. 555 6254

LOST: Horse. Indigo City Mounted Police seeks information on Morgan, last observed tethered to fence near #11 mine. Reward. 555 5671

LOST: Elephant. Beloved circus star 'Jumbo' missing since performance in Bottoms Up 12/13/01. Call Jingle Bros. Circus 555 1872

FOR RENT

SAFE HOUSE. Hole up in comfort! Satellite TV, DSL, EZ Boy. 555 0036

GOING TO THE MATTRESSES? This easily-defended 6-room apartment has beds for 16, modern kitchen facilities. 555 1132

ON THE LAM? We offer different accommodations every night. Box 790

LOCATION, LOCATION, LOCATION! Looking for an atmospheric hide-out that creates just the right image for your gang? How about this massive 12,000 sq. foot warehouse in the Crater Bay docks area? Quiet access by radared watercraft 24/7. Foggy 365 days a year! Even GREYSHIRT will be impressed! Crib Realty 555 8362

PROFESSIONAL SERVICES

FENCE can take hard to sell items off your hands. Hot ice? No problem! Cash paid for jewelry, watches, etc. Reply to Box 438

STORAGE. Going upriver? Call us for five, ten, twenty-year storage in clean, dry facility. Competitive prices or percentage deal. Call 555 9054

LAUNDERING. Too much cash on hand? No amount too large. Foreign currency okay. We can make it spotless! Box 634

TAX PREP. Remember how they got Al Capone? If you expect a large increase in your reportable or non-reportable income, call me. Complete discretion. 555 7895

LOSE A LOVED ONE? We make lavish mourning easy and affordable. Doornail Funeral Home 555 9837

PSYCHIC. Why go into your next job blind? We specialize in entrail readings, omen interpretations. Box 109

GOODIOS ANONYMOUS: Addicted to high-sugar breakfast cereal? Join others in our supportive twelve step program. Box 689

ITEMS FOR SALE

1999 BUMPMOBILE. Supercharged convertible. Used on only three jobs. Minor perforation. Box 740

PERSONAL PROTECTION. We can get it all! Derringers to military-surplus. Box 753

HANDY ITEMS: Brass knuckles made to fit. Blackjacks all sizes and weights. Box 540

MACHINE GUN SPECIALIST! We refit and repair Thompsons. Ammunition clips available. Box 385

COLLECTIBLES

TIJUANA BIBLES. Authentic reproductions of salty 1960s 8-pagers. Cobweb, Tom Strong, Promethea, Johnny Future, Pearl Of The Deep, Splash Brannigan. America's Best Heroes as you've never imagined them before! Box 109

HOODLUM HIT. Complete collection, mint condition. Inspiration for "Carbones" TV series! Box 530

HIGH HEEL SHOE. Authentic COBWEB footwear purchased at charity auction. Signed by Science Heroine. Faint smell of lavender. Best offer. 555 9835

RARE BOOK. Surrealist collage masterpiece "La Toile Dans Le Chateau Des Larmes" by Georges Delcourt. 1928 first edition. Excellent condition. All offers considered. Box 675

REVERSED WRISTWATCH, LETTER. Said to be central to Greyshirt case involving Doctor Crescendo. Sold as is. 555 7843

ORIGINAL COMIC BOOK ART. Kaput Comics, SPLASH BRANNIGAN by Daisy Screensaver. Ink behaves strangely sometimes. Frame at own risk. Call for details. 555 2098

HELP WANTED

BODYGUARDS. James Bond fan w/unlimited funds seeks well-built young women with mastery in martial arts for work/party on 70-ft yacht cruising Crater Bay. Send resume with swimsuit photo, references. Box 784

EXTRAS NEEDED!

Do You Want To Be In The Movies?

Casting Call. Big-budget theatrical release filming in Indigo City seeks extras. We need men, women and children for crowd scenes recreating 1980s Indigo City, etc. Distinctive physical characteristics sought. Bring photos to:

FANMAN PRODUCTIONS
Indigo City Central Station
Thursday, December 20th

SUNSET CLASSIFIEDS

To place an ad call 555-5674 Visa/MC welcomed

The Indigo City Sunset takes no responsibility for the legality of any goods or services offered.

BUSINESS OPPORTUNITIES

HOME BUSINESS. Learn LOANSHARKING! Fun! Profitable. Box 1083

LOTTERY TICKETS! Look real! Suckers go for them every time. By the carton. Box 8906

PHONE CARDS! We print 'em, you sell 'em to the rubes. Box 6724

BE A LOOKOUT! Learn how you can make money just keeping your eyes open! Box 5367

PROTECTION RACKET. Established route. Percentage. Box 4987

YOUR LETTERS OF COMMENT WANTED! Send to Sunset Letters, 888 Prospect St., Suite 240, La Jolla, CA 92037, or email sunset@wildstorm.com. We reserve the right to edit and condense all letters.

ESTATE SALE

Personal effects of Seymour "Spats" Katz

Noted Indigo City gangster Spats Katz, who passed away last year at the age of 84, kept a luxury penthouse apartment on the top floor of the Katz Building for sixty years. Now with the property condemned and set for demolition, and his only heir scheduled for execution, the Mayor has ordered all of Katz's effects sold with the proceeds to go to his long time caretaker, Sonny Rolaid.

Terms: cash or cashiers check

December 21, 2001 9 AM to 5 PM
Corner of Fume and Beryl Streets
Indigo City

Indigo Personals

To respond to ads call 555 0669. You must be 18 years or older. ($2.19 per minute charge applies)

WOMEN SEEKING MEN

TOUGH BUT PLIABLE SWF 27, blonde, stacked, with perpetual sneer seeks muscular no-nonsense SM 25-35 who doesn't take any crap. Ad #3298

KITTENISH
SWF 23, filled out in all the right places. Knows how to keep her trap shut. Seeking sugar daddy 65-99 to provide finer things in life. Ad #9043

EXPERIENCE COUNTS!
WWF 38, well preserved, energetic, intimate knowledge of bank workings, seeks SWM any age to plot future. AD #5320

LUCK BE A LADY
DAF thirty-ish, wants to be hole card to dapper gambler type, 30-40. Ad #1987

MOTHERLY LOVE
WWF 64, experienced in armed robbery and police evasion, expert marksman, seeks three SWM 20-24 to call her 'Ma.' Ad #7927

COUPLES

Masterful, statuesque dark-haired femme fatale with slavish blonde assistant seeks like-minded female, any age/race, to join us in creative play. AD #7982

Masterful, statuesque dark-haired femme fatale with slavish blonde assistant seeks like-minded male, any age/race, to join us in creative play. AD #7983

Masterful, statuesque dark-haired femme fatale with slavish blonde assistant seeks like-minded couples, any age/race, to join us in creative play. AD #7984

MEN SEEKING WOMEN

OLD FASHIONED VALUES
SWM, 36, seeks SWF 25-30 to pick up after me, wash my socks, iron my shirts, cook my meals and look pretty. Ad #3461

GOOD EYE FOR DETAIL
Engraver, 46, seeks SWF with printing experience. Object: counterfeiting. Ad #9528

LET'S KNOCK OVER A FEW BANKS TOGETHER
Ex-con, 36, fresh out of stir, wants to get back into swing of things. ISO frail with a sense of adventure. Ad #3987

I'LL TAKE CARE OF YOU
SM with good head for business, sharp dresser, seeks hard-working women. I can keep you busy, safe, buzzing. Will train. Ad #8467

MEET FOR A DRINK
DWM 38, likes his Jack Daniels ISO honey with a taste for the Mountain Dew. Ad #5498

LONELY HEART
SWM 42, currently in confinement up the river, looking to correspond with understanding SWF, possible visitation rights available. Send photo with letter. Ad #5573

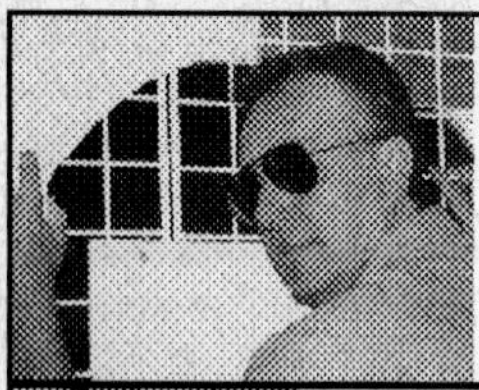

RICK VEITCH
Writer-Artist fingered in swipe scandal! Page 8

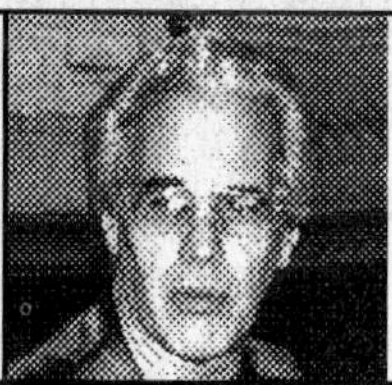

AL WILLIAMSON
Inker aims to be first artist on planet Mongo! Page 9

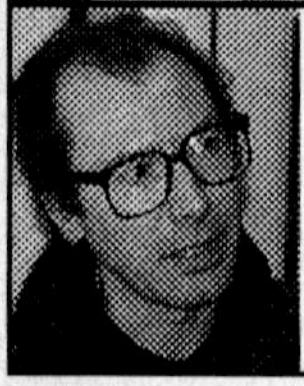

DAVID LLOYD
Cartoonist pulls shade on private life! Page 10

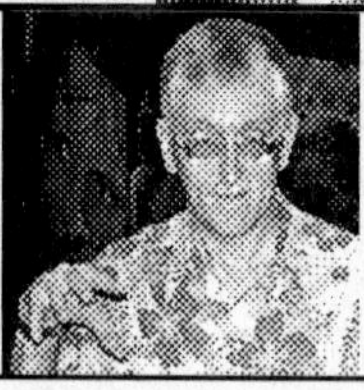

TODD KLEIN
Letterer is true power behind ABC throne! Page 11

WILDSTORM FX: Painting by the Numbers!

ALL THE NEWS FROM DAWN TO DUSK

INDIGO CITY SUNSET

AFTERNOON CITY EDITION

Wednesday, December 19, 2001 Metro Weather – Today: Hazy, Tonight: Murky, Tomorrow: Smoggy

BACK PAGE EXTRA:

SHADOW FALLS ON MYSTERY MAN MONUMENT!

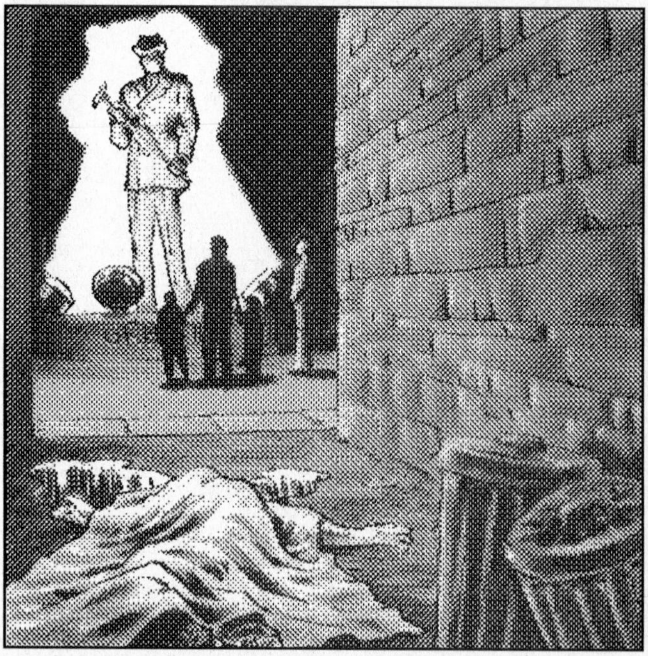

DEATH, CONTROVERSY MAR UNVEILING OF GREYSHIRT SHRINE!

Special to The Sunset
by Geekus Crow

The long-awaited official unveiling of Indigo City's GREYSHIRT monument in Propane Square took place on schedule yesterday, but what was intended to be a day spent honoring the city's favorite son was overshadowed, first by continuing complaints from local residents concerning lighting arrangements, and finally by an unexpected tragedy. While the project has long been dogged by kickback scandals and questions from civil libertarians about the appropriateness of honoring a masked vigilante, no one was prepared for what police found in Sulphur Street, only yards from the ceremony. FULL STORY: PAGE 16

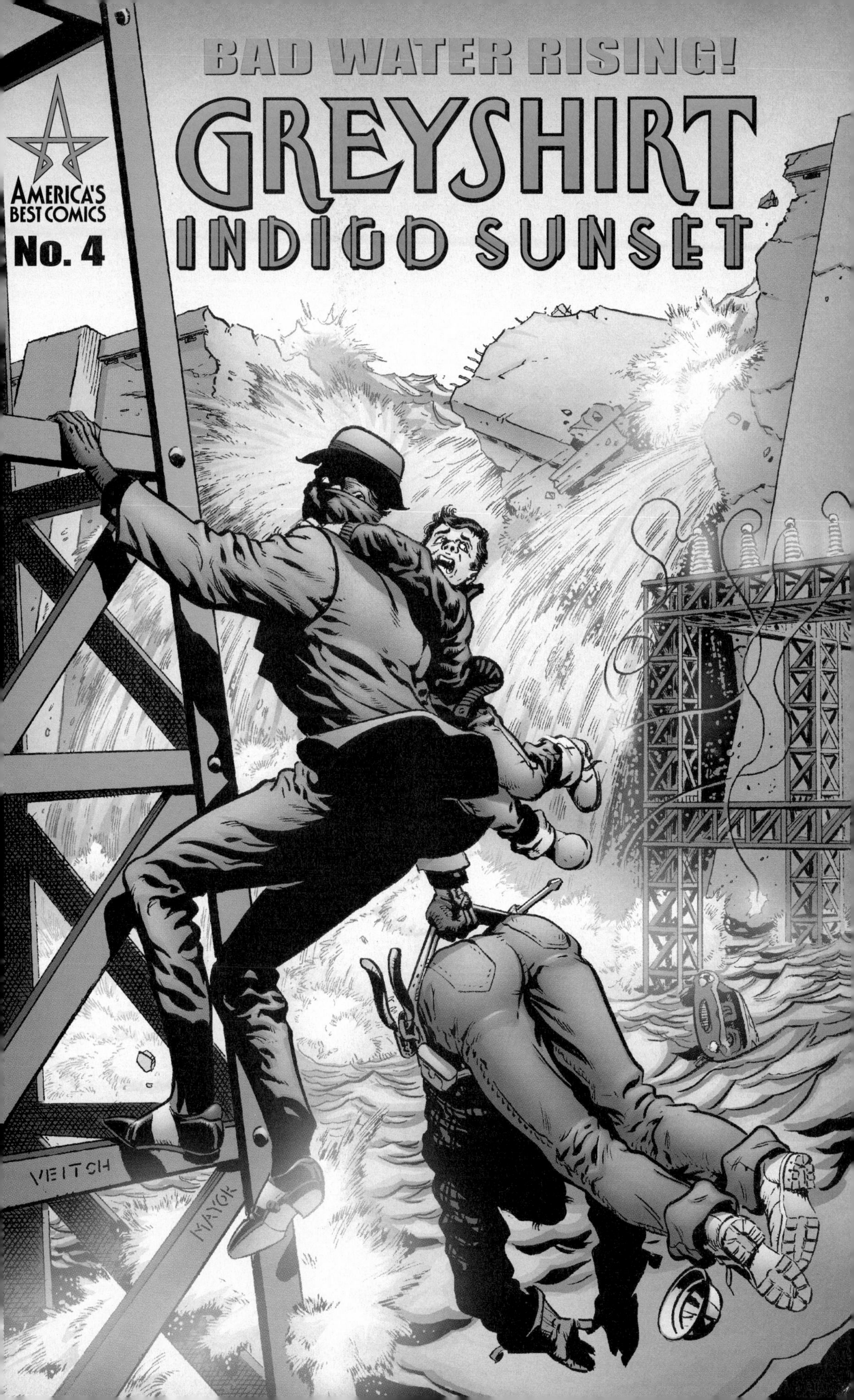
BAD WATER RISING!
GREYSHIRT
INDIGO SUNSET
AMERICA'S BEST COMICS
No. 4
VEITCH
MAYOK

WHAT'S GOING ON? I THOUGHT THIS WAS **LADY L'S** CORNER?

IT **USED** TO BE!

BUT SHE HASN'T SHOWN UP TO OPEN HER NEWSSTAND IN OVER A WEEK.

NEVER THOUGHT **LADY L** WAS THE TYPE TO JUST WALK AWAY WITHOUT NOTIFYING ANYONE AT THE **SUNSET**.

YEAH. DOESN'T SOUND LIKE HER...

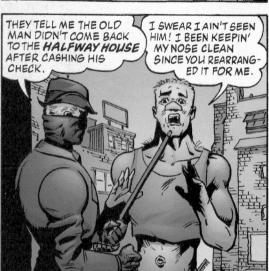

THEY TELL ME THE OLD MAN DIDN'T COME BACK TO THE **HALFWAY HOUSE** AFTER CASHING HIS CHECK.

I SWEAR I AIN'T SEEN HIM! I BEEN KEEPIN' MY NOSE CLEAN SINCE YOU REARRANGED IT FOR ME.

NO DISRESPECT-- BUT HE'S JUST ANOTHER OLD CRIP. WHAT'S HE MEAN TO YOU?

PUT A LID ON IT.

THE PAPERGIRL'S **MISSING?** N-NO WAY WE'D LAY A HAND ON HER AFTER **LAST** TIME!

LOOK AT US! W-WE CAN'T LAY A HAND ON **NUTHIN'** UNTIL THE CASTS COME OFF!

SH-SHE'S A LITTLE SOFT IN THE HEAD, PROBABLY GOT LOST OR SOMETHIN'...

YOU BETTER **HOPE** THAT'S ALL IT IS.

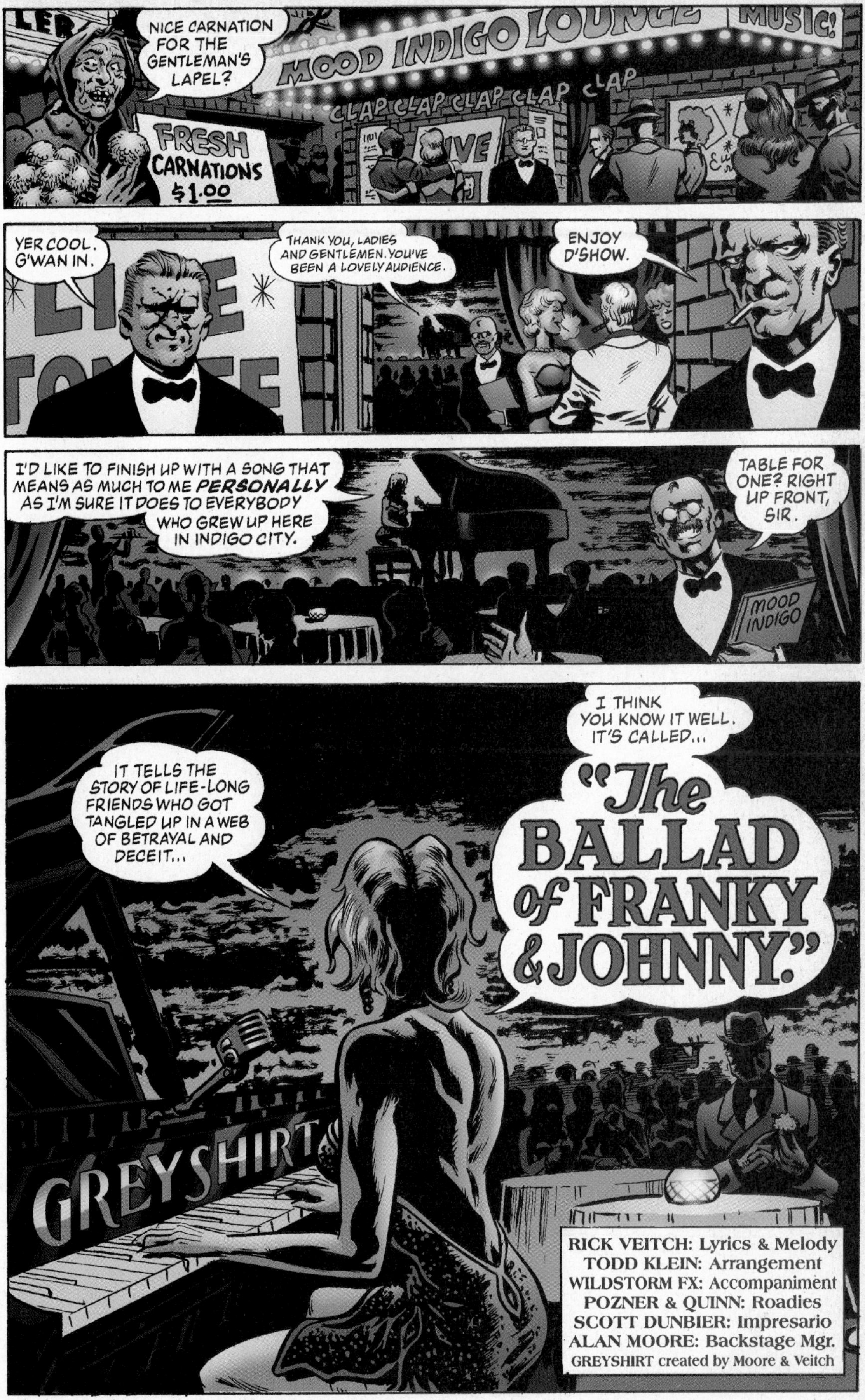
MOOD INDIGO LOUNGE
MUSIC!
NICE CARNATION FOR THE GENTLEMAN'S LAPEL?
FRESH CARNATIONS $1.00
CLAP CLAP CLAP CLAP CLAP
YER COOL. G'WAN IN.
THANK YOU, LADIES AND GENTLEMEN. YOU'VE BEEN A LOVELY AUDIENCE.
ENJOY D'SHOW.
I'D LIKE TO FINISH UP WITH A SONG THAT MEANS AS MUCH TO ME PERSONALLY AS I'M SURE IT DOES TO EVERYBODY WHO GREW UP HERE IN INDIGO CITY.
TABLE FOR ONE? RIGHT UP FRONT, SIR.
MOOD INDIGO
IT TELLS THE STORY OF LIFE-LONG FRIENDS WHO GOT TANGLED UP IN A WEB OF BETRAYAL AND DECEIT...
I THINK YOU KNOW IT WELL. IT'S CALLED...
"The BALLAD of FRANKY & JOHNNY."
GREYSHIRT
RICK VEITCH: Lyrics & Melody
TODD KLEIN: Arrangement
WILDSTORM FX: Accompaniment
POZNER & QUINN: Roadies
SCOTT DUNBIER: Impresario
ALAN MOORE: Backstage Mgr.
GREYSHIRT created by Moore & Veitch

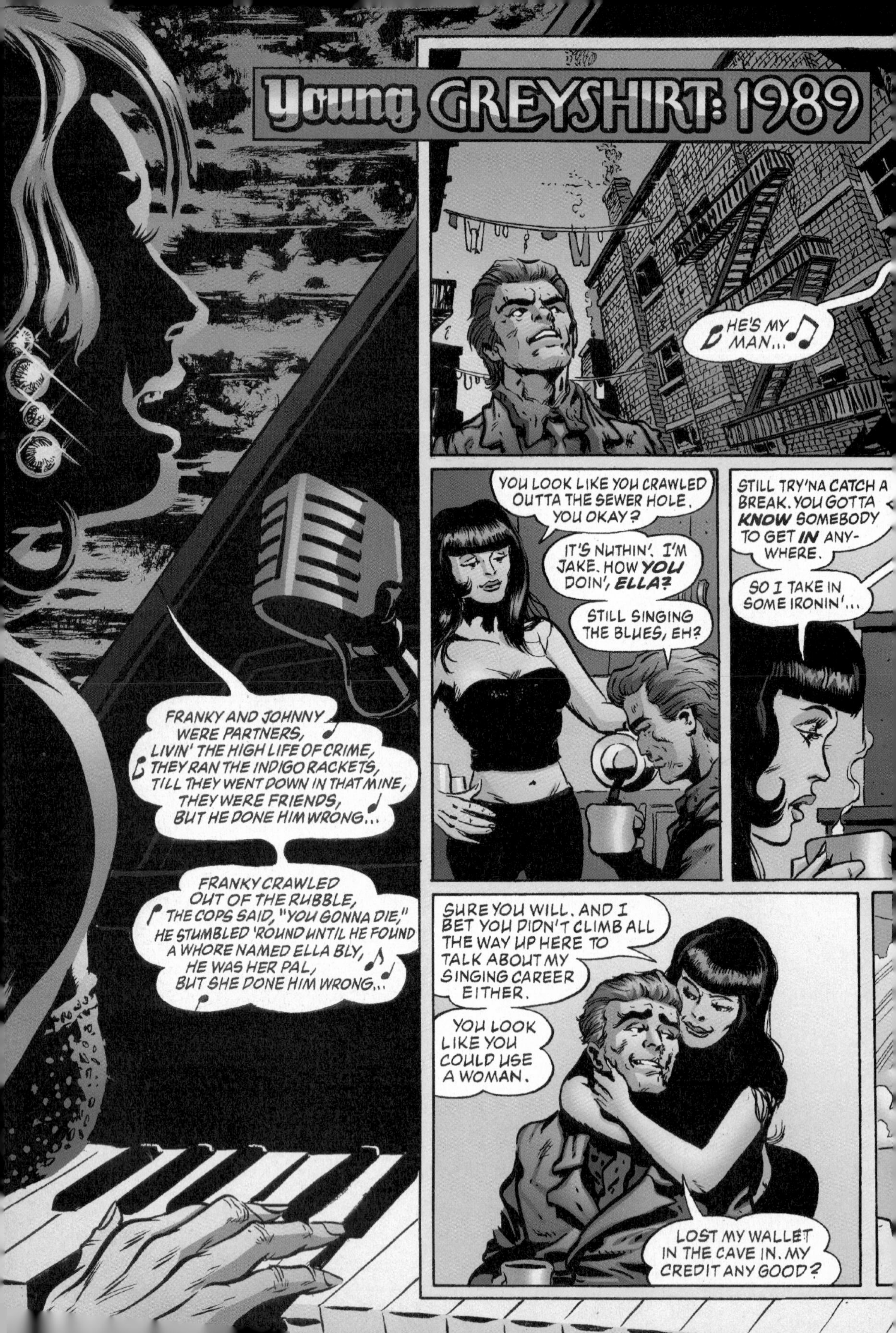
Young GREYSHIRT: 1989
HE'S MY MAN...
FRANKY AND JOHNNY WERE PARTNERS, LIVIN' THE HIGH LIFE OF CRIME, THEY RAN THE INDIGO RACKETS, TILL THEY WENT DOWN IN THAT MINE, THEY WERE FRIENDS, BUT HE DONE HIM WRONG...
FRANKY CRAWLED OUT OF THE RUBBLE, THE COPS SAID, "YOU GONNA DIE," HE STUMBLED 'ROUND UNTIL HE FOUND A WHORE NAMED ELLA BLY, HE WAS HER PAL, BUT SHE DONE HIM WRONG...
YOU LOOK LIKE YOU CRAWLED OUTTA THE SEWER HOLE. YOU OKAY?
IT'S NUTHIN'. I'M JAKE. HOW YOU DOIN', ELLA?
STILL SINGING THE BLUES, EH?
STILL TRY'NA CATCH A BREAK. YOU GOTTA KNOW SOMEBODY TO GET IN ANYWHERE.
SO I TAKE IN SOME IRONIN'...
SURE YOU WILL. AND I BET YOU DIDN'T CLIMB ALL THE WAY UP HERE TO TALK ABOUT MY SINGING CAREER EITHER.
YOU LOOK LIKE YOU COULD USE A WOMAN.
LOST MY WALLET IN THE CAVE IN. MY CREDIT ANY GOOD?

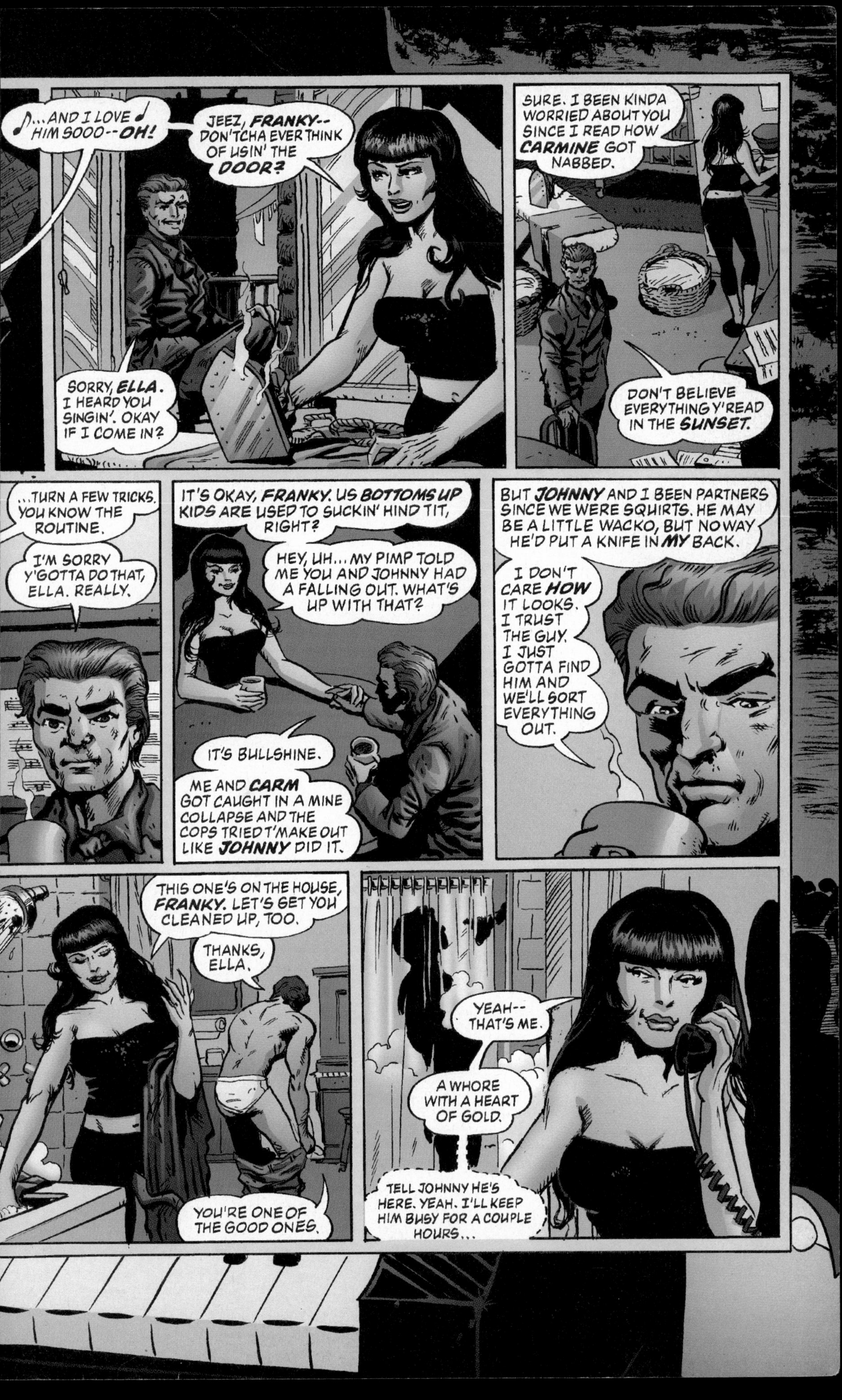
♪...AND I LOVE ♩ HIM SOOO--OH!
JEEZ, FRANKY-- DON'TCHA EVER THINK OF USIN' THE DOOR?
SORRY, ELLA. I HEARD YOU SINGIN'. OKAY IF I COME IN?
SURE. I BEEN KINDA WORRIED ABOUT YOU SINCE I READ HOW CARMINE GOT NABBED.
DON'T BELIEVE EVERYTHING Y'READ IN THE SUNSET.
...TURN A FEW TRICKS. YOU KNOW THE ROUTINE.
I'M SORRY Y'GOTTA DO THAT, ELLA. REALLY.
IT'S OKAY, FRANKY. US BOTTOMS UP KIDS ARE USED TO SUCKIN' HIND TIT, RIGHT?
HEY, UH... MY PIMP TOLD ME YOU AND JOHNNY HAD A FALLING OUT. WHAT'S UP WITH THAT?
IT'S BULLSHINE.
ME AND CARM GOT CAUGHT IN A MINE COLLAPSE AND THE COPS TRIED T'MAKE OUT LIKE JOHNNY DID IT.
BUT JOHNNY AND I BEEN PARTNERS SINCE WE WERE SQUIRTS. HE MAY BE A LITTLE WACKO, BUT NO WAY HE'D PUT A KNIFE IN MY BACK.
I DON'T CARE HOW IT LOOKS. I TRUST THE GUY. I JUST GOTTA FIND HIM AND WE'LL SORT EVERYTHING OUT.
THIS ONE'S ON THE HOUSE, FRANKY. LET'S GET YOU CLEANED UP, TOO.
THANKS, ELLA.
YOU'RE ONE OF THE GOOD ONES.
YEAH-- THAT'S ME.
A WHORE WITH A HEART OF GOLD.
TELL JOHNNY HE'S HERE. YEAH. I'LL KEEP HIM BUSY FOR A COUPLE HOURS...

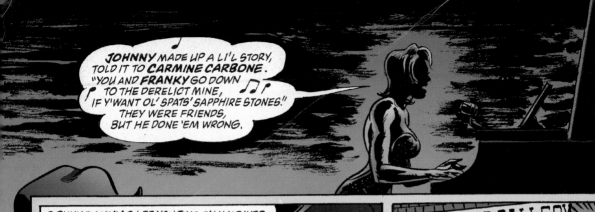

JOHNNY MADE UP A LI'L STORY, TOLD IT TO CARMINE CARBONE. "YOU AND FRANKY GO DOWN TO THE DERELICT MINE, IF Y'WANT OL' SPATS' SAPPHIRE STONES." THEY WERE FRIENDS, BUT HE DONE 'EM WRONG.
I DUNNO WHY I LET YOU TWO TALK ME INTO GOIN' TO A GODDAMN ART OPENING, OF ALL THINGS.
SO, YOU ALWAYS SUCH A *SNIFF* PARTY POOPER, APOLLO?
YEAH, JOHNNY-- LOOSEN UP! YOU'RE A BIG BOSS NOW!
THE SHOOTING GALLERY
POW
SORRY. I DON'T THINK I'M GONNA BE SMILIN' TOO MUCH UNTIL MY BOYS LOCATE FRANKY LAFAYETTE.
GUY MIXING
HEY! THAT'S ME AND FRANKY-- FROM HOODLUM HIT # 64!
WHOEVER PAINTED THIS THING COPIED IT RIGHT OUT OF A COMIC BOOK!
PUH-LEEZ! COMICS WERE THE FURTHEST THING FROM MY MIND...
POW! ART EXPLORES THE PARADOX BETWEEN THE PRETENSIONS OF AMERICAN PAINTING AND OUR ANONYMOUS MACHINE-MANUFACTURED GUTTER CULTURE!
THERE'S MORE OF ANDY SAVANNAH IN THESE PIECES THAN ANY HACK CARTOONIST!
OH, ANDY! YOU'RE SO SLY!
AFTER I WIN THE ELECTION FOR MAYOR, I'M GOING TO BE RUNNING THE WHOLE CITY, APOLLO.
AND I GUARANTEE YOU AND YOUR GANGSTER FRIENDS AREN'T GOING TO LIKE HOW I GO ABOUT IT.
SEE YOU ON DEATH ROW, CANDICE?
I WOULDN'T DO YOU AGAIN EVEN IF I WAS SET TO RIDE ON OLD SPARKY!
HEY--

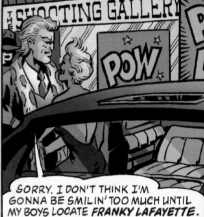

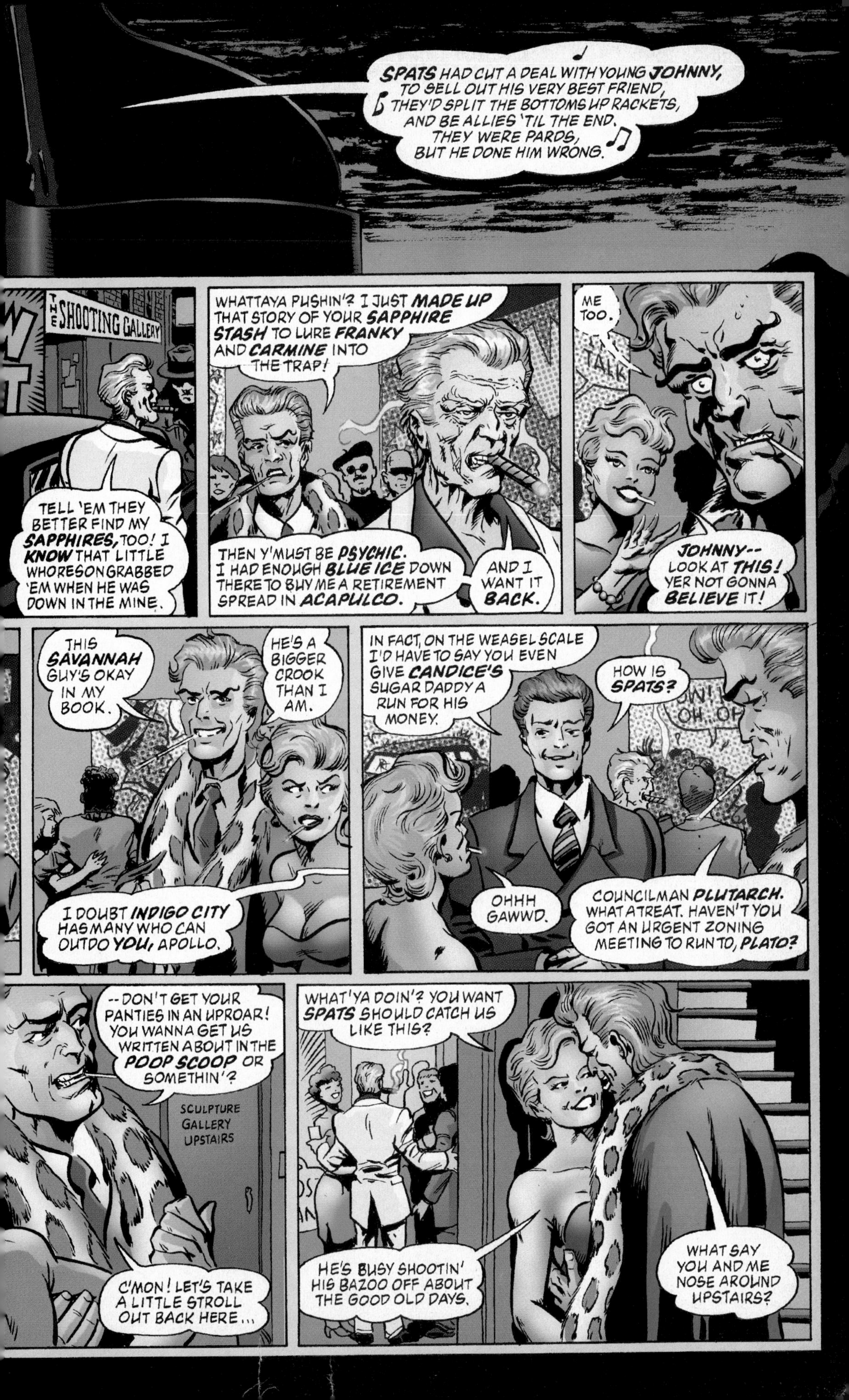

SPATS HAD CUT A DEAL WITH YOUNG JOHNNY, TO SELL OUT HIS VERY BEST FRIEND, THEY'D SPLIT THE BOTTOMS UP RACKETS, AND BE ALLIES 'TIL THE END. THEY WERE PARDS, BUT HE DONE HIM WRONG.
THE SHOOTING GALLERY
TELL 'EM THEY BETTER FIND MY SAPPHIRES, TOO! I KNOW THAT LITTLE WHORESON GRABBED 'EM WHEN HE WAS DOWN IN THE MINE.
WHATTAYA PUSHIN'? I JUST MADE UP THAT STORY OF YOUR SAPPHIRE STASH TO LURE FRANKY AND CARMINE INTO THE TRAP!
THEN Y'MUST BE PSYCHIC. I HAD ENOUGH BLUE ICE DOWN THERE TO BUY ME A RETIREMENT SPREAD IN ACAPULCO.
AND I WANT IT BACK.
ME TOO.
JOHNNY-- LOOK AT THIS! YER NOT GONNA BELIEVE IT!
THIS SAVANNAH GUY'S OKAY IN MY BOOK.
HE'S A BIGGER CROOK THAN I AM.
I DOUBT INDIGO CITY HAS MANY WHO CAN OUTDO YOU, APOLLO.
IN FACT, ON THE WEASEL SCALE I'D HAVE TO SAY YOU EVEN GIVE CANDICE'S SUGAR DADDY A RUN FOR HIS MONEY.
HOW IS SPATS?
OHHH GAWWD.
COUNCILMAN PLUTARCH. WHAT A TREAT. HAVEN'T YOU GOT AN URGENT ZONING MEETING TO RUN TO, PLATO?
--DON'T GET YOUR PANTIES IN AN UPROAR! YOU WANNA GET US WRITTEN ABOUT IN THE POOP SCOOP OR SOMETHIN'?
SCULPTURE GALLERY UPSTAIRS
C'MON! LET'S TAKE A LITTLE STROLL OUT BACK HERE...
WHAT'YA DOIN'? YOU WANT SPATS SHOULD CATCH US LIKE THIS?
HE'S BUSY SHOOTIN' HIS BAZOO OFF ABOUT THE GOOD OLD DAYS.
WHAT SAY YOU AND ME NOSE AROUND UPSTAIRS?

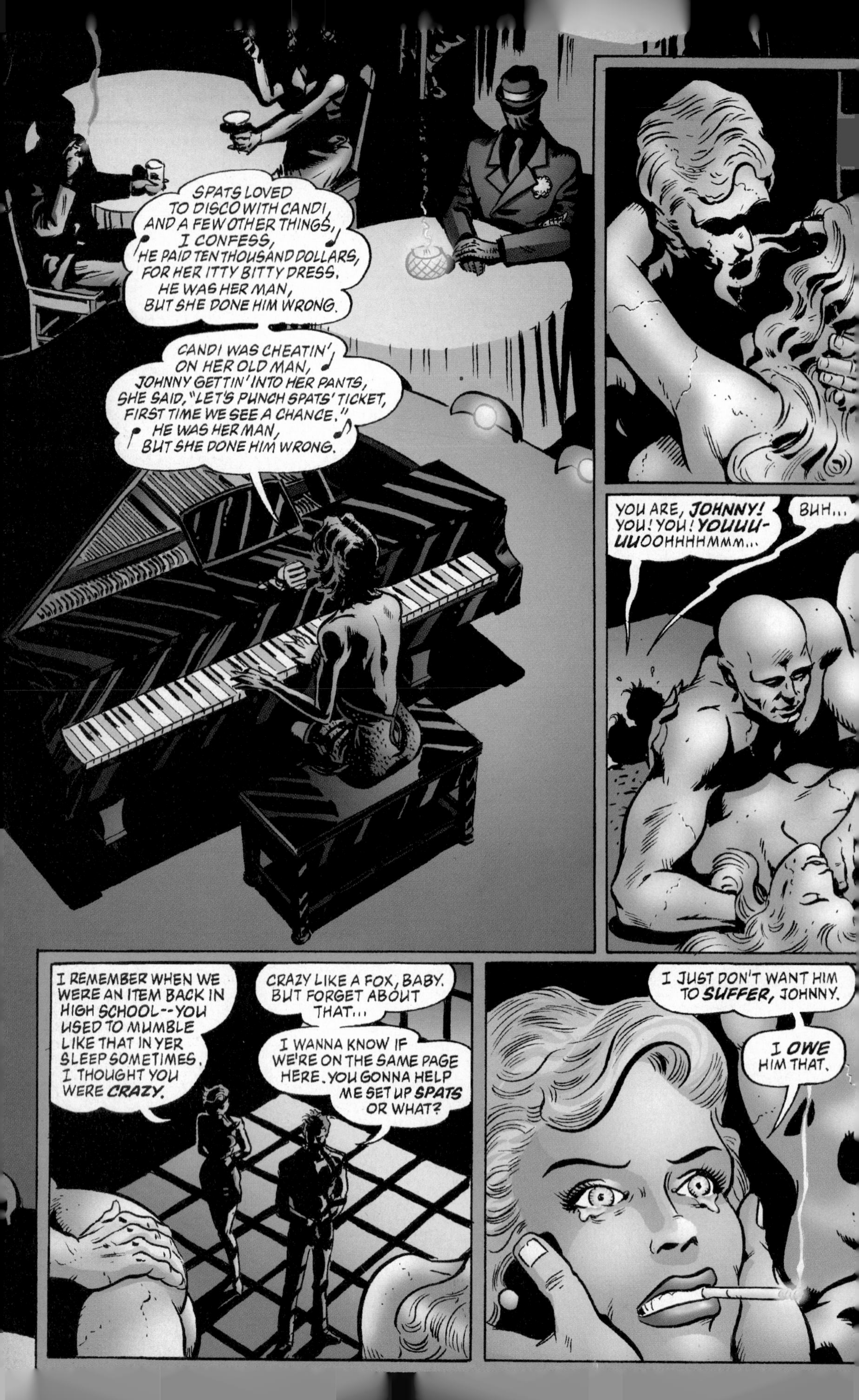
SPATS LOVED TO DISCO WITH CANDI, AND A FEW OTHER THINGS, I CONFESS, HE PAID TEN THOUSAND DOLLARS, FOR HER ITTY BITTY DRESS. HE WAS HER MAN, BUT SHE DONE HIM WRONG.
CANDI WAS CHEATIN' ON HER OLD MAN, JOHNNY GETTIN' INTO HER PANTS, SHE SAID, "LET'S PUNCH SPATS' TICKET, FIRST TIME WE SEE A CHANCE." HE WAS HER MAN, BUT SHE DONE HIM WRONG.
YOU ARE, JOHNNY! YOU! YOU! YOUUU-UUOOHHHHMMM...
BUH...
I REMEMBER WHEN WE WERE AN ITEM BACK IN HIGH SCHOOL--YOU USED TO MUMBLE LIKE THAT IN YER SLEEP SOMETIMES. I THOUGHT YOU WERE CRAZY.
CRAZY LIKE A FOX, BABY. BUT FORGET ABOUT THAT...
I WANNA KNOW IF WE'RE ON THE SAME PAGE HERE. YOU GONNA HELP ME SET UP SPATS OR WHAT?
I JUST DON'T WANT HIM TO SUFFER, JOHNNY.
I OWE HIM THAT.

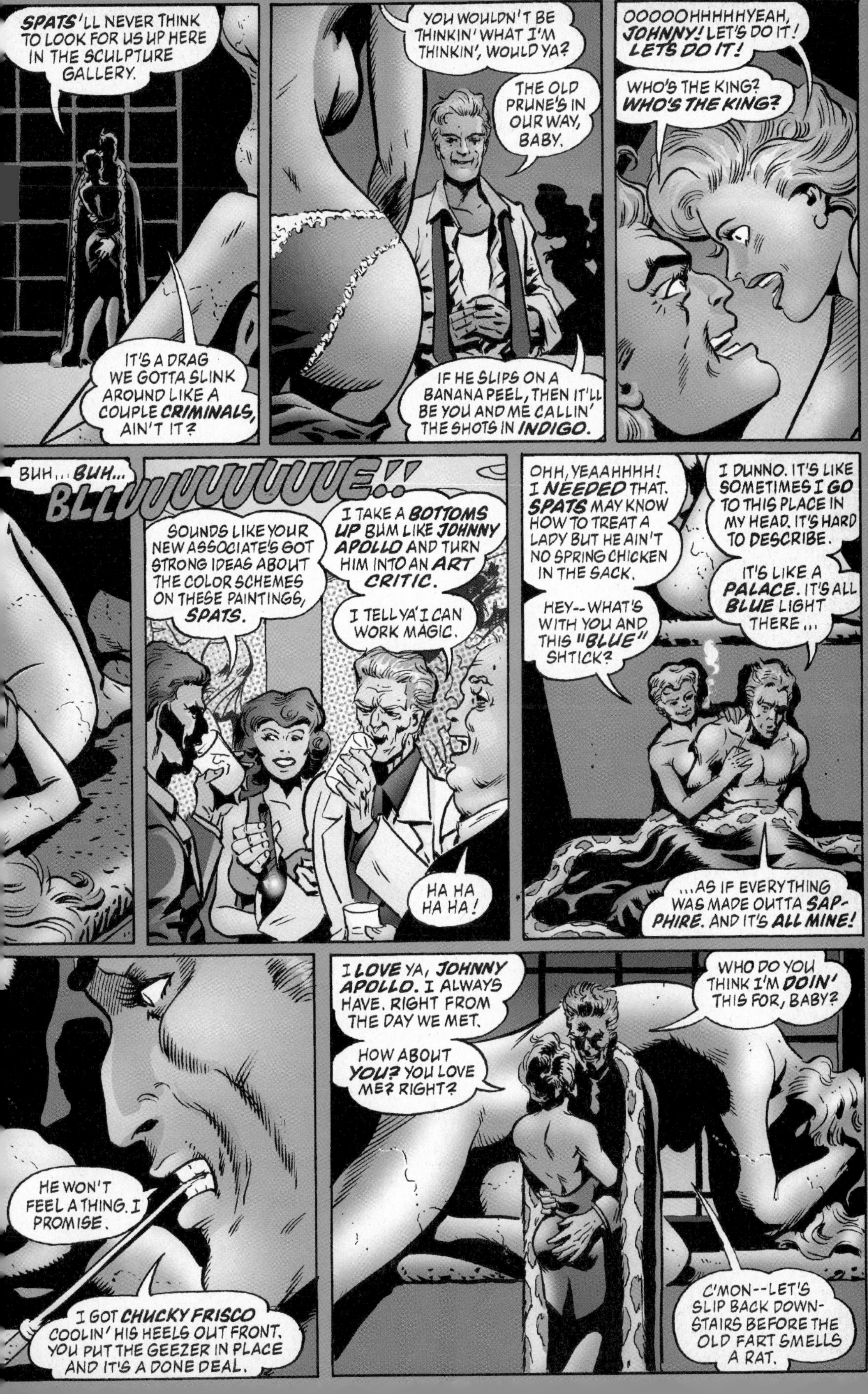

SPATS'LL NEVER THINK TO LOOK FOR US UP HERE IN THE SCULPTURE GALLERY.
IT'S A DRAG WE GOTTA SLINK AROUND LIKE A COUPLE CRIMINALS, AIN'T IT?
YOU WOULDN'T BE THINKIN' WHAT I'M THINKIN', WOULD YA?
THE OLD PRUNE'S IN OUR WAY, BABY.
IF HE SLIPS ON A BANANA PEEL, THEN IT'LL BE YOU AND ME CALLIN' THE SHOTS IN INDIGO.
OOOOOHHHHHYEAH, JOHNNY! LET'S DO IT! LET'S DO IT!
WHO'S THE KING? WHO'S THE KING?
BUH... BUH...
BLLUUUUUUUUUE!!
SOUNDS LIKE YOUR NEW ASSOCIATE'S GOT STRONG IDEAS ABOUT THE COLOR SCHEMES ON THESE PAINTINGS, SPATS.
I TAKE A BOTTOMS UP BUM LIKE JOHNNY APOLLO AND TURN HIM INTO AN ART CRITIC.
I TELL YA' I CAN WORK MAGIC.
HA HA HA HA!
OHH, YEAAHHHH! I NEEDED THAT. SPATS MAY KNOW HOW TO TREAT A LADY BUT HE AIN'T NO SPRING CHICKEN IN THE SACK.
HEY--WHAT'S WITH YOU AND THIS "BLUE" SHTICK?
I DUNNO. IT'S LIKE SOMETIMES I GO TO THIS PLACE IN MY HEAD. IT'S HARD TO DESCRIBE.
IT'S LIKE A PALACE. IT'S ALL BLUE LIGHT THERE...
...AS IF EVERYTHING WAS MADE OUTTA SAPPHIRE. AND IT'S ALL MINE!
HE WON'T FEEL A THING. I PROMISE.
I GOT CHUCKY FRISCO COOLIN' HIS HEELS OUT FRONT. YOU PUT THE GEEZER IN PLACE AND IT'S A DONE DEAL.
I LOVE YA, JOHNNY APOLLO. I ALWAYS HAVE. RIGHT FROM THE DAY WE MET.
HOW ABOUT YOU? YOU LOVE ME? RIGHT?
WHO DO YOU THINK I'M DOIN' THIS FOR, BABY?
C'MON--LET'S SLIP BACK DOWN-STAIRS BEFORE THE OLD FART SMELLS A RAT.

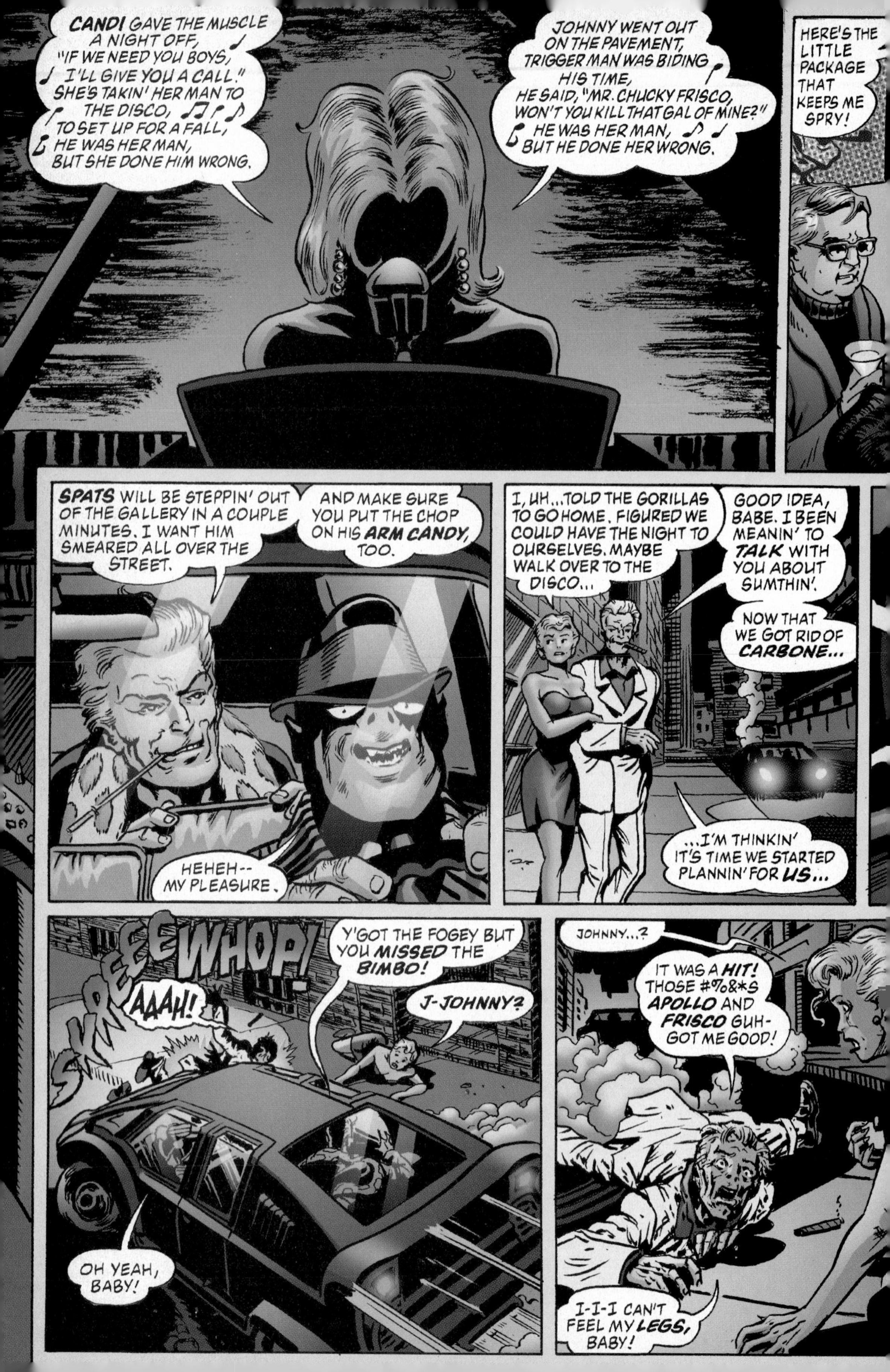
CANDI GAVE THE MUSCLE A NIGHT OFF, "IF WE NEED YOU BOYS, I'LL GIVE YOU A CALL." SHE'S TAKIN' HER MAN TO THE DISCO, TO SET UP FOR A FALL, HE WAS HER MAN, BUT SHE DONE HIM WRONG.
JOHNNY WENT OUT ON THE PAVEMENT, TRIGGER MAN WAS BIDING HIS TIME, HE SAID, "MR. CHUCKY FRISCO, WON'T YOU KILL THAT GAL OF MINE?" HE WAS HER MAN, BUT HE DONE HER WRONG.
HERE'S THE LITTLE PACKAGE THAT KEEPS ME SPRY!
SPATS WILL BE STEPPIN' OUT OF THE GALLERY IN A COUPLE MINUTES. I WANT HIM SMEARED ALL OVER THE STREET.
AND MAKE SURE YOU PUT THE CHOP ON HIS ARM CANDY, TOO.
HEHEH-- MY PLEASURE.
I, UH...TOLD THE GORILLAS TO GO HOME. FIGURED WE COULD HAVE THE NIGHT TO OURSELVES. MAYBE WALK OVER TO THE DISCO...
GOOD IDEA, BABE. I BEEN MEANIN' TO TALK WITH YOU ABOUT SUMTHIN'.
NOW THAT WE GOT RID OF CARBONE...
...I'M THINKIN' IT'S TIME WE STARTED PLANNIN' FOR US...
SKREEEWHOP!
AAAH!
Y'GOT THE FOGEY BUT YOU MISSED THE BIMBO!
J-JOHNNY?
OH YEAH, BABY!
JOHNNY...?
IT WAS A HIT! THOSE #%&*S APOLLO AND FRISCO GUH- GOT ME GOOD!
I-I-I CAN'T FEEL MY LEGS, BABY!

DID'JA LOSE OUR BOY *JOHNNY,* SWEET-CAKES?

ALL THIS CULTURE WAS TOO *MUCH* FOR HIM.

SAID HE HAD TO GO *MEET* SOMEBODY...

JUST GOT A HEADS UP FROM ONE OF OUR PIMPS.

YER BUDDY *LAFAYETTE* IS GETTIN' A KISS AND A CUDDLE OVER AT *ELLA BLY'S* PLACE.

CHUCKY--YOU ARE AS EFFICIENT AS YOU ARE HANDSOME! WE GOT ONE LAST DETAIL TO TAKE CARE OF BEFORE WE PUT *FRANKY* OUT OF HIS MISERY...

WHAT I'M ASKIN', *CANDI...* BABY... IS... WELL... WOULD'JA WEAR *THIS?*

THABUMF

A *DIAMOND?* Y'MEAN...?

AWW, *SPATS*-- I BEEN SUCH A *JERK!*

HEY!

CANDI-- LOOK OUT!

VROOOAAWM!

OH YEAH!

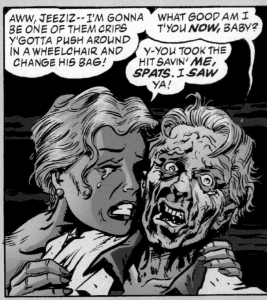

AWW, JEEZIZ-- I'M GONNA BE ONE OF THEM CRIPS Y'GOTTA PUSH AROUND IN A WHEELCHAIR AND CHANGE HIS BAG!

WHAT GOOD AM I T'YOU *NOW,* BABY?

Y-YOU TOOK THE HIT SAVIN' *ME,* SPATS. I *SAW* YA!

DON'T YOU WORRY. I'M GONNA TAKE CARE OF YOU. YOU'LL SEE.

AND BEFORE THIS IS OVER WE'RE GONNA TAKE CARE OF THAT RINGTAIL *JOHNNY APOLLO,* TOO!

AAAAUWWW!

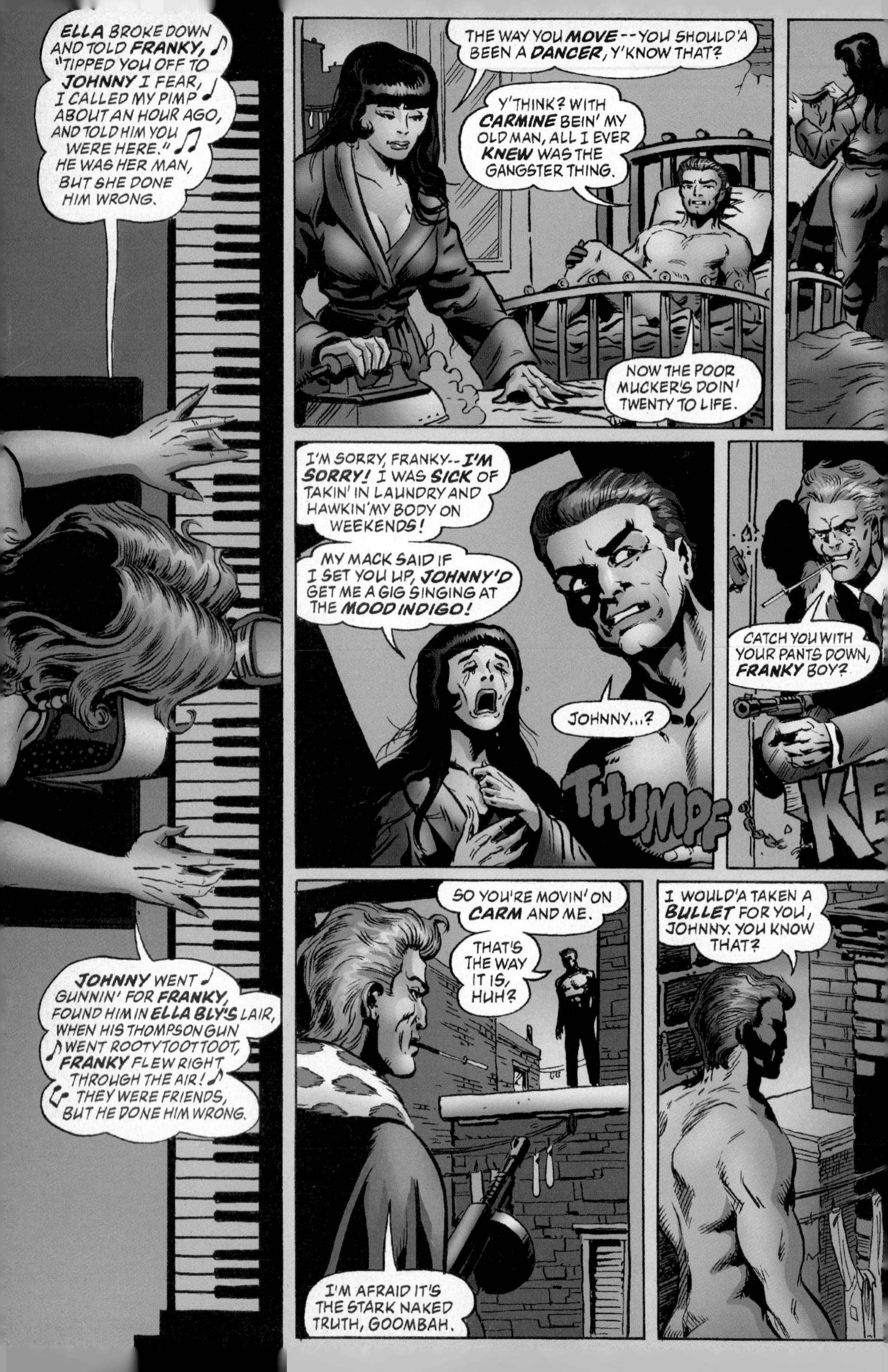

ELLA BROKE DOWN AND TOLD FRANKY, "TIPPED YOU OFF TO JOHNNY I FEAR, I CALLED MY PIMP ABOUT AN HOUR AGO, AND TOLD HIM YOU WERE HERE." HE WAS HER MAN, BUT SHE DONE HIM WRONG.
THE WAY YOU MOVE--YOU SHOULD'A BEEN A DANCER, Y'KNOW THAT?
Y'THINK? WITH CARMINE BEIN' MY OLD MAN, ALL I EVER KNEW WAS THE GANGSTER THING.
NOW THE POOR MUCKER'S DOIN' TWENTY TO LIFE.
I'M SORRY, FRANKY--I'M SORRY! I WAS SICK OF TAKIN' IN LAUNDRY AND HAWKIN' MY BODY ON WEEKENDS!
MY MACK SAID IF I SET YOU UP, JOHNNY'D GET ME A GIG SINGING AT THE MOOD INDIGO!
JOHNNY...?
THUMPF
CATCH YOU WITH YOUR PANTS DOWN, FRANKY BOY?
JOHNNY WENT GUNNIN' FOR FRANKY, FOUND HIM IN ELLA BLY'S LAIR, WHEN HIS THOMPSON GUN WENT ROOTY TOOT TOOT, FRANKY FLEW RIGHT THROUGH THE AIR! THEY WERE FRIENDS, BUT HE DONE HIM WRONG.
SO YOU'RE MOVIN' ON CARM AND ME.
THAT'S THE WAY IT IS, HUH?
I'M AFRAID IT'S THE STARK NAKED TRUTH, GOOMBAH.
I WOULD'A TAKEN A BULLET FOR YOU, JOHNNY. YOU KNOW THAT?

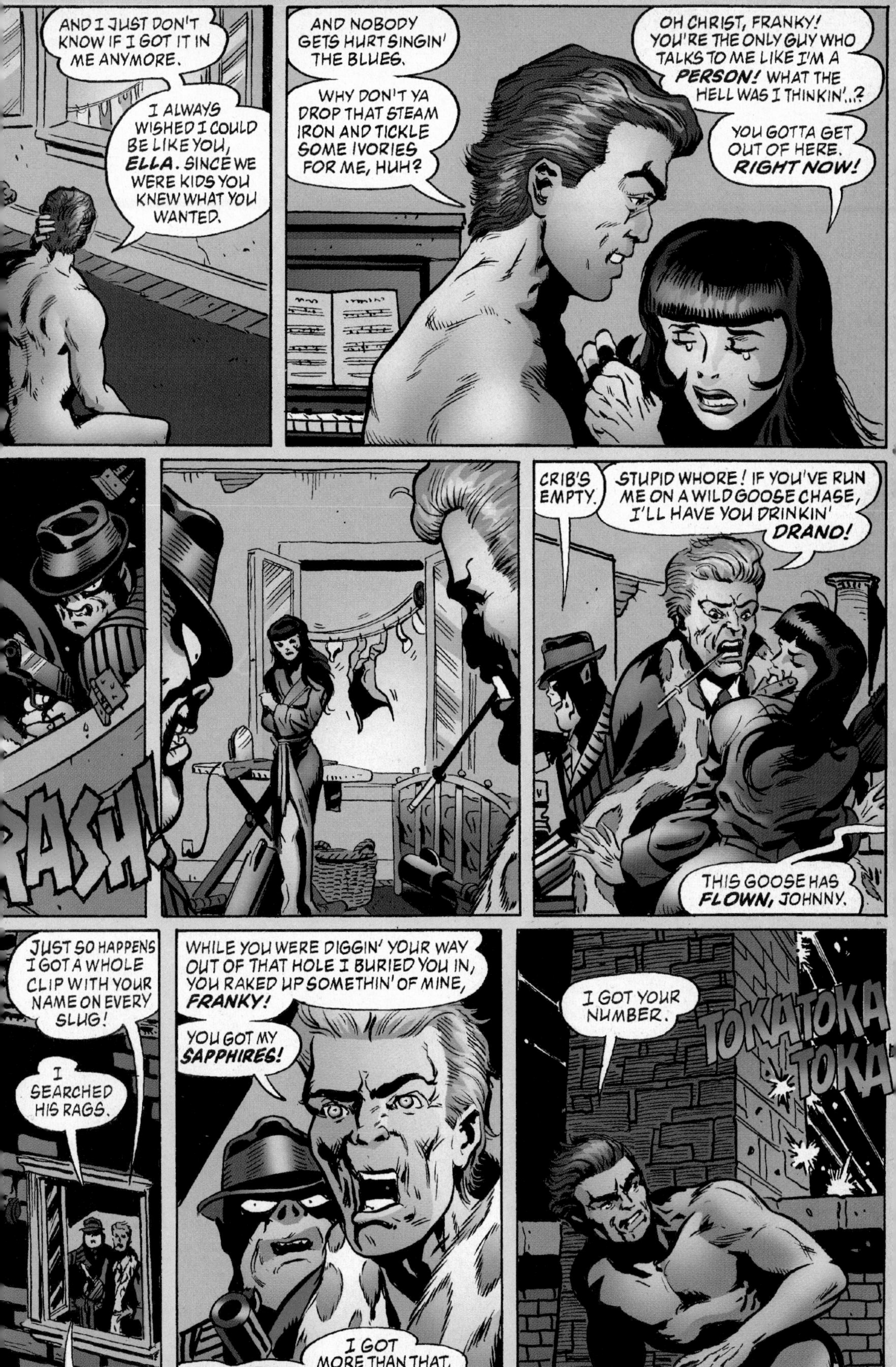
AND I JUST DON'T KNOW IF I GOT IT IN ME ANYMORE.
I ALWAYS WISHED I COULD BE LIKE YOU, ELLA. SINCE WE WERE KIDS YOU KNEW WHAT YOU WANTED.
AND NOBODY GETS HURT SINGIN' THE BLUES.
WHY DON'T YA DROP THAT STEAM IRON AND TICKLE SOME IVORIES FOR ME, HUH?
OH CHRIST, FRANKY! YOU'RE THE ONLY GUY WHO TALKS TO ME LIKE I'M A PERSON! WHAT THE HELL WAS I THINKIN'...?
YOU GOTTA GET OUT OF HERE. RIGHT NOW!
RASH!
CRIB'S EMPTY.
STUPID WHORE! IF YOU'VE RUN ME ON A WILD GOOSE CHASE, I'LL HAVE YOU DRINKIN' DRANO!
THIS GOOSE HAS FLOWN, JOHNNY.
JUST SO HAPPENS I GOT A WHOLE CLIP WITH YOUR NAME ON EVERY SLUG!
I SEARCHED HIS RAGS.
THE STONES AIN'T HERE.
WHILE YOU WERE DIGGIN' YOUR WAY OUT OF THAT HOLE I BURIED YOU IN, YOU RAKED UP SOMETHIN' OF MINE, FRANKY!
YOU GOT MY SAPPHIRES!
I GOT MORE THAN THAT, JOHNNY.
I GOT YOUR NUMBER.
TOKATOKA TOKA

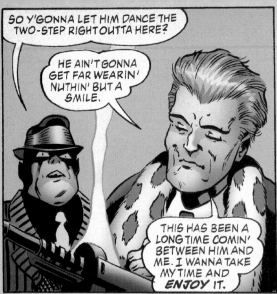

SO Y'GONNA LET HIM DANCE THE TWO-STEP RIGHT OUTTA HERE?

HE AIN'T GONNA GET FAR WEARIN' NUTHIN' BUT A SMILE.

THIS HAS BEEN A LONG TIME COMIN' BETWEEN HIM AND ME. I WANNA TAKE MY TIME AND *ENJOY* IT.

WHAT ABOUT THE BISCUIT?

YEAH, I CAME THROUGH WITH THE TIP-OFF. IT'S NOT *MY* FAULT HE GOT AWAY.

YOU PROMISED ME A *GIG*!

Y'MEAN YOU *STILL* HAVEN'T GOT THAT SINGING CAREER GOIN', *ELLA*? EVEN AFTER ALL THESE YEARS?

NOT WITH GUYS LIKE *YOU* RUNNIN' THE *CLUBS*, JOHNNY! I BEEN PAYIN' DUES ON MY BACK!

WELL, THE *MOOD INDIGO* IS PART OF *MY* TERRITORY NOW. BUT THERE'S MORE TO GETTIN' ON THE BILL THERE *THAN* RAW TALENT OR CONNECTIONS...

SEE, IF YOU WANNA *REALLY* SING THE BLUES...

...YOU GOTTA SUFFER.

NO, DON'T. *DON'T*!

NNOOOAAUUGGHHH!!

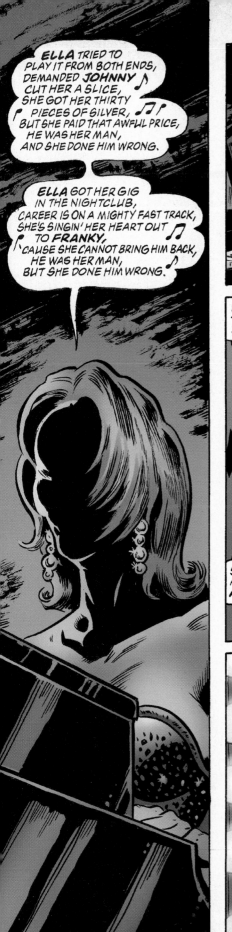

ELLA TRIED TO PLAY IT FROM BOTH ENDS, DEMANDED *JOHNNY* ♪ CUT HER A SLICE, SHE GOT HER THIRTY PIECES OF SILVER, ♪♫ BUT SHE PAID THAT AWFUL PRICE, HE WAS HER MAN, AND SHE DONE HIM WRONG.

ELLA GOT HER GIG IN THE NIGHTCLUB, CAREER IS ON A MIGHTY FAST TRACK, SHE'S SINGIN' HER HEART OUT TO *FRANKY*, ♪ 'CAUSE SHE CANNOT BRING HIM BACK, HE WAS HER MAN, BUT SHE DONE HIM WRONG. ♪

CLAP CLAP CLAP CLAP

THANK YOU, LADIES AND GENTLEMEN, THANK YOU SO MUCH.

GOOD NIGHT AND GOD BLESS.

KEN -- YOU GOT THE LIGHTING JUST HOW I LIKE IT. THANKS!

NO PROB! YOU SOUNDED *GREAT!*

AND SHE'S GOT A *SECRET ADMIRER,* TOO!

THAT MASKED GUY IN THE FRONT ROW TOOK THIS *CARNATION* OFF HIS LAPEL, SAID TO PASS IT ON WITH HIS COMPLIMENTS BEFORE HE LEFT.

AAH... SHOW BIZ.

THERE'S ALWAYS FANS OUT THERE...

...EVEN WHEN Y'GOT A KISSER LIKE MINE.

6

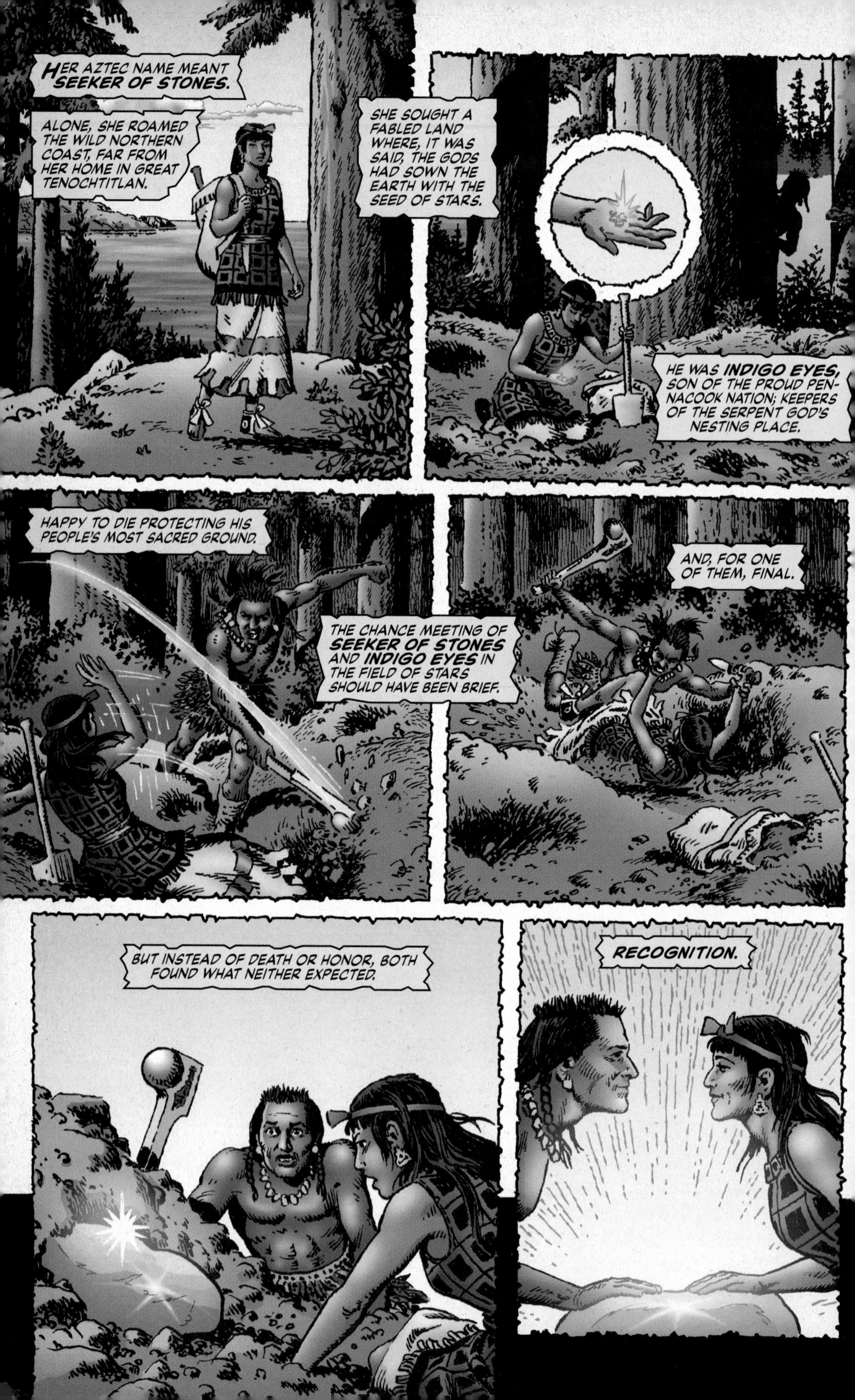

HER AZTEC NAME MEANT SEEKER OF STONES.
ALONE, SHE ROAMED THE WILD NORTHERN COAST, FAR FROM HER HOME IN GREAT TENOCHTITLAN.
SHE SOUGHT A FABLED LAND WHERE, IT WAS SAID, THE GODS HAD SOWN THE EARTH WITH THE SEED OF STARS.
HE WAS INDIGO EYES, SON OF THE PROUD PENNACOOK NATION; KEEPERS OF THE SERPENT GOD'S NESTING PLACE.
HAPPY TO DIE PROTECTING HIS PEOPLE'S MOST SACRED GROUND.
THE CHANCE MEETING OF SEEKER OF STONES AND INDIGO EYES IN THE FIELD OF STARS SHOULD HAVE BEEN BRIEF.
AND, FOR ONE OF THEM, FINAL.
BUT INSTEAD OF DEATH OR HONOR, BOTH FOUND WHAT NEITHER EXPECTED.
RECOGNITION.

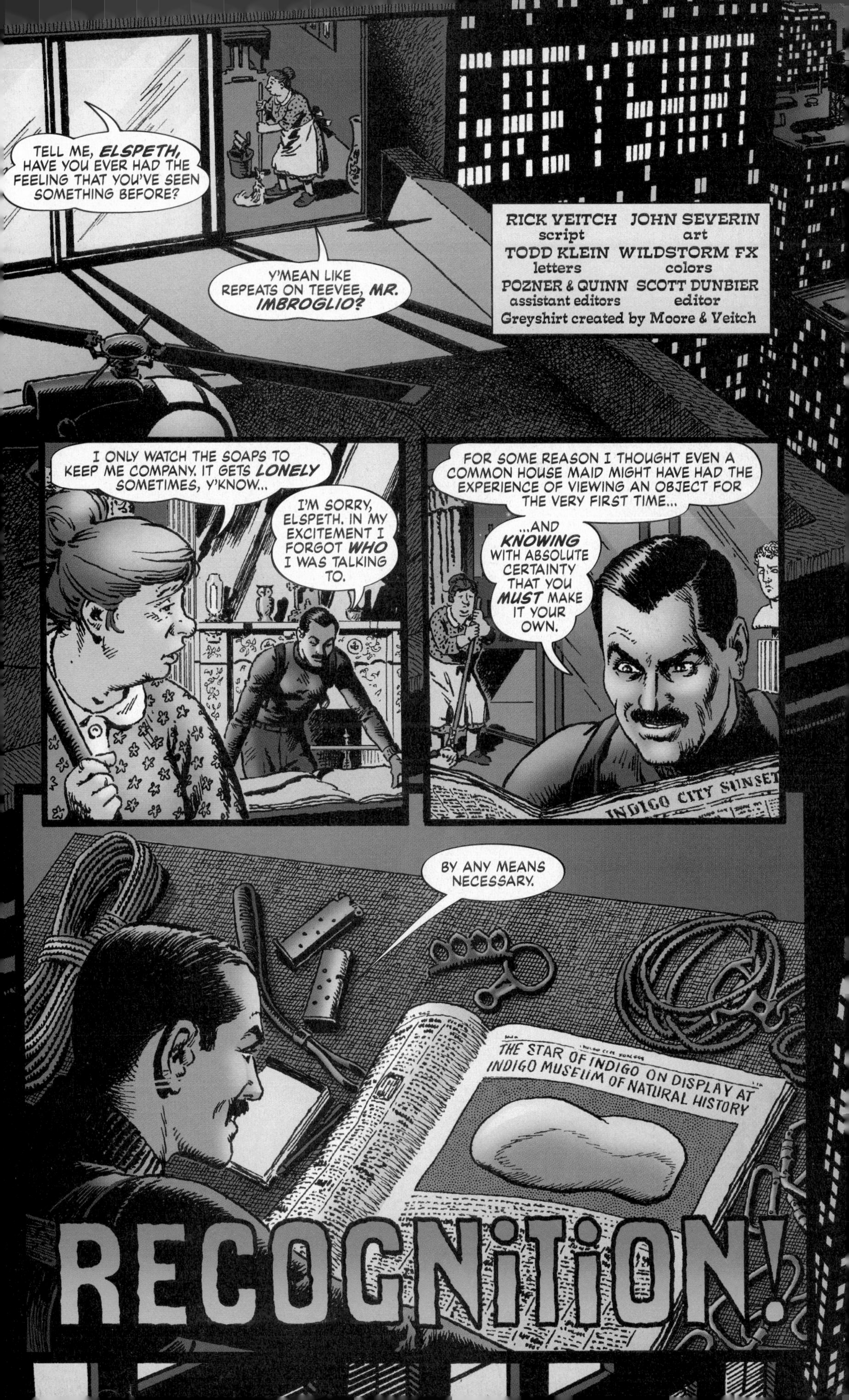
TELL ME, ELSPETH, HAVE YOU EVER HAD THE FEELING THAT YOU'VE SEEN SOMETHING BEFORE?
Y'MEAN LIKE REPEATS ON TEEVEE, MR. IMBROGLIO?
RICK VEITCH script JOHN SEVERIN art
TODD KLEIN letters WILDSTORM FX colors
POZNER & QUINN assistant editors SCOTT DUNBIER editor
Greyshirt created by Moore & Veitch
I ONLY WATCH THE SOAPS TO KEEP ME COMPANY. IT GETS LONELY SOMETIMES, Y'KNOW...
I'M SORRY, ELSPETH. IN MY EXCITEMENT I FORGOT WHO I WAS TALKING TO.
FOR SOME REASON I THOUGHT EVEN A COMMON HOUSE MAID MIGHT HAVE HAD THE EXPERIENCE OF VIEWING AN OBJECT FOR THE VERY FIRST TIME...
...AND KNOWING WITH ABSOLUTE CERTAINTY THAT YOU MUST MAKE IT YOUR OWN.
INDIGO CITY SUNSET
BY ANY MEANS NECESSARY.
THE STAR OF INDIGO ON DISPLAY AT INDIGO MUSEUM OF NATURAL HISTORY
RECOGNITION!

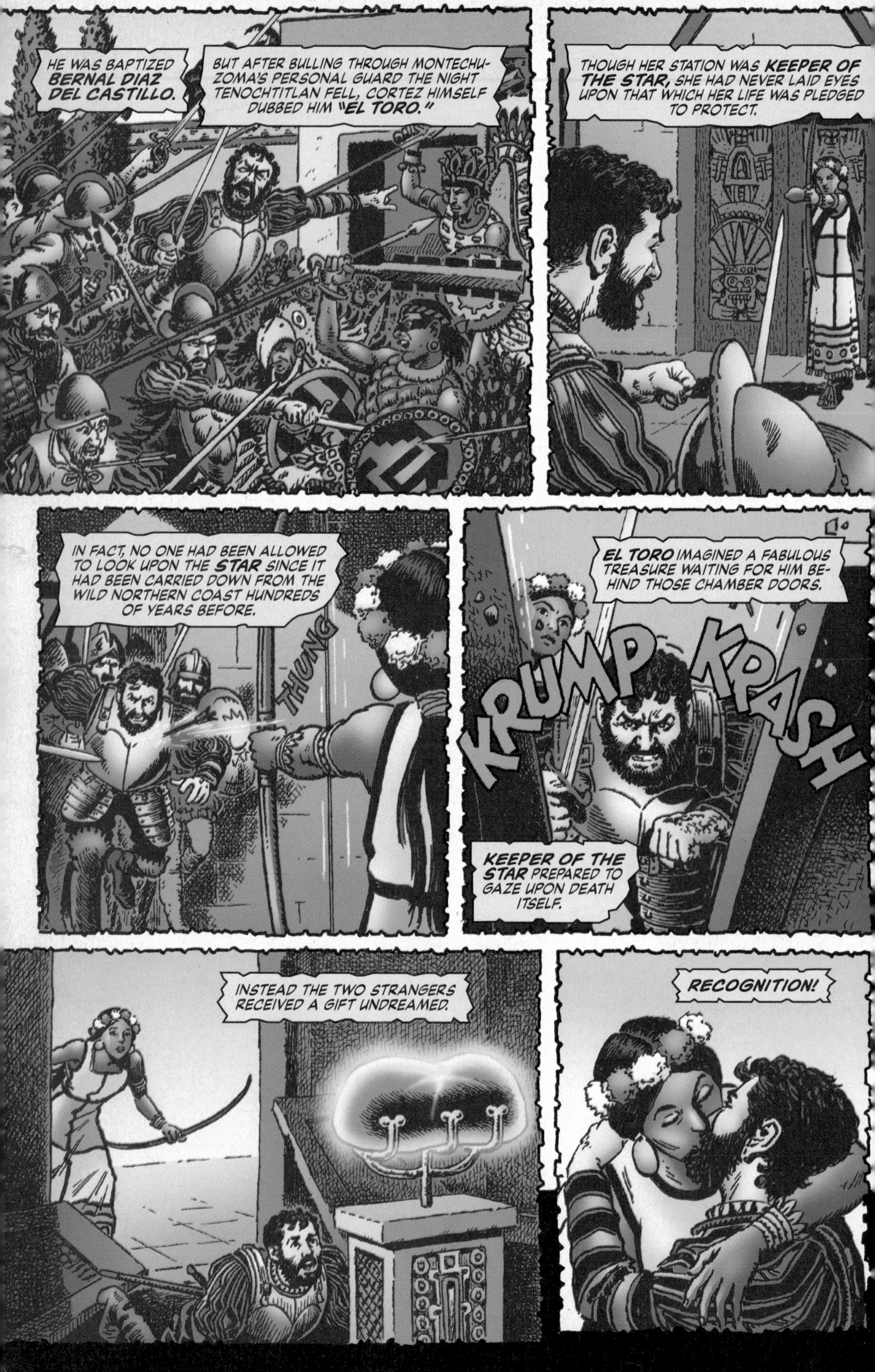
HE WAS BAPTIZED BERNAL DIAZ DEL CASTILLO.
BUT AFTER BULLING THROUGH MONTECHUZOMA'S PERSONAL GUARD THE NIGHT TENOCHTITLAN FELL, CORTEZ HIMSELF DUBBED HIM "EL TORO."
THOUGH HER STATION WAS KEEPER OF THE STAR, SHE HAD NEVER LAID EYES UPON THAT WHICH HER LIFE WAS PLEDGED TO PROTECT.
IN FACT, NO ONE HAD BEEN ALLOWED TO LOOK UPON THE STAR SINCE IT HAD BEEN CARRIED DOWN FROM THE WILD NORTHERN COAST HUNDREDS OF YEARS BEFORE.
THUNG
EL TORO IMAGINED A FABULOUS TREASURE WAITING FOR HIM BEHIND THOSE CHAMBER DOORS.
KRUMP
KRASH
KEEPER OF THE STAR PREPARED TO GAZE UPON DEATH ITSELF.
INSTEAD THE TWO STRANGERS RECEIVED A GIFT UNDREAMED.
RECOGNITION!

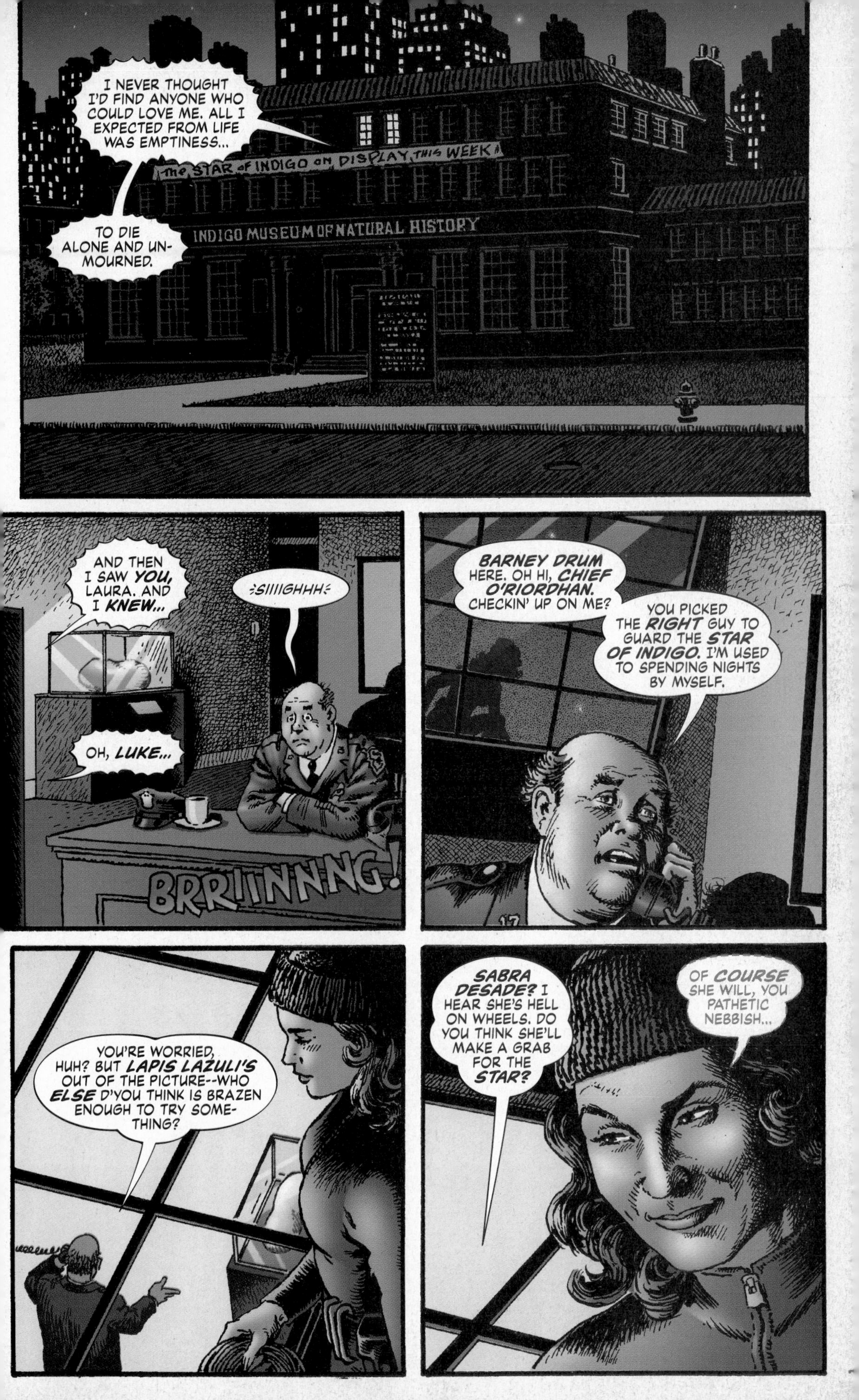

I NEVER THOUGHT I'D FIND ANYONE WHO COULD LOVE ME. ALL I EXPECTED FROM LIFE WAS EMPTINESS...
THE STAR OF INDIGO ON DISPLAY THIS WEEK
TO DIE ALONE AND UN-MOURNED.
INDIGO MUSEUM OF NATURAL HISTORY
AND THEN I SAW YOU, LAURA. AND I KNEW...
SIIIIGHHH
OH, LUKE...
BRRIINNNG!
BARNEY DRUM HERE. OH HI, CHIEF O'RIORDHAN. CHECKIN' UP ON ME?
YOU PICKED THE RIGHT GUY TO GUARD THE STAR OF INDIGO. I'M USED TO SPENDING NIGHTS BY MYSELF.
YOU'RE WORRIED, HUH? BUT LAPIS LAZULI'S OUT OF THE PICTURE--WHO ELSE D'YOU THINK IS BRAZEN ENOUGH TO TRY SOME-THING?
SABRA DESADE? I HEAR SHE'S HELL ON WHEELS. DO YOU THINK SHE'LL MAKE A GRAB FOR THE STAR?
OF COURSE SHE WILL, YOU PATHETIC NEBBISH...

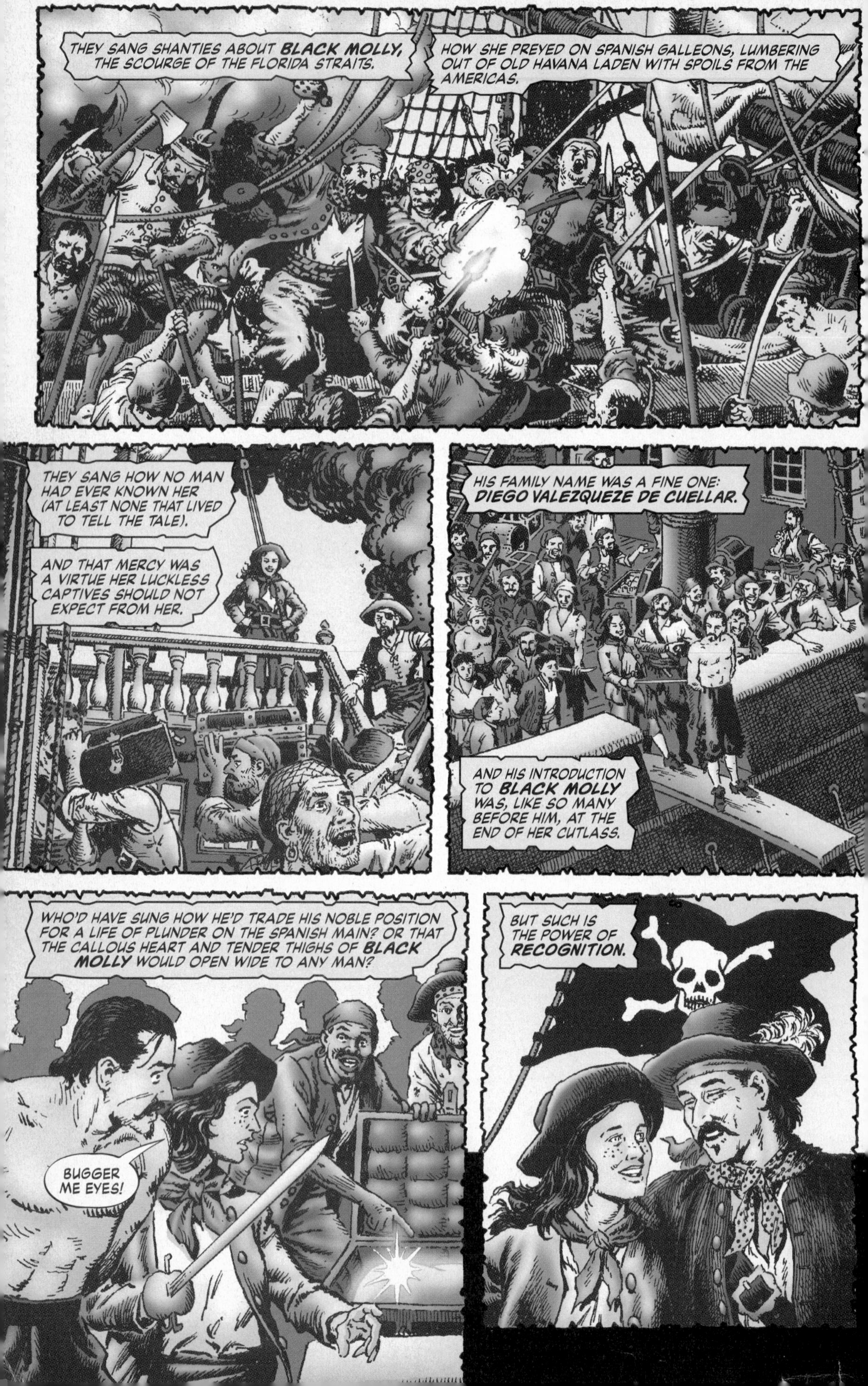
THEY SANG SHANTIES ABOUT BLACK MOLLY, THE SCOURGE OF THE FLORIDA STRAITS.
HOW SHE PREYED ON SPANISH GALLEONS, LUMBERING OUT OF OLD HAVANA LADEN WITH SPOILS FROM THE AMERICAS.
THEY SANG HOW NO MAN HAD EVER KNOWN HER (AT LEAST NONE THAT LIVED TO TELL THE TALE).
AND THAT MERCY WAS A VIRTUE HER LUCKLESS CAPTIVES SHOULD NOT EXPECT FROM HER.
HIS FAMILY NAME WAS A FINE ONE: DIEGO VALEZQUEZE DE CUELLAR.
AND HIS INTRODUCTION TO BLACK MOLLY WAS, LIKE SO MANY BEFORE HIM, AT THE END OF HER CUTLASS.
WHO'D HAVE SUNG HOW HE'D TRADE HIS NOBLE POSITION FOR A LIFE OF PLUNDER ON THE SPANISH MAIN? OR THAT THE CALLOUS HEART AND TENDER THIGHS OF BLACK MOLLY WOULD OPEN WIDE TO ANY MAN?
BUGGER ME EYES!
BUT SUCH IS THE POWER OF RECOGNITION.

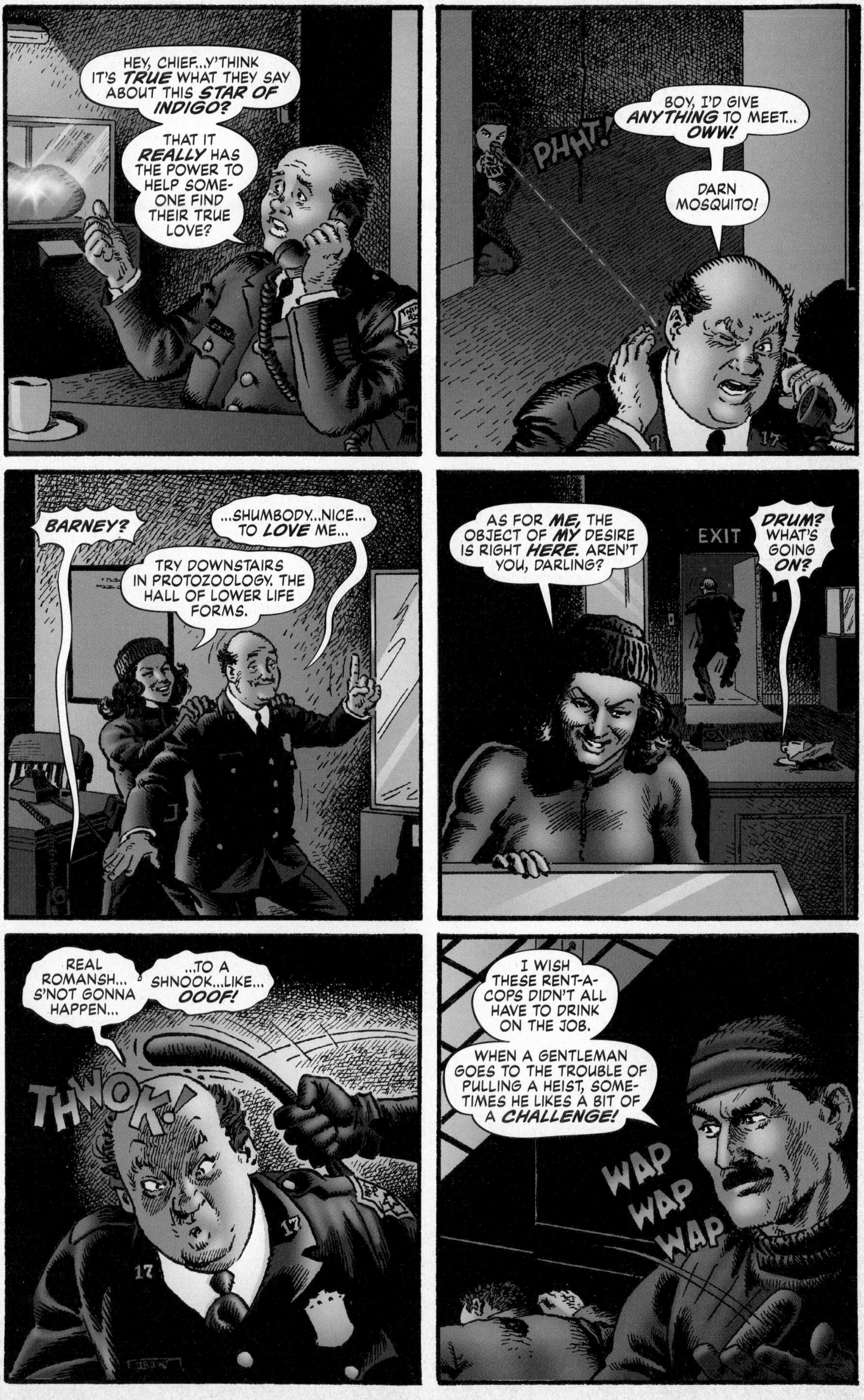
HEY, CHIEF...Y'THINK IT'S TRUE WHAT THEY SAY ABOUT THIS STAR OF INDIGO?
THAT IT REALLY HAS THE POWER TO HELP SOME-ONE FIND THEIR TRUE LOVE?
PHHT!
BOY, I'D GIVE ANYTHING TO MEET... OWW!
DARN MOSQUITO!
BARNEY?
...SHUMBODY...NICE... TO LOVE ME...
TRY DOWNSTAIRS IN PROTOZOOLOGY. THE HALL OF LOWER LIFE FORMS.
AS FOR ME, THE OBJECT OF MY DESIRE IS RIGHT HERE. AREN'T YOU, DARLING?
EXIT
DRUM? WHAT'S GOING ON?
REAL ROMANSH... S'NOT GONNA HAPPEN...
...TO A SHNOOK...LIKE... OOOF!
THWOK!
I WISH THESE RENT-A-COPS DIDN'T ALL HAVE TO DRINK ON THE JOB.
WHEN A GENTLEMAN GOES TO THE TROUBLE OF PULLING A HEIST, SOME-TIMES HE LIKES A BIT OF A CHALLENGE!
WAP
WAP
WAP

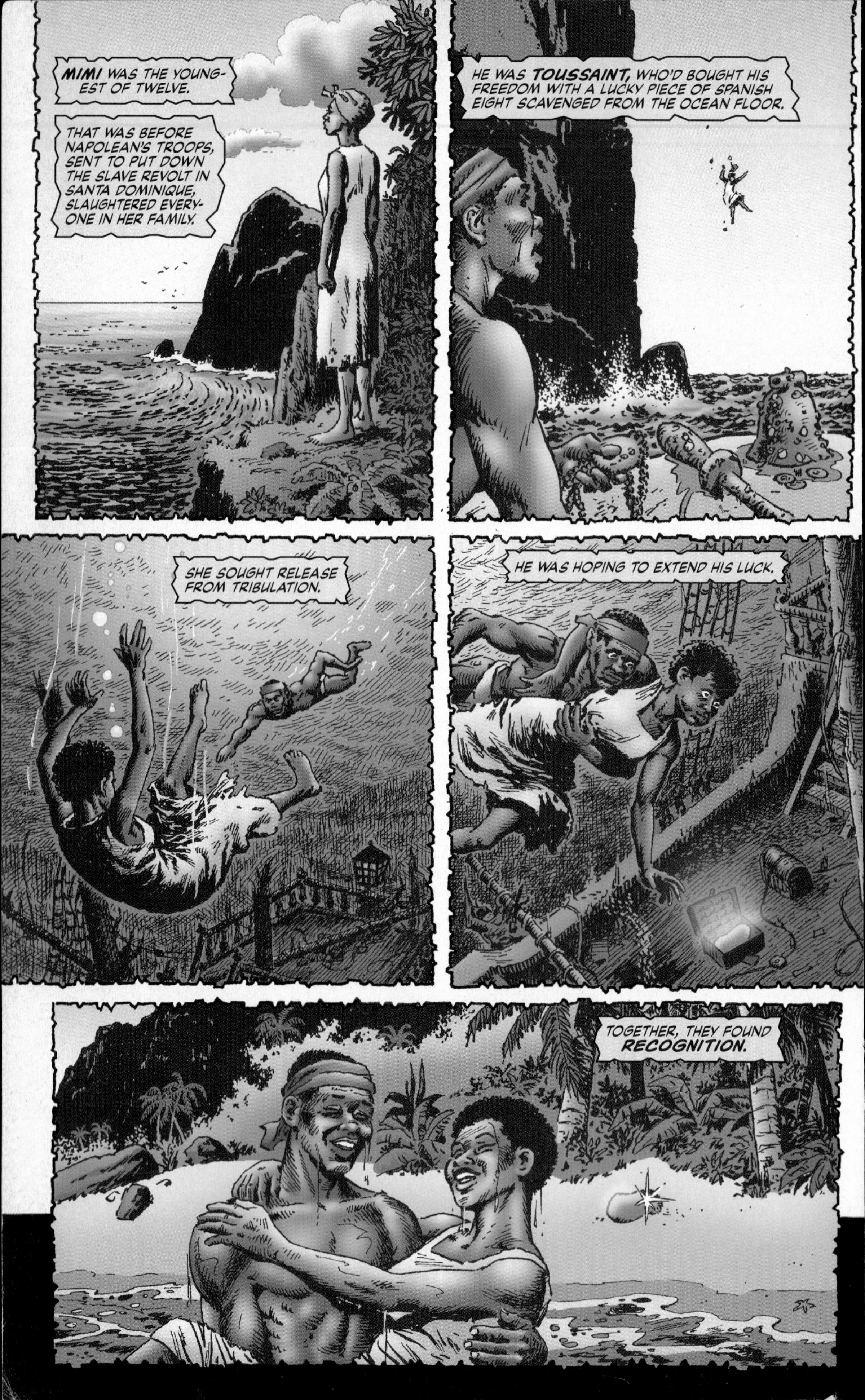
MIMI WAS THE YOUNGEST OF TWELVE.
THAT WAS BEFORE NAPOLEAN'S TROOPS, SENT TO PUT DOWN THE SLAVE REVOLT IN SANTA DOMINIQUE, SLAUGHTERED EVERYONE IN HER FAMILY.
HE WAS TOUSSAINT, WHO'D BOUGHT HIS FREEDOM WITH A LUCKY PIECE OF SPANISH EIGHT SCAVENGED FROM THE OCEAN FLOOR.
SHE SOUGHT RELEASE FROM TRIBULATION.
HE WAS HOPING TO EXTEND HIS LUCK.
TOGETHER, THEY FOUND RECOGNITION.

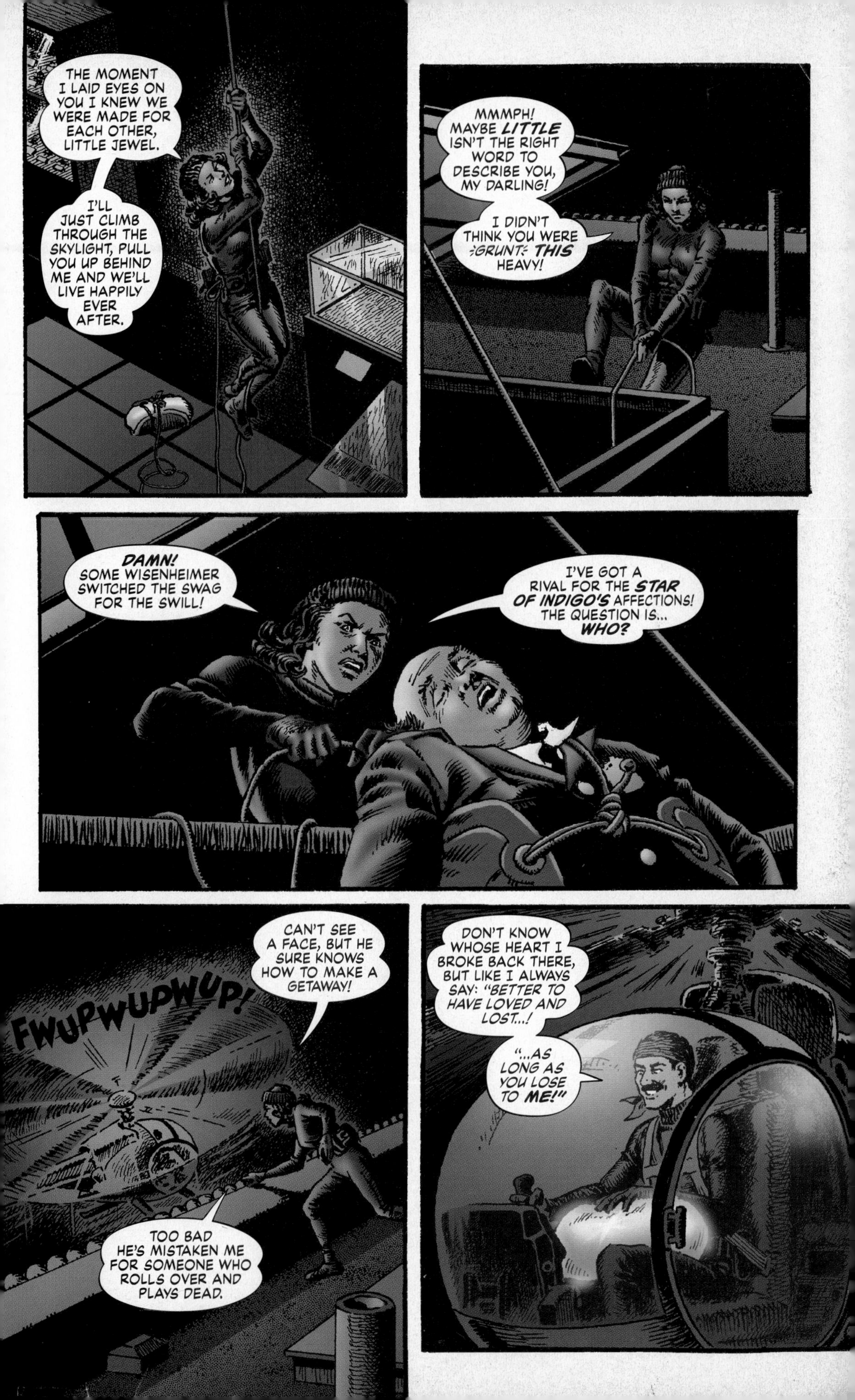
THE MOMENT I LAID EYES ON YOU I KNEW WE WERE MADE FOR EACH OTHER, LITTLE JEWEL.
I'LL JUST CLIMB THROUGH THE SKYLIGHT, PULL YOU UP BEHIND ME AND WE'LL LIVE HAPPILY EVER AFTER.
MMMPH! MAYBE *LITTLE* ISN'T THE RIGHT WORD TO DESCRIBE YOU, MY DARLING!
I DIDN'T THINK YOU WERE *GRUNT* *THIS* HEAVY!
DAMN! SOME WISENHEIMER SWITCHED THE SWAG FOR THE SWILL!
I'VE GOT A RIVAL FOR THE *STAR OF INDIGO'S* AFFECTIONS! THE QUESTION IS... *WHO?*
FWUPWUPWUP!
CAN'T SEE A FACE, BUT HE SURE KNOWS HOW TO MAKE A GETAWAY!
TOO BAD HE'S MISTAKEN ME FOR SOMEONE WHO ROLLS OVER AND PLAYS DEAD.
DON'T KNOW WHOSE HEART I BROKE BACK THERE, BUT LIKE I ALWAYS SAY: *"BETTER TO HAVE LOVED AND LOST...!*
"...AS LONG AS YOU LOSE TO ME!"

THE NEW YORK ORGANIZATION HAD SENT IN *DOCTOR DO.*

HE SPECIALIZED IN *"HOUSE CALLS."* EVEN AS FAR AWAY AS HAVANA.

THE "PATIENT" WAS A CASINO OPERATIVE WHO'D LOST HIS NERVE WHEN CASTRO'S INSURGENTS TOOK CONTROL OF THE COUNTRYSIDE.

WORD WAS HE WAS GOING TO BOLT WITH SOME EXPENSIVE COMPANY PROPERTY.

HER *KGB* HANDLERS CALLED HER *EMPRESS OF ICE.*

HER MISSION WAS TO TAKE OUT MAFIA PARASITES AND ACQUIRE ASSETS FOR THE COMING WORLD REVOLUTION.

VRUMM!

BAM BAM

POW POW POW

SKREEE!

NEITHER *DOCTOR* NOR *EMPRESS* EVER DREAMED THEIR MAFIA LOYALTY AND REVOLUTIONARY ZEAL WOULD ONE DAY EVAPORATE...

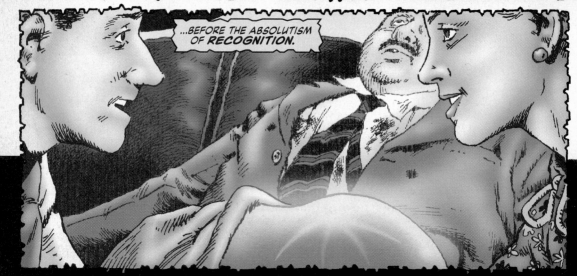

...BEFORE THE ABSOLUTISM OF *RECOGNITION.*

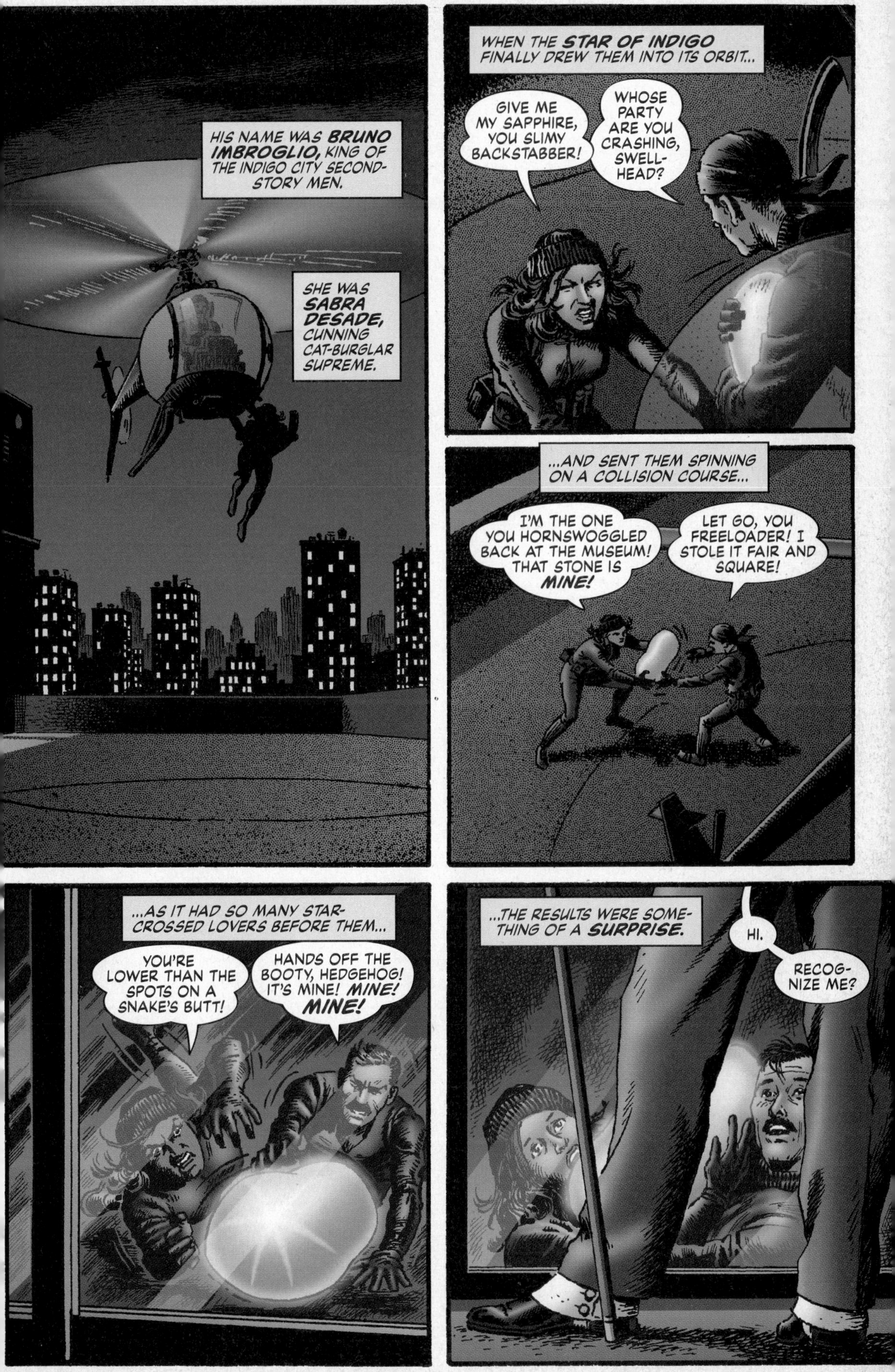
HIS NAME WAS BRUNO IMBROGLIO, KING OF THE INDIGO CITY SECOND-STORY MEN.
SHE WAS SABRA DESADE, CUNNING CAT-BURGLAR SUPREME.
WHEN THE STAR OF INDIGO FINALLY DREW THEM INTO ITS ORBIT...
GIVE ME MY SAPPHIRE, YOU SLIMY BACKSTABBER!
WHOSE PARTY ARE YOU CRASHING, SWELL-HEAD?
...AND SENT THEM SPINNING ON A COLLISION COURSE...
I'M THE ONE YOU HORNSWOGGLED BACK AT THE MUSEUM! THAT STONE IS MINE!
LET GO, YOU FREELOADER! I STOLE IT FAIR AND SQUARE!
...AS IT HAD SO MANY STAR-CROSSED LOVERS BEFORE THEM...
YOU'RE LOWER THAN THE SPOTS ON A SNAKE'S BUTT!
HANDS OFF THE BOOTY, HEDGEHOG! IT'S MINE! MINE! MINE!
...THE RESULTS WERE SOMETHING OF A SURPRISE.
HI.
RECOGNIZE ME?

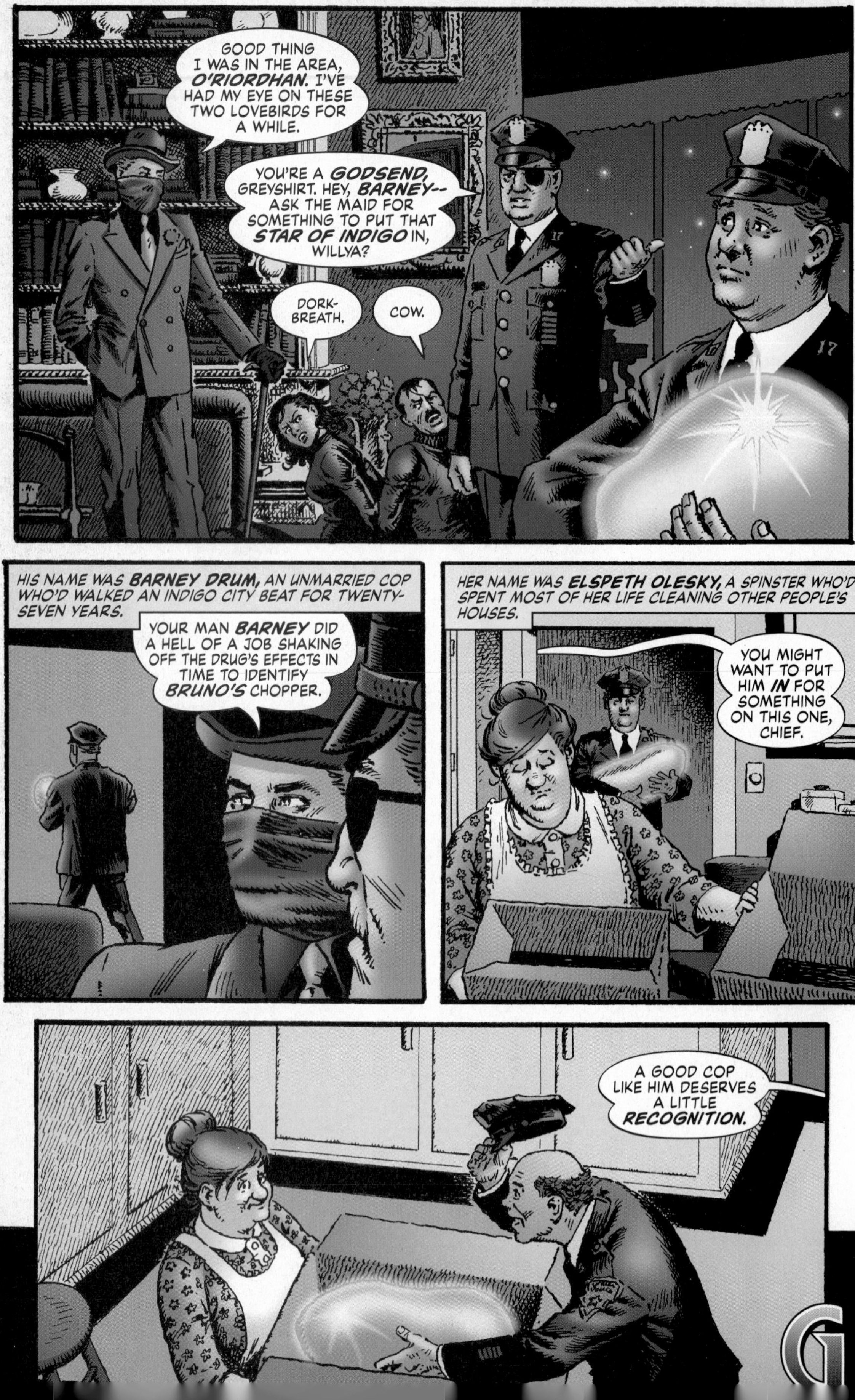
GOOD THING I WAS IN THE AREA, O'RIORDHAN. I'VE HAD MY EYE ON THESE TWO LOVEBIRDS FOR A WHILE.
YOU'RE A GODSEND, GREYSHIRT. HEY, BARNEY-- ASK THE MAID FOR SOMETHING TO PUT THAT STAR OF INDIGO IN, WILLYA?
DORK-BREATH.
COW.
HIS NAME WAS BARNEY DRUM, AN UNMARRIED COP WHO'D WALKED AN INDIGO CITY BEAT FOR TWENTY-SEVEN YEARS.
YOUR MAN BARNEY DID A HELL OF A JOB SHAKING OFF THE DRUG'S EFFECTS IN TIME TO IDENTIFY BRUNO'S CHOPPER.
HER NAME WAS ELSPETH OLESKY, A SPINSTER WHO'D SPENT MOST OF HER LIFE CLEANING OTHER PEOPLE'S HOUSES.
YOU MIGHT WANT TO PUT HIM IN FOR SOMETHING ON THIS ONE, CHIEF.
A GOOD COP LIKE HIM DESERVES A LITTLE RECOGNITION.

ALL THE NEWS FROM DAWN TO DUSK

NOW 75¢

INDIGO CITY SUNSET

AFTERNOON CITY EDITION

Tuesday, February 19, 2002 Metro Weather – Today: Low-lying Mist, Tonight: Deepening Fog, Tomorrow: Pea Soup

DAM FOOLS!

GREYSHIRT SAYS CROOKS CAUSED DAM COLLAPSE!

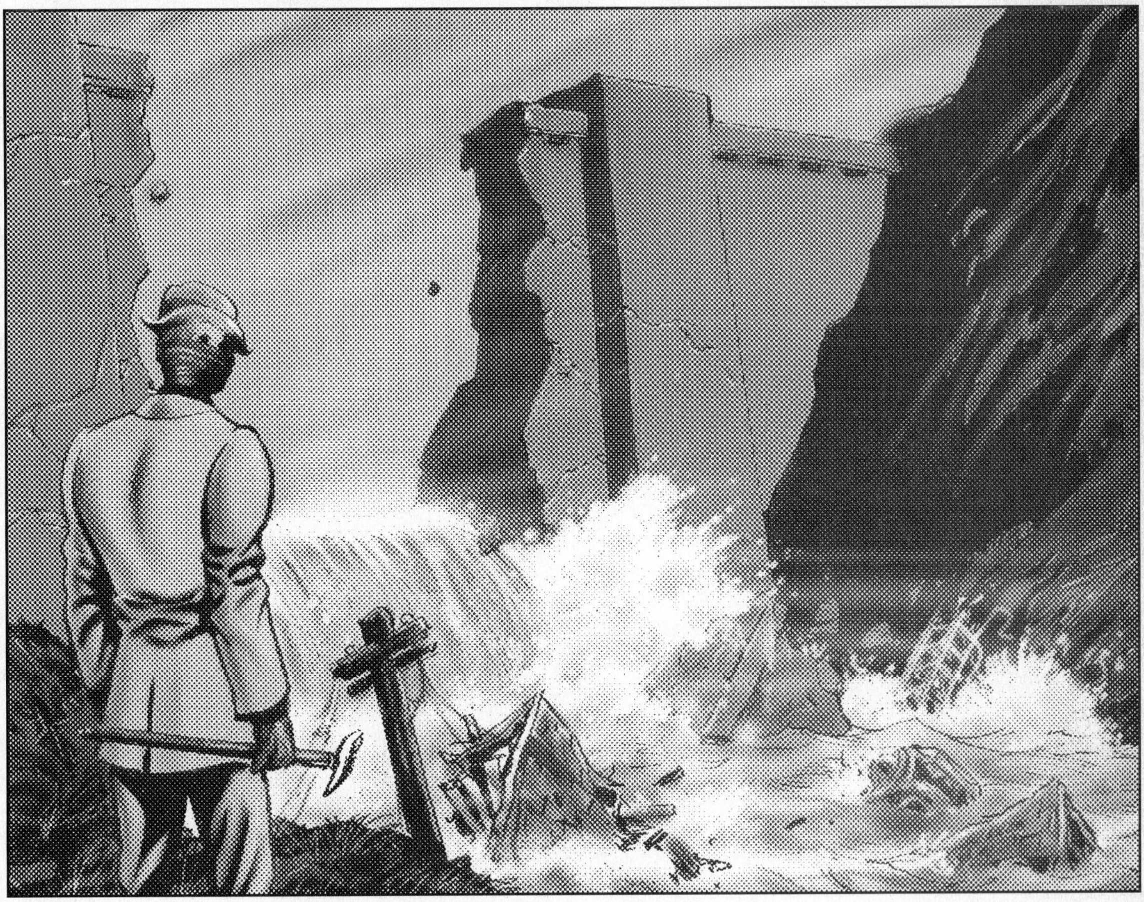

Indigo City: The headwaters of the mighty Turquoise River tore a swath of destruction through a lower Cerulean Valley housing development yesterday after the Bluestone Dam gave way. According to GREYSHIRT, the collapse of the $75 million construction was a result of illegal excavations undertaken by local gangsters that undermined the dam foundation.

FULL COVERAGE: Pages 2 and 3

ELLA'S MOOD INDIGO! Page 28

INDIGO CITY SUNSET, TUESDAY, FEBRUARY 19, 2002

HIGH WATER RISING!

THE HOLE-IN-THE-HEAD

SPECIAL TO THE SUNSET BY SKEETER BACKENBEATER

A slight fog lay over the Cerulean Valley as local residents rose from their beds Monday morning and prepared to get their kids to the school bus and begin their morning commutes into Indigo City. Little did they know that when they returned to their quiet suburban homes that evening they would find a Biblical scene of utter devastation. The cause would be the rupture of the Bluestone Dam, only recently completed, which poured millions of gallons of pent-up fury into the valley below.

While authorities are still trying to piece together the exact sequence of events, a source close to the mayor's office, who asked to remain anonymous, told the SUNSET that the cause of the catastrophe was unauthorized tunneling beneath the dam's foundation.

It appears that the culprits were a gang of small-time Indigo grifters looking for a big score. Somehow they had convinced themselves that a treasure trove of lost sapphires lay hidden in the warren of old mine shafts that pepper the sides of valley walls into which the dam was built.

The leader of the gang was two-time loser, JOHNNY PERROGEY, who was apparently infatuated with the idea that a large stash of sapphires was located in the area. The sapphires were thought to be a fabled treasure trove belonging to celebrated gangster Spats Katz, supposedly hidden in one of the thousands of abandoned mine shafts in Indigo City some time in the 1980s. Katz, who died of a fall out the window of his penthouse apartment last year, was reportedly obsessed with locating the stash of gems right up to the end of his life. Insiders who were close to the paralyzed gangster said he blamed Franky Lafayette and Johnny Apollo for stealing the sapphires from their original hiding place in the #11 mine in the Bottoms Up District. Both Lafayette and Apollo died in a shoot-out and gas explosion in Indigo's Central Station in 1989 and the sapphires were never found.

There has been renewed interest in the mythical Katz sapphires since shooting began on "THE CARBONES: FRANKY AND JOHNNY," a major motion picture telling the story of the two young Indigo gangsters. Sources within the mayor's office tell the SUNSET that Perrogey may have gotten a bootleg copy of one of the shooting scripts for the film, and pieced together what he thought were clues to the sapphires' whereabouts from various parts of the script, not realizing it was mostly a work of fiction.

Perrogey enlisted the help of three Indigo City lowlifes, including con-man Hoagie "The Scarecrow" Jejune, pickpocket Edgar "Fisheye" Bile, and three-card-monte dealer Mike "The Mung" Poodle, promising them a share of the take, which he originally estimated to be in the hundreds of millions of dollars.

The gang took actual employment as laborers with a construction outfit that had a city contract to seal up the scores of abandoned mines in the Cerulean Valley hillside following the opening of the dam. After working full shifts during the day, the gang would hide inside the shafts and continue digging surreptitiously through the night, utilizing the company's construction equipment to search the shafts for the lost gems.

While none of the gang had ever worked real jobs before, they appear to have labored mightily at their task, going weeks without sleep while digging night and day into the hillside. Their motivation

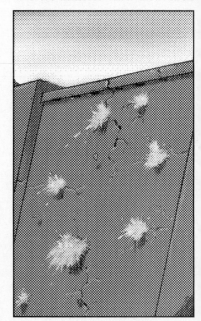

was the sapphire treasure, which grew in Perrogey's imagination to be worth billions of dollars as work progressed.

Problems began about three weeks into the operation when "Fisheye" Bile, careless from lack of sleep and overwork, swung a pickax and inadvertently knocked out "The Mung's" front teeth. Also exhausted, "Mung" lost his temper and proceeded to use the shovel he was digging with to stave in Bile's head. This action enraged "Scarecrow" Jejune, who was Bile's brother-in-law, and he

HIGH WATER RISING!

GANG!

Gang That Couldn't Dig Straight Brings Down Bluestone Dam!

pulled out a pistol and started shooting. "The Mung," also armed, returned fire and both crooks were seriously wounded.

At that point Perrogey was in a lower area of the mineshaft and had unearthed a corner of what appeared to be a cement sarcophagus. Convinced that it held the jewels, he ran up the shaft to inform his three cohorts only to find them all wounded and dying. At first overjoyed that he wouldn't have to share the booty with his soon-to-be-dead partners, Perrogey was then dismayed to discover that their gunfire had riddled the cave wall with holes and water was beginning to pour through the openings.

Perrogey became desperate at this point, realizing that the pent up waters behind the dam were likely to fill the shaft below and cut off his chance of collecting the fabulous treasure trove. Acting quickly, Perrogey positioned his dying comrades near the perforated cave walls and proceeded to use their fingers to plug as many leaks as he could. Cackling with manic glee, he then ran back to what he was sure was the resting place of the sapphires.

Digging frantically, Perrogey raced against the waters rising steadily around his feet until he was again forced to give up his labors and retrace his steps back to where his comrades lay. To his horror, Perrogey discovered large cracks forming near the bullet holes he'd plugged with his cohorts' dying fingers. As he wondered what to do next, a large fissure ruptured and a powerful stream of water burst into the tunnel. Thinking quickly, Perrogey grabbed the moaning Bile and stuffed his entire body into the gushing hole as a makeshift cork.

Another crack broke open and then another! Perrogey similarly sealed these openings with the crying "Scarecrow" and "Mung," then descended back to the lower part of the mine. Throwing all cau-

tion to the wind, Perrogey took a large pneumatic drill and tore into what he thought was the cement sarcophagus, expecting to break it open wide and find his fortune in sapphires inside. Instead of a sarcophagus, Perrogey had cut into the foundation of the dam itself, as he discovered when he was knocked across the tunnel by a firehose stream of highly pressurized water gushing from the hole he had created.

Meanwhile, morning had arrived and the denizens of the Cerulean Valley were beginning their day, unaware that Perrogey was deep in the rapidly filling mine shaft, desperately trying to plug up the ruptures with anything at hand. Finally forced to use his own body as a plug, Perrogey jammed himself into the broken foundation and succeeded in stopping the immediate flow of water. Authorities say this move saved thousands of lives because it held off the then-inevitable collapse of the dam long enough for most of the locals to leave their homes on their daily business.

Sometime about ten in the morning, GREYSHIRT was in the area, staking out a suburban crack house, and heard a strange noise, not unlike a huge champagne cork popping. Looking up towards the dam site, GREYSHIRT witnessed the screaming body of Johnny Perrogey flying out of one of the shafts on a highly pressurized jet of water. First ricocheting off a transformer tower amid a shower of sparks, then becoming hopelessly entangled in high tension lines, Perrogey finally landed like a sack of burning melons in the street nearby. As the ground began to shake, GREYSHIRT immediately grasped the severity of the situation. Heading straight for the control center of the dam's hydro-electric generators, the Indigo Avenger informed personnel of the impending danger and sounded the alert siren.

GREYSHIRT then led an

immediate evacuation effort of the area, even as the earth rocked and ominous cracks began to grow across the face of the dam. Through the valiant efforts of the Indigo Avenger in conjunction with local emergency personnel, all loss of life, other than the hapless criminals, was avoided when the great dam finally let go at 11:36 this morning. As a huge breach opened and massive chunks of concrete were carried down on a deluge of water, GREYSHIRT could be seen scrambling up a transformer tower carrying a frightened child and a lineman who had been knocked unconscious while trying to rescue the kid.

Later, while surveying the swath of damage unleashed by the dam's collapse, GREYSHIRT stood over the soaked and twisted remains of the four criminals who caused the disaster, and grimly quipped, "It just goes to show you can lead a horse's ass to water, but you can't make him think."

SOFTWARE WHIZ KID LIVING IT UP!
Sultry Sirens Help Sixteen-year-old Spend His Billions!

Special to the Sunset by Skeeter Backenbeater

If you were sixteen years old and found yourself with a six billion dollar fortune, how would you spend it? Indigo City software wünderkind Jack Hawkins is faced with that exact problem, but he doesn't seem lost at sea about what to do! When asked how he's going to use his newfound fortune, Hawkins, who doesn't give interviews, replied with a terse one sentence e-mail: "I'm gonna have fun!"

If the reports we're receiving are true, then "fun" isn't a strong enough word to describe Hawkins' day-to-day existence. The Sunset has confirmed that The Indigo City Boatworks delivered a $200 million yacht, outfitted with every luxury imaginable, to Hawkins' software company three months ago. And advertisements seeking a crew of "well-built young women with mastery in martial arts for work-party on 70 ft yacht cruising Crater Bay" that appeared in the Sunset Classified Section have been traced back to the company's post office box as well.

Sources tell the Sunset that Hawkins interviewed dozens of candidates personally before settling on a crew of sexy young coeds to sail his floating pleasure palace.

While Hawkins has succeeded in creating an impenetrable zone of privacy around his party boat as he sails Crater Bay with his crew of sultry belles, the Sunset was able to catch up with some of those who were left behind. Biff Sock, star running back for the Indigo College Weasels, tells us that his ex-girlfriend, Stella Clay, gave up a promising academic career to join Hawkins' epic pursuit of pleasure.

"She was really smart, you know? Only needed to pull six more credits to get her degree in Botany. Then this wimp shows up and starts throwing money around. He's more interested in how she wiggles her butt than her brains," said Sock weepily over a beer in the campus lounge.

A similar story was told by Indigo City police officer Quentin Santiago, who says his girlfriend, Bernice Wilson, was also lured onto the cruise with expensive gifts and promises of a six-figure salary. "She had so much going for her. Now she's just a trinket for this pimply-faced kid with more money than morals. All I can say is he better not double park his limo on my beat!"

As for Hawkins, he doesn't appear to be at all interested in setting foot on the dry land of Indigo's streets these days. The sixteen-year-old genius who made his pile in computer software is staying far out in Crater Bay, playing with his new hires and thumbing his nose at the rest of us poor working stiffs.

ANOTHER SHIP LOST TO PIRATES!
Shipment of Breakfast Cereal Vanishes in Crater Bay!

A container ship, which left Indigo City on Saturday with a shipment of GOODIOS breakfast cereal to be donated to the relief effort in Asia, appears to have been the victim of piracy on the high seas. The Indigo Princess was last heard from Saturday evening, sending a radio message that she was under attack by another ship. Heavy fog prevented the Indigo Coast Guard from immediately rushing to her aid. When authorities did get to her last reported coordinates the following morning, they found the body of one dead crewman and nothing of the ship itself.

Coast Guard Captain Horus Goldenrod held out hope the ship would yet be found, telling the SUNSET: "Crater Bay is one of the foggiest areas on Earth, and can be a treacherous place to navigate in. If she went off course and veered from the normal shipping lanes, we can't rule out that the Indigo Princess might have run aground on one of the many uncharted islands that speckle the bay."

But Indigo's old salts don't accept Goldenrod's possible version of events. In the seedy bars and fetid flophouses that line the Indigo City wharf district, many experienced sailors are convinced that pirates are on the hunt for plunder in Crater Bay. The area was a favorite haunt of pirates in the 1850s due to its craggy coastline and heavy fog, but in modern times authorities say it has been smugglers who have presented more of a problem than pirates.

The Coast Guard is executing a sweep of the area in hopes of finding clues to the fate of the Indigo Princess. In the meantime, the GOODIOS Company has stepped up efforts to collect another shipload of donated cereal for the Asian relief effort.

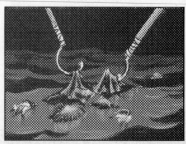

IT IS TO LAUGH!

INDIGO POOP SCOOP! BY IDLE DISH

There's a joke making the rounds of Indigo bars and barbershops concerning a psychiatrist, a gangster and GREYSHIRT that CANNOT be published in a family newspaper. But that didn't stop the distinguished Dr. I. KRAKEM from boring a trapped audience at the Indigo Comedy Club with his pet theories concerning the psychology of humor last night. The good doctor, who is rumored to treat some of the most violent gangsters in the Cerulean City, claims that jokes are merely a mechanism by which we release pent-up emotions and repressed desires. Krakem spent over an hour performing an antiseptic autopsy on the GREYSHIRT joke, eliciting only painful groans from an audience who arrived expecting to be treated to an evening of hearty belly laughs. It turned out that the whole night was a setup, engineered by infamous Indigo practical joker, YUCK UPPEM, who had told the renowned psychiatrist that he would be speaking to a conference of fellow psychologists. But, the joke turned out to be on UPPEM, who, when he finally took the stage and started peppering the room with his trademark rapid-fire gags, found the club empty of any audience except for Krakem, who took it upon himself to analyze all the jokes in Uppem's repertoire ad nauseum.

GREYSHIRT WANNABES? While Indigo City has long been overrun with crazy dames dressing up like mysterious science heroine, COBWEB, now it seems there is a guy or two out there with serious GREYSHIRT fantasies! The Maitre D' at the toney MOOD INDIGO LOUNGE told the POOP SCOOP that a recent performance by diva ELLA BLY was attended by a gentleman gussied up in GREYSHIRT's distinctive Edwardian suit, including mask and cane. The gray-clad clone was reported to be infatuated with the divine Ms. BLY! But then who in Indigo City isn't?

FANMAN TAKES CHARGE! We hear that filming on Fanman Productions' "THE CARBONES: FRANKY AND JOHNNY" was briefly halted last week when the mysterious FANMAN himself decided that certain scenes already in the can needed to be reshot. Sources say director Michael Minstrel had resigned from the troubled bio-pic the day before he died in a tragic traffic accident on Sulphur Street. While no new director has been named, word from deep inside the secretive production is that the elusive FANMAN will be taking a more hands-on approach to completing the film, due for a summer release.

YO HO HO AND A BOTTLE OF RUM! A little parrot tells us that software wünderkind Jack Hawkins has become so obsessed with old pirate movies that he's taken to dressing as Captain Hook and talking like Long John Silver. The sixteen-year-old zillionaire is currently enjoying his fortune . on his 70 ft yacht with the help of a half dozen babelicious young women. No word on whether he's asked any to walk his plank!

ASK DR. SYNTAX

Blackmail Requires Good Manners!

Dear Dr. Syntax: I recently came into possession of some photographs of a well-known Indigo City celebrity. The photos, if they were published in, say, the INDIGO CITY SUNSET, would prove to be very embarrassing (and potentially incriminating) to this person. I'm quite certain this celebrity, who might or might not write a daily column for the SUNSET, would pay handsomely to make certain these photos of him, which could depict him dressed in nothing but a women's caftan and possibly even carousing with farm animals, stay out of circulation.

My question is, what is the correct etiquette when contacting this person to present my demands? Also, is $100,000 in small bills a fair price to ask?--Shakedown

Dear Shakedown: The best way to present demands to potential blackmail victims is with proof that you are actually in possession of the embarrassing material. A good set of prints mailed to the victim's post office box, along with the cash request, is suitable. Most extortion targets are quite willing to accede to reasonable demands if they believe you will act with the proper discretion. When setting a figure, remember that the victim will need all copies of incriminating photos, as well as the negatives, for complete peace of mind.

Dear Doctor Syntax: I was the victim of a brazen daylight robbery recently. The robber held me at gunpoint and was in the process of relieving me of my pocketbook when, by an amazing coincidence, TWO Science Heroes appeared on the scene from different directions. By an incredible stroke of luck, both GREYSHIRT and THE COBWEB had been patrolling nearby and, unaware each other's presence, descended on the criminal and then joined in giving the miscreant a sound thrashing.

While I am grateful for their intervention, I was also a little annoyed at how they proceeded to completely ignore my needs after the crook had been subdued. Even though I was obviously upset, the two of them only had eyes for each other. When I tried to break in and ask for further assistance, they made a lame excuse and hurried off, leaving me to explain what had happened to the police. The last I saw of them, they were ducking into the nearest hotel!

Doctor Syntax, I hope you will print my letter, so other Science Heroes will show more consideration to the victims of crime in Indigo City. Science Heroes may have special powers or be compelled to fight crime, but they mustn't forget that they are still human, as are we all.--Lucky but Peeved

Dear Lucky But Peeved: Perhaps you misunderstood the dynamics of the situation. Certainly such symbols of virtue as GREYSHIRT and THE COBWEB must have been sharing important clues about some impending case. No doubt others were in greater need than yourself; possibly in the very hotel you saw them enter, which forced them to act so brusquely towards you.

SUNSET COMICS

MUSSEL BEACH

By Squid Pro Quo

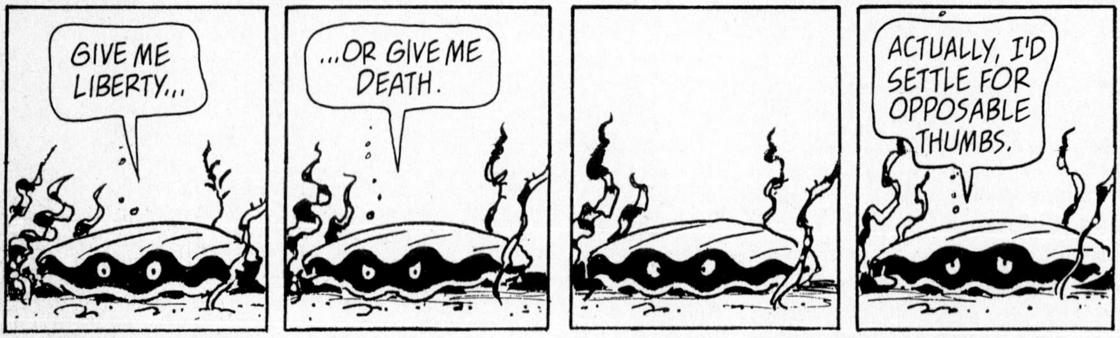
GIVE ME LIBERTY...
...OR GIVE ME DEATH.
ACTUALLY, I'D SETTLE FOR OPPOSABLE THUMBS.

HARRY GEE

By Chet Ghoulash

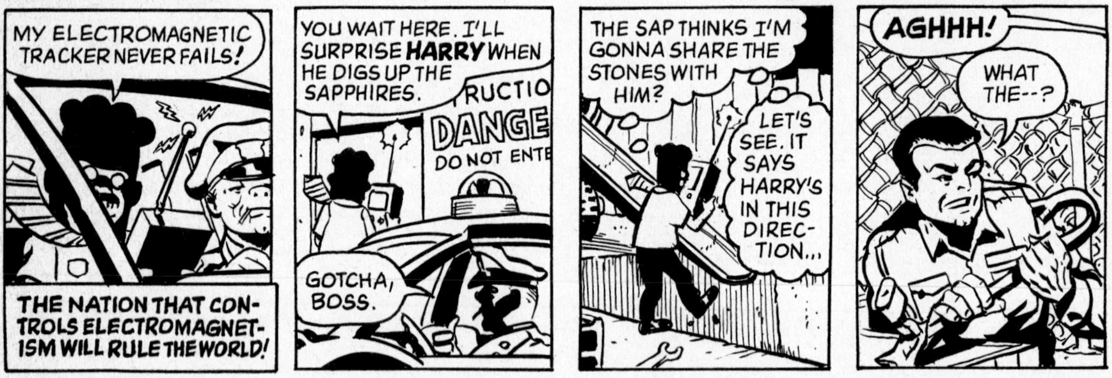
MY ELECTROMAGNETIC TRACKER NEVER FAILS!
THE NATION THAT CONTROLS ELECTROMAGNETISM WILL RULE THE WORLD!
YOU WAIT HERE. I'LL SURPRISE HARRY WHEN HE DIGS UP THE SAPPHIRES.
RUCTIO
DANGE
DO NOT ENTE
GOTCHA, BOSS.
THE SAP THINKS I'M GONNA SHARE THE STONES WITH HIM?
LET'S SEE. IT SAYS HARRY'S IN THIS DIRECTION...
AGHHH!
WHAT THE--?

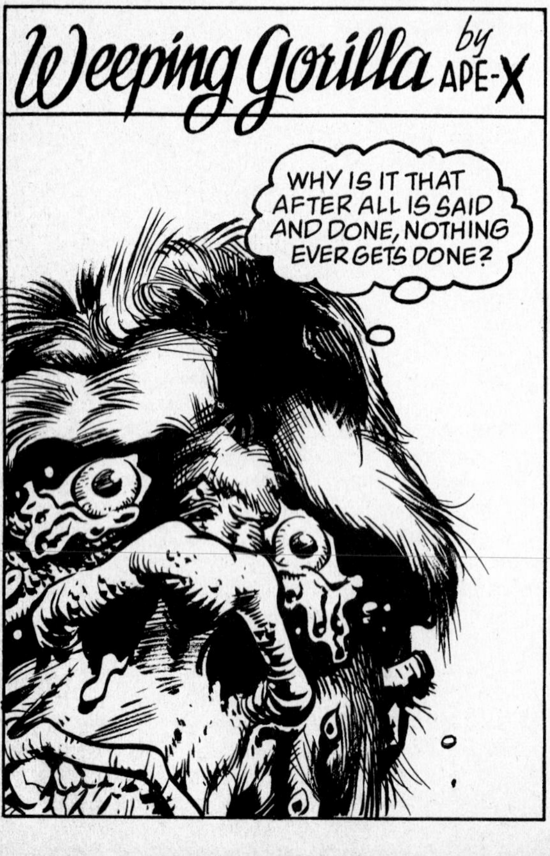
Weeping Gorilla by APE-X
WHY IS IT THAT AFTER ALL IS SAID AND DONE, NOTHING EVER GETS DONE?

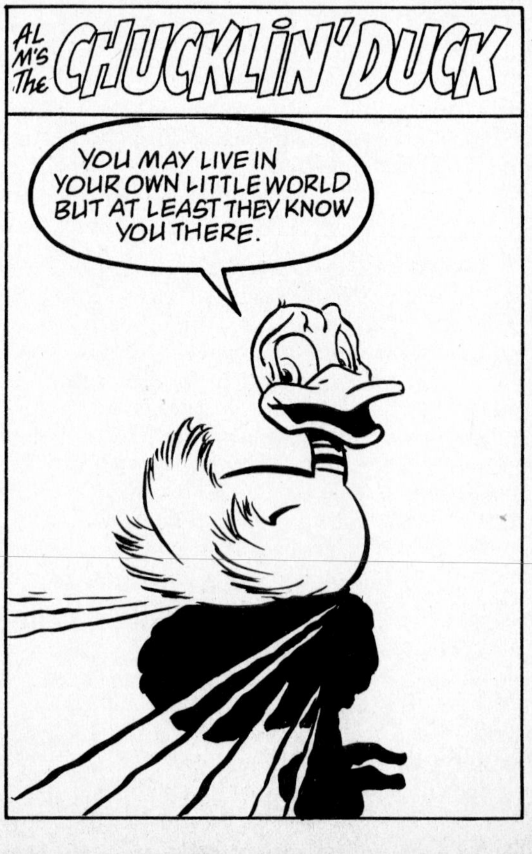
AL M'S The CHUCKLIN' DUCK
YOU MAY LIVE IN YOUR OWN LITTLE WORLD BUT AT LEAST THEY KNOW YOU THERE.

FOR INDIGO KIDS OF ALL AGES!

BOWSER THE SCHNAUZER

By Yowzuh Trousers

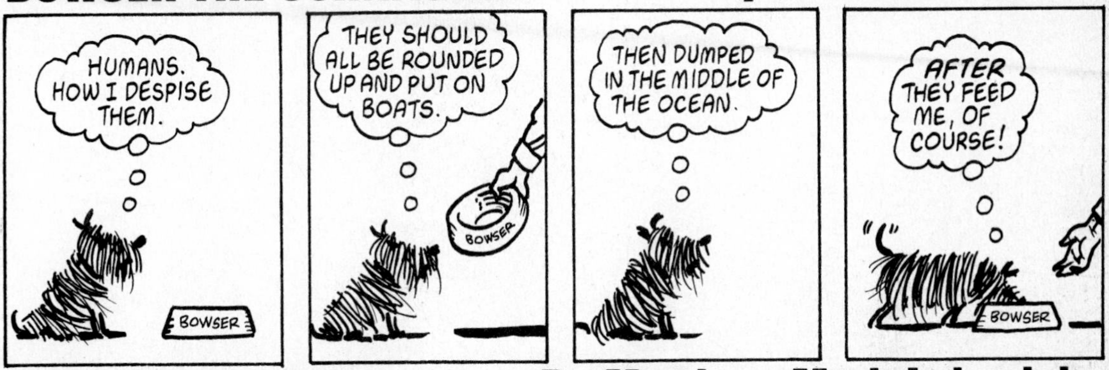
HUMANS. HOW I DESPISE THEM.
BOWSER
THEY SHOULD ALL BE ROUNDED UP AND PUT ON BOATS.
BOWSER
THEN DUMPED IN THE MIDDLE OF THE OCEAN.
AFTER THEY FEED ME, OF COURSE!
BOWSER

MADAM I'M ADAM

By Matthew Mark Lukenjohn

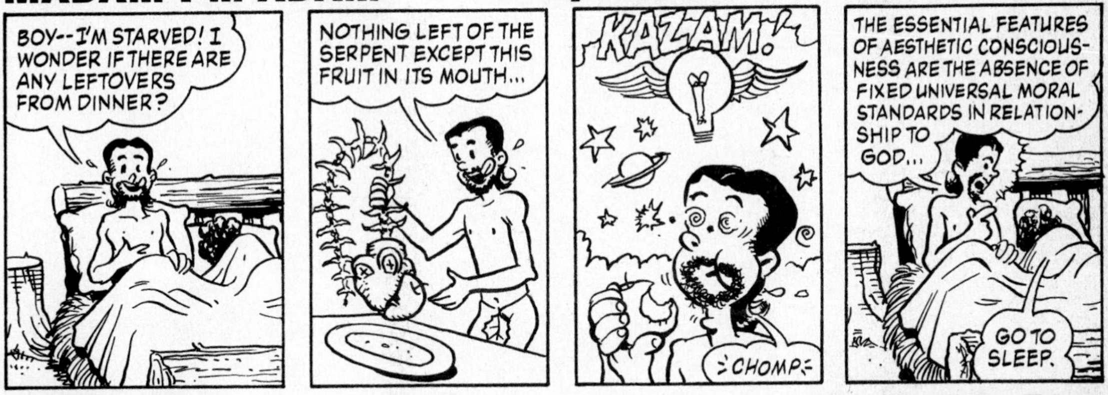
BOY--I'M STARVED! I WONDER IF THERE ARE ANY LEFTOVERS FROM DINNER?
NOTHING LEFT OF THE SERPENT EXCEPT THIS FRUIT IN ITS MOUTH...
KAZAM!
CHOMP
THE ESSENTIAL FEATURES OF AESTHETIC CONSCIOUSNESS ARE THE ABSENCE OF FIXED UNIVERSAL MORAL STANDARDS IN RELATIONSHIP TO GOD...
GO TO SLEEP.

GOODIOS

ADVERTISEMENT

By Buddy Fact

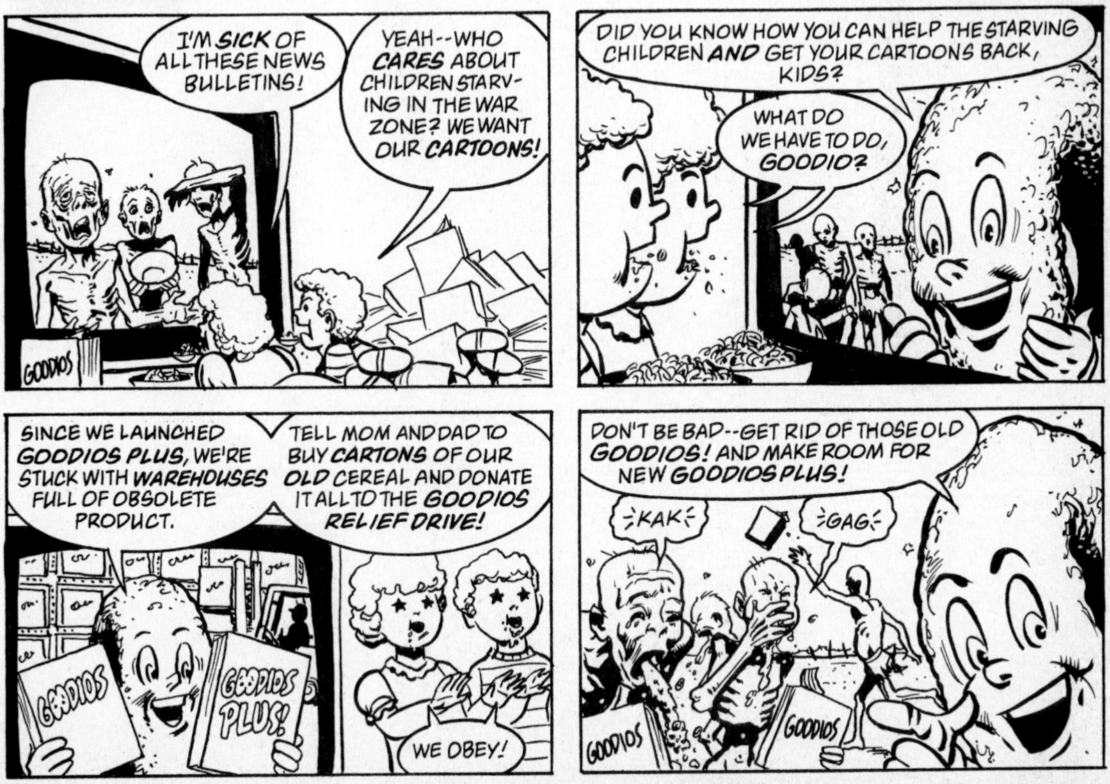
I'M SICK OF ALL THESE NEWS BULLETINS!
YEAH--WHO CARES ABOUT CHILDREN STARVING IN THE WAR ZONE? WE WANT OUR CARTOONS!
GOODIOS
DID YOU KNOW HOW YOU CAN HELP THE STARVING CHILDREN AND GET YOUR CARTOONS BACK, KIDS?
WHAT DO WE HAVE TO DO, GOODIO?
SINCE WE LAUNCHED GOODIOS PLUS, WE'RE STUCK WITH WAREHOUSES FULL OF OBSOLETE PRODUCT.
TELL MOM AND DAD TO BUY CARTONS OF OUR OLD CEREAL AND DONATE IT ALL TO THE GOODIOS RELIEF DRIVE!
GOODIOS
GOODIOS PLUS!
WE OBEY!
DON'T BE BAD--GET RID OF THOSE OLD GOODIOS! AND MAKE ROOM FOR NEW GOODIOS PLUS!
KAK
GAG
GOODIOS
GOODIOS

ELLA! *Indigo's Celebrated Songbird Reflects On Her Life of Triumph and Tragedy!*

She may be one of Indigo City's most sought-after celebrities, but Ella Bly doesn't enter a room the way you'd expect a diva of her stature to arrive. Though tall and shapely, she keeps to the shadows, as if avoiding bringing any undue attention to herself. And when in public she doesn't wear her trademark bleach-blonde tresses with the long bangs that serve to cover her once regal cheekbones. Music lovers who regularly pack her performances at the MOOD INDIGO may think the subdued lighting and extravagant wig are all part of the act, but when one sits across a table from Ella Bly in broad daylight, the reasons for her actions and image are painfully clear. A vicious attack she sustained ten years ago left her beautiful features mutilated beyond repair.

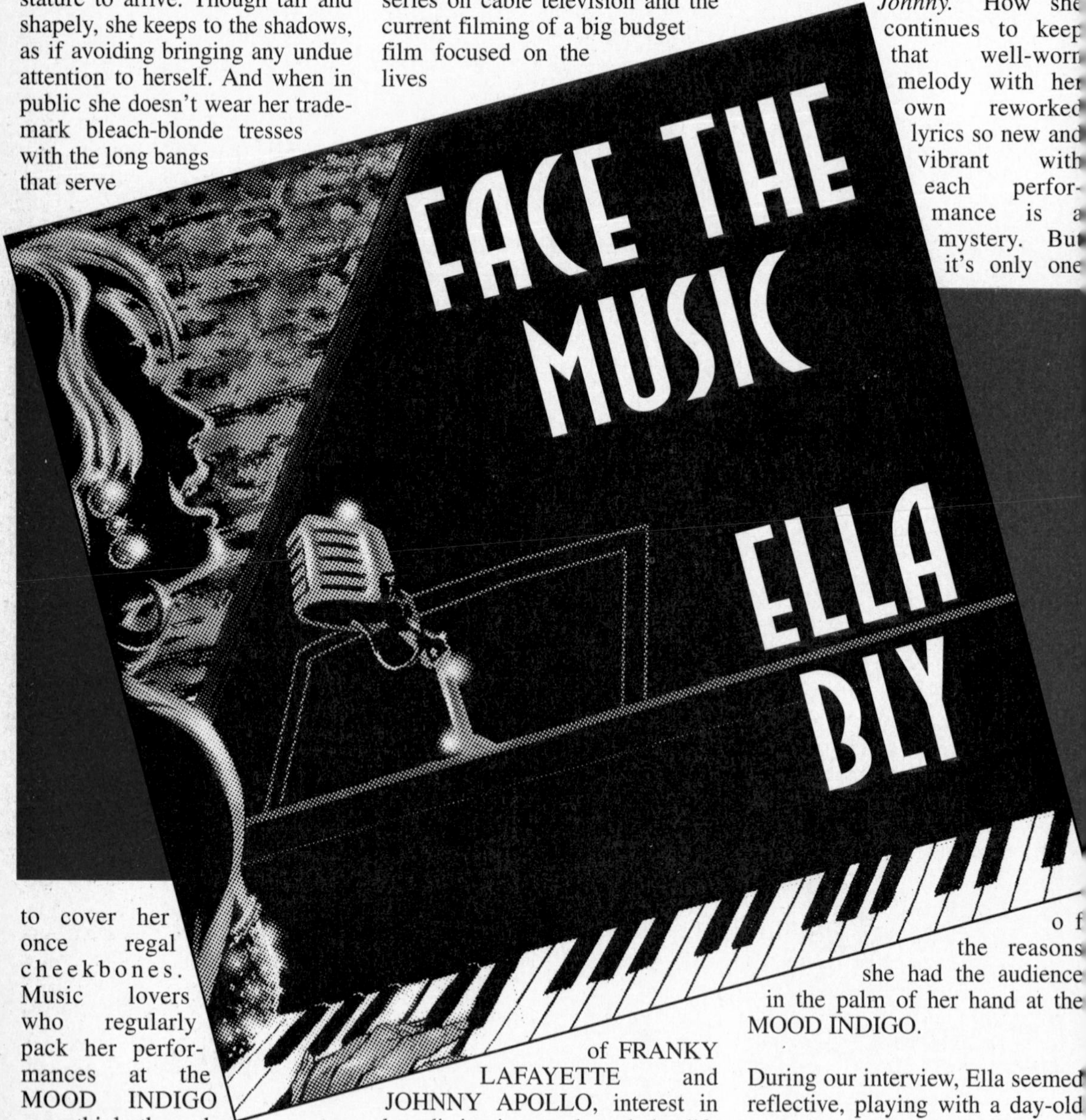
FACE THE MUSIC
ELLA BLY

Since breaking onto the INDIGO music scene with her first hit record, *"The Ballad of Franky and Johnny,"* Ella has never gone out of style. But, with the recent success of the "THE CARBONES" series on cable television and the current filming of a big budget film focused on the lives of FRANKY LAFAYETTE and JOHNNY APOLLO, interest in her distinctive work and the life she led growing up in INDIGO CITY have moved her up to "landmark" status.

The SUNSET caught up with Ms. Bly following another triumph at the MOOD INDIGO LOUNGE. The irony she gave to the Rogers and Hammerstein song, *"I've Grown Accustomed To Your Face"* provided a new and haunting dimension to the old *MY FAIR LADY* chestnut. And she brought down the house when she ended with a soulful, bluesy rendition of *"The Ballad Of Franky and Johnny."* How she continues to keep that well-worn melody with her own reworked lyrics so new and vibrant with each performance is a mystery. But it's only one of the reasons she had the audience in the palm of her hand at the MOOD INDIGO.

During our interview, Ella seemed reflective, playing with a day-old carnation given to her by some lovestruck fan in her delicate fingers. As she spoke of her life and times in Indigo's Bottoms Up district she frequently raised the carnation to the ruins of her face to take in its scent. If a single word could describe this complex star's mood that day it would be "wistful." More than anything, Ella Bly demonstrated that she possesses an inner beauty, forged of tragedy, and that it is more than skin deep.

SUNSET: *Are you surprised by the recent surge of interest in FRANKY LAFAYETTE and JOHNNY APOLLO?*

ELLA: Not much surprises me anymore, I'm afraid. But it is a little strange to see the lives of a couple people I knew being turned into a collective myth.

SUNSET: *How close were you to Lafayette and Apollo? Some say you were born in the same neighborhood.*

ELLA: We all grew up in the BOTTOMS UP district. Went to the same school. I remember those two when they were a couple of juvenile delinquents hawking Tijuana Bibles in study hall. I never liked Johnny that much. He was...not especially nice. Franky was the one I was closer to.

SUNSET: *How close? There are published rumors you and he had a secret love affair!*

ELLA: Franky used to say, "Don't believe everything you read in THE SUNSET!" We were like brother and sister, he and I; not a steady couple. We might not see each other for months, then he'd turn up at my window and we'd pick right up where we left off as if no time had passed at all.

SUNSET: *What was he like in real life?*

ELLA: Franky was a beautiful guy. Very physical. He moved like Nureyev. Not the sharpest tool in the shed, but he had a way of looking at you with those piercing eyes that kind of went right to the deepest part of your soul. And when he went after something, there was no stopping him. He wasn't really a criminal type, either, if you know what I mean. He was always questioning the gangster lifestyle he'd sort of inherited from his father. I think if he'd lived he would have gone on to do something else. Maybe something great.

SUNSET: *Which is just opposite of the way he's portrayed on televi-*

sion. *In "THE CARBONES," he's really the dark side of the Franky and Johnny team.*

ELLA: Yeah, well that's one of the problems I have with the tube version. They make Johnny Apollo out to be some sort of hero and Franky's depicted as this ugly thug. I just hope they don't continue that in the film.

SUNSET: *What was Johnny Apollo really like?*

ELLA: Johnny? Well...he wasn't my favorite human being. I'll just leave it at that.

SUNSET: *But the way Kenneth Fury plays him, we think of him as a misunderstood character; sort of vulnerable and empathic. Are you saying the real Johnny wasn't like that?*

ELLA: Nothing like that. The only way to describe Johnny Apollo is "schizo." He was like two personalities fighting for control of a single body. One minute he'd be nice as pie, then the next he'd be waving a knife in someone's face.

SUNSET: *Will you be providing any music for the upcoming film?*

ELLA: You'd think that with my *"The Ballad Of Franky And Johnny"* gone triple platinum they'd have asked me, wouldn't you? Instead I hear they're going to use the STANLEY AND THE STALEMATES version. I guess Fanman Productions owns the rights, and of course it's aimed more at the youth market.

SUNSET: *You mean the so-called "alternative sound?"*

ELLA: Yeah. Well, it's all a marketing shuck. But I never liked how Stanley And The Stalemates reworked the lyrics from my version. I don't get why everyone wants to make Johnny Apollo the hero of this sordid little tale.

SUNSET: *Speaking of the sordid side of things, there are a number of competing stories about how you came by the scars on your*

face.

ELLA: The official biography is the right version. When I was trying to get a foothold in the music business I used to take in laundry. Some punks broke into my place and attacked me with a hot steam iron. Just another Bottoms Up tragedy.

SUNSET: *How did you cope?*

ELLA: It wasn't easy. At first, I thought that by losing my looks my chances for a singing career were over. But I still had my voice and somehow the experience broadened and deepened my emotional range. I put together some demo tapes and when the record company heard them they went nuts. These were the same guys that told me I didn't have a prayer six months earlier. They released *"The Ballad Of Franky And Johnny"* as a single and helped me put together a stage act so I could appear live without scaring audiences. The rest is history.

SUNSET: *Franky Lafayette and Johnny Apollo perished in an explosion over ten years ago. If you had a chance to say anything to either of them, what would it be?*

ELLA: To Johnny, I'd say "Rot in Hell." If Franky were here today, I'd say...I don't know. "Listen to my song," I guess. That says it all.

ELLA BLY appears nightly at the MOOD INDIGO on Beryl Street and Butane Avenue. Her latest album, *FACE THE MUSIC,* has just been released on LILAC RECORDS. For more information, contact the paper's arts staff at 555-2882:

JIM LEE
Editorial Director
JOHN NEE
VP & General Manager
SCOTT DUNBIER
Group Editor

Or write to SUNSET LETTERS, 888 Prospect Street, Suite 240, La Jolla, CA 92037
email: sunset@wildstorm.com

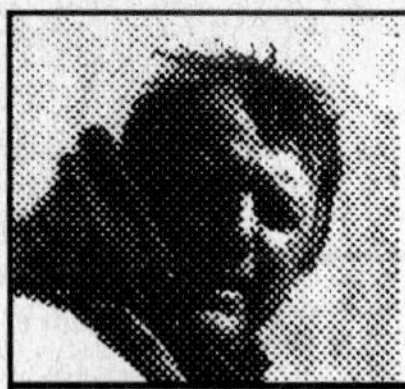

RICK VEITCH
Writer-Artist denies Madonna rumors, Page 12

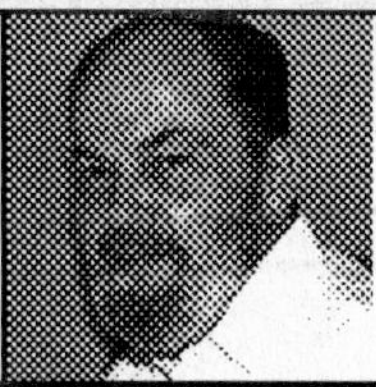

JOHN SEVERIN
Venerable artist proves two fists better than one! Page 14

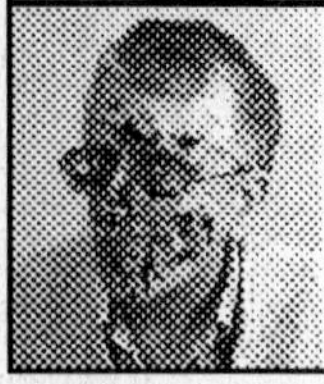

TODD KLEIN
Letterer's leaking technical pen horror! Page 15

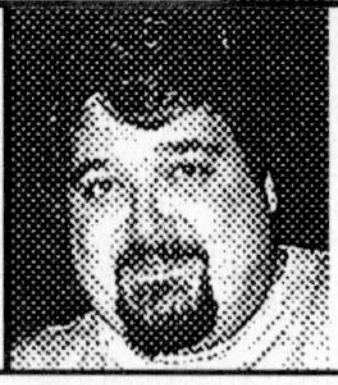

SCOTT DUNBIER
Editor's nose out of joint, demands equal billing! Pg 16

WILDSTORM FX: What color are their parachutes?

ALL THE NEWS FROM DAWN TO DUSK

INDIGO CITY SUNSET

AFTERNOON CITY EDITION

Tuesday, February 19, 2002 Metro Weather – Today: Low-lying Mist, Tonight: Deepening Fog, Tomorrow: Pea Soup

BACK PAGE EXTRA:

CELL MATES OR SOUL MATES?

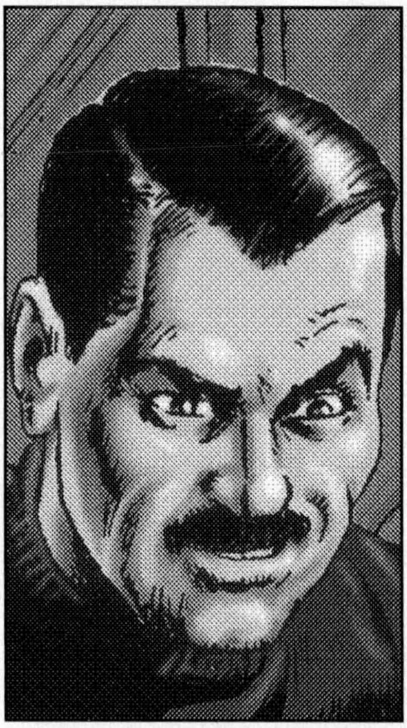

Master Thief BRUNO IMBROGLIO

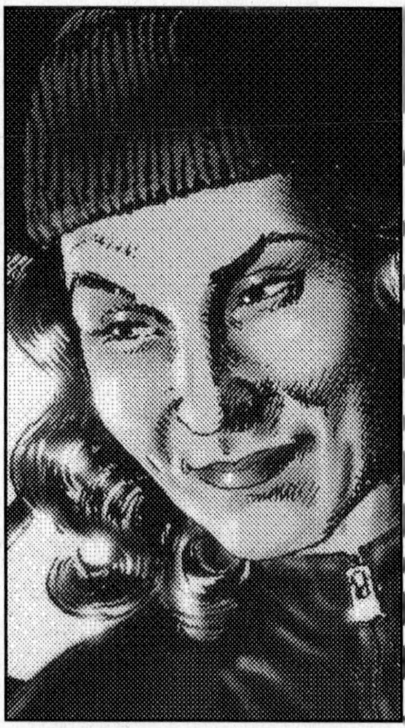

Cat Burglar SABRA DESADE

STAR OF INDIGO HEIST ENDS IN CRIMINAL EMBRACE!!

Special to The Sunset
by Geekus Crow

The fabled Star Of Indigo went on display this week at the Indigo City Museum of Natural History, attracting huge crowds fascinated by the jewel's mythical ability to act as a powerful love potion. The twenty-two pound perfect Star Sapphire, originally unearthed near Indigo Bay in pre-Columbian times, has also enflamed the desires of the city's criminal element. Last night GREYSHIRT and the Indigo City Police surprised two infamous Indigo burglars in mid-robbery and in each other's arms.

FULL STORY: PAGE 20

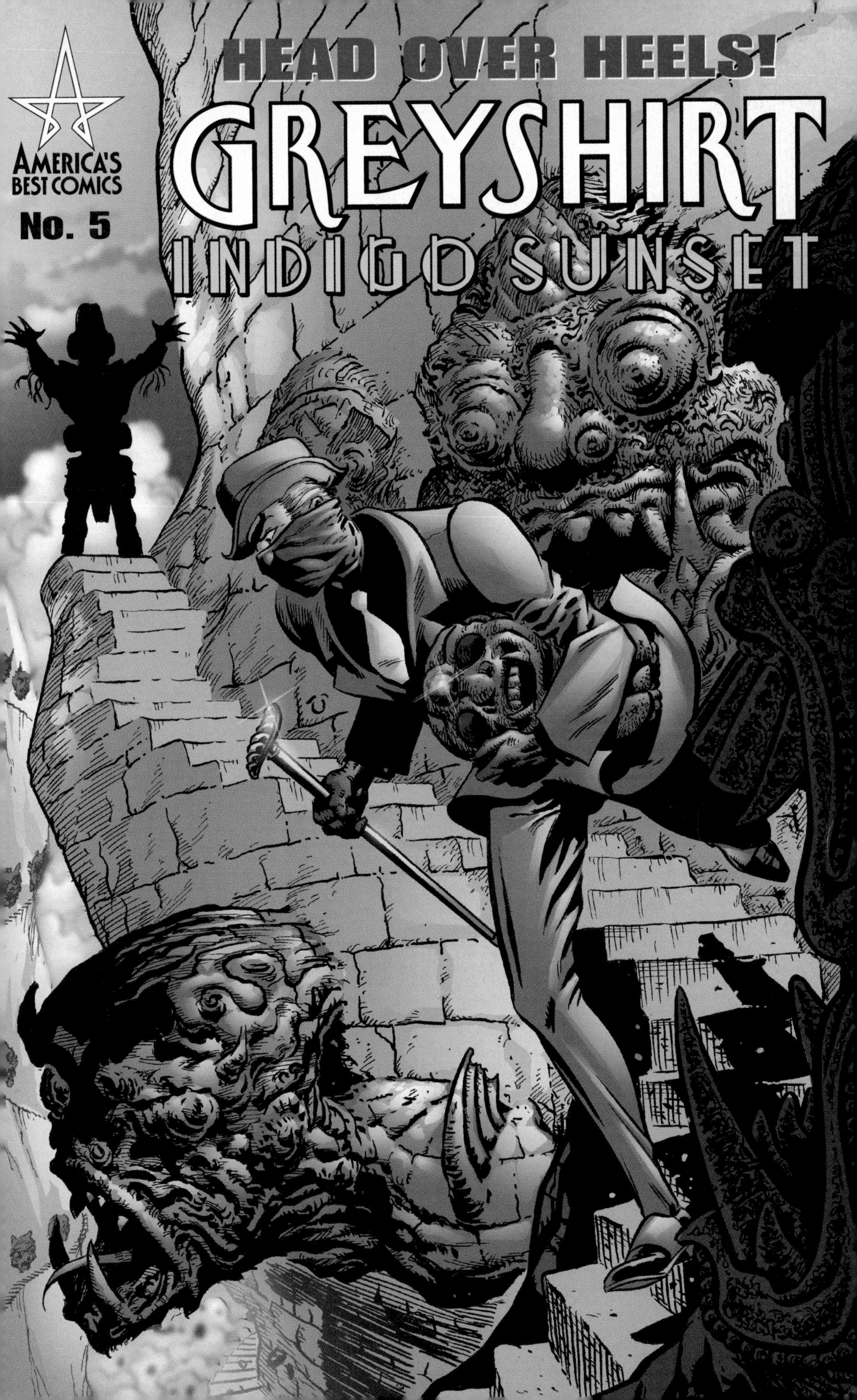
HEAD OVER HEELS!
AMERICA'S BEST COMICS
No. 5
GREYSHIRT
INDIGO SUNSET

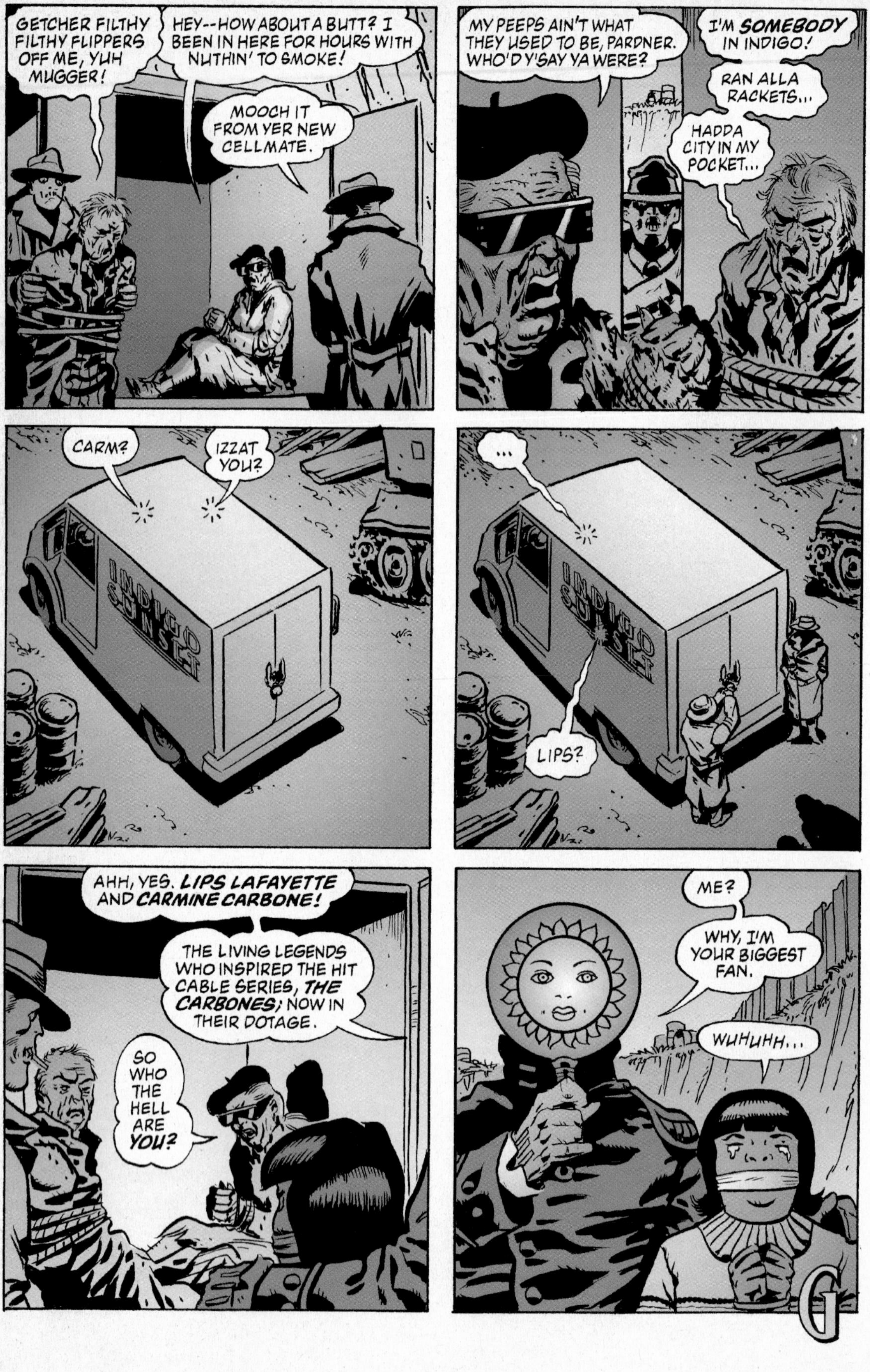
GETCHER FILTHY FILTHY FLIPPERS OFF ME, YUH MUGGER!
HEY--HOW ABOUT A BUTT? I BEEN IN HERE FOR HOURS WITH NUTHIN' TO SMOKE!
MOOCH IT FROM YER NEW CELLMATE.
MY PEEPS AIN'T WHAT THEY USED TO BE, PARDNER. WHO'D Y'SAY YA WERE?
I'M SOMEBODY IN INDIGO!
RAN ALLA RACKETS...
HADDA CITY IN MY POCKET...
CARM?
IZZAT YOU?
INDIGO SUNSET
...
INDIGO SUNSET
LIPS?
AHH, YES. LIPS LAFAYETTE AND CARMINE CARBONE!
THE LIVING LEGENDS WHO INSPIRED THE HIT CABLE SERIES, THE CARBONES; NOW IN THEIR DOTAGE.
SO WHO THE HELL ARE YOU?
ME?
WHY, I'M YOUR BIGGEST FAN.
WUHUHH...

THE CRONE SITS GLOWERING; STONE-FACED AND ALONE.
INDIGO CITY CENTRAL STATION
CAUTION: GAS STORAGE FACILITY HIGHLY FLAMMABLE! OPEN FLAMES FORBIDDEN
FORGOTTEN IN THE RUINS OF HER ORACULUM.
IN A PREVIOUS EPOCH, HER PALACE SERVED THE INHABITANTS OF A GREAT CITY.
HOW THEY LINED UP BEFORE HER! CRIMELORDS JOSTLING PETTY CROOKS, HOUSEWIVES SHOULDER TO SHOULDER WITH HARLOTS, CAPTAINS OF INDUSTRY WAITING PATIENTLY FOR NEWSBOYS HAWKING THE MORNING SUNSET.
COUNTLESS THIN SILVER DIMES WERE SLOTTED INTO HER CASH BOX AS TRIBUTE.
AND TINY PAPER PROPHECIES, INSCRIBED IN 12-POINT BODONI BOLD, WERE SPAT ONTO PALMS ALREADY MOIST WITH WORRY AND DOUBT.
NOW LONG FORSAKEN BY HER PETITIONERS, THE CRONE CAN ONLY SCOWL THROUGH THE POISONOUS FUMES AND AND MEPHITIC EMPTINESS.
THERE ARE NO FATES TO AUGUR BUT HER OWN.
Young GREYSHIRT: 1989
INSERT 10¢ KNOW YOUR FATE
ORACLE: RICK VEITCH
RUNEWORK: TODD KLEIN
WIZARDRY: WILDSTORM FX
HARBINGERS: QUINN & POZNER
DIVINATION: SCOTT DUNBIER
PYTHONIST: ALAN MOORE
GREYSHIRT CREATED BY MOORE & VEITCH

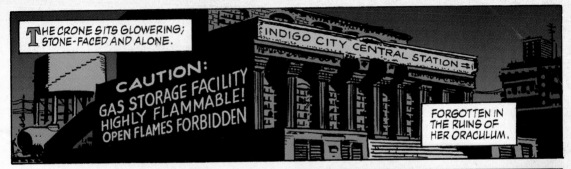

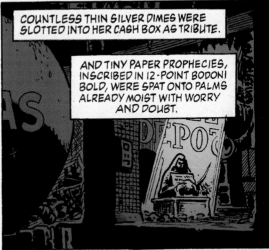

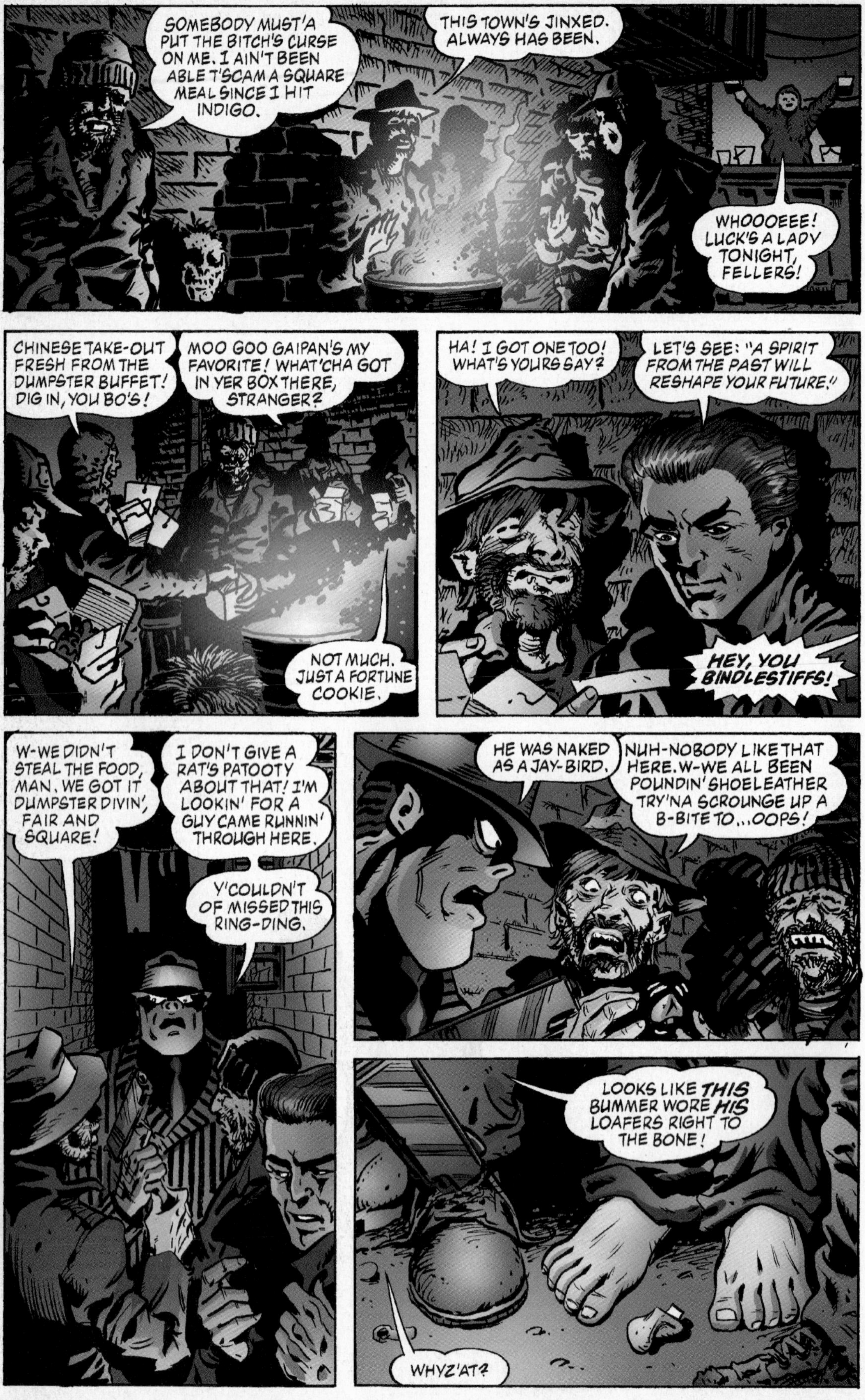
SOMEBODY MUST'A PUT THE BITCH'S CURSE ON ME. I AIN'T BEEN ABLE T'SCAM A SQUARE MEAL SINCE I HIT INDIGO.
THIS TOWN'S JINXED. ALWAYS HAS BEEN.
WHOOOEEE! LUCK'S A LADY TONIGHT, FELLERS!
CHINESE TAKE-OUT FRESH FROM THE DUMPSTER BUFFET! DIG IN, YOU BO'S!
MOO GOO GAIPAN'S MY FAVORITE! WHAT'CHA GOT IN YER BOX THERE, STRANGER?
NOT MUCH. JUST A FORTUNE COOKIE.
HA! I GOT ONE TOO! WHAT'S YOURS SAY?
LET'S SEE: "A SPIRIT FROM THE PAST WILL RESHAPE YOUR FUTURE."
HEY, YOU BINDLESTIFFS!
W-WE DIDN'T STEAL THE FOOD, MAN. WE GOT IT DUMPSTER DIVIN', FAIR AND SQUARE!
I DON'T GIVE A RAT'S PATOOTY ABOUT THAT! I'M LOOKIN' FOR A GUY CAME RUNNIN' THROUGH HERE.
Y'COULDN'T OF MISSED THIS RING-DING.
HE WAS NAKED AS A JAY-BIRD.
NUH-NOBODY LIKE THAT HERE. W-WE ALL BEEN POUNDIN' SHOELEATHER TRY'NA SCROUNGE UP A B-BITE TO...OOPS!
LOOKS LIKE THIS BUMMER WORE HIS LOAFERS RIGHT TO THE BONE!
WHYZ'AT?

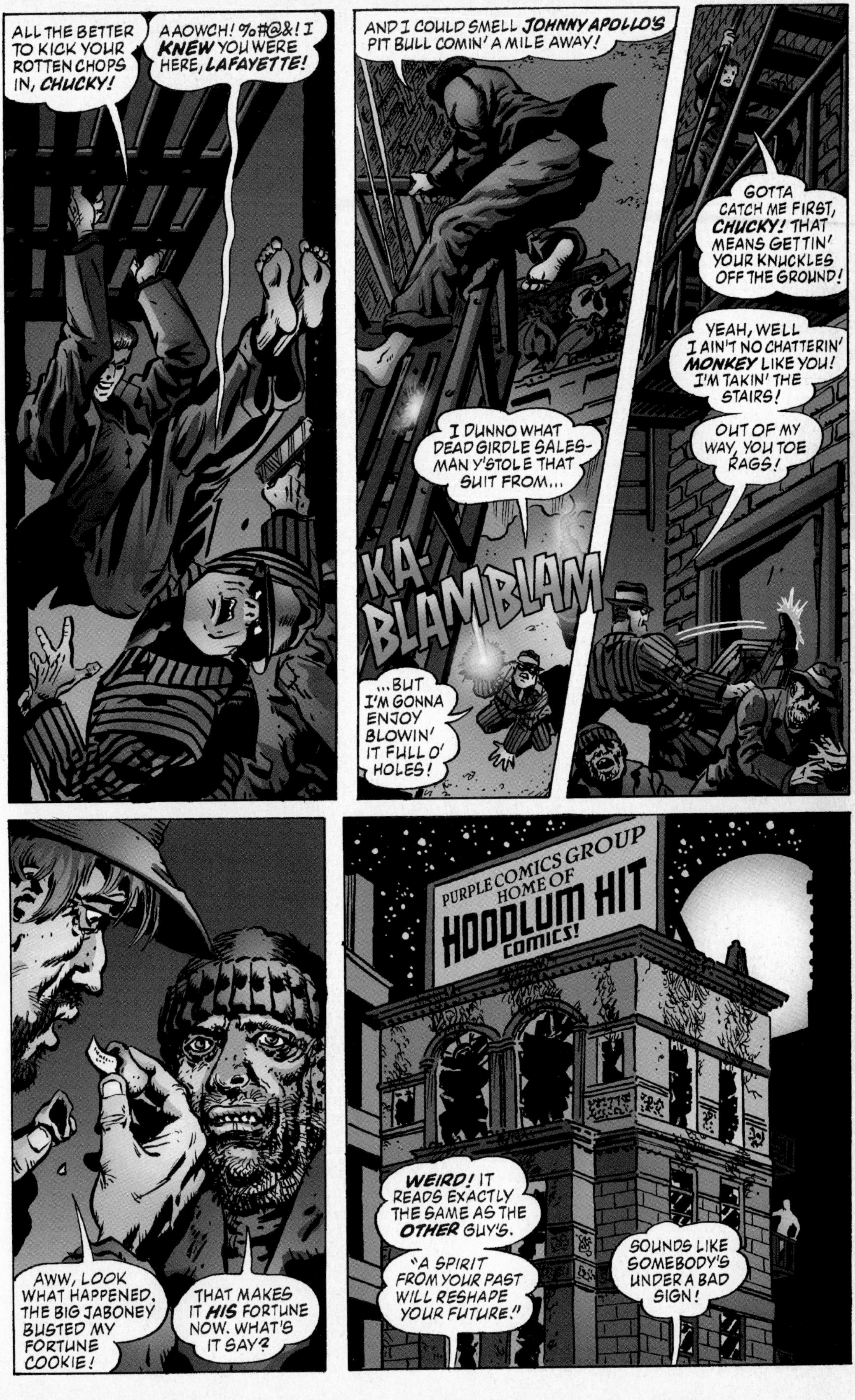
ALL THE BETTER TO KICK YOUR ROTTEN CHOPS IN, CHUCKY!
AAOWCH! %#@&! I KNEW YOU WERE HERE, LAFAYETTE!
AND I COULD SMELL JOHNNY APOLLO'S PIT BULL COMIN' A MILE AWAY!
I DUNNO WHAT DEAD GIRDLE SALES-MAN Y'STOLE THAT SUIT FROM...
KA-BLAMBLAM
...BUT I'M GONNA ENJOY BLOWIN' IT FULL O' HOLES!
GOTTA CATCH ME FIRST, CHUCKY! THAT MEANS GETTIN' YOUR KNUCKLES OFF THE GROUND!
YEAH, WELL I AIN'T NO CHATTERIN' MONKEY LIKE YOU! I'M TAKIN' THE STAIRS!
OUT OF MY WAY, YOU TOE RAGS!
AWW, LOOK WHAT HAPPENED. THE BIG JABONEY BUSTED MY FORTUNE COOKIE!
THAT MAKES IT HIS FORTUNE NOW. WHAT'S IT SAY?
PURPLE COMICS GROUP HOME OF HOODLUM HIT COMICS!
WEIRD! IT READS EXACTLY THE SAME AS THE OTHER GUY'S.
"A SPIRIT FROM YOUR PAST WILL RESHAPE YOUR FUTURE."
SOUNDS LIKE SOMEBODY'S UNDER A BAD SIGN!

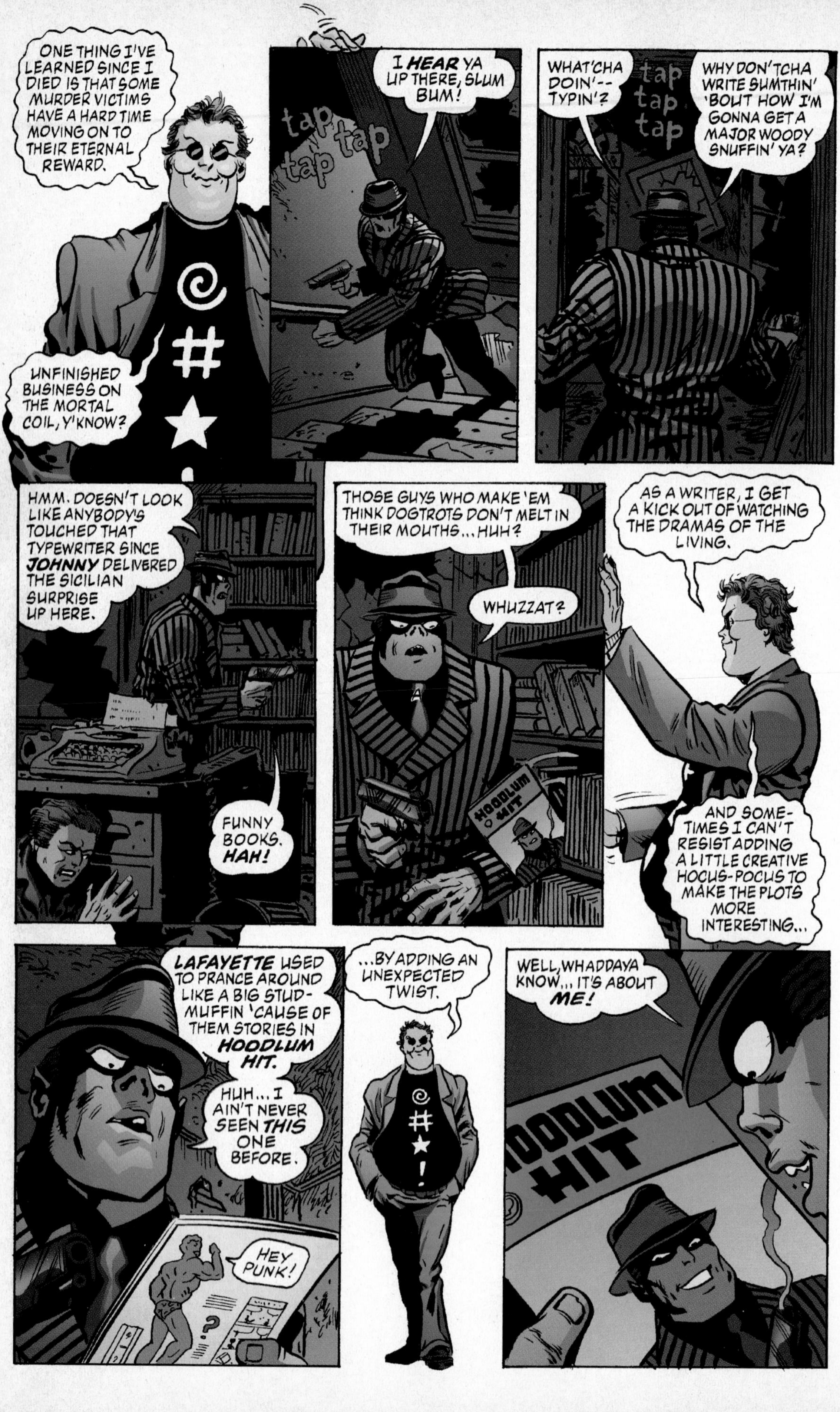
ONE THING I'VE LEARNED SINCE I DIED IS THAT SOME MURDER VICTIMS HAVE A HARD TIME MOVING ON TO THEIR ETERNAL REWARD.
UNFINISHED BUSINESS ON THE MORTAL COIL, Y'KNOW?
tap tap tap tap
I HEAR YA UP THERE, SLUM BUM!
WHAT'CHA DOIN'-- TYPIN'?
tap tap tap
WHY DON'TCHA WRITE SUMTHIN' 'BOUT HOW I'M GONNA GET A MAJOR WOODY SNUFFIN' YA?
HMM. DOESN'T LOOK LIKE ANYBODY'S TOUCHED THAT TYPEWRITER SINCE JOHNNY DELIVERED THE SICILIAN SURPRISE UP HERE.
FUNNY BOOKS. HAH!
THOSE GUYS WHO MAKE 'EM THINK DOGTROTS DON'T MELT IN THEIR MOUTHS... HUH?
WHUZZAT?
HOODLUM HIT
AS A WRITER, I GET A KICK OUT OF WATCHING THE DRAMAS OF THE LIVING.
AND SOMETIMES I CAN'T RESIST ADDING A LITTLE CREATIVE HOCUS-POCUS TO MAKE THE PLOTS MORE INTERESTING...
LAFAYETTE USED TO PRANCE AROUND LIKE A BIG STUD-MUFFIN 'CAUSE OF THEM STORIES IN HOODLUM HIT.
HUH... I AIN'T NEVER SEEN THIS ONE BEFORE.
HEY PUNK!
...BY ADDING AN UNEXPECTED TWIST.
WELL, WHADDAYA KNOW... IT'S ABOUT ME!
HOODLUM HIT

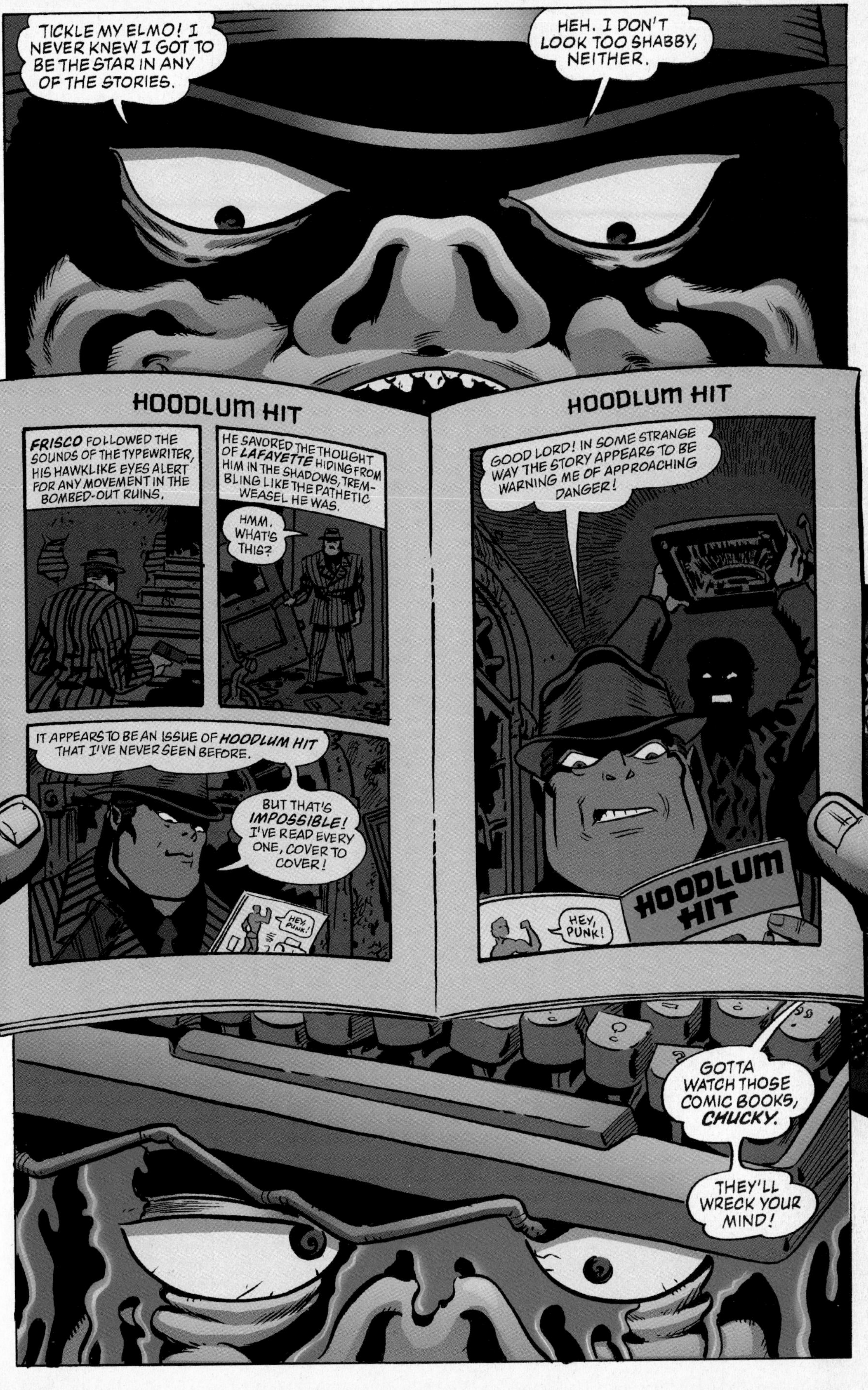
TICKLE MY ELMO! I NEVER KNEW I GOT TO BE THE STAR IN ANY OF THE STORIES.
HEH. I DON'T LOOK TOO SHABBY, NEITHER.
HOODLUM HIT
FRISCO FOLLOWED THE SOUNDS OF THE TYPEWRITER, HIS HAWKLIKE EYES ALERT FOR ANY MOVEMENT IN THE BOMBED-OUT RUINS.
HE SAVORED THE THOUGHT OF LAFAYETTE HIDING FROM HIM IN THE SHADOWS, TREMBLING LIKE THE PATHETIC WEASEL HE WAS.
HMM. WHAT'S THIS?
IT APPEARS TO BE AN ISSUE OF HOODLUM HIT THAT I'VE NEVER SEEN BEFORE.
BUT THAT'S IMPOSSIBLE! I'VE READ EVERY ONE, COVER TO COVER!
HEY, PUNK!
HOODLUM HIT
GOOD LORD! IN SOME STRANGE WAY THE STORY APPEARS TO BE WARNING ME OF APPROACHING DANGER!
HEY, PUNK!
HOODLUM HIT
GOTTA WATCH THOSE COMIC BOOKS, CHUCKY.
THEY'LL WRECK YOUR MIND!

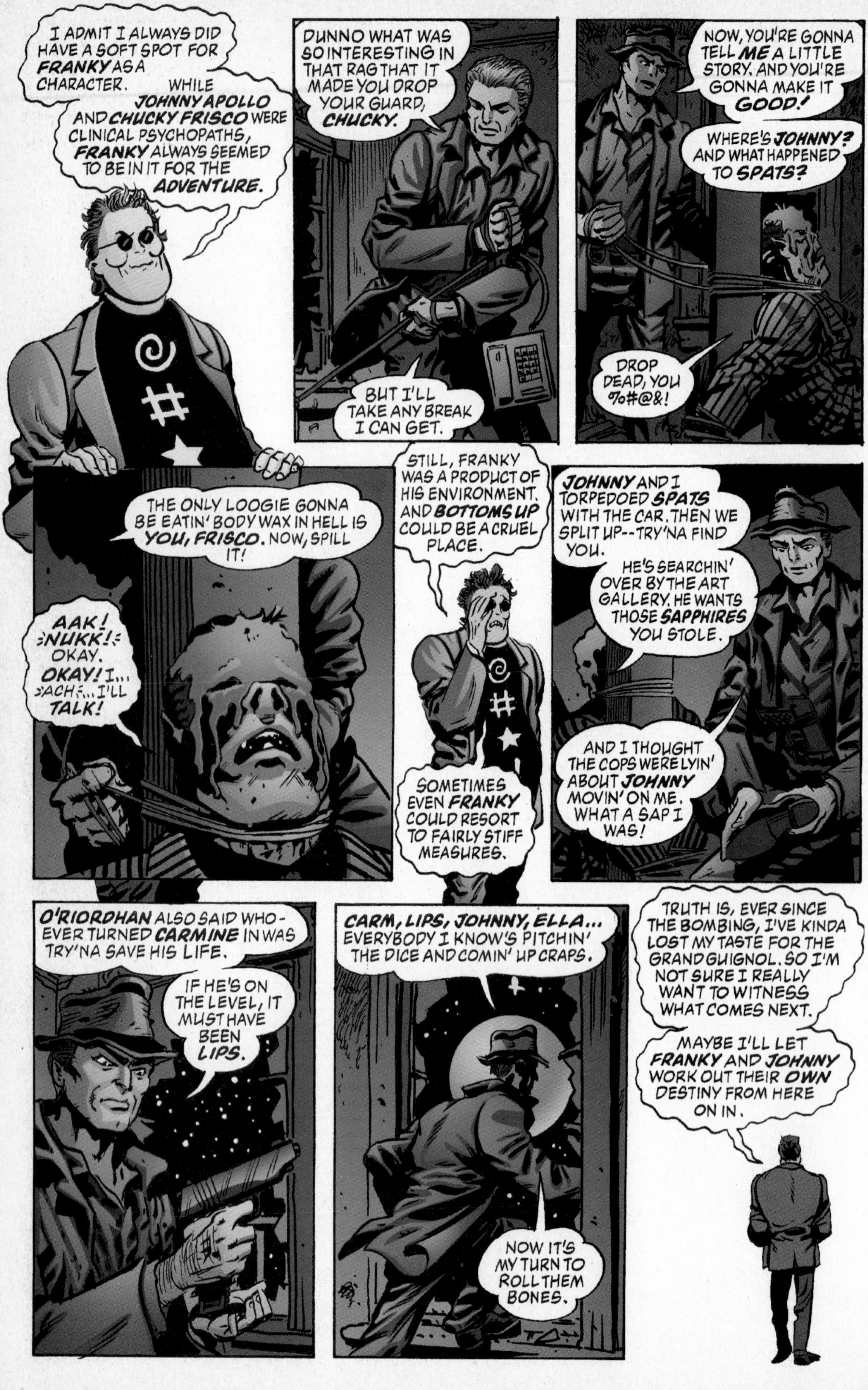
I ADMIT I ALWAYS DID HAVE A SOFT SPOT FOR FRANKY AS A CHARACTER.
WHILE JOHNNY APOLLO AND CHUCKY FRISCO WERE CLINICAL PSYCHOPATHS, FRANKY ALWAYS SEEMED TO BE IN IT FOR THE ADVENTURE.
DUNNO WHAT WAS SO INTERESTING IN THAT RAG THAT IT MADE YOU DROP YOUR GUARD, CHUCKY.
BUT I'LL TAKE ANY BREAK I CAN GET.
NOW, YOU'RE GONNA TELL ME A LITTLE STORY. AND YOU'RE GONNA MAKE IT GOOD!
WHERE'S JOHNNY? AND WHAT HAPPENED TO SPATS?
DROP DEAD, YOU %#@&!
THE ONLY LOOGIE GONNA BE EATIN' BODY WAX IN HELL IS YOU, FRISCO. NOW, SPILL IT!
AAK! NUKK! OKAY. OKAY! I... ACH... I'LL TALK!
STILL, FRANKY WAS A PRODUCT OF HIS ENVIRONMENT. AND BOTTOMS UP COULD BE A CRUEL PLACE.
SOMETIMES EVEN FRANKY COULD RESORT TO FAIRLY STIFF MEASURES.
JOHNNY AND I TORPEDOED SPATS WITH THE CAR. THEN WE SPLIT UP--TRY'NA FIND YOU.
HE'S SEARCHIN' OVER BY THE ART GALLERY. HE WANTS THOSE SAPPHIRES YOU STOLE.
AND I THOUGHT THE COPS WERE LYIN' ABOUT JOHNNY MOVIN' ON ME. WHAT A SAP I WAS!
O'RIORDHAN ALSO SAID WHO-EVER TURNED CARMINE IN WAS TRY'NA SAVE HIS LIFE.
IF HE'S ON THE LEVEL, IT MUST HAVE BEEN LIPS.
CARM, LIPS, JOHNNY, ELLA... EVERYBODY I KNOW'S PITCHIN' THE DICE AND COMIN' UP CRAPS.
NOW IT'S MY TURN TO ROLL THEM BONES.
TRUTH IS, EVER SINCE THE BOMBING, I'VE KINDA LOST MY TASTE FOR THE GRAND GUIGNOL. SO I'M NOT SURE I REALLY WANT TO WITNESS WHAT COMES NEXT.
MAYBE I'LL LET FRANKY AND JOHNNY WORK OUT THEIR OWN DESTINY FROM HERE ON IN.

SO HOW'S LIFE TREATING **MRS. LAFAYETTE?**

IT'S **MISS** LAFAYETTE, AND I CAN'T DECIDE WHETHER TO HANG MYSELF OR SLIT MY THROAT.

HOW'S BY YOU?

OH, UHHH... **MISS.** OF COURSE. SORRY. UMMM... LET'S SEE, NOW...

LOOKS LIKE IT'S A GIRL FROM THE ULTRASOUND. YOU THINK YOU'RE AROUND SIX MONTHS ALONG?

SOMETHIN' LIKE THAT. THIS LAST YEAR'S BEEN PRETTY MUCH OF A BLUR.

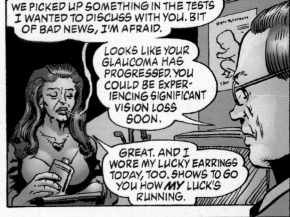

WE PICKED UP SOMETHING IN THE TESTS I WANTED TO DISCUSS WITH YOU. BIT OF BAD NEWS, I'M AFRAID.

LOOKS LIKE YOUR GLAUCOMA HAS PROGRESSED. YOU COULD BE EXPERIENCING SIGNIFICANT VISION LOSS SOON.

GREAT. AND I WORE MY LUCKY EARRINGS TODAY, TOO. SHOWS TO GO YOU HOW **MY** LUCK'S RUNNING.

AND YOU SHOULD BE CUTTING BACK ON YOUR ALCOHOL INTAKE. IT CAN BE A CONTRIBUTING FACTOR IN DOWN'S SYNDROME...

YEAH, WELL, I ALREADY KNOW I'M A LOUSY MOTHER, OKAY? THAT'S WHY I'M HEADIN' UPSTATE T'HAVE THE KID.

IT'S KILLIN' ME, BUT I'M GIVIN' HER FOR ADOPTION.

ARE YOU SURE THERE ISN'T ANOTHER WAY?

WHAT--TRY AND RAISE HER IN **BOTTOMS UP?**

OB GYN

SO SHE CAN GROW UP AND HITCH HER STAR TO SOME GANGSTER'S DREAM LIKE I DID?

INTENSIVE CARE

THAT'S A FATE I WOULDN'T WISH ON ANY JAIL BAIT.

TALK ABOUT YER BAD OMENS!

HOW THE HELL WE GONNA FIGHT A GANG WAR WITH *SPATS* BUSTED UP LIKE DIS?

WHITEY... MUCKSTICK... RHUBARB... ≶KOF≶...

CANDI... AIN'T JUST'A... DUMB BLONDE... ≶KOF≶ LISTEN T'HER.

OKAY-- SO WE FIND OUT WHO IN THE ORGANIZATION FINGERED *SPATS*, RIGHT?

DON'T WORRY ABOUT THAT. DUSTING *JOHNNY APOLLO* IS JOB ONE.

WHATTAYA GOT, *MUCK-STICK?*

A CALL GIRL SAYS *CHUCKY FRISCO* GAVE HER A STEAM-IRON *FACIAL.*

SHE'S DOWN IN *EMERGENCY...*

YEAH...*CHUCKY* RUINED ME--BUT *JOHNNY* GAVE THE ORDER. THEY LEFT MY PLACE IN BOTTOMS UP A COUPLE HOURS AGO.

THEY WERE SEARCHIN' THE BACK ALLEYS FOR *FRANKY LAFAYETTE.* SOMETHIN' ABOUT SOME *SAPPHIRES.*

WERE YOU LIKE, UH... DOIN' IT WITH *JOHNNY?*

NO--I WAS ONLY SWEET ON *FRANKY.* THEN *JOHNNY* PROMISED ME A SINGIN' GIG IF I SET HIM UP.

I'M *TERRIBLE*, AIN'T I? ANY WOMAN WHO BACK-STABS THE ONE GUY IN HER LIFE WHO'S GOOD TO HER DESERVES WHAT I GOT, RIGHT?

I--I DUNNO! I DUNNO NUTHIN' ABOUT NOTHIN' LIKE THAT!

I GOTTA GO!

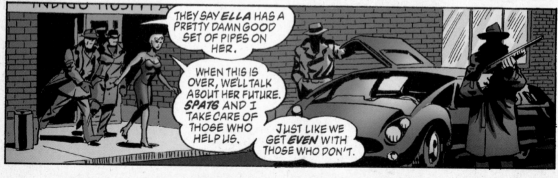

THEY SAY *ELLA* HAS A PRETTY DAMN GOOD SET OF PIPES ON HER.

WHEN THIS IS OVER, WE'LL TALK ABOUT HER FUTURE. *SPATS* AND I TAKE CARE OF THOSE WHO HELP US.

JUST LIKE WE GET *EVEN* WITH THOSE WHO DON'T.

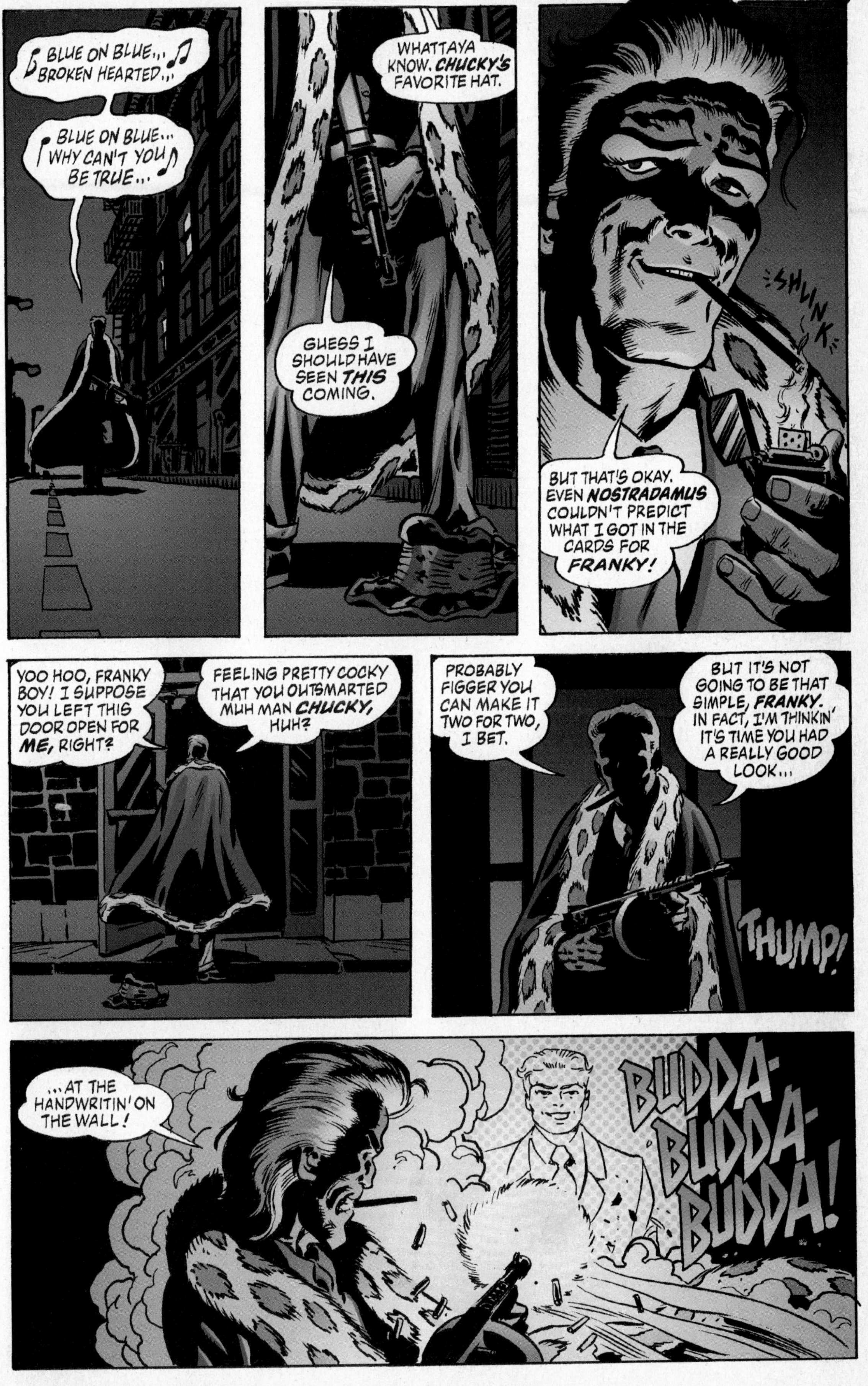
BLUE ON BLUE... BROKEN HEARTED...
BLUE ON BLUE... WHY CAN'T YOU BE TRUE...
WHATTAYA KNOW. CHUCKY'S FAVORITE HAT.
GUESS I SHOULD HAVE SEEN THIS COMING.
SHLINK
BUT THAT'S OKAY. EVEN NOSTRADAMUS COULDN'T PREDICT WHAT I GOT IN THE CARDS FOR FRANKY!
YOO HOO, FRANKY BOY! I SUPPOSE YOU LEFT THIS DOOR OPEN FOR ME, RIGHT?
FEELING PRETTY COCKY THAT YOU OUTSMARTED MUH MAN CHUCKY, HUH?
PROBABLY FIGGER YOU CAN MAKE IT TWO FOR TWO, I BET.
BUT IT'S NOT GOING TO BE THAT SIMPLE, FRANKY. IN FACT, I'M THINKIN' IT'S TIME YOU HAD A REALLY GOOD LOOK...
THUMP!
...AT THE HANDWRITIN' ON THE WALL!
BUDDA-BUDDA-BUDDA!

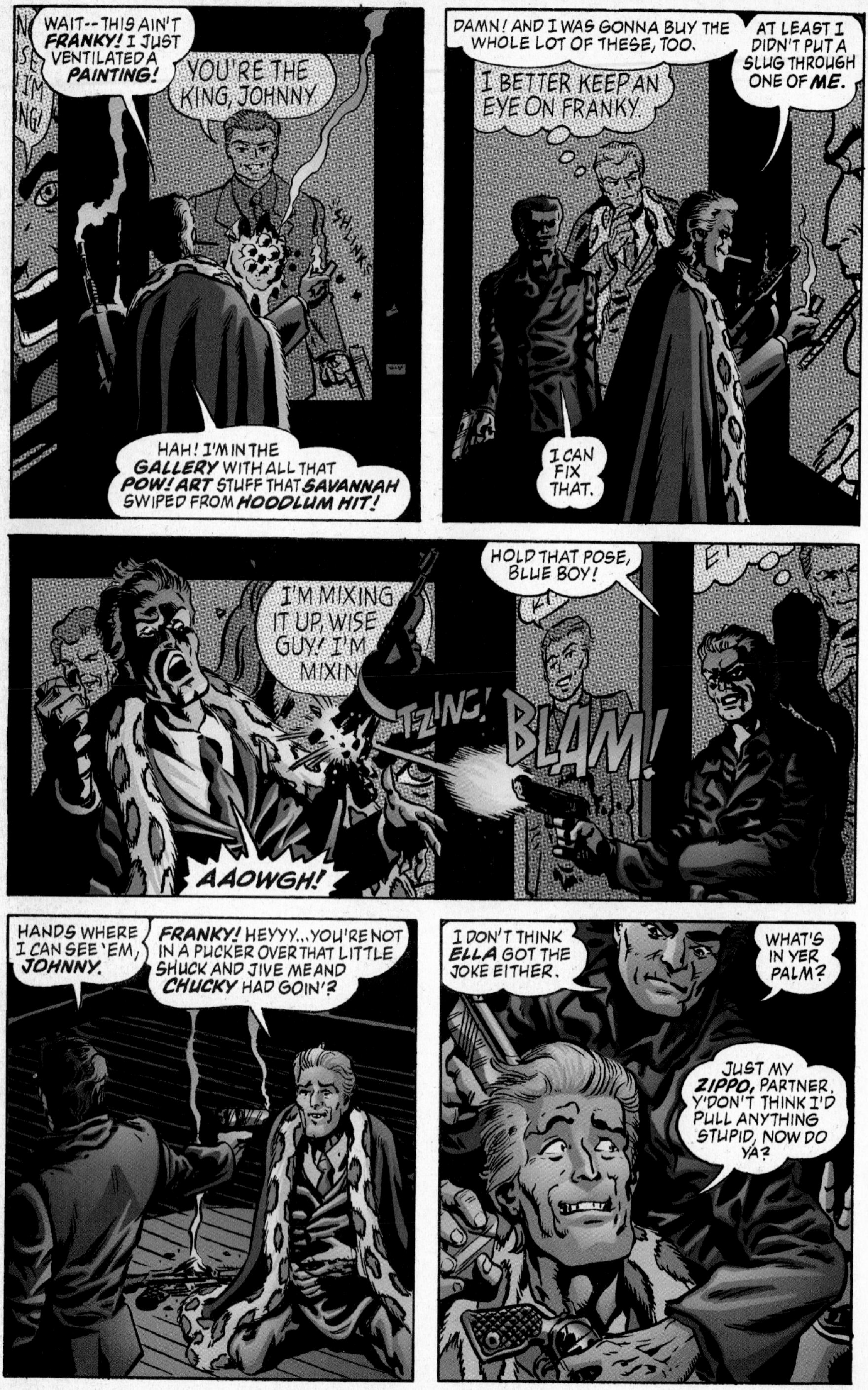
WAIT--THIS AIN'T FRANKY! I JUST VENTILATED A PAINTING!
YOU'RE THE KING, JOHNNY.
SHLINK
HAH! I'M IN THE GALLERY WITH ALL THAT POW! ART STUFF THAT SAVANNAH SWIPED FROM HOODLUM HIT!
DAMN! AND I WAS GONNA BUY THE WHOLE LOT OF THESE, TOO.
I BETTER KEEP AN EYE ON FRANKY.
AT LEAST I DIDN'T PUT A SLUG THROUGH ONE OF ME.
I CAN FIX THAT.
I'M MIXING IT UP, WISE GUY! I'M MIXIN
HOLD THAT POSE, BLUE BOY!
TZING!
BLAM!
AAOWGH!
HANDS WHERE I CAN SEE 'EM, JOHNNY.
FRANKY! HEYYY...YOU'RE NOT IN A PUCKER OVER THAT LITTLE SHUCK AND JIVE ME AND CHUCKY HAD GOIN'?
I DON'T THINK ELLA GOT THE JOKE EITHER.
WHAT'S IN YER PALM?
JUST MY ZIPPO, PARTNER. Y'DON'T THINK I'D PULL ANYTHING STUPID, NOW DO YA?

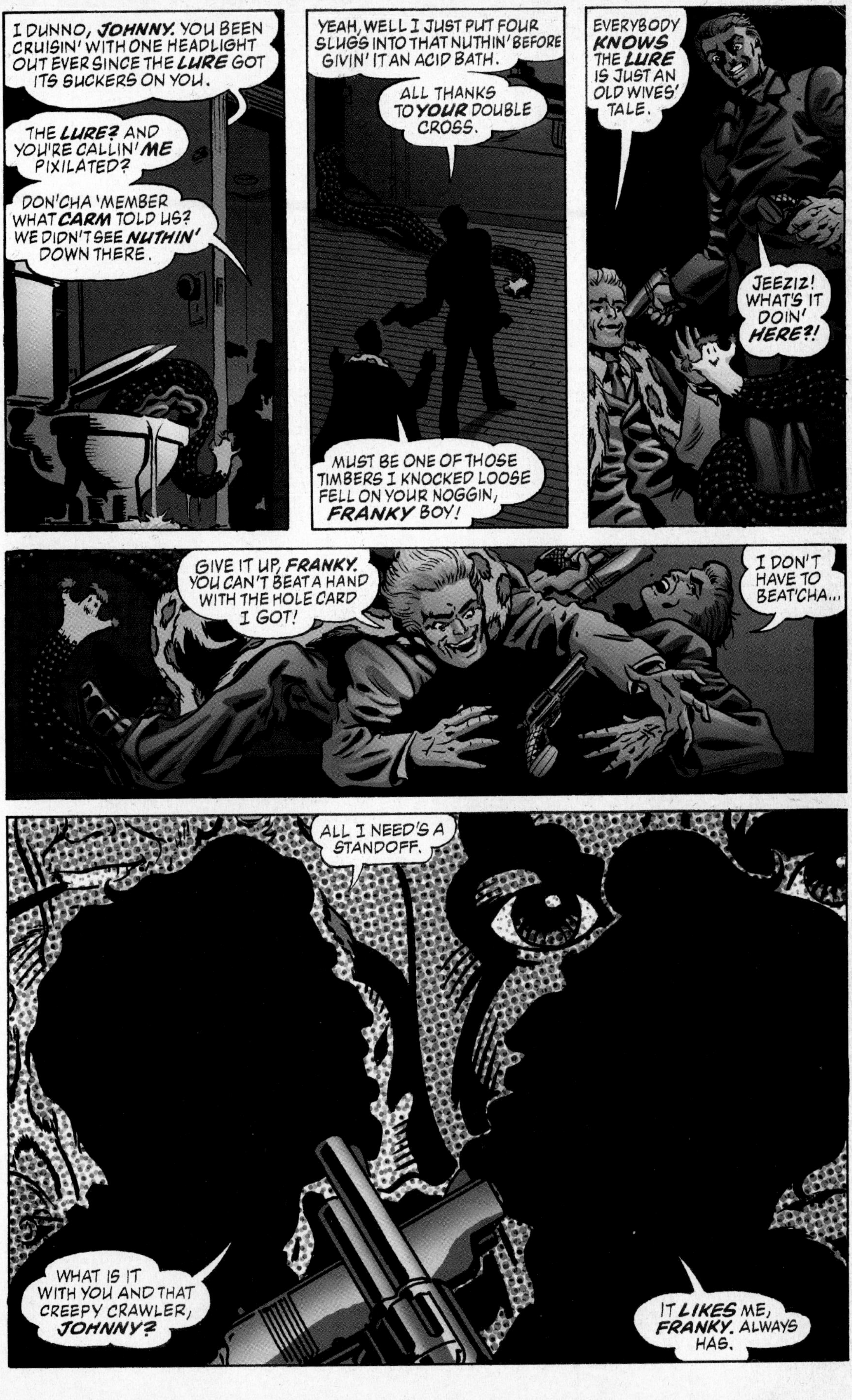
I DUNNO, JOHNNY. YOU BEEN CRUISIN' WITH ONE HEADLIGHT OUT EVER SINCE THE LURE GOT ITS SUCKERS ON YOU.
THE LURE? AND YOU'RE CALLIN' ME PIXILATED?
DON'CHA 'MEMBER WHAT CARM TOLD US? WE DIDN'T SEE NUTHIN' DOWN THERE.
YEAH, WELL I JUST PUT FOUR SLUGS INTO THAT NUTHIN' BEFORE GIVIN' IT AN ACID BATH.
ALL THANKS TO YOUR DOUBLE CROSS.
MUST BE ONE OF THOSE TIMBERS I KNOCKED LOOSE FELL ON YOUR NOGGIN, FRANKY BOY!
EVERYBODY KNOWS THE LURE IS JUST AN OLD WIVES' TALE.
JEEZIZ! WHAT'S IT DOIN' HERE?!
GIVE IT UP, FRANKY. YOU CAN'T BEAT A HAND WITH THE HOLE CARD I GOT!
I DON'T HAVE TO BEAT'CHA...
ALL I NEED'S A STANDOFF.
WHAT IS IT WITH YOU AND THAT CREEPY CRAWLER, JOHNNY?
IT LIKES ME, FRANKY. ALWAYS HAS.

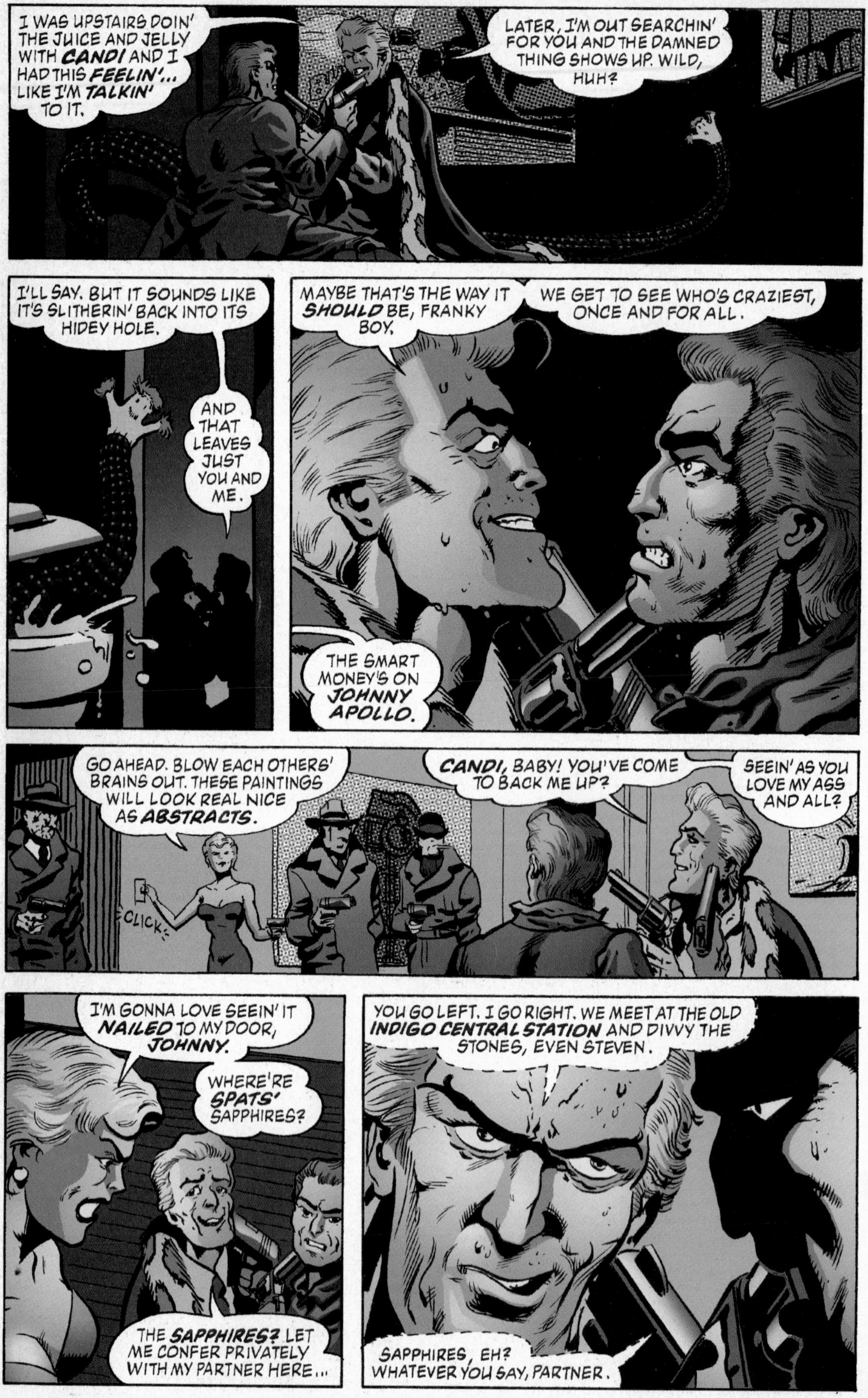
I WAS UPSTAIRS DOIN' THE JUICE AND JELLY WITH CANDI AND I HAD THIS FEELIN'... LIKE I'M TALKIN' TO IT.
LATER, I'M OUT SEARCHIN' FOR YOU AND THE DAMNED THING SHOWS UP. WILD, HUH?
I'LL SAY. BUT IT SOUNDS LIKE IT'S SLITHERIN' BACK INTO ITS HIDEY HOLE.
AND THAT LEAVES JUST YOU AND ME.
MAYBE THAT'S THE WAY IT SHOULD BE, FRANKY BOY.
WE GET TO SEE WHO'S CRAZIEST, ONCE AND FOR ALL.
THE SMART MONEY'S ON JOHNNY APOLLO.
GO AHEAD. BLOW EACH OTHERS' BRAINS OUT. THESE PAINTINGS WILL LOOK REAL NICE AS ABSTRACTS.
CLICK
CANDI, BABY! YOU'VE COME TO BACK ME UP?
SEEIN' AS YOU LOVE MY ASS AND ALL?
I'M GONNA LOVE SEEIN' IT NAILED TO MY DOOR, JOHNNY.
WHERE'RE SPATS' SAPPHIRES?
THE SAPPHIRES? LET ME CONFER PRIVATELY WITH MY PARTNER HERE...
YOU GO LEFT. I GO RIGHT. WE MEET AT THE OLD INDIGO CENTRAL STATION AND DIVVY THE STONES, EVEN STEVEN.
SAPPHIRES, EH? WHATEVER YOU SAY, PARTNER.

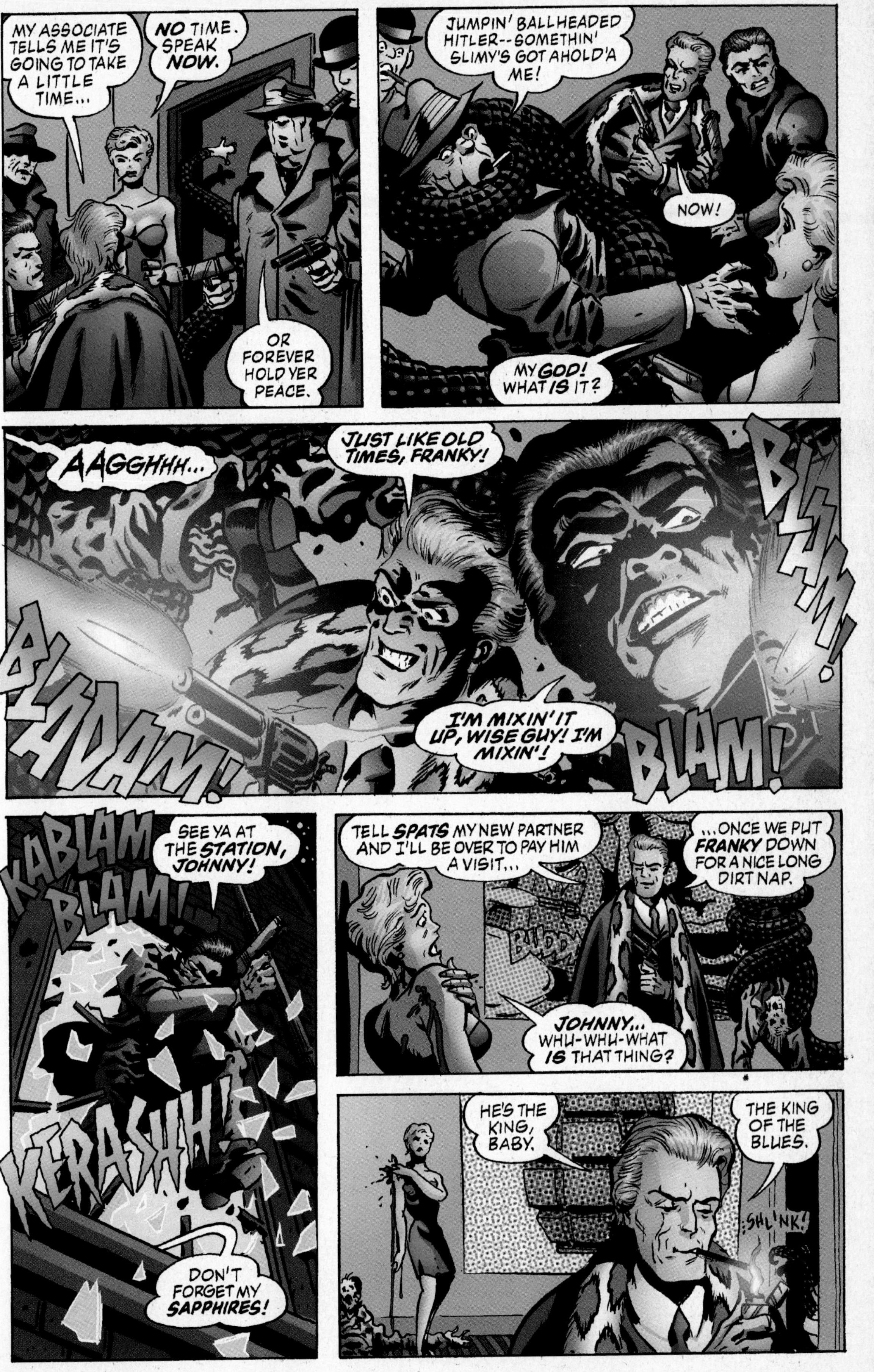
MY ASSOCIATE TELLS ME IT'S GOING TO TAKE A LITTLE TIME...
NO TIME. SPEAK NOW.
OR FOREVER HOLD YER PEACE.
JUMPIN' BALLHEADED HITLER--SOMETHIN' SLIMY'S GOT AHOLD'A ME!
NOW!
MY GOD! WHAT IS IT?
AAGGHHH...
JUST LIKE OLD TIMES, FRANKY!
BLAM!
BLADAM!
I'M MIXIN' IT UP, WISE GUY! I'M MIXIN'!
BLAM!
KABLAM BLAM!
SEE YA AT THE STATION, JOHNNY!
KERASHH!
DON'T FORGET MY SAPPHIRES!
TELL SPATS MY NEW PARTNER AND I'LL BE OVER TO PAY HIM A VISIT...
...ONCE WE PUT FRANKY DOWN FOR A NICE LONG DIRT NAP.
JOHNNY... WHU-WHU-WHAT IS THAT THING?
HE'S THE KING, BABY.
THE KING OF THE BLUES.
SHL'NK!

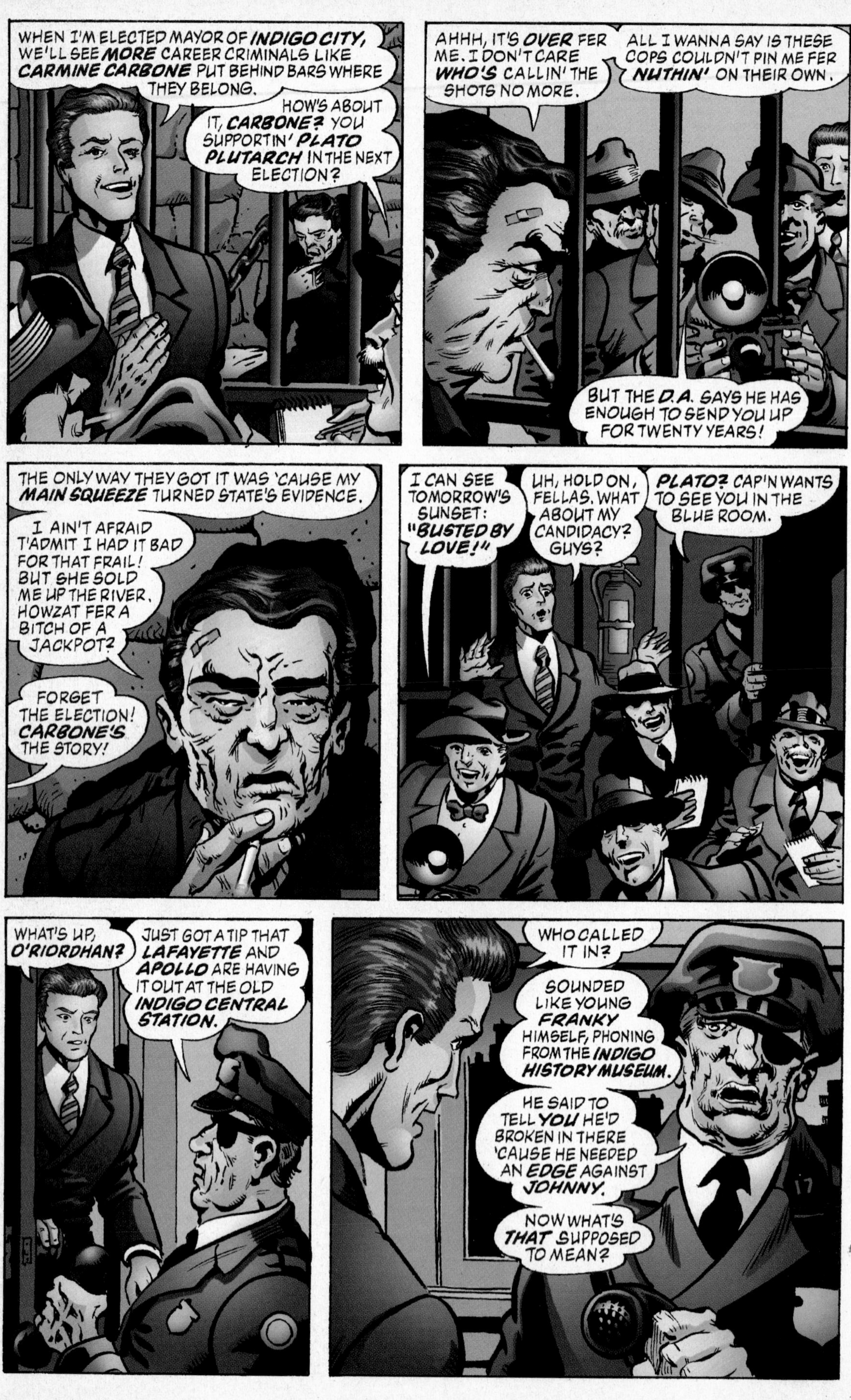
WHEN I'M ELECTED MAYOR OF INDIGO CITY, WE'LL SEE MORE CAREER CRIMINALS LIKE CARMINE CARBONE PUT BEHIND BARS WHERE THEY BELONG.
HOW'S ABOUT IT, CARBONE? YOU SUPPORTIN' PLATO PLUTARCH IN THE NEXT ELECTION?
AHHH, IT'S OVER FER ME. I DON'T CARE WHO'S CALLIN' THE SHOTS NO MORE.
ALL I WANNA SAY IS THESE COPS COULDN'T PIN ME FER NUTHIN' ON THEIR OWN.
BUT THE D.A. SAYS HE HAS ENOUGH TO SEND YOU UP FOR TWENTY YEARS!
THE ONLY WAY THEY GOT IT WAS 'CAUSE MY MAIN SQUEEZE TURNED STATE'S EVIDENCE.
I AIN'T AFRAID T'ADMIT I HAD IT BAD FOR THAT FRAIL! BUT SHE SOLD ME UP THE RIVER. HOWZAT FER A BITCH OF A JACKPOT?
FORGET THE ELECTION! CARBONE'S THE STORY!
I CAN SEE TOMORROW'S SUNSET: "BUSTED BY LOVE!"
UH, HOLD ON, FELLAS. WHAT ABOUT MY CANDIDACY? GUYS?
PLATO? CAP'N WANTS TO SEE YOU IN THE BLUE ROOM.
WHAT'S UP, O'RIORDHAN?
JUST GOT A TIP THAT LAFAYETTE AND APOLLO ARE HAVING IT OUT AT THE OLD INDIGO CENTRAL STATION.
WHO CALLED IT IN?
SOUNDED LIKE YOUNG FRANKY HIMSELF, PHONING FROM THE INDIGO HISTORY MUSEUM.
HE SAID TO TELL YOU HE'D BROKEN IN THERE 'CAUSE HE NEEDED AN EDGE AGAINST JOHNNY.
NOW WHAT'S THAT SUPPOSED TO MEAN?

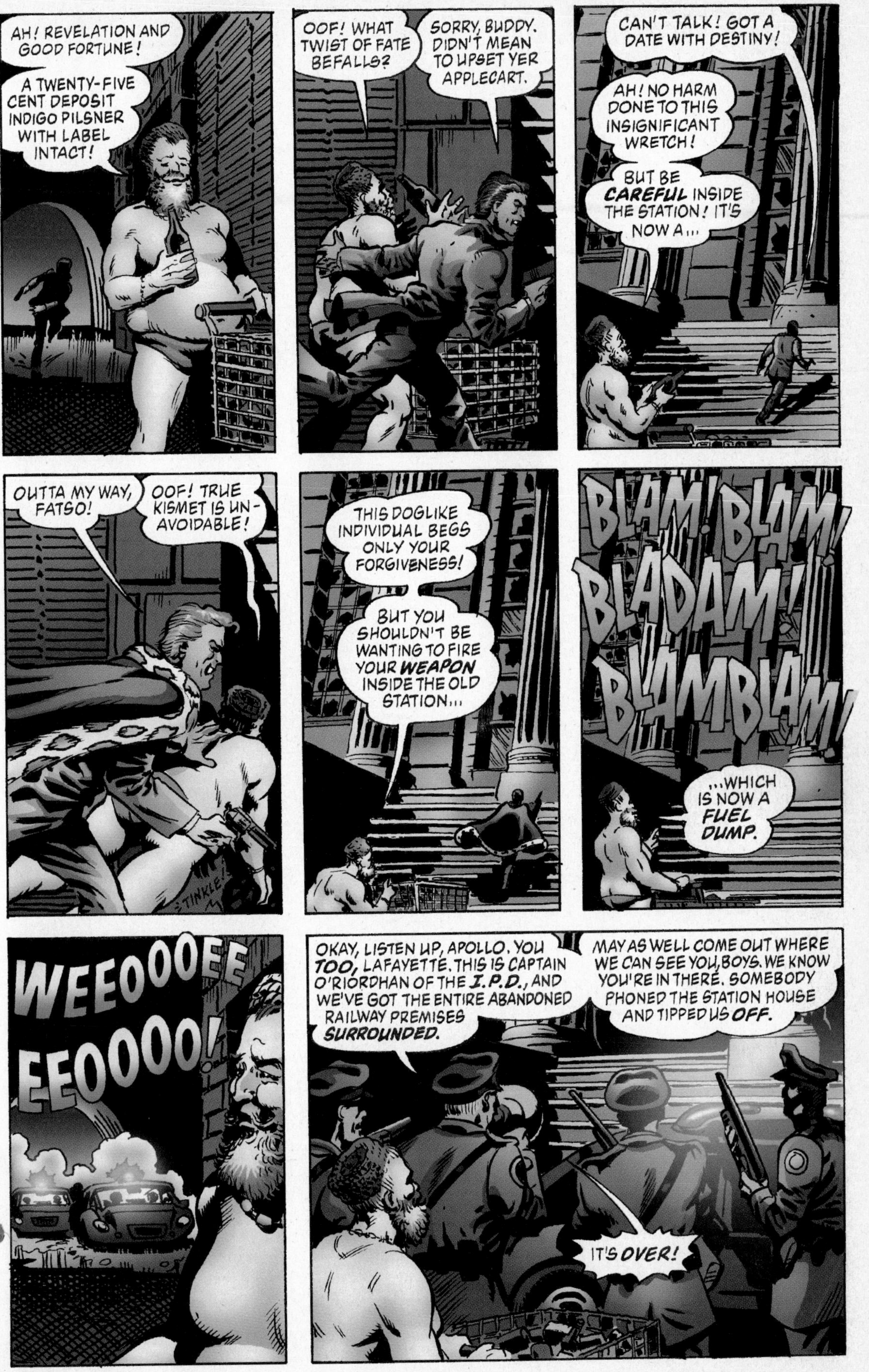
AH! REVELATION AND GOOD FORTUNE!
A TWENTY-FIVE CENT DEPOSIT INDIGO PILSNER WITH LABEL INTACT!
OOF! WHAT TWIST OF FATE BEFALLS?
SORRY, BUDDY. DIDN'T MEAN TO UPSET YER APPLECART.
CAN'T TALK! GOT A DATE WITH DESTINY!
AH! NO HARM DONE TO THIS INSIGNIFICANT WRETCH!
BUT BE CAREFUL INSIDE THE STATION! IT'S NOW A...
OUTTA MY WAY, FATSO!
OOF! TRUE KISMET IS UN-AVOIDABLE!
TINKLE!
THIS DOGLIKE INDIVIDUAL BEGS ONLY YOUR FORGIVENESS!
BUT YOU SHOULDN'T BE WANTING TO FIRE YOUR WEAPON INSIDE THE OLD STATION...
BLAM! BLAM! BLADAM! BLAMBLAM!
...WHICH IS NOW A FUEL DUMP.
WEEOOOEE EEOOOO!
OKAY, LISTEN UP, APOLLO. YOU TOO, LAFAYETTE. THIS IS CAPTAIN O'RIORDHAN OF THE I.P.D., AND WE'VE GOT THE ENTIRE ABANDONED RAILWAY PREMISES SURROUNDED.
MAY AS WELL COME OUT WHERE WE CAN SEE YOU, BOYS. WE KNOW YOU'RE IN THERE. SOMEBODY PHONED THE STATION HOUSE AND TIPPED US OFF.
IT'S OVER!

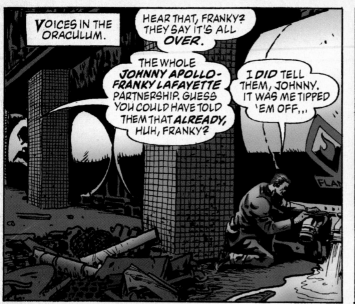

VOICES IN THE ORACULUM.

HEAR THAT, FRANKY? THEY SAY IT'S ALL *OVER.*

THE WHOLE *JOHNNY APOLLO-FRANKY LAFAYETTE* PARTNERSHIP. GUESS YOU COULD HAVE TOLD THEM THAT *ALREADY,* HUH, FRANKY?

I *DID* TELL THEM, JOHNNY. IT WAS ME TIPPED 'EM OFF,,,

...WHEN I FIGURED YOU WERE GONNA DOUBLE-CROSS ME OVER DIVIDING UP THE *SAPPHIRES.*

VOICES CUT WITH MURDEROUS INTENT.

I MIGHTA KNOWN.

YOU KNOW *YOU'RE* GONNA DIE HERE, DON'CHA?

HELL, I KNOW I HIT YOU IN THE GUT ONCE OR TWICE ALREADY.

TINGED WITH FATALISTIC BRAVADO.

YEAH. GUESS YOU DID.

CAN'T SAY I'M BOTHERED,,,

...AS LONG AS I KNOW YOU'RE COMING *WITH* ME!

VOICES CHARGED IN DESPERATE SEARCHING,,,

UH-UH. AIN'T GOIN' *NOWHERE.*

FROM HERE ON, FRANKY, YOU TRAVEL *ALONE.*

BDAMM! BDAMM!

AAAH!

SQUIRMING THROUGH THE LOOPHOLES OF DESTINY!

DID I GET YA THAT TIME? YOU AIN'T SHOOTIN' *BACK.* WHATSAMATTER? LOST YOUR *HEATER?*

SHLINK

LET'S GET SOME *LIGHT* IN HERE. HELP YOU *FIND* IT.

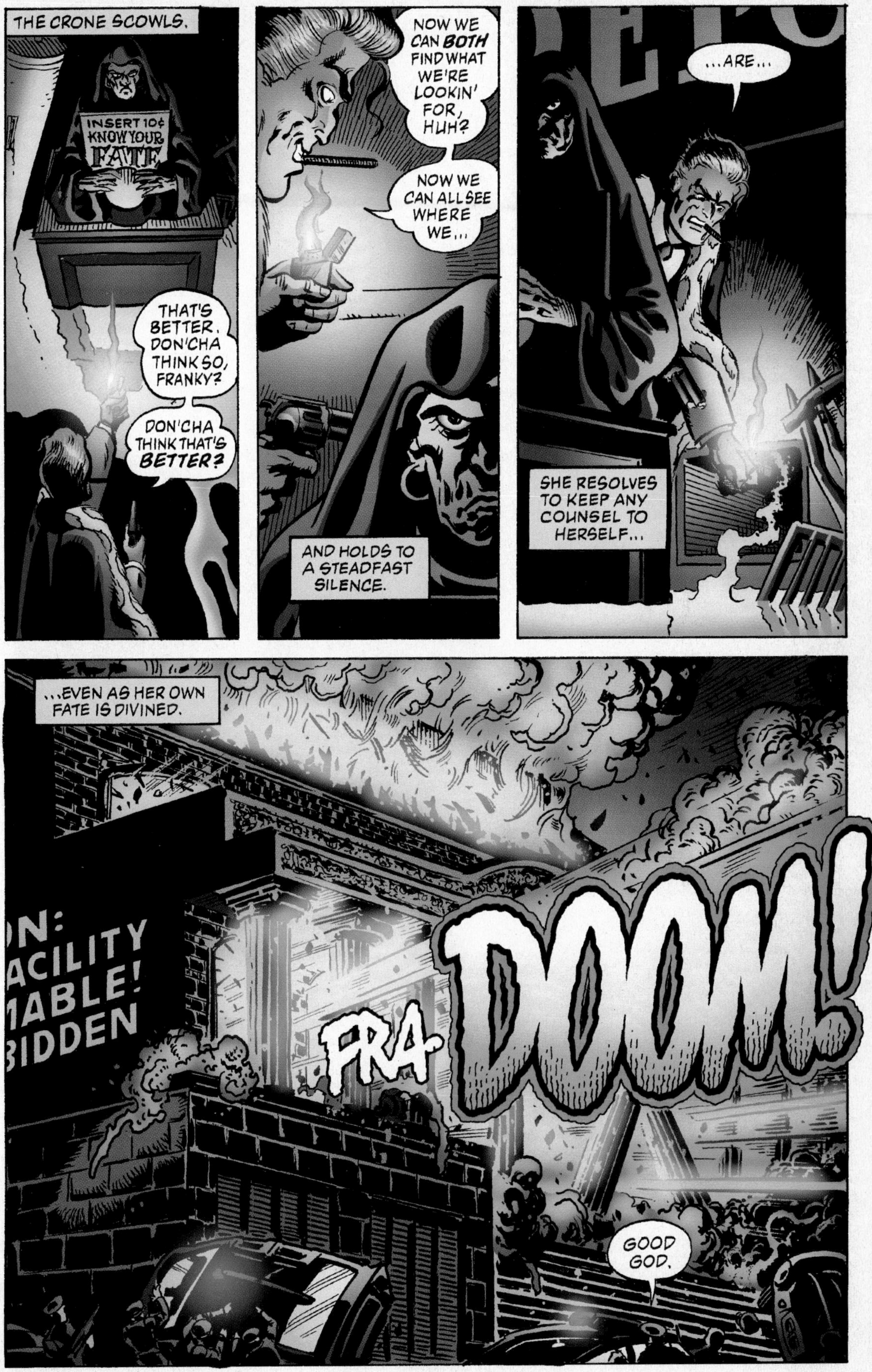
THE CRONE SCOWLS.
INSERT 10¢ KNOW YOUR FATE
THAT'S BETTER. DON'CHA THINK SO, FRANKY?
DON'CHA THINK THAT'S BETTER?
NOW WE CAN BOTH FIND WHAT WE'RE LOOKIN' FOR, HUH?
NOW WE CAN ALL SEE WHERE WE...
AND HOLDS TO A STEADFAST SILENCE.
...ARE...
SHE RESOLVES TO KEEP ANY COUNSEL TO HERSELF...
...EVEN AS HER OWN FATE IS DIVINED.
ON:
ACILITY
MABLE!
BIDDEN
FRA
DOOM!
GOOD GOD.

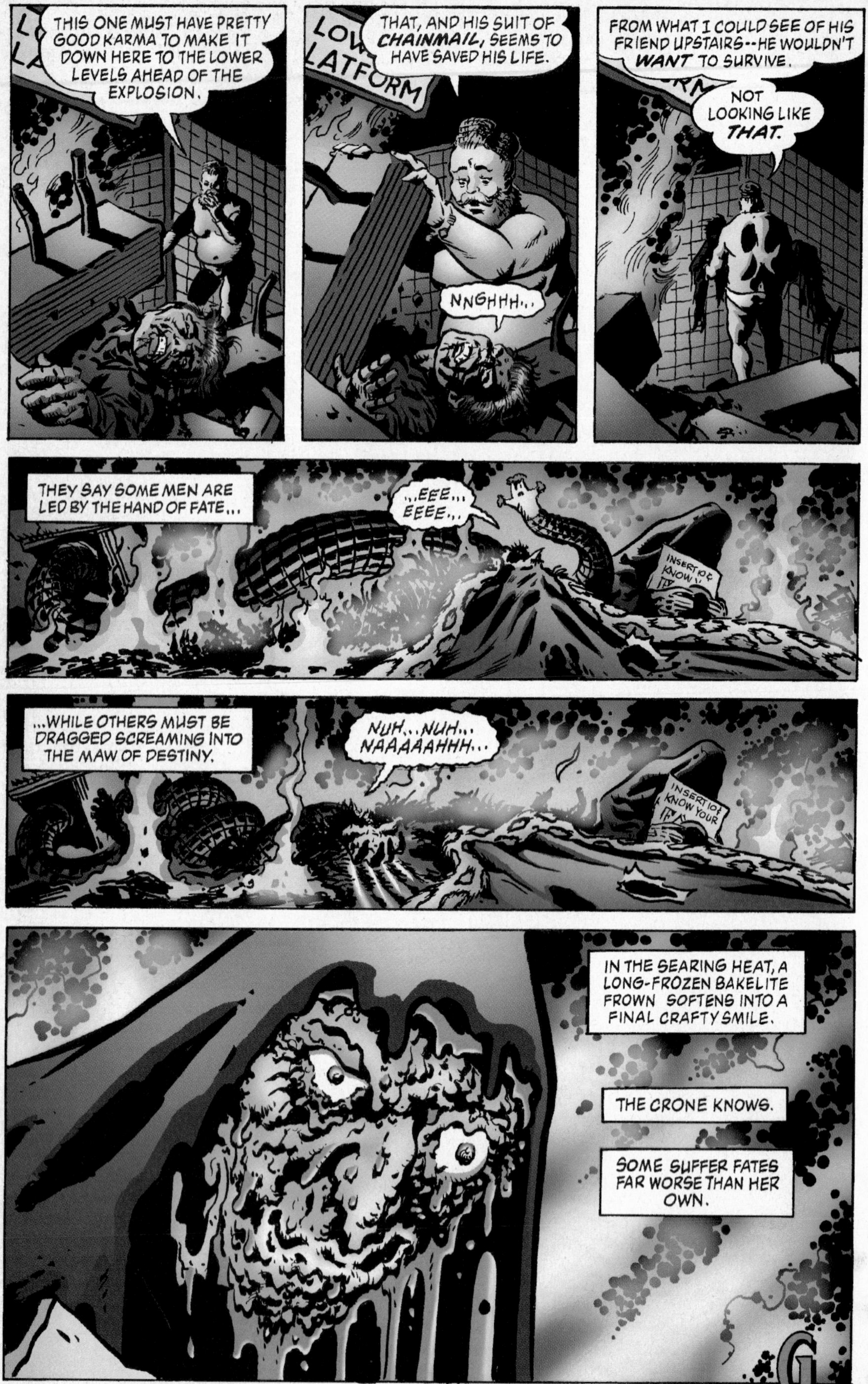
THIS ONE MUST HAVE PRETTY GOOD KARMA TO MAKE IT DOWN HERE TO THE LOWER LEVELS AHEAD OF THE EXPLOSION.
THAT, AND HIS SUIT OF CHAINMAIL, SEEMS TO HAVE SAVED HIS LIFE.
NNGHHH...
FROM WHAT I COULD SEE OF HIS FRIEND UPSTAIRS--HE WOULDN'T WANT TO SURVIVE.
NOT LOOKING LIKE THAT.
THEY SAY SOME MEN ARE LED BY THE HAND OF FATE...
...EEE... EEEE...
...WHILE OTHERS MUST BE DRAGGED SCREAMING INTO THE MAW OF DESTINY.
NUH...NUH... NAAAAAHHH...
INSERT 101 KNOW YOUR
IN THE SEARING HEAT, A LONG-FROZEN BAKELITE FROWN SOFTENS INTO A FINAL CRAFTY SMILE.
THE CRONE KNOWS.
SOME SUFFER FATES FAR WORSE THAN HER OWN.
G

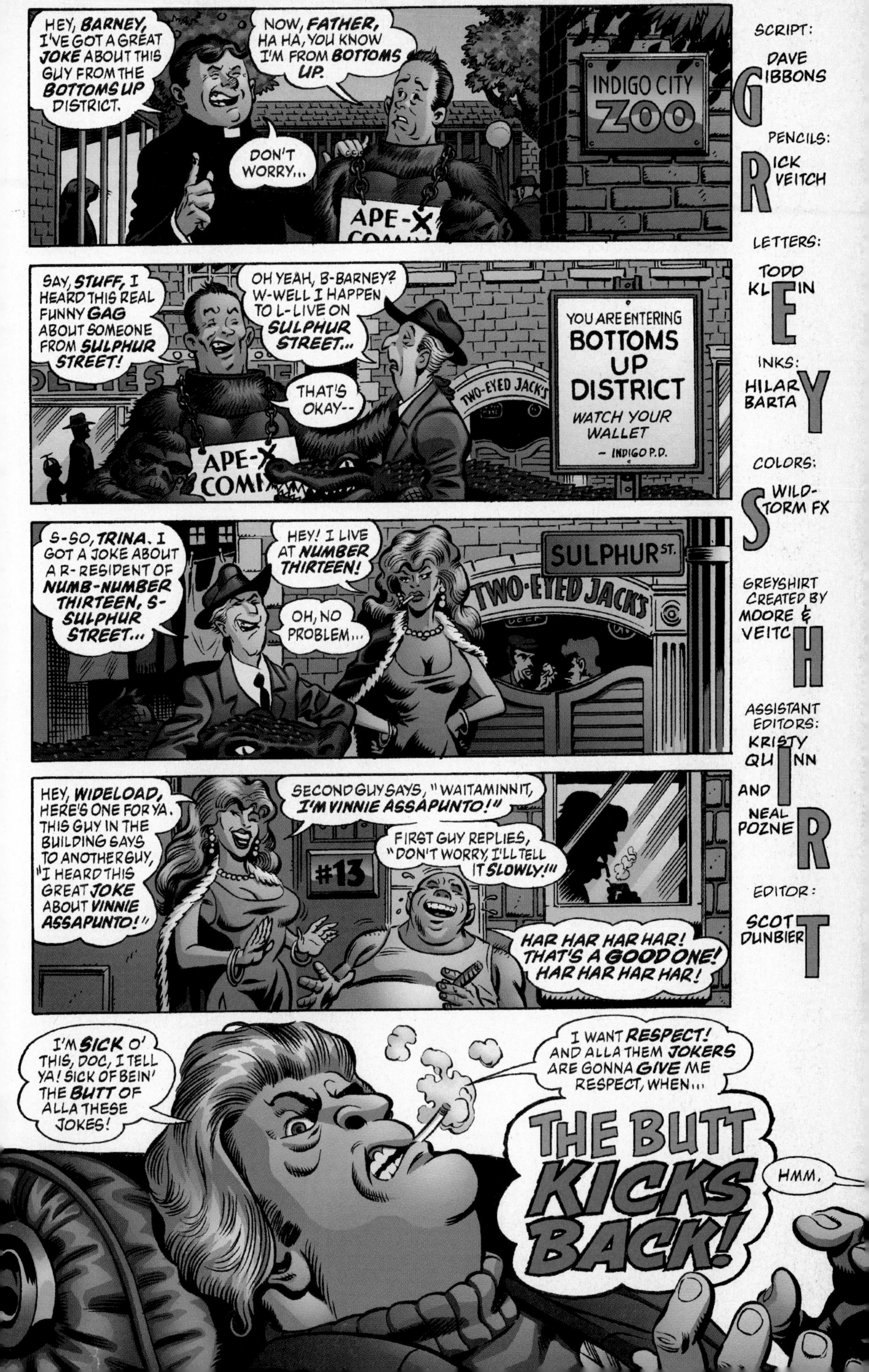
HEY, BARNEY, I'VE GOT A GREAT JOKE ABOUT THIS GUY FROM THE BOTTOMS UP DISTRICT.
NOW, FATHER, HA HA, YOU KNOW I'M FROM BOTTOMS UP.
DON'T WORRY...
INDIGO CITY ZOO
APE-X
SAY, STUFF, I HEARD THIS REAL FUNNY GAG ABOUT SOMEONE FROM SULPHUR STREET!
OH YEAH, B-BARNEY? W-WELL I HAPPEN TO L-LIVE ON SULPHUR STREET...
THAT'S OKAY--
TWO-EYED JACK'S
YOU ARE ENTERING BOTTOMS UP DISTRICT WATCH YOUR WALLET - INDIGO P.D.
APE-X
S-SO, TRINA. I GOT A JOKE ABOUT A R-RESIDENT OF NUMB-NUMBER THIRTEEN, S-SULPHUR STREET...
HEY! I LIVE AT NUMBER THIRTEEN!
OH, NO PROBLEM...
SULPHUR ST.
TWO-EYED JACK'S
HEY, WIDELOAD, HERE'S ONE FOR YA. THIS GUY IN THE BUILDING SAYS TO ANOTHER GUY, "I HEARD THIS GREAT JOKE ABOUT VINNIE ASSAPUNTO!"
SECOND GUY SAYS, "WAITAMINNIT, I'M VINNIE ASSAPUNTO!"
FIRST GUY REPLIES, "DON'T WORRY, I'LL TELL IT SLOWLY!"
#13
HAR HAR HAR HAR! THAT'S A GOOD ONE! HAR HAR HAR HAR!
I'M SICK O' THIS, DOC, I TELL YA! SICK OF BEIN' THE BUTT OF ALLA THESE JOKES!
I WANT RESPECT! AND ALLA THEM JOKERS ARE GONNA GIVE ME RESPECT, WHEN...
THE BUTT KICKS BACK!
HMM.
GREYSHIRT
SCRIPT: DAVE GIBBONS
PENCILS: RICK VEITCH
LETTERS: TODD KLEIN
INKS: HILARY BARTA
COLORS: WILDSTORM FX
GREYSHIRT CREATED BY MOORE & VEITCH
ASSISTANT EDITORS: KRISTY QUINN AND NEAL POZNER
EDITOR: SCOTT DUNBIER

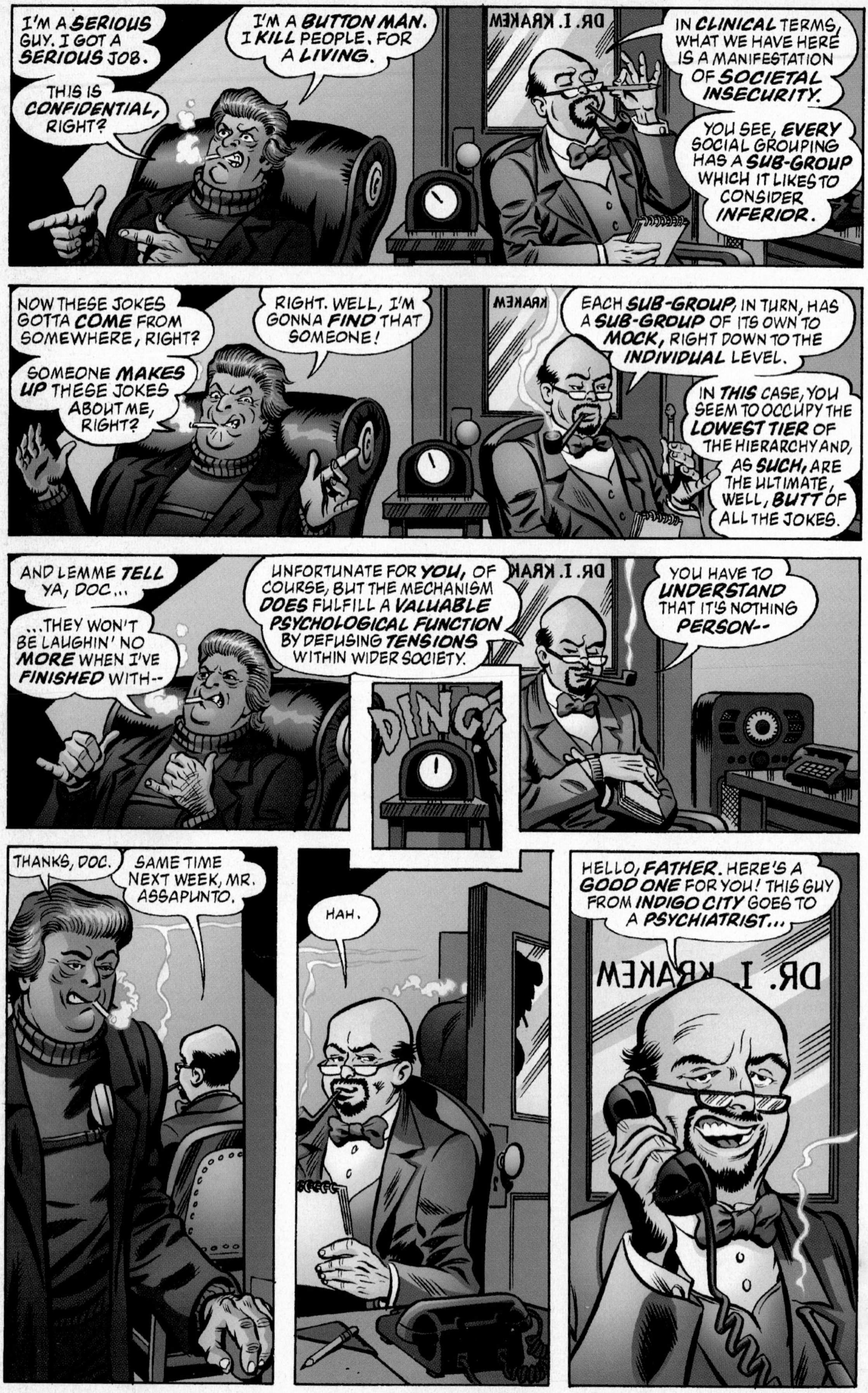
I'M A SERIOUS GUY. I GOT A SERIOUS JOB.
THIS IS CONFIDENTIAL, RIGHT?
I'M A BUTTON MAN. I KILL PEOPLE, FOR A LIVING.
DR. I. KRAKEM
IN CLINICAL TERMS, WHAT WE HAVE HERE IS A MANIFESTATION OF SOCIETAL INSECURITY.
YOU SEE, EVERY SOCIAL GROUPING HAS A SUB-GROUP WHICH IT LIKES TO CONSIDER INFERIOR.
NOW THESE JOKES GOTTA COME FROM SOMEWHERE, RIGHT?
SOMEONE MAKES UP THESE JOKES ABOUT ME, RIGHT?
RIGHT. WELL, I'M GONNA FIND THAT SOMEONE!
EACH SUB-GROUP, IN TURN, HAS A SUB-GROUP OF ITS OWN TO MOCK, RIGHT DOWN TO THE INDIVIDUAL LEVEL.
IN THIS CASE, YOU SEEM TO OCCUPY THE LOWEST TIER OF THE HIERARCHY AND, AS SUCH, ARE THE ULTIMATE, WELL, BUTT OF ALL THE JOKES.
AND LEMME TELL YA, DOC...
...THEY WON'T BE LAUGHIN' NO MORE WHEN I'VE FINISHED WITH--
UNFORTUNATE FOR YOU, OF COURSE, BUT THE MECHANISM DOES FULFILL A VALUABLE PSYCHOLOGICAL FUNCTION BY DEFUSING TENSIONS WITHIN WIDER SOCIETY.
YOU HAVE TO UNDERSTAND THAT IT'S NOTHING PERSON--
DING
THANKS, DOC.
SAME TIME NEXT WEEK, MR. ASSAPUNTO.
HAH.
HELLO, FATHER. HERE'S A GOOD ONE FOR YOU! THIS GUY FROM INDIGO CITY GOES TO A PSYCHIATRIST...
DR. I. KRAKEM

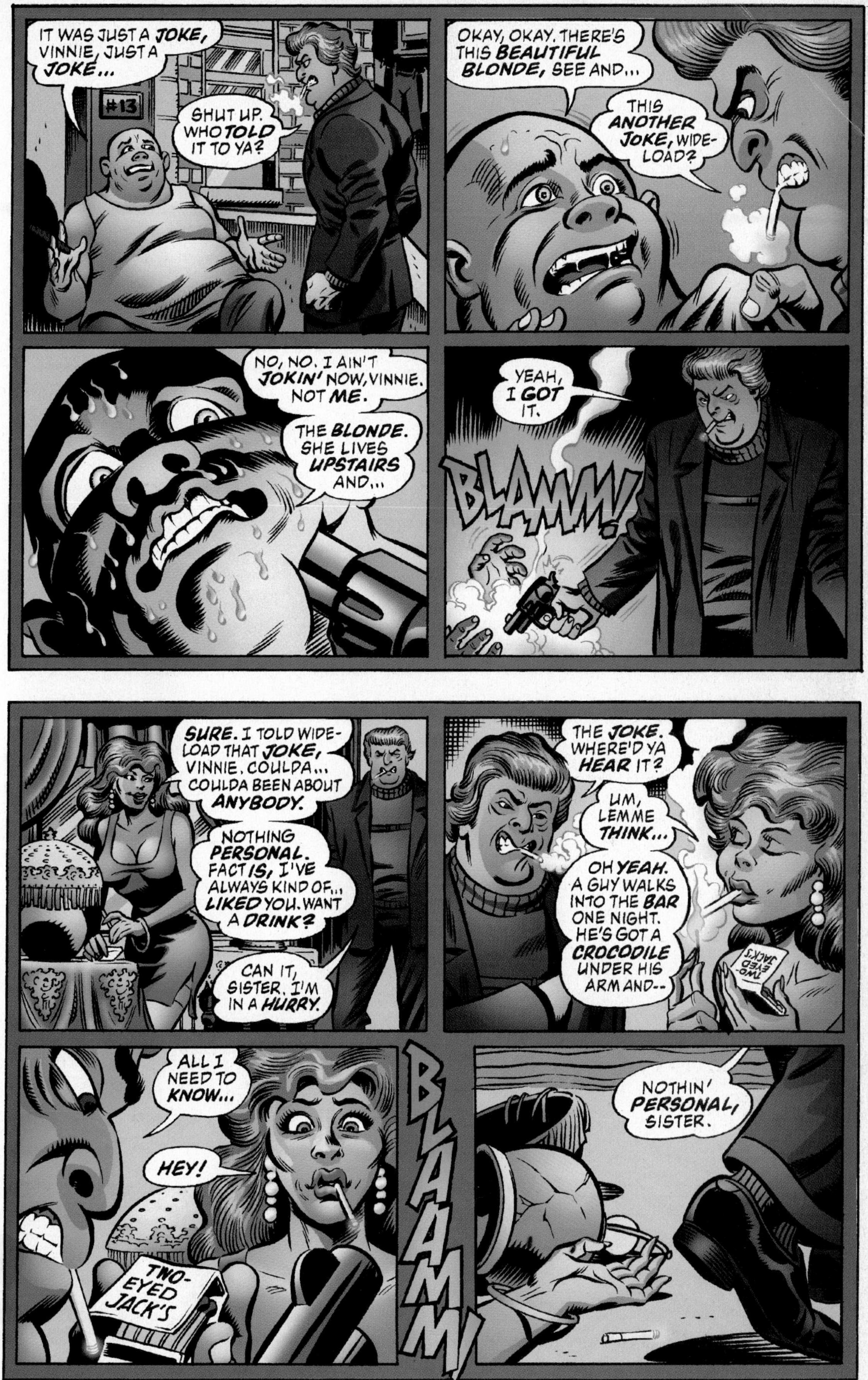
IT WAS JUST A JOKE, VINNIE, JUST A JOKE...
#13
SHUT UP. WHO TOLD IT TO YA?
OKAY, OKAY. THERE'S THIS BEAUTIFUL BLONDE, SEE AND...
THIS ANOTHER JOKE, WIDE-LOAD?
NO, NO. I AIN'T JOKIN' NOW, VINNIE. NOT ME.
THE BLONDE. SHE LIVES UPSTAIRS AND...
YEAH, I GOT IT.
BLAMM!
SURE. I TOLD WIDE-LOAD THAT JOKE, VINNIE. COULDA... COULDA BEEN ABOUT ANYBODY.
NOTHING PERSONAL. FACT IS, I'VE ALWAYS KIND OF... LIKED YOU. WANT A DRINK?
CAN IT, SISTER. I'M IN A HURRY.
THE JOKE. WHERE'D YA HEAR IT?
UM, LEMME THINK...
OH YEAH. A GUY WALKS INTO THE BAR ONE NIGHT. HE'S GOT A CROCODILE UNDER HIS ARM AND--
TWO-EYED JACK'S
ALL I NEED TO KNOW...
HEY!
TWO-EYED JACK'S
BLAAMM!
NOTHIN' PERSONAL, SISTER.

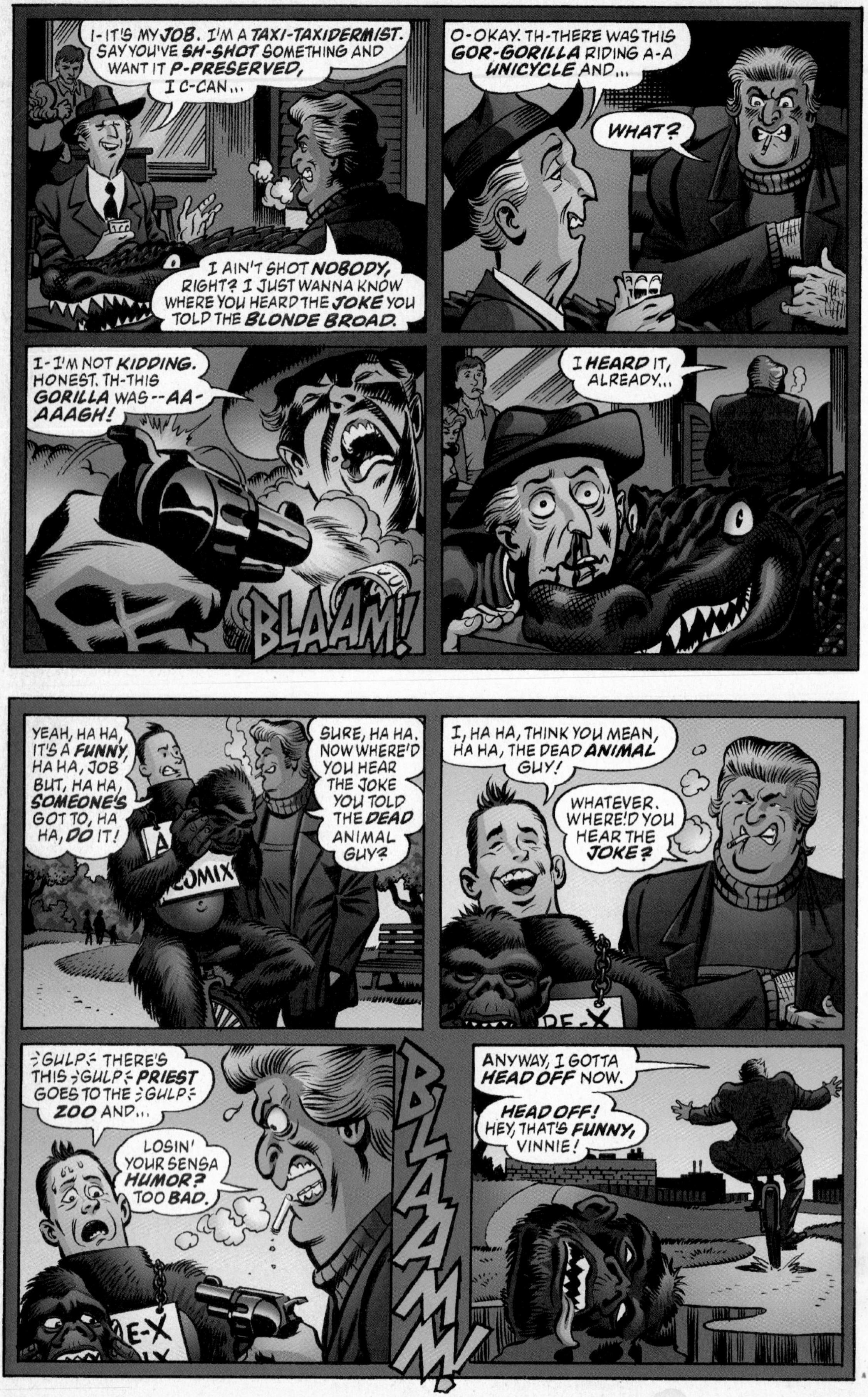

I-IT'S MY JOB. I'M A TAXI-TAXIDERMIST. SAY YOU'VE SH-SHOT SOMETHING AND WANT IT P-PRESERVED, I C-CAN...
I AIN'T SHOT NOBODY, RIGHT? I JUST WANNA KNOW WHERE YOU HEARD THE JOKE YOU TOLD THE BLONDE BROAD.
O-OKAY. TH-THERE WAS THIS GOR-GORILLA RIDING A-A UNICYCLE AND...
WHAT?
I-I'M NOT KIDDING. HONEST. TH-THIS GORILLA WAS--AA-AAAGH!
BLAAM!
I HEARD IT, ALREADY...
YEAH, HA HA, IT'S A FUNNY, HA HA, JOB BUT, HA HA, SOMEONE'S GOT TO, HA HA, DO IT!
SURE, HA HA. NOW WHERE'D YOU HEAR THE JOKE YOU TOLD THE DEAD ANIMAL GUY?
I, HA HA, THINK YOU MEAN, HA HA, THE DEAD ANIMAL GUY!
WHATEVER. WHERE'D YOU HEAR THE JOKE?
-GULP- THERE'S THIS -GULP- PRIEST GOES TO THE -GULP- ZOO AND...
LOSIN' YOUR SENSA HUMOR? TOO BAD.
BLAAM!
ANYWAY, I GOTTA HEAD OFF NOW.
HEAD OFF! HEY, THAT'S FUNNY, VINNIE!

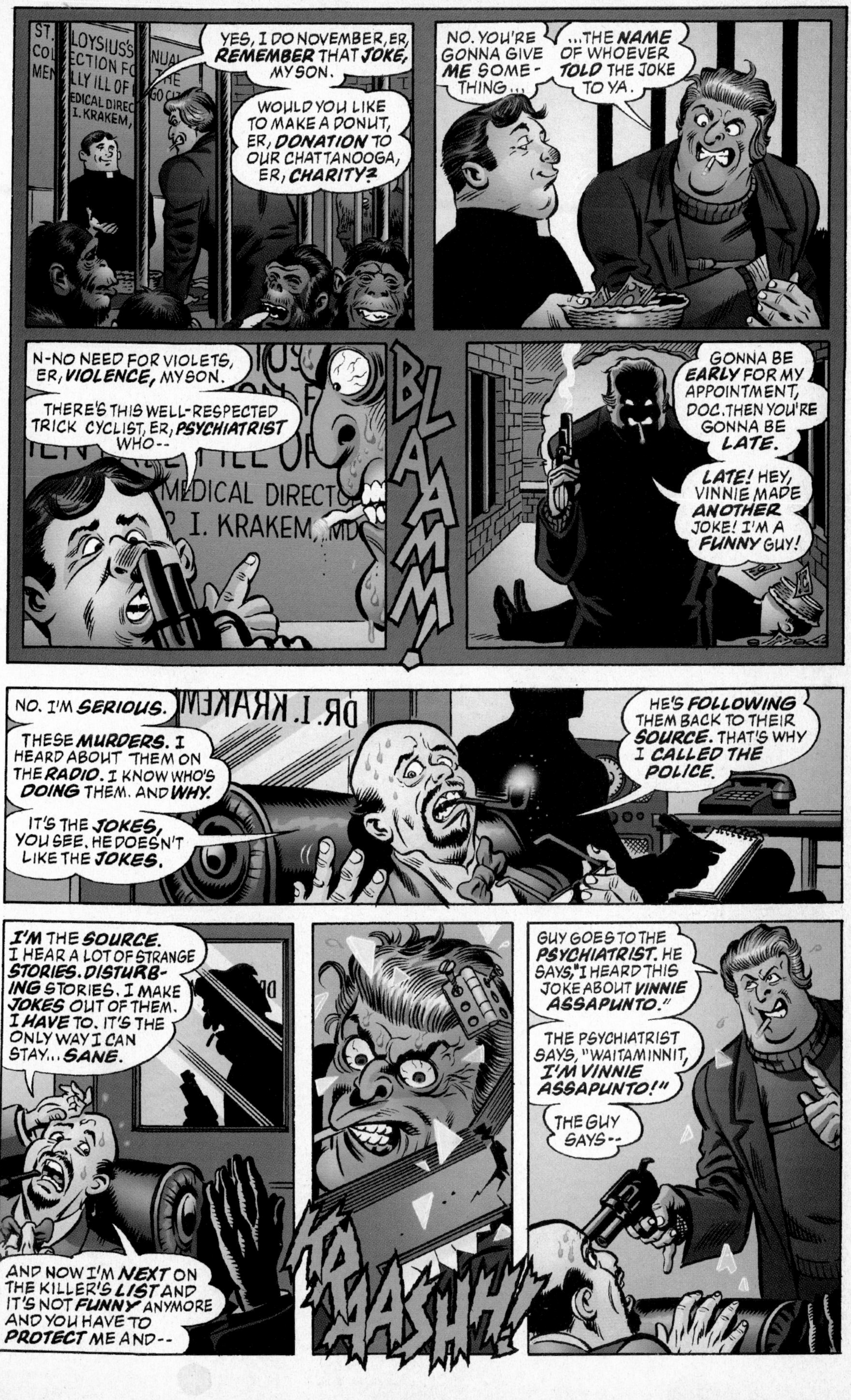
ST. LOYSIUS'S ... NUAL COLLECTION FO... MEN...LLY ILL OF ... EDICAL DIREC... I. KRAKEM,
YES, I DO NOVEMBER, ER, REMEMBER THAT JOKE, MY SON.
WOULD YOU LIKE TO MAKE A DONUT, ER, DONATION TO OUR CHATTANOOGA, ER, CHARITY?
NO. YOU'RE GONNA GIVE ME SOME-THING...
...THE NAME OF WHOEVER TOLD THE JOKE TO YA.
N-NO NEED FOR VIOLETS, ER, VIOLENCE, MY SON.
THERE'S THIS WELL-RESPECTED TRICK CYCLIST, ER, PSYCHIATRIST WHO--
MEDICAL DIRECTO... I. KRAKEM, MD
BLAAAMM!
GONNA BE EARLY FOR MY APPOINTMENT, DOC. THEN YOU'RE GONNA BE LATE.
LATE! HEY, VINNIE MADE ANOTHER JOKE! I'M A FUNNY GUY!
NO. I'M SERIOUS.
DR. I. KRAKEM
THESE MURDERS. I HEARD ABOUT THEM ON THE RADIO. I KNOW WHO'S DOING THEM. AND WHY.
IT'S THE JOKES, YOU SEE. HE DOESN'T LIKE THE JOKES.
HE'S FOLLOWING THEM BACK TO THEIR SOURCE. THAT'S WHY I CALLED THE POLICE.
I'M THE SOURCE. I HEAR A LOT OF STRANGE STORIES. DISTURB-ING STORIES. I MAKE JOKES OUT OF THEM. I HAVE TO. IT'S THE ONLY WAY I CAN STAY... SANE.
AND NOW I'M NEXT ON THE KILLER'S LIST AND IT'S NOT FUNNY ANYMORE AND YOU HAVE TO PROTECT ME AND--
KRAASHH!
GUY GOES TO THE PSYCHIATRIST. HE SAYS, "I HEARD THIS JOKE ABOUT VINNIE ASSAPUNTO."
THE PSYCHIATRIST SAYS, "WAITAMINNIT, I'M VINNIE ASSAPUNTO!"
THE GUY SAYS--

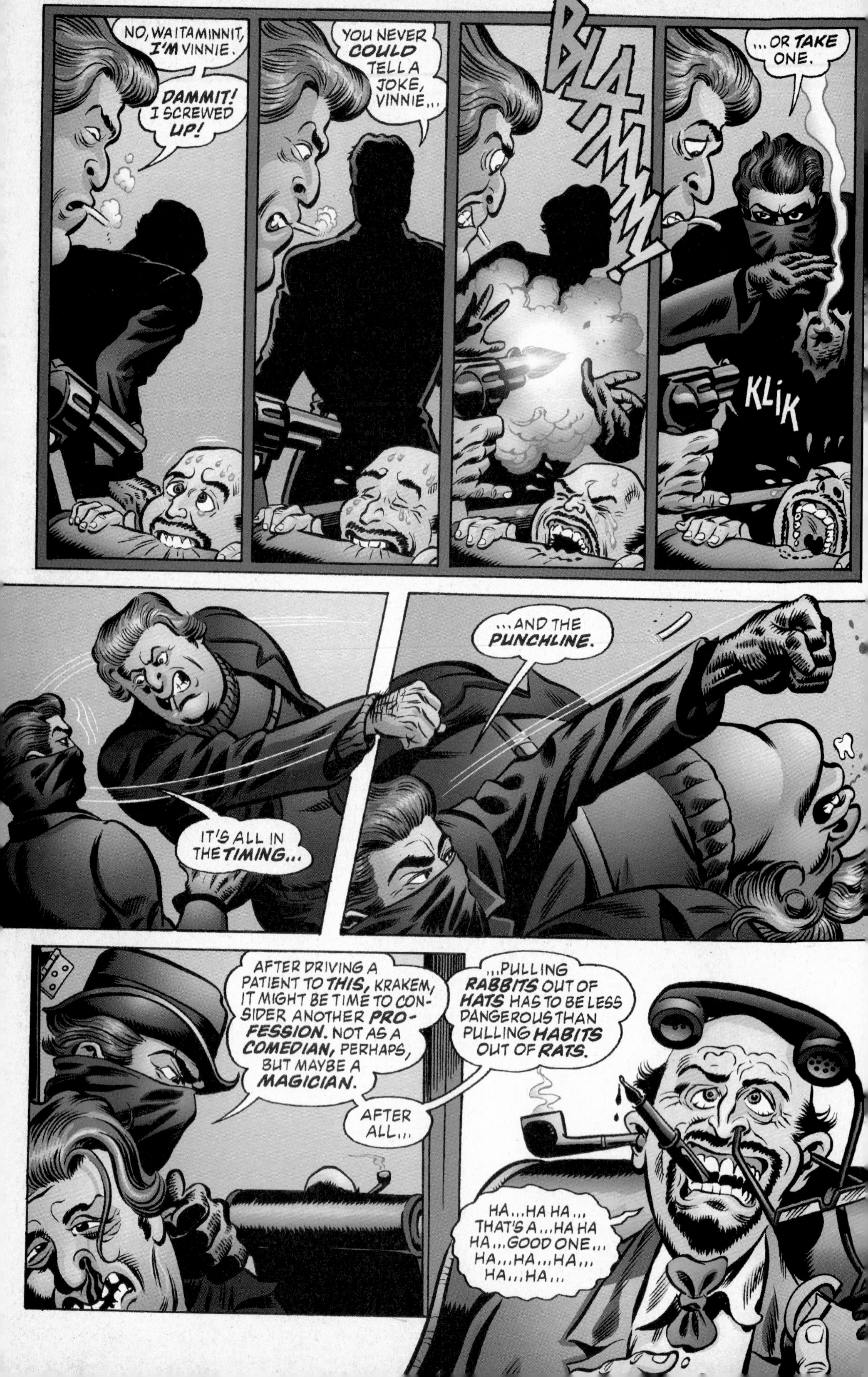

NO, WAITAMINNIT, I'M VINNIE.
DAMMIT! I SCREWED UP!
YOU NEVER COULD TELL A JOKE, VINNIE...
BLAMM!
...OR TAKE ONE.
KLIK
IT'S ALL IN THE TIMING...
...AND THE PUNCHLINE.
AFTER DRIVING A PATIENT TO THIS, KRAKEM, IT MIGHT BE TIME TO CONSIDER ANOTHER PROFESSION. NOT AS A COMEDIAN, PERHAPS, BUT MAYBE A MAGICIAN.
AFTER ALL...
...PULLING RABBITS OUT OF HATS HAS TO BE LESS DANGEROUS THAN PULLING HABITS OUT OF RATS.
HA...HA HA... THAT'S A...HA HA HA...GOOD ONE... HA...HA...HA... HA...HA...

ALL THE NEWS FROM DAWN TO DUSK

STILL 75¢

INDIGO CITY SUNSET

AFTERNOON CITY EDITION

Wednesday, April 17, 2002 Metro Weather – Today: Hazy, Tonight: Soupy, Tomorrow: Won't see your hand in front of your face

EVEN HEROES GET THE HEEBIE-JEEBIES!

GREYSHIRT suffers fever, hallucinations after mission to return stolen statue backfires!

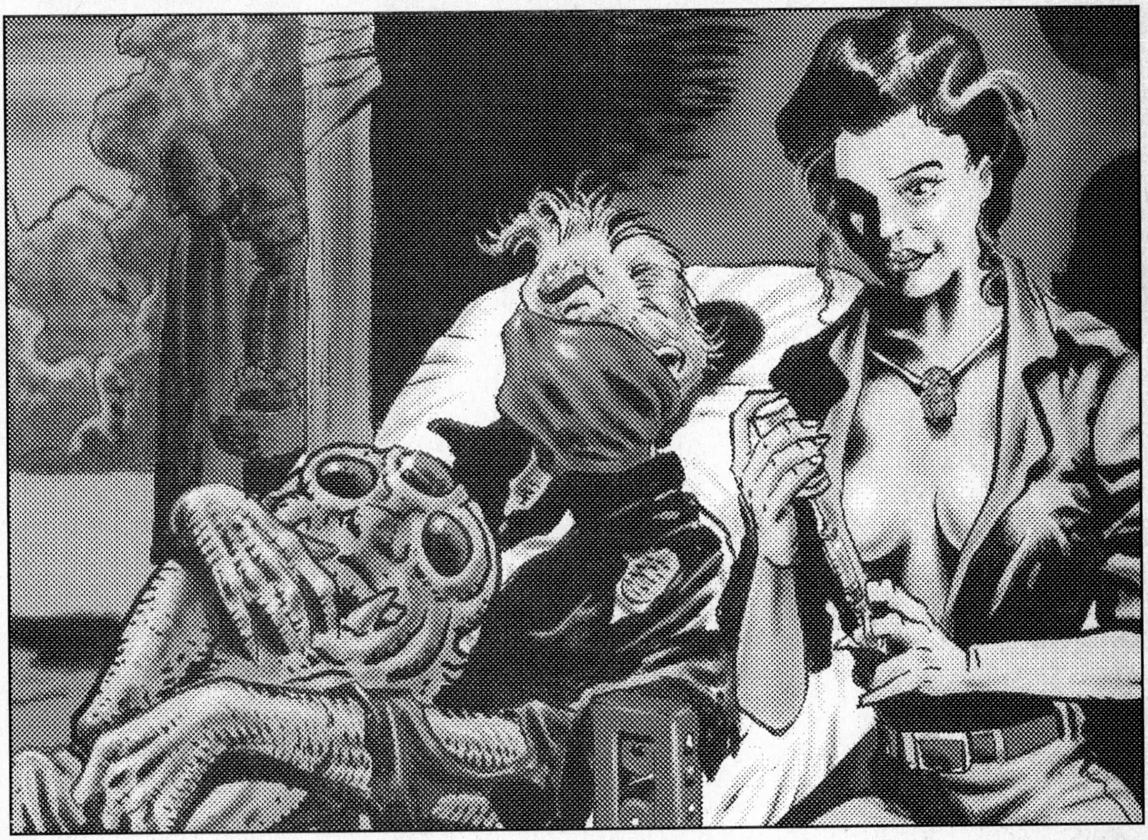

A report out of Chile reveals how perilously close Indigo City came to losing one of its top Science Heroes this week. GREYSHIRT, on a mission to return a stolen statuette to its rightful tribal owners in the Primeval Plateau of the Patagonian high country, was stricken by an extreme case of jungle fever. Saved from certain death thanks to the timely treatment of a mysterious doctor who recorded his fevered ravings, GREYSHIRT is back in Indigo tonight, not much worse for wear but a little wiser about the authenticity of items one might find in museums.

FULL COVERAGE: Pages 2 and 3

FANMAN: FIRST PHOTOS! Page 33

PANDEMONIUM ON PRIMEVAL PLATEAU!

GREYSHIRT BATTLES PHANTOM

SPECIAL TO THE SUNSET BY SKEETER BACKENBEATER

What began as a simple attempt to return a stolen statuette to its original owners on the PRIMEVAL PLATEAU in the Patagonian jungle nearly ended in disaster for GREYSHIRT this week. Reports out of Chile indicate the masked adventurer was discovered wandering through the rainforest, out of his normally steel-trap mind with fever, by local villagers. Nursed back to health in a jungle clinic by a doctor trained in Western medicine, GREYSHIRT returned to Indigo City yesterday, followed by wild rumors concerning his mental health and competence. The speculation was fueled by a transcript of GREYSHIRT's ravings recorded when his hallucinations were at their peak.

The adventure began right after GREYSHIRT succeeded in capturing Bruno Imbroglio and Sabra Desade, two cat burglars who nearly pulled off the heist of the decade by stealing the fabled STAR OF INDIGO sapphire from the Indigo History Museum.

Among other stolen artifacts recovered from Imbroglio's lavish penthouse apartment was a curious bejeweled statuette, which museum directors identified as centermost to the religious beliefs of a tribe of mystics known as the PRIMEVAL people in South America. The statuette had reportedly been stolen from the main temple on the Primeval Plateau seven years ago, causing a deep split in the tribal government with a renegade cult of priests launching a civil war against the rightful queen.

GREYSHIRT, who for his own personal reasons felt he owed the Museum a favor, offered to return the statuette to its rightful home on the plateau and, being a man of immediate action, caught the next flight out of Indigo International Airport bound for Chile.

According to the transcript of his hallucinations, GREYSHIRT claimed he was met in Santiago by a representative of the Chilean government, an antiquities scholar named Estabon Huerchonoto, who had already arranged for a well-equipped small plane to whisk the pair into the remote regions of the Primeval Plateau.

Along the way, Huerchonoto filled GREYSHIRT in on the background of the statuette, to which the native peoples invested deep mystical powers. According to legend, the statuette was the key to accessing another world where the normal laws of physics do not apply.

Huerchonoto asked to see the statuette and when GREYSHIRT pulled it from his bag and handed it to him, the scholar revealed himself to be one of the Primeval Elders. He told GREYSHIRT he was part of a splinter cult of Primevals who planned to use the statuette to destroy the rightful queen, open the doors to this strange new dimension and flood our civilized world with madness incarnate.

It is at this point that the story, pieced together from the fevered mumblings of a hallucinating GREYSHIRT by the woman doctor who treated him, stops making any coherent sense.

According to the doctor's record, GREYSHIRT repeatedly claimed the aircraft he and the Primeval priest were riding in was suddenly transformed, with the windows shrinking into nothingness and the hard plastic interior becoming wet, warm flesh, not unlike the guts of an animal. Trapped in the dark, fetid interior, GREYSHIRT claimed he could feel digestive juices beginning to burn at his clothing.

The priest laughed and, with the statuette in hand, headed towards what would have been the cockpit. The front of the vehicle opened in a strange way and as light burst into the interior it seemed to GREYSHIRT that he had indeed become imprisoned within the stomach of a huge animal. The priest leaped out of the forward opening and GREYSHIRT attempted to follow, but found it closing on him. Thinking quickly, he stopped it from shutting by inserting his cane as a wedge, then looked out to

PANDEMONIUM ON PRIMEVAL PLATEAU!

PATAGONIAN PRIESTS!

But fever dream transcript shows latest foe all in his mind!

view an impossible sight.

He found himself sitting within the open beak of a crow the size of a Piper Cub, or so he later claimed in the throes of his fever. A thousand feet below he could see the priest riding the air currents down towards a fantastic cliffside city of towers and stairways lined with huge graven heads. Desperate to escape the burning gastric juices, GREYSHIRT leapt to the back of the great bird and forced it down towards the city beneath him.

The landing was rough, but GREYSHIRT was able to bring the bird to earth unhurt and unnoticed by any of the other inhabitants of the city, many of whom exhibited traits that could only be described as non-human.

GREYSHIRT later told the mysterious doctor that he was able to surprise the priest and regain possession of the statuette, after which he attempted to escape the plateau by a series of steps carved out of the side of the mile-high cliffs. Here the Indigo Avenger's hallucinations again appear to have gotten the better of him, as he was convinced that the hundreds of fanciful heads carved into the cliff wall suddenly sprang to life at the Priest's bidding, harassing GREYSHIRT as he raced down the innumerable steps. The Indigo Avenger claimed he would have been crushed by the living monoliths had he not threatened to throw the statuette to certain destruction on the valley floor below. When he saw that the stone gargoyles obeyed him, he then ordered them to attack the priest, which some of them did. Other monoliths moved in to protect the priest and a fantastic battle ensued, which allowed GREYSHIRT the diversion he needed to reach the valley floor and escape into the jungle with the precious statuette.

It was a week later when peasants in a nearby village found the masked adventurer wandering through the brush, delirious with jungle fever and still clutching the statuette. They took him to a local clinic where a Western-trained doctor, Magdalena Moreno, had by some coincidence arrived on an unexpected visit. Doctor Moreno was able to successfully treat the ailing crime fighter with antibiotics and record a transcript of his story. His fever raged for three days but he refused to let go of the statuette.

Once GREYSHIRT was well enough to travel, Doctor Moreno took him, still clutching the statuette, down to the tourist section of the little town. There she showed him something that finally loosened his grip on the idol. In the village square were half a dozen pottery shops, all selling exact copies of the statuette he had given so much to protect. In fact, the doctor told him, the idol in his arms was nothing but a fake as well. GREYSHIRT finally gave up the statuette to Doctor Moreno and was put on a plane to Indigo. Local authorities say he's already back patrolling the city's streets.

Attempts by this reporter to locate Doctor Moreno, or the statuette, were unsuccessful. The Chilean government claims that there is no one in the country licensed to practice medicine under that name. Oddly enough, the name of the rightful queen of the Primeval people is listed in local records as the same as the mysterious doctor who nursed GREYSHIRT back from the brink of death and disappeared with the original statuette: Magdalena Moreno.

THE LADY VANISHES!

Colorful Corner Newsy disappears!

One of Indigo City's most colorful street characters failed to turn up at the corner newsstand she's run for almost ten years and both the police and the Indigo City Sunset are at a loss to explain the disappearance. Known only as "LADY L," and famous for her saucy language and independent attitude, the blind newsy failed to open her Ozone Square newsstand last week and left no forwarding address.

The locals at TWO-EYED JACK'S, a nearby saloon, were toasting LADY L long, loud and late last night--with more than one of them imitating her well-known and all-purpose expression, "Kiss my rosy red butt." The saloon itself had been the site of a shooting earlier in the evening, but customers virtually ignored the coroner and clean-up crew, instead reminiscing and attesting to their affection for the curmudgeonly old woman, who was known to frequent the establishment regularly.

Police have no leads and last night were trying to question Rubberneck Crowbar, who rode the Sunset truck that normally delivered the morning edition to LADY L's newsstand. As it turned out, Crowbar was already down at the precinct reporting the fact that his paper truck had been stolen.

Police said there was probably no connection between the incidents. The Sunset will reopen the Ozone Square newsstand under new management as soon as possible.

AGING GANGSTER ESCAPES HALFWAY HOUSE!

O'Riordhan says Carbone "not dangerous to anyone except himself."

Fifteen years ago his name inspired fear and awe in every corner of Indigo City, but today CARMINE CARBONE is a shadow of that former self. His escape yesterday, from a halfway house for elderly felons, elicited only concern that the old man would harm himself. Police said there was little chance he would attack any law-abiding Indigo City citizens.

Carbone was convicted of conspiracy and racketeering charges in 1989 after the District Attorney received overwhelming evidence from an anonymous source. In a dramatic jailhouse interview, Carbone claimed the informant was his own mistress.

Once in prison, Carbone's health and mental state deteriorated sharply and the old man was released into the halfway house program in 1999. He was frequently seen in his pajamas and bathrobe, confused and talking to himself as he pushed his walker through the old Bottoms Up district of Indigo City.

Police Chief O'Riordhan told the Sunset, "Carmine doesn't present a threat to the community. He's just an old man who probably got lost and didn't return to the halfway house at the appointed time. We're not treating it as an escape so much as a lost and found problem."

COPS INVESTIGATE POSSIBLE CHILD ABDUCTION!

Retarded girl fails to finish paper route!

A mildly retarded paper girl is missing and the police are treating it as a possible abduction case. The girl, CATHERINE SMITH is twelve years old and lived at the SAINT ALLOYSIUS'S ORPHANAGE until her disappearance yesterday.

Her bag and undelivered copies of the Sunset were found in a back alley off Helium Street. There were no signs of a struggle, but police clearly suspect foul play. Police said they had received reports that Smith was routinely taunted by some of the young toughs along her route but was known to show gumption, standing up to their bullying. Despite her mental handicap, she was reportedly determined to do what work she could to make her own way in the world.

Anyone with information on her whereabouts should contact their local precinct, or phone the Indigo Sunset news desk at 555-2822.

INDIGO POOP SCOOP!
BY IDLE DISH

AND THE WINNER IS...!

The annual, semi-secret SCIENCE HERO AWARDS were held in INDIGO CITY this week and the SCOOP was able to swing a ringside seat at the exclusive gala festivities (thanks to a certain mayor who shall go nameless.) Many of the country's most infamous Science Heroes and Heroines turned out in their finest uniforms hoping to bring a coveted ALAN statue home to their secret headquarters.

The menu was a surprise traditional potluck supper put on by the citizens of Queerwater, Kansas, who were there in force to cheer hometown favorite, JACK B. QUICK. Many of the Queerwater party ended up with summonses after they attempted to stage a "Running With The Cows" event down Sulphur Street in honor of the boy genius.   Quick received the ALAN award for BEST DEFENSE AGAINST AN ALIEN ABDUCTION after the 10-year-old succeeded in turning a galactic-spanning civilization into a race of hopeless neurotics in perpetual therapy.

Perennial favorite TOM STRONG was a perennial no-show again. The fact that he sent his talking-ape manservant to accept the ALAN for BEST PERFOR-MANCE IN AN INTERSTELLAR ADVENTURE for his work in the Terra Obscura case had event organizers already planning next year's ceremony for Millennium City to avoid future snubs.

Living liquid SPLASH BRANNIGAN was on hand, his nervousness spilling over into a number of telling shapes as his id got the best of his better judgment. When the dribbling dynamo approached the podium to accept his award for BEST PERFORMANCE BATTLING A VERSION OF HIMSELF for the infamous "SPLASH OF TWO WORLDS" case, BRANNIGAN confused and embarrassed everyone by transforming into a shuffling, fawning caricature of TOM STRONG's manservant. We expect it will be the last ALAN nomination the Indelible Avenger sees for a few years!

GREYSHIRT provided the evening's highpoint of Hollywood-style melodrama when he was awarded BEST ENCOUNTER WITH A LONG-LOST LOVE for his work on the LAPIS LAZULI case. The Indigo Avenger had been seated next to his reported new flame COBWEB when the ALAN was announced, causing an immediate buzz through the crowd. For her part, COB-WEB seemed nonplussed and in fact was later seen slipping out early with a Minotaur from Neopolis, leaving her chauffeur to accept her sweep of BEST EROTIC ENCOUNTER in the GOOD GIRL, BAD GIRL and FREEFORM divisions.

Unfortunately the ceremony broke up early when fighting erupted at the podium between FIRST AMERICAN and U.S. ANGEL, who had been awarded BEST PARODY OF A COMIC BOOK ADVERTISEMENT in the so-called "BITTER CRUMBS OF DEFEAT" adventure. The dispute appears to have been fueled by long-standing ill-will between these science heroes over who got to eat the last "Mistress Cupcake" during that particular adventure.

The real buzz of the evening was the recent reformation of AMERICA's BEST HEROES, which came too late to be considered for this year. The POOP predicts a sweep for the ABH at next year's ALAN awards!

ASK DR. SYNTAX

Is Romance for Real?

Dear Dr. Syntax: I'm an unmarried housekeeper who, until recently, was employed by a well-to-do young man living in a luxurious penthouse apartment. As it turned out, my boss was a master thief who had built his fortune as one of the best second story men in Indigo. I didn't know any of this until the police and GREYSHIRT descended on the penthouse suite and arrested my boss for attempting to steal the STAR OF INDIGO sapphire.

As you might be aware, the STAR OF INDIGO is reported to have mystical powers that cause people to fall in love at first sight. Strangely enough, that is exactly what happened to me! I was working in the kitchen when one of the arresting officers came in with the jewel. Our eyes met and instantly I knew he and I were destined for each other. As we spoke it became clear he had had a similar experience when he first saw me.

We began to date and soon became inseparable. He has asked me to be his wife and I have accepted. I am deliriously happy for the first time in my life, but there is a little voice in the back of my mind that suggests my happiness is not real. I'm worried that what I feel for this gentleman might just be an effect caused by the magic of this famous gem.

What should I do?--Elspeth

Dear Elspeth: While experts in the history of the STAR OF INDIGO agree on its power, they are divided on how it actually works. Some say it causes love at first sight, while others suggest that it merely brings couples, who are already destined to meet and fall in love, together. We think you should stop listening to the little voice of doubt and instead pay attention to what's really important. Like, how's the sex?

Dear Dr. Syntax: I'm an Indigo City police officer often called on to stake out criminal activities in a squad car with another officer I'll call "Dick." Dick has a habit of eating beernuts while on the job and this results in constant attacks of excessive flatulence on his part. In the cramped confines of the squad car, I find the odor often-times unbearable. Last night it was so thick and disgusting that it felt like my skin was smeared with ambergris. I've tried to get reassigned to another partner, but no one else in the department will work with Dick and since I'm low man on the seniority pole, I'm stuck with him. What can I do?--Gassed Out

Dear Gassed Out: I suggest a word with your superiors about how they can best make use of Dick's affliction is in order. Suggest that any suspects the department picks up be put in the squad car's cage while Dick is seated up front with a goodly supply of beernuts. If it is as thick as you say in there, those hoods will be pleading guilty to every crime in the book to get out!

SUNSET COMICS

MUSSEL BEACH **By Squid Pro Quo**

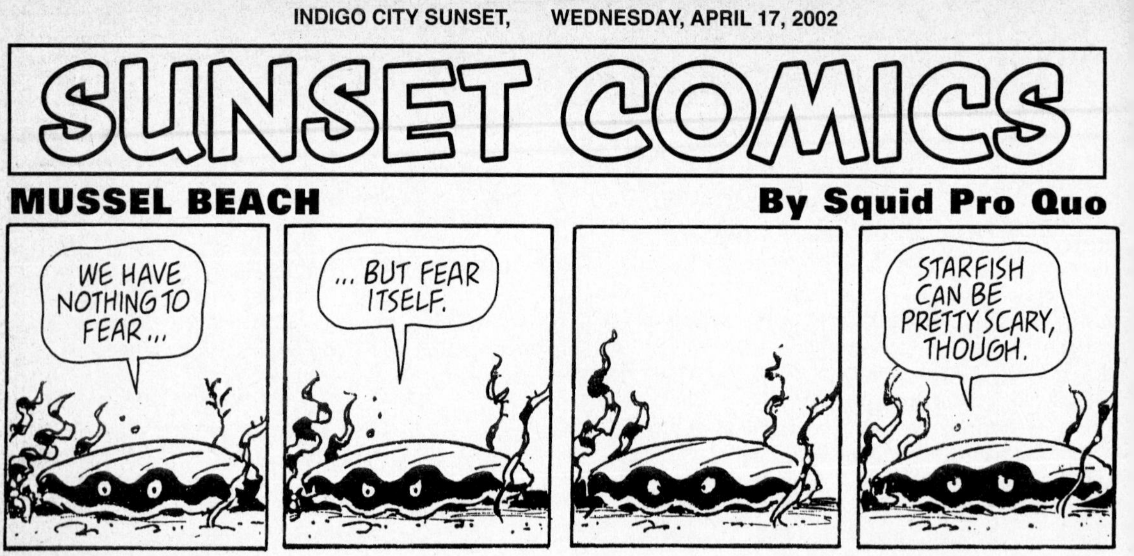
WE HAVE NOTHING TO FEAR...
... BUT FEAR ITSELF.
STARFISH CAN BE PRETTY SCARY, THOUGH.

HARRY GEE **By Chet Ghoulash**

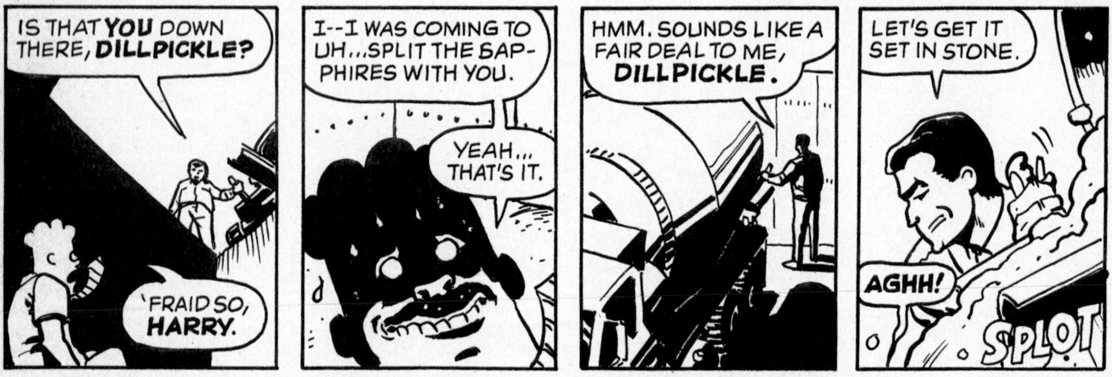
IS THAT **YOU** DOWN THERE, **DILLPICKLE?**
'FRAID SO, **HARRY.**
I--I WAS COMING TO UH...SPLIT THE SAP-PHIRES WITH YOU.
YEAH... THAT'S IT.
HMM. SOUNDS LIKE A FAIR DEAL TO ME, **DILLPICKLE.**
LET'S GET IT SET IN STONE.
AGHH!
SPLOT

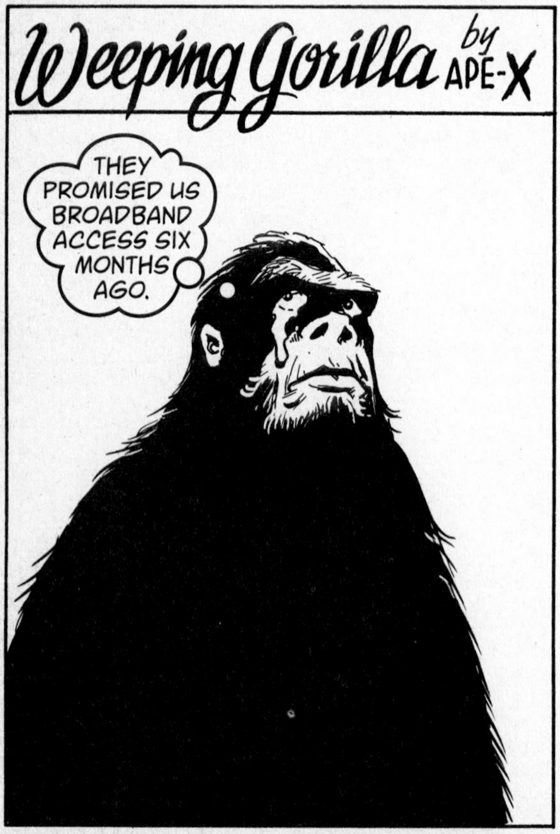
Weeping Gorilla by APE-X
THEY PROMISED US BROADBAND ACCESS SIX MONTHS AGO.

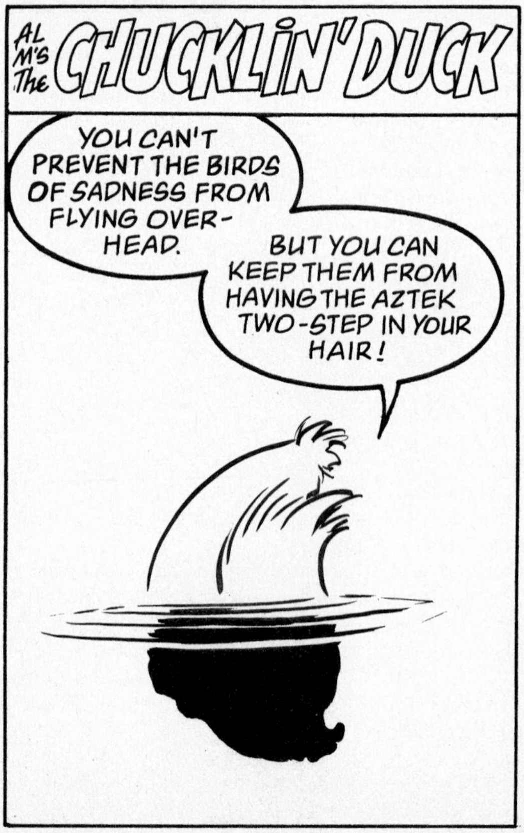
AL M'S The CHUCKLIN' DUCK
YOU CAN'T PREVENT THE BIRDS OF SADNESS FROM FLYING OVER-HEAD.
BUT YOU CAN KEEP THEM FROM HAVING THE AZTEK TWO-STEP IN YOUR HAIR!

FOR INDIGO KIDS OF ALL AGES!

BOWSER THE SCHNAUZER

By Yowzuh Trousers

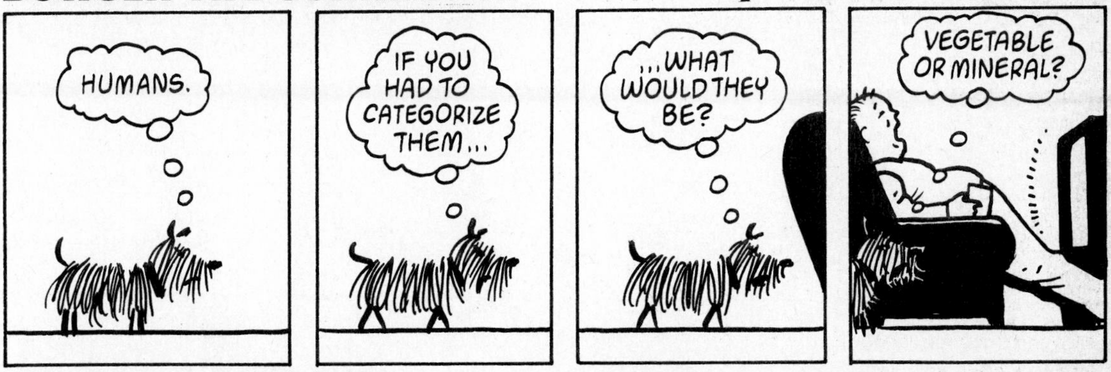
HUMANS.
IF YOU HAD TO CATEGORIZE THEM...
...WHAT WOULD THEY BE?
VEGETABLE OR MINERAL?

MADAM I'M ADAM

By Matthew Mark Lukenjohn

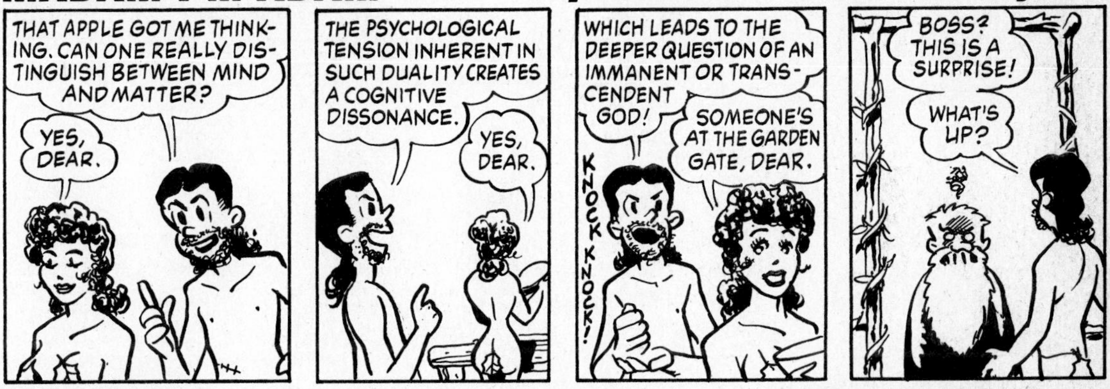
THAT APPLE GOT ME THINKING. CAN ONE REALLY DISTINGUISH BETWEEN MIND AND MATTER?
YES, DEAR.
THE PSYCHOLOGICAL TENSION INHERENT IN SUCH DUALITY CREATES A COGNITIVE DISSONANCE.
YES, DEAR.
WHICH LEADS TO THE DEEPER QUESTION OF AN IMMANENT OR TRANSCENDENT GOD!
KNOCK KNOCK!
SOMEONE'S AT THE GARDEN GATE, DEAR.
BOSS? THIS IS A SURPRISE!
WHAT'S UP?

GOODIOS

By Buddy Fact

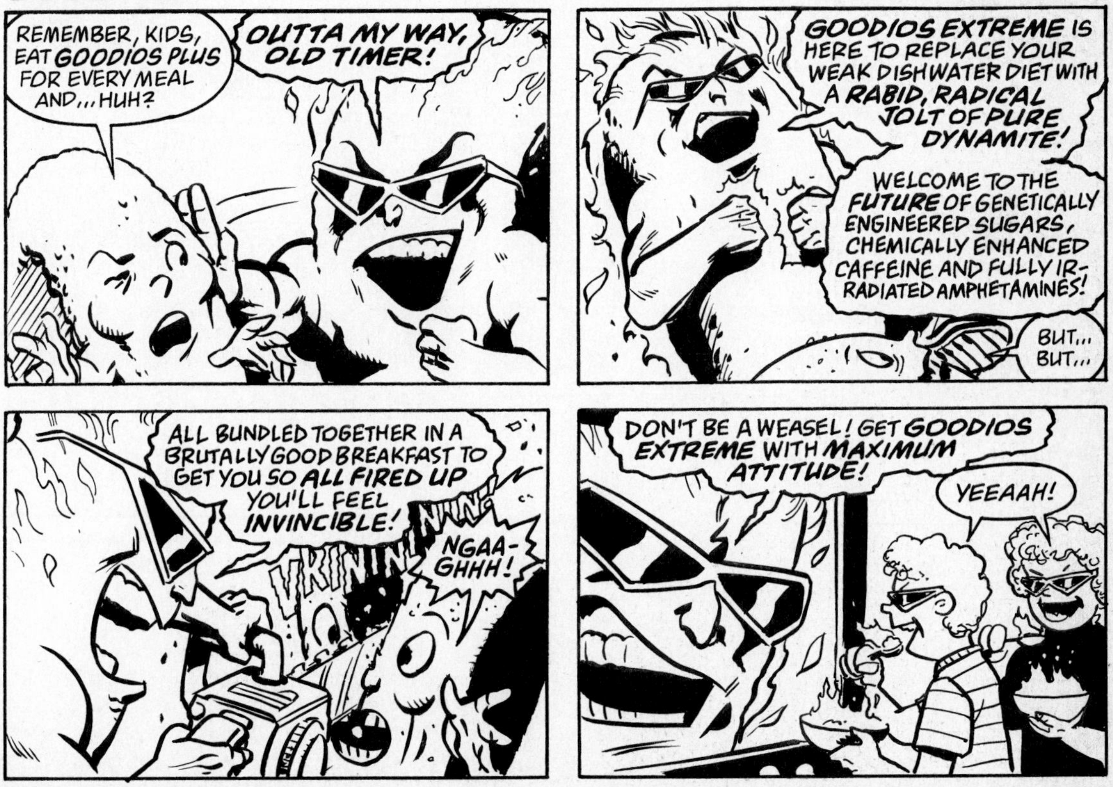
REMEMBER, KIDS, EAT GOODIOS PLUS FOR EVERY MEAL AND... HUH?
OUTTA MY WAY, OLD TIMER!
GOODIOS EXTREME IS HERE TO REPLACE YOUR WEAK DISHWATER DIET WITH A RABID, RADICAL JOLT OF PURE DYNAMITE!
WELCOME TO THE FUTURE OF GENETICALLY ENGINEERED SUGARS, CHEMICALLY ENHANCED CAFFEINE AND FULLY IRRADIATED AMPHETAMINES!
BUT... BUT...
ALL BUNDLED TOGETHER IN A BRUTALLY GOOD BREAKFAST TO GET YOU SO ALL FIRED UP YOU'LL FEEL INVINCIBLE!
VRKINNNNNNG!
NGAAGHHH!
DON'T BE A WEASEL! GET GOODIOS EXTREME WITH MAXIMUM ATTITUDE!
YEEAAH!

 SUNSET HOROSCOPE
By Madame Dagmar

The Stars Reveal Your Destiny!

AQUARIUS (Jan 21-Feb 19): You won't need anyone to stand over you with a truncheon this week, because you're in the mood to take the kind of risks that will either turn you into a rich swell or leave you a pathetic palooka doing twenty to life.

PISCES (Feb 20-Mar 20): You've had your fill of feuding, so tonight's full moon will be the perfect time to get out there and put an end to any bohunk who's been giving you a hard time.

ARIES (Mar 21- April 20): Beware of strangers dressed in gray. Especially wearing a mask.

TAURUS (April 21-May 21): You've cleaned up in the rackets in recent weeks and you may be tempted to to stop where you are and enjoy your gains. But the planets say you should delay any R&R; the best is yet to come.

GEMINI (May 22-June 21): With the sun aspecting Uranus, you better watch your butt.

CANCER (June 22-July 28): Venus, planet of love, moves into your birthsign tonight. For a good time, call 555-6291.

LEO (July 24-Aug 23): If you are awaiting a verdict, then the planets are all pointing towards "guilty." Don't despair, people who never make mistakes never learn. With good behavior you'll be back on the street before you know it.

VIRGO (Aug 24-Sept 23): If you allow yourself to feel threatened, the odds will be stacked against you. Pick a battle you can win and go in packing heavy.

LIBRA (Sept 24-Oct 23): Someone you work with has their hand in the till and your patience is rightfully wearing thin. Mars, planet of anger is squaring up with Jupiter, the planet that makes everything bigger. Drop the hammer.

SCORPIO (Oct 24-Nov 22): You'll be up against someone in authority today, but he's overconfident and will make mistakes you can profit from. Keep your nerve and leave the first move to him.

SAGITTARIUS: If you move too fast, too soon, something unpleasant could happen. The family sector of your chart is highlighted, so don't go up against the Don.

CAPRICORN (Dec 22-Jan 20): Hold out for what you know you are worth. Don't lower your standards or your prices.

IF APRIL 17th IS YOUR BIRTHDAY: You're screwed.

SUNSET PHOTOG DIES!
Tragic gas explosion takes life of Veitichello!

One of the Indigo City Sunset's most versatile news photographers was blown to atoms last night in his own apartment, apparently when a malfunctioning gas television exploded just as the lensman was watching the latest episode of "THE CARBONES."

Ricardo Veitichello made his first splash with the Sunset with a series of pictures illustrating the early career of masked adventurer, GREYSHIRT. Veitichello delivered indelible images of GREYSHIRT's greatest exploits including his rescue of Baby Einstein and his battle with the Robo-Apes of Dr. Heinrich Claw. Veitichello even traveled to Rhajipur when GREYSHIRT and Pandora Siam became involved with a Devil-cult there. Veitichello's most memorable shot was of GREYSHIRT embracing psychopathic murderess Lapis Lazuli just before arresting her on a capital crime.

Ironically, Veitichello's last assignment, completed just hours before he sat down to watch "THE CARBONES," was to get pictures of that hit show's producer, the FANMAN of FanMan Productions. Veitichello had spent weeks shadowing the elusive Hollywood mogul, and was injured in one attempt, ending up hospitalized with a broken nose and slipped disc. The persistence and gumption of this first rate news hound will be missed at the Sunset. His final photos appear next page.

INDIGO CITY SUNSET, WEDNESDAY, APRIL 17, 2002

EXCLUSIVE SUNSET SPY SHOTS!

FIRST FANMAN PHOTOS!

Pix reveal mystery honcho who helms "Carbones!"

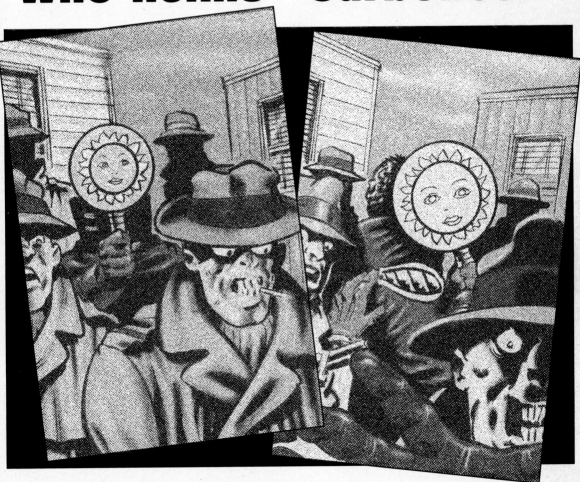

Special photo spread by Ricardo Veitichello

We knew it was only a matter of time before our ace spy photog caught the mystery celebrity who's put Indigo City back on the popular culture map. Here are the first photos ever of the fabulous FANMAN himself, whose hit cable series "THE CARBONES" took half a dozen awards at this year's Emmys. The white hot producer, seen here with his trademark fan shielding his face, has reportedly taken over the director's seat for the big budget "FRANKY AND JOHNNY" flick in the wake of previous director Michael Minstrel's resignation and untimely death in a traffic accident. Word is that the shoot is on schedule and is expected to wrap up location filming in Indigo's Bottoms Up district next month.

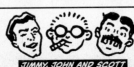

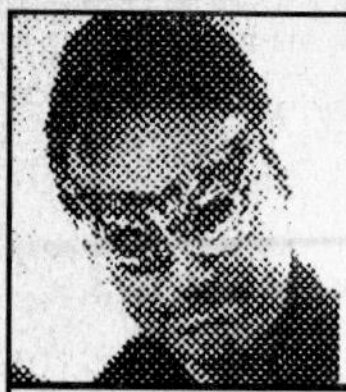

RICK VEITCH
SHOCKER! Writer-Artist's secret identity unmasked! Page 7

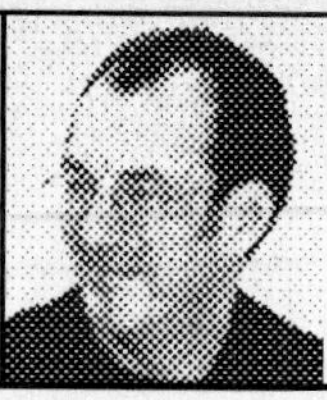

DAVE GIBBONS
Truth about Writer's subliminal doomsday clock plot! Page 8

TODD KLEIN
Letterer admits: "I CAN'T SPEL!" Page 9

HILARY BARTA
Inker's daily Black Magic rituals revealed! Page 10

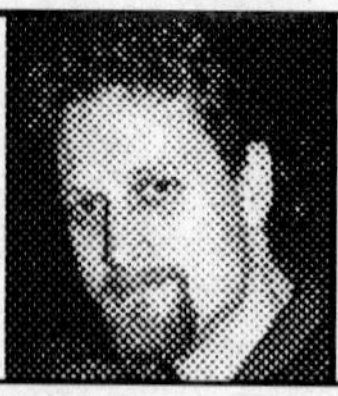

SCOTT DUNBIER
Editor swears "the check is in the mail!" Page 11

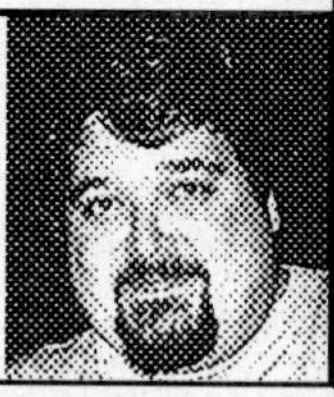

WILDSTORM FX: Color them over-worked!

ALL THE NEWS FROM DAWN TO DUSK

INDIGO CITY SUNSET

AFTERNOON CITY EDITION

Wednesday, April 17, 2002 Metro Weather – Today: Hazy, Tonight: Soupy, Tomorrow: Visually Impenetrable

BACK PAGE EXTRA:

THIS ONE WILL KILL YOU!

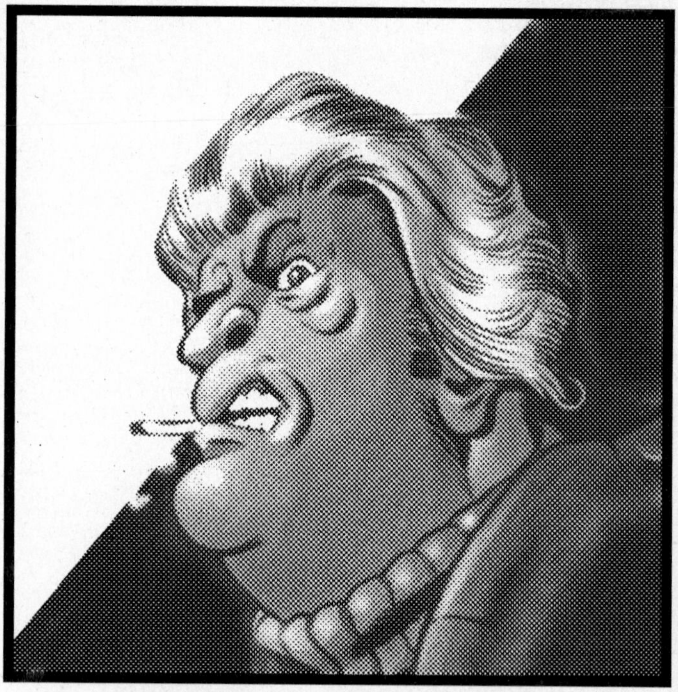

Button Man VINNIE ASSAPUNTO

Lousy Sense of Humor Leads to Rampage!

Special to The Sunset
by Geekus Crow

The streets and tenements of Indigo City's BOTTOMS UP district ran red yesterday as a mob-connected hit man went on a wild rampage that left five people dead. One of the victims was a priest collecting donations at the Indigo City Zoo. The rage of the murderer, Vinnie Assapunto, appears to have been triggered by a gag making the rounds among Indigo wags. Apparently, the beefy hit man was the butt of the joke.

FULL STORY: PAGE 19

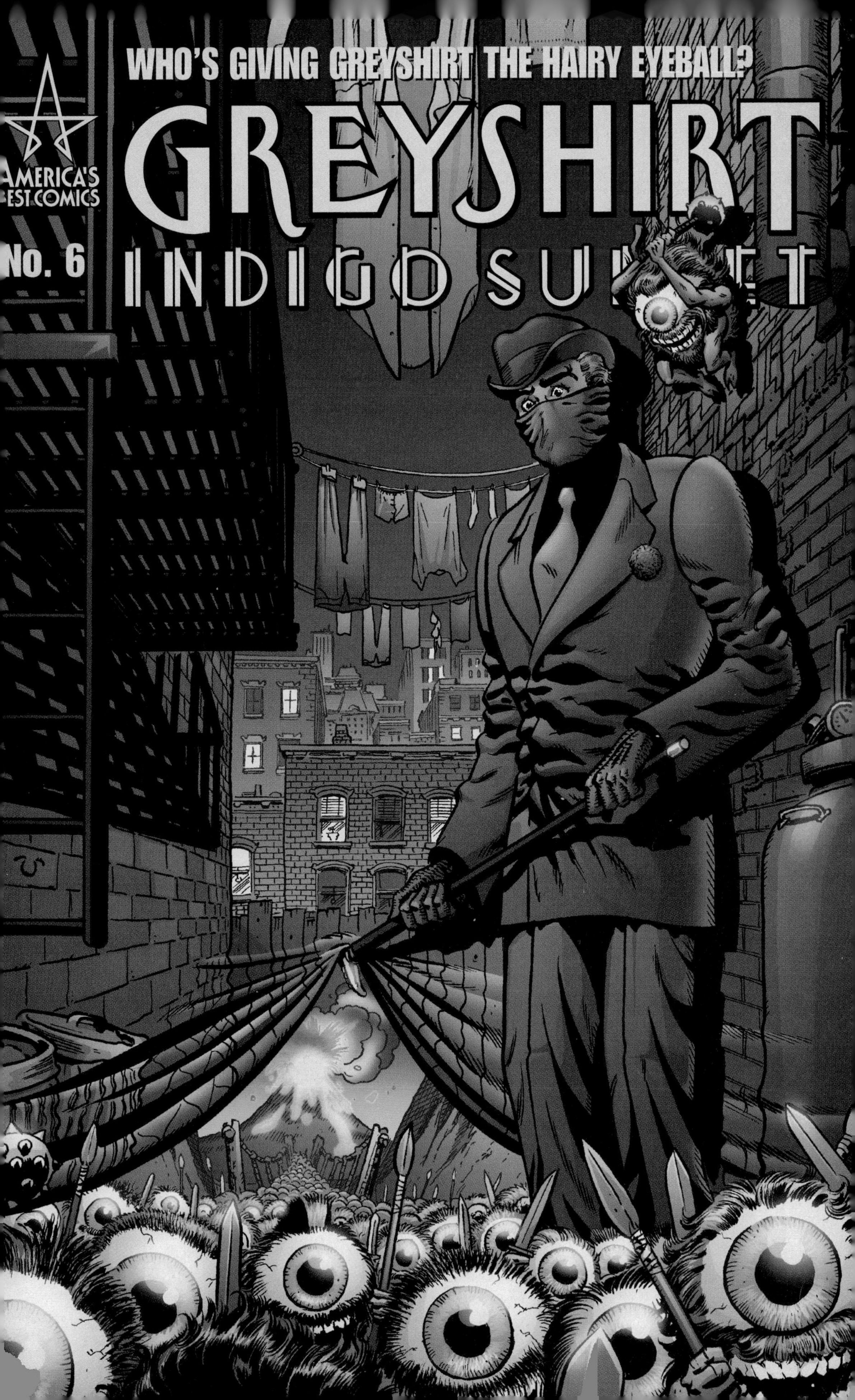
WHO'S GIVING GREYSHIRT THE HAIRY EYEBALL?
AMERICA'S
EST COMICS
No. 6
GREYSHIRT
INDIGO SU ET

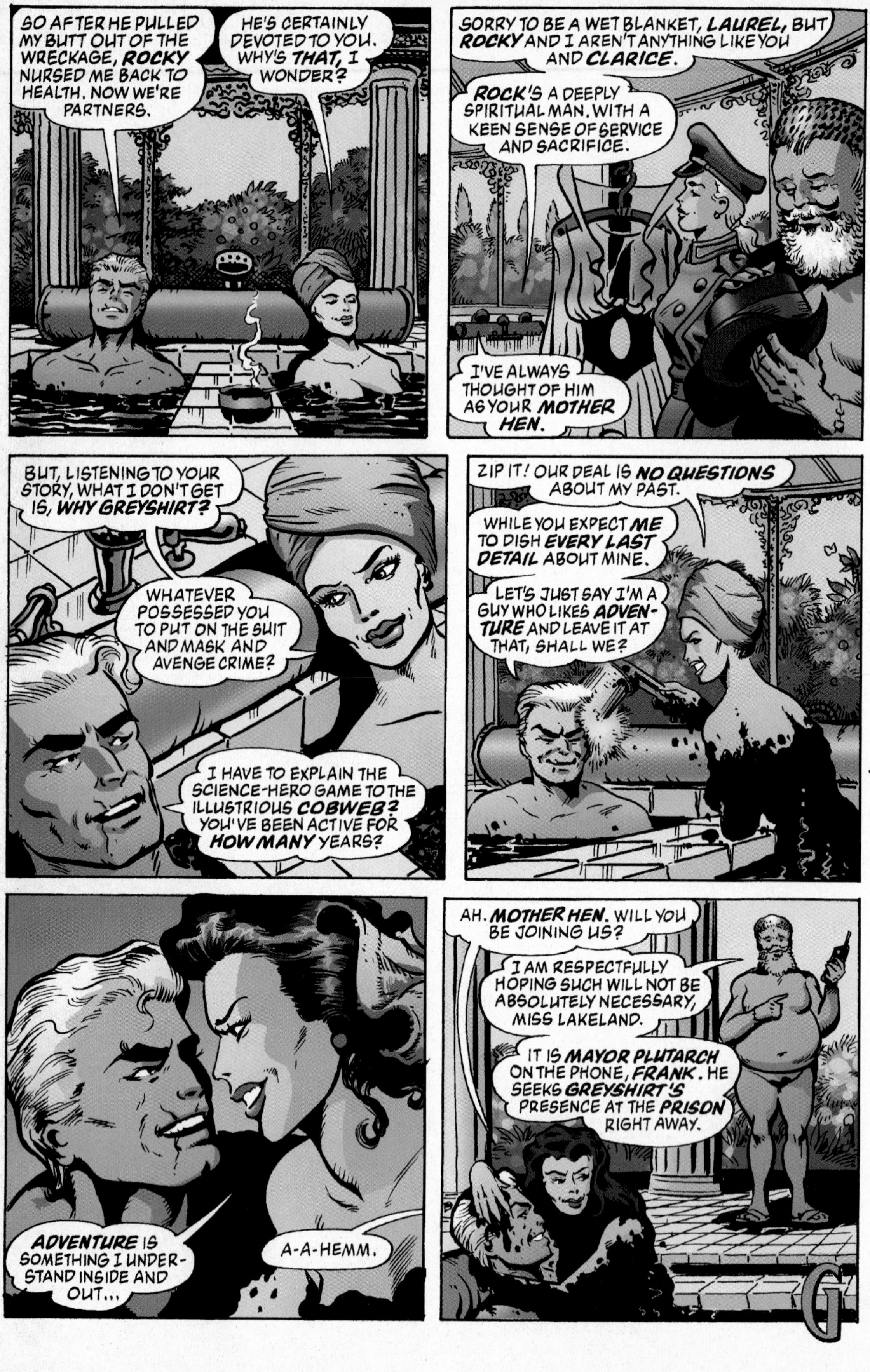
SO AFTER HE PULLED MY BUTT OUT OF THE WRECKAGE, ROCKY NURSED ME BACK TO HEALTH. NOW WE'RE PARTNERS.
HE'S CERTAINLY DEVOTED TO YOU. WHY'S THAT, I WONDER?
SORRY TO BE A WET BLANKET, LAUREL, BUT ROCKY AND I AREN'T ANYTHING LIKE YOU AND CLARICE.
ROCK'S A DEEPLY SPIRITUAL MAN. WITH A KEEN SENSE OF SERVICE AND SACRIFICE.
I'VE ALWAYS THOUGHT OF HIM AS YOUR MOTHER HEN.
BUT, LISTENING TO YOUR STORY, WHAT I DON'T GET IS, WHY GREYSHIRT?
WHATEVER POSSESSED YOU TO PUT ON THE SUIT AND MASK AND AVENGE CRIME?
I HAVE TO EXPLAIN THE SCIENCE-HERO GAME TO THE ILLUSTRIOUS COBWEB? YOU'VE BEEN ACTIVE FOR HOW MANY YEARS?
ZIP IT! OUR DEAL IS NO QUESTIONS ABOUT MY PAST.
WHILE YOU EXPECT ME TO DISH EVERY LAST DETAIL ABOUT MINE.
LET'S JUST SAY I'M A GUY WHO LIKES ADVENTURE AND LEAVE IT AT THAT, SHALL WE?
ADVENTURE IS SOMETHING I UNDERSTAND INSIDE AND OUT...
A-A-HEMM.
AH. MOTHER HEN. WILL YOU BE JOINING US?
I AM RESPECTFULLY HOPING SUCH WILL NOT BE ABSOLUTELY NECESSARY, MISS LAKELAND.
IT IS MAYOR PLUTARCH ON THE PHONE, FRANK. HE SEEKS GREYSHIRT'S PRESENCE AT THE PRISON RIGHT AWAY.
G

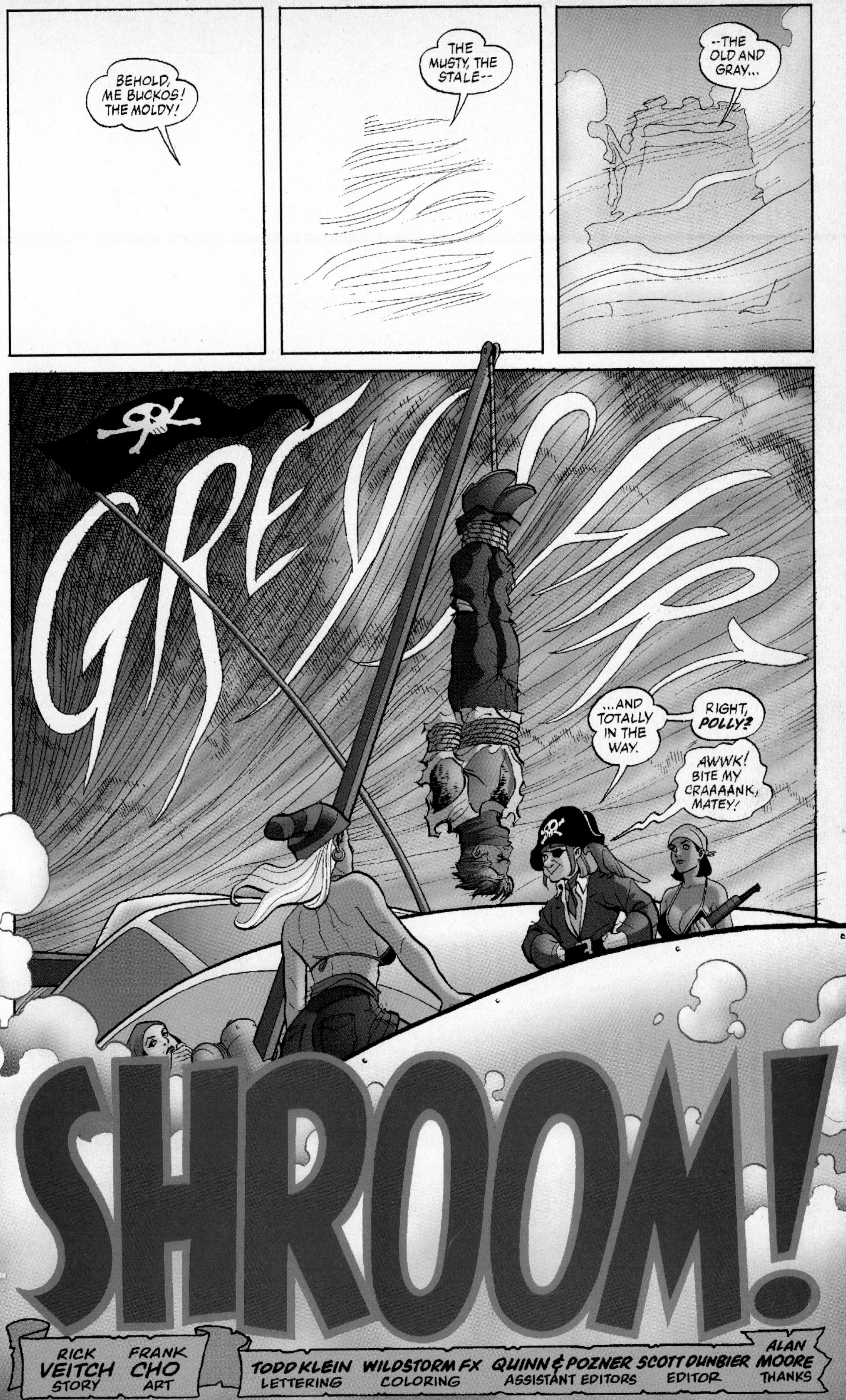

BEHOLD, ME BUCKOS! THE MOLDY!
THE MUSTY, THE STALE--
--THE OLD AND GRAY...
...AND TOTALLY IN THE WAY.
RIGHT, POLLY?
AWWK! BITE MY CRAAAANK, MATEY!
SHROOM!
RICK VEITCH STORY
FRANK CHO ART
TODD KLEIN LETTERING
WILDSTORM FX COLORING
QUINN & POZNER ASSISTANT EDITORS
SCOTT DUNBIER EDITOR
ALAN MOORE THANKS

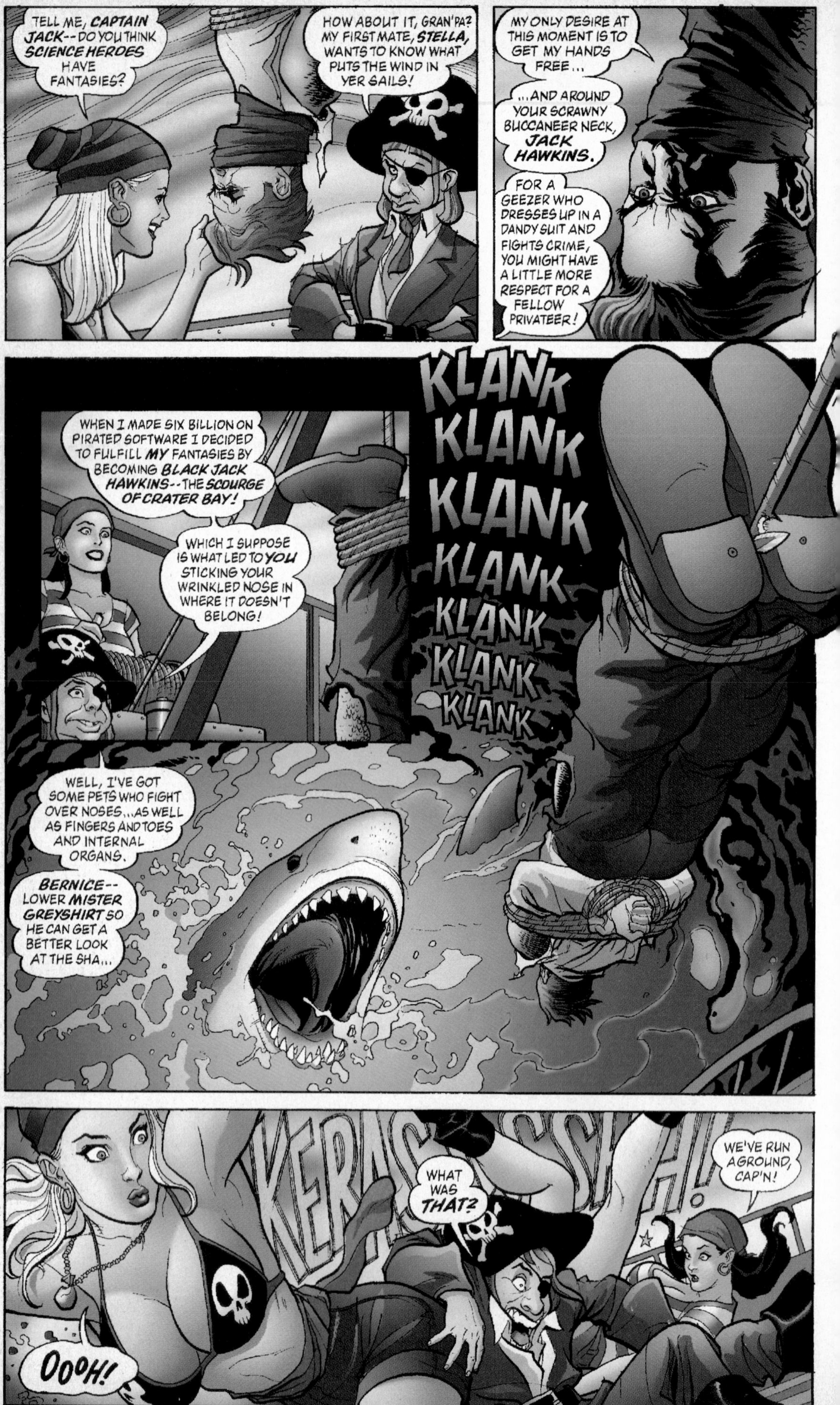
TELL ME, CAPTAIN JACK--DO YOU THINK SCIENCE HEROES HAVE FANTASIES?
HOW ABOUT IT, GRAN'PA? MY FIRST MATE, STELLA, WANTS TO KNOW WHAT PUTS THE WIND IN YER SAILS!
MY ONLY DESIRE AT THIS MOMENT IS TO GET MY HANDS FREE...
...AND AROUND YOUR SCRAWNY BUCCANEER NECK, JACK HAWKINS.
FOR A GEEZER WHO DRESSES UP IN A DANDY SUIT AND FIGHTS CRIME, YOU MIGHT HAVE A LITTLE MORE RESPECT FOR A FELLOW PRIVATEER!
KLANK KLANK KLANK KLANK KLANK KLANK KLANK
WHEN I MADE SIX BILLION ON PIRATED SOFTWARE I DECIDED TO FULFILL MY FANTASIES BY BECOMING BLACK JACK HAWKINS--THE SCOURGE OF CRATER BAY!
WHICH I SUPPOSE IS WHAT LED TO YOU STICKING YOUR WRINKLED NOSE IN WHERE IT DOESN'T BELONG!
WELL, I'VE GOT SOME PETS WHO FIGHT OVER NOSES...AS WELL AS FINGERS AND TOES AND INTERNAL ORGANS.
BERNICE--LOWER MISTER GREYSHIRT SO HE CAN GET A BETTER LOOK AT THE SHA...
WHAT WAS THAT?
WE'VE RUN AGROUND, CAP'N!
OOOH!

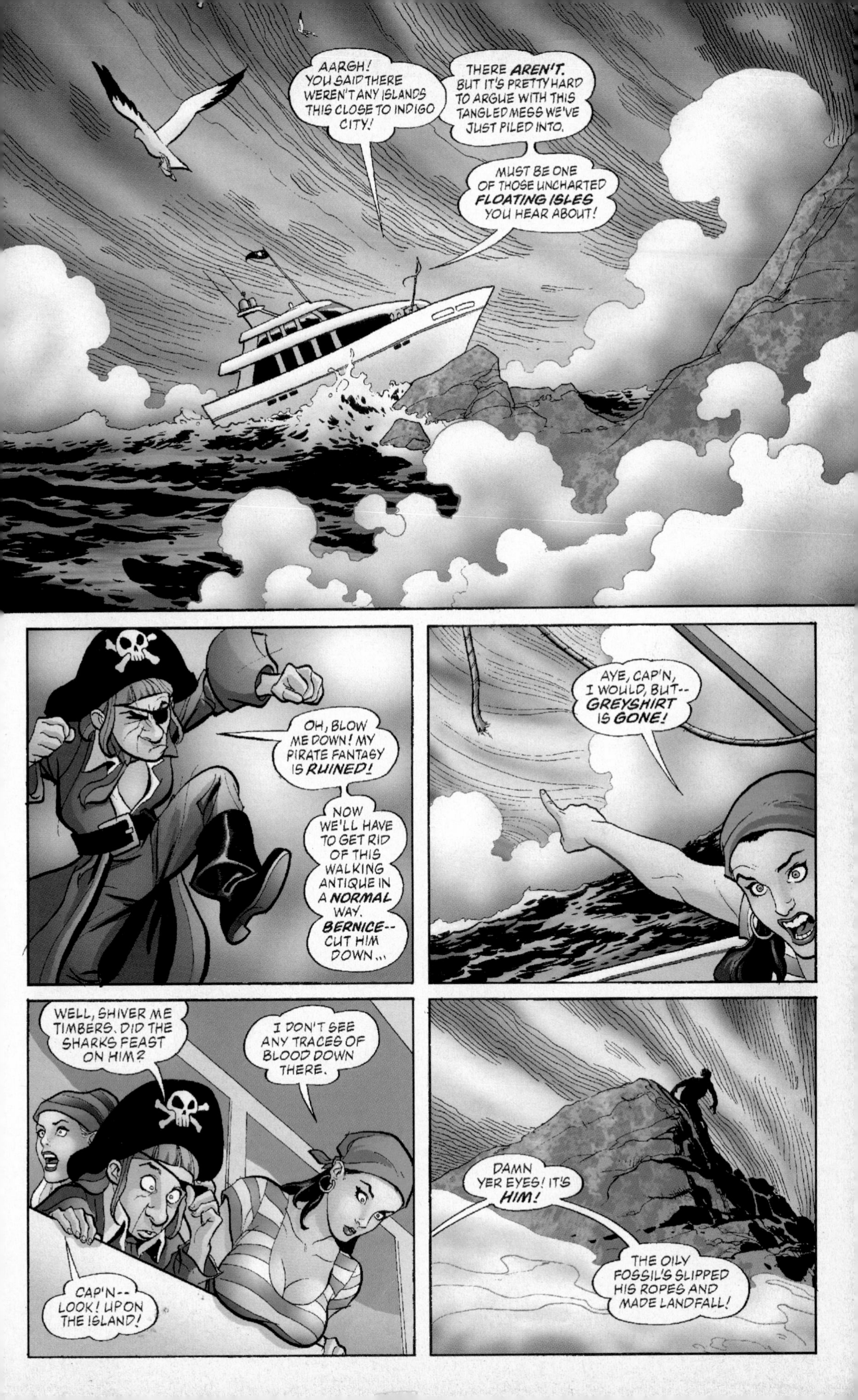
AARGH! YOU SAID THERE WEREN'T ANY ISLANDS THIS CLOSE TO INDIGO CITY!
THERE AREN'T. BUT IT'S PRETTY HARD TO ARGUE WITH THIS TANGLED MESS WE'VE JUST PILED INTO.
MUST BE ONE OF THOSE UNCHARTED FLOATING ISLES YOU HEAR ABOUT!
OH, BLOW ME DOWN! MY PIRATE FANTASY IS RUINED!
NOW WE'LL HAVE TO GET RID OF THIS WALKING ANTIQUE IN A NORMAL WAY. BERNICE-- CUT HIM DOWN...
AYE, CAP'N, I WOULD, BUT-- GREYSHIRT IS GONE!
WELL, SHIVER ME TIMBERS. DID THE SHARKS FEAST ON HIM?
I DON'T SEE ANY TRACES OF BLOOD DOWN THERE.
CAP'N-- LOOK! UP ON THE ISLAND!
DAMN YER EYES! IT'S HIM!
THE OILY FOSSIL'S SLIPPED HIS ROPES AND MADE LANDFALL!

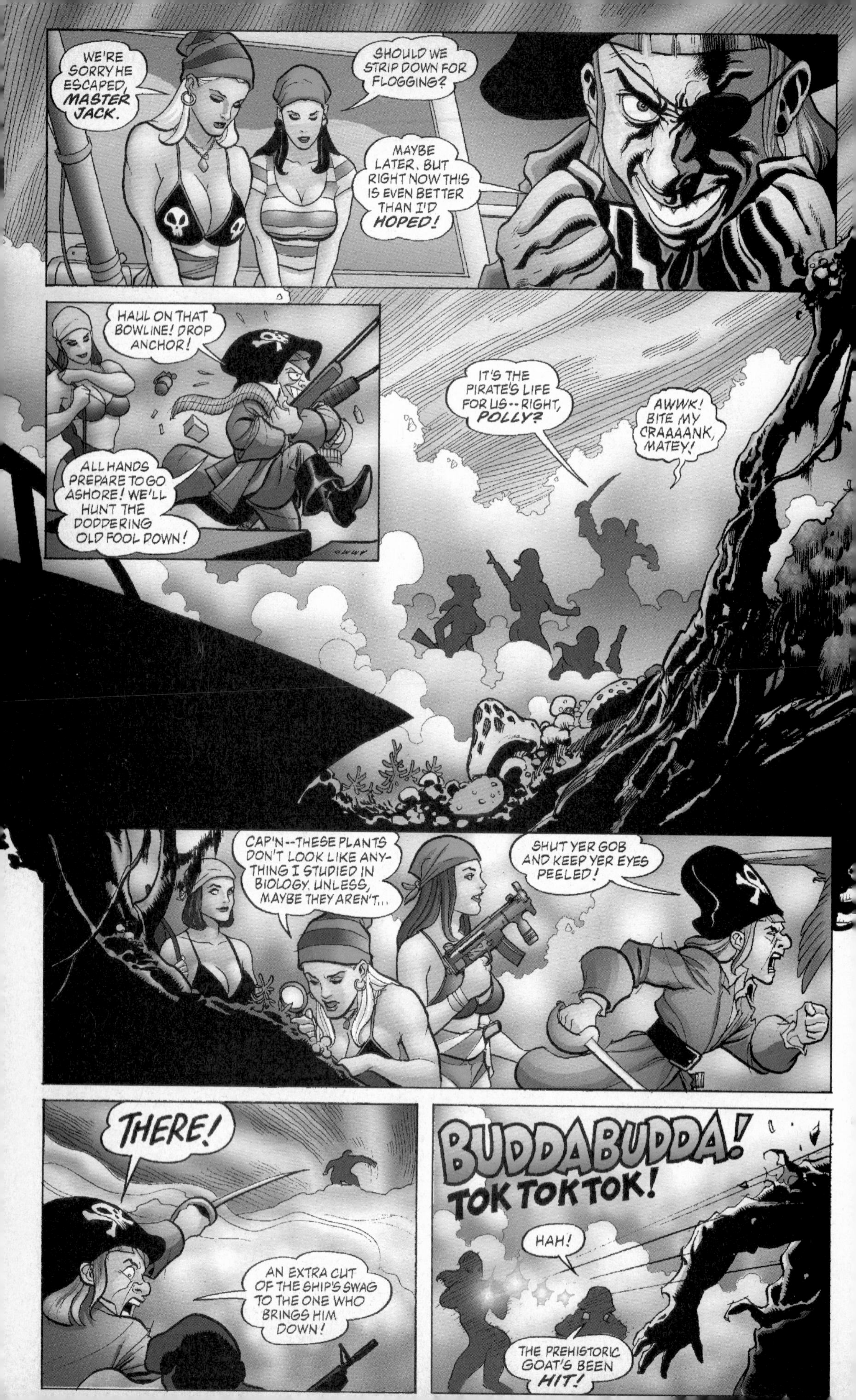
WE'RE SORRY HE ESCAPED, MASTER JACK.
SHOULD WE STRIP DOWN FOR FLOGGING?
MAYBE LATER. BUT RIGHT NOW THIS IS EVEN BETTER THAN I'D HOPED!
HAUL ON THAT BOWLINE! DROP ANCHOR!
ALL HANDS PREPARE TO GO ASHORE! WE'LL HUNT THE DODDERING OLD FOOL DOWN!
IT'S THE PIRATE'S LIFE FOR US--RIGHT, POLLY?
AWWK! BITE MY CRAAAANK, MATEY!
CAP'N--THESE PLANTS DON'T LOOK LIKE ANYTHING I STUDIED IN BIOLOGY. UNLESS, MAYBE THEY AREN'T...
SHUT YER GOB AND KEEP YER EYES PEELED!
THERE!
AN EXTRA CUT OF THE SHIP'S SWAG TO THE ONE WHO BRINGS HIM DOWN!
BUDDABUDDA!
TOK TOK TOK!
HAH!
THE PREHISTORIC GOAT'S BEEN HIT!

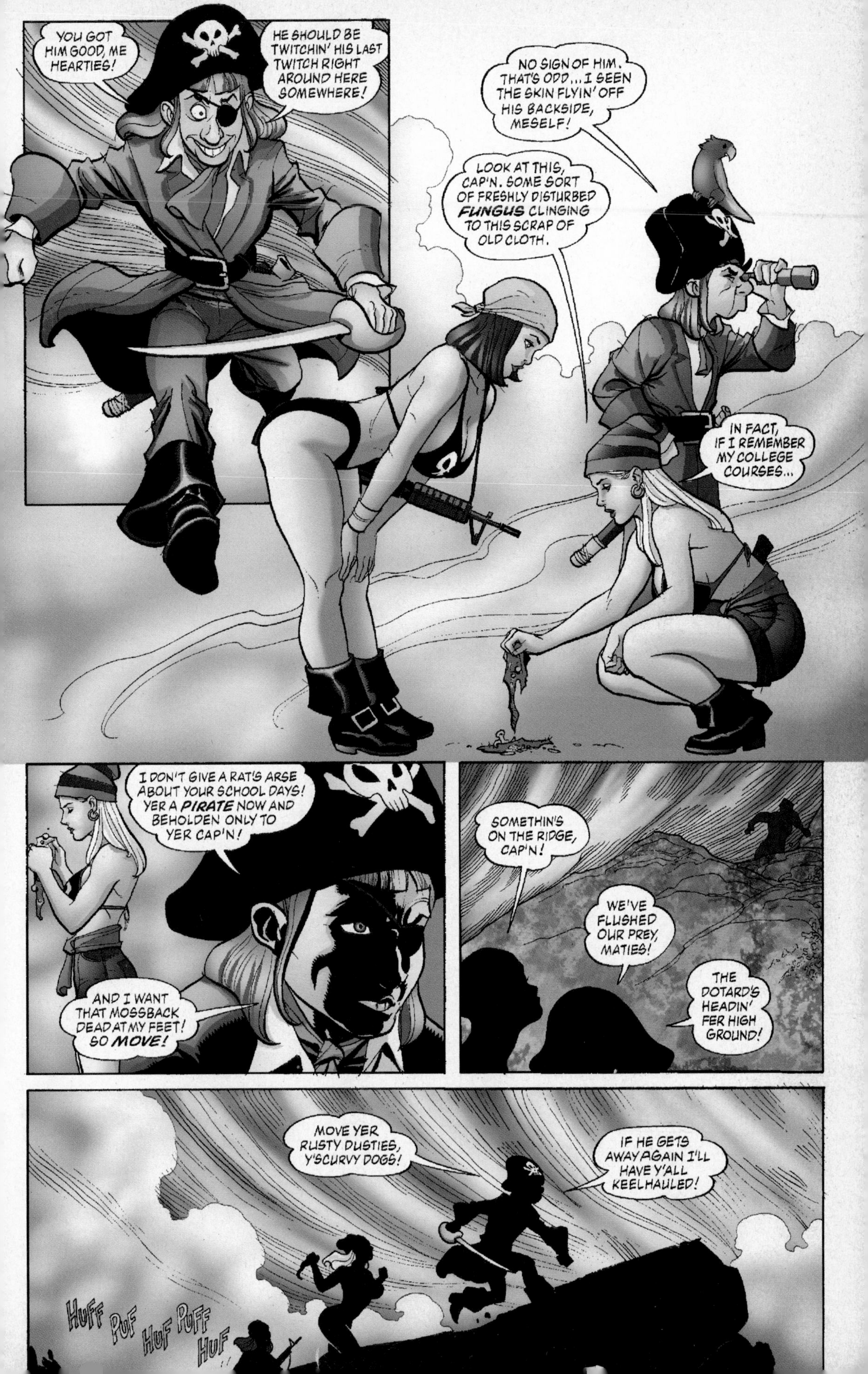
YOU GOT HIM GOOD, ME HEARTIES!
HE SHOULD BE TWITCHIN' HIS LAST TWITCH RIGHT AROUND HERE SOMEWHERE!
NO SIGN OF HIM. THAT'S ODD... I SEEN THE SKIN FLYIN' OFF HIS BACKSIDE, MESELF!
LOOK AT THIS, CAP'N. SOME SORT OF FRESHLY DISTURBED FUNGUS CLINGING TO THIS SCRAP OF OLD CLOTH.
IN FACT, IF I REMEMBER MY COLLEGE COURSES...
I DON'T GIVE A RAT'S ARSE ABOUT YOUR SCHOOL DAYS! YER A PIRATE NOW AND BEHOLDEN ONLY TO YER CAP'N!
AND I WANT THAT MOSSBACK DEAD AT MY FEET! SO MOVE!
SOMETHIN'S ON THE RIDGE, CAP'N!
WE'VE FLUSHED OUR PREY, MATIES!
THE DOTARD'S HEADIN' FER HIGH GROUND!
MOVE YER RUSTY DUSTIES, Y'SCURVY DOGS!
IF HE GETS AWAY AGAIN I'LL HAVE Y'ALL KEELHAULED!
HUFF PUF HUF PUFF HUF

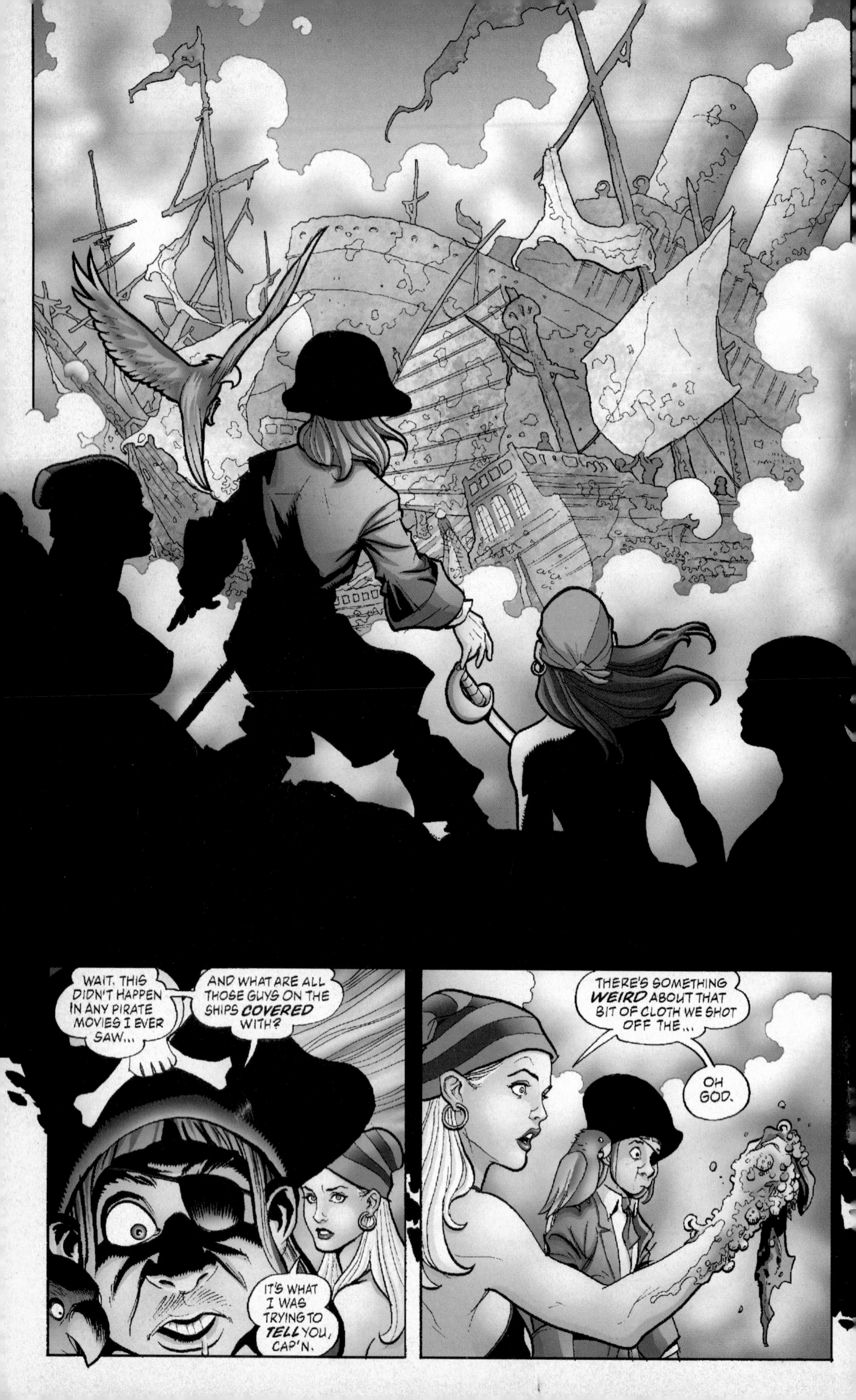
WAIT. THIS DIDN'T HAPPEN IN ANY PIRATE MOVIES I EVER SAW...
AND WHAT ARE ALL THOSE GUYS ON THE SHIPS COVERED WITH?
IT'S WHAT I WAS TRYING TO TELL YOU, CAP'N.
THERE'S SOMETHING WEIRD ABOUT THAT BIT OF CLOTH WE SHOT OFF THE...
OH GOD.

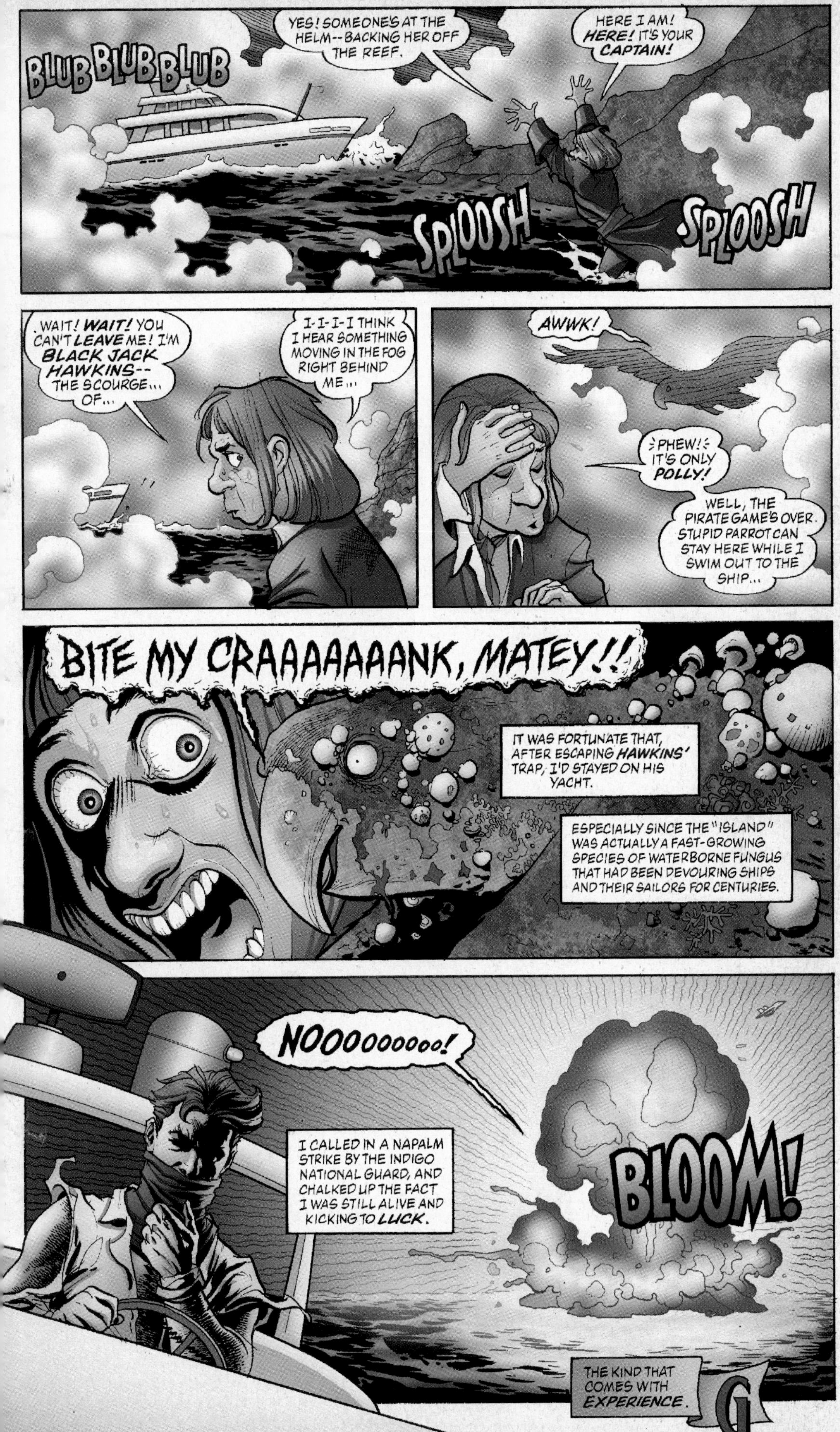
BLUB BLUB BLUB
YES! SOMEONE'S AT THE HELM--BACKING HER OFF THE REEF.
HERE I AM! HERE! IT'S YOUR CAPTAIN!
SPLOOSH
SPLOOSH
WAIT! WAIT! YOU CAN'T LEAVE ME! I'M BLACK JACK HAWKINS-- THE SCOURGE... OF...
I-I-I-I THINK I HEAR SOMETHING MOVING IN THE FOG RIGHT BEHIND ME...
AWWK!
PHEW! IT'S ONLY POLLY!
WELL, THE PIRATE GAME'S OVER. STUPID PARROT CAN STAY HERE WHILE I SWIM OUT TO THE SHIP...
BITE MY CRAAAAAAANK, MATEY!!
IT WAS FORTUNATE THAT, AFTER ESCAPING HAWKINS' TRAP, I'D STAYED ON HIS YACHT.
ESPECIALLY SINCE THE "ISLAND" WAS ACTUALLY A FAST-GROWING SPECIES OF WATERBORNE FUNGUS THAT HAD BEEN DEVOURING SHIPS AND THEIR SAILORS FOR CENTURIES.
NOOOoooooo!
I CALLED IN A NAPALM STRIKE BY THE INDIGO NATIONAL GUARD, AND CHALKED UP THE FACT I WAS STILL ALIVE AND KICKING TO LUCK.
BLOOM!
THE KIND THAT COMES WITH EXPERIENCE.
G

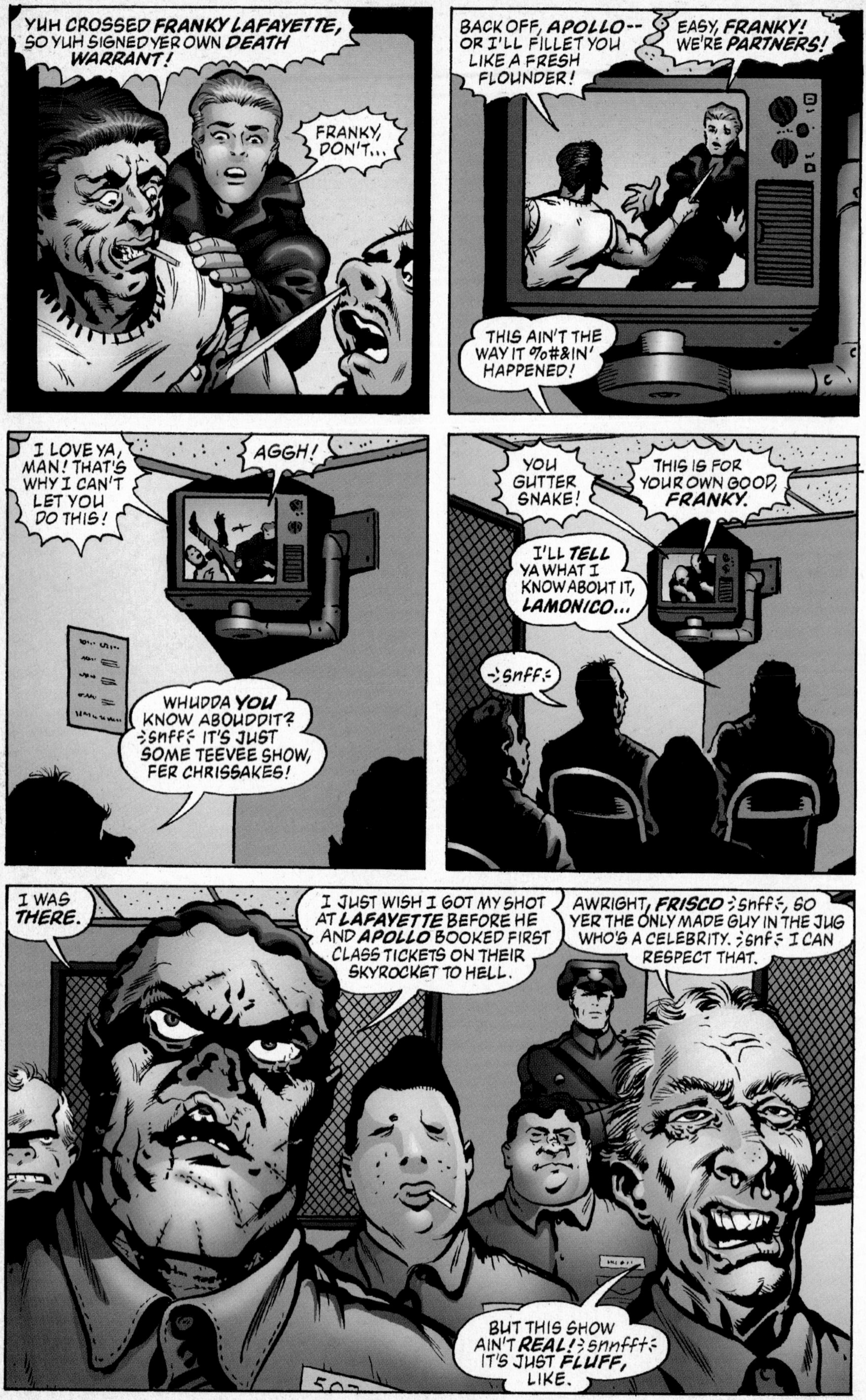
YUH CROSSED FRANKY LAFAYETTE, SO YUH SIGNED YER OWN DEATH WARRANT!
FRANKY, DON'T...
BACK OFF, APOLLO-- OR I'LL FILLET YOU LIKE A FRESH FLOUNDER!
EASY, FRANKY! WE'RE PARTNERS!
THIS AIN'T THE WAY IT %#&IN' HAPPENED!
I LOVE YA, MAN! THAT'S WHY I CAN'T LET YOU DO THIS!
AGGH!
WHUDDA YOU KNOW ABOUDDIT? -snff- IT'S JUST SOME TEEVEE SHOW, FER CHRISSAKES!
YOU GUTTER SNAKE!
THIS IS FOR YOUR OWN GOOD, FRANKY.
I'LL TELL YA WHAT I KNOW ABOUT IT, LAMONICO...
-snff-
I WAS THERE.
I JUST WISH I GOT MY SHOT AT LAFAYETTE BEFORE HE AND APOLLO BOOKED FIRST CLASS TICKETS ON THEIR SKYROCKET TO HELL.
AWRIGHT, FRISCO -snff-, SO YER THE ONLY MADE GUY IN THE JUG WHO'S A CELEBRITY. -snf- I CAN RESPECT THAT.
BUT THIS SHOW AIN'T REAL! -snnfft- IT'S JUST FLUFF, LIKE.

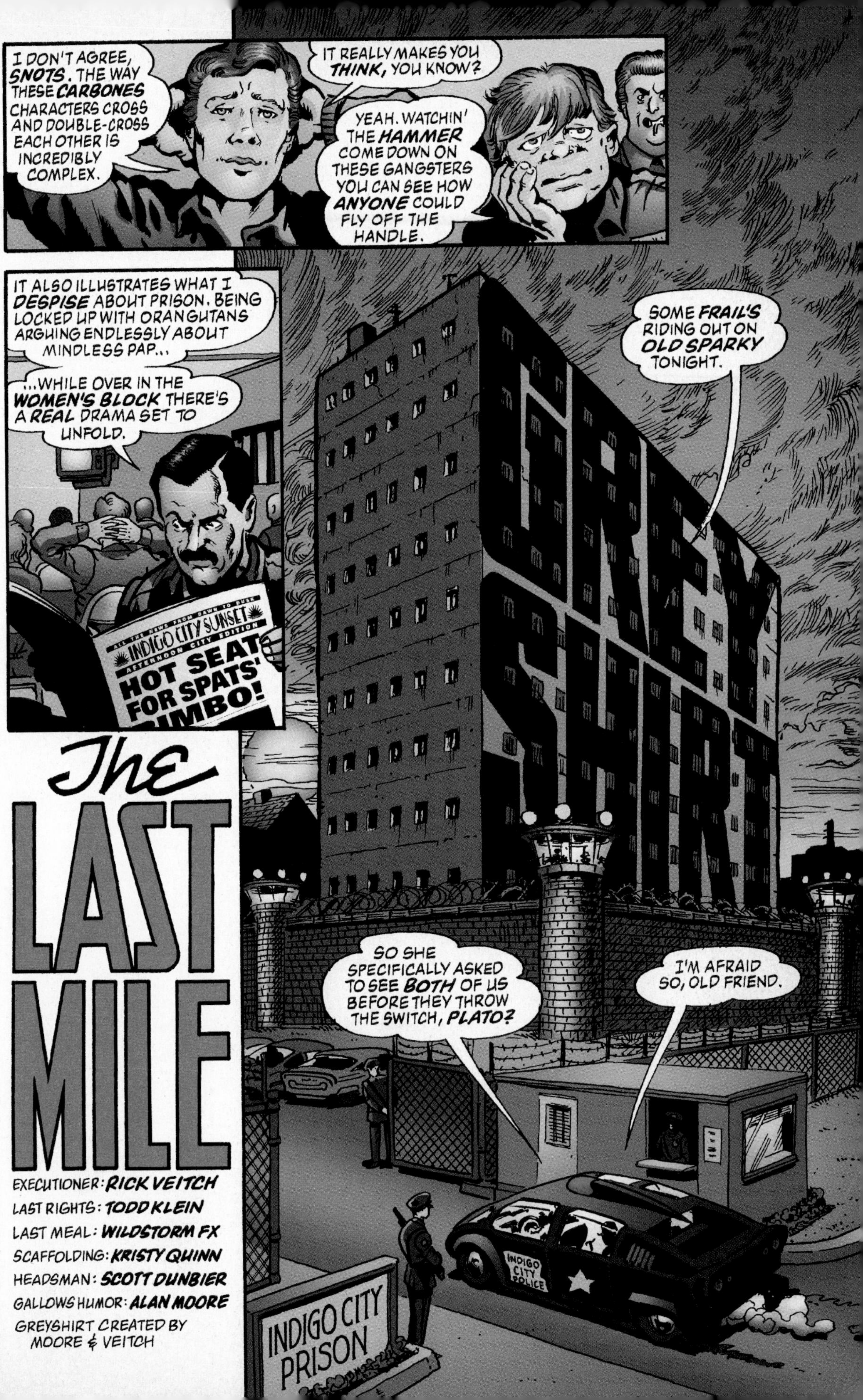
I DON'T AGREE, SNOTS. THE WAY THESE CARBONES CHARACTERS CROSS AND DOUBLE-CROSS EACH OTHER IS INCREDIBLY COMPLEX.
IT REALLY MAKES YOU THINK, YOU KNOW?
YEAH. WATCHIN' THE HAMMER COME DOWN ON THESE GANGSTERS YOU CAN SEE HOW ANYONE COULD FLY OFF THE HANDLE.
IT ALSO ILLUSTRATES WHAT I DESPISE ABOUT PRISON. BEING LOCKED UP WITH ORANGUTANS ARGUING ENDLESSLY ABOUT MINDLESS PAP...
...WHILE OVER IN THE WOMEN'S BLOCK THERE'S A REAL DRAMA SET TO UNFOLD.
ALL THE NEWS FROM DAWN TO DUSK
INDIGO CITY SUNSET
AFTERNOON CITY EDITION
HOT SEAT FOR SPATS' BIMBO!
SOME FRAIL'S RIDING OUT ON OLD SPARKY TONIGHT.
GREYSHIRT
The LAST MILE
SO SHE SPECIFICALLY ASKED TO SEE BOTH OF US BEFORE THEY THROW THE SWITCH, PLATO?
I'M AFRAID SO, OLD FRIEND.
INDIGO CITY POLICE
INDIGO CITY PRISON
EXECUTIONER: RICK VEITCH
LAST RIGHTS: TODD KLEIN
LAST MEAL: WILDSTORM FX
SCAFFOLDING: KRISTY QUINN
HEADSMAN: SCOTT DUNBIER
GALLOWS HUMOR: ALAN MOORE
GREYSHIRT CREATED BY MOORE & VEITCH

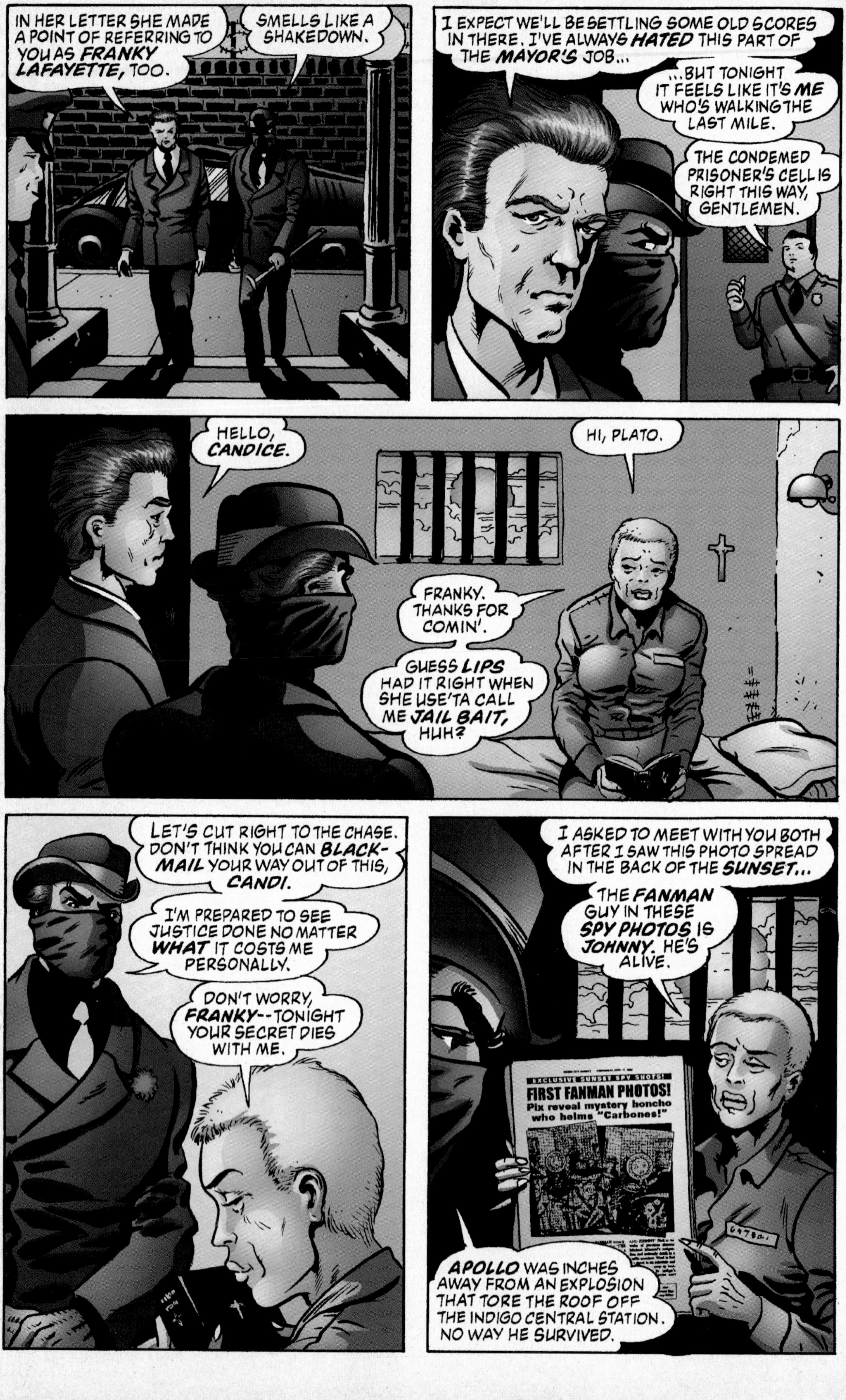
IN HER LETTER SHE MADE A POINT OF REFERRING TO YOU AS FRANKY LAFAYETTE, TOO.
SMELLS LIKE A SHAKEDOWN.
I EXPECT WE'LL BE SETTLING SOME OLD SCORES IN THERE. I'VE ALWAYS HATED THIS PART OF THE MAYOR'S JOB...
...BUT TONIGHT IT FEELS LIKE IT'S ME WHO'S WALKING THE LAST MILE.
THE CONDEMED PRISONER'S CELL IS RIGHT THIS WAY, GENTLEMEN.
HELLO, CANDICE.
HI, PLATO.
FRANKY. THANKS FOR COMIN'.
GUESS LIPS HAD IT RIGHT WHEN SHE USE'TA CALL ME JAIL BAIT, HUH?
LET'S CUT RIGHT TO THE CHASE. DON'T THINK YOU CAN BLACK-MAIL YOUR WAY OUT OF THIS, CANDI.
I'M PREPARED TO SEE JUSTICE DONE NO MATTER WHAT IT COSTS ME PERSONALLY.
DON'T WORRY, FRANKY--TONIGHT YOUR SECRET DIES WITH ME.
I ASKED TO MEET WITH YOU BOTH AFTER I SAW THIS PHOTO SPREAD IN THE BACK OF THE SUNSET...
THE FANMAN GUY IN THESE SPY PHOTOS IS JOHNNY. HE'S ALIVE.
EXCLUSIVE SUNSET SPY SHOTS!
FIRST FANMAN PHOTOS!
Pix reveal mystery honcho who helms "Carbones!"
APOLLO WAS INCHES AWAY FROM AN EXPLOSION THAT TORE THE ROOF OFF THE INDIGO CENTRAL STATION. NO WAY HE SURVIVED.

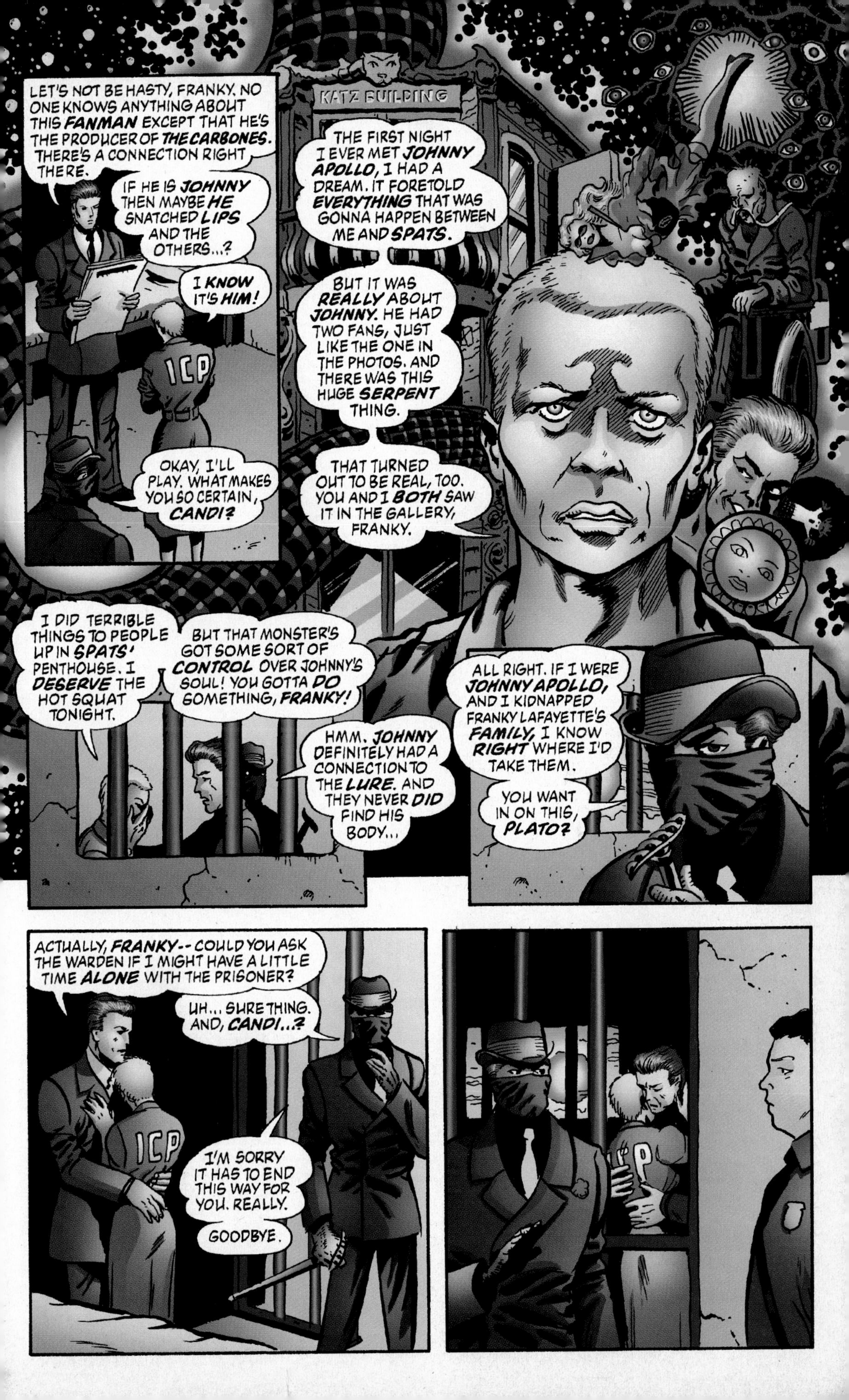

KATZ BUILDING
LET'S NOT BE HASTY, FRANKY. NO ONE KNOWS ANYTHING ABOUT THIS FANMAN EXCEPT THAT HE'S THE PRODUCER OF THE CARBONES. THERE'S A CONNECTION RIGHT THERE.
IF HE IS JOHNNY THEN MAYBE HE SNATCHED LIPS AND THE OTHERS...?
I KNOW IT'S HIM!
OKAY, I'LL PLAY. WHAT MAKES YOU SO CERTAIN, CANDI?
THE FIRST NIGHT I EVER MET JOHNNY APOLLO, I HAD A DREAM. IT FORETOLD EVERYTHING THAT WAS GONNA HAPPEN BETWEEN ME AND SPATS.
BUT IT WAS REALLY ABOUT JOHNNY. HE HAD TWO FANS, JUST LIKE THE ONE IN THE PHOTOS. AND THERE WAS THIS HUGE SERPENT THING.
THAT TURNED OUT TO BE REAL, TOO. YOU AND I BOTH SAW IT IN THE GALLERY, FRANKY.
I DID TERRIBLE THINGS TO PEOPLE UP IN SPATS' PENTHOUSE. I DESERVE THE HOT SQUAT TONIGHT.
BUT THAT MONSTER'S GOT SOME SORT OF CONTROL OVER JOHNNY'S SOUL! YOU GOTTA DO SOMETHING, FRANKY!
HMM. JOHNNY DEFINITELY HAD A CONNECTION TO THE LURE. AND THEY NEVER DID FIND HIS BODY...
ALL RIGHT. IF I WERE JOHNNY APOLLO, AND I KIDNAPPED FRANKY LAFAYETTE'S FAMILY, I KNOW RIGHT WHERE I'D TAKE THEM.
YOU WANT IN ON THIS, PLATO?
ACTUALLY, FRANKY-- COULD YOU ASK THE WARDEN IF I MIGHT HAVE A LITTLE TIME ALONE WITH THE PRISONER?
UH... SURE THING. AND, CANDI...?
I'M SORRY IT HAS TO END THIS WAY FOR YOU. REALLY.
GOODBYE.

STAR-CROSSED LOVERS REUNITED AFTER YEARS OF MISUNDERSTANDING!

CARMINE CARBONE AND *LIPS LAFAYETTE* ARE MEAT AND POTATOES TO A TELEVISION PRODUCER LIKE ME, BOYS.

I NEED TO GO HOME NOW, PLEASE.

AND WE MUSTN'T UNDER PLAY YOUNG *CATHERINE'S* MELODRAMATIC POTENTIAL!

A PLUCKY YOUNG PAPERGIRL WITH DOWN'S SYNDROME IS WORTH SEVEN PRIME-TIME POINTS IN ANY MAJOR MARKET!

BUT MEETING HER *BIRTH PARENTS?* IT'S GOT ME SMELLING *SWEEPS WEEK!*

WHAT THE HELL YOU SPOUTIN' ABOUT *BIRTH PARENTS?*

OH JESUS.

OH SWEET MARY AND JOSEPH IN HEAVEN...

SUMTHIN'... SUMTHIN'...

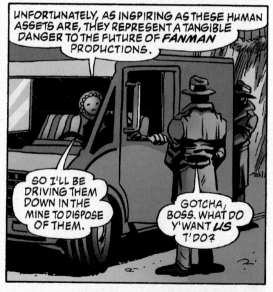

UNFORTUNATELY, AS INSPIRING AS THESE HUMAN ASSETS ARE, THEY REPRESENT A TANGIBLE DANGER TO THE FUTURE OF *FANMAN* PRODUCTIONS.

SO I'LL BE DRIVING THEM DOWN IN THE MINE TO DISPOSE OF THEM.

GOTCHA, BOSS. WHAT DO Y'WANT *US* T'DO?

THERE'S ONE *LAST* JOB FOR YOU BOYS!

VROOOOMM

KR

WHAT JOB'S *THAT,* BOSS?

BOSS?

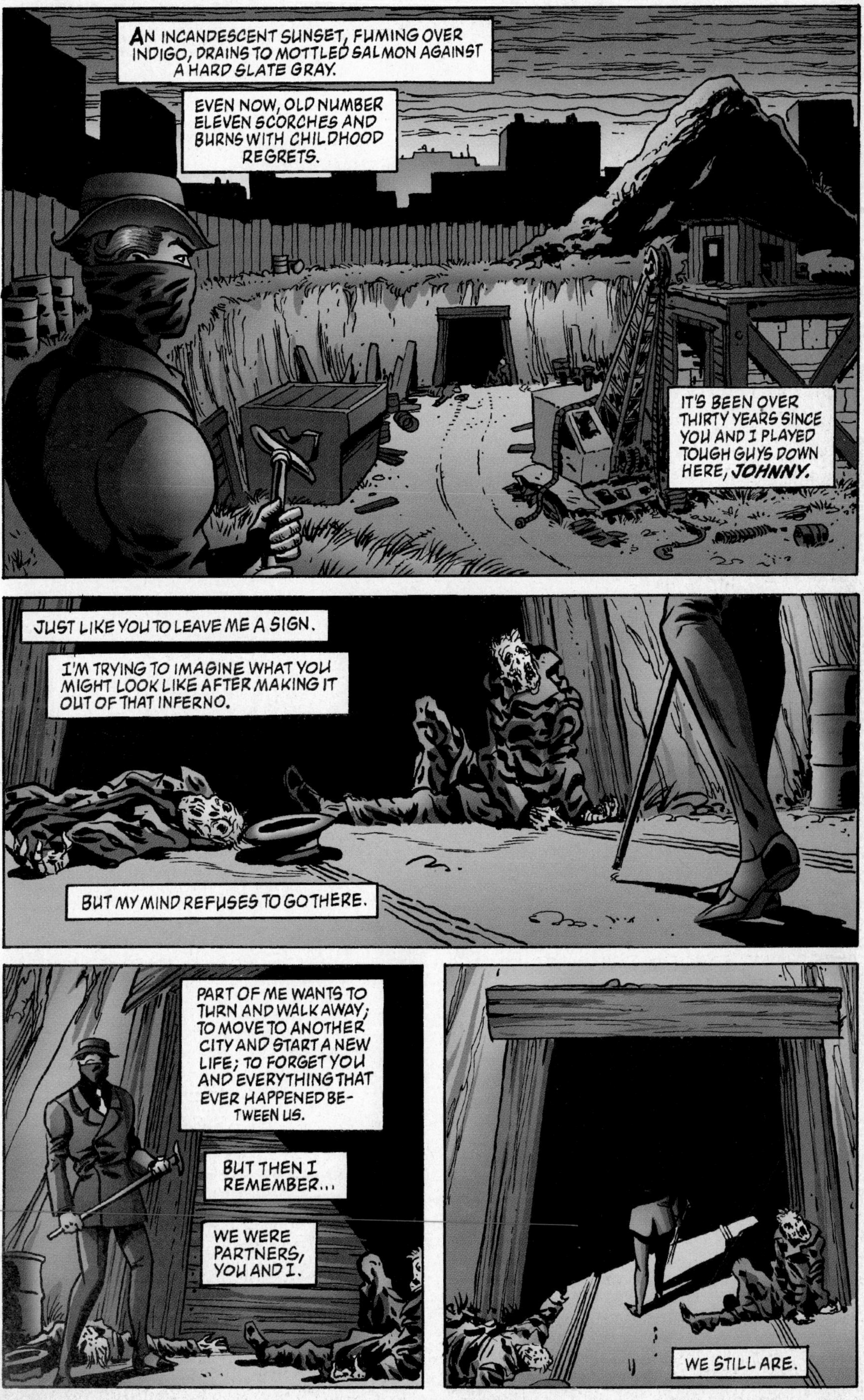
AN INCANDESCENT SUNSET, FUMING OVER INDIGO, DRAINS TO MOTTLED SALMON AGAINST A HARD SLATE GRAY.
EVEN NOW, OLD NUMBER ELEVEN SCORCHES AND BURNS WITH CHILDHOOD REGRETS.
IT'S BEEN OVER THIRTY YEARS SINCE YOU AND I PLAYED TOUGH GUYS DOWN HERE, JOHNNY.
JUST LIKE YOU TO LEAVE ME A SIGN.
I'M TRYING TO IMAGINE WHAT YOU MIGHT LOOK LIKE AFTER MAKING IT OUT OF THAT INFERNO.
BUT MY MIND REFUSES TO GO THERE.
PART OF ME WANTS TO TURN AND WALK AWAY; TO MOVE TO ANOTHER CITY AND START A NEW LIFE; TO FORGET YOU AND EVERYTHING THAT EVER HAPPENED BETWEEN US.
BUT THEN I REMEMBER...
WE WERE PARTNERS, YOU AND I.
WE STILL ARE.

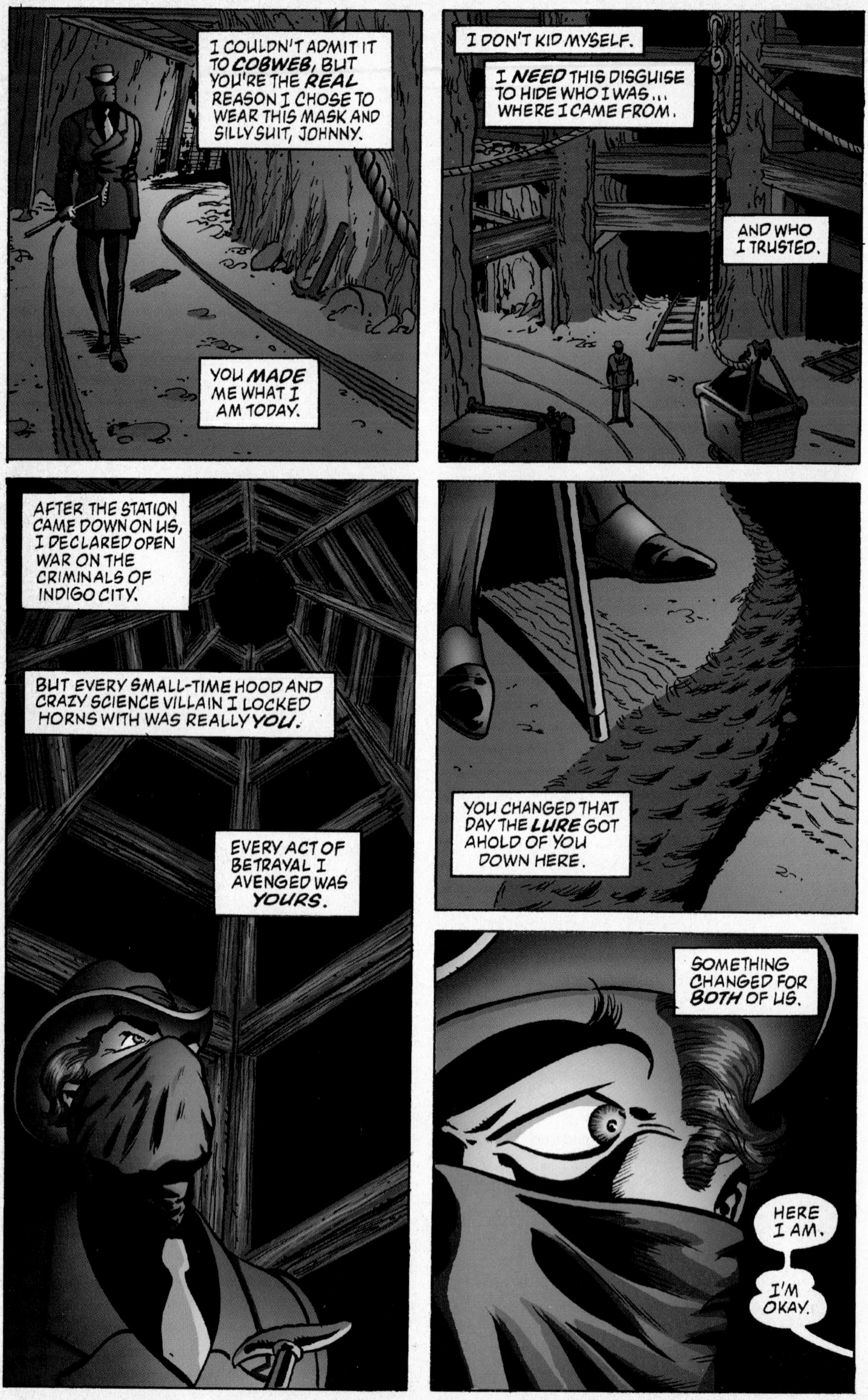
I COULDN'T ADMIT IT TO **COBWEB**, BUT YOU'RE THE **REAL** REASON I CHOSE TO WEAR THIS MASK AND SILLY SUIT, JOHNNY.
YOU **MADE** ME WHAT I AM TODAY.
I DON'T KID MYSELF.
I **NEED** THIS DISGUISE TO HIDE WHO I WAS... WHERE I CAME FROM.
AND WHO I TRUSTED.
AFTER THE STATION CAME DOWN ON US, I DECLARED OPEN WAR ON THE CRIMINALS OF INDIGO CITY.
BUT EVERY SMALL-TIME HOOD AND CRAZY SCIENCE VILLAIN I LOCKED HORNS WITH WAS REALLY **YOU**.
EVERY ACT OF BETRAYAL I AVENGED WAS **YOURS**.
YOU CHANGED THAT DAY THE **LURE** GOT AHOLD OF YOU DOWN HERE.
SOMETHING CHANGED FOR **BOTH** OF US.
HERE I AM.
I'M OKAY.

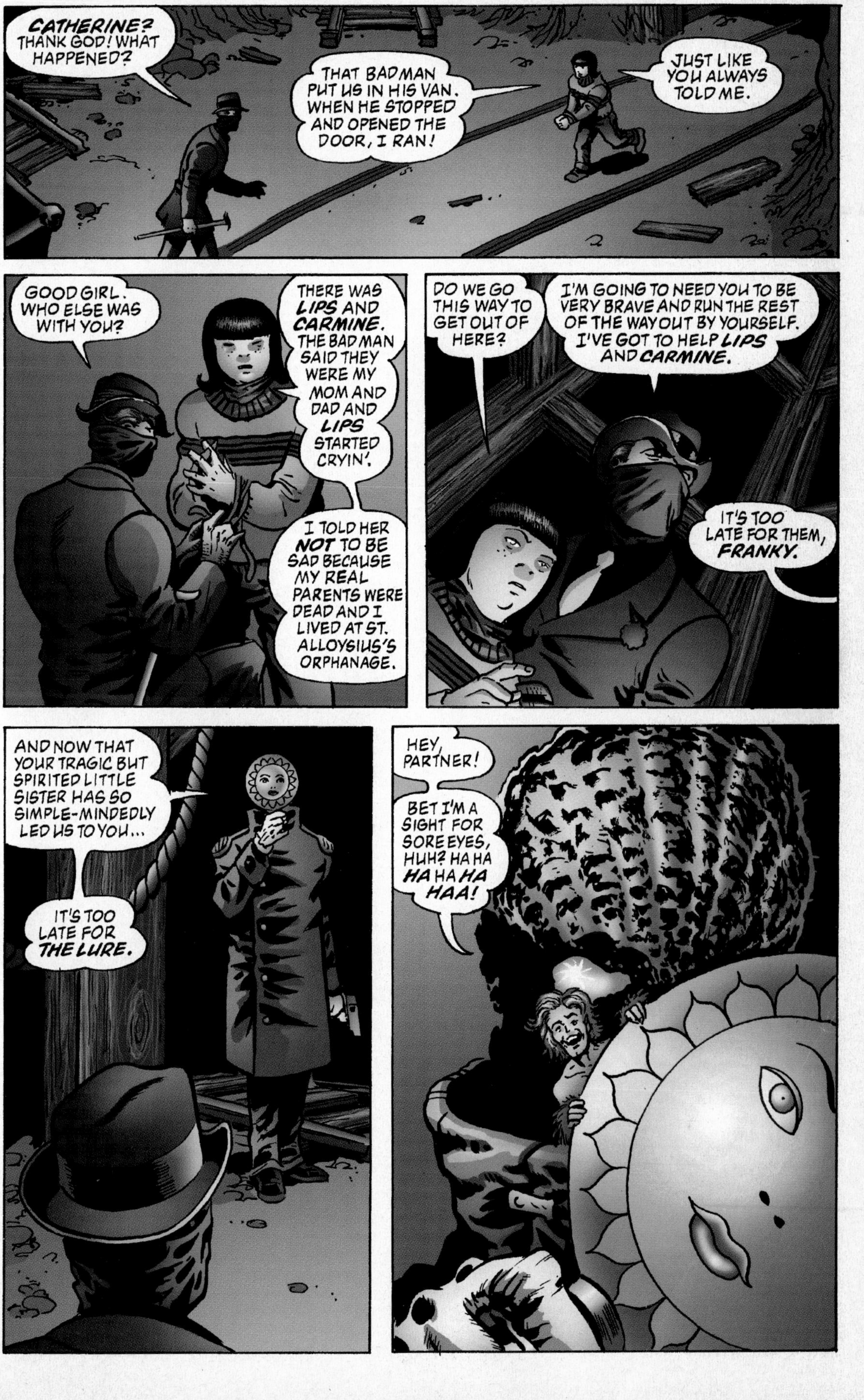
CATHERINE? THANK GOD! WHAT HAPPENED?
THAT BAD MAN PUT US IN HIS VAN. WHEN HE STOPPED AND OPENED THE DOOR, I RAN!
JUST LIKE YOU ALWAYS TOLD ME.
GOOD GIRL. WHO ELSE WAS WITH YOU?
THERE WAS LIPS AND CARMINE. THE BAD MAN SAID THEY WERE MY MOM AND DAD AND LIPS STARTED CRYIN'.
I TOLD HER NOT TO BE SAD BECAUSE MY REAL PARENTS WERE DEAD AND I LIVED AT ST. ALLOYSIUS'S ORPHANAGE.
DO WE GO THIS WAY TO GET OUT OF HERE?
I'M GOING TO NEED YOU TO BE VERY BRAVE AND RUN THE REST OF THE WAY OUT BY YOURSELF. I'VE GOT TO HELP LIPS AND CARMINE.
IT'S TOO LATE FOR THEM, FRANKY.
AND NOW THAT YOUR TRAGIC BUT SPIRITED LITTLE SISTER HAS SO SIMPLE-MINDEDLY LED US TO YOU...
IT'S TOO LATE FOR THE LURE.
HEY, PARTNER!
BET I'M A SIGHT FOR SORE EYES, HUH? HA HA HA HA HA HAA!

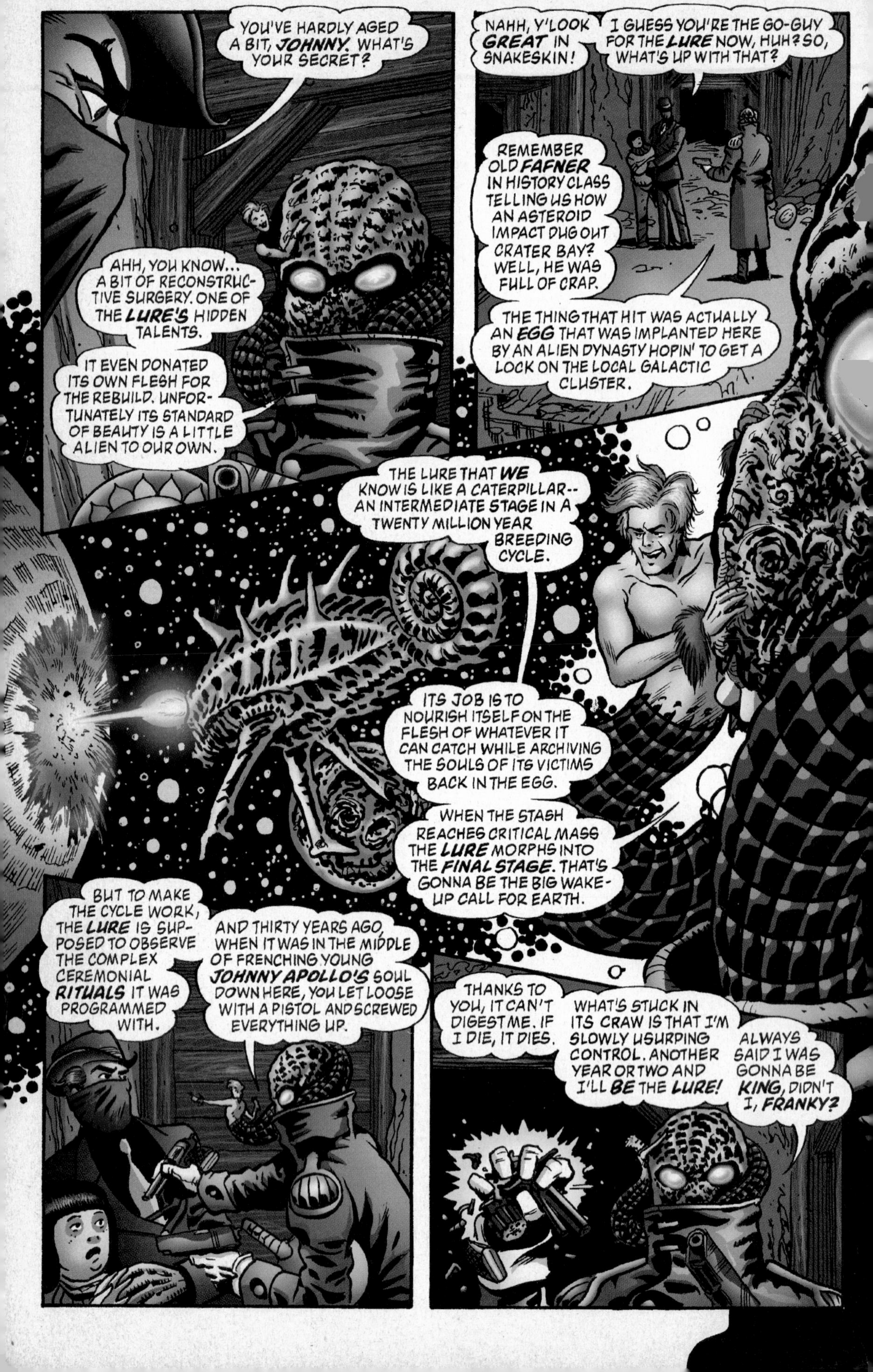

YOU'VE HARDLY AGED A BIT, JOHNNY. WHAT'S YOUR SECRET?
AHH, YOU KNOW... A BIT OF RECONSTRUCTIVE SURGERY. ONE OF THE LURE'S HIDDEN TALENTS.
IT EVEN DONATED ITS OWN FLESH FOR THE REBUILD. UNFORTUNATELY ITS STANDARD OF BEAUTY IS A LITTLE ALIEN TO OUR OWN.
NAHH, Y'LOOK GREAT IN SNAKESKIN!
I GUESS YOU'RE THE GO-GUY FOR THE LURE NOW, HUH? SO, WHAT'S UP WITH THAT?
REMEMBER OLD FAFNER IN HISTORY CLASS TELLING US HOW AN ASTEROID IMPACT DUG OUT CRATER BAY? WELL, HE WAS FULL OF CRAP.
THE THING THAT HIT WAS ACTUALLY AN EGG THAT WAS IMPLANTED HERE BY AN ALIEN DYNASTY HOPIN' TO GET A LOCK ON THE LOCAL GALACTIC CLUSTER.
THE LURE THAT WE KNOW IS LIKE A CATERPILLAR-- AN INTERMEDIATE STAGE IN A TWENTY MILLION YEAR BREEDING CYCLE.
ITS JOB IS TO NOURISH ITSELF ON THE FLESH OF WHATEVER IT CAN CATCH WHILE ARCHIVING THE SOULS OF ITS VICTIMS BACK IN THE EGG.
WHEN THE STASH REACHES CRITICAL MASS THE LURE MORPHS INTO THE FINAL STAGE. THAT'S GONNA BE THE BIG WAKE-UP CALL FOR EARTH.
BUT TO MAKE THE CYCLE WORK, THE LURE IS SUPPOSED TO OBSERVE THE COMPLEX CEREMONIAL RITUALS IT WAS PROGRAMMED WITH.
AND THIRTY YEARS AGO, WHEN IT WAS IN THE MIDDLE OF FRENCHING YOUNG JOHNNY APOLLO'S SOUL DOWN HERE, YOU LET LOOSE WITH A PISTOL AND SCREWED EVERYTHING UP.
THANKS TO YOU, IT CAN'T DIGEST ME. IF I DIE, IT DIES.
WHAT'S STUCK IN ITS CRAW IS THAT I'M SLOWLY USURPING CONTROL. ANOTHER YEAR OR TWO AND I'LL BE THE LURE!
ALWAYS SAID I WAS GONNA BE KING, DIDN'T I, FRANKY?

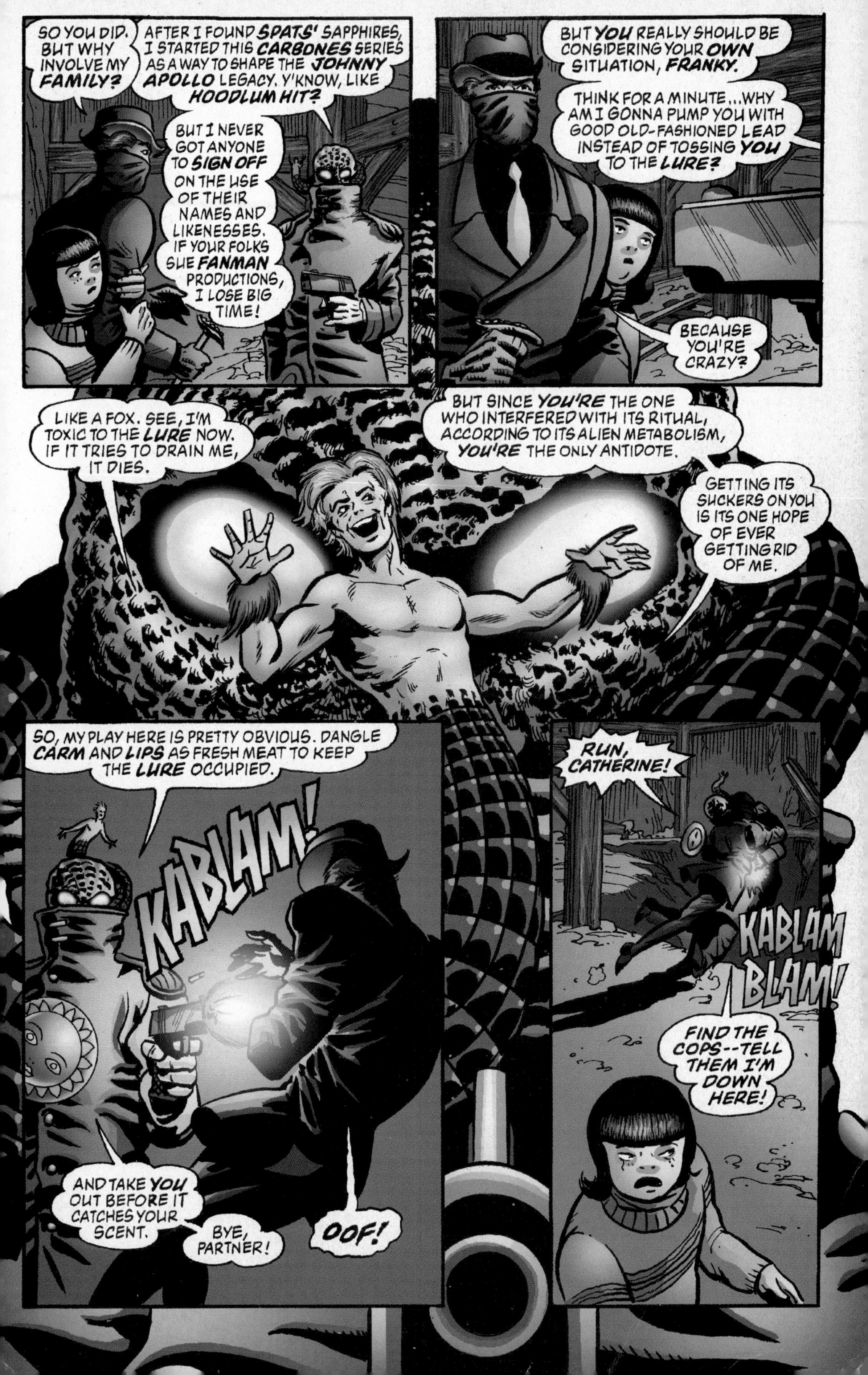
SO YOU DID. BUT WHY INVOLVE MY FAMILY?
AFTER I FOUND SPATS' SAPPHIRES, I STARTED THIS CARBONES SERIES AS A WAY TO SHAPE THE JOHNNY APOLLO LEGACY. Y'KNOW, LIKE HOODLUM HIT?
BUT I NEVER GOT ANYONE TO SIGN OFF ON THE USE OF THEIR NAMES AND LIKENESSES. IF YOUR FOLKS SUE FANMAN PRODUCTIONS, I LOSE BIG TIME!
BUT YOU REALLY SHOULD BE CONSIDERING YOUR OWN SITUATION, FRANKY.
THINK FOR A MINUTE...WHY AM I GONNA PUMP YOU WITH GOOD OLD-FASHIONED LEAD INSTEAD OF TOSSING YOU TO THE LURE?
BECAUSE YOU'RE CRAZY?
LIKE A FOX. SEE, I'M TOXIC TO THE LURE NOW. IF IT TRIES TO DRAIN ME, IT DIES.
BUT SINCE YOU'RE THE ONE WHO INTERFERED WITH ITS RITUAL, ACCORDING TO ITS ALIEN METABOLISM, YOU'RE THE ONLY ANTIDOTE.
GETTING ITS SUCKERS ON YOU IS ITS ONE HOPE OF EVER GETTING RID OF ME.
SO, MY PLAY HERE IS PRETTY OBVIOUS. DANGLE CARM AND LIPS AS FRESH MEAT TO KEEP THE LURE OCCUPIED.
KABLAM!
AND TAKE YOU OUT BEFORE IT CATCHES YOUR SCENT.
BYE, PARTNER!
OOF!
RUN, CATHERINE!
KABLAM BLAM!
FIND THE COPS--TELL THEM I'M DOWN HERE!

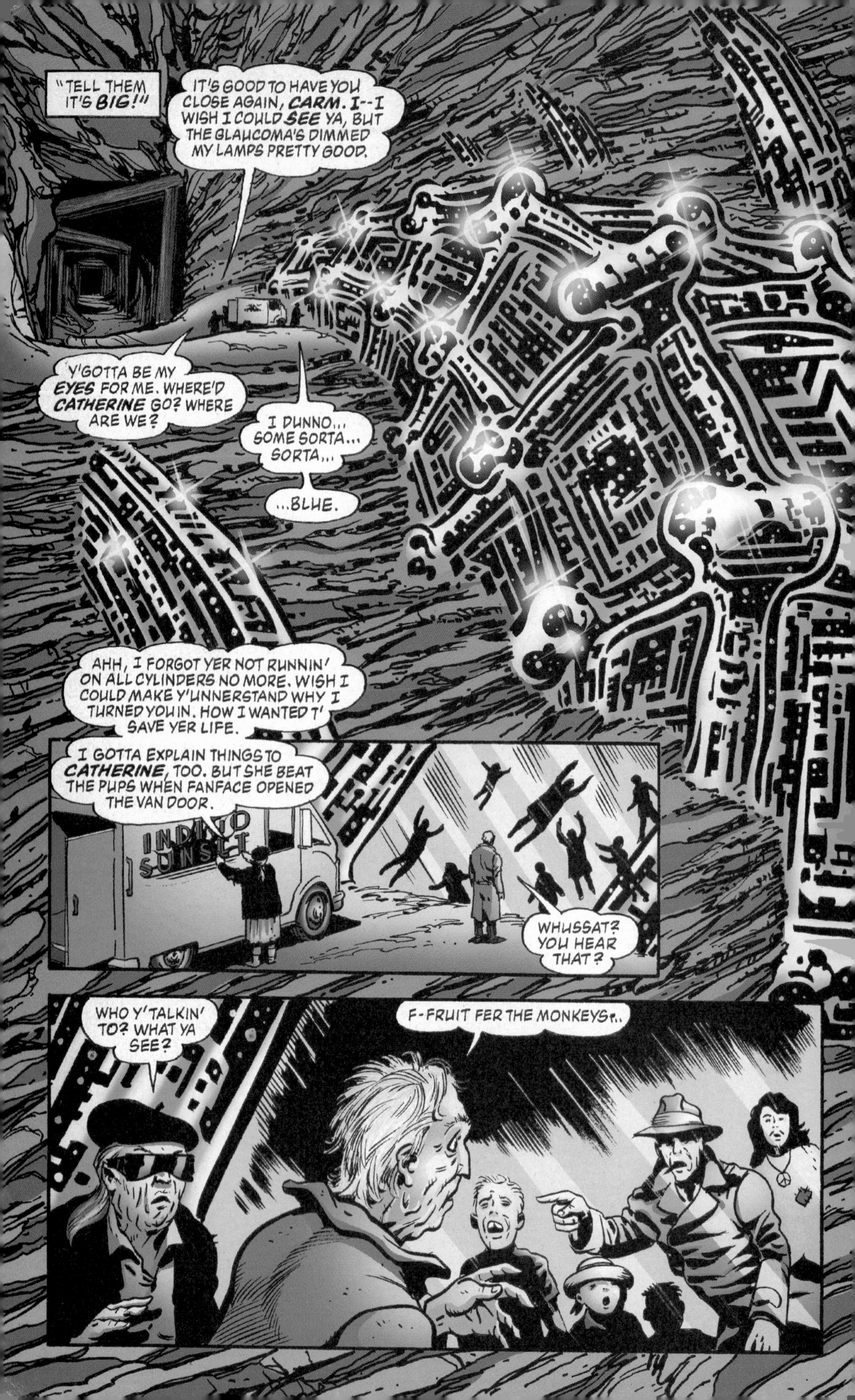
"TELL THEM IT'S BIG!"
IT'S GOOD TO HAVE YOU CLOSE AGAIN, CARM. I--I WISH I COULD SEE YA, BUT THE GLAUCOMA'S DIMMED MY LAMPS PRETTY GOOD.
Y'GOTTA BE MY EYES FOR ME. WHERE'D CATHERINE GO? WHERE ARE WE?
I DUNNO... SOME SORTA... SORTA...
...BLUE.
AHH, I FORGOT YER NOT RUNNIN' ON ALL CYLINDERS NO MORE. WISH I COULD MAKE Y'UNNERSTAND WHY I TURNED YOU IN. HOW I WANTED T' SAVE YER LIFE.
I GOTTA EXPLAIN THINGS TO CATHERINE, TOO. BUT SHE BEAT THE PUPS WHEN FANFACE OPENED THE VAN DOOR.
WHUSSAT? YOU HEAR THAT?
WHO Y'TALKIN' TO? WHAT YA SEE?
F-FRUIT FER THE MONKEYS...

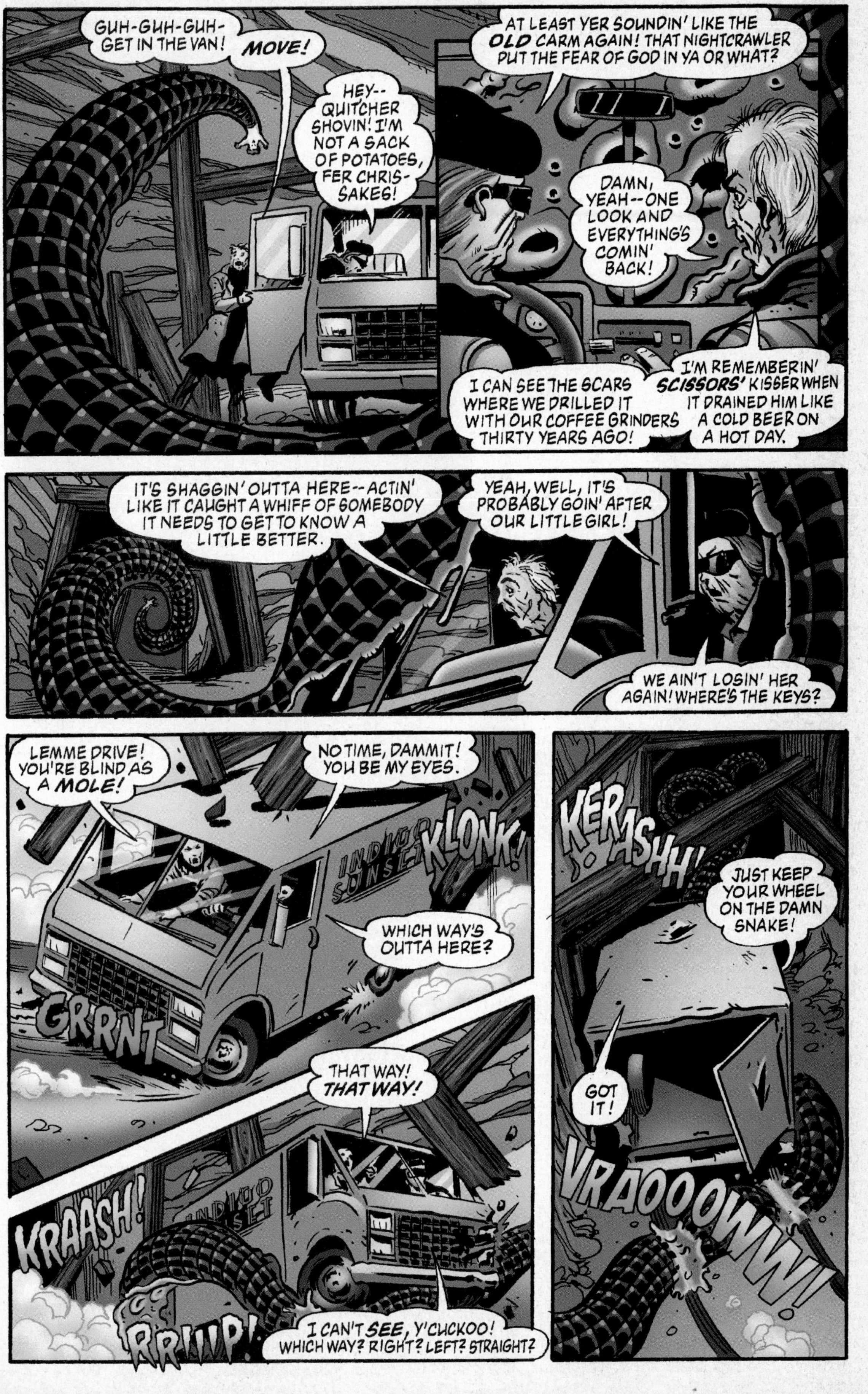
GUH-GUH-GUH-GET IN THE VAN!
MOVE!
HEY--QUITCHER SHOVIN! I'M NOT A SACK OF POTATOES, FER CHRIS-SAKES!
AT LEAST YER SOUNDIN' LIKE THE OLD CARM AGAIN! THAT NIGHTCRAWLER PUT THE FEAR OF GOD IN YA OR WHAT?
DAMN, YEAH--ONE LOOK AND EVERYTHING'S COMIN' BACK!
I'M REMEMBERIN' SCISSORS' KISSER WHEN IT DRAINED HIM LIKE A COLD BEER ON A HOT DAY.
I CAN SEE THE SCARS WHERE WE DRILLED IT WITH OUR COFFEE GRINDERS THIRTY YEARS AGO!
IT'S SHAGGIN' OUTTA HERE--ACTIN' LIKE IT CAUGHT A WHIFF OF SOMEBODY IT NEEDS TO GET TO KNOW A LITTLE BETTER.
YEAH, WELL, IT'S PROBABLY GOIN' AFTER OUR LITTLE GIRL!
WE AIN'T LOSIN' HER AGAIN! WHERE'S THE KEYS?
LEMME DRIVE! YOU'RE BLIND AS A MOLE!
NO TIME, DAMMIT! YOU BE MY EYES.
INDIGO SUNSET
KLONK!
WHICH WAY'S OUTTA HERE?
GRRNT
THAT WAY! THAT WAY!
KRAASH!
RRIIIP!
I CAN'T SEE, Y'CUCKOO! WHICH WAY? RIGHT? LEFT? STRAIGHT?
KERASHH!
JUST KEEP YOUR WHEEL ON THE DAMN SNAKE!
GOT IT!
VRAOOOWWW!

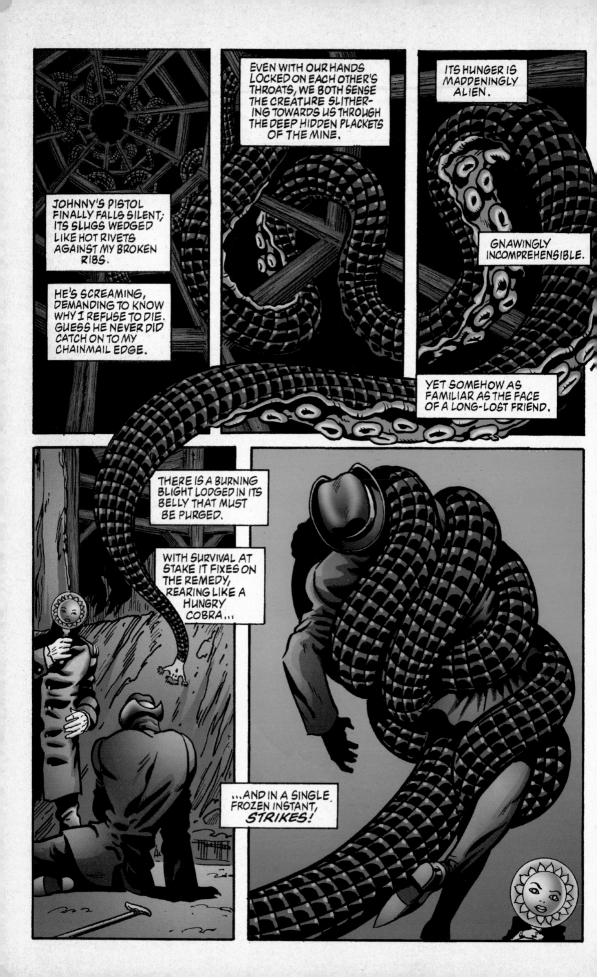

JOHNNY'S PISTOL FINALLY FALLS SILENT; ITS SLUGS WEDGED LIKE HOT RIVETS AGAINST MY BROKEN RIBS.

HE'S SCREAMING, DEMANDING TO KNOW WHY I REFUSE TO DIE. GUESS HE NEVER DID CATCH ON TO MY CHAINMAIL EDGE.

EVEN WITH OUR HANDS LOCKED ON EACH OTHER'S THROATS, WE BOTH SENSE THE CREATURE SLITHER-ING TOWARDS US THROUGH THE DEEP HIDDEN PLACKETS OF THE MINE.

ITS HUNGER IS MADDENINGLY ALIEN.

GNAWINGLY INCOMPREHENSIBLE.

YET SOMEHOW AS FAMILIAR AS THE FACE OF A LONG-LOST FRIEND.

THERE IS A BURNING BLIGHT LODGED IN ITS BELLY THAT MUST BE PURGED.

WITH SURVIVAL AT STAKE IT FIXES ON THE REMEDY, REARING LIKE A HUNGRY COBRA...

...AND IN A SINGLE FROZEN INSTANT, *STRIKES!*

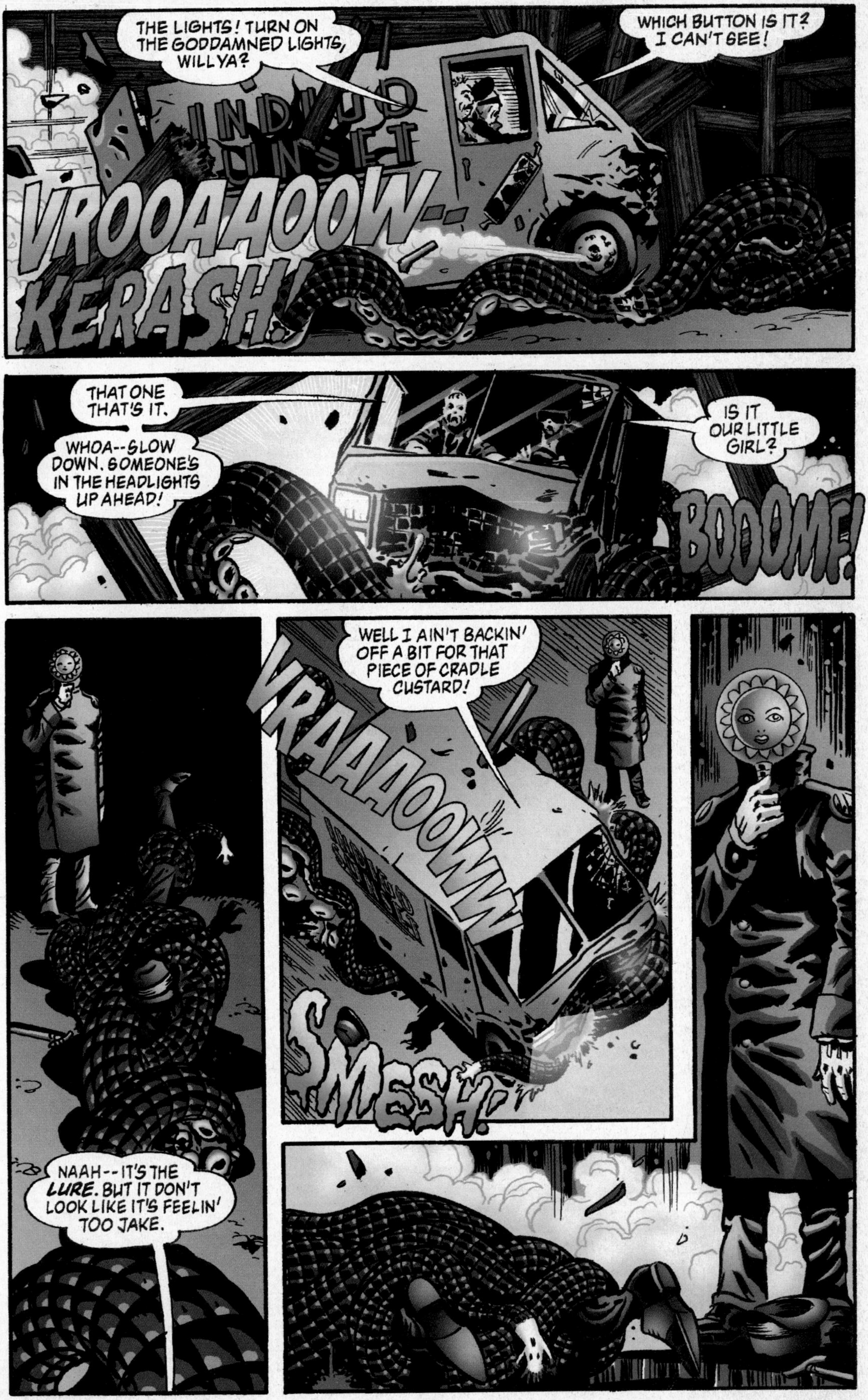
THE LIGHTS! TURN ON THE GODDAMNED LIGHTS, WILLYA?
WHICH BUTTON IS IT? I CAN'T SEE!
VROOAAOOW--
KERASH!
THAT ONE THAT'S IT.
WHOA--SLOW DOWN. SOMEONE'S IN THE HEADLIGHTS UP AHEAD!
IS IT OUR LITTLE GIRL?
BOOOMF!
WELL I AIN'T BACKIN' OFF A BIT FOR THAT PIECE OF CRADLE CUSTARD!
VRAAAOOWW
SMESH!
NAAH--IT'S THE LURE. BUT IT DON'T LOOK LIKE IT'S FEELIN' TOO JAKE.

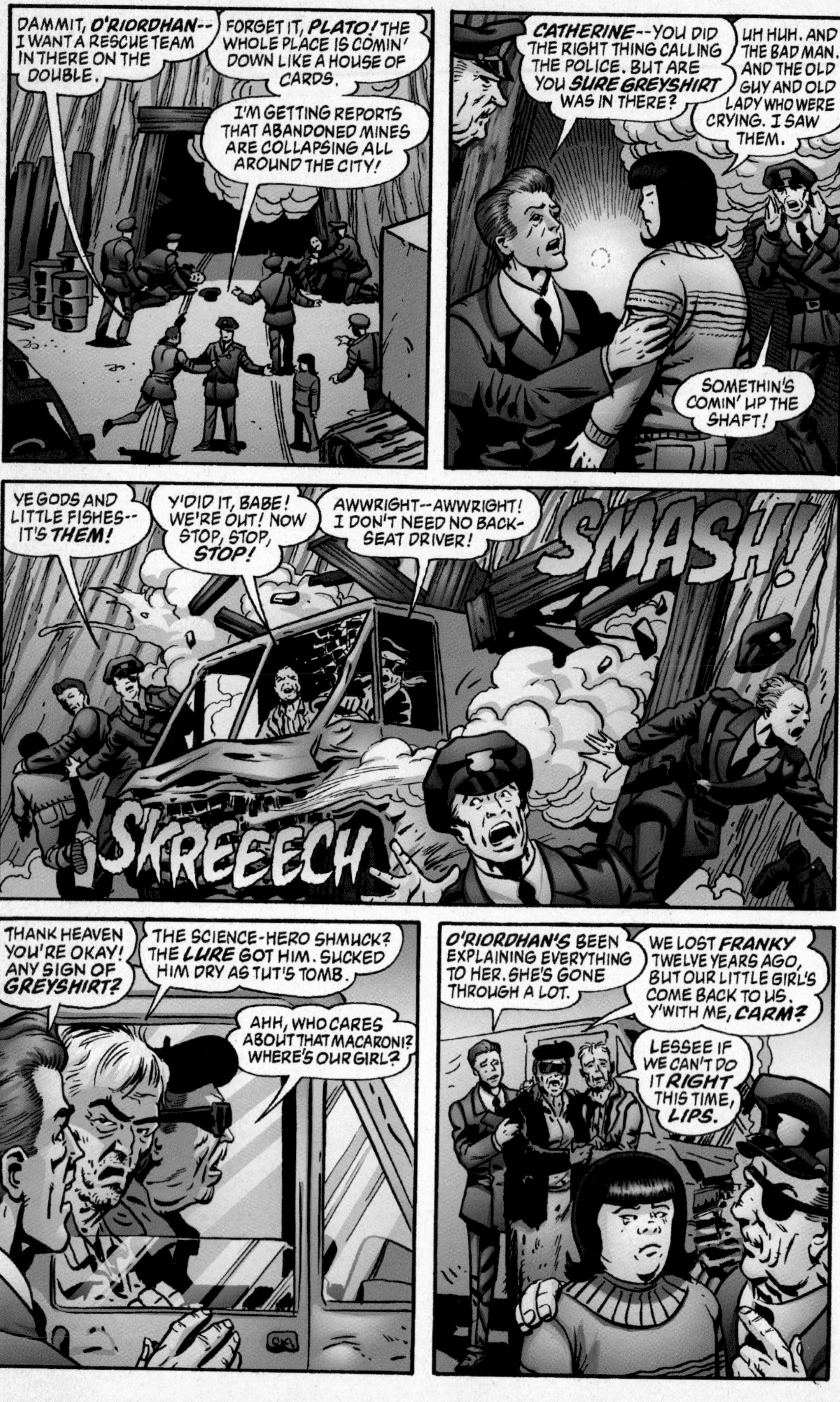
DAMMIT, O'RIORDHAN-- I WANT A RESCUE TEAM IN THERE ON THE DOUBLE.
FORGET IT, PLATO! THE WHOLE PLACE IS COMIN' DOWN LIKE A HOUSE OF CARDS.
I'M GETTING REPORTS THAT ABANDONED MINES ARE COLLAPSING ALL AROUND THE CITY!
CATHERINE--YOU DID THE RIGHT THING CALLING THE POLICE. BUT ARE YOU SURE GREYSHIRT WAS IN THERE?
UH HUH. AND THE BAD MAN. AND THE OLD GUY AND OLD LADY WHO WERE CRYING. I SAW THEM.
SOMETHIN'S COMIN' UP THE SHAFT!
YE GODS AND LITTLE FISHES-- IT'S THEM!
Y'DID IT, BABE! WE'RE OUT! NOW STOP, STOP, STOP!
AWWRIGHT--AWWRIGHT! I DON'T NEED NO BACK-SEAT DRIVER!
SMASH!
SKREEECH
THANK HEAVEN YOU'RE OKAY! ANY SIGN OF GREYSHIRT?
THE SCIENCE-HERO SHMUCK? THE LURE GOT HIM. SUCKED HIM DRY AS TUT'S TOMB.
AHH, WHO CARES ABOUT THAT MACARONI? WHERE'S OUR GIRL?
O'RIORDHAN'S BEEN EXPLAINING EVERYTHING TO HER. SHE'S GONE THROUGH A LOT.
WE LOST FRANKY TWELVE YEARS AGO, BUT OUR LITTLE GIRL'S COME BACK TO US. Y'WITH ME, CARM?
LESSEE IF WE CAN'T DO IT RIGHT THIS TIME, LIPS.

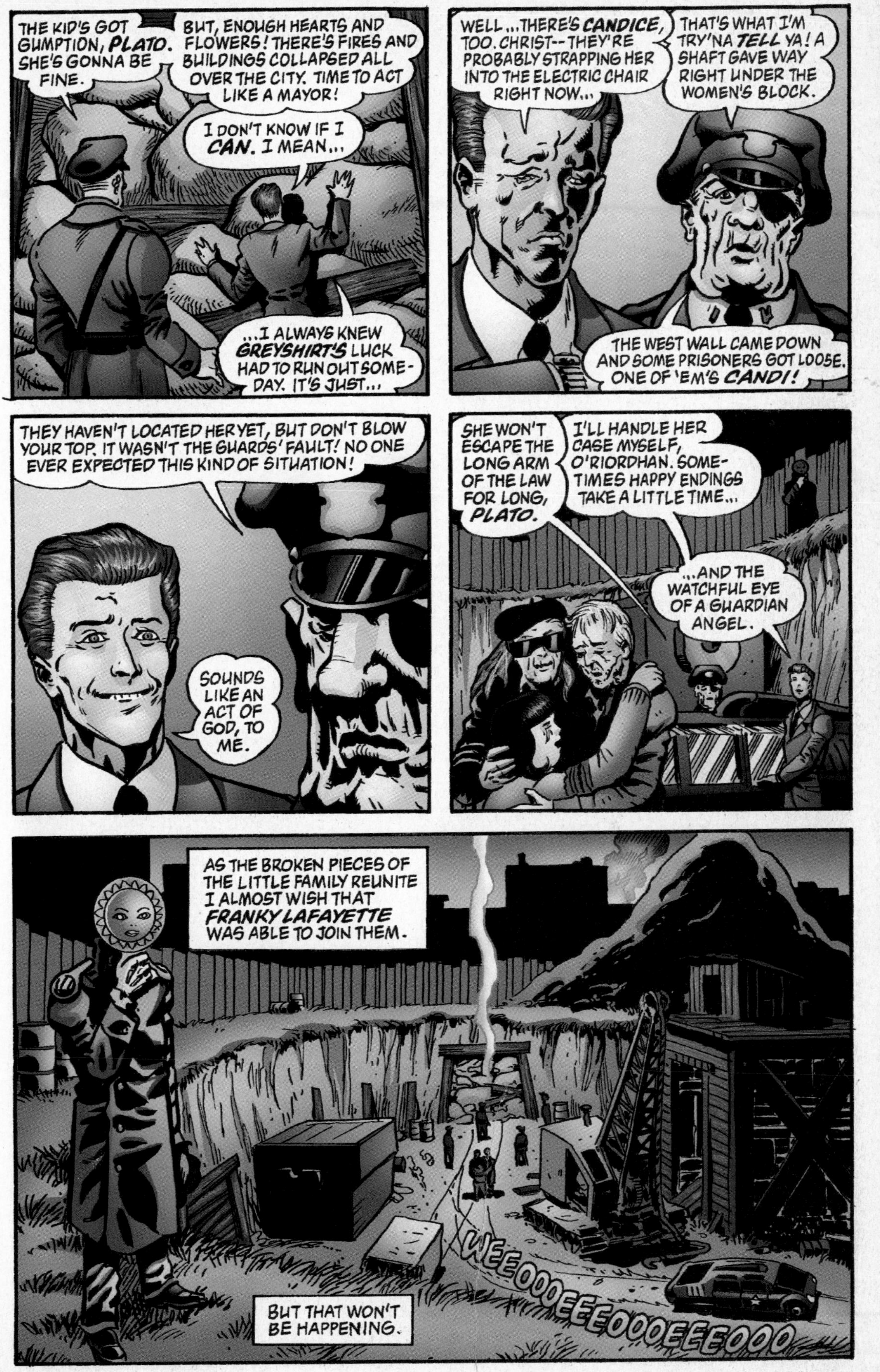
THE KID'S GOT GUMPTION, PLATO. SHE'S GONNA BE FINE.
BUT, ENOUGH HEARTS AND FLOWERS! THERE'S FIRES AND BUILDINGS COLLAPSED ALL OVER THE CITY. TIME TO ACT LIKE A MAYOR!
I DON'T KNOW IF I CAN. I MEAN...
...I ALWAYS KNEW GREYSHIRT'S LUCK HAD TO RUN OUT SOME-DAY. IT'S JUST...
WELL... THERE'S CANDICE, TOO. CHRIST-- THEY'RE PROBABLY STRAPPING HER INTO THE ELECTRIC CHAIR RIGHT NOW...
THAT'S WHAT I'M TRY'NA TELL YA! A SHAFT GAVE WAY RIGHT UNDER THE WOMEN'S BLOCK.
THE WEST WALL CAME DOWN AND SOME PRISONERS GOT LOOSE. ONE OF 'EM'S CANDI!
THEY HAVEN'T LOCATED HER YET, BUT DON'T BLOW YOUR TOP. IT WASN'T THE GUARDS' FAULT! NO ONE EVER EXPECTED THIS KIND OF SITUATION!
SOUNDS LIKE AN ACT OF GOD, TO ME.
SHE WON'T ESCAPE THE LONG ARM OF THE LAW FOR LONG, PLATO.
I'LL HANDLE HER CASE MYSELF, O'RIORDHAN. SOME-TIMES HAPPY ENDINGS TAKE A LITTLE TIME...
...AND THE WATCHFUL EYE OF A GUARDIAN ANGEL.
AS THE BROKEN PIECES OF THE LITTLE FAMILY REUNITE I ALMOST WISH THAT FRANKY LAFAYETTE WAS ABLE TO JOIN THEM.
WEEOOOEEEOOOEEEOOO
BUT THAT WON'T BE HAPPENING.

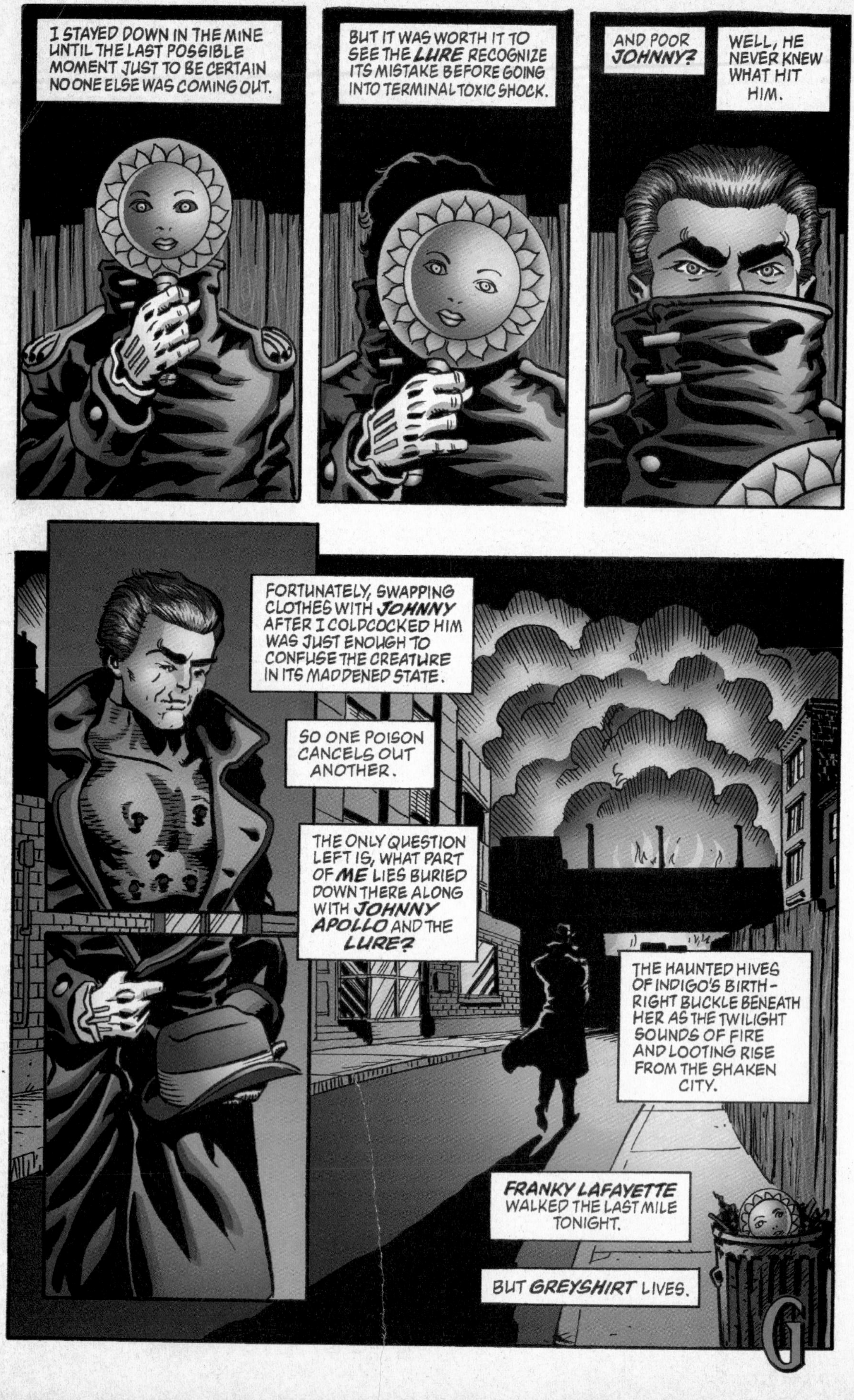
I STAYED DOWN IN THE MINE UNTIL THE LAST POSSIBLE MOMENT JUST TO BE CERTAIN NO ONE ELSE WAS COMING OUT.
BUT IT WAS WORTH IT TO SEE THE LURE RECOGNIZE ITS MISTAKE BEFORE GOING INTO TERMINAL TOXIC SHOCK.
AND POOR JOHNNY?
WELL, HE NEVER KNEW WHAT HIT HIM.
FORTUNATELY, SWAPPING CLOTHES WITH JOHNNY AFTER I COLDCOCKED HIM WAS JUST ENOUGH TO CONFUSE THE CREATURE IN ITS MADDENED STATE.
SO ONE POISON CANCELS OUT ANOTHER.
THE ONLY QUESTION LEFT IS, WHAT PART OF ME LIES BURIED DOWN THERE ALONG WITH JOHNNY APOLLO AND THE LURE?
THE HAUNTED HIVES OF INDIGO'S BIRTH-RIGHT BUCKLE BENEATH HER AS THE TWILIGHT SOUNDS OF FIRE AND LOOTING RISE FROM THE SHAKEN CITY.
FRANKY LAFAYETTE WALKED THE LAST MILE TONIGHT.
BUT GREYSHIRT LIVES.
G

ALL THE NEWS FROM DAWN TO DUSK

NOW $1!

INDIGO CITY SUNSET

AFTERNOON CITY EDITION

Monday, June 17, 2002   Metro Weather – Today: Fog, Tonight: More Fog, Tomorrow: Bad Foggem

SHAKE, RATTLE AND ROLL!

CHAOS AS ABANDONED MINE SYSTEM COLLAPSES UNDER INDIGO!

The industry that built Indigo almost took her down last night, as the vast hive of abandoned sapphire mines beneath the city unexpectedly, and catastrophically, collapsed. Authorities said property damage could run into the hundreds of millions of dollars, but because early tremors forced citizens out of their homes before the worst quakes hit, injuries and loss of life were mercifully low. Mayor Plutarch declared the BOTTOMS UP district, which was hit hardest, a disaster area, while Police Chief O'Riordhan put out an all points bulletin for six prisoners who escaped custody when the west wing of the Indigo City prison collapsed.

FULL COVERAGE: Pages 2 and 3

Happy Ending for Real Life "Carbones!" Page 34

INDIGO CITY ROCKS!

MINE COLLAPSE GIVES CITY A CASE OF THE JITTERS!

SPECIAL TO THE SUNSET BY SKEETER BACKENBEATER

Indigo City's colorful past came up to bite her on the butt last night as the extensive system of mine shafts over which the city was built experienced a sudden and catastrophic collapse. The cave-ins shook buildings and tore up streets all across the city as, one after another, the interconnected hive of tunnels let go in an extended chain reaction.

Most of the damage and injuries were caused by exploding gas mains ruptured in the quakes. Initial reports from the Mayor's office indicated that loss of property and life could have been much worse, but final estimates are unclear with authorities still battling fires and looters late into the night.

The hardest-hit area was the old Bottoms Up district, where scientists believe the first and most devastating cave-ins occurred. Sulfur Street was in a shambles this morning, with regular patrons of its infamous bars and bordellos bemoaning the loss of their favorite haunts. Two-Eyed Jack's saloon had set up a makeshift bar on the sidewalk and was consoling all comers with free drinks and promises to rebuild the venerable watering hole as soon as possible.

Also damaged was the Indigo City Prison, which experienced a catastrophic collapse of the west wing and a mass escape of convicts (see story on sidebar).

On Vapor Street, the Mood Indigo Lounge was evacuated when the first tremors hit during a standing-room-only set by Indigo songbird Ella Bly. The whole night-club collapsed moments after patrons safely exited the building.

The newly dedicated GREYSHIRT monument in Propane Square was reduced to rubble when an emergency vehicle lost control during a tremor and hit

the statue head on. The driver and other personnel escaped with minor injuries.

Other hard-hit areas included Neon Avenue, which saw the collapse of the Purple Comics Building. Reports from the scene were sketchy, but some artists and editors, working late to make a deadline, told this reporter they were warned about the impending disaster by a ghostly presence.

Also damaged was the Indigo Museum of Natural History. The facility was closed for the evening and empty except for a guard. The officer, Barney Drum, was back on his first night of guard duty since his honeymoon and was able to save the fabled *Star Of Indigo* just before the ceiling above the display came down.

Firefighters battled a blaze at the old Cobalt Forge that was still raging out of control this morning. Authorities said the fire was probably caused by super-heated molten metal which was spilled in the quakes.

Morning editions of THE

INDIGO CITY ROCKS!

Damage Heavy, Injuries Light as Shafts Go Down like House of Cards!

INDIGO CITY SUNSET were delayed when the main press was rocked off its foundation in the tremors. Pressmen had the machine back in service within an hour of the first tremor.

Fire in the Shooting Gallery on East Monoxide destroyed the complete life's work of notorious Indigo painter and gadfly, Andy Savannah. The POW! ART paintings had just been moved back to the gallery after a show at the Lakeland Museum of Contemporary Art, which was not damaged.

On Fume Street, the old Katz Building, which was in the process of being prepared for demolition, collapsed. Looters, attracted by stories of the long-lost sapphire stash of Spats Katz descended on the rubble and were seen digging frantically with their bare hands when police arrived to make arrests.

The mine system under Indigo has long been a major concern for citizens and government officials alike. The hive-like warrens, the first of which were sunk in the 1850s, were boarded up and abandoned in the 1930s when the once abundant sapphires began to run out. Dozens of children disappeared in the dangerous pits over the years, prompting calls for action that were never heeded.

The problem has been a hot-button political issue in recent years, with city officials claiming their hands were tied by the legal morass of mining claims and deeds going back over a hundred and fifty years.

This morning, as Indigo cleans up the wreckage, it appears that the mine problem has solved itself with the help of rotting timbers and the forces of gravity. Geologists say it is too early for a definitive analysis, but that it appears all the old shafts have completely caved in, sealing off the dangers to Indigo City citizens forever.

CANDI BEATS THE RAP!
Spats' Bimbo Escapes Date with Hot Seat!

A condemned murderess, just moments away from being strapped into the electric chair to pay for her crimes, was granted a dramatic and unofficial stay of execution by last night's disastrous collapse of the mine shafts under Indigo City.

Candice "Candi" Lovelace, (seen in file photo below) longtime paramour of Indigo gangster Seymour "Spats" Katz, was set to ride out on "Old Sparky" last night. Following a final visit from Mayor Plato Plutarch and Greyshirt, Lovelace was given a last meal and a few moments with a priest to make a final confession and receive Last Rights.

As she was being led to the death chamber, the first quake rolled under the prison, knocking out power and plunging the women's block into darkness. In the ensuing confusion, guards moved quickly to put the facility under an emergency lockdown. But, within minutes, a previously unknown mine shaft directly under the prison let go, bringing down the west wall and causing mayhem among guards and prisoners alike.

Lovelace, along with five other prisoners, was able to exit the prison through the collapsed wall and disappear into the night, escaping her captors, and for the time being, justice itself. All the escapees were still at large this morning and considered dangerous.

Mayor Plutarch issued a statement late last night, saying he would personally head up a special tactical group charged with finding and apprehending Lovelace and the rest of the group.

Lovelace was arrested two years ago after Greyshirt uncovered a crime ring run by her and Spats Katz from their penthouse apartment in the Katz Building. Katz, confined to a wheelchair since an attempted mob hit ten years earlier, died in a fall from the fourth floor of his building. Lovelace stood trial and was convicted of multiple murder, kidnapping and assault charges.

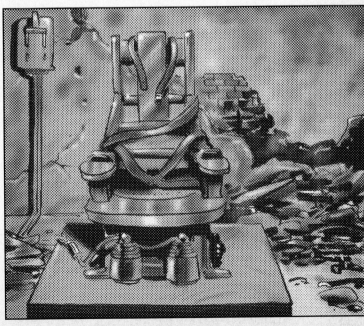

THE EYES HAVE IT!

Greyshirt Blindsides Invasion of the "Eye-Borgs!"

A fantasy role-playing game among scientists at Liverspot National Laboratory nearly ended in the invasion of Indigo City by interdimensional berserkers yesterday. Only quick thinking by Greyshirt saved the city from being overrun by furry and ferocious eyeball warriors that, according to scientists, might or might not actually exist.

The incident began in the SuperString Theory Department headed by Tucker Pinkus of the Liverspot National Laboratory. Members of the department, who are usually engaged in unlocking the secrets of the universe, regularly meet with members of the Quantum Probability Department across the hall in a gaming group. The two departments have long competed in a fantasy role-playing card game called Thaumaturg, which involves imaginary armies of characters pitted against each other in duels of magic and might.

The friendly games have been going on for years without a hitch until this week when an angry dispute over a perceived infraction of the rules erupted between the two departments. The usual jovial atmosphere of the event devolved into childish name-calling and a walkout by the Quantum Probability Department. At that point, according to authorities familiar with the case, Pinkus decided to play a trick on the departing Quantum Probability group and went to his own laboratory to get a top-secret device being experimented on there. The device is said to be a violin-like musical instrument based upon the theories of musician-mathematician Victor Crescendo, who died in obscurity last year.

Pinkus activated one of the strings on the instrument, causing a reality distortion field to ripple across the hallway into the other department. What Pinkus didn't realize was that the Quantum Probability scientists were also unleashing a secret device of their own, aiming it back at the offices of the SuperString group. The second device was a quantum foam unit, which is said to have the ability to open our reality to all possibilities inherent in any given situation.

When the superstring resonance hit the quantum foam, they somehow, unexpectedly, interacted with the nearest fantasy role-playing card causing the imaginary characters depicted on it to come to life and appear in our reality. The characters were so-called "Eye-Borgs," a race of warrior eyeballs from a volcanic dimension.

Fortunately for Indigo City, Greyshirt was on the scene when the creatures first invaded our world. The Indigo Avenger was searching for clues at an unrelated crime scene near the laboratory when he noticed that the alley before him had transformed into a perfectly realized two-dimensional backdrop. Hearing skittering and yammering behind it, he raised the curtain just as thousands of armed eyeball creatures burst through into our reality.

One of the eyeball people immediately struck at Greyshirt, braining him with a mace. The Grey Guardian was somehow able to remain conscious as the invading army swarmed into Sulphur Street like ocular army ants, terrorizing Indigo citizens with their bloodthirsty cries.

Thinking quickly, Greyshirt immediately got the invaders' attention by finding and grabbing the apparent leader of the invading force. Using his cane like a Louisville Slugger, Greyshirt sent the eye king arcing in a long loping fly ball towards the Indigo City Appliance Emporium. As the army of berserker eyeballs swarmed after their chief, they stopped dead in front of the display window of the Appliance Emporium. There in the window, just as Greyshirt had planned, was a new gas-powered wide-screen television playing reruns of *Gilligan's Island*. The warrior eyeballs turned towards the flickering screen and and were soon helplessly trapped by the adventures of Gilligan, the Skipper and the other castaways.

With the invaders completely hypnotized by the situation comedy, Greyshirt had the time he needed to round up Tucker Pinkus and the other scientists at Liverspot Lab, who were able to reset their scientific instruments and send the invaders back to whatever imaginary realm they inhabited before.

As the last of the eyeball warriors disappeared behind the curtain and back into their volcanic realm, the scientists began to argue amongst themselves whether or not the creatures actually did or did not exist. Greyshirt was heard to quip, "Sometimes you can't believe your own eyes in this town."

INDIGO POOP SCOOP! BY IDLE DISH

AMBULANCE CHASING for FUN AND PROFIT!

Indigo is just beginning to dig out from under last night's mine collapse, but legions of litigious lawyers are already descending on the city, handing out cards and promising big-buck settlements to victims of the disaster. While blame for the collapse will be nigh impossible to affix, proving legal responsibility might be an even harder job with ownership of the mines long entangled in a quagmire of claims, deeds and swindles dating back to the 1850s. Those individuals who dug the pits and made vast fortunes ripping cool blue sapphires out of Momma Indigo's bosom are far beyond the reach of the legal system now. The SCOOP hears that the city itself might have to assume fiscal responsibility, but expect years of push-me, pull-you from the usual suspects in City Hall.

THE SMART MONEY!

Meanwhile, word on the street is that the really sharp shysters are maneuvering for a much different, and possibly more lucrative, court-appointed jackpot. A little birdie tells the Scoop that the recently reunited power couple of LIPS LAFAYETTE and CARMINE CARBONE might be holding all the cards in a Hollywood hustle worth hundreds of millions of dollars! While no one has been able to find the mysterious FANMAN since the mine disaster, his Fanman Productions (which has raked in a lot of cabbage producing the white hot *CARBONES* cable television series as well as the *FRANKY AND JOHNNY* box office spin-off) could be facing serious legal complications that might destroy the company. Rumor has it the Fanman's legal beagles never got permission to use the names and likenesses of LAFAYETTE and CARBONE and so the company may be liable for a HUGE court ordered damage award pay out.

****

And what about *FRANKY AND JOHNNY?* The much touted megabuck Hollywood production was in the final stages of filming when sudden disaster struck Indigo last night. Rumors are flying that the mysterious FANMAN himself was killed and that the finances of the big budget bio-pic are up in the air again. We wouldn't doubt that a new hand on the tiller (this will be the picture's third director) will want to go back and reshoot some material to be more faithful to the source. Historians have long taken issue with the series' depiction of JOHNNY APOLLO as a handsome, misunderstood hero. Expect something more in line with the vicious crazy punk who terrorized the town before going up in a blaze of glory in the Indigo Central Station explosion.

AND WHILE WE'RE AT IT!

Let's replace that awful STANLEY AND THE STALEMATES version of *"THE BALLAD OF FRANKY AND JOHNNY"* that was pre-released in the soundtrack album for the film with the real item, written and performed by Indigo songbird ELLA BLY.

ASK DR. SYNTAX

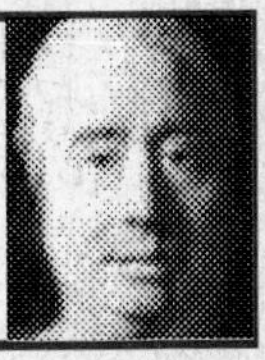

Werewolves of Neopolis!

Dear Doctor Syntax: I'm a middle-aged male with an unusual problem. Right after I reached puberty, I noticed that I had six nipples. I also have unusually hairy palms and a rather extraordinary sense of smell. When the moon is full I am plagued with bizarre dreams that involve sniffing around trees and lampposts and ripping human flesh. While I have been able to keep these afflictions a secret (I've never married and don't remove my shirt in public) I have always felt alienated from those around me. What is wrong with me? — Howler

Dear Howler: I was all set to tell you to that you suffered from lycanthropy and should turn yourself in to the authorities to be institutionalized for the rest of your life. But then I noticed the postmark on your letter. You're from Neopolis. There is absolutely nothing abnormal about you.

Dear Doctor Syntax: Once upon a time, I dressed so fine; threw the bums a dime, in my prime, didn't I? People called said "Beware, doll, you're bound to fall," didn't they? I used to laugh about, everybody that was hanging out. Now I don't talk so loud. Now I don't feel so proud, about having to be scrounging for my next meal. How does it feel? — Like a Rolling Stone

Dear Stone: You have an affliction commonly called Zimmerman's Disease in which the sufferer compulsively views his or her life through the prism of old Bob Dylan song lyrics. You're an idiot, babe. It' s a wonder that you still know how to breathe.

Dear Doctor Syntax: My boss is a woman. The other day at work my office computer broke down, and since she was out of town I borrowed hers. While working on it I did a little poking around and discovered she was a regular poster on an Internet message board devoted to the erotic adventures of Science Heroes. Under an assumed name, my boss admitted that her ultimate fantasy would be to get dressed up like the Cobweb and make love on a rooftop with Greyshirt. It just so happens I've had a Cobweb fetish since I was a kid reading her Tijuana Bibles. While I've never been attracted to my boss before, the thought of her in transparent lavender under an Indigo night sky has got me salivating. What should I do? — Hot and Bothered

Dear Hot: Head down to your local haberdashery and get fitted out in some Science Hero togs. Then send her an anonymous gift of a Cobweb costume and an invitation to an anonymous rooftop encounter. As long as you keep your masks on, the usual rules of office etiquette need not apply.

INDIGO OPINION

"The Lure," We Hardly Knew Ye!

SUNSET EDITORIAL

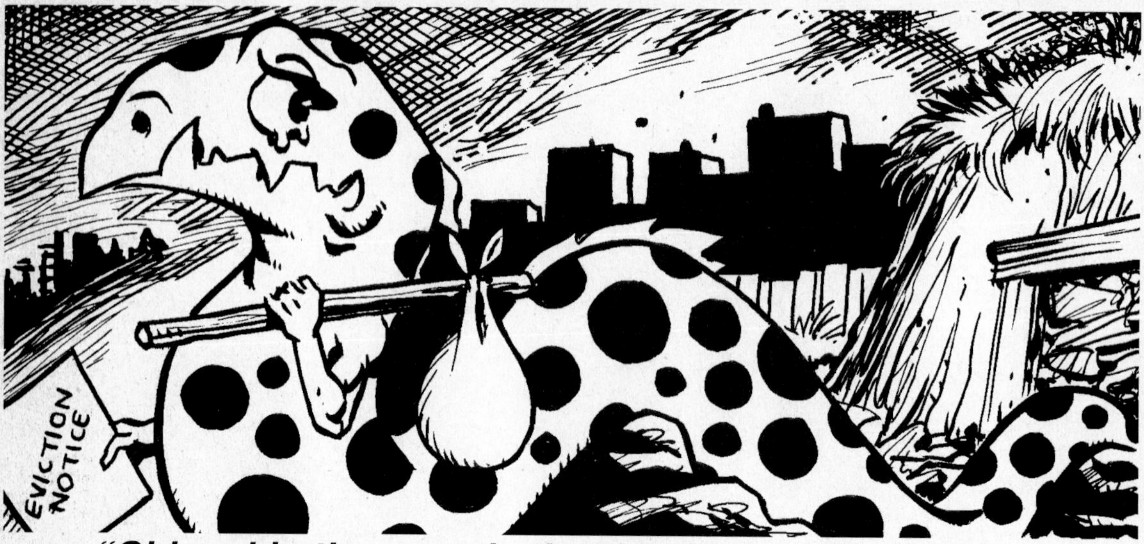
EVICTION NOTICE

"Old and in the way, that's what he heard 'em say..."

While blame for the 2002 Mining Disaster has yet to be apportioned to, or avoided by, the usual suspects in local government, it's not too early to mourn the loss of Indigo's most infamous citizen in the collapse. This particular personage has been an integral part of local culture since time immemorial. History began recording his exploits when old Chief Greylock warned local settlers of a snake-like creature that extended to the center of the earth. When this was followed by reports (in the very first edition of the *Indigo Junction Sunset* mind you) of a huge serpent monster who preyed on unsuspecting miners, the number-one boogie man of Indigo City was born.

We're talking about THE LURE, of course, who is as much a part of Indigo City as the bay, the fog and the sapphire and gas deposits left by an asteroid collision twenty million years ago. Every parent in Indigo City regularly scared the daylights out of their children with stories of the hideous behemoth that preyed on young fools who strayed too close to the abandoned mines. THE LURE that slithered into the nooks and crannies of our imaginations was surely far more fearsome than any poor creature that might actually make its home in those mines beneath Indigo City.

There was method to our parents' madness, though. They needed to scare the living bejeeziz out of us so we wouldn't go anywhere near the hundreds of dangerous mining sites that dot the city.

And now, early reports indicate that the vast warren of rickety mine shafts that presented such a danger to Indigo's children has been obliterated in one wild night to remember. Forgotten in the tragedy is the sad realization that Indigo parents no longer have need for a LURE.

With no dangers to guard the next generation against, Indigo kids will grow up never hearing of THE LURE, never knowing the delicious terror of hiding under the covers wondering if the creature was slithering under the bed or in the closet. And with the mines sealed off, the true daredevils among us will never know what it feels like to ignore the warning signs and fences and slip into those mine shafts that were home to Indigo's most famous son.

So let's give a hearty farewell to THE LURE. Indigo City has outgrown you, old friend. But we'll never forget the shadowy tingle of excitement you brought to our normally humdrum day-to-day existence. — Victer Kich

REAL LIFE CARBONES' HAPPY ENDING!

Gangster, Moll Reunited with Daughter They Never Knew!

Lips Lafayette in 1979

Carmine Carbone circa 1980

THE SUNSET has learned that LIPS LAFAYETTE and CARMINE CARBONE, the real-life inspiration for two main characters in the phenomenal *CARBONES* television series, are not only alive but last night were reunited in a dramatic reconciliation with the daughter they hadn't seen in twelve years.

While details are still murky, the SUNSET has confirmed that colorful newsstand vendor, LADY L, who was reported missing recently, is actually LIPS LAFAYETTE. The 54-year-old LAFAYETTE was engaged in a torrid twenty-five year affair with rackets boss CARMINE CARBONE, who was imprisoned in 1989. CARBONE walked away from a halfway house for elderly convicts not long ago.

In a turn of events right out of an episode of *THE CARBONES*, the two were reunited after a botched kidnapping attempt by unnamed gangsters. Both LIPS and CARMINE were then reintroduced to their daughter, a mildly retarded twelve-year-old living at Saint Alloysius's Orphanage, in an emotional reunion during the mine collapse last night.

LAFAYETTE, whose gangster son FRANKY was conceived out of wedlock with CARBONE, had given the daughter up for adoption in the wake of CARBONE'S arrest and conviction for racketeering in 1989. LAFAYETTE turned state's evidence against CARBONE, who was suffering the early effects of Parkinson's Disease at the time, to protect him from an impending hit. Gangsters JOHNNY APOLLO and SPATS KATZ had formed an alliance against CARBONE and FRANKY LAFAYETTE which ended with APOLLO and LAFAYETTE blown to bits in a final explosive shoot-out in the INDIGO CENTRAL STATION.

Last night, sources close to the action described a tearful reconciliation between LIPS and CARMINE with the old gangster not only forgiving his moll's actions but proposing marriage as well. The source said the couple would take immediate steps to regain custody of their daughter.

With the newly reunited family deciding to make a go of it, Mayor Plutarch announced he will authorize an immediate parole for CARBONE covering the rest of his twenty-year sentence.

LIPS LAFAYETTE told the SUNSET that, "The first thing we're gonna do is get CARM's medication looked at. He has his good days and bad days and we want to make sure he can enjoy what time we have left together."

Rumors are circulating that LAFAYETTE and CARBONE are legally due a portion of the huge profits generated by *THE CARBONES* television series, since they had never signed contracts for the use of their names and likenesses. LAFAYETTE refused to confirm or deny she had hired an entertainment lawyer to file the first lawsuit against FANMAN PRODUCTIONS, but did say, "I wouldn't mind having a few bucks to get my eyes fixed so I can see my own daughter again."

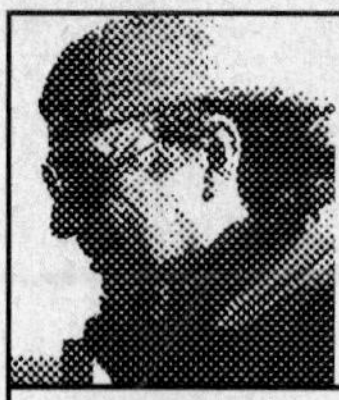

RICK VEITCH
Writer-Artist claims, "I'm channelling Rube Goldberg!" Page 6

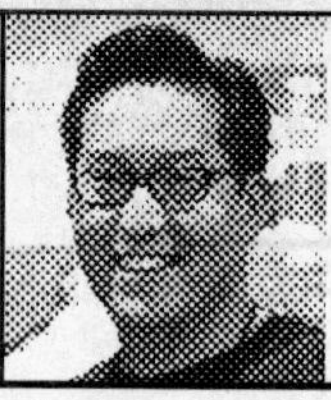

FRANK CHO
Chimp socks artist with defamation suit! Page 7

TODD KLEIN
Why they call him "The Purloined Letterer!" Page 8

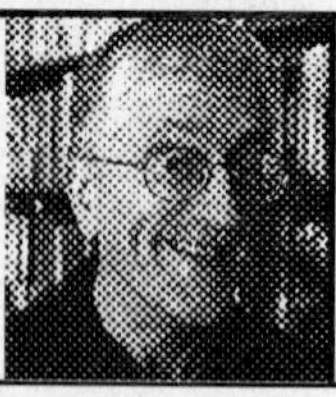

SCOTT DUNBIER
Editor threatens to pen scathing ABC tell-all! Page 9

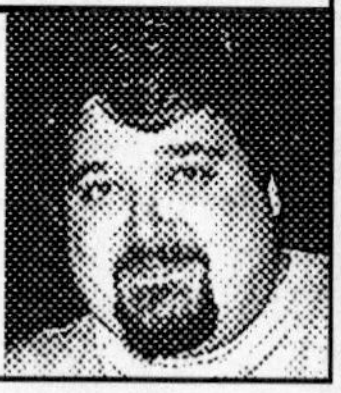

WILDSTORM FX: PASSES WITH FLYING COLORS!

ALL THE NEWS FROM DAWN TO DUSK

INDIGO CITY SUNSET

AFTERNOON CITY EDITION

Monday, June 17, 2002 Metro Weather – Today: Fog, Tonight: More Fog, Tomorrow: You get the idea.

BACK PAGE EXTRA:

MYSTERY AT SEA!

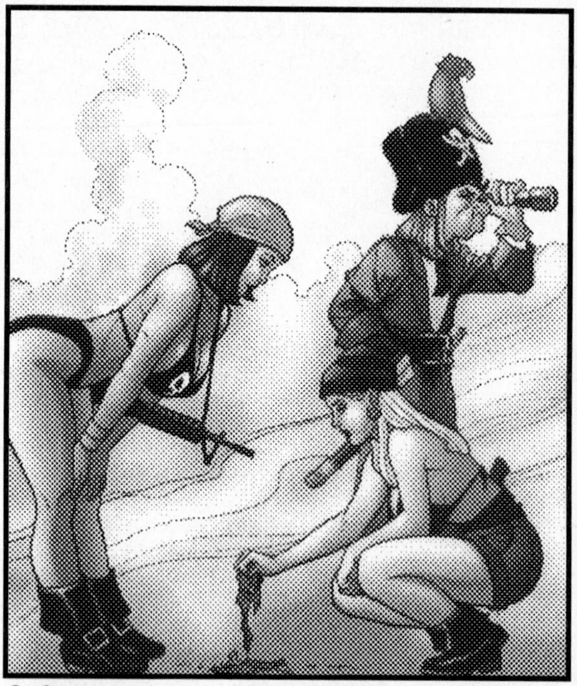

Software pirate JACK HAWKINS and friends

Did Teen Software Pirate Go Overboard with Floating Pleasure Palace?

Special to The Sunset by Geekus Crow

The 70-foot yacht purchased for a reported $200 million by software pirate Jack Hawkins turned up at Pier 3 on the Indigo docks yesterday without a soul on board. Harbor police said the ship was loaded to the gunwales with booty apparently stolen from a number of freighters that were recently reported missing in Crater Bay. One source said the swag even included a shipment of stale breakfast cereal bound for the famine-ravaged Far East. There was no sign of the young billionaire or the crew of buxom babes who sailed the infamous pleasure yacht for the computer wunderkind. Coast Guard Captain Horus Goldenrod said a search of Crater Bay was underway but denied that an unannounced napalm bombing run executed by the Indigo National Guard was in any way connected to the disappearances. FULL STORY PAGE 18

CONTRIBUTORS

RICK VEITCH began writing and drawing comics at the age of six. His first commercially published work was TWO-FISTED ZOMBIES, written by his brother, Tom Veitch, and published by Last Gasp in 1973. Rick enrolled in the Joe Kubert School in 1976, studying under Kubert, Dick Giordano and Ric Estrada, and was part of the school's first graduating class in 1978. While still at school he began his professional career in mainstream comics, contributing over a dozen short stories to DC's OUR ARMY AT WAR. He also met and began lifelong collaborations with fellow artists Steve Bissette, John Totleben, Tom Yeates and Tim Truman. Out of school, the group formed the Flying Duchmasters Studios and began getting published in New York. Rick's work appeared in HEAVY METAL, which led to his collaboration with Steve Bissette and Allan Asherman on the graphic novel adaptation of Steven Spielberg's 1941. He contributed regularly to Marvel's EPIC MAGAZINE, and published his first collaboration with Alan Moore there. Rick wrote and illustrated two early graphic novels for editor Archie Goodwin: ABRAXAS AND THE EARTHMAN and HEARTBURST, before launching a six-issue series, THE ONE, for Epic Comics in 1984. Rick was highly active in the 1980s drawing issues of SWAMP THING, NEXUS, SCOUT and MIRACLEMAN before becoming regular penciller of SWAMP THING, collaborating for a year and a half with Alan Moore before taking over as writer. Veitch's SWAMP THING run ended in controversy in 1989. Rick then created a Teenage Mutant Ninja Turtles graphic novel, THE RIVER, for Mirage Studios. Also in 1989, Rick formed his own publishing imprint, King Hell Press, which released a collection of THE ONE and two new graphic novels, BRATPACK and THE MAXIMORTAL. In 1993 Veitch again collaborated with Moore, Bissette and Totleben on the 1963 comics series from Image. The next year Rick began his most experimental work, RARE BIT FIENDS, a dream diary in comics form, published by King Hell in 21 issues and two collections: RABID EYE and POCKET UNIVERSE. Rick also wrote TEKNOPHAGE for Big Entertainment, and in the late 1990s worked with Alan Moore and Todd Klein on SUPREME and on the launch of the ABC comics line. He and Moore created GREYSHIRT for the anthology comic TOMORROW STORIES before spinning it off into GREYSHIRT: INDIGO SUNSET. He also co-created, with Steve Conley, the internet comics site Comicon.com. Veitch is currently scripting DC's AQUAMAN series with Yvel Guichet on art, and is writing and drawing a graphic novel for Vertigo titled CAN'T GET NO. He lives in Vermont with his wife Cindy and two sons, Ezra and Kirby.

HILARY BARTA has worked as inker and sometimes penciller on a wide variety of characters for many companies, including X-Men, Superman, Spider-Man, Wolverine, Power Pack and others. Though well-versed in traditional action art, he is perhaps best known for his more humorous work in such books as PLASTIC MAN, WHAT THE--?!, RADIOACTIVE MAN and STUPID. Hilary has contributed an EC-Comics send-up to ABC's TOM STRONG in issue 14, collected in TOM STRONG BOOK 2, and with Alan Moore co-created the wacky SPLASH BRANNIGAN feature for TOMORROW STORIES.

FRANK CHO is best known for his highly-acclaimed and multi-award-winning comic strip and comic book LIBERTY MEADOWS, which evolved from a comic strip he created in college, UNIVERSITY², both of which have been collected in book form. Cho's stylish art has also been collected by Insight Studios in the book FRANK CHO, ILLUSTRATOR. He is currently working on SHANNA for Marvel Comics as well as continuing LIBERTY MEADOWS. Frank lives in the Baltimore area with his wife Cari, baby daughter Emily, and his wiener dog Truman.